I0760790

ALSO BY CARMEN ROSALES

The Prey Series

Thirst

Lust

Appetite

Forgive Me For I Have Sinned

Forbidden Flesh

Hillside Kings Series

Hidden Scars

Hidden Lies

Hidden Secrets

Hidden Truths

Cartel Kings Book One

Duets

Giselle

Briana

He Loves Me Not

He Loves Me

Standalone

Like A Moth To A Flame

Delilah Croww Books

Whispers in the Dark

Circle of Freaks

THE PREY SERIES

CARMEN ROSALES

Interior design by Jay Aheer

Cover Design by Carmen Rosales

Art illustration on cover Adobe stock by Maria

ISBN 978-1-959888-59-8

Erotic Quill Publishing, LLC
3020 NE 41st Terrace STE 9 #243
Homestead, Fl. 33033
www.carmenrosales.com
Manufactured in the United States of America First Edition November 2024

THE
PREY
SERIES

THE PREY SERIES

FORGIVE ME FOR I HAVE SINNED

FORBIDDEN FLESH

ENVY

AUTHORS NOTE

Dear Reader,

Please note, the Prey Series may contain themes that can cause triggers for some. Caution is advised.

This is a special edition that contains Forgive me for I have Sinned, Forbidden Flesh, and Envy.

THE

PREY

SERIES

FORGIVE ME
FOR
I
HAVE SINNED

FORGIVE ME
FOR
I
HAVE SINNED

What if everything they thought about you was a lie?

After Victoria's best friend dies, everything around her ceases to exist.

The man she loved all her life didn't want her anymore.

Her world crumbled.

Depression took her under.

All she has left is the will not to let others suffer under the Order's rules, but she has to play the part under the hands of the dangerous and depraved to save them.

It's the end of her senior year, and time has run out. Victoria has to marry under the Order's rules by the time she graduates from Kenyan, and her father has chosen her husband—Her ex-boyfriend's rival.

Alaric is the eldest of the sons of Kenyan, but he is darker. More sinister.

He doesn't play by anyone's rules—Except his own.

Alaric hates what Victoria's become after his cousin's death. He's heard the rumors around campus after he graduated. How dirty and twisted she is.

When he discovers whom she is marrying, revenge has never tasted so sweet.

Alaric has plans for her—Plans she never saw coming.

But what if he was wrong for letting her go, and now it's too late?

VERONICA

Senior Year of High School

"ARE you sure no one will find out if we go?"

Alicia rolls her eyes. "Relax, your parents won't find out. They think you're sleeping over because our end-of-the-year project took longer than expected. My mother assured me it was alright with your mom. You want to see him, don't you?"

"Of course, I do. But I don't want to look desperate or stupid, showing up there uninvited."

Alicia snorts. "If my brother Reid gets to go, I get to go. And that means you can go too. Fuck what anyone else thinks."

I smirk, looking at her through the floor-length mirror in her bedroom. I turn to the side, knowing the black skirt is shorter than what my parents would allow me to wear and the thigh-high socks that stop an inch from the hem are way above mid-thigh, before I turn to face her completely.

"Stop lying," I tease. "You want to go because he'll be there."

Alicia has a major crush on Chase, but Chase is a scholarship student in his junior year at Kenyan and is considered Prey. It wasn't supposed to be serious between them; she isn't supposed to get attached when she has to marry within the Order, but to Alicia, it is, and that is what I'm afraid of, but if he makes her happy, then I'm not going to fill her head with what ifs. Since we both barely turned eighteen, me in August, and Alicia at the end of September, we've waited to go out and hang around college boys because we were both minors and still in high school.

This is technically our first college party and the first party of the year at Ohio University. Only the rich and, of course, the sons of Kenyan are invited. Even Draven, the evil Bedford twin, will probably be there, so they can confuse the shit out of the girls they fuck, thinking there is only one of them when there are indeed two.

"They will both be there, and this is our chance to get them to notice us!" she says with excitement.

"I-I don't know, Alicia. Do you honestly think he'll notice me?"

Pfft. "With those eyes, gorgeous hair, and awesome personality, Alaric would be an idiot not to notice you."

I know she's just being nice and doesn't want me to back out because that would mean she would show up alone like a lamb to a slaughterhouse, but my self-doubt comes from the other times I have seen him at family functions, and he didn't even say hi or notice that I was in the same room. I always blamed it on the age difference and the fact that I was probably too young because I was still in high school, and he's a hot shit college student, powerful, smart, and gorgeous, and one of the sons of Kenyan.

I swear there's never a time when he doesn't have a gorgeous woman on his arm, and that only fills me with jealousy because I want to be the only one on his arm holding his attention, even though I know it's impossible. But I would be happy with just one night with him. One night. It's all I've prayed for every night since the first time Alicia showed me a picture of her amazing cousin on her phone. Alaric Riodrick-Riordan.

Everyone looks up to him like he's a god.

Even me.

"You're my cousin Alicia's best friend from school…Veronica, right?" A warm feeling slides across my skin, hearing my name on his lips. Especially the way he says it.

"Yeah," I say softly, glad he can hear me even with the music blaring from inside the house.

"My name is Alaric."

I smile, trying to hide the nerves causing my heart to beat too fast and the palms of my hands to sweat. Thankful for the light October breeze beginning to caress my skin, hoping he doesn't notice how nervous I am.

"I know."

"How's that? I don't think we've ever met."

I was right. He never noticed me either time we were in the same room or when people talked about Alicia's best friend with the rich father that was a member of the Order. I'm used to it, though—no one giving a shit about me or who I am, except Alicia. To everyone else, I am invisible. But right now, I'm not. At least not to him. And it's all I ever wanted.

Not wanting to sound naïve and boring, I reply, "Then how do know my name?"

He grins. "You are…kind of a smart ass," he says, taking a sip out of a cup in his hand. It's whiskey. I recognize the sweet smell from my father's study when he calls for me. I always hated that smell, but right now, the fact that Alaric smells like it every time he speaks to me changes my perspective.

I glance to the left to see a group of guys who are drinking, looking this way with smirks on their faces. Two girls with them are covering their mouths in a fit of giggles. I'm unsure if they're drunk, and that's the reason, or if they know I'm still in high school and don't belong at a college party. I try not to think that they're judging me because my eyes are too light and my hair is nearly colorless, but most say the color is white.

I used to get teased all the time and sometimes still do. Veronica looks like an old hag with white hair, or her eyes are too light, the color of evil. Soulless. I would complain to my parents when I came home from school, but my father assured me I was beautiful and that having the lightest shade of eyes and hair makes me pure. He would say that it keeps the demons out of my head and not to listen to the kids at school because they are just jealous of me and my last name.

I tear my eyes away from them and look down at my fingers, playing with the hem of my skirt, and ask, "Do you know them?"

He looks up, knowing exactly who *they* are. "Just some friends from school. Don't mind them. They're just being stupid. It's initiation night for all the jocks from both schools. It's one of the few nights we all get along before the rivalry begins when the season starts. Football, guys from the swim team, baseball and basketball players. They all come to this party."

Initiation? "What do you mean?" I ask with a frown creasing between my brows.

"Don't worry about it." He stands up and holds out his hand. "Come on. Let's go somewhere private."

I look at his outstretched hand, and my lips curve into a smile, admiring how the tattoos of bones are drawn over the tops of his hands in deep shades of black and gray, giving the impression that his skin has disappeared. The way the muscles of his lean arms move with effort and his biceps flex by simply holding the cup. My eyes slide to his fitted white t-shirt, unable to obscure the hard body underneath until I reach his sinful mouth and his eyes that are the color of gray clouds.

I recognize a storm in their depths. A storm that calls to me, and I can't stop myself from saying, "Okay." Sliding my hand in his, knowing what going somewhere private means.

He guides me up the stairs, and I avoid the looks aimed my way and the raised brows as we pass. I. Ignore. All. Of. It.

It's my senior year, and yes, I'm still a virgin. So is Alicia.

Her brother scares every guy who tries to show her attention; meanwhile, my parents are hellbent on following the Order's traditions, and their rules, which dictate you have to be betrothed by the conclusion of your senior year of college. Unfortunately, this also means my father forbids me to have a boyfriend of my own choosing for fear of me choosing wrong and the fact that I'm an only child doesn't help because, in my case, it is up to me to form an alliance that is worthy of the Devlin name as the only heir.

Alaric is technically the oldest Riordan, being older than Reid and Alicia, but I haven't heard of him being betrothed to anyone yet and for a girl like me, it gives me hope.

He stops and opens the door at the end of the hall, and my stomach clenches in anticipation. I'm suddenly aware that my skirt is too short and my panties are wet. I wonder if a man like Alaric could tell. Probably.

The room is dark, except for the moonlight coming through the slit in the curtains. The bed is a full size with red and blue sheets. There are football pictures and trophies on a shelf on top of a desk. I stand in the middle of the room, not knowing what to do next. I didn't think that far ahead.

"Have a seat on the bed. I don't bite, Veronica."

I chew on my bottom lip nervously, watching him close the door, and when I do as he asks and sit down, I notice his eyes are on my exposed thighs, making the throbbing between my legs worse.

I slide my hands between my thighs under his watchful gaze and squeeze them together, trying to calm the pulsing that won't stop. I'm obviously nervous, but I don't want to seem like a scared virgin and risk him leaving me here and walking out.

He smiles and hands me the red cup with the whiskey in it. "Here, have some. It looks like you could use it."

I take it because it's where his lips have been. I want nothing more than to drink from him—to be here with him. I take a small sip and feel the liquid burning me from the inside, giving me the courage to relax. I take another sip, and I'm surprised how smooth it is the second time it slides down my throat. Bumps on my skin rise all over my arms under my long-sleeve shirt from the alcohol coursing through my stomach.

I hand him the cup, and he places it on the dresser by the bed. "I'm not twenty-one," I blurt and close my eyes, wanting to kick myself.

"I know. You're obviously not twenty-one if you're still in high school. You're eighteen, and that is all that matters."

I avert my gaze. "Of course."

It's not like I haven't had alcohol before. Alicia and I have snuck some from her parents' liquor cabinet when they went out for dinner. A few sips of alcohol from him will not kill me or send me to hell. I drank from his cup, so I'm sure he didn't lace it with anything. A guy like Alaric Riordan doesn't have to stoop so low to get a girl.

The bed dips when he sits close, and all I can think about is the heat coming off his body and the whiff of his masculine cologne mixed with his scent. A scent I'll commit to memory because I know that whatever happens tonight with him in this room will never happen again, unless he wants it to.

"You know it's a shame."

"What is?" I ask, pinching my eyebrows together a little confused.

He turns slightly toward me, sliding his finger up the side of my thigh, causing the throbbing to worsen by the second between my legs. Shit. "That it is my last year at college, and by the time it will be your freshman year, I'll have graduated."

I let out a slow breath. "Why is that?"

He leans close, his hand sliding over my right thigh, stopping between my legs, and whispers, "Because I won't be around to always do this." He kisses my cheek and the area right under my ear, causing the tiny hairs to rise all over my skin. "Is this okay?"

I nod and let out a slow breath I didn't realize I was holding. Maybe I should tell him it's my first time, but then my mind screams at me that I shouldn't because I would never get a chance with him again if he stopped. This is not the place I planned to lose my V-card, but all I know is that I want it to be him and no one else, which means it's now or never with him.

"You don't have to do anything you don't want to," he says when his lips brush mine.

"I want to," I reply breathlessly.

He smiles, and it's my first time seeing his perfect white teeth. He takes my lips softly and then roughly. One minute he's kissing me, and the next, I have my shirt off and skirt bunched around my waist. The tiny white thong I purchased online without my parents knowing is pushed aside. My freshly waxed pussy glistens from how wet I am for him and drips down my thighs. He holds himself above me without his shirt, and I'm too busy looking at all his ink to care that he's seeing me practically naked.

"Damn, you're fucking hot. Do you know that? Those fucking socks are driving me insane. It's like you're innocent but sinful at the same time."

"Like you," I counter.

He chuckles, and his gray eyes meet my light ones. "We both know there is nothing innocent about me." He unzips his jeans and takes himself out. Fuck, he's huge. He fists himself and I'm mesmerized at seeing him like this. All I can think about is if he will be able to fit inside me and if I can handle what comes next.

I remember overhearing Lindsey and Rachel in the girls' locker room at school during fourth period after P.E. talking about doing It. Lindsay told Rachel that it hurts at first, like a giant sting that burns for a minute, then it feels so good and that it only hurts the first time. After that, it always would feel good, she amended, if the guy you were doing it with knew what he was doing. She said she did it four times with Tristan Minnis, the football team's star quarterback.

Feeling the first brush from the tip of Alaric's cock brings me back to the present. I hear the tear from the wrapper of the condom between his teeth, and his gray eyes flick to mine.

"Are you sure?"

I nod. "Yeah, I'm sure."

Not wanting him to have second thoughts, I slide my hands up the hard muscles on his chest and widen my legs for him while he expertly slides on the condom like he has done it hundreds of times before, and I know he has, but this time, it's with me.

He lowers his head and sucks the swell of my left breast, pulling the bra cup down to lick my nipple. He doesn't suck it like I'm expecting and then does the same to the right, trailing his tongue up between the valley of my breasts and stopping at my parted lips.

For one second, our eyes meet, and I'm lost. I have the man of my dreams looking at me like I'm something special, and he is about to make love to me. I know this means more to me than it does to him, but I don't care.

The head of his cock crowns my opening above my panties when he pushes against me, feeling how hot and wet I am. He closes the space between us, and his lips crash against mine. Our tongues meet, sucking and tasting.

After a few seconds, his lips pull away and his hands slide down my body, my hips lifting off the bed in anticipation. He slides my panties slowly down my legs, leaving me in only my thigh-high socks.

"Open your legs, and let me see your pink pussy," he demands. I open them as wide as my thighs allow and watch his eyes drink me in. "You are so wet, Veronica. Is this for me?"

"Yes," I hiss.

I want him so much. I get wet with just the way he looks at me—like I'm his.

His tongue peeks out and licks his lips while fisting his cock and pushes the tip inside. I close my eyes to brace myself for the sting I know is coming. I'm sure it will be good because Alaric isn't some boy in high school that has only had sex a couple of times; he's a man that knows what he's doing.

He thrusts into me hard, and I gasp from the pain, holding in the sob that wants to cross my lips. It hurts like hell, causing tears to escape my eyes, pooling on my lashes. He fucks me hard like an animal. Thrust after thrust like a man possessed. He isn't soft like I expected but rough.

"Fuck!" he roars. "Your pussy is so tight," he says with a groan, pumping into me savagely.

God, it burns. The sting's not getting any better like I thought it would. My legs shake from the pain, but it must be different for everyone. At least my first time is with Alaric, I keep telling myself.

He's sweating, his hair sticking to his forehead. His tattoos shine from the layer of sweat on his skin. His breaths come in hard and fast. I feel his hand sliding down, gripping my ass between me and the mattress, plunging deeper, causing a strangled groan to escape my lips from the pain. I feel myself stiffen, and something hot floods inside me. I think he came inside the condom. Even if it didn't feel good for me, I blame it on it being my first time, but I was glad I could pleasure him.

When he pushes himself up on the bed, I'm glad it's dark in the room with only our shadows and the moonlight, so he doesn't see the wetness on my lashes or see me wince when he pulls out.

I hear his phone ding with an incoming message. I watch him walk over and fish his phone out of his jeans from the floor and then pull them on after disposing of the condom, admiring the muscles on his back and his trim waist. I push off the bed with my hands and gather my clothes, so I don't look like an idiot lying on the bed with my legs wide open. I didn't have an orgasm, but I don't think I could with how much it hurt.

As I pull my shirt over my head, the bedroom door flies open, and the group of guys that were downstairs are standing at the threshold, laughing and pointing at me. I hastily look around for my skirt and panties, covering myself from their gazes and trying to tune out the abysmal sound of laughter bouncing off the walls in the bedroom.

"I hope she was a good fuck, Riordan. I was wondering who was going to tap that," one of the guys with brown hair says.

I look over at Alaric and can see his lips turn into a frown from the glow of the screen of his phone. Right then the girls that were with the guys walk in and turn on the lights. The brunette points between my thighs with a hideous laugh. I look down between them in abject horror. There's blood. Lots of blood all over my thighs and in between my legs.

"Dude, she had her period!"

The blonde girl pushes the brunette to the side and covers her mouth. "Eww, gross!"

My head begins to spin, but Alaric is frozen, still looking at his phone. His eyes go dark like a storm raging, and it's about to destroy everything in its path. I hear the voices resonating around the room, saying different things about me.

"—Dude, you fucked her on her period—"

I think it was Dorian Black, from the sound of his voice. I remember him from the day we went to a gala, and my father said he went to Kenyan with the older Riordan. The others I don't know, but I can still hear their crude statements.

"—That is so disgusting—"

"—They could have used the shower. What a disgusting whore—"

"—she ruined the sheets on the bed—"

I don't have my period, but it's not like I'm going to scream and tell them I was a virgin. What good would that do? How could a night that was supposed to be unforgettable in a good way turn out to be so wrong in the worst way? Can it get any worse?

I spoke too soon because all of a sudden, they begin chanting, "Whore! Whore! Whore!"

I look up at Alaric and expect him to defend me or kick everyone out, but I'm met with an evil smirk.

"Alaric?" I croak with dread and panic bubbling inside me. He looks over at the group of people, not doing anything to stop them from forming a circle around me as I stand, taunting me as I try to wipe the blood away but fail miserably.

"Stop it!" I scream.

But they don't stop the incantation. The guys and girls by the door and in the hallway begin to chant in tandem. "Whore! Whore! Whore!

Alaric bends down with a malicious smile plastered on his face, picks up my white thong and skirt, and throws it in my face. I flinch when it hits my mouth, falling to the floor at my feet. I bend to pick it up slide them on and grab my shoes to run the fuck out of here. I straighten when the sounds of them chanting begin to subside, but then I hear Alaric when he says, "She was a lousy fuck. All she did was lie there on her back." His hard gaze lands on mine, but I can't clearly see his face because the tears won't stop falling. And his next words slice me deeper than anything ever could, scarring me forever. "It's safe to say that you are the worst fuck I have ever had. Now I have to clean myself by scrubbing my skin from your nasty period blood, you filthy whore." He pauses. "You're so disgusting."

Flailing my arm while holding my shoes with the other, I scramble to leave the bedroom, not caring if my legs are sticky and full of blood.

I run down the stairs, the sobs rising from my throat without restraint. My hair is plastered to my face from the wetness of my sweat and tears. The smell of sex lingers on my skin. I don't look for Alicia or anyone as I run outside, almost face-planting on the sidewalk, falling and scraping my knees and making a hole in my socks. I finally find my footing and run away from the chanting of the word, Whore, and the sound of disgust in Alaric's voice.

I make it home, ignoring every message from Alicia on the way. I took the public bus and sat in the back, ignoring the weird glances cast my way and the embarrassment of having blood smeared on my thighs. It was the first time I met Dorothy. The only person that helped me. She worked in a small restaurant on the edge of town and was on her way to work. She handed me a pack of tissues. I was relieved she didn't ask questions about the blood or the holes in my socks. All she told me was that she lived on the outskirts of Kenyan, and if I wanted a cup of coffee, I could visit her anytime during the night shift at the restaurant to talk. She hated taking the bus, but her license was suspended. My mother never talked to me. That is what I saw in Dorothy even for a moment, a mother figure.

I shut the front door when I make it home and turn, trying to make my way down the stairs to my room, but I pause when I hear my father's irritated voice. "I've been waiting for you, Veronica." I was wrong if I thought this was the worst night of my existence. It was going to get worse. A lot worse. "I got a call tonight," he says in a harsh tone. His hard eyes slide down my tattered clothes until he stops where there's dried blood stained on my skirt. I knew someone from the Order would call him eventually after what happened. There was no way anyone there wouldn't.

"I'm s–"

He backhands me across the face, whipping my head back. Pain radiates on the side of my skull, dulling the burning sensation between my legs.

For the rest of the night, I pray and pay for my sins. I didn't know what he meant when he said the word sin, but I quickly found out, and it's where my nightmares begin. What happened at the frat party was child's play compared to this. Tonight taught me a valuable lesson. I learned how quickly you could yearn for something or someone, only to loathe it and wish it never happened the next.

Which is why I promise myself never to fall in love again.

VERONICA

"WHY ARE you sitting out here alone?" I look up to see Jess standing by my boots.

Looking around at the headstones, I can see why sitting out here by myself on a grave would seem a little odd, but nothing about this place is normal.

My eyes finally rest on her concerned expression, not wanting to tell her why I'm here. "What are you doing walking alone in the cemetery without your future hubby? I thought you would be busy making babies," I tease. She shifts nervously on her feet and all that tells me is that she isn't alone. Reid is probably with her, and she convinced him to let her walk over here.

"I worry about you. I keep thinking about what you said that day in my dorm room."

I wipe crumbs of dirt and leaves off my wool plaid skirt when I move to get up. That was three weeks ago when the cat was out of the bag with Reid, and he finally revealed himself. I shouldn't have said anything. My problems are not anyone else's but my own. And besides, no one can do shit about it. My fate is sealed, stamped, and delivered to the highest bidder who my father deems suitable with the approval of the Order. A nightmare I have to live with for the rest of my life.

I give her a dry smile and do what I do best, lie. "I'll be fine, Jess. It's just an arranged marriage." I look at the gate, not wanting her to notice the headstone I am leaning against and give more of myself away. "You should go. He's overprotective of you, as he should be." She looks over, I follow her line of sight, and I see Reid waiting by the pillar, glaring at me. "He doesn't like me."

He never did.

She waves, and I notice his eyes soften for a fraction when they land on her. "He'll come around."

I laugh through my nose. "No, he won't."

He would rather see me die and be buried here, so he could piss on my grave and take a shit in each flower holder every time he walks through the cemetery to visit his sister. If he ever does. No one comes to visit her. It's too painful for him and his family. Everyone deals with loss and pain differently. Reid deals with it in his way, and I deal with it in mine. But I owe it to my best friend to visit her and let her know I'll keep my promise. Always.

I slide my hair over my shoulder, needing to head home or face my father's wrath. I slide my phone out of my pocket, acting like someone sent me a message. "I gotta go. See you around?"

She nods. "Yeah," she says softly, sliding her hair behind her ear and stepping back. "Do you want to hang out with me and Gia? Maybe go shopping or something."

I hate turning her down when she is trying to be a friend. Even though I don't deserve it for what I did to her, even if my inner motives came from a good place. But in everyone's eyes, I don't deserve anything. Not even a friend. With my best friend dead, I have to agree with them. Jess is better off staying away from me. I did what had to be done— what needed to be done.

I glance down at my shoes that belonged to Alicia, allowing a few seconds to pass so I can paste a fake grin on my face, so the lie that slips off my lips doesn't sit in my conscience like a heavy brick when I look up. "Yeah, let me know, and I'll meet up with you guys."

Making my way down the hallway to the room I call a torture chamber, I check the time on my phone. I have two hours before my late shift at the small restaurant on the edge of town begins. It's been two years, to be exact. I caved one night visiting Dorothy and asked if I could work the night shift during the week and she agreed.

I push the door open, hearing it groan on its old hinges. This house is one of the oldest besides Kenyan. It still has servants' quarters in the basement, keeping in tune with the ancient Victorian era my father refuses to change.

I look to my left and see the man I loathe with every fiber of my being. A man that is part of my living nightmare. "Good, you're here."

His voice feels like a snake's venom sliding through my veins, shutting my organs down one by one. The smell of his preferred whiskey reminds me of the past and present.

"I am," I quip.

I watch as he widens his legs in the chair he is sitting in with a predatory smile, hoping he can find something I did wrong in his eyes.

"You know I don't like to be kept waiting, Veronica. Tell me, how was your day?"

I close my eyes and tell him what he wants to hear. The sins I committed because he loves to make me pay.

"Will that be all?" I ask the couple seated at table fourteen with a smile, placing the plate on the table.

"Yes," the guy says first, as I notice his girlfriend looking straight at him. Probably to see if he's flirting. I hate that feeling. When you like someone so much and hope they are into you the same way you are into them, you're looking for signs because you feel insecure.

I smile at her and avoid looking at her boyfriend to ensure she doesn't feel threatened by me. "We have a new Oreo shake if you're interested. It goes great with the burgers." I smile, looking at her.

She sags in relief, and I make sure to avoid any and all eye contact with her boyfriend. A man that doesn't make sure he only has eyes for his girl sucks in my book.

I glance over at Dorothy as she walks my way and softly says, "Hey, love. Table twelve just sat down, and eleven will be ready to be seated."

I smile. "You got it, Dorothy."

Dorothy knows more about the gossip in Kenyan than I do. She knows most of the parents and the kids who go there. Especially the late Mrs. Bedford, Draven and Dravin's mother. They were fond of each other. I remember the day I found out how close they were when I came to visit Dorothy during her shift, needing a job.

It's funny how a place and its people remind you of certain events in your life that mean the most, but at the same time end in the worst. It didn't stop the night of the party. If anyone mentioned me around Alaric, he would tell people I was a lying whore behind my back and that I was looking to make an alliance because of my father's greed. Alicia told me everything she heard him say about me. Of course, that wasn't true. She was only one person that I confided in and told the truth, and now she's dead.

I pull the ticket off my next order by the kitchen and place the hot plate on the tray. "Is it true you used to be blonde?"

I look over at my friend and co-worker Adam and pinch my brows in confusion for a split second, but then I remember I'm at work, and the fake Veronica Devlin was left home in the dark mansion of hell. "In high school. Who told you that?"

It must have been Dorothy. She is the only one that has seen me with my colorless, platinum-blonde hair. Hair that was dyed because my father liked it the shade of platinum, but hair can only take so much damage, and my scalp could only take so much pain. Now I use pricey extensions and wigs. The only thing my father would pay for, sparing no expense in the way he wanted me to look.

"Dorothy. She said you are one of the few women she knows that can pull off extreme looks like that." He leans close and says softly, "I like your dark hair, honestly."

Adam is about to graduate high school and will be a freshman at Ohio University. It's a rival school, but he doesn't know I attend Kenyan. He also doesn't know who my father or mother is, and I'd like to keep it that way. He started working here his senior year of high school, needing the extra money for college. He secured a scholarship, but he has to pay for additional expenses.

"Thanks," I say, grabbing the tray and heading to the next table.

I place the plates and notice the Ohio State jackets on the two guys sitting across each other in the booth. *Shit.* I don't wear makeup, false lashes, or anything I wear to school so that no one recognizes me when I work here. It is also why I stuck to the night shift on weekdays only.

"Hey, don't I know you?"

I stiffen slightly and look up and meet moss-green eyes. "No."

He points at me when he picks up his fork, but I let my eyes focus on his jacket, so I don't give myself away. "Are you sure? You look familiar, but I can't remember where." I don't answer because I'm sure it's from one of the parties at Kenyan.

"Maybe because you only remember the back of their heads when you fuck them from behind, Matt." His friend sitting opposite him says with a smirk.

Matt shrugs, but I feel the way his eyes travel over my waitress uniform, undressing me with his eyes as I move to the next table. *Dick.* "I haven't fucked *her* because I would have remembered," he says between bites, and I look back with a glare. "There is no way you could forget a girl that looks like that." He pauses and takes a sip of his soda. "I would love to see her eyes when I take her."

Adam slams the plastic tub on the table, making the dirty plates and forks clank inside. "I think you two need to leave," he grits out.

My eyes widen in panic because that would mean I lose tips from a table, or worse, they leave, and I have to pay for their meals.

I walk back to their table and stop next to Matt, who's looking over at Adam. "It's alright, Adam. They must have me confused with someone else. Right, boys?" I purr on the last part.

Matt arches a brow, and Adam looks like I kicked him, but my eyes give him a pleading look.

"Right, gorgeous. How about you let me take you out, and you could be that girl."

I'd rather eat my own vomit.

"I can't; I have a boyfriend," I lie.

Matt looks around mockingly. "I don't see him anywhere, and besides, what kind of guy lets his girl work the night shift at a twenty-four-hour restaurant and not expect guys to hit on her. You're better off with someone like me."

Let me guess, I'll work the dayshift to soothe your ego. I want to say the words, but the fact is, I don't want to lose this job or let Dorothy down.

"Table is ready," Adam says behind me before storming off.

I know he thinks he is trying to be a man by defending me, but you can't change who people are or how they think. I deal with assholes like this all the time. These guys are elementary to what I'm used to dealing with at Kenyan.

"Now that your little boyfriend stormed off. How about it?"

I look down at Matt and his friend, my lips lifting in a sardonic smile. "Is that where I see how big you really are?" I bite my bottom lip and slide my hand down my skirt, watching Matt's eyes widen, my demeanor changing like a flip of a switch. I lean close. "On second thought, I think I'll pass. Taking a girl from behind can only mean one thing. You're a selfish prick that only cares about your own pleasure…which also means—" I pinch my fingers together, leaving a small space in between—"You have a small pathetic excuse of a cock and to be honest, I wouldn't want to look at your ugly mug of a face either while I fake it."

His friend chuckles. "Damn."

I straighten and give him my resting bitch face. "Total waste of my time." When Adam walks back, I place my work face back on, fixing the pin on my uniform and smile. "Will that be all for you boys?"

ALARIC

"AN ALLIANCE between Riodrick and Riordan Holdings and Black Capital investments would benefit the Order, Alaric."

I lean back in the executive chair, looking at the amber liquid in my whiskey glass with three ice cubes, watching it melt, just like my patience as I try to hold myself back from reaching over and strangling Dorian Black. He has something up his sleeve. It is why I accepted this meeting in the first place. Dorian Black is a snake. A venomous one.

But if he's a snake, then I'm the wolf.

I place my elbow on the table and put my forefinger on my lips, acting like I'm considering investing in his piece of shit company that makes in profit what I pay in toilet paper for one of my buildings.

"Send me your Profit and Loss statements. I need to look over them," I state, calling his bluff.

His right eye twitches, and I watch his jaw harden slightly. He won't send it because we both know what I'll find. Loss and little profit.

He needs capital to fund his spending habits, but I'm not the asshole that will support it. Riodrick legacy of hotels comes from my grandmother on my mother's side and the last name Riordan from my father. We use both as a surname interchangeably since my father merged both estates into one and named me and my cousins both Riodrick-Riordan out of respect for the alliance when my uncle and father married their wives. Alliances are everything to the Order and it is how we control the world. In Dorian Black's case, he wants power and money. That much is obvious. He will have to ask the Bedfords to form any business alliance, and good luck with the twins. They will hang him by his balls. Literally.

"What's to think about, Alaric. You don't need P and L's to make a decision. You were summa cum laude at Kenyan, for Christ's sake. We're friends. We go way back...since high school. Then four years at Kenyan." *Yeah, four years of me watching you be a prick.* "We had one fallout." He snaps his fingers, and my eyes harden, hearing the words slide off his lips. "Senior year at the initiation party."

I yawn, feigning boredom. "So," I drawl.

Motherfucker. He wants to throw the steak at the wolf to see if he is hungry so he can bare his teeth. But all I do is give him a grin. I could care less about that party and what happened. It's in the past, and yes, I slipped. Once.

"Get to the point, Dorian. I don't have time for a college reunion. I give three fucks about what happened at that party any more than you do."

"Oh, you don't–"

"No," I grit.

My jaw hardens every time I'm reminded about that night and that lying, manipulative cunt and one of the reasons my cousin Alicia is dead. I could care less about her.

The door to the boardroom opens, and my father and uncle stroll in along with Dorian's father. "Did you two boys wrap things up?" Mr. Black says with a smile.

I'm hardly a boy, but his wife and daughter know that personally. He glances at me when he sits like he won the deal of a lifetime. *In your dreams, asshole.* I will not ever go into business with the Black family in this generation or the next. My father knows that, but he does what I ask, and since my cousin Reid will take over his share of his hotels, he thinks I have a purpose. I do. Just not the way he thinks I do. Keep your moves private. Calculation is key, and timing is everything in business. Like when you want to strangle your opponent, and that someone right now is Dorian. *Not yet.*

"I'm finished," I reply, picking up my whiskey glass and downing the three fingers that are left before getting up.

"Wait!" I look up at Dorian and see the desperation crossing his features. "I-I can get you the reports."

"Riordan?" Mr. Black nudges his head toward me, speaking to

my father like I'm not here. "Talk to Alaric." Like that's going to change the outcome of my decision. Desperate pig.

"I'm afraid it's up to Alaric. He makes all the business decisions, and if he disagrees, I'm afraid it stands, Black," my father replies.

"Alaric?" Dorian calls out.

"The answer is no, Dorian. I have no interest in merging with you because we both know the truth, and I hate wasting my time. You would have sent me the reports if you were serious and a two hundred and fifty million investment is steep, even for you. You and your father can see yourselves out," I say as I move to walk out of the boardroom, hearing his parting shot.

"You will regret it, Alaric. I promise you that!"

"That's enough, Dorian. He said no, and we don't beg," Mr. Black scolds.

That should be the least of his worries. I don't do well with threats.

I walk into my office and shut the door.

"Took you long enough." I turn my head and look at the woman I have chained to the wall, giving her about twenty feet to walk around. And I was being generous. Not because I give a shit but because it gives her the ability to use the toilet. I have no interest in sending someone in to clean up her mess.

"I had a business meeting."

She rolls her eyes. "Of course, you did. You always have meetings. You hold the majority share of both Riodrick-Riordan holdings. Billionaires are found at meetings."

"I'm a busy man," I reply, unbuckling my pants, and watch as she falls to her knees, hearing the chains rattle. She takes me in her mouth, and I hear her moan.

"Can you take it?" I push harder down her throat, making her gag, watching the tears pool in her eyes, just the way I like it. "No?" I grip her auburn-colored hair when she doesn't speak, fisting it in my fingers and looking at the color. Never a blonde or a brunette, unless it is for a reason, but never for pleasure. I pull, arching her neck, so she can take me deeper, watching her eyes roll back in her skull. In three seconds, her air constricts, and if she is as good as she says, she will know to relax her throat and breathe through her nose. If not, she will struggle to breathe. Not my problem. She should have known better than to want to fuck and suck my cock.

I hear her gag and watch the drool slide down her chin while I fuck her face, pulling her hair. I grip the side of her head and pick up speed, fucking her mouth and watching her struggle.

"Just a little more." She nods, but I can tell this is hard for her. She can't take it. Pathetic. All that talk that she can take me. She stops and whips her head back, gasping for air.

"I-I can't," she gasps.

Of course, you can't. You like to fuck rich men for money. That is why she took the job as secretary for Dorian Black. So she can spread her legs and hope to get lucky. I asked her to give me information on Dorian's company, and she thought I was a bigger fish she could catch for a payday, so she folded. The problem is, she didn't know I was an apex predator. I eat the fish and the one trying to catch them.

I pull out and put myself away and step back. "Then get up and get out."

Her eyes look between the door and me. "B-but," she stammers.

I unhook the cuff and chains around her wrist, throat, slide a stack of bills from my wallet, and let them fall at her feet. She looks down at the money with an angry expression. "I'm not a whore," she seethes.

I button my pants, folding my belt, itching to take shower to wash the smell of her off me. "Could've fooled me." I pull the chain and hook it back in place while she tries to cover herself, like she just wasn't prancing around naked in my office, waiting to fuck me like a good little whore.

"Fuck you."

I look up at the ceiling for a second and sigh. "Stop being pathetic. Take the money and get out. It's what you wanted, right? An expensive dinner. Some money to shop to buy a purse and shoes. Except the fucking is obviously off the menu because you couldn't keep up your end, and now, I'm bored." I meet her sour expression while she looks for her clothes. "I have more respect for a prostitute than a gold-digging bitch. At least a prostitute is honest and doesn't hide what she is after. I respect that more than a two-bit lying secretary that spreads her legs for a man in a fifteen-thousand-dollar suit and then gets mad when the guy is being generous in giving her what she wanted all along, even when she couldn't keep up her end.

"You're an asshole."

I walk up and grip her by her neck. "Watch your mouth, Elaine. Don't piss me off. Get up. Get your coin and get out."

She shakes her head in disbelief. Her angry tears run down her cheeks. Tears that do nothing for me.

"You used me."

I did, but I paid her for it. It wasn't like I forced her to do anything. I release her, getting annoyed. "It was nice doing business with you, Elaine."

I sit in my office chair, waiting for her to leave, so I can shower, but of course, she just keeps ranting.

"I didn't think the rumors were true. You are a sadistic fuck. There is no one you care about, is there? You treat all women like animals."

"You should see how I treat men. Count yourself lucky. Here's a tip. You should work on pleasuring a man if you're after his money. Your performance is lacking, and now I have to think of someone else to get off."

She stomps toward the door and says, "Fuck you," before the door slams shut.

I glance at the floor and smile. She took the money. Some people don't like hearing the truth. She's lucky I didn't kill her for her filthy mouth. I should have choked her with my dick, but then I'd have to clean up the mess, and it's bad enough that I need a shower. Besides, I might need her to give me more information on Dorian. I have a feeling he isn't going to let shit go. He likes to dig things up and use it against you. The mention of the initiation party years ago struck a nerve, making my dick twitch in my pants, but that was what he was after. A reaction. One I would never give when it comes to her. She was a one-off. A moment of weakness. And what do you do to a weakness? You destroy it.

VERONICA

"ARE you sure my father left for his trip this weekend?" I ask Marissa, zipping up an overnight bag. I promised Adam and his mother I would babysit his younger sister Melody, so she doesn't get any ideas about bringing boys to the house when no one is around. He has another sister named Madison who started at Ohio State last year, making her a sophomore, and she lives off-campus. This is Adam's freshman year at Ohio State and one of the reasons he feels he had to protect me against those assholes at my table the other day. He said they are on the football team, and off the field, they think girls will just sleep with them.

"Yes, Miss Devlin." I look up, hearing my last name. A name I hate being associated with because of my father.

"Please don't call me that. Veronica is fine."

"I'm sorry, Veronica. You deserve to be addressed with the utmost respect, you know."

In middle school, I used to think I was Cinderella, residing as a servant, and my real mother was the evil stepmother. Except my mother isn't evil. She is just a victim of her own mistakes, and one of them was marrying Charles Devlin. These days she can be found traveling or hopped up on sedatives in her bedroom. She's high most of the time and doesn't care about me as long as I keep Daddy happy. Glancing at the ceiling for a few seconds with the pseudo-redwood and peeling walls I have lived in since I was twelve, I'm reminded of just how messed up my life is.

"Did he say when he would be back?"

"Monday afternoon," she replies, looking down at the uneven floors.

I sag in relief and dread at the same time. He always makes sure he is back by Monday afternoon to ensure I'm home and my heart and mind can break again.

"I'll be back by then. I have to babysit for Adam and his parents. Adam is going to a college party with his older sister. Adam told me Melody is at it again with a boy, and his parents caught him in her room last weekend. His parents are going to visit family and Melody is hellbent on staying."

Marissa snickers. "That child is a wild one. You never snuck boys in your room."

I mockingly point both of my index fingers to the floor and walls. "Look around you, Marissa. A boy wouldn't sneak in a room without windows, and every boy I have encountered is afraid of me. Courtesy of Mr. Devlin."

Her eyes soften, and I hate the pity mirrored behind them. I don't want or need it because that is not how you survive. That is how they destroy you from the inside.

"Do you want popcorn?" I ask Melody, rummaging through the pantry of Adam's house. "We could watch a movie...*Insidious* is streaming."

After I find the packet of microwavable popcorn, I look up to see Melody grinning like she won something on her phone. The boy she snuck into her room last weekend probably sent her a message. When I was fourteen, Alicia showed me a picture of Reid, Alaric, the Bedford twins, and Valen at the lake house they visited that summer. One look at Alaric's perfect face, and I was a goner. Starstruck is what they call it. Alicia and the Riordan's invited me, but I couldn't go. One week without me in the house was a death sentence to Charles Devlin.

I sit down next to her with the bowl of freshly-made popcorn and the irresistible smell has her looking up. Amusement twitches my lips when she tilts the screen so I can't see the text messages on her phone.

"We can watch whatever you want," she finally says.

This means she will be on her phone during the entire movie. As long as she stays out of trouble, then all is good. I could care less what she does on her phone, if her parents allow her to have one. I promised Adam I would watch her, and he promised me fifty bucks for the trouble. I didn't agree because of the money. Well, not entirely. I like being around Adam and his family. I get to be myself and feel...normal.

I find *Insidious* and press play but then notice the grin wiping right off Melody's face and a stream of curse words flying from her mouth.

I raise my eyebrows. "Whoa, do your parents know you use such colorful language?"

"That piece of shit. He lied!" she yells, slamming her hand on the cushions of the couch.

I look at the hurtful expression in her eyes with her ash blonde wavy hair framing her face, hating that someone made her feel this way. Especially some guy that hurt her.

"They all do."

"How would you know?" she snaps. "Adam says he has never seen you even look at another guy since he's known you. I told him it's probably because you like girls."

I snort and almost choke on a piece of popcorn. "I have no issues with people who do, but I assure you, I don't like girls." I tilt my head to the side. "What did he lie about?"

Her eyes are glassy, meaning he either told her he wasn't seeing anyone and he is or that he's somewhere with someone he shouldn't be.

"I can't tell you because you'll tell my brother, and then he'll tell my parents."

I stuff a couple of popped kernels in my mouth and raise a brow. "Try me."

How bad could it be?

She slides a piece of her hair behind her ear, nervously looking between me and her phone. Another message dings on her screen, and she opens it. I watch the fury and hurt swirl in her expression like a tornado at whatever was just sent. The world is crumbling around her in her mind, and she cannot stop it from happening. It's the type of shit that scars you even though those who did it don't deserve you. I sit up, watching her lip tremble, and feel bad for her. The same way I do for all Prey on campus. The ones walking in blindly, only to be slaughtered emotionally by the privileged.

She finally holds up her phone with an audible sigh, and there is a picture of a guy and a girl. His hand is up her skirt, and her tongue is down his throat while she sits on his lap. "He said he was going to sleep early because he had practice in the morning. He's a senior and got a full ride playing football at OSU."

"But you're fourteen," I say. *I think.*

"Sixteen. I will be seventeen in the fall when he starts his freshman year. It's not too much of an age gap, but my parents and brother think he's too old for me."

Her parents and siblings don't trust her to be home alone and now I get why. Guys don't always have a girl's best interest at heart.

I should say she is too young, but then I would be a hypocrite. Alaric was a senior in college when I was a senior in high school, and it didn't stop me. But I was eighteen and a legal adult. I can't tell her that because she will shut down and not tell me. Instead, I go for the let him go. You could find someone better speech.

"You can do so much better."

More tears.

I look at her phone as more messages with pictures come in from social media, with his hand up the other girl's skirt, probably fingering her, and I notice it's somewhere familiar. The outdoor patio. The chairs and benches. A party at a frat house near the college in Ohio. The same one Adam and his sister are probably at right now. I overheard the party was tonight around campus at Kenyan on Friday before the next season starts.

"Does your brother know who he is?" She nods.

Shit.

She looks down, twisting her fingers in her lap as the movie plays. "He snuck in my room, and we…got caught–" she trails off.

"Fucking." I finish for her.

She waves her hand, rolling her eyes and says, "Yeah."

Little shit. I never had a sister. The only one I considered a sister was Alicia. I had no siblings to look up to or to take care of.

I hand her phone back, and she sniffles. "I gave him my V-card. It wasn't like I didn't wait. He said all the right things." It feels like déjà vu.

"That's what some of them do. They're good ones out there, but you need time to figure it out, if not, it can get messy sometimes. He told you that because he knows you wouldn't show up."

She glares. "I would, but you're here."

"So…what…you're just going to show up there and do what exactly? Rip her off of him. The damage is done. You can't take away what you saw on your phone…what everyone saw."

"You're right, but when my brother finds out he's there and what he's doing with whoever, he will kick his ass. He will probably get kicked out of Ohio before he even gets to start football, and my sister will probably do the same to the girl my now ex-boyfriend is currently finger-fucking. It's what I would do."

She's probably right.

I slide my cell phone out and text Valen because I know he is probably there. It's initiation night.

Veronica: Where are you?

Valen: Why do you want to know? Are you all out of fresh victims already?

Veronica: No. I'm bored actually. I wanted to see what you jock losers are up to.

Valen: Ohio frat party. The jocks' initiation party.

Veronica: Why are you there?

Valen: You know why.

Valen wants no-strings sex to feed his addiction. A good-looking guy like Valen and one of the sons of Kenyan will have no issues getting pussy.

Veronica: Be careful. They get attached.

I love teasing him. He thinks it's some twisted scheme I'm up to, but if he only knew the real me, maybe he would think differently.

Valen: Are you coming to rescue me, Veronica? Do you need me to FEED your demons?

Since Reid and Jess happened, Valen has spiraled into a fuck frenzy.

Veronica: You know you couldn't satisfy me. I wonder if your balls ever dropped.

Valen: Come over and find out. Tell me how big they are.;)

He's drunk or almost there. He would have never offered, otherwise.

Veronica: Maybe I will.

Not for what he thinks, but I need to help my friends out before they screw up their lives over some asshole with a hard-on for naïve girls. At least I think they are *my* friends. I glance at Melody, watching her wipe the tears from her red-rimmed eyes. "Did your parents leave the keys to their second car? Can you drive?" I ask.

She nods. "Where are we going?"

"To make sure your brother and sister don't fuck up what they worked so hard for, but I need something to wear to a frat party."

She smiles, her eyes lighting up. "Yeah, I have the spare key to their car, and I have something you could wear, but how are you going to get in? You need to know someone."

"I do."

"Who?"

I don't *really* need to know anyone. My reputation proceeds me, but I can't tell Melody that. Or Adam. Or anyone. I just hope this doesn't blow up in my face. Reid and the Bedford twins don't hang out at parties since their wives are at home. Valen is obviously drunk or on some type of drug. I can use Melody as an excuse for showing up and confronting the little prick before Adam and his sister find out.

It's not like anyone will announce who I am to the entire room like a bunch of idiots. Adam thinks I live in a small house on the outskirts of Kenyan with only my mom. I always make an excuse when he sometimes gives me a ride home because it's raining, and I ask him to leave me at the corner, or my mother will freak out if she sees me alone with a guy. I hate lying, but lies are comfortable to tell because they are easy and hide the truth.

ALARIC

I'M HOME GETTING ready to call it quits from my computer. I've been digging into Dorian Black's finances. He's in the red but barely scraping by. He could turn it around, but he's too stupid to do the work. *Lazy prick.* The last thing you need is a lazy CEO running a business's hard-earned dollars into the ground. Expenditures are through the roof. He wouldn't have to decrease his spending habits if he put in more effort. It is probably why he wanted me to merge with him, so I could be the duck to do all the work while he played.

I've worked my ass off so I was allowed a free pass on the marrying requirement at the end of my senior year in college. Cash is king in the Order's world. And I know how to make loads of it from a laptop.

My phone rings, and I look at the incoming call. Reid.

"What," I answer impatiently.

"I need you to do something for me."

"I have. I got Tara off your back. You got the girl. She accepted your crazy ass and married you. Now what?"

"I need you to go check on Valen. He's at a frat party. Initiation night."

"And? He's a big boy. He can handle himself. We both know why he's there. What's the problem?"

"He's drunk and high, Alaric. After the whole Jess thing—"

"What? He has a problem getting pussy. He'll fuck five more and get over it. He has to marry Melissa. Get to the point," I grit.

I'm annoyed. I'm not his savior. He needs to get his shit together. I lean back, hearing the leather in my chair groan like my patience.

"He's there alone, and I don't trust anyone else to get him out of trouble."

I let out a puff of air from my mouth, pinching my nose. "Fine. I'll go get him but make sure it's the last time, Reid. I don't have time for this shit."

"Not everyone is a killer like you, Alaric."

He means Valen doesn't have a strong mind to handle his own shit because he fell for a girl that wasn't his.

"You know what they say, killers are smart. Most of them are geniuses."

"Whatever, dick." And hangs up.

Now that my night is screwed. I have to get mentally prepared to go to the last place I ever thought I would end up at: an initiation party. Some people might recognize me; some might not. I am one of the sons of Kenyan because my uncle and father are brothers as well as founders of the Order. I just choose to be excluded from the whole Sons of Kenyan dynamic when they all hang out. I'm not in college anymore, but I still have a reputation.

I'm untouchable.

The dealmaker and dealbreaker.

The sinner.

Now I have to help one of our own from doing something stupid he will regret later at a frat party.

I check the time, and it's half past eleven at night. I'm getting dressed like I'm still in college because I can't show up dressed in a suit to a college party, looking like a fucking parent who is searching for his kid.

Heading out in my Ferrari SF90 Stradale, I take the highway, remembering the last time I was at a college party that wasn't in Kenyan, and all I can think about is *her*. Tears falling from her eyes, the color of the clearest blue sky like fat drops on a window pane, play on my mind like a loop and I hate the memory. I grip the steering wheel and shift the car, pressing the gas and hearing it roar down the road.

Follow the rules.

Fuck the rules and fuck her.

She deserved it.

I pull up on the same street, and nothing has changed since I graduated college. People milling about. Cars parked down the road.

The faint thumping music. People with Solo cups in their hands, drunk and high, laughing without a care in the world, except for who they are going to fuck next. Or making sure they have the answers to the next test and work turned in for class, so they can stay and do it all over again the next weekend.

I shut the door of my car and arm the alarm. "Hey, nice car, man," one of the guys says from the porch. "You borrowed it from your dad?"

I almost choke on my spit and clear my throat. "Yeah, man, my parents are divorced 'n shit. My dad lets me borrow it when he's out of town."

"Not a bad way to get pussy."

I walk up the steps and smirk. "Yeah, the car gets the chicks every time."

I can tell the guy is high as a kite, practically falling over the wooden railing.

Fucking idiot.

I'm going to kill Reid. I hate these Ohio pricks. Most of them think they're hot shit and think every girl is a game because they play a sport.

"Go on in, man; there's plenty of liquor and pussy." He laughs. I blink. "Just pick one. This one hot chick came in with another one all pissed and shit. She has dark hair, but she has these eyes. All the guys are going crazy over her."

I raise my brows, pulling open the door. "I bet."

I need to find Valen and get the fuck out of here before I lose it and punch someone, or worse, make them disappear. I just hope I don't find him fucking in a room somewhere.

Making my way through the throng of bodies, I walk toward the back patio, where a group of people are forming a circle around a girl losing her shit and screaming at a guy with a girl in his lap.

"You fucking asshole!" she yells.

The girl sitting in the guy's lap tears her lips from his neck. "Get lost, bitch," she snarls.

The guy angles his head, wide-eyed, and lifts his hands in mock surrender like the girl fell on his lap and he doesn't know how she got there. "Melody, it's not what you think."

Laughter. "Damn, dude," one guy says. "That's fucked up. You got caught. Own that shit."

The girl with ash blonde hair turns around, and I notice that she's young. She has to be fifteen or sixteen tops. This asshole is fucking a sixteen-year-old?

Valen comes up behind me, and I roll my eyes because he keeps looking at a girl with the same ash-blonde hair arguing with a guy on the other side. The guy pushes her to the side when she steps in front of him, but I don't miss Valen's hands balling into fists or the hard set of his jaw. Interesting.

"Adam, stop!" she screams when he lunges toward the guy with the girl on his lap.

He doesn't. Adam walks up and punches the guy in the face, causing the girl to fall off his lap. "You think my little sister is some whore you can play with? Huh, bitch!"

The guy gets up and rushes Adam to the floor, and they go at it. Blow for blow. Fists flying. Flesh connecting with flesh.

"Stop it! Both of you!" I hear a loud voice that I recognize, causing me to whip my head in that direction.

"No fucking way! She came!" Valen points, and I follow, landing on eyes that haunt my dreams. "I dig the hair," he adds.

"Shut the fuck up," I growl.

I don't want her to notice me. Not yet. Why is she here? Veronica looks...different. She's not the same girl I first met and decided to fuck that night. I look around but don't see a guy then I remember what the dork out front said about the girl with the eyes. She came with a female. Putting two and two together. She showed up with the young girl. The question is, how does she know a girl that young, and why the change of hair?

I watch when another asshole from Ohio with a football jacket saunters up next to her. I try to relax when I catch myself grinding my teeth with how he eats her up with his eyes. But what I notice are his hands.

VERONICA

THIS IS EXACTLY why I came. To avoid this crap. I knew this would get out of hand.

"Adam, get off of him," I demand.

Adam looks up, his eyes full of anger, and I notice a cut on his bottom lip already swelling. He might hate me right now, but I'm helping him out. He can get kicked off the team or lose his spot, or worse, get expelled, losing his scholarship before setting foot on campus.

Matt from the restaurant the other day comes up behind me. "You changed your mind, princess?" I flinch at the word *princess*. I turn to face him and watch his eyes slide down my face landing on the swell of my breasts.

He thinks it's cute. To me, it's the same as calling me a worthless whore.

"Fuck off, Matt. She didn't come here for that," Adam tells him, wiping his hands on his jeans.

"I doubt that, Adam. You need to worry about Zack fucking around with your little sister. It's initiation night, and she's fair game. You come; you play."

I glance at Adam, but he looks away. He knew. He wanted me to watch Melody, so she wouldn't show up or find out.

My eyes narrow on Matt, but I plaster a fake smile, making it appear to him that I'm game. Melody steps back and stands behind her brother and her sister, Madison. I reminded Melody right before we walked in that whatever happened and whatever I did, not to interfere.

I lick my bottom lip, scraping my teeth along the skin and pulling it in my mouth, slowly, watching Matt's eyes follow the movement. "Oh yeah? How does that work?" I ask, playing dumb.

I know first-hand how it works, but he doesn't know that, and without my blonde hair and normal clothes, he probably wouldn't know that I'm not from here but from Kenyan. Initiation night at an Ohio frat party means they make men out of the freshman jocks coming in. Testing to see what they can handle and can't. With pussy. Or dick. Or both. It just depends. It also lets everyone know who's easy.

Matt grins and looks around as everyone goes silent, waiting for him to answer. "Depends on what you want and what you can take."

I get closer, letting him think he will get what he wants. "Is that why you invite girls to come here? Get them drunk. Maybe a little high to see how far their legs spread." I close the rest of the space between us, sliding my hand up the stuffed crotch of his jeans, watching the lust pool in his eyes.

When I look behind Matt, I meet gray eyes glaring at me.

Alaric.

My heart begins to beat hard inside my chest. Awareness that he's watching me, causing the nerves to rattle under my skin. Reid must have called him to rescue his friend from fucking everyone inside the frat house. Valen looks between me and Alaric, knowing a storm is brewing. You can feel the tension crackling like static electricity.

I almost laugh because my hand is still on Matt's pegged jeans. I was right. Matt's cock is small, but I'm surprised, he's about six-two. Poor guy. No wonder he treats girls like he does because he lacks in the dick department.

My eyes flick to Matt's, and he has a bitter smile. "Did you think I wouldn't figure out who you were? You're Veronica Devlin and a skank. Everyone in this frat house knows who you are." He lowers his voice. "But I don't think your friends here know that. Do they?"

I'm used to it hearing the rumors about me, but it doesn't matter because I have to marry someone. Even if they don't like what they hear about me, true or not. It buys me time. I stopped caring what they all thought anyway. The man standing behind Matt saw that my reputation here and on campus at Kenyan was tarnished. It doesn't stop the guys wanting to fuck me, though. I just use it to my advantage. Like right now. I don't want Adam and his sisters to know about my past or who I really am coming from these people.

"Tell you what? I'll leave quietly, and I won't tell everyone here how small your hard cock feels in my hand." I lean close and lick his earlobe, causing him to shudder then whisper, "It will be our little secret. Because we both know they will all believe it coming from me. The skaaank."

His eyes darken, and he leans in, placing his lips close to my cheek. "Kiss me. I will make this all go away…if you kiss me. Right now…we both get what we want."

He doesn't want me. He wants to show people he can get any girl he wants, including me. It's all a show. I don't want to kiss him. I want to rip his dick off because guys like him use girls and then talk about them like they mean nothing.

My eyes flick to Alaric briefly and then back to Matt. *Stop thinking about it too much, Veronica. Remember what he did to you every time you see him.* Then the words *whore* and *disgusting* fill my head like a mantra. I look at Matt's moss-green eyes, sliding my hands up his chest. He pulls me closer, and I want to cringe when I feel his small, hard cock on my belly.

He angles his head and takes my lips in a punishing kiss. He tastes like alcohol and pepperoni, and I want to gag, but anyone looking at us would never know it. It seems like I did come here because of him. His hands slide down to grip my ass under my skirt, and my eyes pop open, and I tear my lips from his, taking three steps back.

He bites his bottom lip. "Fuck."

I sink my teeth into the soft skin of my lower lip, tasting blood to mask the disgusting taste of his spit. His eyes are full of hunger and something I recognize. The predatory look that he would force himself on me if I wasn't standing in the middle of the back patio of a frat house full of people. Matt wouldn't ask. He would take.

"Adam, take Melody and Madison home," I say, without looking their way, but from the corner of my eye, I see him push Melody and Madison toward the exit, without looking at me and storming off.

Matt flicks his gaze to Zack. "You're off the team. Get your shit and get out."

"What the fuck, Matt! It's initiation night!"

"I know, and I'm the captain. You're a freshman, and you broke the rules. No girlfriends showing up on initiation night."

"What about her?" Zack points in my direction.

Matt smirks, and everyone snickers. "She's not my girlfriend. She came to play."

I walk down the sidewalk toward the bus stop. I remember where it is and know the route back to Kenyan. My babysitting duties are over, but I dread going home, so I decide to head to the dorms instead. I check the time, and a laugh almost bubbles up my throat. 1:30 a.m. This was nearly the same time I ran out of this same frat house the night with Alaric.

The night my whole world turned to shit and has been since then. My life keeps getting better, but not in a good way. Every time I think I've made friends, it all turns to shit because of my past. Because of Alaric. I tried texting Adam, but he ignored my texts and calls. I probably lost a friend, but if he knew who I really was, he probably would tell me to go to hell and fuck off anyway. *I did what was right*, I tell myself. It felt dirty, but it was worth it.

I hear a roaring engine from a car coming down the street behind me, but I keep walking, ignoring the sound getting louder. I look straight ahead, counting the concrete slabs from the sidewalk in my head, walking past the frat houses on fraternity row.

I watch the sleek black car pull up ahead by the curb. The taillights glow red like evil eyes. I pause for a second but continue to walk and decide just to ignore it. The dark-tinted window slides down when I'm about to pass the car, and I recognize the tattoos on the hands gripping the steering wheel, which only causes me to walk faster.

"Where's your driver?" he calls out.

I keep walking. I've never spoken to Alaric since that night and don't plan to. Ever.

The car crawls forward, but I keep walking.

"Stop being stupid and get in. It isn't safe walking out here alone. I'll take you home."

He didn't care that night, and I made it to hell just fine. This night is no different, but my father isn't waiting to make me pay for my so-called sins this time.

I don't stop and he continues to follow me until I reach the bus stop. I sit and check the time, fifteen minutes until the last bus for the night. If I missed it, I would have to call a cab or an Uber. I like to avoid spending money if I don't have to, so I'll wait for the bus.

"Are you joking right now? The bus?"

Yeah, asshole. It's called public transportation, but a stuck-up dick like him probably has never been on a bus.

"So you're going to sit out here alone until a bus comes with who knows what on it." I roll my eyes and look away. "I'm going to call your father."

My head snaps in his direction as sheer terror flows through my veins. "Fuck off!" I yell angrily.

"She speaks. That got your attention, didn't it? You don't want to piss off Daddy, huh?"

A brief gust of rage flows through me, but I tamper it down. He's just patronizing me. Trying to get under my skin. *Refrain from showing him a reaction, Veronica.*

His gray eyes slide over my crossed legs, making me wish I had pants on. I don't want him looking at me. It confuses me. And the fact that I hated what he did to me doesn't help. I've paid for it with my body and my blood.

"I'm not going to lie and say I wasn't surprised to see you there, but then I saw you with the Ohio State QB, I figured you must have run out of cocks to fuck. I thought you would have toned it down by now, but I guess I was right the first time. You are a whore."

"So I've heard," I reply sarcastically. "Are you done? Because it seems like you love to keep tabs on me since you know how many cocks I take."

"Not at all. That is just what I overhear. I was being generous since I saw to it Valen made it home. I owe it to the Order and all."

"You mean you don't want people pointing fingers if something happens to me and you happened to drive by. Trust me, no one would care."

"That is not true. Your father would be devastated."

A maniacal laugh bubbles out of my throat, and I do what I do best, act like they expect me to, so I don't fall into a self-deprecating puddle of self-pity. I widen my legs so that my panty-covered pussy is exposed. I watch his eyes flick between my gaze and my panties. Maybe he'll leave. "Is this what you were hoping for?" I purr, pasting a fake salacious smile on my lips. "You know, ever since you fucked me like a rabid dog and told everyone what you thought about me, it's made them curious to see if it's true. All they want is to fuck me." I slouch on the bench, widening my legs, and watch him blink in confusion when I finally say, "Thank you for making me their filthy whore. It reminds me of how much I hate you." I snap my legs closed. "Now fuck off."

He shakes his head offended but grinning. "You're just pissed off that you were outed and couldn't trap me. Come to think of it, are you still desperate and fuck random guys on your period?"

I'm relieved the lights of the bus appear, and he will have no choice but to pull away from the curb. After all this time, he still thinks of me the same way. I was so stupid in thinking he was different from the rest. He was a mistake. Poor judgment because I was trying to find someone to feel something genuine with just once. But it's too late for me. The damage is done, because I chose wrong.

I get up when it gets closer and walk toward the curb, not answering him, waiting for the bus to open its doors so I can get on. I sit in the back, relieved there are only two other people on, and watch as Alaric pulls away from the curb, roaring down the street.

I close my eyes and remember the night I walked in on him with another girl. It was at a Kenyan party after a swim meet. I was surprised he showed up since he had graduated. Reid was acting his usual self. It was six months into our freshman year, and Alicia was already gone. They killed her for eloping with Prey. It was a message. Loud and clear, and my father was part of it because he voted like an executioner.

Nothing has mattered since Alicia's death. I hide the pain along with my little notes of self-pity. I have no one but my regrets to keep me company. I should have told Reid when she promised me not to tell anyone she was leaving with Chase, but I didn't. I promised her I wouldn't and that I would make sure Reid found his happily ever after.

After I found out that my father voted for them to kill her, I knew it had everything to do with me. No one knew, but I did. Charles Devlin voted yes because of *me.* If I wasn't her friend to begin with, maybe she would still be alive, which makes it all my fault. I should have known Charles Devlin would take the one pure thing I had: my best friend.

That night at the party in Kenyan, I walked up to the house looking for the bathroom. I didn't think anything of it when Reid looked at me, but I knew it wasn't really Reid. His eyes told me it wasn't. They were dark and malicious with intent. They told me I deserved what I would see and feel. I opened the door, and he was fucking Becca Hales from behind. She hated me. But I'll never forgot the look in his eyes when he saw me standing at the threshold or how he told her she was beautiful and felt good. The way he held her and placed soft kisses on her neck. The way he never was with me—the way no one has ever touched me.

Because girls like me didn't deserve pleasure. They deserved pain.

And I believed it.

I watch the streetlights glow through the big windows of the bus as we pass. My eyes feel heavy, so I decide to close them for five minutes until the bus arrive on campus.

I nod and wash myself, listening to the sounds of his heavy breathing. A cold chill slides down my arms, and a knot forms in my throat, trying not to let the sob escape from my lips as he pleasures himself.

"So beautiful. The devil was the most beautiful angel God had ever created. It is no wonder he would create something so exquisite. Spread your pussy for me, princess," he demands, while he beats his dick faster.

The sound makes me want to throw up. I keep my eyes shut because if I open them, I don't want to cry out and make it worse. I do as he asks and hate myself every time. Every time he makes me bathe in front of him. I just clean myself and imagine there is someone else in the room.

Someone I want.

Who I always wanted.

I say his name repeatedly in my head, trying to picture the only time he looked at me like I was something. I shouldn't because of what he did, but no one has ever looked at me any different.

I jerk, waking up when I hear someone's voice. "Ma'am."

My eyes try to adjust to the bright light. "Huh?"

"This is the last stop. Kenyan."

"Shit." I look around, relieved it's just the bus driver. He looks like Mortimer Snerd sitting behind the wheel.

I walk down the aisle, cursing myself for falling asleep. "Err, thank you."

"Be careful," he says as I run off the bus in front of Drury Hall.

VERONICA

I RUN inside Drury Hall and head to the showers located in the female dorms. I don't want to go home, but I desperately need a shower to scrub my body. If I go home right now, I know I'll fall asleep and I'm afraid I'll have the same dream. I feel numb. Seeing Alaric again and reminding me how he hurt me triggered this need to forget. I keep glancing at the skirt I borrowed from Melody to see if there is blood.

I enter the back door with the skeleton key I found one night in the library when the librarian was busy in the back room and walk down the dark corridor, bypassing the overnight security guard. By the time I enter the shower, I'm out of breath. My lungs burn with trying to stay hidden from security. I close my eyes and look down at my hands. They're trembling.

When I calm down, I turn on the shower, hearing the water hit the tile, and watch the steam from the scalding hot water rise to the ceiling. I remember overhearing Draven saying that his twin hated bathtubs because that is where they found his mother after she slit her wrists. I have to say I agree with him in hating them—especially being inside them. The Bedford twins have their reasons, and I have mine.

After getting undressed, I stand under the spray and look down at the razor blade in my hand. I started cutting when I was twelve. Alicia helped me stop for a while, but after Alaric and then her death, I couldn't stop. Whenever I couldn't cope or hated myself for something I did, I'd cut. It reminds me that I'm still alive—that I'm still here and most importantly, it's pain I can control, making sure it's hidden. The most important part was keeping it hidden from my father by cutting the skin near my inner ankles, inner thighs, or places no one would ever look or notice.

I sit on the tile, push my hair to the side and find a spot near my ankle. I press the tip, closing my eyes, and feel the first sting like the rush of a million needles. I watch the drop of blood flow down my heel to the tile floor. My eyes sting a bit from the heat of the water as I watch the blood flow like a river to the center, gurgling down the drain.

I find another spot when the bleeding becomes too much, watching the blood pool and mix with the water. I slide my fingers down my thighs, seeing the faint bruises, and find a spot scraping the back of my neck with my blunt nails. Tears fall down my cheeks, hating myself like I do every day. I hate my existence, but I have learned to help others in a way. They don't see it, but I don't care.

"Is this how you deal with shit?" I freeze. I look at the blade between my fingers close to the skin on my thigh. "Look at me, Veronica."

I turn around slowly, not caring if I'm naked. *I stopped caring a long time ago.* My dark hair is plastered on the top of my head like a helmet, but I keep my eyes on the tile, watching the blood flow from the cut on my ankle, bleeding out like the tears on my cheeks.

"W-what do you want, Valen? Why are you here?"

"Look at me, Veronica."

I raise my head slowly and see him leaning on the tile far enough so he doesn't get wet, but I don't meet his eyes because that's the last thing I need. Pity.

"Give me the blade."

"No."

"You're stronger than this."

I laugh, baring my teeth, and tap my temple with my finger. "You don't know what I am." I pause. "I-I don't know what I am. The Bible says if you kill yourself, you go straight to hell, but God didn't specify what that hell was." I get up and angle my head, trying not to break down in front of him. The sound of the water gets louder as my heart beats erratically inside my chest.

He tries to move forward, but I step back under the spray, looking at him boldly. "Go home, Valen."

"I'm not. I'm not leaving you here." He rolls his eyes. "Fine," he mutters, removing his shirt, pants, and shoes.

"I'm not going to kill myself," I say with wide eyes, instantly turning around.

"Tell me what's wrong, Veronica. You can't go home like this. I can't leave you like this. Tell me what to do or what you need."

He stands behind me when I turn around and shut my eyes, hoping he gives up and goes away. I don't know why he followed me or how he knew I was here, but it doesn't matter right now. I feel dirty, ugly, and worthless.

"Do you think I'm a good person?" I ask, my voice breaking.

I know he doesn't. No one does, but I need to hear it. I need him to say it. Because one thing Valen is, he's honest. There is no bullshitting with him. He just has a sex addiction. A woman wouldn't know if he wants her for real or if he's just trying to feed his demons, but when he's done, he regrets it as soon as it's over. I've seen how he shuts down right after at Kenyan parties when he comes out of a bedroom after fucking some girl. It's like an off button. Everything shuts down, and the lust in his eyes dies like it never happened, except for Jess. He fell for her, but he saw how Jess looked at Reid and he looked at her. I think we all did.

"I think we all have good in us…you know." I nod. "But whatever you are going through right now, I just need you to trust me. I need you to give me the blade, sweetheart."

I nod again and hand it to him, watching him place it on the brown bench attached to the tiled wall beside his shirt and jeans.

"I'm not trying to kill myself. I need you to know that."

He nods. "You need to feel the pain."

Tears slide down my cheeks because he gets it. He gets me.

"All I've ever known is pain."

He looks confused under the water, causing his hair to stick to his forehead. Water slides down his chiseled chest. Valen is built like a swimmer with little to no body fat on his tall frame. He's good-looking but a heartbreaker.

"What do you mean?"

I cringe inwardly because I said too much. I place my finger over my lips. "Shh." The skin between his brows crinkles, so I slide my finger to my ear and tap slowly and whisper, "It's not what you know but what you see and hear."

"Da-fuq?"

I shake my head, frustrated that he doesn't understand. I look down at my feet, the blood slowing its descent on the tile and walk to the next stall and turn on the water and then the next one, so the sound of water echoes louder against the tiled walls. I walk back, not caring I'm leaving footprints stained with blood on the floor.

He wipes the water from his face and steps close. I place my finger over his lips, telling him to be quiet. I pull his head down, so our lips almost brush and whisper, "They can hear you if they are listening." He raises his brow like I'm fucking crazy, and to most people, I sound like I am. He stands numbly when I turn around and slide my naturally dark hair to the side, and I hear the audible intake of his breath.

My hands begin to tremble at what he sees—what I'm allowing him to see. I turn around to see his expression and widen my eyes while keeping my finger to my lips, so he will remain quiet, shaking my head. His eyes widen in disbelief.

"You can leave now. I need to get back home. You were great, by the way." His lips drop open. "This stays between us," I drone on. "You wouldn't want Melissa to know about us."

Crazy talk. All of it.

But he knows.

He gets it.

He gets me.

And he knows he can't utter a word.

To anyone.

ALARIC

I BANG my fist on the steering wheel repeatedly. "Fuck! Fuck! Fuck!" I look down at my hands smeared with blood from my split knuckles. I lost control. I always lose control when it comes to her. I don't even feel the sting from the adrenaline rush.

"Do you regret it?" Reid asks through the Bluetooth in my car.

Do I regret it?

"No."

"Relax, you didn't kill him, so stop beating yourself up over it."

I slide my black hooded sweater off my head and wipe my hands on it. "Yeah, but I'm trying to *not* kill people."

He snorts. "I hate to break it to you, but that is part of what you do, Alaric."

I let out an audible breath. "Whatever."

"Did Valen get home safe?"

"I'm not an Uber, and he wasn't drunk. He left in his car before—"

"You went back."

"Yeah, and I sent someone to clean it up when I was done."

"Do you need anything from me besides therapy?"

I laugh, and then it fades a little. "I don't need therapy. I need you to handle your boy."

"This is not about him, Alaric. It's about her. It's always been about her for you. Ever since that night, it's like—"

"Like what?" I snap, pinching my nose, not caring if I get blood all over my face. I'm parked in front of my house. I need a shower and a drink.

"Like you feel guilt for once in your life and not the angry kind. Everything that has to do with her is hot and cold. But you don't have to worry for much longer. The next meeting. Her father is going to announce who she's going to marry. Her time has run out. No man or son of one wants to marry her."

Her words play in my head, haunting me. 'All they want is to fuck me.'

Good, I tell myself.

"Jess is worried about her for whatever reason. She keeps asking me if I know who she'll end up with."

"Why the fuck should she care? Whoever the prick picks to marry her crazy ass is doing everyone a favor."

"She won't tell me, but Jess is…delicate."

He told me what happened, and I facilitated the vote, and the Order didn't get involved. I'm on the Consortium, but I have the most influence out of all the members of the Order. I cleaned up the mess.

"It's not our problem. There is nothing we can do. It could be anyone that isn't betrothed."

"Who do you think it is?" he asks, and that funny dread creeps up, but I push it down, like a weakness I must eliminate.

"I don't know, and I don't care. Every time she is around, lives are ruined. No one can do anything about it anyway. Rules are rules." I think about Alicia, and a surge of anger for being unable to save my flesh and blood sparks fury like a gout of flames within me. "Fuck her. I gotta go."

Placing my hands on the tile in my shower, I let the hot water beat down on my back, releasing the tension. The glass shower door opens behind me. Cold hands slide around my waist.

"You need me?"

I don't respond.

I need release. The hard, unforgiving kind. The brutal kind that calms me. I push off the tile and turn, looking at Sasha, my secretary. Her small breasts don't do it for me, but she is nothing I like, which is what I want. To escape from what I like, to focus on what I need. I press the screen, and Disturbed's "Down with the Sickness" plays through the speakers.

I grip Sasha by the throat, guiding her so she can get on her knees. I pump my cock and push the head inside her mouth to the back of her throat, and she takes it.

She takes it all. I fuck her hard, constricting the air from her lungs. Tears are pooling in her eyes. Spit is running down her chin, foaming on the bottom, trying not to choke on my size. I fuck her mouth hard and fast, not caring. Not giving a fuck. I close my eyes and see clear blue, which pushes me over the edge. My fingers fist Sasha's hair, causing her to cry out. The music and water drown out her screams, and then she sputters when I come down her throat.

When I pull out, I hear a string of curses. "You motherfucker! I couldn't breathe."

I walk out after I wash her spit and cum off my cock. "You should've held your breath longer." I grab the towel off the hook and turn my head. "You can see yourself out."

"I don't know why I agree to this shit."

Because I'm a Riodrick-Riordan. I'm a billionaire who can give you what no man can. Money, protection, and a life you could only dream of, and the best part of all, I'm forbidden fruit. The kind you want the most because I'm unattainable. A challenge.

I scratch my left brow as I watch her small, curveless body and small tits bounce with too-large nipples as she scrambles to dry herself and get her clothes on. She knows what I want, and the last thing I need is her running her mouth. I'm not a nice man. I never said I was. I'm not romantic or want more than what I ask. She came here. I didn't force her, but that is the problem with some people who don't know how to take no for an answer when they want more. They expect more because they feel that they can meet your needs.

"Then don't."

She slides her shirt over her almost flat chest. "Don't what?"

"Don't agree to do it. I asked specifically for one thing, you came, and now it's over."

She looks defeated, but that doesn't stop her from sinking her self-esteem even lower. "I'm sorry I overreacted. I'm leaving. I just—"

I stare at the wall, not caring what she is trying to say. I try to keep things convenient with the whole boss and secretary thing because I don't feel like dating women who think I can give them more when I don't. It's not her; I feel like this about every woman. I just like my dick licked. I'm a man. Sue me.

"I will always want more from you, Alaric," she continues. I roll my eyes when I give her my back and wait…until I hear the door shut and watch the screen by my bed as she walks out the front door into her car from the surveillance camera.

Relief.

It's what I feel after she leaves. It's how I feel after every woman leaves when I'm done.

Except for one woman.

And all I can think about is destroying her.

VERONICA

"YOU SHOULD KNOW *by now that I detest having to wait, Veronica."*

My ears become assaulted by the clinking sounds of the buckle, which sound like nails being dragged over a chalkboard. "Get in the bath, Princess."

I take another step forward while observing the heated steam from the ancient tub. I can't help but pray that something will drag me under and drown me once I step inside.

As I undress, taking care not to get any water on the extensions of my platinum hair, my heart beats so hard in my chest, and my voice is screaming inside my head to turn around and run. But I can't. They would just kill me and make it look self-inflicted. Sometimes I wish I had the balls to do it myself.

Sometimes.

The steaming hot water causes me to wince from the discomfort it causes on my skin. I close my eyes as I take the bar of soap in both hands and work it into a lather. The smell of some weird leaves I hate slides over my skin like a ritual.

"You are such a good girl. I love to watch you purge yourself of the wrongs you've done, the sins you've committed, Veronica. You're a sinner because you were consummated by sin—born out of it. In the eyes of God, you are an abomination that is on par with having a kid with a bastard, and I will be your savior, but you must pray for forgiveness."

I look to the corner of the room and see a red dot of light flashing like a tiny beacon. Something was in front of it, but it was unmistakable, and I didn't imagine it. It looks like a recording device.

"What is that?" I ask, pointing to the corner where the light was flashing, making sure to never maintain eye contact. I hate to see the glint of mockery and spite every time I ask about something.

I hear the groaning of the chair but keep washing my skin over and over, acclimating to the heat of the water.

"It's nothing. There's nothing. Now show us how you let him put it in you. What did you say? Everyone knows you're very clever. Like a demon sucking cock to the root. So persuasive in doing what is needed and then expiated…sin is committed because it lives inside all of us. But we have to learn to live sinlessly in a world plagued by demons." I look up and see eyes that glitter hypnotically and a dry smile aimed at my body. "You sin with pleasure, Veronica, and here is where you will repent with pain." The leather belt slaps against my thighs as the sound of my voice gasping from the bite of the sting on my wet thighs fills the room. Rough fingers pull them apart, leaving white marks that then turn red with angry welts on my skin. "He wasn't yours to take!"

I push the wooden door to the confessional, knowing the priest is still here. I keep the hood from my coat in place and the rosary between my hands as if I'm praying.

"Welcome, my child. If we confess our sins, God is faithful, forgives, and cleanses us. But we must confess our sins."

I follow and motion the sign of the cross. "Forgive me, Father, for I have sinned. It's been two weeks since my last confession. I have tried to be good, but the voices inside my head won't stop. They don't help. I want to do good, but I have to repent for the sins I have already committed."

"What kind?"

"Sex. The kind out of wedlock, and I think of sex and what it does. How it destroys. I also keep thinking…what does God think of fatherless children? I mean, if they didn't have one."

"God says he is the father to the fatherless. There is a place for them with the Lord." I wonder where that place is because if he was a father, why do I feel so alone and unloved. Why do I feel so much pain? "Are you fatherless, my child?"

I shake my head. "No. I have a father."

I do, and I don't because he hates me.

"Then you have nothing to worry about."

"What if I feel like he isn't."

"Parents are to bring their child's discipline to the Lord. Now tell me about these voices and thoughts–"

After I've said my prayers, I walk up to the fourth floor inside the left wing on campus and into Dr. Wick's office for my scheduled appointment.

"I'm glad you could make it, Veronica."

"I'm ecstatic to be here," I respond, taking a seat after shutting the door.

She crosses her legs like a queen, but it's mostly because she is squeezed into a black pencil skirt, and there is no other option.

I open the inner pocket of my coat and light a Virginia Slims, taking a drag and exhaling with an audible sigh of relief, watching the smoke in the air like a dark cloud.

"Do you have to smoke in here?"

"I prefer weed. But if I have to be here and they are paying you to, then yes." I tap the middle of the cancer stick with my middle finger so the ash can fall to the floor, hoping I make a hole in the carpet. Maybe she would remember me by the burnt hole and not forget me as soon as she closes the file after telling my father everything I've said because this bitch doesn't know the meaning of patient confidentiality.

"How are the voices? The dreams?"

I take a drag, exhale, and tamp the cigarette on the plastic arm of the chair, and I smile inwardly because she's annoyed. But so am I because it's the same narrative.

"They're still there." I tap my temple and smile. "The voices in my head keep telling me to do stuff."

"Like?"

I watch her solemnly as she waits for my answer. "Like fucking, Mrs. Wick. They tell me to fuck, and then I have these dreams where they tell me that I have sinned. In those dreams, I'm nothing but a sinner."

She shifts in her seat uncomfortably and places her thumb on her bottom lip like she is thinking, but she isn't. She's listening.

"Is that the only time you have intercourse? When the voices tell you to?"

I laugh hysterically. "Well, of course. They tell me who to fuck and how hard I need to fuck them."

"How do you feel after?"

"How do you feel after you fuck, Dr. Wick?"

"We are not discussing me. We are discussing you."

"Of course!" I snap my fingers looking up at the ceiling. "It started when I was twelve, you know—the voices telling me to do it, but it didn't manifest until the sacrifice."

"The night they all ridiculed you at the party?" My head whips forward, and I snap my fingers, watching with glee as she jolts like she is zapped in her chair. "You're really on to something there, doc."

"What am I on?"

"Some good shit. You need to give me some."

"What do you want me to give you?"

"Something to sleep like happy pills. My mother is on them all the time. You should see her. She's perfect."

I need the pills to sleep because I'm tired, not from the night shifts with Dorothy at the restaurant, but from not being able to get actual sleep when I do come home. Nothing has helped. Not tea or reading. Nothing.

I watch her tear the paper off the prescription pad after she writes something on it, so I can give it to the front desk before I leave. She probably gave me tranquilizers, and I need them.

She hands me the script and asks, "Are you sleeping at all?"

"Sometimes. It's why I want the pills."

"I suggest relaxation and massages. A spa to relieve anxiety and thoughts that can cause you not to sleep. I will make a note and send a treatment plan. The sleeping pills will help, but I need you to try to curve your *actions* and avoid what triggers them."

"You want me to avoid being around men, so I don't fuck."

She gives me a pointed look, and I raise my arms and stretch like a cat waking up from a nap. "Alright, doc. I'll avoid all the triggers but can't make any promises." I sigh. "I have to get married soon you know."

"Do you know to who?"

I grin. "Are you asking if I know who will put their semen inside me? The one they call a sinner. Whore. The answer is no, Dr. Wick. I don't know who will make me bleed in sacrifice."

A glimmer of sadness crosses her features for a second, and then it's gone. Her mask is back in place, and I go for the kill because... why not. She doesn't care. She is getting paid to do a job.

"How's your daughter, Dr. Wick? I heard she was going through...a rough patch."

Her head lifts, her eyes flat. "Times up. I will have to see you more often since you're on sleeping medication. If it doesn't work, I recommend observation."

She is trying to deviate from what happened to her daughter. After Dravin fucked her ten ways from Sunday, the girl got attached. Poor thing needs therapy, from what I heard.

"Don't be so hard on her, Dr. Wick." I grin. "We all have voices telling us to do things."

The clink of a marker on the tray attached to the dry-erase board resonates inside the lecture hall. "Whose mistakes caused the tragedy between Romeo and Juliet?" Professor Elliot asks, sweeping his gaze across the room but is only met by silence. He opens his arms wide mockingly. "Anyone?"

I decided to take classic literature as an elective, even though my major is economics, because I wanted it to give me a perspective that I don't have, and one of them is romance, except, Shakespeare's *Romeo and Juliet* is a tragedy, but to me, it's true love.

The professor waits impatiently when no one volunteers to answer. His eyes scan the room once more, so he can call on someone. Garret and Dravin look at each other. Reid and Jess smile when Valen blurts, "Pick someone," then coughs, causing Gia to giggle and the rest of the class to laugh. I was surprised they all signed up for this class, but here we are.

"Mr. Vikiar, since you are so inclined for me to pick someone, why don't you answer for the rest of the class."

"It was Romeo's mistakes that led to the tragedy," Valen responds.

"Good. And why do you think love is the theme? Why is it so different, let's say…than poetry about love?"

Dravin glances at Gia, Reid at Jess. I finally realized why they took this class. It's because they are in love and want to learn something more meaningful. Love is the foundation of why they are here. Valen followed along because he felt the emotion and didn't recognize or know how to act on it.

I raise my hand because I know the answer, having read it fifteen times, looking for the same thing. The good and the simple emotion of love in something. Even if you can't find it in those you want.

"Miss Devlin!" he calls on me. The whole class turns around and my gaze lands on Valen. His eyes soften. His lips twitch, forming a small grin. A direct contrast to the glare aimed directly at me from Reid and Dravin.

I lower my hand, rub my lips together, and answer, "I think it's because Shakespeare didn't want to portray life like a cheesy poem. I believe Shakespeare wanted to write about love in its brutal form. Love is unforgiving. It's not the type of love you see in the beginning when Romeo is in love with Rosaline. It's the all-consuming kind he wanted to write about. For example, when Romeo and Juliet meet for the first time, their love is at first sight, and nothing else matters in that moment or after. Not hate, greed, or acceptance between two families. Everyone makes mistakes, but it was them against everyone, and the only way Romeo and Juliet could be together…was in death."

Professor Elliot pumps his fist in the air. "There you have it, ladies and gentlemen. Miss Devlin is a true romantic." Snorts and snickers can be heard across the lecture hall, but I ignore them. What catches me by surprise is Valen clapping with a smile. Jess joins in, and surprisingly, so does Gia. Dravin and Reid look at them like they grew three heads and have lost their minds, but I smile.

"Alright, I need your short verses for your assignment turned in next time we meet. No exceptions!" the professor announces before everyone gets up to leave.

I'm about to exit, but a hand is placed against the frame blocking my path. I recognize Valen's tattoo peeking out of the sleeve of his sweater. "Come with us."

I shake my head, stepping outside the classroom when he finally lets me through. "I don't think that is a good idea."

"Why not?"

"Because–" I trail off when the sound of my phone pings with an incoming message. I fish my phone out of my bag and look at a message from my mother telling me she made me an appointment for a wax.

"Is it your boyfriend?" he teases. I've never had one, but he doesn't know that. He must think I've had many given my reputation. Sex isn't a boyfriend. It's an act. Sometimes out of choice and sometimes forced. The look on my face swipes the teasing grin off his. "Sorry, I—"

"It's just my mom. I have an appointment at the Galleria."

The Galleria is a shopping venue that also offers different services in the office building attached to the shops, along with exclusive designer boutiques.

"Good, because that is where we are going."

"We?"

"Yeah, the Bedfords, Riodrick-Riordan's, and us."

"I don't think they would like me to come along."

"Jess and Gia want you to come. It can be a girls' thing, saving me from being the sixth wheel," he says, wincing on the last part.

I have to go there anyway. It's not like I'm going shopping there.

"Fine."

"I'll take you. We can ride together."

Walking out in the sunny afternoon toward the parking lot, I keep thinking that ever since my breakdown in the shower, he's been nice. Too nice and it feels like pity, which I loathe. I click the seat belt and sit in the passenger seat of his Mercedes sports car. "You don't have to be nice to me."

He places the car in reverse, following Dravin and Reid in their cars. "I'm sorry, Veronica."

I slide the hood off my head, combing the blonde tresses of my wig with my fingers, listening to him apologize. It's the first time I've heard someone apologize to me and mean it.

"I don't deserve an apology, Valen. I've done things and acted in ways I don't even recognize."

"I don't care about that. A-are you okay? If someone hurt you, you would tell me, right?"

I meet his eyes briefly, and he lets out an audible breath. "That was stupid. What I'm trying to say is, literally."

"No, of course not," I lie.

Why would I tell him the truth? There's nothing he could do about it. He will marry Melissa before he graduates his senior year, and I will soon be married to someone the Order still has to agree to until the next vote—which is next week. But my silence says more than words ever could. It speaks of truths left unsaid. Because we both know I'm part of a bigger game that has been being played for a long time. A game no one saw coming but me. All I can do is sit back and watch who will win or how it will end. All I know is that I will lose.

I make my way to the designer boutique where Jess and Gia are buying clothes to wear to a party Dravin is hosting. I take my sweet time so that by the time I get there, I don't have to watch them shop while I wait because they would find it odd that I can't participate.

After Valen dropped me off in front of the office building and I finish my appointment, the hour spent waxing every pubic hair on my body, I walk by the outdoor café, near the tables and chairs placed under oversized umbrellas. People are chowing down on overpriced salads, deep in conversation.

A man in a suit stands just outside a table with dark glasses and his arms crossed. I immediately recognize his stance as someone's bodyguard or maybe chauffeur because my father has both. A shrill laugh comes from behind him, causing people to stop mid-sentence and look, including me, but what catches my attention is where the laughter is directed. The man seated across from her is sinfully dressed in a white shirt, sleeves rolled up, exposing tattooed forearms, with two buttons undone at the throat, and sunglasses that cost more than my monthly paycheck at the restaurant. His straight jaw, straight nose, and perfect lips make him the complete package.

When I think of a sinner, Alaric is the first one I think about. He's the devil under your skirt. The cause of heat between your legs. The one fallen from grace. A reckoning. His name is a contradiction—Alaric means noble ruler. But even the devil was an angel, and I was his sacrifice.

The woman tries to make him laugh, telling him something, but he's looking straight ahead. You can tell by the angle of his head, he's ignoring her every word. As I get closer, I overhear her talking about a meeting and how one guy was nervous about his proposal. She must work for Alaric or with him. I've never seen her before, but where Alaric is concerned, I stopped noticing. I stopped caring and ignored his existence because I knew better. He's forbidden. The Order's esteemed member can do no wrong in their eyes.

Not being able to keep myself from looking over once more, I feel his eyes on my skin like a burn from the sun on a hot day, even with his dark sunglasses. He pushes his sunglasses on his head, and his gray eyes meet mine. The woman notices and turns to see what has his attention.

"Do you know her?" she asks, her tone dripping with jealousy.

"Yes," I hear him answer her while he looks at my black dress, pantyhose, and black boots. He looks like a model on a magazine cover, and I look like Wednesday Adams with platinum hair.

"I've worked with you for over a year and never seen her before."

She must be his secretary, and she obviously is more than that, but as jealousy creeps in, I have learned that anger feels so much better. I turn and walk over to their table and watch her mouth open like a fish on a hook.

His bodyguard steps forward. The man is built like a brick house, and I stand on the tips of my boots to say softly in his ear, "I'll be just a minute." He looks at the palm of my hand when it lands on his hard chest, and I continue, "We fucked once, but it was messy. I promise to keep things clean this time." He turns to look at Alaric, but I don't wait.

I walk over to their table, ignoring the curious stares aimed my way. "Can I help you?" the woman asks mockingly.

I nervously roll my tongue on my bottom lip, noticing the copper tones in her hair from the sun and trying to figure out why he would find her appealing. Her blouse is unable to flatter her too-small breasts. You can tell she isn't wearing a bra and her makeup is so heavily applied, it looks chalky because of the heat outside from the afternoon sun. "Who are you?" I ask, even though I already figured it out.

She glances at Alaric and places her cloth napkin on the table. "I'm his—Alaric's secretary." The way she says his first name and not his last—hyphenated name, tells me one thing: she's trying to stake a claim and wants me to know that she's fucking him. I'm not sure what my purpose of coming over here is: maybe the lecture on Romeo and Juliet got to me for some reason, or the fact that I will never know what love is truly like, let alone experience it from someone, and I'm a glutton for punishment.

"What can I do for you, Miss Devlin?" Alaric asks with formality.

I look at my short nails like I just had a manicure when I actually need one. "I came to say hi, of course. It would be rude if I walked by without greeting you and your…secretary." His phone rests on the white cloth over the table near his plate.

From the corner of my eye, I focus on the cloth napkin in her lap. She's probably hoping Alaric tells me to fuck off, or worse, that I'm interrupting their time together.

"I'm Sasha, by the way. It's good to meet one of Alaric's… friends," she says, but her eyes say it all. That I'm a threat because that is not what a typical secretary says when she is with her boss.

Her overfamiliarity with him is annoying. She is sitting out in the afternoon having lunch on a beautiful day with the one man I could see myself with when I was young and stupid and thought for one second that he could be the one person that would see me. Maybe save me from the hell I'm trapped in that wants to swallow me whole. I knew the moment I laid eyes on her that I would hate her for it.

I recognize when two people have been intimate. It's probably from personal experience or that my father fucks his own secretary regularly and isn't shy about it. My mother knows and turns a blind eye, pops the next pill to fall asleep, only to wake up, then boards a private plane to visit friends abroad for a brunch date.

A fake grin appears on my lips. I have mastered one for people who show an instant dislike for me. It's sort of an armor I have built, along with my crazy bitch attitude, to hide the way I truly feel inside, that I'm breaking and there isn't much left to ruin.

I have had sex many times and never had an orgasm that wasn't self-inflicted. There was one time I had wanted it more than anything, but it was awful, expecting it to be magical. I was expecting it to be the kind where you have butterflies in your stomach just thinking about it, but instead, it was a horror flick, like a scene that stood out the most when you experienced it the first time, like in the movie *The Exorcist*, and her head spins around. A memory best kept buried that you can't erase because your first time is something you will always remember. The other times I had sex were because it was what needed to be done, and for others. I had no choice, but they all shared the same result. They ended the same, in pain. The only way I have learned to deal with it is acting like it doesn't hurt—like my heart isn't broken into a million pieces or that my soul isn't mine.

My eyes land on Alaric's phone when it vibrates from an incoming message, and I notice she sent him a text. I grip the napkin she placed on the table, watch her mouth open and then close when I tell her, "I think you forgot to clean up your self-worth." I toss the napkin in her lap and tune out her audible gasp when I grab Alaric's phone, toss it in the bucket of champagne with melted ice water, and watch it float like a buoy.

His gray eyes flick up, and I could swear I saw his lips twitch. "It was nice seeing you again, Alaric," I say in a sultry tone, sliding my finger over his busted knuckles, wondering whose ass he kicked or killed, watching the scab turn white around the edges before I walk away, hearing Sasha's raised voice.

"You two have something going on?"

"No, she means nothing," he responds.

The words he uttered are the truth, even if I don't like them coming from him, but it is how he sees me, and nothing I do will change that. I act out to remind myself what I am, by hearing it from his lips. Because the next chapter of my life is the beginning of my sentence.

The rest of my afternoon is spent with Jess and Gia. I'm horrified at how much I envy them that they are in love with someone who can mend them and put them back together. I watch how carefree they are. The way they smile and laugh picking out clothes. How I have to lie and tell them I already have that collection when I don't have anything from this store in my closet. But to them or their husbands, they wouldn't question it. They all believe the lies I spill. The act. Sometimes I wonder how long I can keep it up until it all destroys me.

I am frightened for myself, but thankful for the pills Dr. Wick prescribed to help me get some sleep and not succumb to my dreams. I call them *happy* pills because it's the only time, I don't feel pain. It's the first time, besides the color of my eyes, that I have something in common with my mother. My internal life has become destitute because I revert to fumbling for a token of love from someone who never offers it.

VERONICA

"THANK YOU FOR STOPPING BY. HAVE a nice day."

I pick up my tips left on the table, stuffing them in the small pocket of my apron and hear the plastic tub land on the table for the third time tonight with a loud thud. A thud louder than necessary.

"Dorothy sat the next table down in your section. It looks like they are ready for you to take their order," Adam says in a tight voice.

He's still mad about the initiation party and what happened with Melody and me showing up with her. I don't think it has anything to do with Matt because why would it? Adam never responds to my texts or phone calls so I gave up hoping that with time, he would forget about it.

"I'm on it," I respond.

"On everything apparently," he mutters.

I pause, blinking back the sting of tears, and turn to face him. "You know what, Adam."

"What?"

"Fuck you."

I push past him to wait on my next table and ignore him for the next three hours of my shift. It's Tuesday night and even though this is a small restaurant, On The Edge Diner is open twenty-four-hours and is the hangout spot for both universities when you want something to eat and everything else is closed. That is what brings it success. College kids can hang out and get a bite to eat. It doesn't matter if you're from Kenyan or Ohio State University. It is the middle ground year-round.

Dorothy was able to get the county to approve a license to sell beer and wine. Since the restaurant has a retro theme, no one questions the old cigarette machines hidden in the bathroom that sell

Marlboro and Virginia Slims. There also is an old arcade game and foosball table in the back, so kids can go and play if they are bored.

It's considered a twenty-four-hour hangout mostly for high school seniors and OSU students. Privileged kids from Kenyan have their own hangouts and parties. They don't need to hang out at a retro-themed diner when they have empty mansions to use because their parents are traveling on business or pleasure.

There is a self-serve soda fountain that has all the different flavors of coke that I love. The best part of working here is that no one really knows I work here from Kenyan and I get free food Monday thru Friday. Sometimes, I bring food to the staff my father hired, knowing they are tired of working at the house all day.

When a group of girls with three guys walk in, Dorothy seats them in the back booth in my section. I can tell they are high school kids hanging out way past their curfew or maybe their parents don't give a shit if they are out on a school night.

I check the cup with extra pens by the register, picking one that still has ink when I see Adam approach. "I'm sorry," he says.

"Save it."

"I was wrong. I was mad about what they said about you and I felt stupid for not knowing how to defend you."

"Defend me against what, Adam?"

"All of them because I know that what they said about you isn't true. You're not like that and I get why you did what you did at the party, but you could have let me handle it, even though someone did."

I turn to face him now. "What do you mean someone did?"

"You don't know?" I shake my head raising my eyebrows. "Matt is out for the season— probably can never play football again…at least not at OSU. They named me QB1 as an incoming freshman and I can't be happy about it when someone is laid up in a hospital bed with both hands broken and his face smashed in."

What the hell? I'm not a fan of Matt and I get that he's an asshole with little to no regard for women, but he's hurt and his future is ruined.

"Who did it?"

"No one knows. No one is talking."

"I'm sorry, Adam."

"Is it true that you attend Kenyan?" he asks, then shakes his head. "I don't care about the other stuff. It's all rumors anyway." He smiles. "I know you…and my sisters love you. Especially Melody."

I'm not going to lie to him or keep that part hidden from him or his sisters anymore. It feels good to have friends that think differently when it comes to me.

"It's true, I attend Kenyan. I'm a senior."

He places the plates inside the plastic tub from the bar counter. "So you're friends with the enemy."

"You're still my friend?" I ask hopefully.

He wipes his hands on the towel from his back pocket. "I never stopped. Yeah, I was mad and didn't answer your calls because I felt I wasn't good enough for you to tell me and when I find out who the asshole is behind all the rumors, you can count me in to kick their ass."

I think of Adam trying to kick Alaric's ass, knowing I would never let Adam near him. Adam is a good guy. He's the reason I know that good guys still exist. Any girl would be lucky to have him.

"That would be something, but I wouldn't want you to."

He slides a strand of hair away from my forehead. "I know." His gaze shifts past my head for a second. "I think you need to get to the last booth. They're giving us death glares."

"Does it have anything to do with the girl on the left side?"

I saw the way they looked at each other when she sat down with her friends.

"You mean the one I asked out to prom but won't be seen dead with the bus boy from the restaurant?"

"She said no to you?" I ask surprisingly. He rolls his eyes. "Okay, I take that as a yes. What a bitch."

He shrugs. "It's alright, I won't go."

"Why not ask someone else?"

"Her bullshit reason grew wings and most of the girls I would have asked, felt the same, or already have dates."

I take their drink order, but I don't miss the way the girl sitting next to the one that turned Adam down to prom glances at Adam every time he has his back turned with hope in her eyes that he would pay her some attention. The bitch next to her is pretty, wearing shiny lip gloss and a short top that shows the swell of her breasts. The girl next to her is nothing compared to her with what she is wearing, but I think it's because her friend downplays her looks. Girls can be mean like that when they have competition. Senior prom is a big deal in high school and it's a tradition. Getting asked is a big deal.

I didn't go to prom my senior year because word traveled fast after what happened with Alaric. It's not that I didn't want to go because I did, but I had to turn everyone down that asked. The guys that did asked weren't genuine. You could see it in the way they approached me. It was clear they expected more than a dance. Everyone in my class went and I cried myself to sleep that night and more the next day when I saw the pictures of everyone having fun. I swore to Alicia that I was okay with not going. It was the last thing she dressed up for before she eloped with Chase.

After placing their drinks, I go to place their order in the kitchen when I hear someone from the table ask, "Who is that?" I turn and follow their line of sight behind me and my eyes land on Valen, sliding into a booth and giving me a wink. How did he know I worked here? "He's…wow."

"Hey gorgeous," he says, grabbing a menu like he's here for the food.

"What are you doing here?"

His lips lift in a grin while he scans the menu. "I came to check on you."

I step closer and take out the ordering pad to take his order. "What can I get you?"

He places the menu down and leans back. "Oh, I'm not here for food. I'm here to make sure you attend Draven's little party."

I laugh through my nose. "Yeah, nice try. They would never invite me."

"I'm inviting you and you're wrong. Jess and Gia told me to

invite you because they know you would give them some bullshit excuse for not going."

"I don't belong at Draven's party."

"Why not?"

"You know why? It's...awkward."

He lowers his voice. "I think Gia is over the fact you had sex with Draven. It was before her and I'm sure you weren't the only one."

As much as Draven Bedford is attractive, I didn't want to. It was cold, rough, and impersonal. I didn't get off. I had to fake it and I was glad when it was over.

The girls behind me are whispering and giggling. I look up to see Adam and then turn to look at the girls, contemplating the invite to the party. Valen looks over and shakes his head. "He your friend?"

I slide my tongue over the front of my teeth because I hate catty bitches. Except the girl with the light brown hair is trying to hide her face so that the others don't catch on that she doesn't agree to whatever they are saying. "Yeah. He's a good guy."

"What are you thinking? Who are the girls?" My eyes slide over to his. "Do I wanna know?"

I tilt my head to the side. "If I go, can I bring some friends?"

"As long as they can play ball."

He means no one underage because they sure as hell are not leaving virgins if they go to a Kenyan party. The bell from the kitchen dings, signaling that their food is ready.

Catty bitch number one asks, "You know him?"

"Yeah, why?"

"He's hot."

Yeah, he is and also dangerous with an insatiable cock that breaks hearts.

I smile blithely. "He's a sophomore at Kenyan. He just invited me and Adam to a party Friday night, you girls want to come?" They widen their eyes like I just told them they won front row tickets at a Taylor Swift concert.

"Adam knows him?"

"Of course, he does. Adam practically knows everyone. He's got the QB1 spot at Ohio State. All the girls are going crazy over him, not just me. If you guys are down and of course eighteen, you can come since you know Adam."

"You like him?" she asks, like I know something she doesn't. "You're gorgeous. How could you like a guy like Adam?"

I do and it has everything to do with the fact that he's a nice guy and hell would freeze over before I let this bitch fuck with him.

"What's not to like…umm—" I trail off, waiting for her to tell me her name.

"Jenny."

"Jenny," I repeat. "And you are?" I point to the girl who is secretly crushing on Adam.

"Lizzy," she says shyly. I watch as Jenny shoves her lightly and gives her a what the hell is wrong with you look. *Bitch.*

"I think Adam is hot and so do most of the college girls at Ohio and Kenyan. He works here because he doesn't want his mother to work extra-long shifts so that he can attend college."

It's true, but it's also because Adam's mother doesn't earn enough to cover his expenses.

"Really?" Jenny says surprised.

I write down my number so that Lizzy can call me and I can give her the address to Draven's party. I watch her enter it on her phone, before I move away, watching Adam wipe down the table, casting a nervous glance my way before I say, "Yeah, like I said, what's not to like, I can't believe some bitch had the balls to turn him down for his senior prom. Her loss."

VERONICA

"ARE YOU SURE, MRS. RIODRI. RIORDAN?"

Alaric's mother smiles after I butcher her name when I address her holding the outfit she bought me, after she asked me to stop by her house.

"Could you stop with the formality, Veronica? Claire is fine. Since you were in high school, I have told you to call me Claire."

I remember the first time I met her when Alicia promised to introduce me to Alaric because I had a huge crush on him and couldn't wait until I was old enough to introduce myself. I wanted a fair shot, and being underage wouldn't work in my favor. But I was stubborn and couldn't wait. I wanted to meet him, but I was more surprised to find a mother figure in Claire instead. Her son didn't notice me; I was invisible to him. But she always found a way to bring me dresses and clothes, claiming that she bought them when she was younger and never got a chance to wear them, but we both know that was a lie until she just started telling me she bought it for me. I always wondered why she was so nice to me. Maybe she heard what happened between me and her son but overlooked my behavior afterward. At one point, she thought I was into Reid, but we never had any chemistry and hardly spoke. And after Alaric and Alicia, it got worse. Like most people, he finally opened up with his total dislike for me, and it was open season.

But Claire was one of the few that didn't. Besides the hired staff at home, a few showed me kindness.

"I'm sorry, Claire."

She waves her hand demurely. "Nonsense. I want to know if you like it. I heard Draven is throwing a party and I want you to look your best. Graduation is looming, and I know…you don't have much time before—" She trails off, avoiding my gaze.

"Before I know who I'm marrying," I finish for her.

She presses her lips together, forming a thin line.

"It's okay, Claire. We all have to, right?"

She nods, but I don't miss how she won't look me in the eye, her focus on the short dress with a designer shoe bag attached to the hanger. Claire is one of those women that stays up to date on gossip. She knows practically everything that goes on at Kenyan most of the time.

"It's tomorrow at Thursday's meeting with the Order."

My chest squeezes tightly, knowing that by tomorrow, I will know where I'll be living and the monster who will be keeping me. I'm not a great catch in anyone's eyes or what the Order would consider an acceptable wife. In my case, they only care about an alliance between two families. My father doesn't care about the alliance; he cares only for one thing, power. The power to sway the vote in his favor because the Consortium is a threat to his existence. He needs more power by forming an alliance that favors his ideals.

"I'm aware," I say but don't meet her gaze, afraid of what she might see.

Fear.

"What is she doing here?" I jolt and find gray eyes flash at me in disgust.

"Alaric, you remember Veronica."

His face tightens. "Mother, I know who she is, but that doesn't answer my question. What the hell is she doing here?"

Claire straightens, holding the hanger in her hand. "I invited her here. She was just stopping by to pick something up."

He glances at the dress and then at me. "I will say this once and won't repeat it. You can manipulate and fuck everyone in Kenyan like the whore that you are." I inwardly flinch. He backs me up toward the archway leading to the exit.

"Alaric! What has gotten into you!" Claire yells. But it falls on deaf ears.

"Get the fuck out. You're not welcome here." His jaw is set in a hard line. He opens the front door and almost rips it off its hinges with force.

I should have never come. I keep telling myself to ignore her calls, but it's hard when all someone has done is be nice and give you the most beautiful things because they find they love your company. I remember Claire telling me she wished she was able to have more children. She wanted a daughter. A little girl she could nurture and dress up. Tell her stories about her days in high school and how she fell in love with her husband because she said having a boy was hard. Alaric is not the romantic type by any means. But I would listen to her because I secretly wanted a mother like that. One that would tell me I was loved and that I mattered to her. All my mother did was tell me I was a mistake she wished she had never made, but I could make it up to her by keeping Daddy happy. *Do good, Veronica.*

"I-I'm sorry," I stammer.

"Your kind is never sorry. Stop fucking with my family." He grips me by my throat, and dread fills my veins. The look in his eyes is hard and cold. "Alicia didn't deserve what happened to her. The one thing I wished for is for you to be in that grave instead of my beloved cousin. I thought you should know that."

I couldn't agree more.

"Get your fucking hands off me," I say through clenched teeth, trying to tear myself out of his grip, but he squeezes harder, leaving just enough for me to breathe.

"If you come near my family, I'll kill you, Veronica."

I blink rapidly from the cruelty of his words and begin to shut down. The need to cut taking over like an addict seeking an escape. For some, it's a high, but for me, it's a need for pain. The sting from the wound of a cut bleeding the hurt out of me. Maybe it would be better if he did it. He could finish me off.

"There is nothing I wish for more than for that to happen. I got my spot all picked out. You wouldn't even have to do it, but you see, the funny thing is, it never happens. Because I'm still here. Because they all love to watch."

He shoves me away, and I almost trip on the last step. "The fuck? You're a crazy bitch."

I laugh. It's an ugly laugh that bubbles up my now sore throat as I rub where his fingers gripped me hard and point mockingly at the heat spreading over the area. "You know, my future husband wouldn't like you to fuck up the merchandise."

Everyone will be at the Order's meeting tomorrow night, including him. All members have to attend. I don't care who they pick because it doesn't matter. I have two choices: live with it or die from it.

"I can deal with your little childish games, throwing my phone in a bucket of ice water while you ruin a lunch date with my regular fuck because you're still pissed after all this time that you didn't succeed with Daddy's bidding by trapping me. But I will not let you use my mother. Trust me, the man cursed to marry a bitch like you would expect you to be all used up. I dodged a bullet, but know that everyone who looks at you knows you're just Daddy's puppet. A spoiled little rich girl with nothing better to do than make everyone's life miserable."

I cut myself that night on my way home and when I took the bus after my shift. I had a paperclip in my purse when I received my paycheck the day before. At first, I didn't know why I had saved the silver paper clip in the little pocket next to the bottle of sleeping pills, but deep down, I knew why. It was a band-aid I needed, just in case the wound would reopen, and last night, Alaric's words triggered the wound.

Thursday night would only get worse. I cried in my room before my father was ready to take me to the church.

"I have chosen someone respectable for you, and the members will vote tonight. I'm sure they will have no issues approving the alliance. All I ask, is that you don't embarrass me or your mother. The Devlin name is part of history. You should be honored you are to represent this family as my only heir. You will do as you are told and accept the union. Understood?"

"Yes, Father," I whisper in agreement.

"Good. Don't listen to any of them, Veronica. They might have an opinion of you in a negative regard, but none of them are perfect.

Remember that. No one in that room is a saint. You have nothing to be ashamed of, Veronica."

"Yes, Father," I repeat, knowing deep down that I feel ashamed but have no choice but to agree.

Walking into the church feels like I'm walking into my own funeral. All the members are in attendance, including all of the classmates I grew up with from important families. The eyes of the Bedford twins, Gia, Jess, Reid, Garret, Melissa, and the last person I want to see, Alaric, are all on me. Valen is seated in the corner; his lips turn into a frown when he watches me approach the center of the room by the altar. No one can object to the Order's decision unless they have already taken their family's place and have graduated. They also have to clear up any issues interfering with world leaders. Translation, they need to make sure they are mentally stable to rule in society.

"Welcome, Mr. Devlin. I see you are ready to begin. We have accepted your request and will bring it forth to be voted on. Miss Devlin, will you please remain."

I face the room like I'm in a congregation and respond, "Of course."

Everyone in the room takes in the dress my father selected for the vote. It is black lace with blood-red inserts. It must have cost him a fortune, but it makes me feel cheap with how my breasts are pushed up, almost spilling out of the neckline, and my waist is cinched. I feel like I'm being sold in an auction to the highest bidder.

Jess's eyes soften, and so do Gia's, but I look away, feeling someone's heated stare, and know instantly it's Alaric. Tonight, I'm not lucky like Gia or Jess. They got to marry someone they love and were accepted by the Order. Men that loved them back. Fought to be with them because they mattered. Tonight, my father chose because that was my fate all along. Only one man has the power to override a decision tonight, but like he said, he prefers me to be buried in the cemetery right outside this church. I won't be saved tonight.

"Veronica Devlin is the oldest heir of the Devlin estate, and so it is required, dated centuries before me, that she be married before her graduation at Kenyan University. Since she has no other prospects, it is required for her father to choose a husband so that an alliance can be formed. It has come to our attention that someone has accepted the proposal to wed Miss Devlin." My chest is tight, and I try to breathe and not collapse in front of everyone, waiting to hear my fate. The man that will have my life in his hands. "Dorian Black, will you please come forward."

No! The sound of hideous laughter begins overtaking my senses. The memory of that night and the way he began to chant the word 'whore' replays in my head. My vision blurs and then refocuses, like I'm warping between the present and the past. People are staring at me and the man I hate, as he steps forward, his eyes full of lust, making my skin crawl.

"Does anyone have cause to object to this union?" Mr. Clarence, the oldest member of the Order, announces.

My eyes quickly scan the room, hoping for a miracle, but God has always checked out, and his angels are laughing in agreement.

My eyes land on gray ones pleading, wishing for anything to stop it. For him to say something. To help me. But he stares straight ahead. The small candle of hope I kept in a secret spot in my heart for him dying forever. He could have said something because of that night.

But he didn't.

He let the sound of the wood echo as Mr. Clarence congratulated Dorian Black, telling him he was a lucky man, while my soul shattered into a million pieces when most of the room clapped.

A tiny tear threatens to fall, but I turn my head and wipe my eye like I got something in it and see Valen mouth, *I'm sorry*. Jess's mouth is pinched in a tight line, whispering to Reid, and I watch his gaze land on me, but it's interrupted by the man's voice that will use me to his advantage when the time comes.

"I'm sure you're surprised, but I couldn't resist." He lowers his voice, but I don't miss the evil glint in his eyes. "I'm going to have so much fun with you. I hear you can take pain." I swallow thickly. "It's okay, sweetheart. I can make you bleed too."

"Fuck you. How dare you. You disgust me," I hiss.

He slides his hand behind my neck and grips the skin when he lowers his lips to my ear as everyone begins to leave. "Be careful how you talk to me, wife."

"I'm not your wife," I grit.

"Yet." He chuckles. "I'm surprised no one objected. Everyone must have thought you were a bad lay, but I can work something out with you. Teach you how to pleasure me and whoever I need you to spread your legs for."

"It's gonna be hard with a small dick."

His grip tightens again, and my vision feels fuzzy, but no one can tell because the long blonde tresses of my wig cover his hand wrapped around me.

"Congratulations, Dorian. I'm sorry about your brother." I hear Alaric's voice behind me.

Dorian's hand slithers off my neck and rests on the curve of my ass, and I want to burn it off as he smiles at Alaric, but I avert my gaze. Alaric is nothing to me. Just some stupid girl fantasy that tore me apart.

"I appreciate that. My brother's accident hit us all hard, and when Mr. Devlin mentioned that he needed to marry his daughter off, I couldn't resist. She was always a pretty girl. Everyone thought so." He caresses my ass, and I want to throw up when he continues, "I was surprised she was still available, and listen, I know there is a history, and I have no hard feelings."

I push Dorian's hand off me, not wanting to listen anymore. Fuck them. "If you'll excuse me, I think my father is looking for me."

I run out of the church and notice my father deep in conversation with other members and run toward the cemetery, so I can clear my thoughts. Everything is starting to make sense. I know how my father plans to achieve more power. With me by Dorian's side, he has Dorian's vote and will counter Alaric, Reid and the Bedfords in practically everything before Valen gets closer to graduation. Everyone knows that Dorian Black and Alaric don't see eye to eye. They never have. In business, sports, or at Kenyan. They are opposites, but there is one thing they both are in my eyes, men I hate.

ALARIC

"I CAN'T BELIEVE he can still beat you!" Garret cries, splashing water at Valen.

"What...did you think you pussies could still beat me? I'm the fucking champ at Kenyan all around. None of you have a better time."

"I'll beat you," Valen says with determination.

Out of all the sons of Kenyan, Valen's time is the closest to beating mine. If he would put the work in, he might have a solid chance to beat me and every asshole he goes up against. He might also have a shot of getting on the Olympic team.

"Get wet in the pool, instead of pussy, and you might have a chance," I shoot back.

"I can't believe you can still beat all of us," Dravin adds. "In the same night."

I grin. "I still swim."

"We see that, dick. You still got it," Reid says, shaking his head.

I turn when I hear giggling from the back patio, and my eyes narrow when I spot Gia, Jess, and Veronica with a couple of friends, including the new freshman replacing Matt on the football team at Ohio State.

"Who the fuck invited her to the party?" I ask in a hard tone.

They all give me meaningful looks, knowing exactly who I'm talking about, but Valen's the first one to speak up. "I did."

"Why the fuck would you invite that crazy bitch here with all of us?"

Garret wipes his face and dips in the pool. "Don't call her that."

My head whips like I've been slapped. "Oh...you're going to forget all the shit she has done all of a sudden?"

I know I'm acting childish and shouldn't care, or maybe it's because Garret slept with Veronica and is into her, and…it bothers me.

"I think you have it all wrong about her," Valen adds, looking defiant.

Reid and the Bedfords glance at each other, surprised, probably thinking Valen has gone batshit crazy.

"Let me guess, asshole. You fucked her and caught feelings," I say, leaning forward, making him step toward the deep end of the pool while Garret gives Valen a dirty look.

Garret has strong feelings for Veronica, but she apparently doesn't feel the same way. I don't understand why Valen is defending her, but for whatever reason, the monster within me is rearing its ugly head whenever it concerns her. Last night, I was about two seconds away from punching Dorian Black to wipe the smirk off his face while he pawed her ass.

"She isn't a problem anymore, so why the fuck do you care and for the—" a wave of water splashes on my face, "I've never had sex with Veronica, you jealous fuck. Everyone knows you lose your shit every time she's around."

"Fuck off, Vikiar." I growl, wiping my face.

"Leave her alone," Draven says quietly. "Gia and Jess wanted her to come, and Valen's right; she's no threat to anyone. She'll marry by the time she graduates, and she isn't thrilled about it. So you got what you wanted."

"I never wanted anything. I…she was using me. Reid called me that night—"

"I never called you," Reid shoots back.

I lean back on the wall of the pool. "You called me."

He shakes his head. "I. Never. Called. You. I was looking out for—"

Alicia. He was making sure she was okay at the initiation party. If he didn't call me to warn me about Veronica, then who did? But the text was from him. I remember.

"Stop fucking with me, Reid. You called me that night and warned me about Devlin's daughter setting me up. That asshole has wanted an in since our grandfather and Riodrick Hotels monopolized the hotel industry."

Reid scoffs. "Hey, asshole, I never called you. I knew she had a crush on you. I mean…everyone in our family knew. Your mom knew. Alicia invited her to every family function if her father allowed her to go, and Veronica begged her to introduce you to her, but you never knew she was even there. I get that she was younger than you, and you were fucking your way through college and didn't know who she was or that she existed. That night I figured you didn't like her, and the sex was shit from how you treated her after Dorian walked in on you. Shit got out of hand."

Dorian recorded her bleeding between her thighs because she got her period, her tears, and how she ran home crying after I called her out. It was fucked up, but I was pissed off, and at the time, all I wanted to do was hurt her for thinking I would fall for her mind-fuck games. I got into it with Dorian and made him delete the video and anyone who copied it. Fists were thrown, and threats were made, but in the end, we all turned on her. We fucked with her. Because she deserved it. But if Reid didn't text me that night, who did?

"Then who texted me?" I ask.

"It wasn't us." Garret chimes in. "I didn't know her like that. In high school—" Garret trails off.

Valen's mouth forms a thin line, and he pinches his brows. They both went to high school with her, and so did the Bedford twins.

"In high school, what?"

Draven mutters under his breath, and I'm annoyed they are all avoiding telling me something. Something I don't know because I don't know Veronica like that. Dravin glances across the patio at Gia, deep in conversation with Jess and Veronica, and then shifts his gaze back to me.

"What?" I repeat with my hands spread out in frustration.

"Veronica never had a boyfriend in high school. She only hung around Alicia. Veronica was considered a prude and a stuck-up bitch that wouldn't put out. Every guy tried to nail her but never could, and trust me, they all tried. That's why everyone thought she was into girls," Dravin says.

"She turned down every single guy that tried. After that night with you, it got progressively worse. They called her names like whore, and all the bullshit assholes in high school tell chicks they pick on. It was fucked up," Valen chimes in.

Draven snaps his fingers. "I remember all the guys asked her to prom, hoping they could fuck her, but she ended up not going."

"Yeah, they said someone popped the ice queen's cherry at Kenyan," Garret says mindlessly.

A slow, nagging feeling crawls up my spine. Dread slithers through my veins, and I push off the wall. "What did you say?" I ask Garret.

"What?" he says defensively. "That's what they called her. I know you thought she was easy and was out to trap you, but one thing Veronica never was before that night *was* a slut. To be honest, I don't think it was her period. They called her the ice queen because of her colorless hair and the fact she wouldn't let a guy touch her—"

"What the fuck are you talking about? Are you high?"

Valen rolls his eyes, annoyed with me, but it can't be. I—the way I took her was rough. I—remember that she was just lying there, and then the door flew open. She was horrified to see the blood sticking to her thighs, trying to clean herself. She pleaded for me to do something, but I didn't care. I was staring at my phone with her name and the message Reid sent, or I thought it was Reid. He wouldn't lie. Not about that.

"It doesn't matter. You're off the hook. I'm pretty sure you're the last person she would want anyway," Valen says softly, walking toward the steps and tapping me on my bare shoulder. "That night changed her, but she's not your problem. She belongs to Dorian, and as much as I want to save her from marrying that asshole, I can't because believe it or not, that girl doesn't deserve the shit hand that was handed to her." His face tightens. "I can't believe I'm saying this to you, but I'm gonna say it. Leave her alone. You've done enough."

My fists clench. "You're threatening me, Vikiar?"

"What's going on?" Jess asks when she walks in with Gia and Veronica, along with the friends she invited here.

"Nothing. Valen is just pissed off. I beat his time," I lie.

"Oh. You still swim?"

I look up and smile. "Of course. Someone has to make sure they beat these punks," I tease.

One of the girls that came in with Veronica steps forward in jean shorts and a sweater. "Are you guys like vampires?"

I can see why she would think that. The Bedford mansion looks like Dracula's lair, and the red lights from the pool glow like a pool of blood. The gargoyles add to the whole effect.

"Yeah, be careful. We like to bite," Garret says, mocking with his teeth like Dracula, making her eyes widen.

My gaze lands on Veronica."I need to talk to you." But she looks away, acting like I wasn't speaking to her. A girl with ash-blonde hair steps forward. I recognize her from the initiation party. She was arguing with her brother Adam about the guy playing her little sister with another chick. "She has nothing to say to you," she says defiantly.

"Maddison, could you take me home? Adam will give Lizzy a ride," Veronica says, clearly ignoring me.

A feeling I don't recognize stabs me in the chest. She won't look at me, and I don't know what to do. "Veronica," I call her name, but she ignores me like she can't hear me.

"Please, Maddy. I want to go home," she pleads.

"I can take you," Adam says, stepping forward, but she shakes her head and smiles.

"Take Lizzy, Adam. Maddy can take me. I have a shift tomorrow."

Shift?

"How come you work at the restaurant when you're obviously rich?" The curious one about vampires speaks up in her annoying voice. You can tell she's a bitch.

Work? Veronica works?

Veronica bites her lip nervously, trying to evade the question, and

I usually don't stare at her long enough, but this time, I notice. Fear. "It's for a school project."

I smell bullshit. What is she scared about? Why would she need to work when her father is a billionaire. No school project would warrant a work-study of any kind, except an internship at the end of the semester that she needs to complete, and it's done at one of the family's conglomerates. Not at a restaurant. Adam's confused expression gives it away. She's lying, but why?

I watch Valen and Garret leave the pool, heading for the towel rack.

"Where the fuck are you two fuckers going?" I ask.

Reid chuckles. "They're leaving to make out."

Everyone laughs, but Valen glances at Veronica and Maddy, and I want to pour acid into his eyes. "I'm going to follow the girls to make sure they get home safe."

"Since when do you care if anyone gets home safe?" Draven adds, "I get why Garret is doing it."

"Relax, Veronica and I are actually friends."

"When did this happen?" Draven asks sarcastically.

"After I sucked his cock," Veronica blurts. My nostrils flare when Garret grins and points in her direction and winks. "It was good, by the way, baby. No complaints."

"I'm glad I could be of service," she purrs.

Jess claps her hands together with a grin on her face. I want to pull Veronica into the pool and punish her for giving me a visual of her and Garret, but I surprise myself by chiming in to get her attention, pushing myself out of the pool. "I can find something you can service," I tell her and then turn toward Garret and Valen. "I got her. Make sure Maddison makes it home."

Veronica's eyes go wide in panic. "What are you doing?"

I smirk, quickly dry myself off, slide on sweatpants, and grab my hoodie and wallet from the lounge chair. "You need a ride."

"Not from you."

"I'm not asking, Veronica," I say in a harsh tone. "Let's go." She stomps off, muttering under her breath, and I smile to myself because I love it when she's combative. It makes my dick hard.

"I tell you to stay away, and you do the opposite," Valen scolds.

Not caring that we are in mixed company, I look at the guys, mentally making a list of things I need to do. "Meeting. I will send the invite."

The Bedford twins raise their brows in tandem because I only call a meeting when something is off, and it is...something is way off.

I unlock my car but notice Veronica walking toward the gate. "Get in, Veronica."

"Why, we both know you don't want to take me home."

She's right. I want to take her to my home. Preferably in my bed, so I can punish her.

Walking toward the passenger side, I open the door and wait impatiently. She knows not to push me. She shakes her head, stomping toward my car in her wedge heels. "You want to take the whore home? Wouldn't you be ashamed to be seen with me or that I might contaminate your precious car?"

"How could that be? Won't your daddy be happy that I'm taking you home?" I challenge.

"I can find my way home, and no, my daddy won't be happy if he sees you dropping me off."

My gaze slides down her top, pausing at her plump breasts, remembering how her nipples tasted. Like honey. "Why is that?"

"Because I'm trying to be a good girl, and I don't ride in cars with bad boys," she purrs.

I rub my thumb over her bottom lip and imagine her taking my cock hard and deep. Her eyes focus on me like she can't believe I'm touching her.

"What makes you a bad girl?"

Her tongue pokes out and caresses the pad of my thumb, and my dick twitches in my pants, telling me to take her home, but I can't. Not yet.

"You made me a bad girl, Alaric. So. Very. Bad."

I pull her bottom lip down with my thumb and watch it part submissively, her tongue sliding over it like it's my cock.

"Is that why you bled for me?"

Her eyes flash, but I can't determine if it's anger, lust, or maybe both. Her finger slides down my chest until it rests on my rock-hard cock. She smiles, but it doesn't reach her eyes. "I wanted to know what a cock would feel like for the first time." Her finger swirls and then grips me hard, causing me to grind my teeth when she pulls on it. Then, holding on to the roof of the car, she leans in and says menacingly, "Since then, I've been trying to forget how much I hated it and the nightmares that came with it."

She was a virgin. And I took her like an animal. *Fuck.* She was tight, and she felt good, but it was all ruined by the text message and now Dorian. That motherfucker. But what if this was the plan. Dorian couldn't get me to invest, and now he has Veronica, but whose side is she on?

She releases me, and I push her shoulder, guiding her inside the car and shutting the door. I slide in, fire up the car, and lock the doors. I grip her firmly by the neck.

"What are—"

"Look at me," I demand. Her eyes are full of terror when they land on mine. Her body is trembling. "I guess I will have to change that, won't I? You don't know what's coming, Veronica."

"What's coming?"

My face is void of emotion, and I smile faintly. "Everything."

VERONICA

TAKING the garbage out the back of the restaurant fifteen minutes before my shift ends, I can't help looking back. I keep having the feeling I'm being watched. The tiny hairs behind my neck stand, but I shake it off. That is what I get for watching horror flicks with Melody all the time. I'm paranoid.

Alaric dropping me off and telling me everything is coming doesn't help. It's no secret Alaric is dangerous, if not the most dangerous out of all the sons of Kenyan.

My head turns, and I focus on a dark corner. I could have sworn someone was standing there. I close my eyes and then open them so that they can focus on the dim light from the streetlights and the moon, but nothing. There is no one there, just my mind playing tricks on me.

I walk inside, sliding my sweaty hands over my apron, looking for my bag so I can head home. I have a class in the morning.

"Do you need a ride," Adam asks, looking up from wiping the tables.

"No, I'll be fine." I smile. "She said yes?"

He nods with a grin. "Yes, matchmaker—"

I play dumb. "I don't know what you're talking about."

But I do know. He asked Lizzy to prom, and she accepted. He can go with a great girl, and Adam deserves that.

"She does that, you know," Dorothy says, folding the utensils with a napkin and placing them in the bin. "She loves to make sure others are happy together."

Adam sniggers. "I see that, but who makes sure she's happy?"

"I am happy," I lie.

"Liar."

I stick my tongue out at him. "I gotta go. Bye, Dorothy." I wave and push the door open, letting out a breath and making my way to the bus stop.

There is a full moon in the dark sky, and I look down at the broken cracks on the sidewalk—the orange glow of the streetlights. Only two cars are parked on the curb, reminding me of a deserted town. I check the street to see the bus lights, but it's dark. I check my phone, and I still have five minutes until it's due to arrive.

My phone vibrates, and I check the message.

Dorian: How's my wife?

Veronica: I haven't seen her.

Dorian: I do.

My head whips around, and a wave of dread slides over me. He's watching me. I didn't imagine it.

Veronica: Fuck off, asshole.

Dorian: I'm afraid that's not gonna happen. You belong to me, Veronica. I've been waiting a long time to have you.

Veronica: Get fucked.

Dorian: Good night, princess.

Furious, I get up when the bus approaches the curb—sick bastard.

Dorian Black is repulsive. I can't imagine being married to a man like that. I don't think I can do it. Every time a nightmare ends, a new one begins.

When board the bus, I stop in the aisle and blink hard. A hooded figure sits in the center with a bird mask on. I plop down on the middle bench with my back against the huge window, looking between the driver and the masked figure. The man has his head bowed like he's asleep, but I know better. He's waiting. I look over his sweater, gloved hands, and pants but can't place him.

It could be Dorian fucking with me, or the Order sent whoever is behind the mask to kill me. Tears prick my eyes.

I don't want to die.

I've thought about it...dying or how would they do it. I think about everything, my life or lack of one. I've never been loved, and maybe it gave me the courage to try and love, but that didn't end up as I envisioned it. Perhaps I wasn't meant to be loved, or to be free, but I don't want to die.

I slide my hand inside my apron, looking for the pen I remember sliding in there and grip the top. I press on it with the pad on my thumb, so the ballpoint locks in place, watching the hooded figure. The bus stops moving, and I hear the airlock hiss and the door open.

I run out of the bus, my breath feeling like sharp glass in my throat, running down the sidewalk toward the gates of my house. My lungs burn, but I manage to look behind me. The lights from inside the bus are shining bright, and when I think it's going to shut the door, a gloved hand keeps it from closing, and the hooded figure steps out. My stomach drops, letting the dread seep in when I see him walking briskly toward me.

I turn and run as fast as I can, tears sliding down my cheeks. *Oh God, please. Please.* A gloved hand covers my mouth. I'm lifted off the ground, and the night sky feels like it dropped under me. I feel something sharp and everything goes dark.

I wake up in my bed for what feels like a split second. I look under the sheet. My mouth is dry like sandpaper, and I see that I'm naked, except for my panties. I sit up and place a hand over my forehead. Was it a dream? Am I going crazy?

I check my phone for the time and realize it's 9 a.m. and see a missed text.

Dorian: Don't be a bad girl.

Asshole.

"It is time for your internships. As you may already be aware, they need to be completed at the start of next week. All of you will be assigned a company that is part of a conglomerate to intern. Some of you need a job, and some of you already have jobs," Professor Klein announces to the class.

Professor Klein always wears a suit like he just came from working on Wall Street and fucked his secretary in the lunchroom. His tie is loose, his brown hair looks freshly fucked, and he has a look that screams anywhere but here as he paces with his hands crossed behind him, walking the classroom from end to end.

"A paper is being passed around that includes the contact information, address, and who you will be reporting to for the week. At the end of the week, I want your report on what you learned and how you could improve the company. The CEO will also report on your performance. This is necessary for you to graduate. If you don't complete it satisfactorily, you fail and have to retake this portion of the course in order to graduate."

Good. If I fail, I can buy myself time from marrying Dorian. The paper reaches my desk, and I slide my finger until it stops on my name and follow the dotted line to the company.

Riodrick and Riordan Holdings and Capital Investment.
CEO Alaric **Riodrick-Riordan**
Report to Sasha Barnes, Executive Secretary
216-445-3800 ext. 251
4321 N. Riodrick ***Blvd***
Kenyan, Ohio, 45874

I sag in my chair and look at the paper, reading it in disbelief. He planned this like some sick joke. I don't have clothes to wear to an internship at a billion-dollar company. I've seen how Alaric dresses in suits that cost more than a used car. I only have gala dresses I've acquired for special occasions and outfits to go to parties from Claire or if my mother called the boutique because my father requested it. Dresses are always for a lavish occasion that can't be worn again—like celebrities getting criticized for wearing the same things twice. I always found that stupid, so every time I had one, I would give it away without my parents noticing; I anonymously delivered it to a female Prey that was similar to my size. No one would question a free ten-thousand-dollar dress delivered to their dorm room. Lizzy didn't when I offered to gift her a prom dress by altering it to fit. It felt good to do something nice for someone. Work clothes were never a priority because the restaurant provided the employees with uniforms, so I never had to save to buy them.

After class, I walk toward the cemetery and stop at the entrance to buy flowers for Alicia. It's a beautiful day. The sun is out, but the trees offer enough shade to sit. Springtime in Kenyan is one of my favorite times of the year because it's not too cold or too hot. It's just right.

I bend and slide my hands over the marble of Alicia's grave, removing the dried leaves. Removing a small water bottle, I fill the flower holders to place the red roses in each.

"I miss you…I miss our talks on the phone at night when I tell you everything. I miss your voice and laugh because it was the best sound." I sit cross-legged, not caring that anyone thinks I'm crazy for talking to my dead best friend. I turn my head because that feeling creeps up my neck again like I'm being watched, but no one is there, except the lady with the bucket selling different types of flowers.

Facing Alicia's grave, I sniff. "Guess what? I have an internship, and it's with your cousin, out of all people. I think he planned it to be that way, and to be honest, I'm scared," I choke out. "Every time I'm around him, it gets worse. It's like he's some curse or something, and I need saving. I've had thoughts of running away on my own. I'm saving—"

"Saving for what?" I freeze when I hear Reid's voice. I close my eyes, hoping he didn't hear everything I said.

I look up and meet his dark stare. "Nothing."

He grins, but his eyes tell me I'm full of shit. His hand slides into his pocket and pulls out a thin chain with a silver locket in the shape of a heart holding it out to me. "I think she would have wanted you to have this. I'll admit, I didn't want to give it to you because I wanted everything that was hers to stay within the family."

I squint from the sun's glare as the trees sway with the breeze. "You don't have to give it to me."

He extends his hand, and the locket swings back and forth. "I think you were meant to have this, and she didn't get the chance to give it to you. If anything, it belongs to you."

I take it from him with a smile, feeling the connection from something that belonged to her that she wanted me to have. "Thank you. It means a lot."

He looks away and is about to turn but pauses, his shoulders tensing from the effort. "Whatever you are planning to do, don't do it."

Gripping the locket in the palm of my hand, I give him a tight smile. "I don't know what you mean."

He slides his fingers through his dark hair, like it takes every effort inside him to say what he needs to say. This is the most we have spoken that hasn't included a middle finger or a snarky comment. "She wouldn't want anything to happen to you, Veronica."

I let out a slow breath because I didn't want anything to happen to Alicia and I know she wouldn't want me to suffer the same fate. But I blame myself for not asking Reid for help when I should have told him what she was planning and didn't. He could have saved her.

"I'm sorry." I look at the headstone with her name on it in gold lettering. "It should have been me in there and not her." A tear escapes the corner of my eye, and needles prick my nose. "It should have been me," I whisper.

He pinches his brows. "It's not your fault, Veronica. You didn't kill her. They did."

He means the assholes in the Order that voted for her to be hunted down like an animal and killed along with her boyfriend. Assholes like Charles Devlin who makes it his mission to rip everything I love away from me.

I shake my head with tears running down my cheeks because he doesn't know the truth. It was because of me he voted. "It is my fault, Reid." I sniff, wiping my face. "I should have never been friends with her."

"Why?"

I close my eyes, and my chest tightens. "Because people like me are not supposed to have friends like her." I stand, wiping my hands on the back of my leggings. "I'm no good, Reid. I'm nothing but a worthless bitch that doesn't deserve anything, and I think you were right."

"About what? What are you saying, Veronica? You talk in riddles sometimes, and it makes you sound—"

"Crazy." I finish for him.

"Yeah," he agrees, nodding his head. "It makes you sound crazy." He raises his hand frustratingly, making a fist. "But then there are times where there is something…something about you that is different, like it's all an act or maybe you were like that all along."

He doesn't know and he isn't supposed to know anything about me or what I do and why. "Do you know why I'm interning at Riodrick and Riordan with your cousin? Is this some sick joke?"

"I didn't know. We don't keep tabs on each other with what we do or with who unless it's important to the family business or a threat. I don't believe you are a threat, and for the reason behind you completing the internship there..." he shrugs, "it could be simple coincidence, or…he wants you there for whatever reason."

I roll my eyes dramatically. "Yeah, to finish me off before I graduate. It's not like I'm after him. I have to marry a psychotic asshole before I graduate."

"Who said Dorian Black was the psycho? We both know who is." He leans forward and says softly, "You're not married to him yet, Veronica. You're still game." He arches his neck, covers his mouth with the palm of his hand, and continues, "There is no key to Alaric, Veronica, but you are the door he needs to open."

What does he mean? I don't get the chance to ask because he walks away. All that I got was that I'm still game. It means no one is required to be faithful until the marriage takes place because it was voted by the Order, including me. But there is no end point behind an infinite game, just winners and losers.

VERONICA

"HE IS EXPECTING YOU, MR. RIODRICK," my grandfather's secretary says, standing in the doorway to my grandfather's private offices. I place the magazine I was flipping through on the table and get up.

I don't correct her about using my grandfather's last name and not my father's because I'm part of him too, and so is Reid, and so was Alicia, but he refuses to talk about her. She was the spitting image of my mother, unlike my aunt, who was her opposite, with dark hair and eyes. Alicia and I were the only ones that inherited my grandfather's gray eyes.

Turning the door knob, I enter my grandfather's opulent office. The smell of wood, whiskey, and fine cigars permeate the room's ambiance. "You wanted to see me?" my grandfather says, sitting in his leather chair like a throne.

"Yes, I have something to discuss with you that I trust you have the answers to," I reply, unbuttoning my suit jacket and taking a seat.

My grandfather stepped down as an active member of the Order but still holds power; yet, only a few know he can overrule along with Mr. Bedford, but they rarely bother themselves with Kenyan matters. Mr. Bedford and my father vote on issues involving world leaders.

"I trust this has nothing to do with business matters. Because the hotels and all investments are making billions in profit. You're having an excellent year, so I trust you are here in a personal capacity."

"You know me too well, Grandfather."

"I know you better than most because you think and are ruthless like me, and that is what makes a great leader."

"I want to ask you about Mr. Devlin's daughter, Veronica."

He gets up, walks to the bar, and pours three fingers of whiskey into two glasses with two ice cubes. Giving me his back, he asks, "What about Devlin's daughter?"

"She is my intern for the week before she graduates."

He chuckles and hands me the glass. "You always had a thing for the girl."

I take the glass, but he has a glint in his eyes that tells me there is more. "Thank you. It's not a thing. We both know Mr. Devlin is not our favorite."

He takes a seat. "There are no favorites, my boy. Only players. Mr. Devlin is an atheist at heart. He always hated the religious aspect and history that the Order was founded on, dating back to the eighteen hundreds. His vows on marriage are a lie. Everything he stands for" — he takes a sip and swallows — "is a lie."

"What are you saying?"

"Miss Devlin is not his daughter, Alaric." I almost drop the glass but grip it tightly, almost breaking it in my hand. My chest tightens because that can't be true. "I can tell you are shocked, dumbfounded, but really, did you think a man would let his daughter be what she is?"

I stare at the painting behind him, trying to piece things together in her behavior. "But I thought, er…I don't know—"

"I know you are very fond of the girl, but most of them are."

I frown, placing the glass on his desk with a thud. "What are you saying? Who's Them?"

"I'm not supposed to discuss this, but since you have graduated for some time now and have chosen to remain without a wife, I can discuss matters like this, and you are allowed to explore Miss Devlin, but I feel they won't approve, given her affection for you." I tilt my head to the side, placing my finger over my mouth. My mind is muddled with unanswered questions. "Dating back centuries when the Order was established, they believed in adopting a religion acceptable to conduct meetings inside the church. Rules in those days were adopted under the pretext of religion and the use of the

Bible. In the library, there is a book about the history of Kenyan. It briefly discusses what I'm about to say, but Alaric, it can't leave this room."

"I understand." But I don't. What does Veronica have anything to do with any of this? "Members before us for generations still adopt these ancient rules and still manage to abide by them in modern society, claiming that they are also God's way. Like an eye for an eye and that sort of thing." He takes another sip, but that is the last thing I want, a glass of whiskey. "Are you familiar with the term sex slave or woman used to serve men in higher order just like Hebrew soldiers."

"I've heard of it, but in our case, that is human trafficking and illegal."

He places the glass on his desk with a thud. "That's not what I'm referring to in any way. There were debates in Deuteronomy in modern times, but it was adopted by the Order and still can be used before the Catholic church since it was never voted off because it didn't favor men that had to marry a chosen. It isn't a secret Mrs. Devlin, Veronica's mother, committed adultery with Mr. Bedford."

"Yeah, so. I'm not aware of the details, but they dealt with it. It wasn't like people didn't sleep with each other in college before graduation, so it didn't matter to them." Veronica was born before that, and Mr. Bedford claims his children, so I know she isn't his. She looks nothing like them. The only thing Veronica inherited from her mother were her eyes.

"That is where you are wrong, my boy. It did matter because it wasn't the first time...she is guilty of being promiscuous and a pill popper that lives in guilt with what her husband has done with her daughter."

I slide on the edge of my seat. A wave of blazing fury slides inside my veins, waking up the demon inside me. "What has he done?"

"I'm afraid, with the look in your eye, that I would need to send you to the library where you can conduct research. Brush up on your history and that sort of thing."

"Tell me," I demand.

"I can't tell you, my boy. I've said enough. You need to find this out independently because now she is under your supervision for the week. Make the most of it how you see fit and remember there are consequences for her and what she is allowed and not allowed to do."

"What does that mean?"

He downs the glass of whiskey in one go and stands. "In a few months, she will marry. Everyone else attended the vote; I recall you and everyone else didn't object. I'm sure Dorian Black feels he won something over you since you denied his business proposal when in all honesty, you could care less about the girl."

"What do you mean?" I ask. "He knows how I feel about her."

I don't want to admit I secretly objected but was too hung up about what she did that night at the initiation party. The last person I wanted touching her was that snake Dorian Black, but I kept telling myself she deserves him, but avoided admitting it to myself how I feel about her. I always blamed it on a lustful attraction because Veronica is gorgeous.

"Something you had in the palm of your hand like a gift but then you let it go like a dog, an owner doesn't want, so they put the bitch in the car and drive it to a farm or secluded area to let it out so they could drive off, never once looking in the rearview mirror so their conscience is clean. But to someone else, it seems God answered their prayers." My grandfather slides one hand into the pocket of his pants with ease. "She's not your problem, Alaric. No one cares about that girl." He pierces me with his gaze. "Especially you."

"Is that all you need, Mr. Riordan?" the librarian asks with her wired spectacles resting on her chest.

She looks like she belongs in a haunted library. Her skin is ghastly white and wrinkled, and she looks like she is a breath away from dying.

I flip the leather-bound hardcover book and respond, "That is all."

The last time I was in the library was to fuck in the back by the encyclopedia section. This is the last place I expected to spend my Friday afternoon when I should be going over my financials, but it would have to wait because Veronica is due in my office Monday morning.

It was a dick move to make sure she completed her internship at my office. I was able to override Dorian's request because she doesn't belong to him yet. Some things don't add up when it comes to her. Her eyes continue to haunt me from the minute I felt her in my arms. Her lips are a sweet poison. One look in the cloudy depths of her eyes hypnotized me after tasting her lips, loving the smell of her breath. The memory of the way her lips tasted stayed with me. It hurt to think I was being used because of my name by the man that sent her.

The history of the Order adopted certain rules in the book of Deuteronomy and in the Bible under Exodus. It reads members of the Order adopted beliefs that God could live among the people by cleansing sin and guilt when sin occurs. In Exodus 21, a man can call his daughter to slavery to serve men. I scroll down and find polygamy is allowed, and it's true, Dravin and Draven with Gia. It is all here. The rules in alliances with partners and how sex is allowed between partners.

I scroll down until I reach the term sex slaves, and I feel my blood turn cold when I read the first line.

A man can sell his daughter to another member of the Order if certain obligations are met. Once she is used when given by the hands of God. She is to be beautiful and questioned if she was born out of evil to corrupt. The law of Moses can be adopted when the woman is a virgin, but first must perform a type of ritual for purification for a life as a concubine. After her first taste of flesh, she is purified, and from then on, to serve. Purification is the pain given from the sins committed.

A man can have multiple wives if his brother dies. It also states he can impregnate a slave with no lineage (Prey).

The Prey is marked after the ritual so that there is no question about what she represents among the members. She must perform and be purified from sins committed by the flesh infinitely. She is to serve.

The man she belongs to can marry her or keep her as his concubine and do with her as he wishes until he tires of her and can set her free. If the Prey chooses a master and he has no desire for her and she is set free until she is selected by another, but this must occur before her graduation. Concubines under the rule of the Order are considered Prey and property of their master. She is to serve and obey and provide an heir. Her true master is the first one she serves with children in the eyes of the Order to be deemed abolished for her past sins. She is to serve her true master until her death. If a concubine does not fulfill her duty, she is ordered the penalty of death or sacrifice to eternal damnation, feeding the craving of flesh from man to ward off lust from the legion.

I shut the book and slide my fingers in my hair, pulling at the top in frustration. What. The. Fuck. That is what my grandfather was trying to tell me. Veronica is Prey. She chose me that night but I didn't know. And I set her free. I close my eyes. The word, *whore,* flashes in my mind. I called her a whore. The book talks about a mark, but there isn't a mark on her. I've never seen it.

My grandfather's words replay in my mind. *"No one cares about her. Especially you. He won something."* He won because no one gave a shit about her. She was acting like they wanted her too. Veronica would have never chosen Dorian that night because she chose me and he wanted her. *He played you. He knew what she was.*

Her feelings for me were genuine, and I…let her go. I—

There was no way I knew the truth.

In her eyes, I'm like everyone else in her world.

In her eyes, I'm one of them.

She couldn't be more wrong.

But I am an absolute master in the realms of greed and disgust. Beyond measure. Dorian Black wants to play a dangerous game. I going to give him a war.

VERONICA

MY DOCS THUD on the marble floor of Riodrick-Riordan Holding and Capital Investments' top floor. I ignore the glances at my attire as I walk through the lobby and am shown to the executive offices after giving my name at the front desk. The short skirt, pantyhose, and long-sleeve fitted shirt are what I had, and I wasn't going to waste three weeks of pay on a pantsuit that I would only need for a week.

When I approach the double doors, I reach a desk with a gold nameplate that reads Sasha Barnes. Her smile when she sees me standing in front of her desk is lethal and scrutinizing as her eyes trail the length of me like I'm an insect she wants to swat away.

I give no judgment where it isn't given, but my intuition was right the first time I saw her. She still sees me as a threat, even though he treated me like I was a blood stain on his shirt. I'm not the only one she should be worried about. He isn't tamed. He runs out and picks his prey as he so chooses.

"You must be Veronica. Now that I can place a name to the face. I'll have you know that your attire is not appropriate."

I lean on her desk and tilt my head, letting the platinum locks from my wig brush the surface of her black desk. "Oh, Sasha. You should be rejoicing. You look so sophisticated and older. You can't possibly give a shit what I'm wearing." She's wearing a black skirt suit with sky-high heels, and judging from the red soles, they are Louboutin's. They are gorgeous, but the way she carries herself with her insecurities on her sleeve, they can easily pass for Steve Madden knockoffs. Her blazer is flat, desperately needing a push-up bra.

"I'm afraid it's not the standard here; this is not a college frat party."

"Why don't we let the big man judge." I scrunch my nose like I smell something rotten. "Oh, and by the way, you still smell of inferiority. It's overpowering the room."

Her eyes blaze in anger. Her mouth set in a tight line. "The five minutes you had with him is in the past. You're nothing to him."

She overheard, or he told her. Her words sting. But I'm used to the pain. I've learned to use my words as weapons and know things about Alaric. Things I've overheard pierced my heart, but some things need to be repeated so that they sink in deeper.

"Then why am I here? He has the right to send me away, you know." I turn to her and cup my mouth, lowering my voice. "You need to accept things the way they are, Sasha. You can only suck his cock so much before he gets bored, and then—" I place my finger over my lips. "He sends you home to wash your disgusting spit off his skin." I straighten and smile. "You're not the first or the last he chokes with his cock."

"It tasted great last night," she purrs.

I have a retort on my tongue, but his office door opens, and the man is lust wrapped in a suit you want to suck off. His fitted suit is a dark gray, contrasting with the light gray of his eyes. His crisp white designer shirt is open at the throat, not being bothered with a tie that screams fuck it, I wear what I want. His tattoos are like scriptures you want to read all over his skin, and you need to remove his clothes to discover the secrets of his past.

His eyes flit back and forth between his current fuck and the woman he hates. I know I look childish in comparison. I couldn't keep his attention for five minutes, but I didn't beg him to be here. I'm unsure why I am here if he hates me so much, but I'm about to find out.

"Miss Devlin," Alaric says with formality with a wave of his hand like I'm one of his business associates and has been waiting for me to arrive. Not breaking his stare, he says, "Sasha, hold my calls."

"Yes, sir," she says tightly. His eyes, calm in their gray depths, hold a hidden warning to obey, and I must admit, her last remark stung. I'm jealous. I shouldn't be, but I am.

When I enter, he slams the door shut and pins me to it, holding me by the throat. He has to see the terror in my eyes, but he doesn't waver. He boldly stares at me, rooting me to the spot.

"What are you doing?" I ask.

"What I need to do…" He breathes heavily. "We both know I had a hand in you coming here. And do you know why?"

I shake my head.

"Because I want you to serve me." My eyes widen in sheer terror. "Shh…" he coos. "You will serve me until I decide for you to stop and, of course, before you marry the one that shall not be named because I know Veronica. I know enough."

I'm livid. *Bastard.* Tears sting my eyes as I try to regain my composure. "I hate you," I say through clenched teeth, looking deep into his eyes.

"I won't take you by force, Veronica, but I expect obedience. I won't tolerate you going against what I say. You take what I give and be the good girl I know you to be." His tongue skims my ear and whispers, "You obey, and I will reward you. I can be generous or I can punish you." He slides his hand between my thighs, swiping a finger over the pantyhose and panties covering my slit, and I mewl. "You have the right idea of what I want you to wear when you come to see me, just the wrong fabric"—he slides his fingers deeper between my thighs—"Something so beautiful shouldn't be wrapped in something so cheap."

He pushes off the door, releasing his hand from my throat and between my legs, and then walks toward his desk, picking up his phone and placing a call. I swipe the tears from my face and cross my hands over my chest, feeling humiliated by my reaction to him.

He knows, Veronica.

He knows what I am, and he did nothing to save me.

All I can do is throw him off balance.

What choice do I have?

His eyes meet mine as he speaks into his phone. "Portman, bring the car. Five minutes." He hangs up, opening his suit jacket, sliding it off his strong shoulders, and my mouth goes dry. "From the way you are ogling me, I can tell this isn't hard for you."

I look away, getting caught staring at him because the man is in perfect shape. He's pure muscle with an ideal physique from spending hours in the gym or swimming. My eyes may sell him a fantasy, but my words tell him a different story. "I have had better."

"Sure, you have. I can tell." He places the jacket on his chair. "Let's go."

"Where?" I challenge.

"Wherever I want."

"Right," I answer tightly. "Is there anything I should know? How deep do you want your cock sucked? How wide are my legs to be spread while you pound me like an animal?"

"I'll let you know when I require to be serviced."

He's throwing the same words I said the other day at Draven's party to Garret, '*Serviced.*'

That was different, and it was something horrible that turned into something two single people would do for each other as friends. Even though Garret's father is a prick, Garret isn't a creep like I thought he was.

Alaric walks forward, and I turn to allow him to pass, so he can open the door, but he pauses and gives me an impish smile. "I will be serviced, Veronica." He takes my lips in his, and our tongues meet. Hating him so much but wanting him so bad. He licks, tastes, and fucks me with his mouth, sliding his hand across my cheek, caressing my skin for a few seconds, and I bite him hard, tasting blood before he pulls away, leaving my lips swollen and my head in a daze. His lips break into a wicked smile, licking the blood off from where I bit him.

"I'm different from all the others, Veronica. I'm beyond what is deemed good or evil. You finally did it." Did what? A wave of horror causes the tiny hairs to stand up on my arms at the coldness in his eyes. I'm terrified. He has the power to kill me. "I'm going to enjoy the way you have driven me to insanity." He growls and licks me from my chin to the tip of my nose like a dog. He opens the door when I raise my hand. "Don't wipe it off," he warns.

Dropping my hand, I follow him to see Sasha widen her eyes when he heads to the elevator. "Mr. Riordan?"

He presses the button, turns sideways, and answers her question with a furtive gleam in his eyes. "I'll be out to lunch. Clear my calendar for the rest of the day."

"Yes, sir," she says flatly.

We reach the blacked-out Maybach SUV waiting on the curb. Dark and imposing like the man that owns it. The bodyguard I saw at the Galleria stands with the door open, tipping his head in my direction his eyes sliding over me, but when Alaric looks over, he straightens and looks away.

"I'm glad we understand each other," he says.

"My apologies, sir."

The man, I'm assuming is Portman, shuts the door after we are both inside. Alaric has a hungry sneer on his lips when I cross my legs, and he presses the privacy screen closed. "Take off your panties and pantyhose and put your boots back on."

When I hesitate, he reaches and tugs the pantyhose hard, making them rip. "Off," he demands.

After a few moments of staring at each other, knowing he can force me to do anything he wants, I nod and slide my boots off, not missing the shit-eating grin on his face when I slide my panties over my knees.

"Like this," I say in a taunting voice, opening my legs.

He leans closer to get a look at my waxed pussy. The pupils of his eyes darken, full of thirst. My clit is throbbing for him to touch me, but my mind is telling me not to give in to him, that he is just like all the men in my life. Evil.

He slides his finger on my thigh to my knee, making me squirm. "I want access to you at all times." His fingers grip the tips of my blonde hair. "I don't want this on. I want your natural hair."

"My father will not approve."

"Fuck your father. You serve me now, and I don't want some fake version of you."

I nod because that is the rule, serve and obey. If not, it is the same as sinning. My father will not agree with me parading around members of the Order with my natural hair. It is forbidden.

I glance out the window. "Then I won't be considered pure under his rules."

"That is pointless when I'm going to dirty you, and everyone is going to see it, but like I said before, I need consent before touching you, and I don't need your hair a different shade to think you're pure. I took what was pure about you—"

"And I bled for it," I say quietly.

"I don't regret taking it. I regret not taking it sooner."

Alaric has the driver stop in front of the Galleria, and I don't question why we are here. I also don't miss the way Alaric leans back adjusting his erection in his pants, trying to get a mental image but coming up blank. That night we went right into things, and there was no time to explore his body how I wanted to. All I remember were his rough thrusts that felt like he was splitting me in two. He has a large cock, but I want to know if it's pink at the tip or darker than the tone of his skin and how it would feel on my tongue when he slides to the back of my throat.

Then the part of me that wants to be free of this life kicks in; this man cares nothing for me. He will use me and then hand me over to a man that will make me suffer. This is just a game to him. I'm something to be used. No better than a toy for men to enjoy.

We enter a boutique called Madame with dark lace and sex toys on glass shelves. When the owner of the store notices me with Alaric, she smiles coquettishly. "Is this her?"

"It is."

She undresses me with her eyes, pausing on my breasts, waist, and thighs. "She's perfect."

"I know," he responds.

Some may think it's a compliment, but I know better. Perfect to be his whore and unworthy to be loved.

"Right this way. I have already brought some things out. I just need to take some measurements and I can make anything you wish in her size."

I'm inside the dressing room, and there are different styles of underwear and bras neatly laid out. Black, white, nude, and red.

There are small scraps of lace barely covering anything. I turn when I hear the door shut, but I'm not alone. He's standing behind me and I'm in front of the mirror.

"Take off your clothes."

"Get out."

"I'm afraid that is not the way this works." I gasp when he pulls off my wig and throws it in the corner, tugging my wig cap and releasing my long dark hair. "You won't be needing that anymore." He wraps my hair around his fist and shoves my pleated skirt roughly down my legs.

"What are you doing," I hiss.

"What I asked you to, but you have a problem listening."

"I'm here to do an internship."

He laughs. "Not anymore. Your internship also involves pleasuring me."

"I'm not a whore," I seethe, my nostrils flaring.

He pulls my head back and lowers his lips, licking my earlobe and causing me to squeeze my legs. I can smell his cologne. Spice, man, and sex. "You're my whore now." His hands slide between my thighs, sticky with my arousal. "You're such a bad girl, Veronica. How are you going to try on the lingerie when your pussy is all wet? You'll ruin everything in the store." He swipes his finger over my clit, feeling the evidence of how wet I am. He lifts it up, so I have no choice but to see my arousal on his fingers and then slides them in his mouth, closing his eyes in delight.

I try to get free, utilizing the moment, and surprisingly, he releases the hold on my hair. "You're sick."

He smiles devilishly. "I know. It's what they keep telling me. Try on the black set with the lace."

Once I have the set on, I notice the panties are crotchless. I pick up the nude and the white, and they're all the same. "You realize that the panties are crotchless."

"Yes, I know. I always want access to your pussy. It also makes it easier to slide things inside." I glare at him through the mirror. "You'll thank me when you bleed." I roll my eyes in annoyance.

He opens the door, and I overhear him tell the woman, "I'll take all of it. Two sets of each. Crotchless. I also need the three-prong toys."

He's buying me sex toys.

"All of them, sir?"

"Yes. She will be taking the set she has on now. I also want multiple sets of thigh-high pantyhose."

I've never worn such expensive or intricate lingerie before. There are about fifty different sets and colors. He's gone mad. I'm sure it's not his first time buying them for a woman, and that fact alone gives me the courage to walk out of the fitting room clad in the lingerie. It's not the first-time people have seen me and I want to defy him.

He does a double take, and the woman handing him the receipt raises a brow and smirks. "Get back inside and put your clothes on." He growls.

I lick my lips seductively. "I thought you wanted me accessible at all times?"

His nostrils flare, and I know I'm like a dangling steak to a lion. He rushes me, and I shrink back in fear when he grips my arm, tugging me back into the fitting room and slamming the door shut. He pushes me against the door, breathing heavily. "You're playing with fire. I think you need to be punished."

He pushes me on the shoulder, forcing me to kneel in front of him. He unbuckles his pants, and the sound of the belt buckle causes me to wince. Images of the bathtub flash, and I close my eyes, bringing my hands together in prayer like I was taught. The memory of pain from the feeling of leather smacking against the skin when I didn't obey.

"What the fuck are you doing?"

"I'm sorry I have sinned. Please don't hurt me."

"I'm not going to hurt you, but you're making it difficult for me not to. Open your eyes," he demands. When I open them, his eyes are blazing in fury mixed with confusion. He pulls his hard cock out and begins to fist himself. "Hold on to me, and don't look away."

He strokes his cock from root to tip. I watch as he masturbates, and he's gorgeous. He bites his bottom lip but doesn't stop staring at me. "Pull your tits out of your bra for me."

I obey.

I slide the lace down under my full breasts, so he can see my aroused nipples lifted high and watch him lick his lips like an animal. He strokes faster, his bottom lip jutting out, veins from his strong neck protruding with the effort as he fucks himself faster. I play with my nipples with one hand while holding on to his hips, digging my nails, and leaving half-moon marks on his inked skin with the other. "I'm going to fuck you so hard in every hole in your body. The scent of my cum will be your new scent," he rasps. "If any man tries to smell you, all they will get is the scent of my cum, then I will kill them for trying."

The head of his cock is engorged and full of blood, but I make sure not to touch it. It would mean I'm giving in. Surrendering. And that is the last thing I will do, surrender. I'm on my knees for him because he has done what no other has done in his world, asked for consent. I could say no and I know he wouldn't do it.

I feel him stiffen, his nostrils flare, his breath coming hard, and I know he's coming. "Veronica," he moans my name. Spurts of cum fly out in his hands, on his shaved pubic area, and some even lands on my nipples.

"Lick it clean, like the bad girl you are."

"No."

I won't give in. I can't.

"Fine." He lifts me up and scoops up the cum, flicks it off my nipples, and presses me against the mirror, so I can see him. "Spread your thighs and arch your neck and give me your lips," he commands.

When I arch my neck, he slides his tongue inside my mouth and moans. My hand reaches behind me and cup his cheek, licking the inside of his mouth over his straight white teeth and tasting copper from the cut on his lip. I'm so wet I can feel my arousal sliding down my thighs. "Fuck my mouth with your tongue, baby." He breathes over my lips. It's like we need each other's air to survive.

"Yes." I moan subconsciously, and that's his cue, and I don't realize what I've done until his fingers slid inside me like his tongue is in my mouth. I try to pull away, but his grip tightens, deepening the kiss while his fingers full of his cum slide inside me. He withdraws his fingers and wipes them on my belly. "Next time, it will be my cock fucking you hard."

He puts himself away and exits the fitting room, leaving me standing confused, wet, and full of his cum between my thighs.

VERONICA

"I SEE you have to complete your internship with Riodrick-Riordan Holdings," my father says, nursing his glass of whiskey.

"Yes. I was assigned to his company for the week."

His left eye twitches. "Are you fucking him?"

I lean back like he slapped me. "No."

His phone rings, he looks at the screen and answers. I watch as he listens, piercing me with a look of hatred. "I understand"—he taps the desk and looks out the window—"of course." He tosses the phone on his desk with eyes raging in anger. "You ungrateful bitch!" he bellows, his face turning red and spittle flying from his mouth, making me want to gag. I don't know why he's mad, but I sense it has something to do with Alaric. "You have no idea who you are dealing with, but I promise you, Veronica. You fuck up, and I will punish you. I will inflict pain on you that you might not come back from. You will be his little whore, but you will marry Dorian. I don't care if he has to marry your corpse. Alaric Riordan is going to fuck you like an animal and leave you like the whore that you are. You spread your legs for him, but you come here to purify your soul when the time comes."

This all because he doesn't have another heir, and could not get a woman pregnant out of wedlock, so what would be the point in that. My mother can't have any more children after me. She hemorrhaged after he beat her, and he won't divorce her because no one wants to be married to a defiling atheist. Pig.

"Since you haven't fucked him again and he is a higher member of the Order, you must go to him, but first, you must cleanse. You need to be reminded, Veronica."

I swallow the lump in my throat because this part breaks me

every time. I close my eyes and wait. I pray like the priest taught me to when I need saving.

I open my eyes after a while and turn to see Charles Devlin sitting near an old freestanding tub with brass legs. Dread fills me. "You know I hate waiting, Veronica. I hear him undo his belt.

The clinging noise of the buckle assaults my ears like nails being dragged down a chalkboard. "In the tub, princess."

I flinch, hating the endearment, and step closer, looking at the hot steam rising from the antique tub and wishing something would pull me under and drown me when I step inside.

I remove every article of clothing, careful not to wet my platinum hair or the wig I placed over my head before meeting him. Charles hates my natural hair because it reminds him, I don't belong. I must have gotten the color from my real father. My heart is hammering inside my chest, scolding me for not giving in to Alaric. I want to run out of the room, but the door swings open and three other members walk in and I close my eyes so I don't have to look at their faces. If I attempt to disobey, they will just kill me right here.

Sometimes when they are circling around me, their old beady eyes look at me naked, salivating. I'm not surprised that I recognize Dorian's father. It's the first time I have ever seen him here with my father but nothing surprises me. These are the moments when I think of dying.

But those thoughts come when you want the pain to stop.

I step inside the scalding hot water, wincing when it stings my skin. I grip the soap bar, lather it in my hands, and close my eyes.

"You're such a good girl. Let me see how pretty you are while you wash away the sins you have committed from the past," he says between the clinking sound of metal from the belt buckle. "You're a sinner, Veronica. You were consummated by sin. Born out of it. An abomination no different than a bastard child in the eyes of God, and I'm your savior."

He repeats the same words, reminding me that he isn't my biological father and has groomed me to be a slave serving the higher Order. I'm a Prey born and groomed to do as they ask. I wasn't supposed to be born, so they made me pay for the sins my parents committed. My father in death, my mother in guilt, only to be kept alive if I do as they ask. I'm to be punished and enslaved until a man comes to claim me, and when he does, I have to obey or die. This is my nightmare, and I'm their sacrifice, begging for forgiveness for I have sinned.

After being dropped off by Alaric's driver the day before, I was tired from all the shopping. He picked out all my clothes like I was a toddler. The designer boutiques knew him by name but treated me with respect. The staff took measurements for my clothes and color matched my foundation, and selected makeup.

There were so many packages but they weren't dropped off when Portman took me home. I didn't bother to ask about where he was taking them because I feared what awaited me when I got home. I showered, drank some tea, and slept, dreaming of a different life for the first time since I was eighteen. It was of me and Alaric making love in a bed. The way he looked at me in my dream was how I always wished he would look at me, but then I woke up and was summoned by Charles Devlin. A man I hate with every fiber of my being. A man I have reluctantly had to call father.

I check the time and prepare for my night shift at the restaurant. I couldn't give up my shift because I desperately need the money. Being around Alaric during the day is the same as being at school, so I decided not to take the week off.

"You have a visitor in booth five," Dorothy says, giving me a wink.

I smile and lean back, waiting for Peter, our cook, to hand me the sandwich a customer ordered. As my eyes focus on booth five, the smell of French fries frying causes a cloud of smoke from the heat, making the alarm go off. My stomach drops when I see Alaric sitting alone in the booth with one hand sprawled across the red vinyl bench seat, perusing the menu.

"Why is he here?" Adam asks, standing behind me.

I play with the hem of my apron, wondering the same thing.

"I don't know. Maybe I forgot to do something at the office."

I told Dorothy, Adam, and his sisters that I was interning with Alaric, and they were all surprised that he allowed it. Him being here is for a reason, and I know it has nothing to do with the office.

"Go, I'll take the order to your table."

"Are you sure?' I ask, still looking at the booth behind the counter. I like the fact that I can watch him without him noticing. It reminds me of all the times I would stare, and he didn't know I existed. I always knew it was a pipe dream to be with a guy like him, my time with Charles Devlin and his cronies solidifying it.

"Yeah, go ahead."

I take a deep breath and head over to booth five. When he sees me approach, he drops the menu and slides his gaze up until he reaches my eyes. "How can I help you? Are you hungry?" I ask.

He smiles. "I'm hungry but not for the food. I need you. I need to blow off steam."

He came here like I'm a prostitute, and don't wait tables in a restaurant.

"Isn't your secretary available?" I gift him with a sarcastic smile. "She seems very passionate about her job…and you."

"Is she a problem for you?" he asks.

I think he's asking if I'm jealous or see her as a threat. The truth is, maybe. Do I want to be? No. Not like this. It was never supposed to be like this.

"Do you think she is a problem for me?"

"I don't know." He shrugs. "You brought her up. I didn't."

"Hmm…let me see. Then it isn't a problem with you when I hang around a guy I have slept with daily."

"Have you?" he says, looking toward Adam and then back at me with a hard glint in his eyes.

"Are you asking if I slept with anyone I work with?"

He leans back, sliding his ass half off the bench, and I wait a few seconds, making him sweat. "No," I finally say. "He's a friend, and I help his family out babysitting for his younger sister Melody, so she stays out of trouble."

He laughs, and I swear it's the sexiest laugh. His lips lift in a smile, showing those perfect white teeth, which makes my stomach flip. "You're trouble. How can you keep someone else out of it."

I fidget with the pen in my pocket and nervously click the top repeatedly, making a clicking sound. *Is he flirting with me?*

"I'm not trouble. It seems like I am or that I don't have friends because I had no choice but to alienate people. Most people think I'm some crazed bitch, and I get why they think that. But this is the only time I have to make friends and be myself. It is why I work the night shift when no one at Kenyan is around to see me because they won't be caught dead near Ohio State territory during the school year."

"Is that the only reason?" he inquires.

I'm surprised I'm even talking to him this way. Normally, people from Kenyan could care less about me, and I know why. It is my fault, but the freedom of choice was taken from me way too early. It is easy to say, *stand up for yourself. Run away.* Yeah, where would I go? They have all the resources in the world to find and kill me. My best friend is proof of that, and she simply ran away because she fell in love. Her parents loved her. Her brother and even her dangerous cousin with power and influence loved her, but they all had something in common. They loved her and none of them could stop it from happening. All those thoughts pop into my head when I want to run. The screams from my nightmares telling me to never look back is my inner weakness telling me to give up because I know the end result. It's the same as committing suicide.

"You mean the reason why I choose to work here?"

He nods.

I pull out the pad holding the pen in my hand. "People work because they need the money, and it's a way to survive. Now what can I get you?"

It's a hard pill to swallow, knowing where I live and that I have to work to pay for things I find trivial. The dresses are nice. You'd be surprised how much clothes cost when trying to blend in with rich pricks in high society. I'm Prey, which means I don't have a fat bank account like the other kids. I don't have a fancy car like Reid or Valen—I never learned how to drive. I have to take the bus or catch a ride.

Since I was best friends with Alicia, no one considered it in high school. After I was blacklisted my senior year by the man sitting in front of me and the asshole I'm now supposed to marry, no one gave a shit or looked closely. I was a nuisance. A threat and honestly, they were right. Charles Devlin made sure I was his puppet, ordering me to destroy lives.

"I'll have a milkshake."

"Flavor?"

He looks up. "What flavor is your favorite?"

Those damn butterflies are swarming in my stomach again. *Get a grip, Veronica.*

"Oreo, cookies and cream."

He taps the table with his hands like a drum. "Oreo, cookies and cream it is then," he says with a smile.

I snag my bottom lip with my teeth and write it down, even though it is unnecessary because I won't charge him after he bought me all those pretty clothes.

"I'll be right back."

"Where you goin?"

I blush. "I have to make your milkshake."

"They got you doing that too?"

"Uh…yeah." My cheeks flame like I'm sixteen, and my crush is right in front of me. "I'll be right back."

I scuttle behind the counter to make him the milkshake. "I wish I could make you blush like that," Adam says next to me, placing the dishes in the commercial dishwasher.

"I wasn't blushing," I say defensively.

"You know he keeps looking at me like he wants to murder me every time I talk to you, but I'll die a happy man because it's about time I see you get all girly for a guy."

I pick up the ice cream scooper and slide the freezer door open to scoop the ice cream. "I'm not girly for him." I shoot back, hating myself for reacting this way when I know all he wants is…what they all want, my body.

Adam places the milk on the counter from the fridge. "Then, don't blush, and you practically ran back here like your ass was on fire after you talked to him. He wouldn't stop staring at you at the party you invited me to. I overheard some things—"

I stiffen and place the blender on the machine. "They are all true," I say, turning on the blender and drowning out the rest.

When it finishes, and I am pouring the shake into the fifty's diner-styled shake glass, Adam says softly, "There is one important part that isn't true because I know you—the real you, Veronica. You're none of those things. I hope he realizes it before it's too late."

I grab the glass and look at my friend. "It's already too late, Adam."

Alaric left me burning in the fire twice. The first time I ran, he never went after me. I stumbled, I fell, but he was never there to catch me. The second time I stood, I pleaded with my eyes, my soul screaming at him to save me. He never looked up.

My heart burned inside a church before God's angels praying for a miracle. It never came, and I knew it was because I was unworthy in everyone's eyes.

I place the milkshake before Alaric and slide a straw next to the glass. "Will that be all?"

"What time do you get off?"

"Oh, that's right. You need to blow off steam," I say tonelessly. He frowns at my sudden change in attitude, but I'm glad I found the will to remind myself that I mean nothing to this man. I never did, and my future will never change, but this is the part of my day I control. "I'm going to say this only once." He looks up after sliding the straw inside the cup with a blank expression, but I continue, "Charles Devlin has respected my time while I work in this restaurant at night, and so has everyone else. This is a time that I'm me. A time that I'm not what someone expects me to be or do. It's a time where I'm not a slave to someone's pleasure, and I respectfully request you don't come here asking for something I would never give you if the circumstances were different"—I slam the ticket on the table—"shakes on the house. You have yourself a good rest of your night. Mr. Riordan."

He looks confused when I turn away, but Alaric needs to understand that he doesn't own me or this part of my life because of who he is. I worked hard to find my identity, even if very few people see who I really am.

VERONICA

I'M WALKING toward the bus stop, dragging my feet down the sidewalk in my Crocs with a thousand-dollar tip in my pocket at five a.m. I wanted to give the tip back but couldn't pass up on free money when I needed it. The money would help pay for lunch for the rest of the week, and I could save the rest for Christmas to help the staff with their families at the house. They have children to feed, and every year since I was a kid, they would all manage to get me a gift, and it was the best present I ever got because it was from a special place. A place called kindness, and only some are gifted with something so precious. I was alone during that time of year. Where families would get together and go on trips and create memories.

Every year, Charles made sure he took my mother away to another continent, so he wouldn't have to be reminded of me and what I stood for, infidelity. But in his mind, I would always be called Prey. I would see the sorrow in my mother's eyes, but ignored it because she could do nothing, and there was nothing I could do emotionally. Her fate was in my hands. But I had to admit, I loved Christmas because only those who cared about me the most, remembered that the real me existed.

The smell of morning dew is still in the air, and I knew it would disappear once the sun appeared on the horizon reminding me that day is just beginning. I tried to stay as long as possible at the restaurant because of what happened last time on the bus. I still can't remember exactly what occurred; I just remember waking up in my bed, and when I asked Marilyn, one of the housekeepers, she said she was fast asleep when I came home and didn't hear anything amiss.

I'm not sure if I took one of the pills or decided to stop taking them, even if it risked me getting nightmares. That reminds me...I skipped my visit with Dr. Wick last week and need to make sure I don't miss the next one, or Charles will be pissed he didn't get the scoop.

"Do you always tune out when sitting alone waiting for the bus in the early morning before the sun rises? Anyone can just walk up and mug you."

When I look up, Alaric is in his blacked-out Ferrari, idling at the curb like last time. "I've been watching you for about five minutes, and you didn't notice me."

I didn't notice him. I was stuck in my head like I usually am when I'm alone and have time to think. His last statement reminds me of the hooded figure with the plague mask. I know it's a signature mask from the Order's secret society. Jess described it in detail, and I know they exist because of Reid, but no one questions when and if they appear. But when they do, two things happen, you die, or they want you to know who they are. If they don't, you don't. I'm unsure if he's one of them or maybe he's too close to the top to bother with mundane dealings.

"I don't have much they can take," I say, looking down the dark road to see if the lights from the bus appear.

"Why don't you have a car?"

I glance at him, holding the medium-sized bag I purchased at Target on clearance tight against my stomach, surprised he even asked that question. "You're an intelligent guy. Why do you think?"

"Humor me," he shoots back.

I slide my dark hair over my shoulder and sigh, looking down the dark road again. "Why would I need a car if my chauffeur comes to pick me up? I know when he is always coming with enough room to take all of my friends along with me," I say flatly, turning my head to meet his stormy gray eyes that look almost black under the streetlights. "On gala days or special events, I get a limo that ensures I get home. You know, so I don't look bad, given my last name."

"Is that the truth?" he asks, surprising me again because he can't be so blind. "I want to know why Veronica doesn't have a car?"

"Why?"

"Because I want to know? Why don't you come with me and tell me? We have to be at the office in about four hours. Besides, your shift is over." He came to collect me since he owns my time technically and can decide what to do with it.

Rain begins to pour in sheets without warning, like the sky just opened up in anger.

I get up without having much of a choice. I'll get wet or worse, get sick, and then Marissa would have to stay longer because she refuses to leave me alone when I'm ill. The wind blows, and I gasp when the cold rain hits my uniform. I hear footsteps hit the pavement, and then I'm lifted off the ground bridal style, wrapping my arms around his neck. When he places me in the front passenger seat, I can smell his crisp cologne mixing with the rain and the hint of leather. He leans in, not caring that his back is getting wet, and turns to face me. "You'll catch a cold in the rain." The door slams shut.

He gets in the car, running his fingers through his damp hair and wiping his face. I see the lights from the bus finally pulling up when he drives off. I shiver from the air conditioner blowing over my wet arms. "Are you cold?"

"Yeah," I admit. He adjusts the temperature of the air conditioner so that it shoots warm.

"Thank you," I say softly.

"So tell me?"

I rub my lips together and begin. "I can't afford a car, and it would be pointless to save for one because I never learned how to drive. I only have an identification card. I'm not licensed to operate one."

I hated admitting that to him. I didn't learn to drive because there wasn't a car to practice on. It wasn't like I could ask Charles Devlin to let me borrow one of his, and I didn't ask Alicia because I was ashamed of my situation. When it was time at school to get a license, I opted for ID only and took my picture. No one questioned it.

"Oh…I guess that makes sense."

I glance out the window. "Yeah, you just missed my chauffeur," I deadpan.

He laughs. "I'm sorry. I'm not making fun of you, but I must admit, I thought it was real when you first said it. I fell for it, and then I realized you meant the bus and that you were waiting for one."

"Kind of surprising, isn't it? Everyone thinks I'm this privileged rich girl with all the money at her disposal. When in reality, I sleep in the hired helps wing like a servant waiting to be summoned."

He remains quiet after that statement. I can't blame him. It's sad to be honest. At that moment, it wasn't fun thinking I was Cinderella like I did when I was younger, waiting for Prince Charming. I wasn't Cinderella and I didn't have a Prince Charming or fairy godmother. It's funny when you think you have a person all figured out, only to realize you know nothing about them.

The silence stretches in the cabin of the car. The first time I sat in it at the party, I didn't appreciate the red leather or the beautiful lines on the dash, or how the engine purrs. It must be nice to be entitled to a privileged life. When we approach the light after fifteen minutes, he takes a left turn instead of a right. I crane my neck to make sure I'm not missing something.

I hook my thumb behind me. "You missed the turn."

"No, I didn't."

"I need to get home."

"No, you don't."

"But I need my things. I have to take a shower and change my clothes."

"I have a shower and all your clothes."

The clothes are things he bought because it's what *he* likes. He never asked if I liked any of the items. Most of the them I would only see once they were delivered. He selected everything and then he pulled out his credit card, and that was it, except for Madam's boutique. My cheeks flame when I think of what happened inside the fitting room. It's not that I'm ungrateful for all the nice things he purchased. It's why he bought them— for me to be his show pony. The same way my father has me dressed up to attend his parties or when I have partaken in his games, like sleeping with Draven because my mother slept with his father and had to act like I wanted it. It's all just a bunch of mind-fuck games.

We reach a black double gate with three cameras looking down on a white pillar surrounded by tall hedges on each side. There is a screen on a call box, but it must recognize the car because the gates suddenly open when the vehicle gets close enough. When the car pulls through the long-curved driveway, there is a two-story mansion with gas-powered lamps. The house looks modern but with a hint of warmth. Sophisticated like the man.

"Is this your home?"

"Yes."

"It's beautiful."

It is. The house is white with black accents and clear glass doors that allow you to see the foyer. Seven garage doors are to the left, and each side has those beautiful gas lamps with a single flame burning.

"Thank you," he finally says, placing the car in park.

I reach the side of the door, trying find the latch to open it, but by the time I see it, the door is pulling away from me when he opens it.

Following him inside through the double glass doors, I inhale and smell the hint of spice belonging to him mixed with a vanilla scent. I imagine I'm sitting out back with the view of a cozy beach with fluffy blankets and the sun setting on the horizon.

The farther you walk inside, the vibe of the house changes. It's like the entrance and living room is a mirage, and the farther you go, the darker it gets inside the English-style gothic home with its high, vaulted ceilings and an imposing staircase that spirals upwards like a twisted spine. Opaque, polished oak panels line the walls, contrasting the pale marble flooring beneath. An oversized, ornate chandelier hangs above, casting dramatic shadows across the room. A massive antique mirror dominates one wall, its tarnished surface reflecting the past and the present.

When we reach the master bedroom, it's a sanctuary of luxury and gloom, with a four-poster bed draped in rich velvet curtains and a canopy of dark lace. Moonlight filters through the draped windows, casting a silvery glow on the inky walls. A glimpse inside the en-suite bathroom features a claw-footed tub and a vanity adorned with antique mirrors. A shiver runs down my spine when my eyes linger on the bathtub.

"The bathroom is through that door," he says, but I stay rooted to the spot and gaze at him with wide eyes. "What's wrong?"

"D-do you have a shower…please," I stammer.

He looks in the bathroom, where the tub is trying to lure me in to remind me of how I could pay for my sins, and slides his gaze back to me and nods. He walks inside, and I'm relieved when I see the modern rain shower with a digital screen mounted on the tiled wall.

"Towels are in the towel warmer."

I wait until he leaves and place my bag on the counter, looking at the smudges under my eyes from my mascara running and stringy dark hair badly in need of a wash. Wiping my face with a tissue, I turn the shower on, press the buttons on the screen, and look up when the water comes down like rain. It must have activated the music to turn on because "Concrete Jungle" by Bad Omens begins to play softly, and I smile.

I pour shower gel into my palm from the dispenser nailed to the dark tile and wash my body, basking in the warmth of the water and the clean, fresh scent of his soap. *How could anyone skip a shower?*

A breeze of cold air slides over my skin, causing my nipples to pebble, and I turn to Alaric walking naked inside the expansive shower. "I expected you to use the tub. I always use the shower, but I don't mind."

I want to scream at him and tell him to get out and give me privacy, but I can't. I have no choice but to eventually be his until my time is up and I graduate, or he tires of me. Usually, I play a game my father wants me to star in, and since Gia and Jess showed up, I have turned over a new leaf and prefer to play a game where the innocent win. But this is different.

I stand against the wall watching him under the spray while "Concrete Jungle" by Bad Omens gives way to "Bad Decisions" by Bad Omens and finish washing my body slower than necessary.

He plants his hands above his head on the tile, leaning forward and letting the water run down his perfectly muscled back and trim waist, his tattoos glistening under the bathroom's light. He has ink everywhere, in places I've never seen before. On his neck and shoulders, it stops on some parts and begins on others. Some are scriptures from the Bible; others are skulls and angels. I pause and linger on his impressive cock between his muscled thighs. He's long and thick with a barbell through the tip. I don't think he had it before, or I would have felt something like that the first time.

I have to admit that I'm aroused. I'm wet and want nothing more than to slide my fingers between my thighs and pleasure myself. *It's been a while since I touched myself.*

"Do you like what you see?" he asks, bending his elbows and turning his head to look at me.

I slide my hands down my stomach slowly until I reach the lips of my pussy, washing myself with my eyes closed, letting the water rinse me off. I moan while I rub my clit, not caring if he's watching. It's bold, but this is all I could do without walking over there and touching his thick, long cock, stroking it in my hands, prepping myself for when I take it inside my body. How well will it fit now? I was an inexperienced virgin the first time, but now I could take him fast and hard.

"Do you like what you see?" I say breathlessly, throwing back his own words. Taunting him. I don't know why I say it. Acting like a different person for so long just stuck and became as natural as breathing.

I suddenly feel heat, and something soft touching me. My eyes pop open, and he's so close I see the tip of his hard cock on my lower belly. He pins me to the shower wall with his body, and my fingers stop rubbing myself, staring wild-eyed into the storm of his gray eyes.

"Don't stop," he rasps, his forehead touching mine, water sliding down the sides of his face to his lips. "Don't be scared. I won't hurt you…I want to watch you come." He grinds the length of his hard cock against my stomach, his chest heaving, breaths coming quick and shallow. I can feel his piercing rub against my skin. It must feel good for him because his bottom lip is snagged between his teeth.

I continue to play with myself.

My mouth parts when I hit the sensitive spot I like. The place that will bring me over the edge. He lowers his hand and fists his cock to the same rhythm. I moan, and he grunts, but his forehead never leaves mine.

"Faster, baby. Show me…fuck—" He strokes faster. His eyes pin mine. His pupils are full of something dark and powerful I have never seen or felt before. I can feel my heart pounding inside my chest. His jaw flexes, and I keep rubbing and flicking my clit on the brink of a powerful orgasm. "The day you let me slide my cock between those lips again, I'm not going to stop," he says breathlessly. "If I were to drown, I would want to drown in you." He takes my lips in his. I swirl my tongue, matching the rhythm of my fingers. The pressure begins to build, my orgasm coming hard and fast. He breaks the kiss and whispers against my lips, "I won't stop until you give me the real you, Veronica." I swallow hard and moan when my orgasm crests, and I come sliding two fingers inside, feeling my walls clench. I arch my back as he takes one nipple into his mouth and sucks hard.

I gasp. "Harder." He sucks harder, and I come, stars exploding behind my eyes. "Yes!"

The sound of my moans reverberates off the tiled walls. My fingers grip the strands of his hair hard when he holds me and I must admit, my orgasm felt like the best high.

Alaric is a dangerous drug everyone warns you about. The one that makes you forget that your shitty world exists. A drug that is hard to shake once you're on it. The one that you always end back on because it consumes you and your entire world, promising to make it better, not caring that it could kill you because you know, deep down, you would sell your soul to the highest bidder just to get one more taste of that high, and that is what I just did. I sold my soul, not caring what happens because I am an addict. And he is the drug promising me rapture in my hell.

I slide up the tiled wall, releasing his hair and holding on to his shoulder, my head looking down, watching his thick, hard cock swell, getting ready to spill his release while he fucks himself. His sweet words replay in my head. A dull ache forms in my stomach, shooting up to my head, telling me to ruin them—that they're a trick.

To him, I'm the whore they made me out to be. The one with no choices. *Ruin what he said! Ruin them, Veronica. He doesn't love you! Whore! Whore!* The chant goes on inside my head.

My eyes flick up to him like they're possessed. I grip his cock and stroke it faster, making him grit his teeth when I take over. His nostrils flare until he gives a loud grunt, and cum spurts in strings landing on the tile, my stomach, and fingers.

I tilt my head with a sultry smile and reach for the bath gel to wash his cum off my hands and give him my back. I close my eyes. "I'm glad I could service you in blowing off steam."

I turn, widening my hand full of soap and his cum under the spray of water, letting it wash away like it was something grotesque I touched and wanted off my skin. "Don't worry," I purr, "I won't take what you said to heart. Some things are said in the heat of the moment." *Ruin it!* He blinks. His skin is flushed under the spray. Silent. *Good Girl, Veronica.*

I slide my hair over my shoulder, revealing the mark behind my neck. Small but unmistakable. The mark of Prey belonging to the Order. A skull with a small rose. A cross and an inverted cross right under it. I hear his breaths short and fast. Turning my head over my shoulder, his eyes are hard, and his jaw is tight.

I plaster a fake grin and then lick my lips. "You could whisper sweet words, tell me you like what you see, or how I make you feel, but there is one word I always hear when I look at you or when you look at me. The one word I will always remember. Whore."

He slides his fingers through his wet hair. "Veronica, I–"

I turn around, cupping his cheek and feeling how hard his jaw is set. *Tell him!* "I thought a girl's first time was supposed to be special. If it's her first time or first time with someone she thought was good enough. A crush—girls have those you know—I know for some guys they don't— guys like you. The popular, rich ones." I drop my hand and continue, "My first time was…unforgettable. It reminded me what I was worth to you and every guy I would meet." I audibly swallow and laugh, so I won't cry in front of him because I could never sink so low. He took a lot away from me that night. I wanted that moment to be something to remember—to help drown out the bad that would come. The one thing I begged for when I would look at the stars in the sky. I drove Alicia crazy that summer, trying to be anywhere he would be. I would have accepted him to kiss me goodbye and for him to never talk to me again. I didn't expect a phone call or a repeat. And right now, the last thing I need is for him to see my tears. He wants me here, then I will take what I can from him—time. But I will not give him any more pieces of me.

"Veronica, I—" he tries again.

"I want to go home," I say quietly. I look around the shower like the walls are closing in on me. "I don't want to stay here with you." I cross my arms over my body, like he didn't just watch me finger myself and see me fall apart. I wait, hoping he agrees, watching the water slide down the drain like the moment never happened.

He opens the glass door and relief floods me when he says, "I'll take you home."

We drive in complete silence. My purse clutched to my chest, and a designer shopping bag between my feet with an outfit he picked out that's suitable for the office and some other items he expects me to wear. I was surprised he didn't end the arrangement right then, or maybe he will when he drops me off. He could call someone in the Order who would then call Charles.

Since my hell with Dorian Black is soon to begin, I would have to first purify my soul like the sick bastard he is, and maybe it would be a good thing. I could think of a way to leave and change my identity, like those witness protection programs where people adopt new identities and move to another country where no one can find them.

"Are you okay?" he asks. "You're very quiet—"

"I'm fine."

I keep cutting him off because I don't want to hear his lies, so he can convince me to fuck him. He might say how sorry he was or he didn't know, but he had plenty of time to find out. He's Alaric Riodrick-Riordan. He managed to convince the whole Order for him not to marry and to immediately take over for his father. I am here with him because of some sick joke or game they put him up to or that he wants to be a part of. *He did nothing, Veronica. He watched and did…nothing!*

He pulls up to the driveway, and I'm glad I figured out how to open the door from inside his Ferrari. I step out, closing the door before he can say anything, and walk toward the servants' side door. The front door of the house gives me flashbacks of that night with him and what had happened when I made it home. That was the first time I had to pay for my sins. It was the first time I knew the reason for my existence as a Devlin. Charles would tell me things I didn't understand, but I did—that night.

Since then, I have used the servants' door, which is also closer to my room. He waits until I'm inside and drives off. When the door closes behind me, I let the sobs and tears come. I almost don't recognize the shrill sounds coming from my throat, wishing the words he said to me were true and hating myself for having to ruin them, but knowing I wouldn't forgive myself if I didn't. What I hate the most is that I want him when I shouldn't. After everything he's done, I'm scared I'm still in love with him.

ALARIC

I FRUSTRATINGLY GRIP the strands of my hair, pulling and ripping a couple out as I watch the side door shut and drive off. I was trying to tell her that I— what. That I've never felt so ashamed of anything I've done, but I'm not just ashamed, I'm disgusted with myself for treating her like a prostitute. The solemn look on her face when she told me what I reminded her of, what I said to her that night at the initiation party. She gave me what I just asked of her so freely that night. She chose me.

In her confession, she admitted what I meant to her in the beginning and what I mean to her now. It was heartbreaking to see her fall so beautifully in my arms, only to break seconds later. The words I said hearing her beautiful moans were true. If I were to drown, I would want it to be in her.

The mark on her neck sent a ball of fury inside me, wanting to rip it off or cover it so no one could see it. How could Charles Devlin be such a bastard to an innocent girl? But I know the answer. Because he can. She is nothing to him but a poisonous thorn to his ego. Something he can torture and use to get more power because he is a failure as a husband and a lover, so he wants Veronica to pay for it all because outing his wife would draw attention to his inadequacies as a man. He prefers to cover it up by being ruthless in the eyes of the Order, all to inflate his ego. *Piece of shit.*

I slam my hand on the steering wheel because I know I haven't treated her any better. I saw the look in her eye. I'm one of *Them.* Just another sick bastard using her, watching her like a creep in the diner. I'm not going to lie, what she said, it messed with my head and the way she talked to Garret fucked with my head even more. *Serviced. That fucking word.*

I'm at a red light and I'm still gripping the wheel. The sun is rising, blinding me with a stream of light. Placing my sunglasses on, I turn the wheel, put the car in gear and hear the tires squeal when they kiss the pavement followed by the engine roaring through the loud exhaust.

After the ten minute drive, I reach the bronze gate and it automatically opens because his parents are rarely home and the last four years all the Kenyan parties have been here like his own personal playground. Not giving a fuck that I'm going to be late to the office—I'm never late, I open the front door, letting myself in the grandeur of the mansion, reminding me that vampires must live here because you never see people inside the house during the day.

I walk through the house like I own it, knowing the piece of shit must still be in bed, and take the stairs two at a time. I reach the landing and push the door open with a slam, causing Garret to bolt out of bed. His eyes widening like he just saw a ghost.

"What the fuck man! Really?" he says, sliding his hand over his face like that's going to make me disappear. "You scared the shit out of me?"

That's the idea.

"Why did you sleep with her!" I growl, walking over and grabbing him by the neck.

He holds his hands up in mock surrender and I look down, noticing he's naked and the fact that he does have a small dick winking at me. *Pathetic.*

I must sound like a crazy, deranged asshole, but I don't care. I'm going to dig out the truth and kill who ever fucks with me.

He blinks rapidly, probably trying to wrap his head around who I'm talking about, but he knows because he begins to shake like a dog when it does something bad and its master walks in.

"I–"

"Now is not the time to lie to me, Garret." I squeeze harder, causing him to turn red.

"Please." He struggles, but if I want to know, I can't kill him.

I release him, and he begins to cough in a fit. When he finally gets himself under control. I throw some shorts at him.

"Put those on. I can't take it anymore."

"Fuck you," he chokes out. He slides the shorts on and shakes his head. "I knew it. I saw the look in your eyes when Veronica said it, but it wasn't like that man. I'm in love with her." My fist flies, connecting with his left eye. The sting in my first two knuckles a welcome feeling, telling me it hurt him even worse.

"Ow, man! What the fuck!" he yells, placing a hand over his face and doubling over.

"Wrong fucking answer." I grip him by the hair, lifting his head and watching the swelling get worse around his eye. *Good, I hope it hurts.*

"Speak."

"M-my father arranged it. I had trouble getting girls in high school and after–" I glare, tightening my hold on his hair and causing him to gasp and close his eyes. "Please man. I didn't know you felt anything for her. I thought you hated her because she was trying to get you to marry her or some shit. Every girl wanted you. When I started Kenyan, I had trouble getting girls and Veronica knew. When I tried to go after Jess, Melissa stepped in because she has a thing for Prey because she likes women." He opens his eyes, and I release a bit of my hold, so he can talk. "I didn't hurt Veronica, but she made it seem that Jess was just Prey and we needed to fuck with her like we all do to Prey so she—" he looks away with a pained look in his expression, "I couldn't believe she wanted me like that. She's beautiful and I fell hard for her. My father laughed at me when I told him…I still don't know why she did it, but the next day, she made it known on campus that we slept together and then all the girls wanted me. I threw parties and it was like my flaws were suddenly overlooked, but I didn't want them. I wanted her. Reid and Valen thought I wanted Jess, but in the end, it wasn't her I wanted. Veronica made me feel like I was a man. When I told her how I felt, she didn't laugh—" he looks up at me, scared that I'm going to go after his good eye, but he swallows— "she said we could be friends and that was all. I never touched her after that and I am—"

"What?"

"I'm her friend and if she needs anything I would…do anything for her."

I smile manically. "How charming," I snarl and shove him on the bed.

"I'm sorry, man. I really am. I didn't know and she really isn't what people make her out to be, but I don't know why she doesn't change the way she acts or stop playing these games messing with people's heads."

I have an idea why. He doesn't know what she is to the Order. But I don't tell him that. I pin him with a hard stare before walking out of his room and growl. "Touch her again and I'll kill you."

I pull out my cell phone once I'm in the car and dial Portman.

"Sir?"

"I need you to pick up Miss Devlin at her home and take her to my office as scheduled. Please have her breakfast ready when she arrives in my office."

"Yes, sir."

"Tell her I will meet her there and to wait for me. Understood?"

"Y-yes, sir."

"And Portman?"

"Sir," he responds warily.

"Keep your eyes to yourself."

"Yes, sir. Understood."

I hang up, giving him the only verbal warning I will give when it comes to her.

VERONICA

THE ELEVATOR DOORS OPEN, and I ignore Portman because every time he speaks to me, he stares at the ground like I'm going to hit him, only giving me curt answers. I'm wearing what Alaric picked out for me. A beautiful black silk wrap-around dress and underneath is some type of undergarment. There are actually strings that look like rubber bands made into a monokini with a crotchless panty paired with over-the-knee suede boots by designer Gianvito Rossi. Little lace petals are intricately sewn into the bands that cover my nipples, but the single string that goes between the cheeks of my ass is uncomfortable because it rubs when I walk, making me wet.

I pause at the desk right before the double doors to Alaric's office, and I'm greeted by a man. I expected Sasha and her ironic smile to greet me, and he must know because of the surprised look on my face.

"You must be Verrronica," he says, rolling the Rs in my name. His voice has a feminine tone and you could tell he was gay. His suit is perfectly tailored with a pink flower on the breast of his pocket and a little LGBTQ pin with a rainbow on the collar. It's so cute. To me, a gay man is a girl's best friend.

I smile. "Yes."

"Mr. Riordan hired me to assist you in whatever you wish because I can tell"—he winks—" you will be assisting him with everything he needs."

"Where's Sasha?"

He raises his brows and shakes his head from side to side in a rhythm and lowers his voice. "Sasha, who? This is an opportunity of a lifetime. Please, if I did something wrong—"

My eyes widen in horror, hoping I didn't offend him. "Oh, no. You're perfect." I smile, calming him down.

He places a hand on his chest in relief, breathing dramatically, like he just ran a marathon. "Oh, thank God," he rushes out. "He gave the agency I work for specific instructions when selecting the perfect candidate on short notice and I promised I could assist you with anything you needed."

"What did he do with Sasha?"

He cups his hand over his mouth and whispers, "He fired her." I step back, looking at Alaric's closed office door and then back at him. *Why would he do that?* "I'm Sergio, by the way," he says, holding his hand out for me to shake, and I do. "We're going to get along fine. I see a spark in those beautiful eyes." He lowers his voice again and whispers, "He must go crazy looking at you."

I snort. "You will understand when you see me and him in the same room."

"Well, he's not in yet, but there is a delicious breakfast waiting for you in his office," he says, sashaying toward the door and holding it open so I can walk through.

After eating a sensual breakfast of fruit, eggs, and coffee, I wait for the man in question to appear. My phone goes off, and I look at the incoming message.

Dorian: Is he bored of you yet?

Veronica: What do you want, stalker?

Dorian: Is that any way to talk to your fiancé?

Veronica: You are nothing of mine, and you know I would never choose you. I'd rather die.

Dorian: That can be arranged.

Cold dread sits at the bottom of my stomach, making me nauseous.

Dorian: What's wrong? Afraid, princess. I have so many fun things planned for you.

"Is everything alright?" I drop the phone on his desk. Alaric is standing in a tailored blue suit, freshly-shaven, with a questioning look in his eyes.

I swallow thickly, realizing I'm in his chair like I own the place. "Oh…um…I'm sorry." I stumble blindly, getting out his chair, careful not to drop the plastic-covered plates and trying to clean up the mess.

When I toss everything away and move so he can sit, I notice he's watching me like a lion waiting to pounce. He's quiet, his hands are in his trousers pockets, waiting. For what? I don't know.

"I hire people to clean," he says, before taking a seat. "I had a meeting this morning."

I sit in the chair in front of his desk, and when he places his hands on the smooth glass surface, I notice the first two knuckles are red and swollen over white spots of skin from the scabs I saw at the Galleria that were almost healed. He stares at me when he notices me looking at them but doesn't say anything.

I find the courage to gently reach out with my hands and gently caress the red skin, leaning across his desk. "Getting into trouble," I say in a soft voice. His lips twitch, and I know he wasn't at a meeting.

He probably beat the shit out of someone, and it isn't the first time. When I learned that he existed, I was consumed with wanting to learn everything about him, like every girl does when she is crushing hard on a guy. I wanted to know what he was into, what he liked, where he hung out, if he was single or had a girlfriend—so I could hate her because she was with the guy I considered mine when I would daydream about him in class. In those dreams, instead of him kissing her and taking her out on a date, it was me. I overheard Reid one time complain about Alaric's character but what stood out the most to me was Alaric's bad temper. He would fight with anyone who got in his way or wronged him.

He's as violent and as lethal as they come when you think of the sons of Kenyan. The villain of all villains. The one you don't cross. He is heartbreak guaranteed, but it doesn't keep the girls away; it attracts them even more, even if they know there is no future. Alaric doesn't have a girlfriend or plan to get married like the rest of his generation, but that didn't stop me when I turned eighteen and wanted something bad enough, having waited so long to get it. You don't care. You go for it.

"I caught my hand on a door."

"Did it hurt?"

"You should see the door."

"What did the door do?" I ask playfully.

"It got in my way." He looks behind me, and his gaze slides back on mine. "Lock the door."

I get up and do as he asks, hearing him move around the room behind me. Once the lock is in place, I see hooks on the wall with chains I hadn't noticed before because a wall slides up, hiding the toys hanging behind it. He must not like to take his women home. He pulls the chains, the sound clicking against each loop. There are leather wrist cuffs on each end as he holds them in each hand.

"Come here." I hear the chains rattle. "Take off the dress and leave everything else on."

I untie the dress, letting it fall in a puddle of black silk at my feet. I watch his pants tighten between the space of his suit jacket, right under his belt. *I hate belts.* "Hold both wrists out."

I hold out my hands and watch him fasten the cuffs on each wrist chained to the wall. "Why are you cuffing my wrists?"

He looks up. "I want to ensure you don't leave my office until I tell you to." He leans in close. "I want to see you dressed like this and watch you come."

"What if I need to use the bathroom?"

"Then you'll go, but if you run, I'll punish you."

A chill runs down my skin, my nerves on end, and I look away. "W-with what?"

He lifts my chin with an index finger so I can look at him and frowns. "I would never physically hurt you, Veronica." He cups my pussy, pulling me toward him. "This…is mine…I'll punish you, but I'll make sure you like it."

Mine. I know he means I'm his for as long as he allows it. There is no way he means it permanently. He must see the confusion mixed with the look of terror on my face. "This is not a game." His red knuckles slide up my stomach and stop at the side of my breasts, causing the nerves to tighten all over my skin. My nipples are hard underneath the lace. He stares at my heavy breasts for a couple of seconds and asks, "May I?"

I nod, watching his head dip as he flicks his tongue over the lace petal. Arousal grips me, sending intense pleasure between my thighs. My breath comes in quick when he moves to the other breast. I squirm and it causes the elastic string to tighten, causing heat between my legs and around the lips of my pussy.

"Mmm…" My fingers pull his perfectly-combed hair. "If you're going to cause the mess between my legs, then it's only fair everyone knows what you've been up to." He grins, flicks the lace to the side with his tongue, and holds my breasts with both hands. He traces the area around my nipple in tiny little circles, and when I think I'm going to scream from the intense pleasure, he flicks my nipple with the flat part of his tongue, sucking it inside his mouth and then the other. "Oh, God." I moan, holding his head, so he won't stop. "Please," I beg.

"What do you want?"

"Your fucking tongue, everywhere."

His eyes flick up, and his hand shoots to a button on the wall I didn't notice before, causing the chain to retract. "Stand with your back against the wall."

The cuffs have rings that allow free movement, so I can turn without crossing the chains. When the chains shorten, giving me no choice but to stand with my back against the wall, it causes my arms to spread like open wings at his mercy.

He removes his suit jacket and walks over to a box I hadn't noticed sitting on the couch on the far wall by the bar. He opens it and removes a black leather rabbit mask with a silver metal cross in the middle. "I bought this for you," he says, holding it up.

He walks over, places it over my head, ensuring it fits securely on my nose and the openings around my eyes. Once it's on, he steps back. "It looks gorgeous on you."

"Does it?" I purr.

I step to the side, widening my stance. My pussy is hot and throbbing, wanting his mouth to lick and suck. "I like it on you, but I like that you're at my mercy more." I pull on the restraints, but they don't budge. I can't move my arms down. The chains that have retracted have my arms pinned to the wall by the cuff on my wrist, not letting me pull to release them. "I can do whatever I want to you."

"I can scream."

He shakes his head with a devilish smile. "They can't hear you." I begin to panic. My body feels flashes of hot and cold. He steps closer, giving me enough room so I can knee him in the balls, but what would that do but piss him off. He leans in, and I feel the heat from his chest through his shirt on my wet nipples. "I'm going to make you come, and that is the only scream I want to hear." His lips brush against mine. "Your screams belong to me. Your pain belongs to me—" his hand slides over my throat, cupping my cheek, "your fears…belong to me."

Every breath I take, I take in his scent. The vibrations of his voice embrace my skin, awakening a deep desire. A pleasure he can only give me. I've never had a man give me an orgasm. I tried, but I knew why I couldn't. It wasn't because I was a sinner like Charles said I was. It was because of the man in front of me. He took that from me. Taking it only allowed me to have one if I gave it to myself. It felt like a cruel punishment for what he thought I did.

I want to kick and scream at him for always having power over me.

Over my body.

Over my mind.

The punishment I took for him wasn't why I hate him; it's because it was for nothing. He still thought of me the same way. He could have anyone—any woman he wanted like this, so why me?

"Why me?"

He doesn't answer but takes my lips with his and my face in his hands, sliding his tongue over the delicate skin of my mouth. He pulls back lazily. My eyes follow the backs of his fingers sliding between the valley of my breasts. I bite my bottom lip when he reaches my wet slit, spreading my arousal over my clit in circles, causing a little cry to bubble from my throat. I arch my back against the wall while he plays with me. His other hand lifts my leg over his hip, placing kisses on my throat, not once pulling his hand from between my thighs. The wet sounds of his fingers rubbing my clit are the only ones I can register between the sounds of our breathing.

"When you look at me, and I look at you, and that word possesses your mind—" he slips a finger inside me, and I gasp, "the word whore." My half-lidded eyes widen. "You forgot the rest—" The dark pupils of his eyes darken. "You're *my* whore."

The phone rings and my eyes shoot to his desk, where it's going off, but he ignores it. I'm disappointed when he pulls his finger out and licks it clean. My leg slides off his hip, and I watch as he slowly drops to his knees surprising me. I thought he was going to answer the phone but instead, Alaric is on his knees, lifting one leg over his shoulder and pressing his mouth over my opening and fucking me with his tongue.

"Mmm…" I moan, hoping that the office is soundproof and he isn't messing with me because everyone on this floor will know what the CEO is doing to his intern, and it's not going over financials.

He hums while he takes my clit in his mouth, the vibrations from his throat making me wet, teasing my pussy as he moves faster. "Fuck, yes," I say breathlessly. "More, don't stop…Alaric." I push my hips forward, wanting more and hoping he won't stop when I grind my pussy on his mouth. His lips make kissing sounds with my pussy, and the phone rings again.

"Are you going to get that?" I ask breathlessly.

"I'm eating," he murmurs. "They can wait."

He slides his tongue and fucks me with it. In and out, he sucks and twirls his tongue until I can't take it anymore and come, making a desperate, dirty noise. My pussy pulses in his mouth, but he doesn't stop, causing my leg over his shoulder to shake but not caring if the heel of my black suede boot digs into his back. My breaths are coming out faster than the last as I try to calm myself by closing my eyes.

"I love the way your pussy tastes and your skin smells." He places stray kisses on my inner thigh, my pussy, and my stomach. He rises on his feet and undoes the cuffs on my wrists. The ache from having them up causes tingles that feel like tiny needles. I rub them, watching him walk back from the bathroom to hand me a wet cloth. "Put your clothes on, we have a meeting."

My eyes almost bulge. That is why the phone was ringing, we're late. When we walk in, they will all know or have an idea why and all I can think about is that he didn't stop. He didn't care.

He hands me the dress, and I glance upward to see his reaction from what we just did, or rather...what I let him do. Taking it from him, I hand him the washcloth.

"We're late," he says softly with a grin, causing me to blush. "But I'd do it again."

ALARIC

WE WALK in late to the board meeting, relieved Sergio is behind us, covering for us. I'm sure Alaric couldn't care less what people may think, but I'm here as an intern, and deep down, I know I'm not doing anything related to school.

"Sorry we're late, gentlemen. My lunch ran late, and I have to eat," Alaric announces with a smirk. All the men seated at the boardroom table glance at me and Sergio as we take our seats, while I'm wishing the floor would swallow me whole. Alaric walks to the head of the table and takes his seat.

There are six men in total besides Alaric, Sergio, and me. The first one eyes me with curiosity. He's wearing a brown suit with a pink pinstriped shirt that clashes with his red facial complexion. He reminds me of a pack of Starburst, the pink and red pack where pink and red are the only colors inside. The man seated to his right, who keeps scrutinizing my long dark hair, reminds me of a guy trying to sell a pyramid scheme on an infomercial with a bad haircut because he doesn't want to face the fact that he is balding. The one to the left of Starburst gives me a knowing grin, and the way his eyes linger on me longer than necessary, I know he knows my father, which means he knows who I am.

"You're Devlin's daughter, right?" he asks.

"I—"

"She will be addressed as the Intern in our office and be called as such," Alaric says curtly.

"Oh, well now, Alaric, we can also just call her Veroni—"

"Call her by her first name, and I'll cut out your tongue," he says icily, pointing at him.

The man's face turns white; then gulps and looks away.

"Oh my," Sergio whispers.

"That goes for everyone except Sergio. He will guide my intern while she's here, assisting her with everything she needs. She will be addressed as the Intern. Not her first name or her last name."

Starburst clears his throat. "Intern it is," he says, giving me a nervous smile.

"Veronica, look over page five and give me your analysis," Alaric says.

I turn over the prospectus in front of me and turn to page five. I quickly scan the line items and immediately notice the issue as to why EBITA is higher than in previous quarters. I clear my throat, trying to calm my nerves about being put on the spot, before I respond. "Direct Labor was higher than normal because...um, there are more employees but no reason as to why the company is top heavy when development hasn't commenced to expand for a full quarter in the same positions. When everything else was the same the previous —"

"She's not making any sense," the asshole to Alaric's right interrupts me in a raspy tone. I can smell the stench of old cigars permeating around him like a cloud. I can tell he has something to do with the company's financials because I know I'm spot on. A wave of annoyance causes me to drop the paper from the folder in my hand on the table.

"Interrupt her again, Gino, and I'll pull the funding from your next build."

Alaric is a capital investor and lends money to companies, then takes a percentage of the profits. Page five is a huge problem with a certain investment. But knowing how smart Alaric is, he already figured it out. These men are the ones needing money to fund different projects for companies that Alaric is investing in.

I wanted to avoid coming in with an attitude since I'm just an intern. They know I'm just a senior at Kenyan with no traditional work experience.

Alaric glances at me and says, "Continue."

I lick my lips, pick up the folder, and turn to page five, glancing at Gino. "Your company has hired employees that work in the same capacity, causing the direct labor to increase; therefore, increasing your EBITA instead of decreasing or at least staying the same in the last quarter. There is no reason to increase overhead when you are seeking capital funding unless there is a loss, but clearly there is nothing reported. Increasing your direct labor hurts profits. Is there a reason for the increased overhead when the project hasn't broken ground? It would be detrimental to the company when you do have to hire the employees for the new project after it commences, putting the company in the red and risking not being able to pay back the loan, leaving with interest-only payments."

Gino's face turns a different shade of red. His jaw clenches in anger because I figured it out and it doesn't take a genius to know he's funneling money out in case it goes belly up or he already knows it will. The employees probably don't exist and are ghosts on paper. He would file bankruptcy, and then lenders would get pennies on the dollar when he has to restructure. He will then open another company while he has loads of liquid cash stashed somewhere.

"You're wrong," he barks. He looks at the rest of the men. "She's wrong."

"I'm right, and you know it. I bet those employees are ghosts on paper."

"What would you do, Veronica?" Alaric says in a soft voice. "If you owned my company?"

I stare Gino straight in the eye. "I'd pull the fucking plug on his whole operation and leave him having to get a loan at Wells Fargo, but that wouldn't work because I would place liens on his assets, causing the banks to pay you out before he files and they place it in a REO."

Sergio inhales air next to me, covering his hand over his mouth and stifling a smile as he looks away.

"Congratulations, Veronica. You passed your first test. My senior advisors couldn't find it, but you did in five minutes." I grin, and Gino looks like he's about to blow a gasket glaring at me like I'm the devil that fucked up his plan.

He pushes the chair back and stands up with a snarl. "You bitch. You're nothing but a cunt."

I flinch because I hear the sound of his belt buckle, triggering the mental image of an antique bathtub and the sound of hard breathing. My palms are sweating, and my heartbeat is pounding in my ears. I feel hot, imagining the steam from a hot bath.

"Are you okay?" I hear Sergio ask.

"I need some air," I whisper.

Sergio looks behind me and nods, getting up and guiding me outside the boardroom. The door shuts behind us, and I know I messed up in lashing out at one of Alaric's business associates, but I wanted to tell Gino to go fuck himself, the lying, stealing prick, but the sound of his belt buckle and him calling me a bitch and a cunt triggered the memories I try to forget every day. It also doesn't help when Portman shows up so he can take me home for the rest of the day when it's the last place I want to be.

"How is your internship going? I heard you are interning with one of the most prestigious family's companies," Dr. Wick says with a cold smile, reminding me of Maleficent. The tone of her voice sounds regal. A bitch with a chip on her shoulder because she was fucked over by a man and wants to make other people's lives just as shitty.

"It couldn't be better. I watch old men in suits with a lot of dough, listen to their refined voices, and watch their hard cocks swell every time I walk by in heels. It's quite entertaining. You should talk to the board and get the male doctors to wear suits. I promise you, Dr. Wick, you won't be disappointed."

Her eyes narrow when I pull out another Virginia Slims and light it up just to piss her off. She takes a deep breath before the smell of smoke reaches her.

"How's Mr. Riordan treating you?"

My eyes light up because I expected this question. My father must be curious. I take a drag of the cigarette and exhale, wetting my lips. "He's riding me hard," I say in a sultry voice. "Making sure I get the work done right. I COME…in every day by 9 a.m."

She swallows because I think she gets aroused when I talk about men insinuating how I use their appendages. How hard they get when they see a woman. I don't care if my father takes it out on me later. I'm used to it after so many years and this is where I can vent. When I started seeing Dr. Wick, I secretly hoped she would find me crazy enough and put me in a room in the ward for a couple of days so that I didn't have to go back home and deal with Charles and his rituals.

"What else do you do for Mr. Riordan?"

I snuff out the cigarette, adding to the holes in the carpet under the chair. "Oh, a lot of things. The first week, I had orientation." I lick my lips seductively. I inwardly laugh when a flush rises on her cheeks, and she shifts in her seat. "Does Mr. Wick…fuck you hard. Not those lazy fucks, you know--" I wink, "a good solid hard fuck. The kind that makes your toes curl?"

Her face turns red in lust and anger. "Leave."

"Just tell him, Dr. Wick." I lower my voice. "Tell him to fuck you with his tongue. You won't be so uptight."

"Leave!" She raises her voice, pulling the neck of her blouse, and I notice she isn't wearing a bra. Her nipples are hard, and she's aroused. Good.

"I need to change my medication. The one you gave me messes with my memory."

She tears a script off the pad after she scribbles something on it the way doctors tend to do, like five-year-old's writing in a notebook, and only a pharmacist understands.

The door opens, and another doctor walks in with dark hair and a medium build. "Excuse me, Dr. Wick?" The color in Dr. Wicks's face turns pink. Her eyes widen. The pen falls from her fingers, and I smile when she smooths her skirt and rights herself.

"Yes?"

"I need you in room four," he says.

"I'll be right there," she says softly, but I don't miss how her eyes betray her.

She's fucking him.

She hands me the script and turns toward the hallway but then turns with her hand gripping the door. "Same time, Friday."

Turning in my seat, surprised she still wants to see me after she asked me to leave. I give her a knowing smile. "Remember, what I said."

"I gotta go."

She closes the door, and I hear her heels click-clack on the floor heading down the hallway, then, "You needed to see me, Dillon..." The sound of clothes being shifted, heavy breathing, and a grunt fill my ears until the closing of the door shuts off the rest, so I turn and make my way out to the receptionist.

"Is that all?" the receptionist asks.

"I also need my monthly birth control refilled."

She looks at my name, and she freezes for a moment. She looks up with wide eyes and smiles. "I'll be right back. Let me fill those for you."

Weird.

She comes back after five minutes and hands me both filled prescriptions. "Did Dr. Wick need you to come in again?"

"Yes."

"Date and Time?"

"Friday at Four."

"Perfect."

"Let me get her to sign off, and you should be all set." She moves to get up, and I don't stop her when she walks down the hallway looking for Dr. Wick.

I walk out, not feeling bad about her getting caught fucking Dillon. Bitch fucks with plenty of lives.

ALARIC

I'M BROODING in my office, seated at my desk, contemplating after I let Sergio escort Veronica out of the meeting and had Portman take her wherever she needed to go. He notified me she wanted to be dropped off at campus. I can't get the traumatized look on her face out of my head when Gino called her a 'bitch' and a 'cunt.' It was as if she shut down entirely, her body tense and voiceless. It was also as if an invisible curtain had fallen over her.

Something triggered it, but I couldn't understand what or why. People have called her worse, but I've never seen her shut down like that. I expected a fast retort on her end but nothing.

She was magnificent in there. She is brilliant, with her sharp mind and astute responses. She knew what the right decision was. It was spot on to what I had concluded myself. After she left, I pulled the plug on Gino's' funding and terminated all his contracts with my company, but I wasn't done with him. I wanted to go after her, but I had something to take care of. Something that couldn't wait. My phone buzzes on the glass surface of my desk from an incoming message.

C: Ready when you are.

A: On my way.

I rise from my desk, casting my gaze at the wall to where I had her restrained, recalling the taste of her on my lips. Yet, an invisible chain bound her to a hellish realm—a nightmare created only for her. An inferno where she remained ensnared, devoured from within, and I couldn't reach her.

Once on the highway, I accelerate the car, hurtling into the darkness for the twenty-minute drive. Drizzling rain obscures the illuminated streets as I reach the ancient house nestled in the woods.

Concealed behind trees, the house appears abandoned, deliberately crafted to avoid attention. Only a barely visible black road hints at its presence, either concealed by the speed limit or by those already acquainted with its existence. Only the Consortium visits this place. The house has a wood wrap-around porch missing two slabs of two-by-fours and an old, rusted swinging bench. The house might look abandoned to some, but out here, that's the look we were going for, so it's not easy to find.

There are sixty-six members, but only ten I truly trust concerning Veronica.

I walk up to the door, and it opens with a scream from the hinges. "Where?" I ask.

I follow him inside, where the old fireplace is burning, casting the only light in the room. Ten cloaked figures with plague masks encircle a man confined to a chair.

A cloak and mask are promptly placed in my hand. I quickly pull it over me, ensuring my anonymity as I step into the circle. Gino is bound and gagged, attempting furtive glances and struggling against his restraints. Faint red marks on his wrists reveal his prior struggles. His muffled screams fill the room as I near.

Extending my hand, I receive a pair of black leather gloves. Slipping them on, I permit the removal of the gag, granting him speech. "Who the hell are you?" he gasps; voice hoarse from his screams.

Dressed in his work attire, his shirt stained and evidence of incontinence at his feet, he trembles in fear. His panicked eyes dart around the room, his demeanor a stark contrast to the arrogance that once resided in them.

"Gino, Gino, Gino," I echo mockingly. "What shall we do with you?"

"Alaric, you son of a bitch! I–"

"I would watch your tone and choice of words. Such impudence led you to this predicament like calling someone a bitch and a cunt."

"You can't be serious!" He laughs hysterically, but I see the fear in his eyes. I'm feeding off of it.

"I'm afraid not."

"She's just an intern! I get it, you're sleeping with her, but she ruined my company–"

"You did that all on your own. I'm not here because of your company. What your company is worth is nothing to me. Her actions in those five minutes surpassed your two decades in this business. The issue, however, is your blatant disrespect for what belongs to me."

"I-I didn't know," he stammers. "I heard she's nothing but a bitch and a whore."

The contemptuous words kindle a fiery rage within me. Valen hands me a sharpened butcher knife, and the man's eyes widen in horror. "P-please. I'm sorry," he pleads. "P-please, please. I promise not to say anything. I saw nothing. Just…release me."

"My concern for your future utterances has waned, Gino." Raising the knife, its gleaming blade catches the firelight. "Your fate was sealed the moment you insulted her."

I bring the blade down repeatedly; each strike a visceral manifestation of the trauma she endured. The splatters of blood decorate my mask and gloves, echoing the rhythm of my swings. The memory of her face, that vulnerable expression, fuel my unrelenting fury. I continue until my arms can no longer bear the strain.

"Jesus," Draven says when I'm done.

"Jesus isn't going to help anyone that has hurt her. I suggest you spread the word. Veronica is mine."

Returning to the campus library, I delve into the history of Kenyan and the Order. Victoria's induction into the Order wasn't due to birthright; I look up and stare at the old wooden shelves. The library is dark except for the light in the hallway and the small lamp I have on by the brown desk in the corner, casting shadows on the leather-bound books, their words akin to scriptures. I recognize how history underpinned governments and beliefs, ours veiled within cryptic texts penned by the privileged. Countries adopt them to create a way of life, but ours is a secret, hidden in riddles inside books penned by assholes with fat bank accounts. Temptation, greed, gluttony, and sin. A way to cover it all when it's committed. It's all a prophecy, you're born or married into it.

Charles Devlin adopted Veronica because she isn't his biologically, so that means she is no different than Prey. Only children fathered by a man born into the Order are members automatically and the ones that are not mentally stable attend here. The question is, what is her mental instability that was strategically put in place to be accepted here as the heir of the Devlin estate? It had to be manifested. She has to see a doctor on the fourth floor to be screened. Dr. Wick is the only shady bitch that's heartless enough to have medical notes of her patients' progress, offering band-aids to the problem Veronica would have.

I sit back in the uncomfortable wooden chair, scanning the gold spines before me. *She's Prey,* I think to myself. Prey chooses. I read that she was enslaved as Prey and she must have gotten the mark when initiated. I close my eyes, trying to remember what she said in the shower. Her gaze lingered on the claw-footed bathtub. That same fearful expression returned in the boardroom. She didn't have the mark when she chose. She chose me that night at the initiation party.

The spine of a book with three words in Latin catches my attention, Praeda Litatio Captura. They all mean Prey in Latin. I know that because my grandfather made sure I learned Latin. Turning its pages, dread tightens my gut at the sight of the mark—the same one I saw on the back of her neck. I turn the page, and I want to throw up. Disturbing images fill the pages, depicting ritualistic horror. Illustrations of a woman standing in a Victorian-era bathtub with men around her. They have whips, and she's naked. *Do you have a shower?* The way she looked at the claw foot bathtub. It was the same look I saw in the boardroom. Fear.

The bottom of the picture reads Peccator (Sinner) Rituale (Ritual). Not being able to read more, I close the book like it's the Antichrist. I slide my chair back with force, causing it to fall back, wanting to kill them all, but knowing I can't. There's more of them and not enough of us. The Consortium knows there are sick bastards at the top, but this is some archaic sick shit that they have done to her.

I pinch the bridge of my nose and close my eyes. *Oh, baby. I'm so sorry.*

I need to get her out of Charles Devlin's house. He delivered her on a platter because of his bitterness. His hate. The purpose behind all of it, is for her to find the realization that she is fundamentally animalistic, repulsive, and putrid. Unworthy. Cleansing herself under the pretense of abuse and repeating the same thing over and over until ultimately, she gives up.

I look around and place the book back on the shelf, knowing I can't come back. They will know because someone is always watching and you can't trust anyone. I'm walking out to my car and dial Portman.

"Is this a new thing?" I look up from the menu when I hear her voice. "Spying on me while I work?"

My gaze returns to the menu. "I'm here for a cookie and cream milkshake. I liked it the last time I was here."

She shakes her head and writes it down. "Anything else I can get you?"

"Yeah, when can I take you out on a date?"

She takes the menu from my hands, and I meet her clear blue eyes when she says, "I think we're past that."

I shake my head. "I don't think so…no…not at all. Have you ever been on one?"

I watch her swallow when she looks out the window with an expression between doubt and uncertainty for a few seconds. "No," she finally says.

"Me either. It will be both our first time then."

Her gaze shifts to mine. "Why?"

"Because I never got the opportunity to ask you."

"I think that ship has long since sailed. You don't need to take me on a date or go through all the trouble. Under the circumstances, I'm a sure thing."

"See…that's the thing. It's not what I want."

She places the ticket on the table. "Stop it…stop playing games with me." Her eyes get glassy. My stomach turns into knots because I'm not playing a game with her, but in her mind, I am not to be trusted. I get it. I've been an unredeemable asshole to her, and I don't deserve her. But fuck I want to make it right. "I'll be right back."

I'm about to go after her but don't want to push her. I don't want her to go back home after her shift, so I wait. I hear the blender turn on, and when it stops, it's not Veronica but Dorothy bringing me the glass with a straw. She looks older than I remembered. She has wrinkles around her mouth from years of smoking. Her skin looks like paper when it's been in your pocket too long. Her hair is dull and stringy with streaks of gray, but she's a good woman and stays on top of all the gossip from both schools. Last I heard, she was friends with Mrs. Bedford before she died. I've overheard my mother mention her once or twice. Her father left her this diner last year after he passed away, and she made it into a retro restaurant open twenty-four hours.

"Funny seeing you here, son. I'm surprised to see you in this neck of the woods," she says in a raspy voice, placing the glass on the table.

"I came to see someone."

"Ahh, Veronica. She's a looker, but I gotta say…you're wasting your time."

"Oh, yeah. How's that?"

I'm curious. I want to know what she thinks of her and the reason behind saying that to me. I'm sure Dorothy can tell me more about Veronica than her mother ever could. The only person that knew her was my cousin—her best friend, but she is dead. I think she was the only person who knew Veronica inside and out. I wasn't very close to Alicia, but I respected her and thought if she was best friends with Veronica, there was a reason.

That night at the party, I tried to blame Veronica, but the reality was, I wanted a reason. A reason not to feel a certain way for a girl and I used it. It was easy to accept the worst and not fight the feelings with my inner self so I could open my eyes and see her for what she really is, an innocent woman.

"She doesn't give any of the boys that come in here the time of day. They come in here like hound dogs every time they see her. Adam is always giving them looks when they give her a hard time."

"Who gives her a hard time?"

She snickers. "The boys. Why…you goin' kick all their asses? I see the way you look at her. You're Claire Riodrick's boy." I'm not surprised she recognizes me. "A Riordan because of your father." She leans her hip on the table and lowers her voice, making it sound raspier. "I know who you are, and I can guess why you're here, but I do know that girl isn't for the likes of you. She's kind. Whatever business you have with her, leave it at Kenyan or at work where it belongs. This is the only place I have seen that poor girl smile and be herself. So don't you come in here messing with her head," she warns.

"I think you got it all wrong. It's not like that."

She scoffs. "Oh, you goin' to marry her?"

My eyes widen in horror at the sound of the word marriage. I don't believe in it.

Is she insane?

"That's what I thought. I know about your little deal with the big dogs. I got ears. I've heard plenty about you, Alaric. I know she is interning at your company because she told me but refused to give up her shift here at the restaurant. She likes working here. She works hard and I'm tired of her getting treated like a piece of meat all the damn time. I'm sure you have plenty of women that would love to play games with you, so you can toss them aside when you're finished, but Veronica isn't one of them," she says morosely. She's about to leave but pauses. "Say hi to your mom for me. She's a real nice lady." And then walks away to take other orders, leaving me stunned by how she defended Veronica.

I cast my gaze toward the kitchen, where a hand can be seen banging a silver bell, and watch Veronica prepare her orders. She said she would be right back but sent Dorothy because she's afraid. I know I get under her skin and don't care if I look like an idiot staring at her. She's a mystery I want to unravel. She's too smart to be working in a restaurant, and most people from Kenyan wouldn't be caught dead working here. It's obvious she's different and has learned to play both sides, but this is the side she prefers because it's where she feels important, valued and loved by the people working around her. I don't want to take that away from her. It's humbling, but I'm determined to get my date with her, and I won't take no for an answer.

VERONICA

AFTER MY SHIFT WRAPS UP, I find myself walking the familiar path toward the bus stop. An unsettling sensation of being watched clings to me like a shadow, causing my nerves to prick. I can't shake it off, even though every time I glance around, the empty streets at four in the morning reveal no one lurking in the shadows. I could've stayed at the diner until five, but I'm tired, and the thought of a hot shower followed by a brief nap is all that fuels me, especially when I'm done at his office at nine-thirty. I didn't expect him to see me at the restaurant after I told him not to go there when I was working or that he would ask me out. He, of all people, dared to ask me out on a date. I can't deny a small blossom of hope unfurled within me. The way he looked at me when he posed the question was a puzzle—a mixture of sincerity and confusion.

Alaric Riordan is a man who doesn't bend, who doesn't apologize or acknowledge regret for any of his actions. And certainly not for the torment he subjected me to. If there's anyone on this earth for whom he'd reserve even a whisper of remorse, it's not me.

I hear a purring of an engine, and from the corner of my eye, I spot his Ferrari, but I ignore it and keep walking to the bus stop.

"So, what time do I pick you up on Friday?"

I stop and turn to face him. "You don't take no for an answer, do you?"

"No. When I want something, I get it."

"Of course, money is no object to someone like you, and because you have so much of it, you get what you want. It doesn't matter what anyone thinks. Money…power and all that."

"This has nothing to do with money or power. Just a man asking a woman out on a date."

"What for? You've already had me; the last time I checked, I didn't meet your standards. If you want a date so badly, ask Sasha or Tara. Last time I checked, you were fucking her and did your cousin a favor. Go ask them; I'm sure they will oblige. Maybe both of them at the same time. It all depends on your kink."

"I don't want them."

"I don't think you have trouble finding a woman, Alaric. After all, you have me for your little sick game for a while. The only reason I talk to you is because you have the decency to give me a choice and don't have to fake it."

"Did you the first time?"

I pinch my brows together, rub my arms, and stop walking to face him. He applies the break, and I ask, "First time?"

"The night at the party. I'm not talking about sex. Did you fake it?"

My instinct is to tell him yes, but the truth is, it would be a lie because everything I felt that night was real. It was the last time I felt like myself. It doesn't matter if I tell him the truth because it's too late. "No," I say and keep walking on the sidewalk.

"Get in, Veronica," I hear him call out. "You're not going back there. You're staying with me."

I pause a step. "But–"

"Don't piss me off," he warns. "Get in the car."

He jumps out and walks around, opening the passenger door, and waits for me to enter. I could run, but what would be the point. He will find me; the last thing I need is a pissed-off Alaric. In my mind, I want him to get annoyed with me and end this little game. I would go back, and the real nightmare would begin, but deep down, I want him to keep me like this, belonging to no one. Dorian can only interfere if I'm playing a game with Alaric, but how long? A cynical voice in my head drowns out the faint hope. *This is how to get back at you*—a strategic move to infiltrate my thoughts and emotions. If he had truly cared, truly understood the depth of that night, he would've seen through the lies they said about me. He would've sought me out and attempted to hear my side of the story. But he didn't. His inaction spoke louder than words ever could.

The drive to his house is silent. We don't say a word to each other the whole way.

As we pull up, he graciously opens the door for me, and I step into his home, mirroring the scenario from the first time. The opulence of the surroundings is as overwhelming as before, everything unchanged except for one conspicuous detail: the bathroom. Its centerpiece—the bathtub—is now conspicuously absent.

A cold tremor traces its way down my spine as I catch sight of the pipes, now tightly sealed, starkly reminding me of what used to exist there. A mixture of relief and unease washes over me. While seeing it is a chilling reminder, I'm grateful I don't have to look at it.

"I had it removed last night," he says, standing behind me. "I'm sure you would prefer the shower." He knows. I nod and look away. "I'm not a fan of them either, to be honest. It's like bathing in your own dirty piss."

"Is that supposed to be funny?"

He shrugs. "It's the truth. I never used it. It came with the house."

"So you're just going to leave it empty like that?"

"What would you like me to put in its place?

I look around and notice the shower has glass doors—"What if the entire bathroom was an open shower. No glass doors but had an area to sit and lie down like you were bathing in the rain."

"Is that what you would like to do? Bathe in the rain."

"If it was warm with the sound of thunder minus the lightning," I say mindlessly. He steps close behind me, and I can feel the heat of his body. I must smell like food. "I should take a shower. I must smell like fried food," I add, changing the subject.

"I don't mind. I'm kind of hungry," he replies. All I can think about is yesterday when he ate my pussy in his office, and we were late for his meeting. The sounds that escaped my mouth. I always thought that women sounded like that when they had an orgasm because they were faking it or it was staged. I guess not all the time. He places his hand on my waist and pulls me toward him so my back can feel how hard he is for me. "Are you hungry, Veronica?"

My thighs clench. My pussy throbs hearing the timbre of his

voice. The heat from his hand on my waist. The scent of his cologne. "How did you know about the bathtub?"

His lips are close to my ear. "You said you preferred a shower?"

He knows, but he won't admit it, and I'm unsure if I'm grateful or upset. He brought me here to show me. My head is pounding at the same time my body is aroused. Confusion, indecision, and want swirl inside me.

He turns on the shower and slowly unzips the back of my uniform. "Let's take a shower. You look tired, and you've had a hard day."

He faces me naked in the shower, and I can't keep my eyes from wandering between his legs. His dick is perfect. It's thick and long, even when it's not hard. His stomach is chiseled, and he has those deep V's that disappear like deep valleys. When my eyes trail up, he has a gleam in his eyes; he places gel in his palm and begins to wash, stroking his long shaft.

He turns around, and I can't help but admire his ass and strong legs. There isn't an ounce of fat on his frame. He looks perfect, and he knows it. The water slides over his muscles, and the smell of his shower gel permeates the air. I place shower gel in the palm of my hand and take the opportunity to wash myself, closing my eyes under the spray and wetting my hair.

The third time I close my eyes to rinse the conditioner from my hair, the energy inside the shower shifts like an impending storm, and I know he's right in front of me. When I open my eyes, I can't help how he stares at my body like a piece of art.

"I love to taste you, but I want to be inside you." He pulls my bottom lip, pressing his thumb into my mouth. "I want you to suck my cock."

This is what he wants, but secretly, so do I, and there is nothing more satisfying to a woman than when she enjoys the man she has sex with. He pulls his thumb out, and I drop to my knees, slowly noticing his jaw tensing in anticipation. His nostrils flare when I touch his shaft, feeling it rapidly growing in my hand. I stroke it once, then twice. I lick my lips, look up, and slide his engorged cock into my mouth. I hear him hiss through his teeth when I take him deep, hitting the back of my throat. I relax and breathe through my nose, trying to accommodate his size.

His hands slide to the back of my head, threading his fingers in my wet hair. I dig my nails in his thighs when I bob my head. Faster and faster. "I love the way you take my cock. I'm going to fuck your throat hard… until you give me that pussy."

I want him to, but I know, deep down, why I won't give in to him so easily. My mind can tell me otherwise, but I know. I fear he will end this, and I don't want it to end. I want to stay with him. I prefer him to punish me than to return home to what awaits me. For the first time, I have to admit I am scared. I am afraid I will die in Dorian Black's hands.

I take him deep, loving how his length feels in my mouth and throat. He fucks my mouth hard, almost choking me, but I love it. The feel of him and the power I have to make him lose control. I almost can't breathe, but he's close, and I want to taste him. I grip his ass, pushing him deeper into my mouth.

"Take it, baby. You're so good." He growls, biting his bottom lip and holding my head, moving faster. He's panting by the time he shoots his cum down my throat. I sputter, trying to swallow it. It drips down my chin, dropping between the valley of my breasts. When he pulls out, and I shoot him a glance, he cups my face. "You're mine," he says breathlessly.

He lays me on the soft bed after we dry off, hovering over me between my legs. His elbows are resting on the mattress on both sides of my face. My eyes are trying to adjust to the darkness of the bedroom.

"Are you okay?" he asks, his eyes trailing my mouth, and I respond with a simple nod. My jaw is a bit sore, but I liked it. "When you decide to let me have you, and only when you decide, I want you to be sure. I want you to want me because it's what you want." He presses his warm cock between my legs. A whimper escapes my throat at how good it feels, and he looks down where he's pressed against me. "Because I'm not going to stop once you let me, but I do like that sassy mouth."

I place my palms on his chest, lift my chin, and whisper, "Are you telling me you want to be friends?"

"Are you being funny?" I giggle, and he smiles, placing a kiss on my forehead. "Let's sleep; I have a meeting in a few hours."

VERONICA

AFTER WAKING up in the most comfortable bed, I take a shower and notice everything he picked out that day we went shopping is in his closet. All the clothes take up residence on an entire wall. He has a note on a black double-breasted blazer that reads, "Wear this."

When I open the bottom drawer where the shoes are neatly placed, there is a lingerie set, also black, and a note that reads, "I want to see how bad you are."

No, you don't, I tell myself. He doesn't want to see how bad I am because every time I have let that side out, it has been because I have had to act that way. At first, it was hard, and I felt a certain type of guilt that always came after every penance in the form of a ritual. It always boiled down to that event, like a turning point. I was now one of them. A hypocrite. I hated how they began to make fun of me everywhere I went, at school or a party. It became easier after Alicia passed. There was no one to talk to or trust with all my secrets. That side of me became a weapon, and Alaric wants to see it in its pure form.

The elevator doors slide open. "Twentieth floor," the voice from the elevator announces. When I walk toward the reception area, Sergio practically jumps out of his chair and rounds his desk. "You look gorgeous," he says, clapping his hands excitedly and checking out my outfit. "Dolce & Gabbana blazer dress and those ankle boots are perfect."

"Thank you."

"He's in his office. He's in a meeting, but I think they should be wrapping up," he says, but I don't miss the way his lips turn slightly into a frown when he finally says, "Go on in."

I stare at Alaric's door, the butterflies in my stomach dying slowly. He left early for a meeting. The alarm I set on my phone is what finally woke me up.

I turn the handle on the door without knocking, and the sound of female laughter hits me like a slap in the face. "Alaric, it was just breakfast–"

Tara is sitting with her legs crossed in a short skirt. She crosses and uncrosses her legs to attract his attention. Her blouse is open, revealing the top of her bra, screaming I'm a desperate bitch and want to fuck.

My eyes lift and land on Alaric. He looks relaxed without his suit jacket, sporting a blank expression, and I instantly hate that I'm wearing the outfit he picked. My eyes flick back and forth between them. How comfortable they look sitting in his office. He must have taken my advice and took Tara out for breakfast.

"I trust you had a good meeting or…breakfast. Is there anything you need me to work on?" I ask formally.

"Veronica, I heard about your internship here," Tara says in a catty tone.

"I'm sorry about your engagement with Reid."

She smiles dryly. "It worked out alright, I guess. I was dating Alaric, if you can call it that. I think we were better suited than Reid and I were. Arranged marriages work out like that sometimes, and I guess me and Alaric have something in common. We aren't committed. I did hear about yours. Dorian Black. Congratulations. I'm surprised he hasn't swept you away yet."

Bitch.

Tara's father was brought into the Order years ago, but they didn't require Tara to attend Kenyan. She inherited her father's company and has been doing business with the Riordans for years. It was the reason behind the initial arrangement that she and Reid were supposed to be married. Tara has been dying to be tied to one of the sons of Kenyan. She failed with Reid and is trying to get Alaric to commit.

"I'm hard to please," I reply, giving her a closed-lipped grin. My gaze lands on the time from the phone clasped in my hand. Five hours. Five hours and I can get the fuck out of here, and then there is one day left, and I don't have to step foot in his office again.

"I trust you already had breakfast. Ours was great. We went to this little café down the street after our meeting," she drones on, my gaze now locked on Alaric. "The pastries are so good—"

My gaze serenely swings to Tara. "Are you trying desperately to tell me you two are still fucking?" I walk slowly toward the corner of his desk and lean on the edge, watching her raise a brow. Alaric is silent. I swing my long hair to the side, letting the side of Veronica that everyone expects to show up. "Let me guess, he chained you to the wall over there." Her eyes shift to the wall where the chains and different cuffs hang hidden from view, and I know I'm right. "You sucked his cock; he may have...sodomized you, breath play, or chained you." Her eyes light up in recognition while she relieves those moments with Alaric. I hear him clear his throat, but I ignore it. "He does that to every woman, and you're no different. You just... think you are."

"How would you know?" she asks cynically.

I lean close, placing one hand on the arm of the chair she is sitting in, my lips inches from her ear, and say in a soft sultry voice, "It sucks to suck, doesn't it? It must be exhausting trying to fuck your way into an alliance."

I lean back, and her lip curls in a snarl. "Funny coming from you because everyone knows you're a twisted...sick whore probably on meds. I'm surprised Dorian agreed to marry you when no one wants you. You crazy bitch."

"That's enough," Alaric barks.

I let out a sardonic laugh. "It's okay, Alaric. She's right. She's just mad that so am I. The only difference is, I don't give a fuck, and she does." I push off and walk toward the door.

"Where do you think you're going?" he asks in a hard tone.

I ignore him, walking out his office door, my skin on fire, wishing it would melt the clothes he bought me and, like an idiot, I'm wearing. I close the door and meet Sergio's surprised expression.

"Is everything alright?" Sergio asks.

I walk to the elevator pressing the button repeatedly. "Everything is fine."

"Of course," he mutters.

I pull out the Uber app and order a ride, not caring if I don't complete the internship. What are they going to do, fail me? Alaric would give them a bad report, my professor will fail me, and I won't graduate. Who gives a shit. It's not like I have a promising job when I graduate. It will give them all something else they can criticize and use to make fun of me.

"You know I don't need babysitting anymore. I've learned my lesson from Zach," Melody says, plopping on the couch with a bag of freshly made popcorn. It's Friday night, and I shut off my phone and asked Dorothy for two nights off, promising her I would take the late afternoon shifts to make it up to her, avoiding contact with anyone at Kenyan.

"I know, but maybe I needed to be around a friend for a change."

"It's Friday night," she says, while I'm scrolling through the streaming apps, looking for something to watch. "You're over twenty-one. You could be at a dance club with a hot guy or on a date. Yet, you're holed up here with me. Maddison said you have hot friends."

I pause my fingers on the remote. "Trust me. You are better company…and…those aren't my friends."

I hear the front door open and slam shut, but I continue scrolling, looking for something to watch in the horror section.

"Of course, they are your friends. Maddy said they want to hang out, but you always refuse their offer."

I cringe inwardly because Jess did point that out the night of Draven's party, but I shrugged it off and changed the subject. Melody has no idea about Kenyan or the things I've done.

"They aren't," Adam says, plopping beside me on the couch.

Melody gives a side glance. "How would you know?" she asks between bites.

"Because I know, and that is all I'm saying. I've worked with Veronica for almost a year and have never seen them show up until recently. Take her word for it"—he leans forward and snatches the popcorn from her hand—"we are more her friends than they are."

"I was eating that," she snaps.

"Sharing is caring."

"Why are you here and not on a date with Lizzy?"

"Because I wanted to hang out with my friend Veronica. Besides, Lizzy can't go out tonight. Her parents are a little strict." He hands me the bag. "Why did you take two days off?" he asks me.

"I needed a break."

He nods. "How is the internship going?"

"I wouldn't know because I left Thursday morning and haven't returned."

"Is that why you have your phone off?"

I haven't told anyone what happened or how I felt seeing Tara in Alaric's office or the fact that he took me up on my advice and went on a date with her after his meeting, like those cliché dates where a guy asks the girl to go out with him for coffee. What's worse, I lashed out and acted like a jealous idiot when there was nothing to be jealous of because I was there for two entirely different reasons, and none of them had anything to do with dating or a serious relationship. I turned him down when he asked, but seeing and hearing about it by the horse's mouth hit home. *"You're getting married to Dorian Black in two months, Veronica. You never meant anything to him, and you never will."*

I scroll and land on *Nightmare on Elm Street*. Perfect.

"Really, that one?"

"Yeah, why not."

"It's scary and messes with your head."

"That's exactly what I was going for, and it's not scary."

"I heard it was based on a true story where the guy couldn't sleep, and he checked himself into a psychiatric ward and was found dead, clawed to death or something."

"He must have fucked up somewhere."

Adam laughs, but then there is a knock on the door. He glances at Melody and then at the door when the knocking becomes louder.

"Are you expecting someone?" Melody asks.

"No," Adam responds, getting up to open the door.

Boom! Boom!

"Shit."

Adam opens the door, and I hear a familiar voice. "Where is she?" Alaric's voice sounds like he wants to murder someone and is on a rampage.

My heart hammers inside my chest, and my head pounds from how much I have hidden my emotional torment for the past two days. I haven't slept. I took an Uber to campus, then sneaked into the dorm room showers, slept last night in an empty dorm, took the bus to work, and ended up here after calling Dorothy and Adam. I never went home. I stopped at Target on the way here to buy some clothes from the clearance rack so I didn't look like a homeless person that hasn't changed their clothes. I learned what it felt like to air dry your underwear after hand washing it in the dorm room shower sinks.

"She's on the couch," Adams says, eating popcorn like nothing is happening. "We were beginning to watch *Nightmare on Elm Street*." He moves past Alaric and sits right back next to me, holding the bag of popcorn out to me so I can have some.

I avoid meeting Alaric's gaze, slide my hand, and grab popcorn while the opening credits roll up. "You're going to sit there and ignore me. I've been looking for you. You didn't come back—"

"You were busy, and I didn't want to interrupt your date with Tara. You two had a lot to catch up on. I ate breakfast on my own and figured out why should I go back. The internship was over anyway."

"It wasn't like that, Veronica. It wasn't a date."

Melody shakes her head in annoyance and mutters, "Guys are so stupid."

"Some…not all," Adam points out.

Alaric snorts and plops himself down between Adam and me, pulling me toward him so I have no choice but to lean on his side. "You didn't come home. You don't answer my calls because you shut your phone off, and you are not working at the restaurant. I had to beg Dorothy to give me Adam's address to find you."

"So," I quip.

"So…I was worried you didn't come home."

"Your home is not my home. What do you want?"

"I want you."

"So," I repeat.

Melody raises her brows when Alaric gets up, and when I look up, arousal spreads through me. He's wearing a fitted black hoodie that reads Saint across the front. His tattoos on his neck give him that bad-boy sex appeal he knows how to pull off when he is not in the office.

"It was nice seeing you and your sister again, Adam."

He picks me up and throws me over his shoulder, holding me by placing his palm on my ass.

"What the hell, Alaric!"

I watch Adam, the traitor, open the front door for him. "See you later, Veronica. Looks like you have a date for Friday night, after all."

"Traitor!" The front door slams shut.

VERONICA

"I KIND OF LIKE you like this," Alaric says, palming my ass. "Feisty."

"Fuck off. Put me down."

"In a minute."

He walks over to a black Bentley, which unlocks when he places his hand on the door. He finally puts me down and slides into the driver's seat, pulling me in his lap. "What are you doing?"

"What does it look like? I'm driving."

"But I'm on your lap."

"Because you are driving with me."

"Are you crazy?"

"I don't know." He fires up the car and buckles us both in the seat. "That's what they say, but who knows, are people that kill others crazy?" He adjusts the mirrors. "Let me know if you can see through the rearview and side mirrors."

I nod. My hands tremble slightly because he is pulling out onto the road, and I have never been behind the wheel of a car before.

"Relax. I will never let anything happen to you. I've been worried about you. I thought–" he trails off.

"You know where the gas and the brake are?"

"I know the basics, just never been behind the wheel."

He maneuvers the car to an abandoned lot. "Alright. Try it out."

"I-I'm going to mess up your car," I say, stammering nervously.

He slides the palms of his hands over mine and rasps against my neck, "I have more." He slides my hair over the opposite shoulder. "I picked this one because it's a smoother ride and not as intimidating."

He removes his hands, and I panic. "No…no…put them back."

I hear the smile in his voice. "Alright." I close my eyes when I feel the heat of his hands over mine.

"Don't let go."

He kisses my neck. "Never." His mouth wanders over my skin, causing a chill to slide down my back. "Relax, baby. I'm right here. You scared me. I couldn't find you, and what you saw wasn't how it was made to be. I had to get rid of her and sever ties with her company."

"Why?"

"Because she was a game, Veronica. It was the only way Reid could marry Jess."

That is probably why he didn't interfere in her little jealous rant in his office or didn't go after me when I walked out. Reid wanted Jess but was betrothed to Tara since they were in high school, and Alaric was the only way he could sway the Order and blackmail her. Since her father wasn't initiated into the Order by birth, his daughter had no freedom to sleep around before marriage. That was only reserved for offspring born into it.

I press my foot on the gas, and the car lunges forward, and I laugh when he grips my hands tightly over the steering wheel, the car picking up speed. "Slow down, you little speed demon." I let my foot off the gas as we come up on a turn. "Okay, slow down." I apply the brake harder than necessary, and he holds me so I don't fly forward. "Not so hard. You're doing good."

"Liar."

"You are. Turn the wheel to the left and let your foot off the brake. Don't press the gas until you get the hang of it."

"I want to go faster."

I did. Going slow is like sweet torture. I want to feel the rush of being scared but knowing he won't let anything happen to me. I love feeling safe in his arms.

Once I straighten the wheel, there is nothing but an open parking lot about a mile long. No car in sight. Just the moon in the dark sky and the yellow-orange glow from the streetlights.

"Alright. Press the gas."

"Hard?"

"However you want."

I press the gas and floor it, hearing the engine rumble and the tires screech on the pavement. My heart is beating so fast as the car picks up speed. Adrenaline surges through my veins, putting every cell in my body on alert, but I know nothing will happen—nothing will happen as long as he is with me because I know, deep down, he won't let it. The lights fly by like straight lines, and I can't see the end of the street.

"Let go of the gas." I do. "Now Brake!"

I brake, and his arm feels like steel wrapped around me, holding me to his chest. The seat belt locks us both to the seat. The screaming sound of the tires fill my head. I'm panting by the time the car makes a complete stop.

I lean back and feel him kiss my head. "You did well. Did that feel good?"

"Yes."

I have to admit that it felt good. I felt like all my problems faded in those seconds. In those seconds, Alaric found a way I could feel free.

"Let's do it again."

We do. He teaches me how to turn the car around and apply the brake in different scenarios. How to park and parallel park for the next five hours.

"Thank you," I tell him, seated in the passenger seat.

"Anytime. We'll come out here whenever you want, and I'll teach you."

I look down at my hands and slide my thumb over where he held them on the steering wheel, wishing his words were true because I know there wouldn't be a whenever.

"Hungry?"

"Yeah."

"I know this place that makes a great sandwich, and they have ice cream shakes."

I smile. "Okay."

We pull into an All-You-Can-Eat diner the next town over. The Bentley sticks out in the parking lot with the regular working-class cars like Hondas, Toyotas, and Fords. The place is really half diner and half gas station. When you walk in, three aisles have quick essentials like a convenience store. The rest of the place is a diner with eight booths, four on each side. They have a soda machine like in Dorothy's diner, but this place has a jukebox that you don't have to pay to play a song. You can send a text, and it will give you a list of songs you can play.

When we walk in to be seated, some kids, who look like they're still in high school, are sitting in two booths next to each other.

After we place our order, I ask, "You come here a lot?"

"When I want to think. When I need to get away from it all. I come here and eat like the common folk."

"I never would have thought you ate at a place like this."

"I did in high school and freshman year of college."

I imagine him sitting here like those kids in the back booths laughing and making jokes with their arms around a girl. How I wished my life were so simple.

"That must have been fun."

"Not really. Not when you were destined to be the first of your generation to be the greatest. Reid, Alicia, Valen, and the twins. They were all younger than me. I had to prove to everyone that I was better and that the other members attending Kenyan weren't. No sweat."

"That must have been…stressful."

"Yeah, and then the whole marriage thing didn't appeal to me either. Everything was thought out and chosen to benefit others; you were just created to follow it. I honestly thought I had it bad. Until..." The waitress sets our meals along with our cookie and cream shakes on the table and walks away. "Until you.

He means finding out that I'm Prey and the shit I was forced into.

"There is nothing I can do about it. It's done. In two months, I belong to a different type of monster."

I slide my phone on the table with the text message open, letting him read Dorian's texts. He picks up my phone and scrolls through them, and his expression turn furious.

He places the phone on the table and slides it back across the table. "I'm sorry."

I lock the screen on my phone, wondering if he's sorry because I have to marry that asshole Dorian or if he's sorry about that night. It doesn't matter; nothing does. But I am grateful that I don't need to go home. That act alone is worth its weight in gold.

"I'm sorry about everything, Veronica."

"Is this your 'I misjudged you making your life miserable, and I feel sorry for you' speech."

He shakes his head after placing his shake down. "No, this is a I know I fucked-up speech, and I want to fix it."

There it is. The guilt and the pity.

"There is nothing you can do to fix it. Some people are destined for a great life, to fall in love, be happily married or happily single, and have gorgeous children. I'm not one of those people." I look at the high school kids laughing like they're in slow motion. The helpless feeling I hate making its way under my skin. "I've tried everything, and it all boils down to what I'm destined to be…unworthy of having anything good."

"I don't think that."

A laugh bubbles out of my throat, causing me to drop the sandwich. "A few days ago, I found that highly unlikely. You threw me out of your mother's house because I was there when she called me, so I could pick up a dress she bought, saving me from having to buy one because—" I trail off.

"Because?"

Rolling my eyes, I finish what I was about to say, "Because I'm broke. I make twelve bucks an hour plus tips. Do you know how much they take out in taxes or how much one of those dresses costs when you make peanuts?"

"Charles Devlin doesn't buy you clothes?"

"Ha! Unless it's out with him for some stupid ball or to sell me off. Oh…I can't wear the same thing twice because, God forbid, I embarrass the sick bastard. The only thing I do have is a roof over my head with utilities included."

I don't tell him I shower in the dorms because Charles found it amusing to install only bathtubs in the entire mansion to punish me.

"Stay with me."

I lift my gaze and see in his expression that he's serious. "Why?" I shake my head. "It won't change anything."

"There is something I want to change."

What would he want to change? In my mind, there is nothing that could, except my existence.

"What is that?"

"Our first time."

ALARIC

RELIEF SETTLES INSIDE ME, seeing her in the passenger seat of my Bentley. I went crazy looking for her since yesterday, after telling Tara to never contact me again and that I was terminating any business we had from her father's company. She accused me of using her, but the truth was, she had an expiration date, and it was passed due. What I fear happened when Veronica walked in. I couldn't panic, but I did after Tara stormed out.

I looked for her everywhere. I even called Valen, who told me to check the dorm showers, but I couldn't. It was too early, and I was not a creep looking in the women's showers, knowing they would be occupied. I decided to give her a day and would try again today until I had to bribe Dorothy to redo her kitchen so she would give me Adam's address. I swear that woman hates me.

"I missed you," I tell her.

I did. I couldn't sleep last night. I never thought I would ever need a woman to fall asleep, but I find that I need her. I want the warmth of her hair and the smell of the shampoo I bought her. The feel of her skin on mine, her lips parting when she is in a deep sleep. Lips I kiss when she isn't aware that I'm doing it.

After we shower, I drape a towel over my neck and notice her splayed out on the bed in one of the sets I bought her.

My cock instantly goes hard when my eyes slide over the slit between her legs from the crotchless panties that attach to the lace pieces on her hips. She's holding herself up with the palms of her hands behind her as her dark hair falls like a waterfall down her back.

I swallow hard. "You're gorgeous."

She always was. I walk over to a drawer and open it, pulling out the thigh-high socks similar to the ones she wore that night.

I watch her eyes widen when she spots them in my hand. "You weren't kidding."

"No. I'm not," I answer, handing them to her, so she can put them on and I can watch.

I wish I was a superhero with powers that could take us back in time. Because that night was a setup. They ruined us, and I was too blind to see it. I can still see the terror and horror in her beautiful innocent eyes replaying in my mind on repeat. The look she gave me screamed for help, but all I could see was betrayal. Her father had people watching her every move, but so did I. Except yesterday, and I was terrified. Sometimes it takes a person to disappear for a moment, knowing you might not get them back to realize what the mystery of death means. The end of the world you're currently a part of.

When she slides the last sock over her soft thighs, I kneel on the bed, feeling it dip with my weight. "Is this okay?"

She knows what I mean. I want her to want this as much as I want it. I slide the towel off my neck and kneel, completely naked, between her thighs.

"Hard or soft," I ask.

She smiles, and I think I just saw what an angel would look like. It would look like her. Because God could have only been the one to create something so perfect.

"How would you have wanted our first time to feel like?"

I knew the answer before she asked, but I wanted to ask her anyway. It's because the more I hear her voice, the more I can tell myself this is real. It isn't another woman touching me, so I won't have to close my eyes and imagine it's her.

She's here.

In my bed.

With me.

I slide my hand behind her neck and pull her to my chest. I kiss her, taking my breath away like the air thinned and I need oxygen. Our tongues search like they're seeking each other's secrets, and there is only one way to hear them, to consume them. I've never made love to a woman before, and now I know why. It's because of her.

If there is one part of my life I would redo, it would be the first time I looked into her eyes because I could convince myself to never let her go.

She pulls away, panting, her chest rising and falling. She lies back on the bed, her legs open wide like the first night. I dip my head, sliding my hands under her legs and gripping her hips, then lick her clit.

"Alaric…mmm." She moans.

Her sweet little cries slip through her lips every time I lick, careful not to suck. I want her to want me as much as I want her.

I slide my tongue and suck the soft skin of her inner thigh and notice the faded cuts she tries to hide. I lick and suck them, hearing her gasp. She arches her back, causing her full breasts to push out. She holds my head when I slide my tongue to her clit and finally suck, holding me to the spot she loves. I slide my tongue inside, fucking her pussy. She grinds her hips, fucking my mouth.

"Mmm…yes…" She mewls. "I need more, Alaric." I pull the crotchless panties open, hearing them tear. "Please."

I glance up, and the pupils of her clear eyes darken, following me when I hold myself over her, stroking the tip of my cock over her clit. "Right there?" I ask, playing with her clit with my piercing.

She bites her lip, gripping my shoulders. "Yes…more."

I tilt my head, holding her gaze, and push the tip inside her tight pussy. I almost bite my tongue at how good she feels. She falls back on the pillow, and I slide the rest of the way inside her in slow, smooth thrusts, holding her gaze and getting lost in her.

"I'm drowning," I whisper.

That is the most I have ever said to a woman, and I mean it. It's my first time—our first time. I slide all the way out and push in as deep as I can, filling her, stretching her.

Her hands slide down my back and grip my ass, pushing me deeper. Her legs are spread wide. I hook each of them over my arms, holding her, and I watch as my cock disappears inside her in measured thrusts. My cock swells with each thrust. My balls draw up, and I know I'm about to come, but I hold out for her.

"Come for me, beautiful."

Her hands slide down my chest then back up to my neck as she pulls me down, taking my mouth with hers and whispers, "Fuck me…fuck me hard, Alaric."

My nostrils flare, and I place one hand on the mattress and the other around her neck. "You don't know what you just asked for."

Her lips lift in a seductive smile. "You're the only man that can make me come. Now make me come," she says, licking her lips.

She whimpers when I enter her again. Over and over. Harder and harder. Holding her neck in the palm of my hand, I squeeze, allowing her just enough space to breathe.

"Harder." She moans.

I go even harder, fucking her like an animal. She comes with a scream, her pussy contracting, but I don't stop impaling her. It spurs me on, and I go harder, gripping her throat, my hips move faster and my ears ring, warning me that I am going to come hard. I know I'm constricting her air, but she keeps meeting my thrusts, and when we can't take it anymore and it becomes too much, she comes a second time. When I ease my grip on her throat, I come on a roar, watching her take gulps of air. We're exhausted and spent, her beautiful dark hair sticking to her neck. I push it away, still inside her, filling her with cum, licking and sucking her neck, leaving marks.

My tongue traces her ear as I slide out of her and whisper, "Turn around, beautiful. I'm not done."

She turns around with her ass in the air on her elbows, and I slap her hard on her ass, making her yelp. My cum leaks out of her swollen pussy lips with every slap. I grip her by the hair hard and slide my finger up her slit, lubricating her tight hole with my cum. "Can I have it?" She mewls when I play with her tight hole. "Is this your first time?" She nods. "Good, I want all of your firsts and I'll take your lasts too. They think they have you but they don't know that you have always belonged to me."

"Alaric," she calls out my name breathlessly when I push in the tip of my finger, stretching her little by little. She's so tight.

"Play with your pretty pussy and lick your fingers." She slides her fingers inside her pussy and a sweet little cry escapes her lips.

"Mmm..." She moans when she slides them out and puts them in her mouth. "Your cum tastes so good in my pussy."

My fingers slide and entwine with hers around her clit, and I push them together, fucking her pussy and pressing my cock into her tight hole. She is so wet and swollen, but that doesn't stop her from pushing my fingers inside her cunt. Squeezing my cock deeper into her tight ass, she whimpers.

"Breathe, baby."

"You're so fucking big, and I feel so full." I push deeper, holding her by the hips and matching the speed of her fingers playing with her pussy. "It feels so good." A filthy noise escapes her lips. I pick up speed, ruthlessly fucking her in the ass. I pull my hand away and grip her by the hips, our skin slapping against each other, making clapping sounds. My heart is beating fast, and my chest tightens when I begin to come.

"Oh God...Alaric...I'm coming."

"Me too, baby." I pull her by the hair and lick the mark on the back of her neck while my cum fills her tight hole. "Mine." I growl.

VERONICA

AFTER CLASS ON MONDAY, I head over to Babylon, the bar across the street from campus. Alaric is at work, and I want to avoid showing up at his office and raising questions. The rest of the weekend, we spent in bed, ordering takeout and watching horror movies. He told me about his childhood and the pressure his parents' expectations put on him. He showed me how sorry he was by worshiping my body.

The change in his behavior toward me could be because of guilt. His possessive words and how he brands my body make me crave him more than I should. My heart is reckless in holding on to the attention, enjoying the moment, knowing that it will all end at one point. *It will end, Veronica.*

I'd heard about life's guilty pleasures and thought they never existed for me, but it takes one person to show you everything you're missing. Then you realize how wrong you were and that it was because you were in the wrong room at the wrong time. If someone were to tell me that I could be set free but that I would never experience what it was like in his arms, I would prefer to be chained in a life of sin, suffering penance, because my life wouldn't mean anything without being in the arms of the man of my dreams.

My eyes adjust to the bar's darkness when I walk in from the afternoon sun, hearing the jukebox blare Nirvana's "Heart-Shaped Box." My eyes scan the pool tables, and I find Garret, Jess, Gia, and the Bedford twins, along with some of the guys from the swim team gathered around the table while Valen and Reid play a game of pool.

Jess waves at me from across the room to head over.

"Hey, I heard the big bad wolf has you holed up in his lair."

My cheeks heat, and I roll my eyes, trying to play it off. "I've been studying."

Gia bursts into laughter. "Is that what you call it, studying."

"Higher learning," I shoot back.

I walk over and grab a pool stick. "I got next."

"We were just finishing a game, and Valen lost."

I jut my bottom lip out when he grimaces a bit. "Poor baby, you lost to the big boys." He hates losing.

"I wouldn't necessarily say they're big," Valen teases.

"We are all bigger than you ass-wipe," Dravin chimes in, and I laugh through my nose.

"You should ask Jess. She knows," he retorts.

"Fuck you, dick," Reid barks.

Gia is trying to calm the situation down because Garret is also within earshot, and he is really quiet, while Jess nervously chews on her lip. "I can attest to that. He can hang," I add, setting up the pool table and lining up the break. He does have a bigger-than-normal cock.

Everyone swings their gaze to Valen with a questionable expression. Looking up at Reid, his dark eyes meet mine, surprised that they're not full of contempt. "Ladies first," he says.

I smile, lining up the shot; carefully, so my ass isn't hanging out of my pleated skirt.

"Hey, just because she's seen it doesn't mean she's touched it," Valen defends.

I feel a warm hand slide up my thigh, causing the nerves in my heart to tingle. "Seen what?" I hear Alaric's deep voice behind me.

I almost drop the pool stick between my fingers when I feel the hard ridge of his cock pressed on my backside through his pants.

"Nothing," Valen responds.

His lips skim my ear. "Are you being a bad girl, baby?"

Electricity runs over my skin, causing me to look up at our audience nervously. He's here. "We were discussing how big Valen's dick is compared to the twins and Reid."

"Hmm, is that so," he says with an edge in his tone.

With a smile, I line up the ball to break and shrug. "I've only seen it. I've never touched it." I shoot the ball, hearing them hit. I straighten, but his hand is under my skirt and over my panties, holding me against him.

Reid proceeds to line up his shot.

"It's okay, baby. I think everyone has seen Valen's dick." Jess and Gia laugh, and the twins snort. How he calls me baby makes me dream and wish that this is real, and I'm truly his girl.

When it's my turn, he lines up with me on the pool table, but I feel something soft and rubbery between my legs. I pause, and then I feel the vibration of a vibrator. My mouth drops open when the first wave of arousal slides between my thighs. My eyes widen. "Take the shot," he whispers.

I can't without missing the ball entirely. It feels so good, but I can't grind my pussy against it without everyone noticing. I shamelessly widen my stance and hear the small chuckle from his throat. I grind my teeth every time he circles my clit, stifling a moan. Gia and Jess are watching with raised eyebrows. Reid is smirking, and I want to flip him off. "I can't," I whisper.

"Mm…yes, you can."

I'm about to face plant on the pool table as a moan escapes my lips from the sweet torture. I wiggle his hand away, but his finger slides the vibrator inside me.

"I'm—I'm," I stammer, pressing my lips together, trying to focus on the shot.

Reid gives me a sly grin, dark eyes pinning me to the spot. "Take the shot. We're all waiting, "he says.

Time seems to slow down. The music fades in the background. The sound of Nirvana makes its way to Bush's "Glycerine." All I can feel is his hand fucking me with the vibrator. My chest rises and falls, pushing against my bra. Gia leans back on both twins, her lips mouthing, 'She looks so hot.'

Alaric's lips brush against the spot under my ear, and the pool stick almost slips from my grip. My eyes roll when Bush's "The Chemicals Between Us" begins to play. The little voice in my head whispers, *Play with him, Veronica. Be a bad bitch.*

I blink, gaining control, and when my eyes flick up to everyone watching me, my lips curve in a sultry smile. I slide the pool stick back and forth between my fingers like I'm stroking a long cock. I push my ass out and grind my hips against him.

"Deeper," I moan, not caring who's watching.

"Oh fuck," Valen says softly. "That's so hot."

I push the end of the pool stick while Alaric slides it deeper inside me, my climax building, and I'm about to come. I feel his other hand grip my hip. I shoot the ball in the corner pocket when I fall over the edge, coming on the vibrator around his finger. I bite my lip, and a little mewl crosses my lips; I drop the pool stick on the table. Alaric pulls it out of me and lifts me so I'm sitting on the edge of the pool table, wrapping my legs around his hips. He lifts the small vibrator on his finger, pushing it past my lips. "Mm…" I whimper, sliding my tongue and sucking it into my mouth, tasting my arousal. He pulls it out and slides it into his mouth with a groan.

"You two are so hot," Gia says.

I smile, resting my forehead on Alaric's black dress shirt. The first three buttons open at his throat. I close my eyes, breathing in his spicy scent.

"Fuck the game. It's more fun to sit and watch them."

Alaric raises his hand, flipping Draven off, and I want to die of embarrassment. I still feel awkward in front of Gia when it comes to Draven.

After the game of pool is over and Reid lets me win, I'm sitting in the booth with Jess and Gia, nursing a beer with a plague mask on it.

"It's good, and…it's cheap," Jess says with a smile.

Word must have gotten around about my money situation. Alaric must have told Reid. I heard that Jess and Gia didn't come from money, but Prey usually don't because they get in through scholarships, and they don't live in fancy apartments or mansions, except me. Since they married, their money problems evaporated like a cloud of smoke. There is nothing their men wouldn't buy or do for them, and they deserve that.

"It is," I say, taking a pull.

The back door by the exit near the restrooms opens with a screech, followed by a slam when it closes. My eyes swing toward the hallway, and my stomach flips with dread. Dorian walks in, eyes scanning the entire place until they land on mine with a malicious gleam.

Jess's gaze swings over, watching him approach. The guys are still playing pool in the back, and I want to jump over the booth and run toward Alaric, but that's what he would expect. Me to run away like a helpless animal.

"I thought I might find you here," he says, sliding in beside me.

"Why is he here?" Jess asks in a snarky tone.

Dorian looks between Jess and me in mock surprise. "She hasn't talked about me?" Gia shakes her head, glancing at me. "My name is Dorian…Dorian Black. I believe we haven't been formally introduced. I'm Veronica's fiancé."

Anger spirals underneath my skin at that word. It is the last word I want to be associated with when it comes to Dorian Black.

"I missed you in your class. I wanted to take you out to lunch."

I inch away, sliding farther into the booth. "What for? You know the rules, Dorian."

"I don't think it matters, princess." He lowers his voice. "It wasn't like lover boy over their objected to the vote. He couldn't care less. After he's through fucking you out of his system, you belong to me. In sickness and in health."

I'd rather in sickness so I can die.

"I think you need to leave," Gia snaps.

He slides a black box on the table, and I look away. "In a minute, Mrs. Bedford, I want to give my future wife her engagement ring. She will be mine in every sense of the word in two months."

"What the fuck are doing here, Dorian?" Alaric asks in a harsh tone.

"I came to see my future wife and..." he flips open the black velvet box, revealing a black marquis cut engagement ring on a platinum band, "surprising her with her engagement ring."

My lips form a thin line. The ring is hideous; it reminds me of him, fake with no class. The center diamond is huge and oppressive. I remember seeing a pin on Pinterest of ugly engagement rings, and I saw one similar to this one.

Reid leans on the table to take a look. "Dude, that shit's ugly."

"I agree," Dravin chimes in, leaning over. He glances up at me. "It looks like a ring you find in a 'This shit is ugly store,' and no one wants it."

Jess looks away in disgust, and Gia blows a puff of air out of her mouth when she takes a look. "Who would wear that thing?" Jess says repulsively.

Dorian takes it out, and I hide my hands under my thighs. "She will. Because she will wear whatever I tell her to. In two months, she's mine." He turns to Alaric. "It wasn't like you cared so much about her. I didn't see anyone lining up to take her hand. They do like to have fun with her, though." I look away because as much as I hate him and want it to be a lie, it's the truth. But right now, he can't do shit about me being with Alaric, and I'll die before wearing his ring or going anywhere with him before I have to.

Alaric's jaw is set, and his eyes are full of rage. The little muscle in his jaw ticks rapidly back and forth. "You're just mad because I would never choose to be with you. I'd rather die than spread my legs for you."

Dorian's lip curled. "Too bad, I'll enjoy spreading them for you."

"Touch her, and I'll cut off your hands. I would be careful what I do next if I were you," Alaric warns.

Dorian leans back in the booth, as my eyes dart to Alaric. His gray eyes provoking Dorian. You couldn't see a crucial flicker that he wasn't serious.

"You're gonna threaten me for touching my wife."

"She isn't your wife, and I've done worse for much less."

Dorian smiles. "Like Gino? I heard he went missing."

Valen clears his throat. My stomach rolls over thinking about that day when he called me a bitch and a cunt. What did Alaric do?

"I don't know what you're talking about. I...canceled his contract."

Dorian moves to slide out of the booth. "Canceled his contract." He repeats like he's thinking it over. "I like it. Well, I gotta go. I have a business to run." He glances around until his eyes reach me. "My lawyers will be in touch, princess."

Dorian starts to move away, but then turns and comes back. I reach for the ring and throw it at him, causing him to flinch when the ring drops to the wooden floor like a nickel. "I knew you were coming back because you forgot something."

He knows I would never want to marry him after what he did. He made sure kids in school would put tampons in my locker. I overheard Crystal Mathison say it was Dorian Black that told the incoming freshman football players going to Ohio to do it. I thought Alaric was behind it, but Alicia said he wasn't. He just wanted nothing to do with me. Dorian never had a reason. When the Order voted for him to marry me, I knew something was behind it because I would never go out with him or give him the time of day. Dorian Black and his father are like a disease. There is no cure for their form of cancer. They just keep coming back.

Dorian's eyes are slitted, unemotional, aimed right at me, promising me that he will make me pay. He doesn't bend to pick up the ring; he simply smiles. A smile that doesn't reach his eyes. "You're mine, Veronica. And deep down, you know it."

"Yeah, I can tell she is ecstatic," Draven says morosely. "Get off of it, man. Everyone knows she wouldn't look at you if things were different. It's bad enough we have to listen to you. Take your ring and get the fuck out of here before we all lose our patience."

Alaric slides into the booth beside me and cups my cheeks, bringing my lips to his and kissing me savagely. "Let's get out of here."

When we leave Babylon, it is already well into the evening. Stars are in the night sky, and half the moon shines brightly. The guys, Jess, and Gia are all heading home, and it's just me and Alaric alone in the parking lot.

"It's been a while since I've hung out at a college spot."

I'm surprised he doesn't mention Dorian and his delusional behavior, but I feel he held himself back. I know how angry he can get. Then what Dorian and Alaric said about Gino and canceling his contract tumbles into my head.

"What did you mean when you said you canceled Gino's contract?"

He opens the passenger door of his Ferrari, and his eyes touch mine. "I severed business ties."

I slide inside the car. Before he closes the door, I notice him ogling the exposed part of my thighs between the hem of my pleated skirt and the tops of my thigh-high socks. "Really?"

He shuts the door and rounds the car sliding in, thinking that is the only answer I am getting, but he surprises me when he says, "You were exceptional at the meeting, and I would never let someone get away with disrespecting you. You were right, and I was the only person that caught it. No one that worked with me was able to, but you did. In five minutes."

No one has ever praised me. Not my parents for something I did. No one has ever thought I was smart. I just trucked along and went from graduating high school to beginning college. No one cared about my grades because no one asked. It feels good for someone to say that I am exceptional.

I blush and look straight ahead. "Thank you."

"I think you're very smart. I have looked at your essays on financial analysis, and they are good—really good."

"Thank you. It means a lot coming from you," I say in a very low voice, my heart fluttering in my chest, hoping it doesn't fold in on itself from falling deeper in love with him.

I recognized the feeling this morning when he kissed me passionately and then had Portman drop me off at school before he dropped him at work. The butterflies take flight when I think of all the dirty things he's done to me. How sore I am between my legs. The delicious sting I'll feel when he takes me again.

"I forgot to ask how your little hole is. I know I took you hard."

"It's sore but in a good way."

He glances down at my thighs and places his hand over them. "Why aren't you wearing the clothes I bought you? I love the socks, but I mean the other stuff. It's been more than a few days since you touched anything in the closet. "

After the incident with Tara, it reminded me why he bought me the clothes, and I didn't want to spoil what was blossoming inside me for him. I didn't want to cloud it with negative thoughts from my subconscious. I wanted him to desperately see the real me with the little time I had left.

"I didn't pick them at the store, and you always left a note telling me what you expected me to wear that day."

"That's because I thought it was better to buy you everything in the store so you could choose whatever you wanted."

Dumbfounded, I reply, "Oh."

I didn't see it that way. I just thought he wanted to control what I wanted to wear. Like Charles did.

"I only said that I preferred the crotchless panties because all I could think about was being inside you. I didn't want to shred every piece of lingerie you wore."

"You were so sure I was going to give in, huh?"

"Honestly, I have never been rejected before." He glances at me briefly. "You're the first."

After having dinner at an Italian restaurant and making it home, it's already nine-thirty, and I'm following him out to the backyard to the oversized swimming pool, glowing like a pool of blood.

"What is it with you guys and the red light in the pool?"

"It's a Kenyan thing. A signature for the team. Our logo has red in it, and the color of blood is red and rich."

"Like the sons of Kenyan."

"Yeah, like us."

He slides his shirt off his shoulders and removes his pants and boxers, standing completely naked at the edge of pool and facing me. His naked body is sculpted like a perfect statue. His strong arms and thighs, chiseled abs, and his large thick cock hanging between his legs.

"Swim with me."

"I'm super slow. All I can do is keep myself from drowning."

"That's okay. I'm a good swimmer."

He swims competitively and has a spot on the Olympic team, but he refuses for obvious reasons. Do I want to get in his pool with him? Of course, I do. But I'm scared. Scared that when this is all over, I won't be able to breathe without him. He is becoming the air I need so I can live another day, so when I fall asleep in his arms at night, I can wish for it to happen all over again. To be consumed by him.

I nod and slowly remove my clothes until I stand naked before him. He calls me over with his finger.

"Look at me," he says, touching my shoulders. I raise my chin up, and he kisses me fully. It is desperate but soft, full of a promise I can't figure out. Something is happening between us, or maybe it was already there waiting for us. For the right time.

I shiver when a light breeze hits my skin when he pulls away. His gray eyes hold mine when he whispers, "Swim with me. The pools warm."

He swims laps for the next twenty minutes. He's like a machine, his arms perfect, cutting through the water with measured strokes. I sit on a built-in ledge watching in fascination how perfect he is. His back muscles bunch with the effort. The temperature has dropped because a light fog is coming from the pool's heat, skimming the water's surface.

In the springtime in Ohio, the days are hot, but as night falls, so does the temperature, especially when you're naked in a pool. He stands between my legs while I'm seated on the edge of the pool's built in sun deck, sliding his hands over my thighs and stopping at my waist.

My head tilts, and I look up at the dark sky, watching the stars wink at me from above. If I could look up at the sky every night, I would want it to be with him.

Sometimes you wonder how someone you love could hate you. How could they hurt you or break your heart when you only wanted the opportunity to love them.

"What are you thinking about?" He rasps into my skin. His lips wandering down my throat.

"How much you hate me."

"Does it look like I hate you?"

"I don't know. Do you?"

His tongue slides up my chin, his lips ghosting mine. My nipples pebble from the breeze. "Let me show you. It's why I took you to my favorite place…a place I love the most. You can look at the dark sky you love so much," his thumb caresses my cheek, and he's staring deep into my eyes, "and let the angels and Gods watch us from above while I make you mine."

His hard cock crowns my opening, the air thickening around us with every breath I take. We're in a bubble, and nothing can break it. He slides inside me, stretching me inch by inch, never breaking eye contact. His soft lips skim mine in sweet torture. Tears prick my eyes at how smooth and gentle he is with his words, like a balm to my inner wounds. "I love you," he says softly.

A single tear slides down my cheek, hearing him say it. Those three little words mean so much.

"You're on a mission."

"How is that?"

I blink the tears away. "To steal all of my firsts," I say softly.

He nods, the skin between his brows pinching together like he's struggling with his emotions. He slides his fingers into my wet hair, holding me, sliding deeper inside, moving slowly.

Under the stars, we make love, but I can't say the words back. In my mind, it is too late. He…is too late. But those words have never been said to me before by anyone, and I want to savor them. Because I know what my future holds, and love isn't part of it. But I feel it, and that's all I ever wished for.

VERONICA

DOROTHY PLACES the stack of clean plates on the serving counter with a clink. "You have a visitor in booth eight, Veronica."

I look over and notice Dorian seated in the booth, watching me with rheumy eyes, reminding me of his father. "Yes," I say faintly.

"I got to tell ya, Claire's boy is better looking than that piece of work right there. Alaric's a ball buster, but the way he looks at you... ain't no man ever looked at you like he does."

"Are you sure it isn't because you got a new kitchen out of it?" I tease.

She leans close. "Nah, I would have told him where you were. It helped that Alaric's a tycoon. He could help an old lady out. Now that animal seated in booth eight gives me bad vibes. I think I heard about him a few years back when he was still in college. A few guys came here one night and said he was a real asshole. It's a shame he was like that to the girls too. He's a looker, but you can see it in his eyes when he looks at you."

"Me?"

"Oh yeah, I see it. I'm not sixty-eight for nothin'."

"What do you see?"

"Desperation."

A feeling of cold dread creeps down my legs because I can see it.

"Let me go see what he wants."

"Scream if you need anything. He looks the type."

If you only knew.

"What are you doing here?" I ask angrily.

He just wants to annoy me by showing up here.

"Is that any way to talk to your husband?"

"You're not my husband," I say through clenched teeth.

I hate every time I look at him; it reminds me of that night he flung the door open at the party. He had no right. It doesn't excuse Alaric for how he treated me, and I get that he's apologized, but what was Dorian's excuse? I never did anything to him.

He straightens the salt and pepper shakers, but he's trying to get under my skin. "Not yet." He slides his gaze over my uniform crudely, and I want to rip his eyes out. "You know, you don't have to work here. I think it's a waste of your time—"

"Save it."

"I can find other things you could be useful in doing. I have learned a lot of things about you, Veronica."

Creep. I don't miss the meaning behind his words, and I can't stand him. The way he looks at me makes my skin crawl. But the apple doesn't fall too far from the tree. Does it?

"How creepy of you. I'm sure you learned a lot from your father. He's disgusting and pathetic, just like you."

He smiles, but it doesn't reach his eyes. "I would be careful if I were you. You should be nice to me because *he* won't be able to save you. Once he is done with you, you must be cleansed of the filth." Fear sneaks its way in when I'm reminded of how this ends. The bathtub and the sound of water haunt me, no matter how hard I try to escape it and the memories it keeps. The heavy breathing…the pain from each strike, enough to hurt but not enough to leave a mark. He chuckles. "What's wrong?"

"Leave me alone." I turn, but he grips my wrist hard. I can feel my bones grind. I try to rip my wrist from his grasp, but he pulls me toward him. "You're hurting me."

He loosens his hold a bit. "Not yet. Soon. But I forgot to tell you, my secretary was upset."

"And? What did you do to her? Fuck her without asking," I retort.

He laughs, but it falls off. "Oh, I fucked her, but so did Alaric. I guess he can't help himself. He fucks everything that moves. She was upset he was a little rough on her throat the last time. The chains in the office didn't help either, but none of that surprises me. He did however tell me he doesn't give a shit about you before he turned down my business proposal. He's just using you to get to me because

I'm marrying you. See, I always wanted you, Veronica. No guy could get the high school senior, but everyone with a dick wanted it. I admit I acted childish when I saw you two that night. I wanted to hurt you." I snatch my wrist from his grip in hurt and revulsion. "But when my father told me how special you are." My blood turns cold, and my skin feels numb. "I knew you would be perfect."

My jaw hardens. "You're sick, just like the rest of them."

His eyes gleam. "But I'm the only one that will fight to keep you. They…just use you, Veronica, but they have no plans to keep you. No one wants you but me."

"I hate you."

"I'm going to make you my whore, and you'll like it."

My hands shake.

"Is there a problem here?" Adam asks, walking up to me with a rag in his hand.

Dorian turns his head to look at Adam. "Hey, man. I was just here to check on my girl."

Adam swings his gaze between Dorian and me with a confused expression, and I shake my head slightly. Dorian slides out of the booth. "I'm trying to convince her to stop working here. She doesn't have to, but you know how girls are. Stubborn. I can provide for her, but she stuck in her ways."

"She likes working here," Adam says in a serious tone.

Adam would know if I was seriously dating someone, and the only guy he has seen me with is Alaric. I look over when a couple walks in, needing to be seated.

"Dorian was just leaving."

Dorian winks at me, and I want to throw up. "I'll see you later, babe, and remember to call me." He gives me a peck on the lips before I can turn my head, and I wipe my mouth in revulsion. "You'll owe me for that one," he says through his teeth.

"Have fun jerking off," I snap back. "I'm sure you're used to it." He grins and points at me while walking backward toward the exit with his jeans and sweater, looking like a trust fund reject.

• • •

When he walks out, I watch him cross the parking lot to his ostentatious-looking car, a gold McLaren sports car that looks like a shiny easter egg. Hideous, just like the owner.

"Who is that guy, and why did he say you're his girl?"

I glance up after peering through the window, making sure he leaves. "I'm not. Not yet."

"What do y—"

"Long story. If he comes in again, let me know so I can hide in the bathroom and tell him I'm not here."

"Want me to kick his ass?"

"No!" He raises his brow at my outburst. "Look, he doesn't play by the rules, Adam. He's well-connected and has all the money and resources in the world to—" I trail off.

"To what."

I sigh in defeat. "To make shit disappear like rich people do. He hates Alaric. He's trying to mess with him by using me," I lie.

I'm not sure about anything. I don't know what to believe, but what Dorian said about his secretary and what Alaric told him about me felt like getting stabbed with a hundred knives. They all burned because the truth hurts. I have to marry Dorian.

"Fine, if he comes back. I'll make sure to tell you and ask him to leave."

"Thank you," I say nervously.

"No sweat."

After my shift, I take the last trash bag on my way out. I texted Alaric and told him that my shift would run a little later and not to pick me up. I want to confront him, but what would be the point? He would continue with his life, and I would be trapped in my hell or… I could run. I have money saved. They would vote, and all would be in agreement to end me. I've thought of it a lot this past week. I could just take a bus, leave and go somewhere far away, and not tell anyone. It would give me time. I always wanted to leave Kenyan and go somewhere warm like California. Maybe Texas.

I toss the trash bag in the huge bin and freeze. I blink hard a couple of times. The exit to the left and right are blocked by three men, all wearing plague masks. The first time I saw one on the bus, I thought I was dreaming, but it was real because six are standing right now like the people in the movie the Purge. Disturbing.

It's still dark at 4 a.m. Two lamp posts are the only lighting in the back of the restaurant, and no one comes back here. I look to my left and right, backing away toward the door. "What do you want?"

My palms are sweating, and my hands are shaking. I clutch my bag under my arm, knowing they are not here to mug me. They stand rooted to the spot, looking like human-sized birds. A spine-chilling fear grips me as they move forward in unison like walls closing me in. I can't see their eyes. The eye sockets on the mask shine with the reflection of the lights. The black cloaks conceal their bodies. It could be anyone under those masks. They could kill me, and no one would know who did it. Tears prick my eyes.

"What do you want? I repeat.

Silence.

"Stop fucking with me!" I yell.

They shake their heads slowly, and my fear contorts to anger. "I'll fucking scream, and everyone will come out."

They don't respond. *Bastards.*

They keep walking toward me like they don't care if I scream for help or call 911. I reach into my bag, searching for my cell phone, trying to unlock it before pulling it out and dialing 911 while I scream at the top of my lungs. There are six of them and one of me. There is not much of a chance, and the back entrance to the restaurant is behind me. I would have to run screaming and dialing 911 all at the same time to give me a fighting chance.

My heart is beating wildly in my chest. My fingers are trembling, and the hair is sticking to the back of my neck. There is a sheen of sweat on the top of my lip. I'm terrified, but I can't show them fear.

I turn to run with my phone in my hand, trying to dial for help and screaming.

"Adam!"

I hear the sound of heavy footsteps as a gloved hand covers my mouth, and I'm lifted off the ground. I struggle, but whoever it is, is too strong. I hit the side of the mask and hear a loud grunt. I try to kick and scream, but it's no use. A large blacked-out SUV pulls up, and I'm shoved inside.

"You son of a bitch! Adam! Adam! Help!" I scream. The door slams shut. They place a dark hood over my head, and I try to kick and push when they tie my hands and feet together.

"Help!" I'm breathing fast, and my chest hurts. My voice is hoarse, and my throat burns. I feel something hard being stuffed in my mouth and a piece of rope tightening across my face. I have no choice but to breathe through my nose. I can feel the car moving and rustling on the road.

Tears prick my eyes when "Closer" by Nine Inch Nails begins to play. Tears crest on my lashes because I can't undo the ties from my hands or feet. I panic trying to slide my hands free. When I see that it's no use, sobs tear through my chest.

I can feel a hand on my shoulder, and I jerk away and bump into something hard and solid to my right. It takes a moment to realize that I'm sitting in between two of them. They were sent to kill me. Tears are falling with every sob that bubbles up, muffled because of the ball of fabric in my mouth. I think of Alaric, hoping he finds out that I was taken by the Consortium. I feel stupid for telling him I would get off an hour later.

I close my eyes and pray.

After twenty minutes, the SUV stops, the engine cuts off, and I hear doors open and close. I try to jerk away when someone's hands touch my shoulders. Then I'm grabbed. It's dark, but whoever is carrying me is strong. To him, it's as if I weigh nothing.

I try to see through the hood over my head to find out where they are taking me, but it's too dark. No light filters through, and when they put me down, I try to take a step to see if I can run, but it's no use; I fall hard to the ground and hit my shoulder.

It was stupid, but I had to try.

I'm picked up and carried, hearing his footsteps. I hear a door swing open and more footsteps, and I'm placed on what feels like a bed. Dread snakes through me, wondering what they will do and why.

After ten minutes, the rope around my head is removed,

releasing the gag, and the hood is snatched off my head. My eyes try to adjust to the gloom of the room. I blink a few times, trying to acclimate my eyes. There is only a stream of light from the window coming from an outdoor light, and when my eyes finally focus, a cold knot forms inside my chest, sinking to my stomach.

The six men in plague masks and cloaks are standing at the foot of the bed, watching me. I'm not one to beg, but right now, I can feel panic gripping me in its clutches, telling me to plead.

"Please," I whisper. "If you're gonna kill me. Make it quick," I say in a shaky voice. Tears slide down my wet cheeks, mixing with the ones dripping from my nose.

They all shake their head. Sobs begin suffocating me. One of them reaches out with a gloved hand, and I shrink back in fear.

"No, don't touch me." I sniff. "Please…leave me alone."

Five of them walk out, closing the door. Now there is just one standing in the middle of the room at the foot of the bed. He reaches out, grips my ankle, and pulls me so I slide down to the foot of the bed. I can scream, but they will re-place the hood and gag me again. When his gloved hand slides up my leg, I kick out with both feet, hitting him in the chest. I hear him grunt. He removes his mask, and relief, mixed with a new fear, causes my blood to turn cold and my face to drain of its color. I wipe my face with both hands tied together.

"Why?" I ask.

"Because I'm one of them."

ALARIC

"YOU CAN GO RIGHT IN, Mr. Riordan," my grandfather's secretary says when I walk in.

"Thank you."

When I walk in, my grandfather is seated at his desk smoking a cigar. A plume of smoke hovers around his desk, nursing a scotch in his right hand, the gold ring from his pinky finger catching the light. The same one that is given to all the sons of Kenyan. The same one was given to me once I graduated with the Order's crest engraved on the top.

"You wanted to see me, Grandfather?"

"I did."

My grandfather called me while I was in my office, and there are only two reasons my grandfather would summon me here, death or money. No one has died in our family, so I will choose option two.

"Have a seat. We have much to discuss."

I sit and unbutton my suit jacket as he taught me as a formality. My grandfather preferred to teach me how to be a ruthless businessman. He didn't let my father teach me because he considered me *his* apprentice. The oldest Riodrick-Riordan had to set an unprecedented example for this family. One person to look up to, including my cousins and the other families.

"What do we need to discuss?"

I watch the ash fall in the ashtray from his cigar as it burns. The smell permeates everything it meets. Cigars in my grandfather's world signify power, success, and wealth. The more expensive, the better.

"I trust you went and did your research because I have found that you have terminated contracts. Tara called her father, and her father called, but I wasn't surprised since Reid refused to marry her because he grew a conscience and fell for Prey. The other," he smiles with the cigar between his teeth, "disappeared."

"He did."

He means I killed him, and he fell from the face of the earth.

"Did this have to do with Miss Devlin?"

"I would prefer you not address her by that name, but yes, sir. With all due respect."

He chuckles. Takes a sip of his scotch, setting the glass on his desk. "They think you are fucking her under the pretense of her belonging to the Order for some time before she marries Dorian Black."

I blink. "I am."

"She's your whore."

"She's mine. Period."

The glass clinks when he slams his hand on his desk. "Do you know what you're doing, Alaric! You took an oath to not have a wife. You can't keep her."

"I am, and I will. Whore, wife, slave, or whatever the fuck they want to think of her as. She's mine. Besides," I undo the buttons on my wrists and roll my sleeves up, "they broke the rules. She was mine to begin with. Before."

"You figured it out."

"I did."

He rolls the cigar between his fingers, lost in thought. "Then I have to give you something that arrived today from the Riordan estate under Alicia's last wishes before she died."

I take a deep swallow because out of all of us, Alicia was the most doted on by my grandfather. She was the apple of his eye. The one that could do no wrong, and like all of us in our family, we couldn't save her.

He takes out a folder and slides it across his desk. "Open it."

I open it, pulling out two sheets of paper addressed to me and one to Veronica Devlin in Alicia's handwriting.

Alaric,

Every language is silent.

Every prayer is heard.

Love, Alicia

Confused, I turn the sheet of paper over. Nothing, that is all. Two fucking lines.

I read the second one, not caring that it's addressed to Veronica, and it isn't for my eyes. Still, I read it before giving it to her because I want to know everything.

Veronica,

If you are reading this, I am dead. I gave specific instructions to have this delivered to you before your graduation. You entrusted me with your secrets and gave me your love unconditionally. I am forever indebted to you for always keeping mine and giving me your promises. The world needs more people like you. Strong, full of love, and witty. You are the best friend I could have ever wished for. The greatest love I have ever seen and felt in someone's heart was yours. It was a shame having to watch something so precious not be embraced by others around you. They judged when what they needed to do was save you.

I'm so sorry for failing you and for not telling my promises to you when I should have. I wrote you this letter to be handed to you before your graduation because we both knew what would happen. What they did to you. I'm sorry for not letting you leave with me when you begged me to, but I want to remind you that I love you more than you would ever know, and please don't cut that pretty skin when you feel nothing. I bet you have a grave all picked out next to mine because I know you. You believe in love when others think you believe in hate. That's because they don't see the beautiful person you are. The one screaming on the inside to be loved. To be saved.

I promise to keep a petal for every flower you leave on my grave in my magic garden. I know you want to lie beside me, but there is someone who needs you more. He just doesn't know it yet, but he will. I promise. He will see what I see, and when he does, God help them.

I love you, Veronica.

Till death do you part, I will forever be in your heart.

Until we meet again,

Alicia.

I slide the paper inside the folder.

"All is well?"

"No. I need to hurt some people."

"You have my support."

"I need your vote and Mr. Bedford's."

His eyes flick to mine when he snuffs out his cigar. "Done. I trust you need time to put everything in place."

"I'm working on it. I just need time before she graduates."

"I'm going to warn you. There are things you are going to see. Things that have circulated, but you can't lose your head. You can't kill everyone, Alaric."

"Just a couple."

"Alaric," he warns.

"It's about time I take out some of the trash."

"What are you going to do with Devlin?"

I glance at my watch and get up to button my suit jacket. "She doesn't belong to him. Veronica belongs to me. Rules are rules."

There is a gleam in his eyes when I throw their words right back. "Yes, they are. You know what this will mean for her. Don't you?"

"Your granddaughter made her a promise."

"I see that. And?" he says promptly.

He's asking what I plan to do with Veronica. The truth is, I don't know exactly. But I know one thing…

"I'm in love with her."

He looks at me steadily. "You have always been in love with her, son. It's why you never took another to be your wife. Show her. Even if it's too late and she won't believe you, like I said. There will be things about Veronica you need to be prepared to deal with. Remember, even the devil knows the Bible."

"It's a good thing I know both."

It is nine at night when I walk out of the Riodrick building. The yellow streetlights flare on the pavement when I pull out of the garage. I smell like my grandfather's cigars, and I'm starving, but I need to see the Bedford twins, and it can't wait.

I'm at the Bedford estate after the twenty-minute drive from the city into Kenyan. Draven still lives here, and Gia and Dravin live in a modernized mansion behind it. It makes sense, I guess. Gia is the mistress of both properties, and the twins share the same woman. I always wondered who got Tuesdays and Thursdays but to each his own.

If I think of sharing Veronica with another man, rage filters inside me, and the only thing I can think of is killing someone. It's bad enough I have to stomach her fucking Garret and Draven, but I would be a fucking hypocrite because I have slept with other women. One of them, in fact, hated Veronica, and she walked in on me at a Kenyan party. Thinking about it makes my stomach turn cold in shame, making it seem she wasn't special. The words I said and the things I did to her.

"I hope you didn't come to see me so you can punch me in the face like you did, Garret," Draven says when he opens the door.

"Do you love her?"

"Hell, no. I'm a married man. I love one woman."

"Then all is good. I'm sure Veronica feels the same way."

"Trust me. It was weird, and now that I know the truth, I get why it happened. No offense, but at the time, I'm a man, and she is a beautiful woman. I don't think you could blame me if she had come on to you the way she did. Fucked with my ego."

Draven is a confident guy. I'm curious at what he meant about her messing with his ego, so I ask, "Ego?"

"She didn't get off, dude. It was like a switch," he snaps his fingers, "Just like that. It was over. It was weird. That is all I'm gonna say. It was a game, and she plays it well, but I must warn you."

I slow down in front of his father's office door. "Warn me about what?"

He pinches his nose like I've seen his brother do countless times. It's like watching a clone but with a different demeanor.

Draven looks grimly at me. "What I'm going to show you, all I have to say is…I'm sorry."

A feeling of unease sweeps over me. It feels like I am looking down, and I'm not sure how hard the fall will be if I jump or if there is another way down, so it doesn't hurt as much when I fall. Whatever it is he needs me to see, I am not going to like it.

It is mainly the reason he wants me to come here. He said he needed to show me something when Reid dug into Veronica's past. Whatever it was, Reid couldn't show me. He said he couldn't, meaning...it's bad.

"Alright."

He opens his father's study door, and Mr. Bedford sits behind his desk. He has a sharp look in his gaze when we both walk in.

"Alaric."

"Mr. Bedford," I say, shaking his hand.

He takes a deep breath and I take a seat, but I don't miss how he moves irresolutely back to his desk, like he isn't sure if he should leave me with Draven and let him show me what I need to see or if he should stay.

"I'm going to make this quick. I have never seen this before because I don't partake in these things. This is more for the generation before me."

He means my grandfather's generation of sick fucks. Our generation fucks girls in college, knowing our lives after we graduate are to serve the Order with a wife in our arms. Chosen by us or not. We play games and don't take them seriously, but who in college does? Frat and college parties are full of college kids, getting drunk and high, having the occasional coke habit, and fucking girls. Not these guys. They're more sadistic and take shit to a new level of fucked-up. I read the book on their history.

Mr. Bedford glances at Draven and then at me. "I'm sorry, Alaric."

He turns the screen, and I see her, and my blood turns to ice. My eyes sting, and I suddenly feel hot. I see the men around her, their faces, and what they are doing, and I imprint it into my memory. The ritual. But I can't get the image of her face out of my head. The look of agony. The pain, her skin and the way they touch her, the way they masturbate like the sick fucks they are.

"It started—" He trails off because even for a man like him, it's difficult to watch an innocent woman being treated that way. "After the night with you. This is nothing compared to the so-called sin she committed. It was never supposed to be you she ended up with.

Everyone knew how she felt about you, and the only reason it's allowed now is because they know she can't marry you."

I swallow the lump in my throat. "I can only use her."

"Right," his father says. "You have to let her go, Alaric."

"I'm not."

"Do you know what you are saying, Alaric? She belongs to the Order and to Dorian Black. I hate to say it, but he played you. He played the game and knew where to aim. He wants her and has her."

I glance at Draven as two tears escape down my face. "I need all the names and locations of those men in that video." He nods.

"Are you out of your mind?"

I turn to Mr. Bedford. "Shut it off," I demand.

He turns the video off and says, "You can save her from them, but you can't erase the damage that was done, Alaric."

"We're all damaged, Mr. Bedford. Fucked-up even."

"You're just going to find and kill them, and then, they will vote to kill you too. The higher Order. I can't vote against it, but—"

"They were all dead the second they touched her. They made a promise to themselves the second they looked at her."

"Well, you won't have to worry about her mother. Obviously, Devlin isn't her father, unless he's a really sick bastard and jerks off to his own flesh and blood, but we both know the truth because I slept with her mother. More than once, in fact. I knew that girl wasn't his. You could see it in her mother's eyes when she looked at Veronica that she was a mistake. A mistake she wished she could erase. A beautiful mistake."

"Father," Draven scolds.

"I'm not going to hide that that young lady isn't beautiful. Everyone knows it, you did, too, and I think that saucy bad bitch attitude only adds more to her appeal. Now that we know the skeletons she hides underneath. She's Prey."

My Prey.

VERONICA

"HOW DOES IT FEEL?" I ask, watching him untie my hands and feet.

"How does what feel?"

"To be a lying sack of shit."

"Go take a shower."

I pull my hand back and slap him hard on his face.

He covers his cheek with his hand and grimaces. "What the fuck, Veronica!"

"You lied!"

"I was protecting you."

"From what?"

"Them!"

"Aren't you a little savior!" I marvel.

"Look, I'm sorry."

"Whatever, Adam."

I can feel my cheeks flood with color at how angry I am at him for lying to me this whole time.

"Was any of it real?"

He sighs, and I watch my handprint turn red on his face. "All of it was except that I needed the money to work at the restaurant. I was sent there because of you. I'm attending OSU, and everything else was real. I'm still your friend."

"I was screaming for your help," I say, trembling. I feel so stupid. I feel betrayed. They are always two steps ahead. "I'm going to die, aren't I?"

"People are going to die; you're just not one of them."

"Where am I?"

"Somewhere safe."

I look around and see that the room's walls are painted black with wood furniture. There are three floor-length mirrors. A chandelier over the four-poster bed with wood carvings in intricate designs. "What the fuck is this place?"

"Rich people have more than one house, I guess."

"Who?"

"I am not allowed to say, but you will find out."

"Just please go take a shower. I hate to say this, but you look like shit."

"Gee, I wonder why."

"Bathroom's that way." He points to the left, and a door leads to the bathroom, and the light is already on."

"Where's Alaric?"

"On his way."

My heartbeat begins to calm down, but my legs feel like rubber when I try to stand. My throat is still sore from all the screaming, and my chest hurts when I take deep breaths from all the crying. I'm going to kill him.

When I walk into the bathroom, I sigh in relief when I don't see a bathtub, and it's just a shower with no doors. The dark porcelain tile is everywhere. A white marble vanity is to the left on the walls and floors. I notice a red robe placed neatly on the side with shampoo, conditioner, and bath wash in clear bottles with red bows.

When I look at myself in the mirror, I see that Adam wasn't kidding. I look like shit. There are dark circles under my eyes. I'm a mess. I can't stop shaking, and I know what is to come. The numbness. The need to feel. I look around and notice a razor. I pick it up and take it with me.

The steam comes from the shower like a sign that I'm home. A shelter to drown my pain of being alone, but I learned that sadness needs company too, and depression is its best friend. The pain is its food and tears its ocean.

The waterfalls are like acid rain on my skin. The steam is a storm cloud of my emotions, taking away cold air to breathe. I wash my body. I wince at my wrist. There are fingerprints under the redness from the rope where they tied my wrists together. My fingers grip the razor. It's new, and I know it will cut if I angle it just right. I crouch on the tile and let sobs rack my body. The sound of defeat echoes in the shower like a warning. I angle the razor on the inner part of my ankle.

"You shouldn't damage something so pretty." I jolt, dropping the razor, hearing it clink on the tile and watching him pick it up. I didn't notice him come in. I was so lost in my head.

"Give it back," I croak. "I need you to leave me alone."

"I can't do that. If you need to cut, you cut me." I glance up, confused. My eyes trail down his naked body. "Here," he holds the razor near the skin on his chest, "cut me." He wipes a tear from my cheek with his thumb. "I'll bleed for you." My bottom lip trembles.

"Why are you doing this to me?"

"I'm not. I'm saving you."

"I can't be saved."

He steps forward, throwing the razor on the ground until we're inches apart. In a split second, Alaric lifts me in his arms, his hands gripping my butt and wrapping my legs around his waist. I have no choice but to wrap my arms around his neck. "I'm sorry. I had to have them take you the way that they did."

"Why? I was so scared."

He looks down between us and feels it. "You're trembling."

"I can't make it stop. I need to—" I trail off.

I hate admitting to him that cutting makes it stop, but my whole body is shaking. "Fuck. I'm so sorry. He was watching you, baby. Dorian was watching you after he left the restaurant, and Adam told me what he did. What he said. I'm so sorry you had to find out this way. Look at me, Veronica." I pull back and see pain mirrored in his eyes. "I know this sounds fucked up, but I need you to trust me. Can you do that?" I look away. Every time I trust someone, they fuck me over, or they die. "You're going to stay with me. You're not going back. Ever." I nod because I don't want to go back. "Answer me."

"Y-yes."

He pushes me against the shower wall, my legs slide down, and I wait until I can stand. He wraps his hand around my throat, and arousal shoots between my legs. "Let me wash up."

He washes us both and it soothes me at how gentle he is. He

makes sure the shaking stops, warming my skin before rinsing us both off.

After he dries us both, he carries me bridal style into the bedroom and places me in the center of the bed. "You have a thing with chains."

There are chains anchored to the wall. Three separated inches apart.

"I do. I like them, but I like them better on you." He pulls the middle one, with a leather collar attached, and fastens it on me. He slides his thumb over my lips and whispers, "Beautiful."

"Where are your chains?"

He smiles, lifting an eyebrow. "Is that what you want? To chain me."

"I would. Naked."

"That can be arranged, but I think you would like it better when I do it to you."

"Why is that?" I purr, arching my back on the bed.

When I turn my head, his eyes never leave my body. "You're not trembling anymore."

How could I tremble when he is more dangerous than anything I have seen or felt. Nothing can hurt me when the man holding me in his arms has no fear in his eyes - only fury and desire.

"No. Not with you."

He kisses my lips, pulling the chain behind me, causing my neck to arch. "You'll tremble but for a very different reason."

"Do your worst."

The light filtering through the window is bright enough that I can see his body. Perfect with his hard cock jutting out between his thighs, kneeling on the bed.

"If I touch you right now, I won't stop. I'm going to fuck you. Hard."

Our eyes battle between lust, control, pain, and pleasure. "Then, fuck me. Make me sin."

"Then we are both going to hell." He grabs my legs, pushing them apart. My pussy dripping wet for him. I arch my back, waiting for it. The pleasure of pain. He warned me that it wouldn't be soft, which is the last thing I want. I want it fast and hard.

He strokes his cock, gripping it at the root, watching my pussy. When my fingers trail around my clit, his nostrils flare, knowing that is all it will take. He rams his cock inside me, hard. I gasp, and he freezes while holding me by the hips. My hands are holding me upright behind my back. The collar pulls tight around my neck, and he pushes into me and then begins to pound me harder. Faster and faster. It is raw and powerful.

The chains rattle, and I let out a high-pitched moan. "Mmm, yes!"

His hand grips the leather collar, and his eyes blaze like he is possessed. You can hear our skin slapping between the rattle of the chains in a series of claps. My tits bounce with every hard thrust. It feels like he is splitting me apart, and I know that I won't be able to walk when he's done. I want more.

His chest heaves when he pulls out and then slams into me again. I fall on the pillows, my hands unable to hold me up. He pushes my legs over his arms and clings to me. My legs are shaking. His hands span my waist, pushing me toward his hips with every thrust.

"This is mine." He growls. His jaw is clenched hard. "Come on my cock, baby."

I can feel how hard he is inside me. "Mmm, harder!" I scream, losing my breath.

"You were made for me. This is the only pussy that can take my dick."

My orgasm is cresting and coming in fast from his words. "You're about to come. I can feel it."

I claw at his chest when I come, my orgasm exploding like a storm destroying everything in its wake. He pushes harder, and I feel him come on a roar, filling me with his cum. We are both sweating, but he makes no move to get off me. He stays inside me, gripping my thighs and lifting them over his shoulders, pushing himself deeper.

"I love you so much," he says.

The words don't cross my lips, but I hope he can see it when he looks at me. I just can't say it. I need him to feel it. The way I feel it when he's inside me.

"I'm sorry for everything I have ever done to hurt you. You deserve all the beautiful things in this world. If you don't have them, I will swim in the stars to find them for you if I have to."

I slide my fingers over his cheek, pulling him down for a soft kiss, our foreheads touching. "I have only ever wanted…just you."

He looks down at my wrist and sees the fingerprints. His mouth pulls into a frown. "What's this?"

"Adam told me—he hurt you."

"I'm fine. It's just a little red and sore. The ropes—"

He nods, but I see the little muscle in his jaw tic. His gray eyes go dark. He pulls out of me and undoes the collar on my neck, lifting me off the bed and taking me to the shower.

"Alaric?"

Silence.

ALARIC

WALKING OUT THE BACK PATIO, I reach the fire pit out back. Garret is the first to spot me. "Dude, this house is sick. You slaughter anything, and no one would know."

I had it built on the edge of Kenyan when I bought the land as an investment. No one knew this house existed until now. It was the best place to take Veronica from the diner. Adam texted me what happened when Dorian showed up.

"That's not why I bought it, but if you're thinking like that, I suggest getting checked out with Dr. Wick."

"Touché."

I notice Valen rubbing the side of his face. I smile, having a good idea. "What happened?"

"I think the blind date was a bad idea," he grimly says.

Draven chuckles. "I told you not to grab her like that. She packs a punch."

"At least I didn't play Closer like a psycho in the car on the way here with a hood on her head. Way to go, dick. You fucking scared the shit out of her. She's a cutter."

"She hit you?" I ask Valen to change the subject. I don't want anyone to think she is weak.

"Yeah, man. Look!" He points to the side of his face, moving into the light of the fire. It's red and will leave a bruise.

"He got slapped," Garret says, pointing to Adam.

I glance at Adam; sure enough, he has a red handprint on his face.

"That's what I get for lying to her."

I feel bad for him because he is a good friend to her, but he's one of us. My mother and grandfather's idea. I wasn't surprised my mother set that up. She was always fond of Veronica and Alicia's relationship. I was just too stupid with my head up my ass regarding Veronica. I wanted her but hated what they made her represent, and it was all a lie.

"We had to come out here," Valen says.

"You needed to come out here. I was fine hearing them go at it," Draven says.

Veronica is very vocal in bed.

"Dude, is it always like that?" Adam asks.

"No. Only with him," Draven replies.

Good. At least Draven stroked my ego burning with curiosity.

"Where's Reid and Dravin?" I ask.

"With the girls."

They got Adam up to speed on most of the details with Veronica. He's aware of my plan. They all are. I get goosebumps thinking about her.

"You finally fell, huh," Valen says with a smirk. "You're in love with the little hellfire."

I am, but the look in her eyes tells me she can't say the words back. I don't expect her to for all the reasons she shouldn't. Sometimes damaged people can't feel how you want them to because you have to put them back together differently. I have to be patient with her, and I'll do whatever it takes.

Draven scoffs, rolling his eyes. "It's about time. You always carried a torch for her."

But I don't miss the hurt look on Garret's face when he looks around and licks his lips, avoiding everyone's gaze. He'll get over it.

"We stick to the plan?" Adam asks.

"Yeah," I reply.

Veronica is no longer working at the restaurant, and Adam is only too happy to quit. I ensured Dorothy would be okay, and she was relieved Veronica was taken care of. She said she would get a shotgun and shoot me if I hurt her. I let her slide because she cares for Veronica and sees her like a daughter.

The next day, Veronica has class. I already sent the report to her professor, who agreed she is an exceptional student, but I didn't miss the little gleam in his eyes when I first mentioned her name. I threatened him that if he looked at her in any way that wasn't customary for a professor, I would end his career. He thought it meant he wouldn't teach at Kenyan and would get fired. He didn't know what I planned to do with his eyes for looking at her incorrectly. He still sputtered his way out of the situation like an asshole that got caught with his pants down.

I have eyes watching her. Dorian is a threat, but he doesn't know I know his sick game with Veronica or what I have planned for my girl. She is sex in a pair of heels, and I am crazy about her.

It is three in the afternoon on a Wednesday, and I am waiting for my girl in the quad with a basket. College students are milling about talking shit. For a moment, I wonder if things were different. If I was four years younger and attending Kenyan. Would I kiss her before and after class? Make sure my schedule was aligned with hers? Live off campus with her, share a house, and wake up with her in my arms?

"She doesn't come out here, you know." I glance up and see Jess standing with Gia.

Dravin walks up, slides his hand around Gia's waist, and places his hand over his lips, trying to stifle a smile when he sees me with a picnic basket. *Dick.*

"Try the cemetery. It's her favorite place."

A sense of fear grips me when I think about what Alicia wrote to her in her letter. She knew exactly how Veronica would take her death. It's what I'm afraid of, her not wanting me enough to stay around. I grip the handles and stand.

"Thanks."

"She likes red," Jess says with a smile. "She's always wearing it somewhere."

"Yeah," Gia swallows, then rubs her lips together like she just remembered something. "She loves those black Docs, and I notice they have little red beads through the laces. Simple stuff like that. She only acts sassy when—she has to, but she is always in the cemetery with her best friend."

A woman sells flowers at the entrance, and I pick out two bouquets. One with different colors and another with red roses. I spot her immediately. Sitting on Alicia's grave, the letter clutched in her hand, tears falling like rain, and my heart breaks for the first time. Her pain is the only thing I can feel. I'm afraid she will give up, and I can't live without her.

She looks up, her beautiful clear blue eyes like water from the cleanest ocean. She is gorgeous, with her long dark hair catching in the wind. Those ridiculous old boots that belonged to my cousin.

"I bought you new ones, you know."

She knows I mean her boots when I place the basket on the ground and sit beside her.

"You're going to ruin your dress pants."

I shrug my shoulders. "I have a lot of pairs."

"Sure, you do."

"Shorts and shirts, too," I tease, handing her the colorful bouquet. "Those are for Alicia." I give her the red roses. "These are for you."

She grabs them, sniffing the scent of the rose petals, trying to compose herself and wiping at her face. "They are beautiful. I would have thought you were the black roses type."

"I like them red. It reminds me that you bled for me like I would bleed for you."

A pink stain appears on her cheeks when she blushes. I turn, opening the basket. "I brought you lunch," I say, pulling out expensive cold-cut meats and cheeses. A bottle of sparkling water and two glasses with another bottle of wine.

"Isn't that a bit much?"

"There is nothing as too much of anything."

"I must admit, it's my first time eating with the dead."

I look around, and it's not exactly romantic, but it's us.

"It's a first for me too, but I keep taking them."

"Taking what?"

"All of your firsts. They're all mine."

"That's not fair. What do I get?"

My eyes fix on her mouth as she eats a piece of cold meat with cheese. Her tongue swipes across her bottom lip. Her eyes are still watery from crying. "You have what no one else will."

Her other hand begins to pull on the blades of grass, ripping them out next to Alicia's grave. I lean close, sliding a piece of meat inside my mouth. "It's not your time, my love. I have things I want to do for you. Places I want to take you. If it comes to that, I'll bury myself with you and die a happy man." My lips are inches from hers, my cock screaming in agony, wanting to take her somewhere, but I can't shake the feeling I have inside when I look at her. The expression on her face tells me what all the words in the dictionary couldn't. That she loves me, but she's afraid.

"What are you afraid of?" I ask. I break off a rose from its stem and trace it on the smooth lines of her cheekbones. "Tell me so I can take it away."

She smiles in the way she did when we first met. Gone is the Veronica with fire on her tongue. I like both versions of her, but when we have these moments, moments like the first one we had four years ago, I like this version of her. It's private in that way. Lovers have secrets only the two of them share. A look or a smile.

"You think you can just save me, don't you?"

"I do."

It isn't a lie but a promise. No one will touch her ever again.

"I'm afraid they will take away the one moment I had with you. The one where you told me you loved me for the first time."

"You're the only one that could make me feel, and no one can take that from you. You chose Veronica."

Tears slide down her cheeks. "I did."

"Prey choose," I whisper. She nods. "Don't cry." I lean in and lick her tears. She wraps her arms around me, and we stay sitting on my cousin's grave, and the two sentences she wrote me on a simple piece of paper make more sense than anything ever could. Every language is silent. Every prayer is heard. "Every language is silent. Every prayer is heard," I repeat out loud. "I hear you calling for me, my love. I hear it now." Her sobs rip through her, and then I hear it. Her whisper.

"I love you."

"Then, stay with me. It's not your time to go yet. I need you."

I never thought I would fall in love, but I knew I did that night. Veronica is my first love and my last.

I feel it while looking at Alicia's grave as Veronica waits for me at the cemetery gates. I swear I can feel her energy. Her words were written in letters to both of us, full of love for her friend, completing a promise she never uttered. Death is a mystery. But there is a way to communicate between the dead and the living. They say math is the universal language to solve everything. Books are written about religion to maintain morals and instill faith. But love is and always will be the universal language. My cousin found and risked her life for the one she loved because, without it, you're dead anyway. Love is universal. It is said in prayer because love is all we need and want. Love is what we kill for. Every language is silent because love is all that needs to exist.

I kiss the palm of my hand and place it on her grave. "I'll take care of her now. I promise. I love you, Alicia. Thank you for bringing me happiness." I look over at her boyfriend Chase's grave. "You take care of her now." I look up, and a crow lands on his grave. Its shiny feathers and black beak make a cawing sound.

"Are you sure we can't stay?"

"There is no way to take a shit or use the shower. I'm remodeling all the bathrooms."

"You didn't have to."

I place the fourth suitcase inside the Rolls trunk and press the button so the door can close automatically. I reply, "I did."

"The other house is quieter, and you can study for your finals in peace and no bathtubs."

I made sure all my homes were remodeled with showers and threw out every belt buckle I owned.

She smiles, but I don't miss the whimsical eye she gives when she passes the garage that houses the blacked-out Bentley she practiced on that night. She passed the written driver's exam, and she was able to get her learner's permit last week. I slide my cell phone out and dial my driver. She glances at me and sighs, walking toward the Rolls Royce.

"Take the Bentley to my estate, please," I say into the phone, watching her eyes widen as I open the door, so she can slide in the passenger seat.

There is nothing I don't notice when it comes to her. She likes sex before bed and in the morning when she wakes up. Hard and fast at night, full of chains and an occasional anal. Soft and slow in the morning after I eat her pussy.

She's perfect.

Sometimes it's what scares the shit out of me the most. How perfect she is. There are two sides to her, and I can't figure out which side I like better. Like a precious coin, you can flip over and over and can't decide, so you admire both sides as much as possible.

"You didn't have to take the Bentley."

"It's your favorite. Why not. Do you like specific colors?"

"I like that one."

"You don't want a new one?"

She shakes her head. "No, I like that one because it reminds me of you and the first time I drove it."

"Got it."

I slide my hand in hers, letting that tingling feeling over me, touching her hand in mine. "I'll transfer it in your name. It's yours."

"But—"

"Don't. I want to give it to you."

"It's expensive."

"I can afford it."

"Cocky much."

"You should be proud; your man is loaded. I got bank."

She snorts. "Oh, God. I am proud, but not because you have money."

"It's because I have a huge dick. You can't live without it."

She shoves me, and I laugh, but her face suddenly goes white, and I panic.

"Veronica!"

She holds her stomach and grimaces. "I think I'm going to be sick." Her face turns an ashen color, and I stop on the side of the road. She undoes her seat belt and opens the door and starts to vomit.

"Fuck."

I jump out of the car, and she's retching on the side of the road. I hold her hair back. "It's okay, baby," I say softly. "Get it out. Is it something you ate?"

Her eyes are watery from the effort, but she manages not to get any on her clothes. "I don't feel well," she sputters.

"Can you make it if I drive to the gas station? I can get you some crackers and water."

She nods.

After getting Veronica some water and crackers, I call the doctor so he can take a look at her at the house.

"I'm fine, Alaric."

I'm not taking any chances with her. Maybe she caught something at school or at work. She worked the night shift, and the guys told me she threw the trash out back. Those days are over for her. I'm not going to have my girl work in a restaurant when she could be in our bed watching her favorite horror flick after a day at the spa.

I kiss the top of her hand. "I want to make sure you're okay. I love you."

She looked pale when her body was doubled over, half hanging out, gripping the car door, and the sounds of her vomiting. Her face went white like chalk, but it regained some of its natural color after she ate the crackers and drank some water.

"I'm okay. Maybe it was something I ate," she says with a wane smile.

But she hasn't eaten much. I noticed that these past couple of days, she has left food on her plate, and when I ask if she is hungry or wants me to take her to dinner, she refuses or says she already ate.

"The doctor will run some tests just to make sure."

But I have a feeling I know why. It's all coming together.

VERONICA

"YOU'RE PREGNANT," Gia says with a smile, sitting in front of me.

We are at the Galleria with Jess and four bodyguards standing around us like we are celebrities or something.

Portman gives me a side-eye when Gia giggles.

"What is so funny? I'm not pregnant."

"Oh yes, you are. You don't eat. You sleep all the time or,"—she winks—"not sleep. I know this because I'm pregnant."

My eyes widen. "Oh my God, Gia! I'm so happy for you." Then a thought pops into my head.

"I see that look."

"What look?"

"The same one Jess is giving me."

"It doesn't matter who. We talked about it already. It won't matter anyway. Whoever has one first, that child inherits. It's good that it comes from me and no one else."

I can see her point by looking at it that way and falling in love with twins. "How is it?" I ask.

"How is what?" she asks curiously.

Jess snickers and drops a piece of bread on her plate. "She wants to know how it feels to be fucked by twins."

I laugh when Portman and the other two bodyguards stiffen.

"Oh."

"Who takes the front and who takes the back, or do they take turns?" I ask.

"Take turns doing what?" Dravin asks, sliding into the seat next to Gia and kissing her lips.

"Fucking your wife," I answer.

Jess tries to stifle a cough, placing her hand over her mouth.

"Hmm, I see bad Veronica is coming out to play today." His eyes lower to my stomach. "How are you feeling?"

My eyes narrow. "Why do I feel you know something I don't."

"I don't know what you are talking about. Alaric said you weren't feeling well these past couple of days, and this is your first time out in like forever." His light eyes tell me they hold a secret. A big one.

"Liar."

"What did the doctor say?" Jess asks.

"The results should be in later today. It's the third day." I turn to Dravin.

"It depends on the mood."

"It's his," I blurt, looking at Gia.

He grins. "She told you, and you don't know that."

"She married him legally. You made sure the first child was yours. Fair is fair."

He shakes his head like what I said is crazy, but I know Draven. He's been fucking Gia and pulling out or giving her anal so his brother can have his heir. Poor Gia will be pregnant again when the kid turns one, or should I say lucky.

"Either way, I'm happy for you three." I turn to Jess. "Why is Reid taking so long?"

She knows I mean for her to get pregnant with a little Riordan.

"He's waiting for you and Alaric."

"I'm not married and—" I trail off, rubbing the back of my neck where the tattoo was placed. A reminder of what I am in the grand scheme of things.

I still have to marry Dorian at the end of graduation. I'm not free.

Dravin clears his throat. "We'll see."

After class on Friday, I head over to Babylon to meet with Jess and Gia. We began a sort of routine after school since I got the results from the doctor. I'm pregnant. I don't know how if I'm on birth control. I didn't miss a pill and have been keeping up with filling my prescriptions.

When I walk in, it's packed. There needs to be a seat at the bar. Three bartenders are running around serving drinks. The pool tables are all taken. My eyes scan the booths, looking for Jess and Gia in their normal spot.

I know I've found them when Jess smiles and gestures me over. A hand slides around my waist as I enter the crowd. "Where are you going, princess?" My body stiffens, and my chest tightens as fear grips me when I hear Dorian's voice over Seether's "Fake It."

I pull away. His smile is full of capped teeth glowing white under the dim light of the bar. He's wearing a white t-shirt under a leather jacket, trying to fit in.

My eyes sweep over him in disgust, reminding me of something foul. Like the smell of trash when you walk behind a building. "What are you doing here, Dorian? This isn't your crowd. Aren't you too old to hang out with college kids?"

"Alaric does."

I bare my teeth. "That's because he fucks me better than they do."

"I can do better."

I snort. "I think I'll just ask your secretary. She obviously got bored of you."

It bothered me that Alaric slept with her, but I'm a big girl, and I've done bad things. It's all in the past, and right now, I carry something more important than regrets and hate inside me.

Dorian gives me a wintry smile that suddenly turns into a frown. "You're a long way from the city, Dorian. I didn't think you hung out here chasing college pussy," Valen says behind me.

Dorian glances at me and then at Valen, then back at me. "I don't. I prefer real women. The kind that don't fuck little boys. I'll just have to show you, Veronica."

My lips turn into a salacious smile. "Oh, Dorian. You couldn't make me come the way they can, but I prefer chains to warm baths. Just ask your perverted dad. He can tell you all about it. How much I hate baths."

Dorian's nostrils flare when Alaric shows up with the twins, and Adam overhears the last part. "Damn, Black. You keep it in the family. It's kind of sick." Alaric leans closer. "I know all about it. It's pathetic that your daddy had to pick your wife for you, too, getting off with his three-inch dick, but don't worry, I have something special lined up for you both." Alaric slides his hands protectively over my waist, erasing Dorian's touch and kissing my neck hotly. "And for the record, I'm not a little boy."

"Have fun with your daddy," I chirp.

Dorian's jaw hardens. His eyes seem desperate, but he gives a sharp laugh. A laugh when someone doesn't get their way but knows he's outnumbered and can't do shit about it. I would be afraid of him if I wasn't in a bar full of people and if the sons of Kenyan weren't all around me. Protecting me.

When I slide into the booth next to Jess, she asks, "What did that pathetic piece of shit want?"

"To get under her skin by showing up in random places everywhere, like the creep he is," Gia says, popping a French fry in her mouth.

"The guys should get rid of him," Jess chimes in.

"I'm working on it. It's going to be a real party," Alaric says, sliding into the wooden booth beside me. "How are you feeling?" I turn to Gia, but he's looking right at me.

"He's asking you, not me," Gia says with a smile. "You think he wouldn't find out?" She snorts. "They know everything."

"We do," the twins both say in tandem.

"You knew."

"I did."

"I'm scared. When he touched me—"

"I was there. I saw it," Valen says. "We won't let him hurt you, Veronica."

My heart begins to beat faster, and my stomach has those little butterflies that swarm. I read that some women can experience those kinds of things in early pregnancy. When I found out, I immediately began Googling pregnancy and what to expect. I was happy, nervous, and afraid.

"Fuck," I blurt.

"That's how it starts," Adam teases.

I laugh. "What now?"

Alaric curls my dark hair around his fingers and says softly, "I take you home, and we celebrate."

"How can you be so calm?"

But the intense look in his eyes tells me he has a plan.

He always has one.

Walking out of the restroom, I bump into a hard chest. The spicy scent of Alaric's cologne causes me to smile, knowing it's him. When I glance up, his mouth lifts into a grin.

"Ready to be my bad girl?"

"Always." He pulls me toward the back exit and pushes me gently against the brick wall of the building. He lifts me, my legs wrap around his waist, and my arms around his neck. My pleated skirt is rudely shoved around my waist. My ass is in his hands, his eyes focused on my mouth as he takes my lips. His cock crowns my opening, the crotchless panties he prefers for me to wear, allowing him access whenever he wants. His slides inside me. "Mm."

I'm so sensitive and horny. I'm already wet and ready for him when he plunges deep with a growl. "Fuck."

"Mm, right there," I say breathlessly when I move faster, hitting me in the spot that drives me over the edge. I want to come. Every time we have sex, I come more than once. Sometimes two and three times.

My fingers grip his hair when he goes harder. Pumping inside me with everything he's got. I realize that any moment someone could walk up and see us, or they could exit the same way we did, getting a front-row show of us fucking like rabbits against the building.

"Someone might come and see us," I whisper against his cheek, loving the feel of the stubble from his facial hair.

"Let them see what a bad girl you are," he says between breaths.

My head dips, and I lick his lips like an animal. I grind my hips and hold myself up against the brick wall, glad I'm wearing a jacket and don't feel the rough texture every time he thrusts into me. My hands slide up the wall, and our eyes lock; I bite my bottom lip when the first orgasm rips through me, knowing he won't stop. The door screams open, and Gia and Jess are the first to step out, followed by Reid and the twins.

"Damn. They couldn't wait to get home and celebrate." I think that was Draven.

"She looks gorgeous," Gia says softly. "Take me home."

"I want to watch," I hear Jess tell Reid.

I pull Alaric's cock out and unwrap my legs from his waist and slowly kneel on the ground and take him in my mouth. I give a loud moan tasting myself and his salty precum from the tip. I run my teeth over his piercing. "Fuck, you're such a bad girl," he says with a groan, placing his hand against the brick wall and holding himself steady. I take him deep, relaxing my throat. I glance up, tears sliding down my cheeks. "You're so beautiful. Marry me."

"Let's go. He's proposing," Jess says.

"I want to see if she says yes," Reid teases.

I almost choke when I hear the twins. "Me too."

I pull him out, licking my lips, and he turns, putting himself away. "I love you."

"I think that was a yes," Jess says.

VERONICA

"HOW DID you get into the Consortium?" I ask Adam, placing the clean plates on the serving counter.

It's my last day at the restaurant. I wanted to help Dorothy and Adam out until Melody can start part-time tomorrow. She needs to get into college and wants to save money and her brother wants to help her out.

Adam clears his throat, closing the door to the dishwasher after loading the cups. "Valen came and offered me a sweet deal."

I draw my eyebrows together because the sons of Kenyan don't ordinarily allow anyone into the Consortium that isn't from the Order.

"How's that? You attending high school then OSU."

He smiles. "I'm not the only one, Veronica. They have people everywhere and only the loyal ones are allowed in." He lowers his voice. "If you fuck up, you're dead. How did you think I got the QB1 spot?" He leans close. "Perks of taking care of their girl."

I shake my head in confusion. He rolls his eyes. "The night of the frat party. I was already one of them, Veronica. Alaric showed up and the rest…I can't go into detail. That is all I'm allowed to say."

Adam was one of them the whole time?

"Did you know I went to Kenyan before?"

"What do you think?" he asks, moving to the napkins and rolling them over the silverware.

He did.

"I think you are more involved than what you're telling me, but I get it. You're sworn to secrecy or they will cut your head off."

He nods. "I'm glad you understand." He looks toward the window. "Do you need a ride?"

"Nope. I'll wait for Alaric's driver." I bend and grab my bag. "I'll be off."

"Are you sure?" I reach on my tippy toes and give him a peck on the cheek. "Yep."

I walk over and give Dorothy a tight hug.

"You be good now," she says in a raspy voice.

I look up and scrunch my nose. "I will if you promise to stop smoking."

"Stop stealing my Virginia Slims and I won't buy more cigarettes."

I raise my hand in the air before pushing the exit door open. "Excuses excuses. Bye. Love you guys!"

I walk down the three steps, looking left and right for the familiar black SUV, but I don't see Portman. I pull out my phone, sliding the text app open so I can text him, and walk deeper into the parking lot. I hear footsteps. When I look up, a large hand clamps over my mouth. I try to take gulps of air and thrash my arms dropping my phone. I kick my legs, trying to get free, but I can't. I can hear breathing from behind me and then something black covers my nose that smells funny. Adrenaline floods my veins in panic when my vision goes dark.

I bolt upward needing oxygen and feel the clinking sounds of chains. My arms feel heavy. I blink rapidly, my eyes trying to focus. The smell of dirt filters my nose. It's dark. I blink a couple of times, trying to get used to the light.

"It's about time." I hear Dorian's voice.

I close my eyes, trying to calm the racing of my heartbeat. I glance down and I'm lying in a dirty bathtub. A shudder runs through me. I begin to gag.

"It's normal. Halothane can cause nausea after it's inhaled."

I look up and see the pathetic piece of shit sitting in a chair. Another chill washes over me, and when I look down, I notice that I'm naked. My wrists are bound and the clinking was from the chains rubbing on the edge of the tub.

"Where am I?" I croak.

"Wouldn't you like to know."

"Let me go." I look at him defiantly. "He's going to kill you."

He leans forward in the chair, causing it to groan. "Oh, you mean your little boyfriend." He chuckles. "I was wondering when he would fuck you out of his system and let you go, but I think he's getting attached. Again." He slides his finger over my arm and I pull my arm away, causing the metal to bang. He chuckles harder. "You'll get used to my touch. I wonder if he'll still want you after I fuck you?"

I take three calming breaths. *He'll come for me. Alaric will come.*

I smile and allow a little laugh to escape, wiping the one off his face. "Is that what you think? Honestly?" I get up on my knees. "Do you know how many men I've had to fuck? Pussy I have licked?" I use the pad of my forefinger to make little circles over the white porcelain tub. "And you're worried about little insignificant you." I laugh. The sound echoing.

"You bitch. You're nothing but a whore."

"But you want to marry me. The woman your own father jerks his wrinkled cock to while I bathe myself."

He walks up and yanks the chains so that I'm facing him on my knees. He undoes his belt and I inwardly cringe, hearing the sound of the belt buckle. He pulls himself out and rubs the tip of his penis near my mouth. "Suck it," he demands in a lethal tone.

My eyes flick up. My lips break into a smile. A flicker of confusion crosses his expression. I'll take my chances. Fuck him. His grips my hair, wrapping it around his fist and pushing his hard cock into my mouth, making me want to gag, but I don't. He pinches my nipple, but I block out the pain of the sting.

"I've always wanted you like this. I've been waiting a long time to have you, Veronica. Do you know how it feels to watch someone get everything, including the woman he wants."

I open my mouth and he slides his pathetic excuse of a cock in my mouth and I bite down. I bite down hard with my molars.

"Aahhhhhh! Ahhhhh! You bitch!" he screams.

The taste of copper fills my mouth. He releases my nipple and tries to push me off his cock, but I lock my jaw. He manages to push me off him in one hard push, but I feel my teeth scrape his shaft. His eyes widen when he looks down at his mangled cock. Blood is dripping everywhere. Down my chin. All over his thighs.

"Oh fuck!" His voice croaks on the last part. "You bit my dick"—he grabs it, doubling over— "You crazy bitch."

I spit the blood from my mouth at his cock in that way I 've seen football players do on the football field. "That's just a preview. The next time I'll bite it off." I smile. "Don't worry. You'll get used to my touch."

The sound of a boom from a door opening comes from behind him. My heart is beating like a wild racehorse. A chill racks my body, hoping there isn't someone else with him. I hear footsteps behind him coming from the shadows. Dorian slides his pants on and runs into the darkness in the opposite direction. There is only a small construction light shining down on me like a spotlight, but it's keeping me from seeing. My eyes try to focus.

I hear Valen's voice. "Veronica?"

I sag in relief, crying and laughing like a mad woman. When I see Alaric rush up behind him, looking at the chains binding my wrist, he lifts my chin to see if I'm bleeding. His brows are furrowed and his jaw is clenched.

"Are you hurt?" he asks. "Tell me where?" he says while his eyes inspect my face and body.

"No." I sigh with relief but feel a wave of dizziness when I take a deep breath.

"I can get the chain off from the back," Valen announces behind me, hearing the sound of the chains rattle against the tub.

"You're bleeding," he says while removing his t-shirt. "What did he give you?"

I shake my head softly. "The blood…It's not mine. He drugged me…made me smell…something."

"Motherfucker."

"I got it," Valen says out of breath. My arms sag when the chains are released and Alaric loosens the metal rubbing on my irritated wrists. "Get her in the car and I'll go see if I can find this asshole."

"Alright but be careful."

"Where am I?" I ask.

"Abandoned house four miles from Kenyan," he replies, placing his black shirt over my head, beyond glad that is falls right above my knees.

He picks me up and I wince at how dizzy I feel once the adrenaline wore off.

"How did you get blood all over your mouth and chin?"

"I…bit his…dick."

"Good," he says in a hard tone and I'm glad I don't have to explain further.

The scene he and Valen walked into doesn't have to be explained.

"Did he…" He trails off, carrying me into a dark hallway that feels like a maze, reminding of a dark haunted house.

"No…you came in time but he ran."

"Don't worry, baby. I'll get him. You're more important than revenge right now. The doctor is on the way."

I close my eyes and lay my head on his shoulder, relieved that he came for me. *He came.*

ALARIC

I LEAN BACK in the driver's seat of my car and let out a deep breath. The doctor said she was fine. The baby has a strong heartbeat and whatever Dorian gave her was not enough to cause any issues with the pregnancy.

I hear the passenger door open and look to see Draven slide into the passenger seat. "She's good, man. Don't worry. Gia and Jess are with her."

I look at my hands, feeling the leather under the palms of my skin from gripping the steering wheel. The feeling of needing to kill someone for hurting her growing with every second that goes by.

"He's at the church with his father and some other members of the Order. Most likely in on all the shit that her piece of shit stepfather has her involved in." I nod.

That's why he came here…to tell me. "What do you want to do?"

I turn my head. He throws a t-shirt and I catch it, not realizing I was still shirtless. All I could think about is the woman I plan to make my wife. The one carrying my baby. The one they almost took from me. Sliding the shirt over my head, I reply, "What would you do, Draven?"

He scoffs. "The same thing that must be going through your mind right now. Put the car in drive. The guys will meet us at the church. I'll send a clean-up crew when we're done. After all this shit, you're going to marry that girl and we'll fuck up whoever has a problem with it."

"D-do you think she really wants to marry me?"

I'm nervous. I put her through so much shit, I wonder how she could ever forgive me for being the biggest asshole who never fought for her.

"I'm not going to lie and say I don't feel a sense of guilt for what she's been through. I didn't know, but I think she's been in love with you since she was in high school. I also think she's been waiting for you to save her. So…fucking save her, Alaric."

"You're right."

After the ten-minute drive, I park my Ferrari in the visitors' parking lot by the right side of the cemetery. We walk by the side entrance and already see Dorian's father in deep discussion with the fake priest the Order assigned to make sure no one enters the church after hours, except the members of the Order to conduct their meetings.

"We had him make something up so they wouldn't get inside. The rest of the Consortium are waiting for us. Come on," Draven whispers, pulling to the front of the side entrance.

Once the door slides shut behind us with a soft click, Valen walks up and hands us our robes and masks. "Come on, he can't hold him off any longer."

"You all planned this."

"If you didn't come, I would've killed them myself," Valen says, handing me my knives and a rosary.

I hold up the knife, making sure it's sharp enough. "One way to kill a snake is to start at the head and work your way down, splitting it open and making sure it's dead." My eyes flick to Valen. "You know how I feel about snakes and you damn well know what I'll do for her."

"Took you long enough," Valen says with a smile. "Let's get these sick fucks."

I walk down the aisle and look up at the black cover covering the cross, taking a seat in the middle. The ten members, including Adam, sit in the scattered in the pews facing forward still as a statue. Five members on each side with plague masks on their faces.

Waiting.

I grip the knife in my hand under my cloak. My head is pounding. I can hear roaring in my ears, but when I blink behind the mask, all I hear is the sound of footsteps as the main door of church opens and closes. I can sense them. Six men to us ten.

"What the fuck?" I hear one of them say.

None of us move.

Not yet.

I feel a buzzing sensation in my hands in anticipation. Every time I kill, I feel it. The numbing. The roaring in my ears right before it happens. The manic episode is what they call it. The doctors call it an episode derived from explosive anger derived from a motive. My motive is fear of losing the one thing I value most in this world.

Her.

"One is moving! Ahhhhh!" Mr. Black is the first to scream, drowning out the first rumble of thunder as the main door of the church is shut.

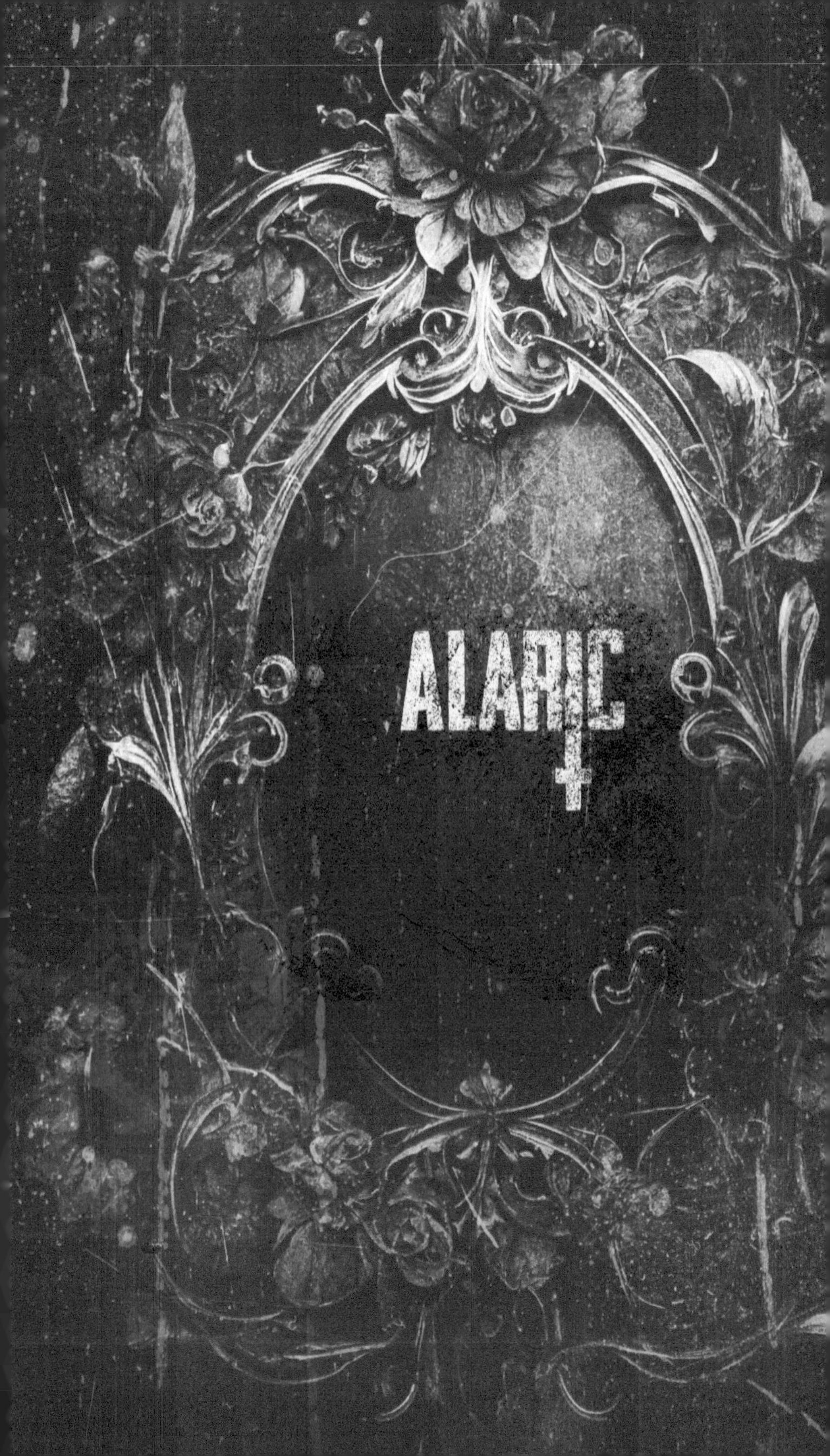
ALARIC

IT'S ten o'clock on a Sunday night, and I'm pacing back and forth. "Relax, sir," Sergio says, before stepping out to see if Veronica needs anything. I can't. I want it to be perfect. Tonight, has to be perfect. I close my eyes and let out a deep breath.

"Cold feet?" Draven asks behind me when he walks in, closing the door.

"It's not mine I'm worried about."

"She's here, and she isn't going anywhere," he assures me.

"I know that, but what if she remembers all the fucked-up shit I've done to her and changes her mind."

"I have already told you, she's loved you since she was in high school. She's done things she's had to do. I see the look in her eyes when she looks at Gia and Jess. She's ashamed. It doesn't matter how often we tell her it wasn't her fault, but one thing she isn't and was never ashamed of was being in love with you. Everyone knows that. There's one man in this world Veronica loves, and that man is you. It was always you, Alaric. Since the first time she laid eyes on your sorry ass, she knew."

"I know, but I didn't fight for her when she needed me."

He steps closer, fixing the red rose on my tux. "You are now. Right now, this moment." He looks up, a fierce look in his eyes. "This is how you show her you're fighting—for both of them. It's not just her you're fighting for. You're fighting for your future with…her and your child."

I nod, my heart filling with an emotion I can't describe. Tonight, I'm marrying the woman I love, and I don't give a shit about rules or what the Order thinks.

After a few seconds, he slaps me on the shoulder, trying to comfort me. "Come on, man. We're starting."

The church is decorated with black and red roses. I asked the priest to marry us, and he approved when I mentioned who I planned on marrying. He got permission from the church without the Order finding out on such short notice. Graduation is looming in one week. The cathedral was cleaned, and it smells of hundreds of candles and roses and a perfumed scent. Nothing at all like death; it's filled with the promise of life.

The pews shine with all the members of the Consortium in attendance. Sixty-Seven, including Adam. His sisters, Dorothy, and the wives of the sons of Kenyan are all seated. Reid is standing to the side, waiting with Jess as the best man. Jess is in Alicia's place. My chest is tight with emotion, and needles prick my throat. Not of sadness but a distinct happiness I have never felt. If I think about the best night of my life, this sums it up. I'm marrying the woman I love, making it my mission to steal all her firsts. Her vows in return for making all of her dreams come true.

I swallow, hearing a click in my throat. "If anything happens to me, she gets everything, Draven. If I live or die, she will be Mrs. Riodrick-Riordan."

He nods. "I know. It's done."

I stand to the left side in front of the priest waiting…waiting for my wife to walk down the aisle.

Evanescence's synthesis version of "My Immortal" begins to play; everyone stands, and she takes her first steps in black and red silk with a dark laced romance dress. Her dark hair is in waves down to her waist. Her eyes are like clear blue diamonds, almost aquamarine, under the candlelight. She looks breathtakingly beautiful. Her waist is still small despite being pregnant with our child. I could not hold back the tears watching my wife come to me. My chest is thick with emotion.

We can't stop staring at each other, lost in our world the whole ceremony. We almost don't hear the priest when he says it's time to say our vows.

"Please," the priest says softly.

I hold her hand and look into her eyes, sliding the halo cut, ten-carat solid diamond with hidden black diamonds around her finger.

"With this hand, I shall bear the weight of your sorrows, lifting them as if they are feathers carried by the wind. Your cup shall remain forever full, for I am to be the crimson essence that fills it - a dark and intoxicating wine of companionship. I will light a candle, and its gentle flame shall illuminate your path through the labyrinthine corridors of darkness"— I slide the ring on slowly— "This ring, a circle unbroken, symbolizes my desire for you to stand by my side, an unbreakable union. As twilight embraces the day, your life with mine, forging a bond as timeless and impassioned as love itself."

Tears shine in her eyes when I glance up, and it's her turn. She takes my hand in her delicate one, doing the same with the platinum band on my finger. She begins, "With the grace of my hand, I shall lift the burdens that weigh upon your heart, holding them delicately like fragile petals in the breeze. Your cup shall know no emptiness, for I shall pour into it the essence of my devotion, a love that overflows endlessly. I accept your ring, a symbol of eternity." She slides on the ring. "I present this ring as a token of my deepest longing, heart, and soul. With the twilight stars in the night sky as our witness and in the eyes of God, I ask for your hand in a journey where our souls intertwine in love as profound as the eternal night. Life is where we love amongst the living and in death where we sleep amongst the rested."

"You may now kiss your bride," the priest announces.

I take her lips, placing my one hand softly on her womb, one hand cupping her cheek and kissing her passionately. The church erupts in applause and sniffles.

I pull back, whispering across her lips, "I love you, Mrs. Riordan."

ALARIC

I WATCH the bastard sitting in his office with his horned-rimmed glasses. Lighting up a cigar, reading something on a piece of paper. I wait a few seconds and then walk inside.

"Who let you in?"

I sit unbuttoning my suit jacket. "I think you have an idea."

"You think because you have my daughter, you can waltz in here like you own the place."

"In a fashion. Yes, and we both know she is not your daughter."

"My name is on her birth certificate."

"I could put Al Pacino's name on her birth certificate. It doesn't mean she is his daughter."

"You're a cocky little shit."

"I am, and I'm not little. Ask your stepdaughter."

He chuckles, puffing on his cigar. You can tell he's a prick, even in the way he holds it in his fingers.

"You've been having fun with her. I can tell."

A message comes through on his phone. He picks it up, and a wicked gleam crosses his eyes when he opens the message. He holds it up, and it's a picture of a young woman with her legs open, showing her unshaven pussy. "Now she has an amazing pussy."

"Let me guess, she's French. And you fucked her without a condom," I answer dryly.

He guffaws, throwing his head back. When he calms down, he opens a little drawer in his desk, takes out a little bag of coke, snorts a line with a hundred-dollar bill rolled up like a straw, and holds it out to me.

"I'm good."

He shrugs. "It's all just a little fun, and you're right. She is French.

I met her in France while the wife was sleeping in the hotel room. I went to have a drink after a meeting, and she offered.

"How much did you pay her?"

He doesn't answer and smiles, but it doesn't reach his eyes. No man likes another one to point out that he has to pay for pussy.

"Why are you here, Alaric?"

To kill you.

I lean forward. "I need the names of the men who attend your little rituals," I say confidently.

I have them, but I want him to know that I know. I'd like Charles Devlin to know why he has to die. The smile slides off his face, his expression cold with hatred. I'm sure no one has ever asked who the bastards are that jerk off and hit my wife with their belts while they watch her bathe. Telling her she needs to be cleansed of her sins.

"I'm afraid that is above your head, even for you."

"I'm afraid," I mock, "I have been above your head since the day I was conceived. I don't think you understand. I want all the names. I know Dorian Black's father is one of them. Just like I know you jerk off to your stepdaughter, watching her bathe herself and then beat her with a belt, careful not to leave marks on her skin."

I watch his face turn ashen when I pull out a serrated knife and slide it into his throat, blood spraying all over his desk. His eyes bulge, quickly filling with blood. The copper smell mixes with the cigar now dropped to the floor. Gurgling sounds can be heard as he chokes on his own blood. His arms twitch like a mechanical robot. "We all have to pay for our sins, Mr. Devlin. Your first one was the day you touched my wife." His eyes roll to the left full of blood. "Don't worry; this is just the beginning. Oh, did anyone mention that I have a thing for knives?"

Walking inside the church, I had the younger members cover Jesus nailed to the cross and the altar. The higher leaders of the Order take their seats. There are eight chairs with an oversized black cloth covering each seat.

"Where are the rest?" old man Caruthers asks out loud.

Mr. Bedford, my father, grandfather, and uncle remain quiet. Gia,

Jess, and Veronica are all home with armed security. The sixty-seven members of the Consortium file in each of the pews, wearing plague masks just like mine. I'm one of the few that announce that I'm part of it.

"Why are we here, Alaric."

"In front of you..." I pause when I hear grunts and rustling of paper. "I apologize, it is not Page Six with some juicy gossip but something that pertains to someone very important to me."

I hear chuckles. "We see," Caruthers says.

They don't, but they will.

"What are you doing?" Dorian asks in a hard tone, sitting sideways in the pew.

I inwardly smile. "Canceling your contract," I reply. "Didn't you hear, I kill people?"

I copied pages from the book in the library with the rules on Prey and the rituals, passing them to the higher members of the Order. I can tell which ones are aware, which means they have seen them. You can tell from their expressions when they look at something familiar. Something they have seen. But like my grandfather warned, I can't kill everyone. Not yet, anyway, just the important ones.

Strategy is key.

"Veronica is Prey and wasn't born into the Order as some may think."

"He's lying!" Dorian bellows.

"Son." Caruthers points at Dorian sitting in the front pew. His face is so red; he looks constipated, trying to take a shit, but I don't miss the way he tries not to grimace from the pain. "One more outburst, and I'll throw you out." Caruthers turns to me. "Continue."

"Even if she is recognized by a member of the Order, she is still Prey, and Prey chooses."

"That's true."

"Well, it is well-documented the night she lost her virginity that she chose as Prey without the mark. It means she's mine. Some of you have stood by and conducted rituals for sins committed by coercion and manipulation of Prey, which is forbidden in the Order."

"I'm afraid it's too late, son. She has the mark and has been initiated for years."

I nod, so the twins remove the coverings and hear gasps and coughing. "Son, are you insane?" Caruthers snaps. He's the oldest member on the voting board of the Order.

"I'm afraid Dorian's father, Mr. Devlin, and his cohorts have been busy with their pricks in their hands." I point at Caruthers's wrinkled face with his eyes full of anger. "To answer your question, I'm afraid I am," I smile, "but you already know that."

"Riodrick," Caruthers calls on my grandfather.

"It's justified. He already married her, and she's pregnant with his child."

"I see," he says solemnly.

I smile like watching all of the old farts trying to avoid looking at the eight men with their cocks stuffed inside their mouths and their eyes missing from inside their skulls.

Dorian is kneeling on the floor, watching his father's head with his cock stuffed in his mouth with tears running down his face. He looks up at me. "You motherfucker."

"I've been called worse, but I'd be careful if I were you." I look up at the higher members, addressing them with the facts. "Dorian Black knew she was Prey that night when she chose and interfered with a higher member's decision and then had you all vote under false pretenses. She has been enslaved as Prey under manipulation. Our law states either way that her true master is the one she bears a child to or is impregnated, so I married her. She's mine and a Riodrick-Riordan by law. Married in this very church. The death of the eight was voted in favor by the founding fathers. I just sped things along."

"Is this true?" Caruthers asks, turning to our fathers.

They all nod in agreement, and the gauntlet is thrown.

The Consortium members walk outside the church silently, and I follow, watching Dorian hastily head toward the parking lot with a limp in his step.

"What do you want to do to him?" Valen asks.

"Let's cut off his hands and make sure he chokes on tampons when he dies."

"Tampons?" Valen says, with a muffled laugh under his mask.

"Yeah." I turn to him. "Hang him from the cross outside Kenyan Preparatory High School."

"Alright. Who's driving?"

"I am," Adam says, walking up to us.

VERONICA

"POLICE ARE INVESTIGATING the crime scene at Kenyan Preparatory High School where a man was hung from a cross, both hands severed and his mouth full of feminine hygiene products." I shut off the local news, tossing the remote on the bed and biting my bottom lip.

Alaric walks in fresh from a shower, his body dripping wet with a towel around his neck. "Was that you?" I ask.

"It was."

"Are you going to stop or should we move on to the secretaries too," I say sarcastically.

He's killed almost everyone like a serial killer on the loose out for blood. I can't sit here and say they didn't deserve it because they did.

He looks up and grins, stopping at the foot of the bed. "If you want. I'll hold, you kill. I suggest we make it quick before our child arrives," he says like we are deciding what color we should paint the nursery, but I know he is dead serious.

"It was a joke."

He grins showing white teeth. "Lie down on the bed, gorgeous."

I lie down on the bed and he kneels between my thighs. "What are you doing?" I ask.

He glances up from between my legs, holding them wide open. "Worshipping you."

THE PREY SERIES

FORBIDDEN FLESH

FORBIDDEN FLESH

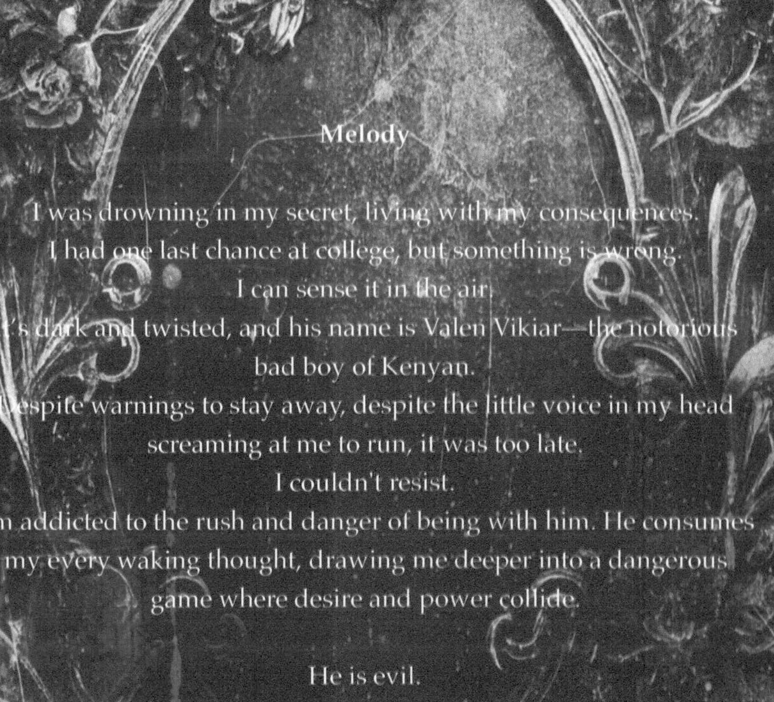

Melody

I was drowning in my secret, living with my consequences.
I had one last chance at college, but something is wrong.
I can sense it in the air.
It's dark and twisted, and his name is Valen Vikiar—the notorious bad boy of Kenyan.
Despite warnings to stay away, despite the little voice in my head screaming at me to run, it was too late.
I couldn't resist.
I'm addicted to the rush and danger of being with him. He consumes my every waking thought, drawing me deeper into a dangerous game where desire and power collide.

He is evil.

I am...forbidden.

VALEN

I WALK into Dr. Wick's office, close the door behind me, and sit, late for my first therapy session of the year since the semester started. Everything is riding on this year. I'm captain of the swim team. I have to get married once I graduate to a bitch I hate.

"So you've started school, and it's your senior year here at Kenyan."

"It is."

"How are you doing?"

I grin. "You mean, how many random women have I fucked?"

"If that is how you like to refer to it, then, yeah. How are you coping with your impulsivity?"

"By coming, Dr. Wick. I cope by coming on a woman's face, stomach, or throat." I chuckle. "Kind of like you and Dillion." She squirms in her chair, but I don't miss how she squeezes her thighs. I notice she wears pantyhose that hide the little varicose veins on her legs to appear younger and the short skirts she wears just for me.

"I'm not here to discuss me, Mr. Vikiar."

"Oh, Dr. Wick. We're past last names. Except I like yours. It rhymes with dick."

"How clever. Did you think that up all by yourself?"

"I did. Did you know that a male sex addict is a master in making himself come to reach euphoria? Like your pussy, it gets wet every time I'm in here, and you begin one of our sessions, so you go back and take it out on poor Dillon, thinking of all the ways I could fuck you. I bet you think it's me sometimes fucking you with your legs over the handles of this chair spread open while I go to town on that middle-aged cunt of yours, making it come so many times you pass out."

"I think this session is over."

"I think not… I need something from you."

"What can I do for you?"

I lean my head back on the wall, looking at the ceiling. "So there's this girl…"

MELODY

THE SUN IS SETTING by the time I pull up to the dingy old trailer I'm renting two miles from Kenyan University.

After the second day of sleeping in my car, I was driving down this road looking for a cheap spot to eat when I saw the old trailer with a FOR RENT sign stuck on the grimy window. I pulled off the road when I saw Mr. Colby outside. I struck a deal for four hundred bucks a month, *as is*.

I turn right on the graveled drive and spot Mr. Colby working on his old car. His stringy hair barely covers the bald spot on his head. His gray beard is long. You can tell he doesn't like it, but he doesn't bother cutting it.

Brock Colby looks about to get ready for his sixty-ninth winter. He glances around the raised hood of the old car. His black pants are held up with suspenders, and his old tank top has seen better days with a stain of sweat that looks like the Panama Canal down the center.

"Melody," he says, right before the scream of shutting my driver's side door, followed by a loud clang.

"Mr. Colby," I say, greeting him with a smile.

He has grease up to his elbows from trying to fix the old Plymouth on his cracked driveway. The burnt grass fills the veined empty spaces. It looks like he's been working on the car since I was nine from the chipped paint on the hood.

"How was work?" he asks.

I look down at my red-and-white diner uniform and then meet his brown eyes. He's squinting at me from the sun's glare.

"Besides smelling like a cheeseburger, I'd say it's as good as any day."

He hooks his thumbs in his suspenders with a line of dirt under the bed of his fingernails.

"I could get you a job at the hardware store if you're interested," he says, looking down at the ground like he's thinking. "Maybe knock a hundred bucks off the rent on the trailer since you fixed it up and all."

"Oh, I don't know," I stammer.

A hundred bucks sounds like a great offer. Since the fall semester started, most of the customers at the diner are from Ohio State. I'm not making enough tips, thanks to the assholes on the football team.

I get discounted meals at the diner, which helps me cover meals, but I'm making less and less each day.

Mr. Colby smiles, his yellow teeth making an appearance, but there is a gleam behind his eyes like he's evaluating my decision. I can't be ungrateful and refuse his offer. It would be rude. Maybe he's full of shit and can't get me a job at the hardware store and thinks he can.

Once he tells them I'm turning nineteen with no retail experience, they probably will tell him they'll think about it to be nice. If he does come through, I'll have no choice but to accept.

"Alright, Mr. Colby. You got yourself a deal. If you can get me the job at the hardware store, I'll quit the diner and take you up on the offer of rent being three hundred instead of four."

"It's Brock, and don't you worry," he assures me. "You'll get the job at the hardware store. The afternoon shift until closing time," he says with conviction. "I can guarantee you that. I know you got school."

My smile falters a bit. I haven't told Mr. Crosby that I'm not in school anymore.

"Will that be all?" I ask, placing the check on the table.

Silence blankets the booth. All four football players from Ohio look up. My heart sinks to my stomach. Instant dislike rises in my throat like acid. I was hoping they wouldn't recognize me, but I'm not that lucky.

The one to the left picks up the check and scans it. "Aren't you that girl who got Zack kicked off the football team his freshman year?"

"I don't know what you mean," I say awkwardly.

The one with blond hair sitting across from him wearing the same Ohio State football hat smirked at me. "We know it's you; it's why we came."

"You fucked up our season that year and the one after that," the blond jock seated on the right accuses.

The person closest to the wall gives me an unwavering stare, their eyes penetrating into mine with steadfast determination. "You think you can hide from us? Zack told us how bad of a lay you were. It's why he didn't stick around for round two, and you know, had to get someone more experienced."

My face flushes with heat, and a surge of frustration rises, urging me to scream. "You have me mixed up with someone else," I assert firmly, my voice strained with indignation, before walking away.

It's sickening how they cover up for each other. All they care about is their precious football season. I thought they would let it go after I didn't report them for what they did.

"They keep giving you crap."

I retrieve the ticket and load the tray for the next booth.

I give Dorothy a fake smile. "Nothing I can't handle."

"You don't have to put up with it, Melody. I could—"

"It's okay, Dorothy."

"They can't come in here and harass you. If they do it again, I'll ask them to leave."

"I can't scare the customers away." I grab a spoon and a small stack of napkins for the couple in booth two. "I need the money," I admit. "I'll let you know when it becomes too much."

I know those assholes won't leave me a tip, but I can't be a problem for her business. My biggest fear is for her to let me go because I'm driving the customers away. It sucks, but business is business. She's not running a charity.

"I promised Adam that I would keep an eye on you, sweetheart. Boys are stupid when it comes to pretty girls."

I snort. The last thing I would call myself is pretty. I had to learn this lesson the hard way. Don't fall for a charming smile and be fooled by the wetness between your legs. It's biology. Hormones. The kind that clouds common sense and blocks comprehension.

I lift the serving tray. "That would be the case if I were."

Pfft. "You're pretty enough."

Older people say this just to be nice. To them, being young is beautiful. Like babies, no one points out how weird they look when they're born. No one says you gave birth to an alien. It's a human life. They are all cute and beautiful.

After I drop off the food at booth six, I walk to booth eight. I begin to clear the table and stack the plates when I see the bill with the exact amount. No tip.

"Assholes," I mutter, but that's not the worst part. It's what they wrote on the bill.

WE ALL HEARD YOU CRIED LIKE A WHORE

The plate rattles in my hand. A butter knife slides to the edge. A fork drops with a clank, sliding under the table.

"Shit," I grumble, placing the stack of plates on the table.

As I bend to retrieve the fork, sudden movement catches my attention—a tattooed arm sliding past me beneath the table. Fascinated, I follow the intricate design inked onto the skin, a sinister skull perched atop a hand. My senses reel as the arm emerges, offering the fork.

My nostrils flare involuntarily as the scent of a woodsy cologne engulfs me, momentarily eclipsing the smell of food.

"You dropped this," says the voice that sets my heart racing.

I straighten and look up at familiar intense hazel eyes, like pools of liquid amber flecked with touches of gold and chestnut softened with a veil of cerulean blue. My eyes slide over his gorgeous face. Straight nose and masculine lips (not too plump but not too thin). He has a symmetrical square jaw with a defined edge that complements his features. Perfect-shaped brows that could only be inherited by a beautiful woman.

His brow lifts. "Your fork?"

"Oh, thanks," I stammer, hastily taking the fork from him. "It's not mine. It's dirty. I was." My words stumble over each other.

A grin tugs at the corners of his lips, amusement twinkling in his eyes as he watches my flustered reaction.

I release a nervous breath, the fork clattering clumsily onto the plate as I hastily gather what I can from the table, desperate to escape the awkwardness. With a quick sidestep around him, I make my way to the wash station, but his scent lingers in my nose.

The man has the effect of a tornado when it touches down. You could only stare in awe as it destroyed everything in his wake, and no one could stop it.

Valen Vikiar is the swim captain at Kenyan University. Rich, dangerous, and a heartbreaker. The first time I saw him, I couldn't look away. I kept watching him from across the room. I was young and underage at a college party. People were drinking and doing things a sixteen-year-old girl had no business seeing, but I couldn't help it. At that moment, Zack was a distant memory. I had never seen a guy who looked like him.

He had his tongue down some random girl's throat. The way he kissed, the way he could fuck a girl's mouth with his tongue would make a girl reconsider watching porn and watch him instead. I didn't ask who he was, but I heard someone call his name and say he attended Kenyan University. That was all I knew about him. I have never seen him again until now.

MELODY

AFTER MY SHIFT, I couldn't get him off my mind. The guys from Ohio were forgotten. The note on the bill was a distant memory. I was relieved when he ordered his food to go with Dorothy at the register. I had already made a fool of myself by stammering like an idiot and knew it would get worse if I had to talk to him again.

I turn the key in the *hand-me-down* Mazda my parents bought me when I was sixteen. I was bummed when they said it was my birthday present. It wasn't because I wasn't grateful, but because I knew, what it meant. I was not the favorite even though I was the youngest. My brother Adam got a shiny new truck when he graduated. My older sister, Maddy, got a brand-new Honda. I didn't complain, but I knew that out of the three of us, Adam was the perfect child in my parents' eyes. The perfect son while I was the hard-to-deal-with daughter who fucked up. I was the outcast. The one they had to make sure they kept an eye on because she didn't know any better, and Maddy was the perfect daughter who didn't cause my parents any trouble.

After Zack and his friends orchestrated my expulsion from Ohio State two weeks ago, falsely branding me as the "crazy ex-girlfriend" who stalked him, I knew I had to leave. Their disappointment was palpable, their questioning gazes piercing through me as soon as they learned of my expulsion. The weight of their accusations hung heavy on my shoulders as I packed what I could.

In their eyes, I had confirmed their worst fears, proving them right in their belief that I was spiraling out of control. It was a bitter pill to swallow, knowing that my own family couldn't see through the facade constructed by Zack and the guys on the football team. They only worried about how I could have ruined my brother Adam's future on the football team.

My brother felt bad and got me his old job at the diner after my parents wouldn't give me gas money so I wouldn't have a way of sneaking out.

Apparently, after hanging out with the rich guys from Kenyan, he didn't need the job at the diner anymore. He had a scholarship to play football and had enough money to pay for all his expenses. Then my sister Maddy moved out. She dropped out of college and left with her girlfriend for New York at the beginning of my senior year.

My parents respected her decision. They respected my siblings but not me. I was already blacklisted when they caught me and Zack fucking in my bedroom my junior year. At the time, I didn't care. I was tired of being caged. I had hearts in my eyes. Zack was my first boyfriend. He said all the right things, and I wanted to know what being in love felt like even though I didn't know what that meant.

After I convinced Veronica to take me to confront Zack when I found out he was a lying piece of shit, my life turned to dog shit. I was made fun of at school. I was threatened my senior year by the guys on the football team and the frat guys from Ohio State. I thought what they did to me right before I graduated from high school was enough. I thought it was over, and they got what they wanted. I couldn't tell my parents. I couldn't tell my brother. I couldn't tell anyone. You have to be a sick group of guys to do what they did to me.

After a bracing cold shower, I settle onto the worn sleeping bag Mr. Colby lent me from his shed, a makeshift mattress in my run-down trailer. The one that had been here before was a relic, yellowed and infested with bugs from years of neglect.

My damp hair sends shivers down my spine, a reminder of my forgotten blow dryer, left behind in the rush to escape my parents' house. It's a stark reminder of the chaos that almost cost me graduating from high school, as I barely scraped by in the final weeks, missing countless days of school.

As my phone rings, my brother's name flashes on the screen, signaling the inevitable conversation ahead.

"Yeah," I answer, bracing myself for the barrage of questions sure to come.

"Hello to you too, sis," he quips in response.

"You're calling because Mom and Dad have been blowing up your phone," I state flatly, already knowing the reason for his call.

I stare at the bold words on the bill. It's a warning. A checkmate. They haven't forgotten, and neither have I.

I pull the phone away from my ear as my brother's voice blasts through the receiver, echoing his frustration. "They have, but I'm also calling because I care. School is important, and as much as I want to k—kick that piece of shit's ass, it's not going to change the fact that you were kicked out of school."

I notice the hesitation in his voice, catching the word he almost said. He's probably surrounded by people; their murmurs audible in the background.

"They denied the appeal. I can't go back," I admit, cutting straight to the point. It's better to rip off the Band-Aid while the wound is still fresh.

I hear a locker door slam in the background, and the silence on his end is palpable. "Damn," he finally murmurs. "That's it, then?"

"Yep," I confirm. "I can't go to Ohio State, and because I took out school loans for the semester, I'll have to pay out of pocket somewhere else. The process of appeal caused the withdrawal date to lapse, and there's nothing they could do."

"But you didn't do anything. I don't get it. They don't have proof of anything. It's all baseless," he protests.

I glance at the cracked mirror in the bathroom from where I'm sitting. "It's obvious... I don't play football, and that's what this is all about. The team, the coaches, and people with power. And it doesn't help that they have a video of me screaming and attacking him at a party the night I caught him cheating on me. It's uploaded to social media." I inhale sharply. "I don't have to go to college, Adam."

"Yes, you do. What happened to writing? You wanted to write or teach literature."

"I'll have to wait. I can go to the community college next semester. It's not that big of a deal."

"It is," he growls. "Look, I'll figure something out." And with that, the line goes silent.

I stare at the phone, making sure the call didn't drop. The plan is thirty-five bucks a month for unlimited calling, but the service sucks. I hardly have a signal out here in the trailer.

Adam has every reason to hate Zack and is stuck in a hard place having to play with him on the field, but his future is safe, and that's all that matters.

MELODY

THE FOLLOWING WEEK, true to his word, Mr. Colby got me a job at the hardware store. Five days a week, from five o'clock to close. It would have been great if I was still in school, but I didn't have the heart to tell him the truth.

My first two weeks at college ended quicker than it took to apply for admission. After speaking to Adam the next day, I called the school again, hoping they could refund my loans to the lender and make an exception, but I was past the withdrawal date and would have to pay the money back on top of coming out of pocket to retake the classes. I couldn't return my books either. I was screwed.

I didn't have anything to do with Zack being kicked off the football team. It was Matt and what he did to Victoria. Zack was guilty by association, and I was just collateral damage.

"Will that be all, sir?" I inquire, scanning the hammer and box of nails as the man with dark hair and freckles approaches the counter.

"I'm going to need to refill two propane tanks as well," he states briskly.

I ring him up, the card reader turning bright green as he swipes his card. "I'll need your driver's license so I can give you the key to the propane out front," I request.

With an annoyed sigh, he hands me his driver's license. I slide the key across the counter, along with his receipt. "Let me know if you need any help. Ariel would be glad to assist you out front."

"I got it," he snaps, snatching the key from the counter and crumpling the receipt along with it.

Dick.

He's not the first male customer to be an asshole when I'm trying to help. Some men think a woman working in a hardware store is an idiot.

The bell from the door rings, signaling that someone has walked in. I look up and inwardly sigh, regretting telling Adam where I am.

My brother walks up to the counter, sidestepping the *dick* carrying the key.

"What are you doing here?" I ask.

Adam looks around the hardware store. It's old and looks like it belongs in the middle of a cornfield in Nebraska.

His gaze lands on my blue polo shirt with the hardware logo engraved on the right with a disapproving look. "Why did you quit the diner last week to work here?"

"Mr. Colby said he could get me a job here and would knock a hundred bucks off the rent." I shrug. "It was a better offer."

He scoffs. "I bet. He's taking advantage of you and probably feels guilty about it. Everyone knows no one would rent that piece of crap trailer. It looks like a rotting coffin."

Adam is probably right, but Mr. Colby treats me with respect and doesn't judge. Not like my parents and not like he is right now. I can see the judgment written all over his face at how shitty my life has turned out. He's never had to prove himself to our parents. They don't question him or think his goals are stupid. They don't judge him. I've always been the one who's a problem.

"Maybe. But I have a job, a roof over my head, and I did it all on my own."

He rubs the back of his neck. "It's not a roof, Melody. It's a piss-yellow trailer with black smudge on bricks. A roof is when you rent an apartment. Renting a room in someone's house is a better option. Why don't you go back?"

"Why? So Mom and Dad can harangue at me? Tell me, 'I told you so' after they treat me like I'm some inmate in a jail cell. I can't go anywhere without them breathing down my neck. They hired a babysitter when I was sixteen," I vent, frustration dripping from every word.

"That was for your safety."

"I'm not going to stick a fork in a socket, Adam. I can eat, bathe, and dress myself without supervision. I don't need parental guidance. I'm not a toddler," I assert, my tone laced with defiance.

"I know that, but you can't alienate yourself from us—from me," Adam pleads.

"You're here." I point out. "I'm talking to you."

"Because I show up. I blow up your phone. I care," he insists.

The guy with dark hair returns with the key to the propane lock and tosses it on the counter. I hand him back his driver's license. He takes it, muttering under his breath as he exits the store.

I raise my eyebrows. "School?"

The bell from the door chimes, and Ariel walks in. Ariel's face suffers from severe acne.

According to Mr. Colby, he's twenty, and his dad owns the store. Ariel glances at Adam with curiosity but then looks away, returning to stock the shelves.

"What time do you get off?" Adam asks, staring at Ariel.

"Closing time is nine o'clock."

He turns. "I'll meet you at your..." He pauses, his hesitation palpable. "House," he says hastily, brushing off the word that nearly slipped past his lips. But I choose to overlook it, too preoccupied with the urgent question burning in my mind. I want to know how the hell I'm supposed to have class tomorrow.

"Fine. Now go before I get fired in my first week and have to sleep in my car again."

His eyes soften, and pity sets in. Pity is the last thing I want.

After Adam leaves, Ariel walks up and asks, "Was that guy bothering you?"

"Huh?"

I heard him, but I'm not sure if I should tell him that he was my brother.

"His name is Adam, right? Plays football for Ohio State?"

"Everyone knows my brother plays football for Ohio State. It's not hard to recognize him since he's the QB1.

I never got to see him play college ball after everything with Zack happened. I watched him play once at a college bar. It was a twenty-one and older joint, and they kicked me out when I admitted I didn't have an ID. I don't have a TV in the trailer or a subscription on my phone to watch him play, so I rely on the stats I find online.

"Yeah, that's my brother."

Relief washes over his features, followed by a hint of surprise. "Oh, is everything okay?"

I return the propane key to its hook. "He likes to check on me," I explain, hoping he changes the subject.

I have a hard time trusting people.

Ariel stares at me for a second too long. I always try to avoid his gaze. I don't want him to think I'm interested in him when instead I'm counting the pimples on his face. I'm not judging him for it. It's a fucked-up thing to do. He is kind of cute. He tries to hide the emo look when he's at work. He would look better if he would take care of his acne.

All the dust and dirt working in the hardware store doesn't help the cause, but I can't help it when he's talking directly at me. I count the red dots. At least they aren't infected, full of puss, or anything. I think he's self-conscious about it with the way he averts his eyes when someone stares straight at him.

The echoes of past words and actions cast a heavy burden of insecurity. It's a shared affliction, I believe, gripping most of us in its suffocating embrace. Yet the roots of insecurity vary, with each person carrying their own unique burdens hidden behind veils of silence. We all bear different scars, silent testimonies to the battles we've fought, the wounds we've endured, and the fears we dare not voice aloud.

I don't like looking at myself in the mirror.

Ariel doesn't like the acne on his face and how people might think it's gross.

"You like working here so far, right?" he says, pushing his hands into the front pockets of his jeans.

"Of course."

"If a customer gives you a hard time or anything, you can call me. I'll come right over," he says.

He's trying to be nice, Melody. Give him a break. This is work.

I smile politely. "Thank you, Ariel."

He smiles. "Anything you need"—he points his thumb to his chest—"I'm your guy," he says, with red blotches appearing over his cheeks on the last part.

After my shift ends, Ariel stands at the door while I walk to my car, taking longer than necessary to lock up. Or maybe it's all in my mind, and I'm being paranoid.

I head to the trailer three miles down the road. It's dark, with the silvery glow of the moon peering through the dense canopy of trees. I pull into the rocky driveway and spot Adam's truck.

I pull up beside him, get out, and open the door to the trailer, not bothering to wait for him to get out. I don't want to hear more about my living situation. I want to know what he meant when he said I had school tomorrow.

I place the keys on the peeled-off Formica top. I left the door to the trailer open behind me. Adam takes two steps and ducks inside.

He looks funny inside the small trailer. My brother is six-two and wide compared to my five-foot-one small frame.

I place my hand over my mouth to stifle a laugh. "Oh, you think this is funny," he says with a smile.

"I would love to see you try to get in the bathroom."

"I'll pass. You would probably have to call the fire department to get me out." He looks around. "This thing is a hazard to humans."

"It's been fine so far."

He snorts and bumps into the ceiling when he tries to run his fingers through his hair.

It isn't ideal, but no one knows where I am except for Adam and Mr. Colby. It isn't pretty to look at, but it's my hidden oasis. A place where I can lick my wounds in private.

He clears his throat. "I pulled some strings and got you back in school."

I sit on my sleeping bag. "You got me back in all my classes?"

He winces. "Not…those same classes, and it's not at…Ohio."

"Where?" I ask, confused.

"Kenyan."

It feels like all the air has left my lungs. My heart is hammering inside my chest. Kenyan? How the hell...

"Victoria?"

He nods and hands me the folder. "Alaric is one of the founders and talked to the Bedford twins and got final approval from the founding families. It was all arranged. I told them Ohio State didn't take what happened with Zack too well and how he blamed you for getting him kicked off the team."

"They made an exception for me?" I look up. "A favor?"

"Yeah. You don't have to worry about paying tuition. They have the same classes, but better. Kenyan is an Ivy League school, Melody. It's the ideal opportunity." He takes a breath. "Screw Ohio. Kenyan can open doors that Ohio could never do for you."

I look over the admissions papers. All that is great, but I've heard the rumors about the way rich guys treat the less privileged.

I have a scholarship I never applied for. Classes I never selected. It's like I never missed school. Then a thought pops into my head. The memory of *him*. The memory of his scent is like a flame burning in my skull.

"What if the guys from Ohio..."

"They can't do anything to you, Melody." He lowers his voice, like he's telling me a secret. "Valen Vikiar is a senior."

"I know who that—"

"Stay away from him, Melody," he warns. "He's changed since I first met him. He's older. He's not..."

"Not like the guys I'm used to. Victoria told me a couple of things about the guys from Kenyan."

"I'm sure she has, but not about Valen." He steps closer. "Promise me, Melody. This was the only way I could help you without involving Mom and Dad. I don't have the money for you to go anywhere else. I still have two years left before I can go pro if I get drafted or get a job."

"You didn't have to—"

"I did it because I love you. I did it because that is what an older brother does when his sister messes up."

"Gee, thanks," I say sarcastically.

He sighs. "I didn't mean it in a judgmental way. You're not the first girl to pick the wrong guy and get caught up." *If you only knew.* "I don't want you to think you did anything wrong."

"You just said I did," I point out. "You said I messed up."

He pinches his nose. "Don't…"

"Okay, fine. Valen Vikiar is off-limits," I say slowly.

"His friends, too. Scratch that. The whole swim team is off-limits. Don't go near them. They are not…"

"What I'm used to."

"If you think guys like Zack are bad, you have no idea what these guys are capable of."

"You mean Valen?"

"Especially him."

I raise my hands with my palms facing up. "Alright. Valen. Swim team. Stay away. Got it."

"I'm serious, Melody. You're a freshman, and this is your last opportunity."

"Then why pull strings to get me in if you're so worried?"

"I'm…"

He looks around the trailer, and it all clicks into place. He was hoping I would go back home if he got me back in school with a full ride. My parents would be happy, and all would be the way things were before, as if nothing happened.

"You thought I would move back home."

He nods slowly.

"You don't understand, Adam. I don't want to go back home. I'm not happy there."

"You *were* happy."

"How would you know?" I say irritably. "You were too busy at football practice and worried about getting into college. You worked at the diner to make sure you had enough money in case they didn't give you a scholarship. You didn't know what it was like for me to live with Mom and Dad when you left."

"What was it like?"

"I felt like I was in jail," I admit. "I couldn't do anything. They question everything I say. Everything I did."

"They felt like they couldn't trust you after they found you."

"Fucking." His eyes widen. "You can say it. I'm a big girl. I couldn't go on a date. I couldn't do anything."

"They didn't want you to grow up so fast."

"You mean, they didn't want me to have sex or become a woman? They gave me shit because they didn't want me to grow up at all. I had to have straight A's. I had to dress a certain way. I couldn't get a piercing. I couldn't listen to certain music."

He smirks. "You did, though."

"I had to sneak out and do it behind their backs."

I got my belly button pierced and forgot to take it off when we went to a family get-together at the lake the summer before my junior year. Everything went downhill from there. They acted as though I was addicted to drugs or something.

"I admit I rebelled, but I pushed because I felt caged."

"You were always the rebel out of the three of us."

"Thanks." He thinks I'm thanking him in a sarcastic way, but I'm not. "I'm thanking you for getting me back in school. For putting yourself out there for me. I know it wasn't easy to ask a favor from your friends."

His eyes soften. "That means a lot, Melody. Thank you."

I look at my class schedule and smile. "The schedule is good, and I can still work at the hardware store. Mr. Colby made sure I got the best shift."

Adam nods, but I can tell he doesn't approve of me continuing to work there or living here. I can't go back home. My room evokes memories of Zack, reminding me of what they did.

"Alright, call me if you need anything. Anything at all, and I'll come."

"Okay," I say with a smile. Even though I'm screaming inside because I can't tell him what they did or how sometimes I can't sleep.

I give him a hug, knowing deep down I did the right thing. As much as he thinks he's saving me, I'm saving him from the guilt if he finds out. He has a bright future. I would rather suffer in silence than drown him in the guilt of my mistakes because he would feel responsible. He would feel that he had failed me.

For a split second, I thought of turning down the offer to go to Kenyan, but he did this for me, so it's the least I can do for him. The last thing I want him to feel is that he couldn't help me when I needed him.

After he leaves, I lock the door. He tugs on the latch to make sure it's secure, and I wait until his truck drives off to let the sob gripping my throat escape.

After I take a cold shower, I sit cross-legged on my sleeping bag and rub my eyes to soothe the sting from crying.

I grab my phone. It's been a while since I've looked him up. I was tempted after the fork incident at the diner, but I didn't. It was better to assume he was like those bastards from Ohio and forget about him. He's friends with them after all. He goes to their parties, and I have to remind myself that he hooked up with girls when I was there.

I type in Kenyan University and his name. Pictures of him pop up. He has blond hair and eyes that captivate you. The kind where the world stops when you stare into them.

He's gorgeous.

I swipe and notice the pictures are almost two years old. His swimming and lap times are the more recent ones. I swiped once more and found one from last year. Shirtless. His jaw is sharper. The expression in his eyes harder. Darker. He looks older. Gone is the playful smirk he wore that night. He has more tattoos on his chest, torso, and neck. His body is hard and ripped. His shoulders are broader. His stomach is more defined compared to when he was a sophomore. His biceps bulge when he breaks through the water. There are more veins on his forearms. The look in his eyes when he thinks no one is looking, or maybe it's the pictures. People look different online than in person.

At the diner, I didn't get a good look at him. All I remember was the tattoo of the skull on his hand. I was stammering like a dork, embarrassing myself.

My brother hints that he's dangerous, and I believe him. For the first time in my life, I don't feel like rebelling and going against him.

I replay the conversation with my brother about my parents caging me at home. Maybe they sensed something bad would happen to me, like a sixth sense. The feeling you overhear parents talk about when they predict how their kids will turn out if they don't discipline them in a certain way.

I didn't listen when they said to stay home and not go out, not to trust boys, or to do things without their permission.

I wasn't supposed to confront Zack that night. The plan was for me to remain at home. I was angry that they hired Veronica to babysit me like I was a child. At the time, I thought it was stupid. Maybe it was, but I convinced Victoria to take me to confront him at the frat party.

I was angry and stupid. I didn't think anything bad would come of it. I was pissed off like any girl my age would be after a boy lied, cheated, and risked your parents' trust. I was excited when the popular quarterback said I was pretty. He had me wrapped around his finger, with stars in my eyes. At school and at his games, he kissed me every time we were together. He said he would wait until I was ready. He wasn't like the other guys. Everything was perfect until I allowed him to sneak into my room and let him fuck me. He had me when he said I had a beautiful body.

When my mom walked in on us, it was too late. The deed was done. He practically flew out of the window. It was awful. My parents, and to be honest, the sex. I didn't feel anything I read or heard about. No butterflies fluttered in my stomach.

The next day, he bragged about it with his friends. All the things he said to me before were bullshit. He said I was it for him. That he never met a girl like me before. That I was different. It was all lies, and I fell for it.

If your parents warn you about boys, listen. If they want you back at a certain time, listen. If they tell you that you are too young for something, listen. Because when shit happens, it's too late to go back.

Don't trust a man when he says you're beautiful. It means he wants something from you. When things don't turn out the way he planned, he does something worse.

Like Zack did to me. He did the unthinkable. He didn't care if I stopped breathing or if my hands shook. He got what he wanted.

Now I feel useless, drowning in a sea of my own tears from the pain and rejection.

Everything I felt came in an exact order after he fucked up my life.

After the lie, the consequences.

After the consequences, the pain.

After the pain, the tears.

After the tears, the damage.

After the damage, nothing is left, and I can't go back to the way I was.

It's too late. Now, I'm someone else.

MELODY

I'VE NEVER BEEN on Kenyan's campus before. It has a Gothic Revival-style that was popular in the 19th century. I widen the picture of the school map on my phone with two fingers to try to find building four. I walk past the old cemetery, hoping I'm heading in the right direction on the narrow cobblestone pathway through campus, bordered by rows of ancient trees whose gnarled branches cast eerie shadows upon the ground.

Despite its age and aura of mystery, the campus is a bustling hive of activity. Students hurry to and from class.

A magnificent cathedral-like church with pointed arches, stained glass windows, and flying buttresses dominates the campus. It looks like they conduct rituals instead of prayer inside.

I have to admit, the campus is beautiful. The leaves and trees add to the effect. It looks like I'm inside the set of a fictional novel where this is a school for vampires and werewolves.

Massive, aged stone buildings stand above, their spires extending upward like fingers stretching to the sky. It's old but prestigious.

Graduating from Kenyan is like graduating from any other Ivy League school, except you are guaranteed a job through connections. There is no fancy football team like in Ohio. Swimming is the sport of choice, and its legacy is their culture. I'm sure it's due to the history of the school.

I look around to familiarize myself with the campus.

I check my phone to see what other places it has to offer wishing I could stay in one of the dorms. I locate a local spot on the map named Babylon, marked with a food symbol.

I turn left and make my way around the buildings, bypassing the female dorms, followed by the male dorms.

One guy walks out in front, pauses for a second, and gives me a once-over. He nods, but I ignore him and keep walking. I turn right until I see the neon sign and cross the street.

The place is buzzing once I'm inside. Students walk in and out of the exit, laughing with their friends. Others replace the spot they just vacated.

This is a Kenyan hangout. The school's accolades hang on the walls. The school insignia and past presidents. The numerous swim championships and famous people who have graduated from here.

I scan the rest of the place. It looks like a dive bar. Pool tables are to the left. College kids occupy the four arcade games available.

"Comedown" by Bush is playing from the jukebox. People form a line for drinks on the left side of the bar. The booths are all taken except the one for three to the right in a secluded corner.

A lady walks up with pink hair, a short skirt with holes in her tights, and combat boots. She appears to be the hostess with the way she keeps waiting for me to say something.

"Table for one," I tell her.

She nods, points at the empty booth, and hands me a menu. "Someone should come by to take your order. In the meantime, you could get yourself a drink at the bar and take it to your table."

"Thanks," I say, taking the menu.

I don't want to look stupid and order a soda or a glass of water at the bar. I don't have a fake ID, and this place is right off-campus. I'm sure they will ask me for one.

I sit at the booth and people watch. I thought it would be a good idea to scope out the campus and see where everyone hangs out. What they're like and what I should expect. I'm glad I did. The people here are nothing like the normal college students from Ohio or any other college I've ever seen.

It's like watching college students in a time machine. Alternative rock styles—emo, goth, and preppy—from the 1980s and 1990s are evident among the people walking around. The way they wear their clothes. Different hairstyles exist. You can tell the people here are all from different places, but one thing doesn't go unnoticed: social classes. You can tell who comes from money and who got lucky for the opportunity to go here.

My eyes scan the pool tables when a group of girls walks over, and then I see him. He's hard to miss from any distance. He's leaning over the pool table in concentration and taking a shot to the corner pocket.

The muscles of his arms bulge when he pulls the pool stick with his hand, sliding it between two fingers. I can't make out the color of his eyes because it's dim. My eyes admire how strong his back muscles are and the way they flex when he hits the ball with the pool stick.

"Valen," someone says. I look over, and a girl with soft pink hair slides on the bench in front of me. "Sorry," she says with a smile. "I saw you sitting here by yourself and figured you could use a little company. My name is Rose, by the way."

I don't, but I don't want to be rude.

"I'm Melody."

"You're new here." She squints her eyes like she's figuring me out. "Freshman."

I don't confirm or deny—it's not hard to guess, especially since I don't have a beer or cocktail in my hand. My gaze swings back to the pool table just as Valen takes another shot. Girls gawk at him from the other side, their cheers echoing the balls smacking together.

His smile lasts only a fraction of a second before a serious expression wipes it away. There's something powerful about watching him without his knowledge as if I'm observing through a looking glass.

"You like him?" she inquires, her smile betraying her interest.

My eyes snap to hers. "No."

I don't know him. He's nice to look at. It's normal for a girl to appreciate a good-looking guy.

Her smirk deepens. "Oh, come on. Every girl finds him hot. The problem with him is," she continues, lowering her voice enough that I can hear her over the music, "he doesn't want anything to do with a girl once he's done. No girlfriends. No relationships. He's just a hookup."

"And you," I probe, my interest piqued. "Do you think he's hot?"

She pinches her brows like I'm blind. "Of course, I think he's hot. Valen is the hottest guy on campus. The last of the sons of the founding fathers. I heard the others married right before graduation." Her gaze flickers briefly toward the group of guys talking to Valen, then back to me with a hint of skepticism. "But Valen. I don't think he's the type to settle down." She leans in. "I heard he's a good fuck and doesn't plan to slow down. I mean, he's fucked all the hot girls on campus. Two, three, sometimes four at the same time."

"You mean orgies. Did you sleep with him?"

She shrugs, a playful laugh escaping her lips, igniting a flicker of jealousy within me. "If you want to label it that way, sure. And no to your second question. He definitely has a preferred type."

A wave of relief washed over me when she admitted she didn't sleep with him. I think about Jess and what Veronica said about her. She was the closest Valen ever came to wanting something serious with someone, but she married his friend instead. That means she fucked them both. Rose says he has a type. Jess was blond, but I don't want to tell her that because that would mean I pay attention. It would mean I care and I'm interested.

Rose is pretty but is on the skinny side. You could tell by her arms. They are very thin, like a person who has an eating disorder. I'm not one to judge, but she would look healthier if she ate a little more.

"What's his type? I don't really care, but there is no one here right now that is interesting to talk about, so enlighten me."

"Nothing that resembles me," she replies, her eyes losing some of their brightness. "I'm too skinny. Back in high school, guys would tell me, 'Go eat a cheeseburger.' Some think I'm pretty but too bony. I think they were trying to be nice."

"I'm sorry," I say, knowing firsthand how that feels.

She waves her hand like it's no big deal, but I can tell it is. It's a very big deal.

"I think he likes blond girls. I heard he liked this blond girl his sophomore year because he was around her more than the others. I think she was the only one he slept with more than once, but the other guys were here around that time until they graduated. They were older, and now it's just him."

I turn my head and catch a girl whispering in his ear, but his expression is hard as if he's annoyed.

"Who's that talking to him?"

"That's Melissa. Senior. Stay away from her. They have something going on that no one knows the details about. She loves to play games, and according to some of the girls in the dorms, she's bi and loves pussy."

I raise my brows. "You think they…"

"Oh yeah." She nods. "They've known each other since high school. She comes from money. Her dad is some investor, I think, or an exporter. I'm not sure, but her family is connected. She's a real conniving bitch and loves his leftovers."

"Leftovers?" I ask, confused.

I knew Veronica didn't tell me the whole story, but this is new. This is weird. This entire school and the people who go here are fucked up. It's like opening Pandora's box and finding a whole lot of dark and crazy.

"She fucks all the girls he fucks. It's a game for her. I'm not sure if they still sleep with each other, but I think he's annoyed by it yet does nothing about it. Rich people shit."

"And you?"

"My sister graduated last year, and I was able to get a scholarship."

"That's impressive. It sounds like she got something worthwhile from this place."

"Sure, if you overlook what she went through."

I'm about to probe further when the server arrives. I order a basket of fries and a Coke. She opts for a Sprite. Once the server departs, she leans in slightly.

"She left with more than just a degree—and also a broken heart."

I nod, sensing the weight of her words. Curiosity piques me, but it feels too personal to pry.

Her gaze suddenly fixes on a new arrival. "See the jerk at two o'clock? That's Garret. The very definition of a rich asshole. Throws wild parties when his parents are out of town. And yeah, that was the one who shredded my sister's heart. He slept with her, then pretended she was invisible. Just another reason to stay away from them."

"I know. I heard," I say insentiently.

"I hope they drown," she teases.

I can't help but chuckle. "I heard demons can breathe underwater."

"You're kinda funny. Which dorm are you staying in?"

"I'm not."

"Ah, rich parents, then?"

"Hardly. I live off-campus. I could only score a scholarship for tuition."

"That's rough."

"Yeah. It's because I'm a transfer from Ohio."

"Ohio State?" Her tone registers surprise.

"The very one."

Her curiosity deepens. "Why did you transfer?"

A wave of discomfort washes over me, a pang of regret for letting that detail slip. I fidget with my fingers, trying to keep the burgeoning memories at bay. It's like trying to peer through a dense, black curtain.

The arrival of the server with our food is a welcome distraction. "Who else should I steer clear of?" I ask, eager to shift the focus.

Rose's attention locks on something—or someone—behind me. "All of them," she states flatly.

I sneak a glance back. Garret fixes his gaze on Rose, giving his gaze a hard edge. Off to the side, Melissa is gone. Instead, a blonde stands in front of Valen, her back to us, clad in a skirt that leaves little to the imagination, deep in a one-sided conversation. Valen's gaze is adrift, ignoring whatever she is telling him.

Then as if drawn by some silent alarm, his eyes meet mine. I hold his stare, finding an unexpected steadiness within. The sensations that once fluttered through me at the sight of him are conspicuously absent—no butterflies, no tinge of envy.

My brother's voice is telling me to stay away. Rose's warning—they've doused any spark that might have lingered.

The girl places her hands flat against Valen's chest, her red nails making a vivid proclamation. He glances at her hands, then returns to me. Redirecting my attention, I join Rose in focusing on the fries.

"He hasn't looked away," Rose murmurs, her voice low after taking a sip of her Sprite.

Whether it's recognition or curiosity in his eyes, I can't distinguish. So I dismiss it, saying with casual indifference, "He's probably wondering why I was staring."

She sneaks another peek. "He's still watching."

I place the fries back in the basket, my fingers brushing the napkin to rid them of grease. "Excuse me for a moment. I need the restroom."

Desperate to divert the conversation away from him and to avoid the temptation of looking back, I slip out of the booth and make a beeline for the restroom marked "Females Only."

Inside, after using the handicap bathroom and washing my hands, a scream pierces the silence as the door swings open. I pause, waiting for the newcomer to choose a stall so I can leave discreetly. Tilting my head, I try to catch a glimpse of their feet but see nothing. After a fruitless minute, I unlatch the stall, and the world plunges into darkness.

Panic surges as I blink, futilely willing the lights back on. "Hello?" My voice echoes. "The lights are off. Could you turn them back on, please?"

Silence is the only reply.

Enveloped in darkness, my eyes fail to adjust. Footsteps creep closer. I lurch out of the stall, colliding with a wall—someone. My hands shoot up, grasping at empty space.

"This isn't funny," I snap, my nerves fraying. "What the hell?"

A single "Shh..." sends a wave of dread through me, heavier than the darkness itself. I'm trapped. Each attempt to move is blocked.

"Is this some twisted joke, some freshman hazing?" My voice is a mix of anger and fear, the latter winning as I'm met with silence, thick and unyielding.

Memories of that horrific night begin to replay in my mind, my ears ringing with the echo of that night. Then, mercifully, the door creaks open, casting a feeble strip of light from the hallway. But there is no one.

I fumble along the wall, my fingers finally flipping the light switch. I wince as the harsh fluorescent lights flicker to life, taking a moment for my eyes to adjust. Tentatively, I look into the mirror and freeze. Scrawled across it, written in red:

WHO SAID I WAS A GIRL?

MELODY

I MAKE it to building four and walk into the creative writing class I'm assigned to. I look around the stadium-style seating to find an empty seat. I tried to think about the message in the mirror last night. It must have been a prank, but what if it wasn't?

Adam texted me this morning to make sure I showed up to class and asked if I needed anything. He assured me that I would be able to catch up and the professor would allow me extra time to submit any missing assignments. I hope he's right.

I was going to call Victoria this morning but decided against it. I didn't want to make a big deal about what happened in the bathroom at the bar. I wouldn't know what to ask her. What would I say? Hey, Victoria, did girls from Kenyan act like psycho freaks, turning off the bathroom lights and trying to scare people while they were using the bathroom? She would think I was crazy. She's married to the love of her life and is happy. She doesn't need my baggage to cloud her mind. Knowing her, she would want to meet up to check on me, and I would have to lie to her too. She would want to know how I've been, if I'm dating, or if I have any friends. You can tell only so many lies before the cracks in the truth begin to surface. Knowing her, she would see them. She would sense something was up.

Students file in and take their seats. I choose a seat in the top right corner, away from everyone but where I can *see everyone*.

A man walks in with a suit and tie and a Starbucks coffee in his hand. I can only gauge that it's the professor. A huge contrast from Ohio. He looks like he belongs at a law firm in New York City. Like those guys in the show *Suits*. Black suit, white shirt, light blue tie, and haircut parted on the side.

I notice everyone pulling out a composition book, so I take out a blank sheet of paper. I make a note of what is required for each class and hope I have enough in my account to cover it.

A group of guys walk in; you can tell by the way they draw everyone's eyes that they are popular. Even if they weren't, their looks are enough to take notice. They are good-looking, and judging from the shirts that read *Don't Drown,* it gives it away.

The girls seated closest to the door stare. Some giggle. Some whisper among themselves. The door opens, causing the room to feel devoid of air. Everyone's head lifts, and conversations stop. The sound of my heartbeat pulses in my ears. It amazes me that he's in this class. Not because it is a writing class. It is an elective, which means seniors and freshmen can take it. What surprises me the most is that *he's* in this class with me.

Valen Vikiar.

I swear my heartbeat slows down when he walks farther in the room and then begins to beat frantically when he takes a seat on my side next to his teammates, but I'm relieved that I chose to sit in the last row where no one is seated next to me and I have a clear view of them four rows below me.

The professor looks down at the podium.

He clears his throat. "Before we begin, we have a new student who transferred in from... Ohio State but missed the first two weeks of class due to a family emergency." My stomach clenches. These people are better liars than the devil. People *boo.*

"Settle down, settle down," the professor says, "none of that. She saw her mistake and is now doing the right thing." I roll my eyes at the jab. "Miss Melody Price," he calls out, and he scans the room along with everyone else. A set of hazel eyes meet mine, causing the room to sway before my eyes. I didn't think he noticed I was here.

My brother must have talked to him. I didn't think he knew who I was. He's never said two words to me. I feel like the new kid in elementary school.

I shift in my seat. "Here," I say, loud enough for every pair of eyes in the room to land on me.

"There you are, Miss Price. Welcome to Kenyan," Professor Owens announces, his smile failing to mask the undertone of formality. "If you need to catch up, feel free to partner with someone or see me after class."

"I'll do it."

"Ah, Mr. Vikiar. How noble of you," the professor says with a touch of sarcasm.

All eyes dart between Valen and the professor.

Slowly, Valen's smile unfolds, a calculated display hinting at the sharpness beneath his exterior. "We both know there is nothing noble about me, Mr. Owens."

Everyone laughs. The professor turns bright red and looks uncomfortable. I press my hands into my lap. Shit.

"Of course. Uh, Mr. Vikiar." Professor Owens gives me a sympathetic smile. His smile tells me I have no choice but to get the missing assignments from the devil himself. "Miss Price, Mr. Vikiar is volunteering. You will find that he is always erudite. He's a senior and is well-informed about the material."

"Good to know. Thank you."

My brother's warning about him goes off like an alarm in my mind. The room's focus returns to the professor, yet a palpable tension persists, akin to the quiet before a storm. Amid the sea of faces pointedly focused on the lecture ahead, I dare to glance to the left. My breath catches. The air between us crackles. Valen's eyes meet mine, his look piercing and unyielding, a silent challenge that leaves the weight of his attention both unsettling and undeniable.

As the professor begins the day's lesson, all I can think about is the way he looks at me. It's like he can see inside me. Like he's rummaging in the dark, knowing where everything is, and making sure everything is where it should be. Or maybe he's trying to intimidate me because I messed up, and my brother needed a favor for his wild little sister that he can't keep out of trouble.

I stare right back.

My junior year in high school, I thought he was a god the first time I laid eyes on him at the college party. After my sister, Madison, stopped me from tearing Zack and that tramp's eyes out, I wasn't aware I was fighting for a boy who would end up ruining me.

Not when I was lost in hazel eyes across the room. Eyes that told me I was fighting for the wrong guy. I was mesmerized by how gorgeous he looked, but at that moment, I begged him with my eyes to take me with him.

I was confused. It wasn't my sister who got me to stop. It was him. I knew he was older since he was at a college party, but I didn't care. I didn't even care if he had a girlfriend.

In those days, I was fearless. I wanted to explore, have sex, and fall in love.

All it took was one look, and he had me.

Too bad I'm not the same stupid girl he thought he could fool.

I watch his tongue rub slowly over his piercing on the corner of his lip. Any girl would fall for him. He is sexy. I don't miss the way the girl to his right sneaks an appreciative glance every few seconds. He must be used to the attention. In the diner, at the party, in this classroom.

She isn't the only one sneaking a glance at him or giving him a knowing smile. His eyes are telling me what I don't need to ask. He's fucked almost every girl in this room, but I see something they don't. I see a face on the other side of the mirror.

There is always a Jekyll to Mr. Hyde. An ugly side to a beautiful one. Valen has both, and no one realizes it until it's too late.

Once the other side appears, run.

After algebra, I walk out to the quad. I take a seat on the bench at an empty table and pull out a bag of chips and a can of Coke I purchased at the gas station for seventy-nine cents, compared to two dollars and fifty cents on campus. It isn't much, but it's what I can afford right now.

I pull out my schedule for my other three classes when I feel the bench vibrate. A shadow falls over the paper in my hand. I look up and see the same group of guys from earlier in the creative writing class. The guys on the swim team.

"It's the new girl," the one with brown hair and brown eyes says.

I pop a chip in my mouth and ignore them, hoping they will go away or ignore that I'm here.

"Leave her alone, Charles. You can tell she doesn't like dick," the guy with dark hair seated to his left says.

The other two chuckle. "Yo, Garret. Where's Valen?"

That has my head snapping up at attention. My eyes land on Charlie. His eyes gleam with amusement. "Hmm, we have a winner. I'm not surprised, though."

Garret walks over and sits next to Charles. I remember my brother mentioning his name around Victoria once. She said he was nice. He wasn't a bad guy.

Garret's dark green eyes meet mine, and he says, "Leave her alone, Charles. I know her brother."

Curiosity washes over Charles's expression. "Who's her brother?" he asks, looking straight at me.

"Adam Price. Quarterback for Ohio State That's his little sister," Garret replies.

"Shit. I thought you were the other one," Charles teases with a wink. He leans over the table and whispers, "The one who likes pussy." My jaw tightens.

I hate the way he talks about my sister. Joking about her sexuality and assuming I was her.

The other two guys sitting on Charles's right look at me with a glassy type of interest.

"Charles," Garret says in a warning tone.

I feel the bench vibrate again, and then someone slides into the seat to my right. I don't have to look to know it's him. I can smell him. There is nothing like it. His distinctive scent stays in my nose and refuses to leave, like a memory.

"Having fun, Charles?" Valen says with an edge to his tone.

The chips I ate turn into a ball at the bottom of my stomach. I'm not sure if he's mocking him or angry that Charles is giving me a hard time.

"I was getting to know the new girl. I figured out what she likes," Charles says with a smirk.

"And?" Valen asks, like he gives a shit what he thinks. Talking about me like I'm not sitting here is not rude.

Charles lets out a nervous breath. "She likes…dick."

I stand, having heard enough. The last place I want to be is with a bunch of guys who have the power to make me disappear. I need to leave.

Valen looks up, and our eyes meet. "Sit," he commands.

It's the first time he's said anything to me. He doesn't introduce himself and isn't polite. He's an asshole, just like his friends.

I grab my bag, leaving the chips and can of soda on the table, and turn to Charles. "Fuck you," I spit, and I walk away.

Laughter trails me, but I don't look back.

I walk into the hardware store for my shift, glad I didn't run into *him* again. I make my way to the back, where there is an old punch-out machine drilled into the wall. I take the brown card from the slot, hear the stamp, and place it back.

I didn't think businesses used these anymore, but this store is old. I'm surprised they have a card reader to accept payments. I walk to the only register to relieve Ariel so he can stock shelves and help customers on the floor.

"Hey, Melody. How was school?"

I pinch my brows in confusion because I didn't tell anyone I was going to school today. I found out last night. How would Ariel know?

Ariel reaches behind me and grabs a bag. "This was delivered right before you walked in." He holds up the takeout bag, and the smell of french fries drifts toward me from the diner. "There is a note."

MELODY, CALL ME FOR THE ASSIGNMENT 614-233-6708.

"Oh," I say, taking the bag.

"I figured you were in school because of the note attached."

I open the bag, pulling the handles apart, and the staples give way. There is a cheeseburger and fries with the same brand of soda I left on the table, along with a brand-new bag of chips.

I look up. "Who dropped this off?"

I know who it's from. But how did he know where I worked? I never said a word to anyone. He doesn't know me, and I don't think my brother would be stupid enough to tell him I worked here.

I stare at the number like it's a creditor out for blood. Valen knows I need the assignment to pass the class. But why didn't he write the assignment down on a piece of paper and slip it inside the bag instead of having it delivered?

I was told to stay away from him, but how can I if I have to call him for the assignment?

Ariel shrugs. "I was in the back. I heard the bell above the door, and by the time I walked by the register, it was here. I didn't see anyone."

I look into his eyes to see if he is lying, but I don't know him enough to know for sure.

When I get home, I type the number four times on my phone, delete it, and start over. It's my sixth time entering, and if I want to catch up in the class, I have no choice but to call. If not, I would have to explain to the professor why I couldn't get the assignment from him.

I stare at the numbers on the screen, the pad of my thumb hovering over the keyboard. I look out the small window at the dark sky. A cloud passes over the bright moon.

It's just a text, Melody.

He probably won't text back right away and wait until morning. I'm sure he's hanging out with his friends or with a girl.

"I'm losing my mind," I mutter.

It's not like I'm going to hear his voice or anything. He might not even recognize the number and leave me on read.

I let out a puff of air. My stomach turns into a knot.

Melody: Hey.

One.

Two.

Three.

I hit send and wait, staring at the screen like a bomb about to go off.

He's not going to reply. It's taking too long. I'm about to place my phone on the charger when it rings.

The phone slips from my hand and falls to the floor with a thud.

Shit.

I pick it up and look at his number flashing on the screen.

Oh. Fuck. I was expecting a text, not a phone call.

I hit accept.

"Hello," he says darkly.

Fuck. His voice sounds sexy over the phone.

"H-hi. Um, this is..."

"Melody," he says.

He knows it's me. *Hey* could have been sent by anyone. A random girl he slept with. He's rich, gorgeous, and popular.

Get a fucking grip, Melody.

He didn't give you his number to ask you out on a date.

"Yes," I say breathlessly. "How did you know where I worked?" I rush out.

I squeeze my eyes shut. My heart is pounding. I'm hot. My hands are sweating. I can't believe I said that.

"I took a wild guess," he says, but we both know it's a lie.

The more he talks, the richer his voice is. Deeper. Darker. It's not playful. In the back of my mind, I don't remember him being so serious. So brooding. I thought he was putting on a show in the quad and the classroom, but he isn't.

"How?"

"It's not important right now. It doesn't change the fact that I know, does it?"

He's right. So what if he knows?

"Why?"

"Why what, Melody?"

"Why did you volunteer? Why did you buy me food?"

"Because I want to, and I can."

"What's the assignment?"

The faster I end this call, the better.

Sweat drips down my neck. I need fresh air, but I don't want to go outside in the dark or turn on the small air conditioner.

"How was the food?"

"It was good. Thank you," I stammer.

"Hmm, it's a shame. I would have loved to see you eat it."

"A cheeseburger?" I ask, confused.

Who the hell wants to see someone eat a cheeseburger? They're big. Greasy. Messy.

"I would have loved to see how wide your mouth can go when you take a bite."

Oh fuck. I squeeze my thighs together. My inner thighs are wet, and I know it's not sweat. I'm wet and aching.

"You like to watch people eat? Is that your thing?"

He chuckles. "I want to watch *you* eat."

"That's kinda…weird."

"Would it be weird if we both watched each other eat?"

"That wouldn't happen," I say quickly. "What's the assignment?"

"I have to see you to give it to you."

"Why?" I ask, confused.

He could just tell me. Why is he playing games?

"It's complicated."

"It can't be that hard."

"It's better if I tell you in person."

I sigh. " Fine. You could give it to me the next time we have class."

"How about lunch tomorrow? Meet me at the quad, same table."

On campus. Nothing can happen to me on campus. There are students everywhere.

"Alright," I agree.

"Noon, Melody."

"Alright," I repeat.

I pull the phone from my ear to hang up.

"Melody?" He says my name slowly.

I place the phone back in my ear. "Yes."

"Be there; don't make me find you." And he hangs up.

I stare at the phone like he's going to crawl out of it and grab me.

What the hell have I gotten myself into?

MELODY

AFTER HISTORY CLASS, I walk toward the quad through a river of students. Some give me brief glances that are sharper than glass. Knowing grins flicker across faces, igniting a trail of anxiety that coils in my stomach. My hands get clammy waiting for the laughter that doesn't come, or is it something darker, a prelude to a torment I can't see?

I'm paranoid. I have anxiety. Get a grip, Melody. It's not going to go away. Deal with it.

I grin back, refusing to show my inner turmoil. I have to stop thinking about the past.

But when I arrived on campus, I changed my mind. I thought I was crazy to even think I could.

What if they know people from Ohio? My brother knows Valen and the other sons of Kenyan. They go to parties, hang out, and date. It's not uncommon. I've seen it with my own eyes. Other people from Kenyan could have been there that night or heard the rumors they spun about me. Even recognized me the same way Valen did.

I push the doors to the exit. The wind is cool against the skin of my cheeks. The sky is overcast. The church looms, casting a shadow on the cobblestone pathway leading to the tables. The wind causes the trees to groan and drags the leaves across the grass.

A sign that fall is coming.

My throat goes dry when I spot Valen sitting on the bench. My steps slow, giving me time to look at him before he spots me walking over. Charles sits across from him facing him. Garret is saying something I can't make out.

My eyes slide over the tops of his tattooed hands, roaming over his face with a predacious smirk aimed right at Charles.

Getting a good look at Valen, the pictures don't do him justice.

Every time I see him, I find something else that is perfect. You could stare at him for hours, trying to find a flaw, but would come up empty. His jaw is more defined. His shoulders broader. He's not as lean but bulkier. He put on more muscle, and you can tell by the definition of his shoulders that he's strong. His messy blond hair and lip piercing add to his appeal. I observe that he has painted his nails black. His bottom lip is a shade darker than the top.

My boots sound like bricks hitting rock with every step I take. The crunch of leaves with every stride. Hazel eyes, with a hint of blue, land on me. It feels like a hammer hitting a high striker at a carnival game right to my brain. His eyes drop to my black boots and slowly rise, pausing by the hem of my skirt like he is waiting to see if I'm bare or wearing panties.

As I approach the table, my gaze immediately finds Charles, my hand flying to cover my whisper of disbelief. "OhmyGod."

Charles's face is swollen, with hues of black and blue marring his face and blood veining the white of his eye. A cut on his top lip. He looks like he was attacked.

Turning to Valen, the question spills out, "What happened?"

Valen responds with a rapacious smile. "He slipped in the shower when he was bending over."

Charles's eyes dance between me and Valen nervously. Then to Garret. The two guys seated across and back to me.

"It happens," Charles explains, "when the tiles are wet. I slipped and—"

"Landed on your face and busted your lip at the same time," I interrupt, not believing it.

Valen grins. "He likes cock, Melody." He turns to Charles. "Isn't that right, Charles?" he muses. "You weren't thinking when you got hot and heavy with your boy toy."

"You're gay?" I ask Charles.

Charles shakes his head in a silent plea and winces when he remembers his face is all banged up. "No," he says solemnly.

"Yesterday, he was," Valen says with a dark resonance.

"You were there?" I ask with a flicker of curiosity.

Is Valen bi?

"No, but you heard what he said. The tiles were wet, so..." He pauses for a moment. "Let's go."

Panic sweeps over me when he stands, his movements fluid and deliberate as he swings his leg over the bench.

"That's okay. You can give me the assignment, and I'll be on my way," I suggest in a feeble attempt at control.

He draws near, his voice low and seductive. "Now, what would be the fun in that?"

The tiny hairs on my body stand. The air around us thickens, leaving his scent. My heartbeat syncs to an unknown rhythm.

Words fail me. My mind tries to scramble for a response, but I come up empty. No, yes. Fuck off. I don't want to go anywhere with you.

Fear and excitement amalgamated in my veins. If I say the last part, he will know the truth.

I'm afraid of him.

That he affects me.

I can't make sense of what I feel, but I'm attracted to him.

I lick my lips nervously, regretting choosing tights with a black skirt to wear this morning. They cling too tightly, not allowing the heat between my thighs to cool. It feels like I have a furnace between my legs when Valen is near me—intense and unyielding.

His gaze intensifies, the blue in his eyes dissolving into a stormy gray. "What do you want to eat?"

I want the ground to swallow me. His smile widens, fully aware of the turmoil he's causing, sending a flush of heat that seems to ignite every nerve ending, the sensation centering with an almost unbearable intensity of heat spreading around my clit like gasoline in a fire.

"I have plenty of places in mind," he says, "not too far, not too close." He steps forward, the chain dangling from his jeans with every stride. I find myself looking up, craning to meet his gaze, feeling dwarfed by his height. His eyes roam down my frame like he's measuring, assessing my size and how it compares to his.

"Where do you have in mind?" The words escape me, betraying me.

I can't believe I said that. I'm encouraging whatever he is trying to do. But this time, I'm different. I don't fall for fairy-tale bullshit or sexy smirks promising forever.

"Let's go," he says, turning around.

Casting a glance back at the table, I catch Charles's worried expression, which does nothing to ease my nerves.

I follow Valen, noting that he ignores all the appreciative glances from the girls who pass by. The head nods from the guys who know him. He's like a god walking across campus. I also don't miss the glances everyone gives me when they notice me following Valen to the parking lot. Like it's normal for a freshman to follow the most popular guy on campus. It's like they know something I don't. A huge secret I'm not privy to.

The lights flash from a blacked-out Porsche. He walks to the passenger side, opens the door, and gestures for me to get in with the palm of his hand.

I cross my arms over my waist.

"I'm not going to bite, Melody." His grin reveals a hint of darkness that sends a shiver down my spine. "Unless you want me to." I freeze, and he laughs. "I'm kidding." I step close to get in but pause when he leans in and says, "You should have seen your face. It looked like that is exactly what you needed."

"And what is that?" I say defiantly.

His nose barely inches from my ear, his breath a warm caress on the skin beneath my hair. A shiver mixed with heat and a pulse of desire that contradicts my rational mind slices through me.

"For me to remind you that you still exist, you can still bleed."

"You're crazy."

As I slide into the passenger seat, he pulls back, a shadow of amusement flickering in his eyes. "So I have been told." And he closes the door with a definitive thud.

We walk into an upscale steak and seafood restaurant on the outskirts of a designer strip mall called Legion. The server walks up, and he orders me a glass of white wine and himself a glass of water. I'm about to tell him I'm underage, but he winks at me and orders two lobsters.

When the server leaves, he smiles. "It's our little secret."

"What if I don't drink wine?"

My rebellious days are over, but I have. When I was fifteen, I tried every bottle of alcohol stashed in the house. Wine, liquor, and beer. I wanted to know what I liked so I wouldn't look like a prude when a guy asked me out to a party. Now, I stay away from anything involving alcohol. I know we're in a restaurant, and I don't think they drug their customers to fuck them in the back.

"What do you drink?"

"I drink what tastes good."

"You'll like what I ordered you."

"Don't get so cocky. I might not like what you give me," I shot back.

"You would have to try it first."

"I think I'm full."

"Satiety is ephemeral."

I lean back, trying to cool my inner turmoil. He's intense.

I take in the opulence of the restaurant. The restaurant adorns each table with pristine white tablecloths, the soft glow of faux candles flickering in their centers against the contrast of elegant black cloth napkins.

An array of blown glass fixtures crowns the bar above, their intricate designs casting a kaleidoscope of light across the polished surfaces. The waitstaff, in their crisp white shirts and black slacks, move with a practiced grace. The men in tailored suits, their conversations low and self-assured; the women in designer dresses, diamonds sparkling at their ears with every tilt of their heads. The air is thick with the scent of gourmet cuisine and the subtle undercurrent of affluence.

For me, this level of sophistication is uncharted territory. My parents considered a night out at Outback or Olive Garden the pinnacle of dining—places where our birthdays and graduations were celebrated, where family stories filled the air. Except for my graduation. I didn't get a graduation dinner. I was too busy finding a place to live when I left three weeks before graduation.

"What's on your mind?" he inquires, his gaze piercing as if he's trying to unravel the threads of my thoughts.

"I'm thinking this place seems...extravagant to just give me my assignment."

"You don't like it?"

"I didn't say that. It's more than I'm accustomed to."

"Have you ever been to a place like this?"

"Honestly, no. Your car costs as much as the house I grew up in."

He looks at me beneath his lashes. "Are you always this judgmental?"

"Do you always beat up your friends?" I blurt.

His eyes flash in amusement. He likes that I know he kicked Charles's ass.

"You caught that?"

"I did."

As our drinks arrive, he leans closer, the space between us charged with an unspoken tension. "And do you understand why, Melody?" He taps his finger on his temple, inviting me to delve deeper while he stares at me. "Think about it for a second. You're a smart girl. You can read me."

Can I?

"I've made you cathartic."

His teeth scrape his lips. "You're so hot. So, so close."

Jesus.

It's so hard not to think about sex when you're around him. He's like a walking sex object you want to stick up your pussy. Every word he utters has a double meaning, or he wants me to think it does. He could be playing around, but why me? He could fuck whoever he wanted. There is not a living, breathing female on campus who wouldn't fuck him. It's written over their faces when girls look at him. Hunger. Hope.

I know why he fucked up Charles. He fucked him up because of what he said. Because he made me uncomfortable.

"He said something that made me uncomfortable. He said he knows I like—"

His mouth rises. "Dick. He imagined you taking one."

"You're going to beat up everyone who says I'm taking one?"

He leans slightly over the table. "Is that what you want?"

"No."

I'm confused. Did he mean if I imagined his dick or any dick? I have to read between the lines. Everything he says has a purpose. Strategic. Like a maze, you have to figure it out.

"You imagine yourself taking cock, Melody? Is that too dirty for you?"

"What are you, my big brother?"

"No. You already have one of those."

"Are you asking me if I want to fuck, Valen?"

"Do you want to fuck, Melody?"

"Do you, Valen?"

I can play his game. I've been fucked over by worse assholes.

"I live and breathe to fuck. It's engraved in my soul."

"Then you don't need me. You have plenty of girls around to fuck with."

"What if I want to fuck you?" He leans closer to the table and lowers his voice. "Will you let me?"

"No," I say. "I have no interest in letting you fuck me, Valen."

He flinches like I slapped him. He's used to women opening their legs like a free ticket to a ride because of who he is and how hot he looks.

"How come?"

"I'm not your type."

I'm no one's type, but I don't need to explain myself to him.

"How do you know what my type is?"

"Blond, beautiful, with curves in all the right places." He pinches his brows, and I continue, "I'm none of those things, and I'm not Jess."

His nostrils flare.

I hit a nerve. The one he thought I didn't know existed. Ears were made to listen, and I've heard that he fucked her. How he felt about her. She is all the things I mentioned he likes and more. She married his best friend. She made her choice. He probably carries a torch for her.

I'm the opposite of what she looks like. I'm fucked up, and the faster I get away from Valen, the better my chances are of saving myself.

I get up and drop the napkin on my table. Not caring, I almost spill the untouched glass of wine. I was never going to drink it anyway. I don't drink around men. I learned my lesson and paid handsomely for my mistakes.

"Where are you going?"

"I'm leaving." I lean in, my voice low but firm. "And a word of advice—whatever game you think you're playing, count me out. I'm sure plenty of girls will take you up on the offer."

I expected him to be surprised and shocked, but he isn't. He stares at me with a promise.

A silent vow that this isn't over.

VALEN

I WATCH the way her hips sway when she walks away. The way the globes of her ass lift with each step she takes in her short skirt. I came on too strong. I shouldn't have been so direct, but I couldn't help myself.

I want to fuck her. She doesn't know her brother sent her to a school full of predators. He thinks convincing me to grant her a scholarship is based on his being part of the outer ranks of the consortium. He thinks it grants her immunity. He doesn't realize you have to be born into one of the founding families or promise to be a member of the Order. He thinks she is safe here.

Melody Price is Prey, and everyone in Kenyan can see it. They smell it.

My cock screams for me to do whatever it takes for her to let me split her pussy and take what I want.

My balls ache, needing release. I stare at the glass of wine. The one she didn't drink.

Bringing her here was a test. She didn't touch the expensive wine. Another girl wouldn't have thought twice about a place like this or left before eating the two-hundred-dollar lobster I ordered. I was trying to showboat, and I failed miserably.

Melody Price cannot be bought with fancy dinners or expensive cars. She also can't be bought with promises of love and devotion.

Someone broke her, and it wasn't because her ex-boyfriend kicked her out of college the second she set foot on campus. I recognize that look on her face. The one she's hiding under the mask, but from what, or more importantly, from who?

I was surprised when she mentioned Jess. I would have never guessed she knew of my past or how I erroneously thought I was in love. Caring for and loving someone are two different things. I don't have the capacity to love when all I think about is my next pussy fix.

It's like snorting a line of coke and chasing a white horse that seems like a mythical creature of satisfaction. There for a moment, and then gone the next.

I don't know why I have this thing for Melody. When I first saw her at a party my sophomore year, trying to beat up her cheating boyfriend, I was amused. I wanted to kick his ass, but I wanted her more. I was filled with guilt because she was sixteen. I shouldn't want a girl that young.

When our eyes met for the first time, I didn't miss the way her eyes begged for the same thing that was going through my mind. She didn't love that asshole. I knew it. She knew it.

The second time I saw her was at a party a few months ago. She didn't see me, and at the time, I was on edge. I didn't like where my mind went, knowing she was so close. She was barely eighteen, and I didn't trust myself.

I left with Rachel and took it out on her at the closest motel. She didn't mind. I've been fucking my way through college, feeding my addiction. It's no secret, but I had no business having these thoughts for a girl fresh out of high school.

I could see it in her eyes. Melody wants the feeling of euphoria she thought her little boyfriend could give her. She knew, from the way I looked at her, that she didn't have a clue what it really felt like to break apart repeatedly. Hard. Rough. Pain. Pleasure.

I was angry when she left the table on campus. Her eyes no longer hold the fire they once did, which is the source of my concupiscence.

The server comes with our plates of lobster.

"Sir," the server asks with her brows raised, glancing at the seat in front of me like Melody is going to pop out from under the table.

"Please have her plate delivered with two cans of soda and a bottle of water," I instruct. "Make sure the lobster is warm with fresh bread. Also, include a message along with a wineglass." I hand her my black card. "Charge it to my card."

"What would you like to have it say once it's delivered?" she says, handing me a pen and paper.

I write on it and hand it to her. She doesn't look at it. At least not in front of me.

The chef rushes out nervously. A line of sweat drips from his forehead.

"Mr. Vikiar, was there something wrong with the lobster?"

"Everything was fine, Gerald. My lunch guest had an emergency. It's why I'm having it delivered. Please send a female courier."

He bows. "Of course, sir."

I look up, and the chef I hired from Italy gives me his full attention. "Don't be late. The hardware store closes at eight. I want her dinner there at six; no exceptions."

"Of course, sir."

By the time I walk out of my restaurant, she is already gone. Not how I planned things to go. The hostess indicated she took an Uber.

"Valen?"

I turn. Hate almost blinds my vision when Melissa walks up with Rachel. Her flavor of the week. Also, the same girl I fucked the night at the party, trying to forget the one I was thinking about.

"Melissa," I say in a tight voice.

She smiles with her red-painted lips, which does nothing for my cock. My balls dry up like prunes.

"I thought it was you." She turns toward Rachel. "This is Rachel. Rachel, this is my fiancé, Valen."

I grind my teeth. Melissa knows I fucked her. It's not like I hide it, but she likes to make a point.

"I'm not whatever she says I am."

Melissa gives me a tense smile. "It's our senior year, Valen. We both know what happens before we graduate."

"I get to continue fucking all of your friends."

Rachel gives me a once-over like I'm a porterhouse steak she wants to take a bite out of. Again. She doesn't like fish all that much. Too bad she poisoned herself with Melissa's smell.

"Hi, Valen. It's good to see you again," she says demurely. "We should hang out again sometime. Melissa talks so much about you."

"Does she?"

"All the time. She always reminds me how lucky she is."

"Well… I wouldn't call it lucky. More like... out of luck."

Melissa glances between Rachel and me. Anger flashes across her features at Rachel's flirting. Normally, I would let her think I'm going to fuck her and her friend but end up fucking her friend in the ass while Melissa eats her pussy, and then, when I'm done, come all over her face.

I haven't fucked her. I haven't since high school, and I never will. Especially after what she did to Jess.

Melissa is bi, but I think she's more of a lesbian. She wants me to hide it from her father, or he will disown her if I don't marry her.

Melissa has claws. Sharp ones. She will destroy everyone who thinks they have a chance with me.

She likes that I have a sex addiction because she doesn't have to worry about me falling in love with someone and voiding the whole arranged marriage stipulation our parents made when we were younger, per the rules of the Order.

"Why do you have to open your mouth?" Melissa says in a menacing tone.

"The same way you do... to get what I want."

"And what is that?"

Melissa gives me a once-over, not hiding the fact that I'm her exception to her every rule when it comes to sex.

"To avoid you. Like right now."

She smiles, but I can tell by the way she blinks that my words cut deep. The way her breathing turns shallow from the blow.

"Who do you want to fuck?" she asks, glancing at Rachel.

She thinks I want Rachel, and she is so pathetic that she would let me just to satisfy me.

"Not you." I glance at Rachel. "And not her."

Rachel's face falls. Melissa's eyes narrow. She senses something is up. She knows it's not in my character to turn down fresh pussy.

"Switching teams," she says, fishing for the truth.

"Enjoy yourself, Melissa. I'm sure Daddy would approve," I say, my words laced with a hint of irony. As I turn to walk away, I catch a glimpse of the storm brewing in her eyes.

Hate for what she can't have.

Melissa wants me, and she compensates by fucking women. She will do anything if it means she gets to keep me.

Too bad I have other ideas.

Swim season is underway. I'm at the very top of my game. My lap time in freestyle swimming is better every time I hit the water.

I pull myself out of the pool and catch Charles's gaze. "How's the face?"

He looks around and sees all the guys standing around with smirks on their faces. They know not to get involved.

"It hurts," he admits.

"That's a preview. Talk about her like that again, and I'll make sure the other side matches the right."

Charles comes from a family of wannabes. His father has money like most of the assholes in the Order, and was allowed in. He's not born into it.

"What is with you and this girl?" Garret asks.

I give him a glare. He nods, a silent acknowledgment that misses the mark. He assumes it's because she's just another Prey in my eyes. But it's more convoluted than that.

Garret is the last of his generation and treads lightly around me. He's acutely aware of the tension that simmers beneath the surface, a tension rooted in his past actions with Melissa and Jess. He said he didn't have a choice. He apologized. Veronica vouches for him, but he isn't a saint. He isn't a monk. Like all the rich kids sent here by their families, he enjoys getting his dick wet.

I didn't miss the way Charles was eye-fucking Melody, and I thought he was funny. I wanted to kill him. I thought of so many ways after she left. I kept staring at him with a murderous rage. I liked watching him squirm. I didn't like the way he said *dick* in front of her. He was picturing her in his mind. The way he gazed at her sent a direct message to his cock, causing his brain to shut down and any sense of morality to evaporate. When he is in that state, there is only one thing that pops into his brain: to fuck.

The first thrust and the last one are what take you over the edge. It disturbed me in ways I never dreamed of. The sensation of his hands on her skin was akin to a burning sensation, and I desired to evoke the same sensation in him. If I killed him, she would know, and I didn't want to scare her. Yet.

So I settled for the locker room shower, bashed his fucking face in, and sent a message. Don't think about touching her, and what would I do if a man uttered the word dick and her name in the same sentence.

"I-I'm sorry," Charles stammers. "I didn't know how you felt about her, man."

I grab a towel and dry off, heading to the locker room. "How do I feel, Charles?"

He walks behind me. "I don't know…um…you like her…more than like her. Obviously, we are protective of her."

I want to burst out laughing. He's afraid to say that I want to fuck her and get his skull crushed. I think he knows that I would kill him and have him buried in the cemetery on campus.

Garret walks in and looks worriedly in my direction. He's afraid of me these days. He thought Alaric and the Bedford twins, or even Reid, were psychotic. I'm in a whole different class of fucked up. He's never seen me fuck someone up for a girl I haven't stuck my dick in before. It's new. To anyone, that doesn't make sense. A sex addict who is protective over a girl he hasn't fucked. A girl he doesn't really know.

"Are you going to the frat party tonight?" Garret asks, changing the subject.

Charles, James, and Spencer look up with keen interest. They want pussy, and they know I'm the guy who could take them to the Promised Land.

"I'll meet up with you guys there."

Garret raises a brow. "I thought we would ride out together?"

"Ride with Charles. He has a blind spot on the side of his face."

Spencer laughs, and the whole locker room joins in. The right side of Charles's face turns red, and he looks funny.

MELODY

AFTER ENJOYING the most delicious lobster, Valen sent it with a note inside that read,

I want to feed you so you will never feel hungry. Fill you so you will never feel empty. I want to live inside you and hear you beg me for more.

V

I couldn't resist when I opened the container. The smell was heaven. I was ravenous and shamelessly horny, thinking about what he wrote. The chef had created a menu and a form where I could list my favorite meals, allergies, and the types of food I disliked. I filled it out and handed it to the older lady who delivered the food.

Ariel raised his brows in surprise when he saw the name of the restaurant printed on the bag. He asked if I was seeing anyone in Kenyan. I said no, but he wasn't convinced. He looked nervous but went back to work. I thought it strange but didn't trust him enough to ask.

After my shift, I walk to my car. My phone dings with an incoming text.

Valen: Look to the right.

Awareness prickles my spine, knowing he is here. I look to my right, and there is a blacked-out SUV with pitch-black tinted windows parked near the brush of trees. My phone dings again.

Valen: Get in.

Melody: So you can kill me?

He thinks I'm a stupid freshman who is going to fall for his crap.

Valen: If I wanted you dead, you would be.
Get in, Melody.

Fear curls in my stomach, but he's right.

I hesitate.

I look at my car and then at the black SUV. He bought me dinner. He said creepy shit with a double meaning, but for the most part, he hasn't been a total dick. He beat up a guy for saying I liked dick. It's a little over the top and a little red flag, but my brother said he would look out for me. I don't think Adam would allow me to be around a guy who would kill me.

A tense click resonates from my throat as I swallow hard, my steps automatic as they draw me across the cool pavement toward the SUV. The night comes alive with the chorus of crickets, their song intensifying with each step I take. The hum of the engine and then the fan when it clicks on those sounds like a breathing dragon.

The back passenger door swings open, spilling a soft, inviting light across the darkened ground. Hesitantly, I peer into the cavernous luxury of the car's interior, the rich scent of leather and a familiar woodsy cologne enveloping me, pulling me into its embrace. I slide into the plush captain's chair, my movements hesitant, only to meet the steady gaze of hazel eyes that hold a patience I can't fathom.

"I'm not going to hurt you, Melody," he assures, his voice a deliberate calm in the storm of my mounting anxiety.

"Then what are you planning to do?"

Everything happens fast. The back passenger door slams shut. The door locks, the driver slides in, and the car lurches forward.

"I need your help," he begins, the words catching me off guard. "I'm taking you somewhere to gauge your reaction. An experiment for my therapy."

"Therapy?" My voice echoes my confusion, the word hanging between us.

I wouldn't be surprised if he saw a shrink. He's a bit unhinged. Not normal by any means, but Zack and his friends weren't either. They didn't come with a warning label. At least with Valen, he gives you a hint.

"Yes," he confirms, his voice steady. "I want to see how you respond and what you think.

"Why would you care what I think?"

Where is he taking me, and why?

"Because… I don't know you the way I want, and you don't know me the way you wish you did."

"I..." I begin, hesitant, grappling with my thoughts. "I'm too young for you. I'm a freshman, and you're a senior."

"You're an adult, Melody. Legal, and will be turning nineteen in a month. I'm twenty-two. We are not that far apart in age."

"How do you know my birthday?"

But I do know. I think…

"Because you are in an Ivy League school because of me. Who did you think approved your scholarship?"

"My brother…"

"Doesn't know who did. He thinks what I want him to think. He made a request, and I honored it."

"Why?"

A moment of pause lingers. My palms sweat. I'm here because of him. He holds all the power with my future in his hands.

"I don't have to turn in the missing assignment, do I?"

He chuckles. The sound vibrates through me like a tug on a guitar string. This is not about the assignment. He wouldn't go through all this trouble.

"You can turn it in if you want. It doesn't take too much time to complete. One is to write about a summer, and the other is a creative essay on anything you want to write about. I want to see it before you turn it in, though. If you decide you want to do it."

I take in his charcoal-colored jeans and black shirt with holes. I think they are supposed to be there. It's ripped on purpose. Everything he does is deliberate. Calculated.

"Why did you help get me into Kenyan?"

"Because I can, and I wanted to."

"You can do whatever you want."

He nods slowly. "For the most part, yes."

I watch the play of shadows over my hands, a distraction from the escalating tension. Suddenly, the interior light snaps on, and he hands me a bag. Inside, I find a cute cropped top, a perfect complement to my skirt and tights, and, notably, in my exact size. My gaze flickers to the driver, then back to him.

"Pull over." His eyes lock onto mine, unyielding. The car stops on the side of the road. "Get out." The driver gets out and shuts the door. "He's gone."

"But you're still here."

He closes his eyes.

A smirk plays at the corner of my lips. "You'll just open them the moment my shirt comes off."

"I won't," he vows, and the steadfastness in his tone almost convinces me. Almost.

"How can I trust you?"

"Trust is not earned, Melody. You have my trust, and I have yours. It's what we do to lose that trust—the actions that shatter it. Change."

"If that's the case, then why did you tell the driver to step outside?"

"You don't want to see what happens if he breaks my trust, Melody," he says with his eyes closed. "It will be bloody."

"You would kill him?"

"If he sees you change your shirt without my consent, I'll kill him. I don't think you want to see that. I want you to trust me. It's safe for you to change."

I look around. I wave my hand in front of his face, but he doesn't move. He doesn't flinch. His eyes are closed. The only light is from the dim light coming from the floorboard and the strip of light on the door panels.

I take a second to admire how beautiful he is. My eyes trail over his ripped arms, memorizing the tattoos of skulls and crows. My eyes find the piercing on his lip. The glint of the small diamond piercing his nose. His lashes are long and dark despite his blond hair.

I pull the polo shirt over my head. I can see the grin playing on his lips. I lean close to check if he's trying to steal a glance.

"Are you wearing a bra?"

I grab the black cropped top from the bag. "Yes."

"Color?"

"Black."

I pull the shirt over my head. Over the swell of my breasts. The fabric is soft and tight. It's comfortable and smells like a boutique store.

He sticks his hand out. "Give me your hand."

His eyes close when I lean over and slide the palm of my hand into his. His hand is large, warm, and strong. The smell of his cologne makes me dizzy. I reach out to steady myself.

My eyes pop open. I was too busy admiring the feel of his hand, not realizing I was touching the crotch of his jeans. His cock is hard.

"Valen," I whisper.

"I don't have to see you to know that I want you, Melody. The thought of you in a bra with my eyes closed is enough." I snatch my hand back. "Is it safe for me to open my eyes?"

He didn't see me. If he did, I'm sure he wouldn't feel the same way.

"Yes."

I look out the window. His driver leans with his back against the car, scrolling through his phone. Valen taps the window, signaling that it's safe to come inside.

We arrive at a frat party. The last place I would agree to go, but for some reason, walking in with Valen has me at ease. Maybe it's because he could have taken advantage of me inside the car, but he didn't, or because I'm attracted to him.

He doesn't stop to chat and ignores everyone trying to get his attention. One of the girls, sipping a beer in the corner, directs a seductive smile at him. Some I've seen walking around campus. Some are from my class, and others I have never seen before.

He heads down a hallway, opens a door, and steps aside to let me through.

"Why are we here?"

"So I can show you something," he says.

Panic sets in when I see a bed. I whirl around, but he blocks me. "That is not for you. I didn't bring you here to do something you wouldn't want to do. I'll explain."

"Explain what?" I say harshly. "I didn't agree to this."

"I get that, but I want you to understand me."

"What? You're a creep."

He smiles and pushes me against the wall.

My eyes go wide. It's dark. "Please," I plead.

I don't know what I'm asking. I don't want to walk out of here without him in the crowd of people. I also don't want to be alone here.

I close my eyes. "Melody."

"Yes," I whimper.

"Are you wet?"

I nod. Fuck. What is wrong with my body? When I'm around him, I can't think straight.

The sound of a door opening has my eyes snapping open. Two girls and a guy walk in.

They spot Valen, and then they glance at me.

The blonde smiles in my direction. "She can join if she wants."

"She's here for me," Valen says in a curt tone.

The brunette next to her pouts. "Oh, that's too bad."

The guy looks away when he spots Valen shielding me from his gaze.

Are they going to fuck? The guy kneels on the bed while both women undress. The man takes off his clothes. He is muscular and good-looking. He's not old. None of them are. They look around the same age as Valen, but I don't recognize them from school.

The brunette starts sucking the guy's cock while the blonde eats her ass. They both moan, and it's hot. It's like watching live porn.

Valen stands behind me, and I can feel his erection on my lower back. Jealousy rises like a rash over my skin, wanting him to be hard because of me, and I hate myself for it. I'm so messed up. How can I feel this way after what happened?

His breath fans my ear, and he whispers, "I have a sex addiction, Melody. I'm addicted to pussy," he admits. "I like to watch and fuck. It's my high. My fix. My need." He grinds his cock on me.

He pulls my hair over one shoulder. The cool air kisses my skin. His breath warms it back up. I'm about to catch fire. My nipples ache, my pussy drips, and I want his cock to be where the blonde has her tongue—in my cunt. I want him to fuck me, but I can't. I'm afraid to experience sex again.

The brunette continues to suck the guy's cock and dips her tongue into his balls. The blonde slides her fingers into the brunette's cunt and continues to tongue her ass. The brunette hums on the guy's balls, and he grunts with pleasure. As he pulls her hair and thrusts his cock deep into her throat, she gags. Saliva drips down her chin. He fucks her mouth, and she moans.

He pulls out and comes on the brunette's face. Her tongue is out, lapping it up, and I'm hot and wet.

I shamelessly push back against Valen's erection. His mouth is near my ear, and his hands hold me steady at my waist.

"Do you like it? Do you like feeling me hard while you get wet watching them fuck?"

"Yes."

"You want me to do that to you, don't you, Melody? Since the day we first laid eyes on each other."

There's a whimper, and it's coming from my mouth. "Um…"

I can't think.

The brunette opens her mouth, cum dripping on her face. She lets out a moan as she orgasms from the blonde sucking her cunt.

"Tell me," he says, "you wanted me to suck your cunt when you first saw me. Tell me the truth, Melody. I remember the look in your eye, but we couldn't. I wanted you, but I couldn't touch you. I couldn't ask you what you wanted. I had to... forget you." He pushes his dick against my ass over my skirt. "I thought I could ask. I thought I could, but it wasn't right." His body trembles behind me like he's holding back. "But now I can." His lips brush over my skin.

"Show me how wet your pussy is for me. How much it needs to be filled. Fight whatever it is that holds you back."

"Who are they?"

The blonde pulls away from the brunette's pussy and licks the cum off the brunette's face, then sucks the guy's dick.

"Rich college kids that like to share." I slide my hand between my legs, and I'm soaked. "Let me see."

I hold up my hand, my fingers glistening from my arousal. He slides his tongue between my fingers and sucks. A wave of pleasure shoots straight to my clit as I watch him close his eyes, savoring the taste. The feel of his soft tongue over my fingers. It's a drug for him. The way his breathing silently gives him away at how much he enjoys the taste of me thrills me.

I look over my shoulder, and the two girls are getting dressed. Their fuck session is over.

"Valen, they are leaving."

His eyes open, and he smiles. "So are we."

Relieved that we aren't staying, I follow him down the hallway to a side door that leads outside to the awaiting SUV.

VALEN

WE SIT in the back of the car on the long bench. She's behind the driver's chair, and I'm sitting in the center. I don't want to tempt the driver into looking at the rearview mirror when she is wearing a skirt.

She doesn't realize how beautiful her body is. How perfect her ass looks or how high her breasts sit in the top I bought her. She doesn't think she's beautiful.

The way she mentioned Jess told me all I needed to know. Melody doesn't think she is attractive, but she is also jealous of the thought of me with someone else. I could see it in her eyes when she mentioned her. I felt it when she thought my cock wasn't hard for her.

"Why are we sitting back here?" she asks.

I stretch my legs out and lean close. "Because you're wearing a skirt, baby. I don't want anyone to imagine what you look like between your legs."

She glances at the driver. "Just you?"

"Only me."

"How presumptuous of you."

"You'll get used to it."

She scoffs. "Who do you think you are?"

I lean closer and reply softly, "The one you think about when you play with your pussy. I'm the man you fantasize about when you imagine yourself to be a whore. I'm the man who has libidinous thoughts about you."

"You're crazy."

"Am I? All women do it. The virgins. The moral wives of men while their husbands are philandering behind their backs. All women wonder what it would be like if they weren't judged so harshly for liking sex the same way men do."

"But you have a problem," she whispers.

"You mean my satyriasis."

I find it amusing that she thinks people don't know—like my driver. He's been driving me around since I was twelve. He's seen my bare ass pump inside countless women.

"Don't worry, Melody. I'm not going to fuck you if that's what you're worried about. I'm not going to do anything you don't want."

"Why?"

My lips skirt the edge of her shirt right above her left breast, watching her nipples go as hard as rocks. I love working her up. I want her to feel how beautifully her body responds to me. I get off on it.

"Because I need your consent."

"To what?" she asks, confused.

"To fuck you, Melody. I need your consent to fuck you like you want me to. I want you to smile when you see me naked between your legs. Your screams when I send you over the edge, and your vision blurs with how hard I pound into your tight cunt, but I don't want to take if you don't want me to."

She leans over my legs, and my cock hardens painfully inside my jeans. Fuck, fuck, fuck. I want to fuck her so bad, but I can't.

Her eyes fall to the piercing on my lip. The one she looks at like a snack she wants to try. I flick my tongue over it. My cock is wet. My balls ache. Desire runs like fire inside my veins. My fingers clench my thighs.

"Melody," I whisper.

She looks between my legs. It's dark, but she can tell by my voice that I'm on the edge. My eyes almost roll to the back of my head. I love her hair. It's a different shade than my own, and I like how soft and shiny it looks. I want to feel the tips on my skin while she rides me.

"I don't want to fuck you, Valen." Her words stab me in the chest. "I don't want to have sex."

Is this how it feels to die?

She steps over my legs. Her ass brushing past my face.

She reaches for the door handle and then opens it. I look out the window, and we are at the hardware store.

The door slams shut, and I watch her run to her car. The driver knows to wait until she starts her car and safely drives off.

The piece of shit Mazda looks like it's fighting to breathe when it makes a noise after she places it in drive. The yellow lights glare past us like two flashlights when she turns on the road.

I place my cell phone over my ear. "Follow her."

My driver looks at me through the rearview mirror. "Where to, sir?"

"Home."

I want to follow her myself, but that would scare the shit out of her. She's resisting me, and it's something I'm not used to. It's refreshing but gutting me from the inside.

I can't think.

I can't breathe without having her near me.

I swipe my hand down my face. I'm losing my fucking mind. Porn doesn't do it for me anymore. I'm trying to hold back and not play with her head. She is the only woman who gives me the control I've wanted since I was a teenager and knew the feeling of what it was like to come. Since I've laid eyes on her now that she is an adult, all I can think about is her.

The SUV pulls through the gate of my father's estate. The darkness my father prefers is like a velvet cloak, smothering most of the light coming from the trees in the red spotlights.

The path to the house is a flickering dance of light and shadow, with fire torches lining the way, casting long, twisting shapes against the backdrop of ancient trees. At the heart of the driveway, a grand fire blazes like a beacon for some arcane ritual. My father has always been drawn to the flame, claiming it mirrors the fire within us all—that primal force fueled by desire and disdain, capable of making our blood sing with heat. And now, as I think of Melody, I understand those words with a clarity that pierces through the darkness. My desire for her is a relentless flame, an insatiable fire that courses through me, demanding attention and action.

I walk inside and don't miss my father sitting in the huge wingback chair with two women sucking his cock. They both look up, their mouths glistening. Something I've gotten used to since my mother died.

My mother was the first Prey married into the Order. The love of my father's life. She died giving birth to my brother, which is a silent testament to the life my mother once carried. Disowned and disparaged, he's a living reminder of the loss that broke him. He is three years younger than me, and my father banished him because of his hatred. My father forbids him from leading a life of privilege and hates his existence. He blames my little brother for my mother's death, and no one can speak of him. It's like he's a bastard child with no rights. No luxuries. No college education. No money or chauffeurs.

My little brother exists because of me.

He eats because of me.

Through it all, my brother loves me. I'm god in his eyes. If he only knew, he is the best thing in my life, and I feel guilty that I can't do more.

"Did you come from seeing the maggot?" he says, his voice dripping in disdain as he adjusts his pants.

The women scurry out of the living room.

After my mother died, Vance Vikiar turned into a womanizer. His only love is in a grave. No one speaks about it. No one mentions it. Everyone acts like my parents are both alive and well. It couldn't be farther from the truth. My father taught me not to love a woman. He warned me that losing her would ruin me forever.

My father didn't set foot in a church after my mother died. Not a real one anyway. The church in Kenyan is not a real church. As the sun sets, evil unites, turning the cross upside down.

"No," I reply, sidestepping the question.

"Well, where were you?" He sneers, eyeing the deliberate tears in my shirt.

Another thing he hates. The way I dress.

"Are you out of money?"

"No, why?"

"Then why do you have holes in your shirt? Have you no shame?"

I want to laugh in his face. My shirt cost more than his shoes, but I see that he doesn't understand fashion. My father adheres to traditional values. He prefers suits and aged scotch. Gold instead of brass. I'm surprised he doesn't have a gold toilet to take a shit on.

"It's designer."

"It's pedestrian, Valen. Is that what women like nowadays? Men fucking them with holes in their shirts?"

From my recent experience, no. But I don't tell him that.

"I don't think women care what you're wearing when you fuck them."

"Don't be funny, Valen. How's Melissa?"

"I wouldn't know, and I don't care."

He chuckles behind me as I walk toward the kitchen.

"You know she doesn't care about your sexual proclivities. She's perfect for you, Valen."

"No, she isn't. If you think she's so perfect, why don't you marry her?"

He wouldn't because he isn't into young girls around my age. It's not his thing. He's against remarrying. Re-committing.

He leans on the counter, watching me make a cup of coffee. "You know how I feel about that, so don't test me. What is going on with you? You've been acting strange since last year. You don't partake in your usual fun."

He means orgies.

"I'm taking a break."

He laughs. "Who's the girl?" he asks quietly.

"There isn't a girl."

"You don't think I could tell when my son is lying?"

I shrug. "I wouldn't know. You have two sons."

He slams his fist on the counter. "I have one son," he yells, then straightens his shirt.

I hate reminding him of my younger brother, but I don't want him to know about Melody. No one can know, or she will become a target.

I have enough with guys trying to fuck with her on campus. I see the way they look at her, which invokes the demon inside.

She was forbidden then, and she's forbidden now. She was too young at the time, and I'm betrothed to a woman who would do anything to make her disappear if she found out how much I wanted her. Melody has no protection on campus. I can't make her want me. I can't claim her if she doesn't consent. Rules are rules.

I've already broken so many when it comes to her.

I pull out my phone when a text comes through. I see the pin on her location when she makes it home, and a picture.

Fuck!

MELODY

"LOOK AT HER. SHE WANTED IT."

I jolt awake, a strangled gasp tearing through the silence, a scream clawing its way up my throat, threatening to choke me. I cough, desperate for air, my hands frantically wiping at the imagined moisture on my neck. My fingertips come away damp—not from sweat but from the tears that have carved paths down my cheeks.

It was only a dream.

For the first three months, I had them every day. I was glad I wasn't in my room, or my parents would hear my screams.

I look around and see the rough plastic that makes the interior walls of the trailer. I scrubbed them the best I could the first day, but the yellow sheen still bleeds through.

It smells like grass and leaves from the small opening of the vent I left open to let the cool breeze in.

My throat is sore. I must have been screaming because it feels like I swallowed rocks.

I open the small fridge I bought on sale at Walmart for twenty-five bucks with the blue Pepsi logo on it. It doesn't hold much, but I don't have much.

I kneel and look out the small window to see if anyone is outside. I used to love scary movies and watched them whenever I was bored and home alone. Funny how you stop watching them when you live like you're in a set on one.

When I slept in my car, I imagined a serial killer dragging me out and mutilating me. When I slept in the trailer for the first time, I thought a man with a mask would come and get me with a butcher knife. The jitters set in, like the first night. I look left and right, and the branches sway, followed by the chirping of crickets. A coyote howls, probably because of the full moon.

I'm peering out the window for a minute or two when my phone rings. I look over at the bright screen lighting up. I reach over and answer, placing it on the speaker, then wait for my brother to speak.

"Hello, Melody?"

"I'm here."

"Hey."

"Hey."

Silence.

"Umm, how are you? How's school?"

Your rich friend wants to fuck me.

"It's good. Everyone is nice."

"Listen, um… I wanted to ask if you could come and watch me play on Friday. It's our first game, and I really want you to be there."

I sit and pull my knees up. "Um…"

"Mom and Dad can't go. They have this thing they have to go to for Dad's work, and I thought—"

I close my eyes. They will be there. I want to kick myself for telling Adam that the whole Zack thing was in the past. It was a stupid high school mistake. I left the house for this reason. So they wouldn't find me. At Kenyan, they would be too busy with practice and school to show up on campus. There's security. There is… Valen.

"Melody?"

"Yeah, yeah. I'm here."

"Will you go?"

My hands are sweating and shaking. All my saliva has dried up in my mouth. I feel hot and cold. My vision blurs, and I can hear my heart pounding. The beginning of a panic attack.

I started getting them after that night. I googled the symptoms after the third time they came around. I usually get them when I'm alone or when something triggers them. A sweaty odor from a locker room or a gym. The smell of spit or a man when he sweats. The dark.

I read there was medication doctors prescribed for it, but I can't go to the doctor. I don't have my insurance card, and it would mean

I would have to ask my parents for it, which I refuse. I close my eyes, hoping it's a quick one this time.

"Melody, are you alright?"

"I'm fine," I say, blowing out a slow breath. "I'll go," I agree.

"Don't worry about a thing. I got you a ticket," he says. "I'll text it to you. It's going to be fun," he says with a smile in his voice. "And don't worry, no one on the team knows you'll be coming to see me. I really want you to be there."

He means Zack.

Zack will be there with the others. I need to stay hidden in the crowd. It shouldn't be too hard. I'll wear a black hoodie over my head and black pants.

"Okay."

"Thank you. It means a lot to me that you're there for my first game."

After we say goodbye, I sit in the same spot on the sleeping bag after a cold shower. My hair is wet, cooling my flushed skin. I close my eyes, willing sleep to come. I try to think of anything but that night. It comes in and out. Like the air from my lungs. In and out, in and out. Just like my memories. It arrives in fragments. I don't want to make out each voice, but I know I have to at some point.

They took turns.

It was five or six, maybe. I could have sworn I heard a female voice, but it could have been the drugs they slipped into my drink that night that distorted my hearing and vision. I blacked out at some point from the pain between my legs, and then everything went numb. It felt like I was on a rower, sliding up and down.

It felt wet, hot, and then cold. The smell of sweat and their sex. Musk. I heard a few names, maybe three. My head was fuzzy. Jacob, Sam, and Zack.

After it was over, I became a college statistic. The victim in a horror story is a girl attending a college party. Guys who drug a girl to take advantage of her.

But you let those things slide because you think there's no way it can happen to you.

You graduated from high school. You're an adult. You're fearless.

You have a big brother who goes to the same school. A sister who accepts and loves her sexuality and isn't afraid to show the world that she is comfortable. You're smarter than they think you're capable of. You have overprotective parents, and you don't think it's fair that they don't let you go out late because they are trying to keep you safe. You start to resent them because there is a boy who smiles the right way and tells you the things you want to hear. You don't want to believe what they are capable of. What they can do when you don't give them what they want.

I had a stable home with perfect siblings, but I wasn't careful about exploring love, sex, and friendships. The guy I gave my virginity to absquatulated; he treated me like a cherry-pick, and I ended up being caught in a web of assholes who took advantage of me. Monsters of the worst kind. They ripped any notion I had about love and exploration of my sexuality from underneath my skin without a clear memory of how they did it.

I grab a pen and paper and begin to write.

Hopefully, I will have something to turn in tomorrow for class. It's a good thing there is nothing to distract me. I don't have a TV and need to charge my phone to wake up on time in the morning for class. I'm sure I'll be swamped with homework for the next three days. Valen said I didn't have to do it, but then the professor would know.

I don't want special treatment or for everyone to think I fucked Valen. It would mean Zack and his friends were right.

My thoughts go to the bedroom where he took me. The two girls and the guy having sex in the room while a party was going on outside. The way he was hard when he was standing behind me showed me the sexual exigency his body felt. The smell of his cologne. The way his lips ghosted my skin. I wanted him at that moment more than anything I have ever wanted, and it clouded my judgment.

I remember the movement in photographic detail. His breath on my neck tickled my ear. The eroticism of his touch. The need for him to taste me the same way. To be his, but I knew being his would mean I would have to share him.

The other part of me screamed in warning. I wasn't beautiful like those women he was hard for. I wasn't blond or pretty. I didn't wear makeup or have pretty tanned skin. I didn't have a body like theirs either. I didn't have confidence or self-esteem. Predators take what you can't easily get back. Your life. The ability to trust someone again. Your sexual prowess.

VALEN

I'M SITTING in class next to the seat Melody was in on Monday. The guys sit on the same side, below me. They don't say anything when I don't sit with them because they know not to. They know I'm interested in her. But who isn't?

I'm interested in her in a different kind of way. I want to fuck her, but not just once. I want something real. I want to be around someone for once who doesn't look at me like I'm a sex-crazed freak who is only good for one thing. Sex and money. I want someone smart like me. A person who looks at things differently. I checked her school records. She was valedictorian, but what doesn't make sense is that she almost didn't graduate for missing school.

I watch people file in and take their seats. Girls I have slept with in the past give me a wink or a knowing smile that I don't return. I fix my gaze on the door, observing each individual as they walk by.

Adriana spots me and walks up the aisle. She's about to take the seat next to me when I announce, "This seat is taken." She looks up in surprise. "I'm waiting for someone."

"Come on, Valen," she says coyly. "We can get something to eat after."

Before Melody showed up, I would have taken her up on her offer, but I'm not interested. I'm hungry, but it's not for her.

I wave my hand, shooing her away, when the door opens and Melody walks in. She looks gorgeous in ripped black jeans, a cropped sweater, and black combat boots. Her hair falls around her shoulders like silk.

I ignore Adriana and gesture for Melody to sit next to me.

She looks at Adriana's stank face with uncertainty and resigns, taking the seat in front.

"Prey," Adriana says, softly shaking her head in disbelief.

My Prey.

I ignore Adriana, but she doesn't move. I look up, annoyed. "What?"

"She isn't interested in you, Valen. Be a good boy and take what's right in front of you."

"I'm not interested," I say in a flat tone.

"Aren't you too old for her?"

"Aren't you too old to act like you're in high school? Desperate for the popular guy to notice you."

Her face turns red, and she storms off, looking around, hoping no one heard me insult her. Adriana's father is in the Order, but a low-key member that helps export whatever the fuck we want in and out of where we see fit. She's a kleptomaniac. She steals for fun and only pays if she gets caught.

Professor Owens walks in, looks at the podium, and picks up a paper I didn't see there when I walked in.

"Miss Price," he calls, looking around the room.

She raises her hand. "I'm here," she says and lowers her hand.

"Would you read it to the class? It's part of the assignment."

I see her stiffen. She hesitates for a split second.

She remembered the assignment. I wonder what she wrote about one of her summers. I told her to let me see it before she turned it in, but she didn't.

She doesn't trust me.

I wonder what she did that I'm not privy to. I want to know what she likes. Her college applications said she aspires to be a writer, which is one of the reasons she is enrolled in this class.

She gets up and takes the paper. She goes back to her seat, making it a point not to look at me.

Her gaze sweeps the room. Everyone looks in her direction. She looks down at the paper and begins:

"For some, summer is warm. It can be a time when you fall in love. The nights are longer. When you're asked out by someone who says you're special, you look up at the dark sky, see the stars, and hope you can burn together and become one. You trust him because he said you could. He's my person in him. It's one of those moments you think is perfect. The kind that

you replay in your mind before you fall asleep. The kind that gives you dimples on your skin from goose bumps. The kind that makes you feel liquescent, glistening under the stars.

But my last summer wasn't warm. It was cold. Wounds would turn into deep scars, bandaging my heart. He wasn't my person. He was a lie. There were no stars in the dark sky. No wishes to burn as one.

There was laughter. He expressed how he thought of me. How ugly I looked. How nasty I felt. I would do anything to fit in. Reminding me that everything I thought about love was a lie. My body was just currency for a sick, twisted game.

I looked up, not knowing what was happening all around me. All I remember is how my breathing stopped. How my hands shook when he laughed about the way I looked without my clothes. It was the summer I would never forget because I lost so much. You see, I was so desperate to live life and fall in love. I didn't know everything I wished for would be taken from me. My confidence. The spark behind my eyes when I looked in the mirror. The beauty I thought I possessed. The love I thought I had. I fell.

I fell into a dark hole, and now I'm here."

She puts the paper down. My hands are numb from how hard I'm gripping the edge of the table.

Silence stretches throughout the room.

Professor Owen clears his throat. "Thank you, Miss Price."

Garret glances at her and then at me. My eyes land on the back of her head, and I know after hearing about her summer, she won't turn around. How could she? Someone hurt her, and it wasn't just one asshole. There were more.

She couldn't breathe.

Her hands shook.

How ugly I looked.

How nasty I felt.

Who would laugh about how nasty someone felt? I'm trying to piece together what she read aloud in my head, searching for clues like shifting puzzle pieces. The pieces are trying to fit. To make sense of it.

How nasty I felt.

How ugly I looked.

Laughter.

Not, he laughed.

I think of Jess. Veronica. Different scenarios are all pleating together.

When?

How?

Time passes in a blur. I remain seated after everyone files out of the room, including Melody. She kept her head down the whole time, avoiding eye contact with me.

Garret walks up. "Hey, man. I…"

"I'll see you at practice. Watch her for me until I come back," I tell him.

He nods. "Alright, Valen."

"What brings you to my office today, Mr. Vikiar?" Dr. Wick inquires, her tone striving for professionalism yet carrying a hint of performative courtesy.

"I'm here because I need to talk, Dr. Wick. Isn't that the crux of your profession? To listen to those of us grappling with our minds, even when the solutions seem elusive."

I notice she's somewhat disheveled today, her usual attire replaced by less formal clothing, perhaps caught off guard by my unexpected visit. Her attempt to cross her legs discreetly in her pantyhose—a vain effort to conceal the varicose veins that betray her age—doesn't escape my attention.

"What seems to be the problem today?" she asks, adjusting to the shift in our usual dynamic.

I settle into my chair, stretching my legs, and without much thought, I light a joint and take a slow, deliberate drag. The smoke curls and dances under the fluorescent lights—a visual echo of my search for the right words.

She's stopped protesting. I'm over twenty-one. It's legal to smoke weed recreationally now in the state of Ohio, so there isn't much she can do about it.

"I've been experiencing certain episodes," I finally say, watching the smoke linger in the air.

"What type of episodes are you referring to?"

I hesitate, then admit, "Episodes filled with intense desire... lechery, lasciviousness."

"I see. Recognizing these patterns is crucial. Would you say these are fantasies driven by an underlying compulsion?"

"It's like hunger. The same way you feel the need to cheat on your husband with colleagues, Dr. Wick."

I like to remind her that she is no different from my *'Don Juanism'* when she's impulsive. She shifts uncomfortably in her seat. She is on the fence about me knowing about her little problem of promiscuity. She wants me to know because she imagines it is me that she fucks. I see the hungry glint in her eyes when she looks at my crotch. She is curious about the length of my cock. What color it is, girth, or if I'm circumcised.

"What are you hungry for? The chase? The high?"

My eyes flick to her, and I see her throat move as she swallows. "Prey."

Her nose flares. "I see."

"I want her."

"Is this the same girl?"

"Yes. She's here."

"How did you..."

"I brought her here."

"Why?'

"You know why?"

"Does she have any romantic feelings toward you, Valen? If this is purely physical…"

"No… I'm not sure, but I'm working on it. I don't know how to."

"What do you want with this girl besides the obvious?"

She knows I haven't fucked, or I wouldn't be here. She's my control, and it's slipping.

"I want her to like me. I want her to see me as her god. I want to own her. I want to fuck her everywhere."

"Do you pleasure yourself?"

I chuckle. "All the time, Dr. Wick. My cock has more ladders than a hardware store."

"To her."

"Five times this morning."

"Have you had sex with anyone else since she's been here?"

"No."

"I see."

"She doesn't want me."

She sits up in her chair. "This is a first for you."

I nod. "I can't think unless I have her, but I want her to want me and only me. She's my obsession."

"No other girl will do."

I shake my head. "I don't want another girl. I want her, Dr. Wick, and I'll do anything to have her, but I don't want to hurt her."

"You have to try, Valen. Meaningful relationships are hard for sex addicts. In your case, you have a strained relationship with your father because of your mother's death. The only thing you have learned when it comes to relationships with women is what your father has taught you." I grin, and she continues, "What do you plan to do with your fiancée?"

I burst out laughing. "Oh…Dr. Wick. You still think I'll be a good husband?"

"Why not? Your father thinks so, or he wouldn't have secured an alliance."

She thinks I would tell her my plans and incriminate myself to the Order. How clever.

I widen my smile. The one that makes her sweat.

"I don't plan to do anything with her yet."

"I see… What do you plan to do about this girl?"

"I want to go on a date," I say simply.

"Then ask."

"I tried, but..."

"She turned you down?" Her eyes light up with interest.

I lean back in my seat and look straight at her. "She did."

"Hmm… try harder… or maybe she doesn't like you."

"She does."

"How do you know?"

"I know," I say quietly.

"Change the narrative. Change what people say about you. Show her the person you want to be with her, Valen. Who do you want to be when she looks at you? The sex addict with a temper, or the perfect guy in her eyes."

"How?"

"Talk to your friends." She means to talk to Reid, Dravin, and Draven. I want to laugh and throw up. Imagine me writing love letters.

"Valen?"

I blink twice. "Yes?"

"If you want to show her and are really interested in this girl, find out what she likes without talking about sex. Learn to control your impulsivity. I think this will be good for you. I like this girl already."

"Because she turned me down?"

She uncrosses her legs and smiles. "Especially because she turned you down. Have you used drugs?"

"No."

She looks up, writing in my chart. "Last time?"

"Party about six months ago."

"The one where you were trying to forget..."

"Yes."

"You're a smart young man," she continues, "very smart. Genius even. I'm surprised you haven't graduated early." She pauses for a moment, like she just realized something. "You…"

"Waited," I finish for her.

"For her."

"I did," I admit. "I waited for her."

"Why?"

"It's what I'm trying to figure out."

MELODY

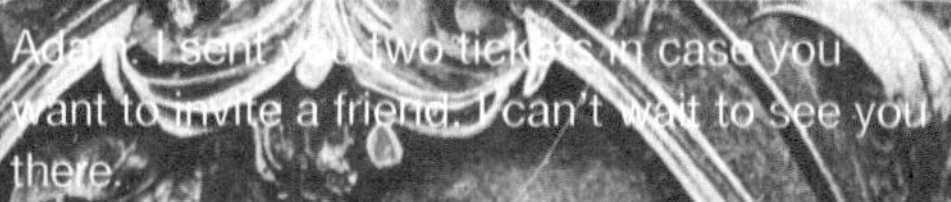

HE SENT me two tickets to see if I made a friend or had a boyfriend. I look up when I hear Ariel help a customer out the door.

He turns around, and our eyes meet. "Hey, Ariel?"

"Is everything okay?"

He's not used to people talking to him unless they need help around the store.

Adam: I sent you two tickets in case you want to invite a friend. I can't wait to see you there.

He sent me two tickets to see if I made a friend or had a boyfriend. I look up when I hear Ariel help a customer out the door.

He turns around, and our eyes meet. "Hey, Ariel?"

"Is everything okay?"

He's not used to people talking to him unless they need help around the store.

"Are you doing anything later?"

He shifts nervously on his feet. He blinks a couple of times. I don't think anyone has ever asked him to go anywhere. A girl even less with the way he is looking at me. Nervous and indecisive.

"No."

"My brother sent me two tickets to the Ohio football game, and I was wondering if you want to go with me."

He stuffs his hands in the pockets of his stonewashed jeans and looks at his dirty work boots. "You want to go with me?"

"Why not?"

He shrugs. “I thought you had a boyfriend. The one that sent you food.”

I can understand why he would think that. Also, the car that waits for me after work.

Valen has a driver wait for me until I get home. I tried to ignore it and thought it would stop after a few days, but it hasn’t. I also thought if I ignored him in class, he would get the hint that I wasn’t interested.

“I don’t have a boyfriend.”

He looks up. “You're not seeing anyone?” He shakes his head. “I don’t want any problems.”

I give him a reassuring smile. “I’m not, and it’s not a problem. I don’t want to go alone, but if you don’t want to go, I understand.”

His eyes widen. “I do,” he rushes out. “I’ll go.”

“Alright,” I say with a smile.

After taking a shower, I meet Ariel back at the hardware store. I’m surprised when he pulls in the lot in a brand-new black raptor. It looks pricey and not something he could easily afford working at the hardware store. I didn’t see it in the parking lot, or it must be new.

“Nice truck,” I point out after closing the door.

His hand grips the steering wheel, looking out the windshield. "Thanks," he replies, his voice carrying a hint of pride and a small smile lifting the corners of his mouth.

There's a subtle scent that seems uniquely his, comforting and inviting. Casually dressed in blue jeans and a gray sweater, he has a flush to his cheeks, a rosy hue suggesting he was trying his best to fix his complexion.

To be honest, I'm not into football. I'm here for my brother—he's playing," I explain, hoping to make him feel more at ease with the situation.

"That makes sense," he responds, with a note of relief.

We fall into a brief silence, the kind that feels like it's waiting to be broken.

"So..." I begin, unsure of where to steer our conversation next.

"My name isn't actually Ariel," he admits.

"Oh?" Of all the things he could have said, this was the last I anticipated. "Why does everyone call you Ariel, then?" I ask, curiosity piqued.

He chuckles lightly. "Well, when I started working at the hardware store after school, Mr. Crosby had trouble pronouncing my real name. He started calling me Ariel instead, and it just stuck. I've been working there since I was fifteen, so after a while, I just got used to it," he explains.

"My real name is Azriel," he reveals.

"Azriel," I say, testing it out. The name rolls off my tongue with a sense of familiarity and identity that 'Ariel' never quite captured.

It is an unusual name. Mr. Crosby is an old timer, and it would make sense for him to have a bit of trouble pronouncing it. I like it.

"I like Azriel better."

"You do?"

"Actually, I prefer Azriel to Ariel. It suits you better."

He nods, with a hint of relief. "Outside the hardware store, everyone calls me Azriel. I just wanted you to know in case we bumped into someone I know. It might be confusing to hear them call me something different," he explains. "I've never really liked 'Ariel,' but Mr. Crosby has been like a mentor to me, so I never corrected him."

"Mr. Crosby is a stand-up guy. He helped me find a job and a place to live when I was in a tight spot," I share.

"How come?" he asks.

"It's a long story," I reply, my gaze drifting out the window mindlessly. "I had to leave my parents' house." No wanting to open the door that leads to too many questions. I ask, "Do you live with your parents?"

"No."

"Oh..."

"You go to Ohio?" He asks, obviously changing the subject.

"No... I...well... I used to and then transferred to Kenyan."

The car jerks slightly as he finds a parking spot, the mention of Kenyan drawing a surprised reaction. "Kenyan?

"Yeah."

"Wow. I-I mean, that's great, but how?"

"I got a scholarship."

"Oh, that makes sense. It's expensive."

"And you, do you go to school?" I ask, turning the focus back to him as we park.

He shakes his head as he turns off the ignition. "School's not for me," he says, stepping out of the truck.

I hop out of his nice truck and see the crowd of fans walking hastily to get to their seats. Azriel walks with me side by side, trying to hide the uncertainty that snakes around my chest. They can't see me in the stands, but that doesn't mean they won't know. My brother might say something, but at least I'm not here alone.

After the game, my brother meets up with us in the parking lot. The entire game left me on edge. I was terrified that the rest of the guys would notice me. Adam looked up at the stands but kept looking at Azriel curiously from the sidelines. I think he was surprised I would bring someone.

"Hey," Adam greets, his eyes flicking between us. "Wanna grab something to eat?"

I look at Azriel, but he's looking around at the crowd of people walking out of stadium getting inside their cars. Some meet up with friends; others drive off.

My brother played great, just like I knew he would, and Ohio won. I cheered despite the fear clawing in my gut, hoping Zack and the others wouldn't recognize me. I sat down the whole time and only stood up when my brother threw the ball, which was caught by one of the guys. It was hard, but I was glad Azriel was here with me.

Azriel smiled, and I noticed he would look good if his acne didn't cloud his face. He has natural blond highlights in his hair. When the light shines, it looks brighter. He has broad shoulders. He's lean and tall. Maybe a good skin routine is what he needs to clear his face a bit and boost his confidence. I think it would make a huge difference. I noticed he likes to put the hood of his sweater over his head to hide the side of his face when he's out in public.

"Yeah, sure. If it's okay with Azriel," I say, hoping he's up for it.

Adam extends his hand. "I'm sorry. I'm Adam."

Azriel shakes Adam's hand. "Nice to meet you. I work with Melody at the hardware store."

"Oh…yeah. I remember seeing you at the hardware store with Melody.' My brother glances at me in surprise and says that it's the same guy he saw when he visited the first time. "I thought you guys went to school together?"

"I'm not cut out for college," Azriel says.

"Ay, man, that's cool. Schools are not for everyone," Adam says, lightening up the mood.

Azriel smiles.

"Want to hang out with us, Azriel?" My brother asks, lightening up the mood.

"Sure," Azriel agrees.

We are seated in a corner booth at the diner. Dorothy smiles and waves at me from behind the counter.

It's a bit crowded with all the Ohio students and the fans from Colorado.

"You guys' obliterated Colorado," I tell Adam, not caring much about the win, but I want my brother to know I support him. I don't want him to worry about how I feel that Zack was on the same team, and I'm hung up about it.

"Yeah," Adam says with pride.

The door of the diner swings open, and in walks Zack and several teammates—a sight that sends a chill down my spine. My gaze darts around, trying to identify any of the faces from that night, but recognition eludes me.

Zack strides over. "What's up, man? "You were on fire out there," he booms, slapping Adam on the back.

I shrink in my seat.

Zack's gaze eventually finds me, and it's like a spotlight I can't escape. There's a look in his eyes—a knowing glint that sets my heart racing, dread coiling tightly in my stomach.

I force myself to look away, focusing on the saltshaker on the table, as Adam engages in a curt exchange about the game. My hands slide under the table, clasping each other to keep them from trembling.

"Who's your friend?" Zack asks with amusement in his tone.

My eyes lift, and I realize it is why he came over. He wants to know who Azriel is and to give him a hard time.

"I'm Azriel, but I didn't catch your name," he says with gravity, his gaze steady.

Azriel reaches for my hand, bringing it to the table and intertwining his fingers with mine. The gesture, both bold and comforting, anchors me, slowing my racing heart to a steadier rhythm.

Zack's gaze flickers to our joined hands, a flash of surprise crossing his features before he masks it with indifference. "Zack," he finally says, his eyes shifting between Azriel and me.

I want to throw salt in his eyes, hoping it will burn. I'm surprised at how well Azriel is dealing with him. I thought he would be nervous, but he's calm, supportive, and collected.

"Oh, that explains a lot," Azriel says.

Zack glances at him. A challenge in his eyes. "Explains what exactly?"

Azriel points to the large booth at the other end of the diner. Seven other football players are looking over here with smirks on their faces.

Zack glances at the table with his friends, then returns his gaze to Azriel, a smirk on his face. "You should get that fixed. Visit a dermatologist. Your face reminds me of burnt pizza."

"Fuck off," I snap. "Go sit with your girlfriends. He's not your type, Zack."

Zack laughs, but I know he's holding back because my brother is here.

"I think you should go, Zack," my brother says. "I'll catch up with you at practice."

"It's all good, Adam. I'm just messing with him, giving him a hard time." —he looks at Azriel—"I still have a soft spot for Melody, and she knows that." He gives me a wink and then turns to Adam. "Not coming to the party, dude?"

"Nah, I'll pass," Adam says in a tight voice. "I'm trying to spend time with Melody."

My brother is two seconds from telling him to fuck off. I know he is trying to be civil, but he knows that Zack has everything to do with me being kicked off campus. Zack and the rest of the team got what they wanted. Adam needs to be a team player. I can let my mistakes get in the way of his game or hinder his future.

I give Adam a grin, letting him know that I'm fine. Everything is good. I wish the lies I spilled were true. I wish I didn't have to lie to save my brother's dreams. I kept a secret that could destroy him, but I need to save him. Some secrets are better left unsaid, so the truth doesn't destroy the happiness you're trying to preserve.

"Alright, man," Zack says, "I'll catch you later."

"Yeah, you do that," Adam says in a hard tone.

"See you later, Melody." I roll my eyes.

"Hey, Az… whatever your name is. I was just messing around."

"It's Azriel." Azriel releases my hand and places his arm behind me along the edge of the booth. No problem, Zack. Have fun eating with your boys. Celebrate the win."

Zack's jaw hardens, and then he walks away.

Adam grins at Azriel. "Thanks, man."

"No problem. That guy is a dick. I'm surprised you have to play with that asshole."

"Trust me. It's not easy, but Melody doesn't want me to break his face. Trust me, I tried to convince her, but she doesn't want me to mess up my chances playing ball and lose my scholarship over it."

"That sucks, but I get it. College isn't cheap."

"Dude, neither is life. Nice truck."

"Thanks," Azriel says, and he picks up the menu.

I don't think he wants to talk about how he could afford it.

After we eat and Azriel surprises me and my brother by paying the bill, we say goodbye to my brother, promising to catch up next week.

Azriel walks me to his truck and says, before opening the door, "Your brother is cool."

"Yeah, I'm lucky to have him," I admit before getting inside.

He shuts the door, and I wait for him to get in.

My heart skips as the driver's side door remains closed, an uneasy feeling creeping over me. Turning towards the rear window, the muffled sounds of confrontation reach my ears before my eyes confirm my worst fears. Zack and four of his teammates have cornered Azriel.

As I force the door open, my adrenaline surges and I murmur "Motherfucker."

Rounding the back of the truck, the scene before me sharpens into focus—Azriel, standing outnumbered.

"Stop it. All of you. Azriel, get in the truck," I command, my voice ringing with authority I barely recognize.

"Aww. You need a girl to save you, bitch," one of them sneers.

"Melody, get in the truck," Azriel counters in a firm command. "Now."

"It's all good, Melody. We're just having a friendly chat," Zack claims, his smile stretching wide and a hollow promise hanging in the air. "Trust me, baby."

"You sick bastard," I scorn.

Zack blinks like I slapped him.

The rumble of Azriel's truck starting cuts through the tension. The remote start's growl is a stark reminder of the odds stacked against us. It's evident from the predatory gleam in their eyes—they're not here for words. Azriel is their target because of me, and I can't let that happen.

I pull my phone out and dial. "Who is she calling?" one of them says.

"Call the cops, and I'll spin this on you, Melody," Zack threatens, confident in his ability to manipulate the narrative. "They'll take my side."

Asshole.

He's right, but I'm not calling the cops. I'm calling someone I never thought I would call.

He answers on the second ring. “Where are you?” He demands.

“On the Edge Diner. My friend is with me, and we’re in trouble. I need you. Please,” I plead.

Tears sting my eyes. I would never be able to forgive myself if something happened to Azriel.

He hangs up, and I stand in front of Azriel.

“What are you doing, Melody?” Zack asks.

Azriel gets closer and whispers, “I got it, Melody. Take my keys and get back in my truck. If anything happens, you drive down the road and call the cops.”

“I’m not leaving you here,” I assert, looking at them defiantly.

I feel like I’m in one of those movies where the bullies surround the new kid to beat him up.

“You think this is funny?” I challenge.

"Yeah, we think it's hilarious," one of them retorts, arrogance dripping from his words. "Your little boyfriend here thought he could step on Zack and us."

“Zack came to our table, not the other way around,” I counter, desperation creeping into my voice as I assess the daunting physical disparity between Azriel and them. These guys are built for the gridiron—broad shoulders with muscular builds. Despite his own physical capabilities, Azriel is outnumbered and outmatched. The reality of the situation is a heavy weight in my chest—it's five against one.

Suddenly, a familiar voice cuts through the tension: "Catch the game tonight?"

They all look up and step back.

“Shit,” Zack mouths.

The other three guys give each other hurried glances that spell, Let’s get the fuck out of here.

I turn to see Valen approaching, his presence like a beacon in the darkness. Clad in black, from his jeans to his sweater, he moves with purpose, his wallet chain swaying with each step.

“What’s up, man?” One of the guys says recognition is flickering in his eyes.

“Nothing,” Valen replies casually, but he makes a point not to look directly at me. “I came to get a bite to eat and saw you guys out here.” He looks at Zack. “What the fuck is going on?”

“Let’s go,” Azriel says softly.

I don’t think twice, walk briskly to the truck, and get inside. They know Valen, and that's one of the reasons I don’t trust him, but his showing up as soon as I called means a lot right now. I think it means he wouldn’t let anyone hurt me.

As we drive away, the silence between us is heavy. I don’t know what to say. You were great. Thanks for coming. I’m sorry my ex-boyfriend and his *ropy* teammates wanted to kick your ass for being around me.

"I'm sorry... for everything that happened back there." I finally break the silence, my voice barely above a whisper.

“That wasn’t your fault.”

What bothers me is that he didn’t ask about Valen or who he was. Does he know who he is? Kenyan is an old town with an even older school that is the center of it all. He grew up here and knows Mr. Crosby. I’m sure he knows who Valen is.

These people have wealth and control. It’s probably why he didn’t ask or hesitate to get the hell out of there. He’s probably afraid of him too.

"It feels like it is," I confess, the guilt casting a constant shadow. "I should have considered the possibility of running into him... I just didn't think."

Azriel's insight cuts deeper than I expected. "He's not over you—that much is clear," he observes, reading the situation with an acuity that surprises me.

His words are a balm and a reminder of the complexities of human emotions—of Zack's twisted version of love, of my own traumas, and of the invisible scars that dictate my every interaction and my every fear.

I snort. “Love is a strong word. It's more like he wants to make me pay for getting him kicked off the team his freshman year and most of his sophomore year.”

“He’s older?”

“Yeah, he graduated a year before me. We dated in high school and snuck around after my parents caught him in my room one night." I pause. "He cheated on me, or I thought he did, at the initiation party with some random girl." I shake my head. "He doesn't love me, Azriel. He wants to hurt me."

"That's not what I saw. Not the way he was looking at you when you weren't looking. He's in love with you on top of whatever sick game he's involved in, but the good part is that he's out of your life because you're smart enough to keep him out."

If he only knew how injudicious I am. How impetuous and messed up my decisions are.

I can't have sex. I can't bring myself to orgasm without thinking about what they did to me. I'm messed up. Even thinking about a guy touching me, I freeze. My belly turns into knots.

Except with Valen.

After I picked up my car from the hardware store, Azriel insisted he follow me home. He pulls on the dirt road behind me, leading to the trailer.

When I get out, he rolls his window down, angles his head, and looks at the old rectangular box on the bricks.

"I think you should move from here. Mr. Crosby is old and might not get to you in time if someone were to break in. I don't think it's safe."

He means Zack and his teammates. He does have a point.

I'm safe until they find out where I'm staying. It's one of my fears. What keeps me awake at night? It doesn't help the triggers for my anxiety. The thoughts that pop up in my head. The way I felt that night when they loaded my drink and, in my absurdity, drank it without a second thought. I never expected them to do what they did.

There are times when I can't get the smell of their sweat out of my mind. How they used my body. How they broke me. How did Zack let them?

They say you never forget your first love or who you lose your virginity to. I didn't have a first love. I had my first real nightmare, and it derives inside my head, gripping me in a vice and making me want to let go. It doesn't matter how hard I try. I feel, but I can't see.

Like a smoke screen was placed in front of my eyes, I heard voices coming in and out.

"Yeah, well. I don't have another option. I can't go back home. I can't find rent that cheap anywhere else."

He pushes the hood off his head. "Why don't you stay at my place? There's a spare room. It wouldn't be any trouble. I'm clean—I have someone who helps me, and I'm not a creep or anything."

I want to laugh and hug him at the same time. He's so sweet and brave. It's a nice offer, but I don't know him. Plus, I don't know where he lives.

"I can show you where I live to ease your mind."

"Thanks, Azriel. I appreciate the offer, but I can impose it on you."

He lowers his gaze in defeat. "I don't want those guys to find out where you are staying, Melody. I didn't like the way they looked at you. You're better off at my place. I don't go out much. I don't really have friends because they all moved or are in college. I don't drink or throw parties."

I unlock the door to the trailer and look back. "I'll think about it." He nods, but I don't miss the worry in his expression. "Bye, Azriel, and thanks for following me home."

"Bye, Melody."

MELODY

THE NEXT DAY, the air was thick with fog. The overcast was sullen. Last night, Azriel's offer weighted heavily on my mind. It was a nice offer, but I don't know him enough, and I'm not the best judge of character. I sent a text to Valen thanking him for saving me and Azriel last night but received no response. It left me with a lingering doubt.

What happened? Did he play it out? Did he say something to them about me?

I parked in the lot but didn't miss the crowd gathered in the mist of the dense fog. A guy runs to the male dorms. One of the female students is sobbing, while another is holding her hand as they walk away from the crowd. Another screams. Girls are crying with trembling hands covering their mouths. Tears run down their cheeks.

When the crowd parts, the swirl of fog goes with them. I see a dead guy sitting at the foot of a tree. His throat was cut. His eyes were staring into nothing. His mouth widened unnaturally due to the split. A pool of blood was underneath him. He is wearing an Ohio football sweatshirt. I recognize him from the Ohio football team. The words written over the white part of the sweater are in his own blood.

GOOD GAME

People begin to fire questions at me.

"Do you know him?"

"Who is he?"

"He doesn't go here. He's from Ohio. Football team, I think."

All I can think about is that he was with Zack last night. In the parking lot after we left the diner.

He's one of the guys who surrounded Azriel to beat him up.

I don't know him.

I was there, but I don't know him.

By the time I walked out of my last class, there was a swarm of police cars. State, campus, and local police surrounded the area. Some are by the tree near the dorms.

Everyone had to show their ID when asked. The discovery of a dead student in front of a tree has sparked a frenzy on social media. The irony that the tree was near the church and the cemetery gives it an eerie feel to the whole thing. No one on campus really knew who he was after reading the breaking news article. His name was Gary Clark, and he was the starting tight end for the Ohio State football team.

I called my brother, and he said he couldn't talk. He did say that the entire football team was being questioned. They went to a party last night around the time I was home. I was relieved because that would mean it happened after he was seen at the party, and who knows what those guys were into? Adam assured me that he was good and had nothing to do with it. No one liked Gary except his teammates. Adam mentioned he was a hard-ass and drank a lot. He was considered a party animal.

"Hey." I turn around and see Rose standing behind me. "Did you hear about that guy?"

"I saw."

"Damn," she says, surprised. "Sucks."

I don't want to tell her that I saw him last night at the diner. I don't want anyone to know it now, or people will talk and ask questions. Questions I don't have the answers to.

You didn't know him, Melody.

"I want to go to Babylon. I'm not hungry," she points out. "But it beats being alone in the dorm, and the cops are everywhere."

I don't want to be alone right now. I agree.

"Alright."

We walk in, and people are hanging out in tight groups. Most likely talking about the dead Ohio student. It's being aired on the big-screen TVs hanging over the bar.

"No one knows who did it. No suspects, and you can bet even if anyone in Kenyan did, they would be tight-lipped about that shit around here."

I take a seat in the farthest booth toward the back. "What makes you say that?"

"You know… bad rap for the school. They keep everything that has to do with this school under control."

I nod, and I couldn't agree more. Most Ivy League schools do. Like the people who go here. The rich kids who come here have more secrets than the government.

"What do you think?"

She scans the bar and then the door, like she's thinking about it. "I'm not sure, but it was obviously a message."

"Like what?" I asked curiously.

"Whoever did it wanted someone here to see it. That much is obvious."

"But who knew him?"

As soon as the words leave my mouth, the door to the bar swings open, and my answer walks in. They know who that guy is, but they stroll in like it's just another day at college and a dead football player from a rival school wasn't scraped off the bark of the tree across the street.

Valen, Garret, and the rest of the swim team walk in, heading toward the pool tables.

"Is that all they do?" Rose asks. "Play pool?"

"I guess there isn't much to do after school. They don't strike me as the type of guys who play video games."

Rose snorts, looking over her shoulder directly at Garret while he chats up some girl with dark hair to her waist and low-waisted jeans who does nothing to hide the string of her panties over her hips.

I glance at the TV to avoid glancing at Valen. He didn't answer my texts, and I don't want him to think I showed up here because I'm stalking him. A picture pops up of Gary. It looks like a high school picture. He looks nothing like the asshole I saw in the parking lot, but he is a good all-American high school kid who has loved playing football since he was five. It's interesting how people tend to portray someone's life story after their death. This good guy had a future. All I can remember of him was being an asshole and wanting to beat up another guy because another asshole on his team said it was a good idea. There are more highlights and a clip of his parents crying and pleading for justice for their innocent son. I was hoping they could find the killer.

A male voice interrupts my inner thoughts. "Did you see what happened?"

I look to my right. Valen and Garret stand beside the wood table. "Who hasn't?" Rose replies. "It's all over the news. Melody saw him all cut up, sitting against the tree."

"Whoa. That must have been intense," Garret says, his face pallid, sliding into the bench across from us.

"Go right ahead. Have a seat," Rose says sarcastically.

"I thought you wouldn't mind since you've been watching me since we walked in," Garret says.

Rose rolls her eyes. "You're so full of yourself. I wasn't looking at you."

"Who were you looking at then?" he challenges.

"Not you," Rose fires back. "I was looking at your friend. The one with the dark hair and piercings. I think he's hot."

She wasn't, but I don't miss the way Garret's jaw hardens or the way he glares at the guy currently playing pool with the rest of the guys.

"Are you alright?" Valen asks.

He means if I'm okay seeing Gary dead.

"Why would you care?"

"Not everyone takes seeing things like that very well."

"He's dead. I don't think you're supposed to."

"Do you want to talk about it? Alone," he asks suggestively.

Silence blankets between us for a beat. The tension grows thick.

"Go ahead. I'll catch up with you later," Rose says, breaking the awkward tension.

I slide out of the booth and follow Valen through the back exit.

"What?" I snap, leaning on the brick wall.

"Why are you mad?" Valen says this in a soft voice, placing his hand flat on the wall above me.

"I'm not mad."

"Scared?"

"I'm not."

His head dips. "You're mad at me."

I look to my left and right and notice we are alone. The sun is just beginning to set. I'm trying to hide the fact that I am upset that he didn't text me back after last night. He didn't tell me what happened, but in a way, I'm glad he didn't because one of the guys ended up dead.

"I'm..."

"You're mad because I didn't call you back. I was...busy."

A chill runs down my spine. He couldn't mean what I think...

"Doing what?"

He chuckles lightly. "I was doing homework."

"Homework?"

"I had a paper due. It's my senior year."

Fuck, right. Homework. What I'm supposed to be doing instead of worrying about why he didn't call me. Walking on campus and finding a dead body, not knowing if it's connected to me or not.

I sigh. "I know. I'm sorry. You don't owe me."

"Why didn't you ask me to go with you?"

"You mean to the game?"

He nods.

"Jealous?"

"Maybe?"

"He's just a friend from work. I didn't think football was your thing. Adam never mentioned you going to a game. I didn't think you were interested."

"I'm not. I was interested in going with you."

A flush creeps up my neck. Is he flirting with me?

"Maybe next time."

"How about I take you out?"

"When?" I find myself asking.

"Right now."

"Where?"

"I was thinking away from here. There are cops everywhere."

There are. The investigation has prompted the state police to step in, and chaos is currently raging on campus. I'm sure rumors will be running rampant by the same time tomorrow if they haven't found who did it.

"Alright."

"Alright," he repeats, lowering his head.

I look up, and before I know what is happening, his lips find mine. His hand wraps around my throat. We kiss. His tongue slides past my lips. My hands land on his hard chest. My tongue flicks the piercing on the corner of his lip. His hand wraps around my throat.

When we break the kiss, I'm stunned that it happened—that he kissed me.

"Let's go," he says softly, walking away.

My fingertips touch my swollen lips as I watch him walk toward his black Porsche. When the lights flash in greeting as he unlocks the car and opens the door, I drop my hands.

He drives away from campus. Away from the flashing lights and caution tape tied around the tree and the light post.

"It's crazy."

"What is?" he asks, looking straight ahead.

"That he died." I glance at him. "The way he died."

"Shit happens."

"It doesn't bother you?"

"I mean… It's fucked up. I didn't know him. All I know is what everyone else does. That he played football for Ohio."

"You didn't know him like you do Adam?"

He shakes his head. "Nah, not like that." He glances at me briefly. "You?"

I shake my head. "No. All I know is that he played football with Adam and hung around Zack. He was an asshole. I thought you would know more since you hung out at their frat parties."

"Is that what you think? That they are my friends."

"Aren't they?"

"No. Just because you saw me there when you weren't supposed to be there doesn't mean I'm friends with them. We don't go fishing together."

"It's no secret why I was there. I think everyone there made the fact that I wasn't supposed to be there a bigger deal than what it was."

"I'm glad you were there."

I furrow my brow. "But I thought you said..."

"If you weren't there, I wouldn't have known you existed. It wasn't like Adam would have introduced me to his much younger, underage little sister." He laughs. "I was glad Zack cheated on you, though. I know it sounds fucked up, but it's the truth."

"Why would you say that?"

"Because I'm fucked up, Melody."

"What do you mean?"

"I think you know."

"I don't."

I do, but I don't want to admit that part to him. I don't want to admit that part to myself.

"Do you like burgers?" he asks, changing the subject.

"Burgers?" He turns right into a fast food drive-through. "Yeah, who doesn't?"

He buys us both burgers. Then he drives down a secluded road, turns left, and stops in front of a lake.

"Why are we here?"

He pushes a button, and the car's rooftop retreats, revealing a sky so densely sprinkled with stars that it nearly swallows the dark. "You said you liked the stars in the summer sky. It's not summer, but it's the best I could do."

I want to melt. I want to cry. He heard every word.

Maybe that's why he wanted to read it before I turned it in to the professor. He wanted to read my thoughts.

I look up and smile. "Thank you."

"For?" He pauses between bites, his casual demeanor belying the depth of the moment.

The stars gleam with a brilliance that seems to intensify with each passing second. I pivot in my seat, facing him fully. "For listening."

"Is that what you like... for me to listen?"

"It's part of it, but I'm curious... why me?"

His response is to sip from his drink. "You'll find out soon enough."

"Is this your way of trying to get me to sleep with you?"

He's smooth; I'll give him that. He has this way of making me forget everything else. I want him, but I know it's dangerous to want someone like Valen. He's dark and unpredictable.

"Is that what you want?"

"It's obvious that's what you want." The accusation hangs between us, presenting a challenge.

The corner of his mouth lifts into a sexy grin. "Why lie? But I didn't bring you out here to fuck you."

"Why did you?"

"Because I wanted to be the one you spent your time with under the stars," he teases with a playful lilt in his voice.

My heart flips. A little laugh escapes my throat. "You want me to fall in love with you?"

His gaze lingers on my lips, intensifying the moment. The food forgotten, my heartbeat seems to echo above the wind's whispers and the distant chirps of crickets.

As the silence stretches, my thoughts wander to the reflection of the moon on the lake, casting a silver glow that dances across the water's surface. The soft ripples, the wind's caress, the memory of a kiss that left tingles lingering on my lips. But then...

What am I doing?

A guy like Valen must have countless girls fall for him. He could never fall in love with a girl like me.

Sleep with me, maybe?

Say the right things, always.

It's what guys like him do. It's in their DNA. We both know I'm not his type, and I'm sure it's one of the reasons my brother warned me to stay away so I don't end up being one of the girls he leaves depressed with a broken heart. It would make sense for my brother to worry after the way I reacted to Zack.

"What are you thinking about?"

I inwardly cringe within myself. He purposely ignored my last question. Of course he would.

Don't fall for it, Melody?

"I'm thinking… It's getting late, and I should be heading back."

His gaze drifts to the lake, contemplative, as if weighing his next words. I should have never left with him. I shouldn't have let him kiss me.

But I did.

After he follows me to my trailer, I push down the embarrassment that he can see how I live.

"You should really think about moving," he suggests.

I snort. "You sound like my brother."

"And I'm sure everyone who visits you."

I open the small door. "Except my landlord."

He looks toward the old house, with the broken-down Plymouth still parked over the cracked driveway and overgrown grass.

"He's still alive?" he teases. "I thought old man Crosby kicked the bucket."

"You know him?" I asked, my curiosity piqued.

"Who doesn't. He's like a hundred years old, but a nice old man. He likes you if he lets you stay on his property, and he likes the fact that you're paying him. I hope he isn't hustling you."

I shake my head. "Why does everyone have a problem with where I live?"

"Why did you move out of your parents' house?"

"The same reason all kids leave their parents' house."

"Ahh, rules and freedom."

"Do you live with yours?"

"No."

"How come? Rules?"

"Something like that."

"We aren't that different."

He looks at the trailer, then back at me. "Stay with me."

I look up at the star-lit sky and laugh. "Nice try, but I think I'm safer in my banged-up old trailer."

"Are you afraid of me, Melody? I promise not to bite."

It's me I don't trust, but I don't tell him that.

"I don't know... do you, Valen?"

His smile is enigmatic, but he plays dumb when he says, "I'll bite if you want me to and to ease your mind. You shouldn't be afraid of me. It's pointless."

"Oh yeah."

He nods, confident. "I get what I want, Melody. And what I want, you'll see."

"What is it that you want, Valen?"

He nudges his chin. "Get inside. It's getting late."

MELODY

"WHAT MOVIES DO you like to watch?"

Azriel shrugs, placing the batteries back on the shelf, his attention only half on me. "Whatever's interesting, I guess."

"Horror? Action?"

"I like horror. If it's good."

"You?"

"I like scary. When I could watch it."

"How come?"

I glance away, the question more loaded than I intended. "I had to move out of my parents' house. The constant fighting and the suffocating rules were too much. I'm not exactly the favorite, as you can tell."

"Brother can do no wrong?"

A laugh, bitter and short, escapes me. "Exactly."

"I know how you feel. Hey, want to watch a movie tonight? After work? I think Netflix added the latest *Friday The 13th*."

"Do you want me to come over to your place?"

He looks up in surprise. "You want to see it?" Azriel stammers.

I shrug. "Sure. If you promise not to be a murderer."

"Alright," he says with a smile.

He places the car in reverse and backs out of the parking lot of the hardware store. He said I could pick up my car later, and he would drive me home. I didn't want my brother stopping by and finding my car there, knowing I left with someone else in their car. It's Friday night. I'm sure he's out doing something, or maybe not. With one of the guys found murdered, I'm sure they are on lockdown anyway. Which means so are Zack and his stupid friends.

"I have plenty of room. Mrs. Mallory will stop by in the morning.

She always drops in on Saturdays to clean and make me breakfast," he rambles on nervously.

I don't think Azriel has many people coming over to his house.

"Who is Mrs. Mallory?"

He scratches his brow and keeps one hand on the steering wheel. "She takes care of the house. She's kind of like a mom slash grandma. You'll really like her."

"You live alone?"

He nods. "Most of the time."

He presses the music app onto the screen. Three Days Grace's "Never Too Late" begins to play.

We drive past Kenyan and notice an uptick in campus security in an upscale neighborhood behind the university. It's secluded and dark.

He makes a right, then a left, and drives down a dark road to a large metal gate. No houses are on either side, hidden behind thick greenery, ancient trees, and sprawling branches. There are two black lampposts on each side of the large pillars. He pushes one of the three buttons on the visor. The gate swings open, and he drives through the winding path leading to a large modern home.

"Wow," I whisper in awe.

The house is gorgeous. Well-lit with white walls and black windows. Clear-encased light fixtures separate all six garage spaces.

"You live here?"

"Yep. I told you I had a lot of space."

"How…"

But I stop myself. It's none of my business. I think Mr. Crosby said his father owns the hardware store, but I have never seen him. Maybe he left the business to Azriel. It's not far-fetched. Azriel is what? Twenty-one. His parents must have had money or something. Everyone born in Kenya has money. They have history.

"Don't worry. I'm not a drug dealer or anything. I swear. You can check."

I grin. "I believe you, Azriel. I never expected this. You have a nice home."

He smiles at the compliment. "You should check out the inside. I have a pool. You can jump in if you want. It's heated." He gets out.

I don't think Azriel hangs out with people all that much. He keeps to himself, and maybe he is better off with people who love him. Veronica has had her share of assholes with the life she has lived, and she has lived here all her life. I don't know all the details about her husband or exactly what went down, and Adam doesn't tell me much.

All I know is that she had it rough before she married her husband, Alaric. I kept in touch until the night when my life turned upside down, and I changed. It's like I stood in the middle of a blackout when the light turned back on, and everything shifted focus. My perception is different.

I stopped calling. I got a new phone. I moved out of my parents' house. Everything happened so fast in the past seven months. I can't believe I'm here and not in my room planning how I'm not going to tell my parents I'm going out to a party to find a cute boy I want to fuck.

He opens the door with his phone and lets me walk in first before he closes the door behind me. I'm greeted with whitewashed hardwood floors, nude-colored walls, and modern furniture. The red-lit pool is clearly visible through the floor-to-ceiling windows. The house smells like vanilla and cedarwood. It's clean and comfortable. It's probably the nicest house I've ever been in.

I like that it's hidden. It's like a celebrity lives here. Safe and sophisticated. It looks like nothing Azriel would pick out for a home.

When I glance at him, I see his innocence, but I can tell there is also fearlessness about how he does things. The way he stood up for me against Zack and the guys. He held my hand when he knew I needed it at the table in front of my brother. He didn't hesitate. The way he talked to Zack. It showed me he cared. It showed me he was my friend, and I shouldn't be afraid.

"Azriel?" I call out.

Lost in my thoughts, I didn't see where he went. The lights turn on, eliminating the darkness in the huge kitchen with white marble countertops and white wood cabinets.

He opens the fridge. "Yeah," he says, reaching inside.

"Thank you for bringing me here. For sharing your home with me."

He hands me a bottle of water. "No problem," he says, lowering his gaze.

"Hey, are you okay?"

He gives me a small smile. "Yeah, I'm not used to having anyone over."

"Oh," I say, bewildered. "Well, I'm glad you invited me."

He gives me a tour of the impressive home but respectfully leaves out his bedroom and the main bedroom. He shows me the guest bedroom. It has a queen bed with two large nightstands and a walk-in closet. A large floor-length mirror was nailed to the wall. It has access to a bathroom with a free-standing tub and double vanity.

"You can stay in this room. No one has ever used this room. It would be a shame to have you stay in the trailer instead of here. It's perfect, and I think you'll be safer. And…"

"You won't be alone."

"I guess we both get something. You get a place, and I get someone to hang out with after work. There's internet and a study to do homework. I hope I'm not offending you with where you live, but I thought— "

"You've thought this through," I tease him, playfully lightening the mood.

He flicks off the light in the bathroom. "I didn't give it much thought because I didn't need to."

My chest squeezes.

"Thank you, Azriel. I'll think about it."

"Take all the time you need. It's here if you want it."

I feel like I'm floating. I'm warm. I feel safe, like nothing could get me. Not the nightmares. Not the memories that plague me or the need to run. The weird smell on my hands from scrubbing my skin instead causes tingles like feathers, awakening all my nerve endings.

I don't know where I am, and then it all comes back to me. The popcorn. The scary movie I couldn't say no to when Azriel suggested watching *The Conjuring* after *Friday, the 13th*, and I ended up falling asleep on the loveseat.

I peel my eyes open. My tongue stuck to the roof of my mouth because of all the popcorn, soda, and candy Azriel offered. It was like he had a snack machine. He had every candy there was.

When my eyes adjust to the stream of light coming through the curtains, I recognize the linen curtains. I'm in the guest room.

I feel something large and hard next to me. My head snaps to my right, and my heart drops. Hazel eyes look straight at me.

"You're beautiful when you sleep."

I scoot to the edge of the bed and look down. I sigh in relief that my clothes are still on. The only thing missing are my shoes.

Panic sets in my veins.

"How did you...?"

"The same way you did, the front door."

I look around. "Where's Azriel? If you hurt him, I'll—"

He chuckles. "He's sleeping in his room." He places the palm of his hand under his cheek and holds his head with his elbow bent on the bed. "He likes you, and that's a lot. He doesn't like anyone."

I'm standing on the side of the bed when I ask, "How do you know him?"

"Get back in bed, and I'll tell you."

I shake my head. "I can't."

"I've taken care of my hard work three times. All in your name. I'm good for a while."

"Very funny," I mock.

"I don't joke when it comes to getting away from the thought of you. Get back in bed, and I'll tell you."

I sit on the bed and mimic the way he is stretching out on the bed.

He pushes off and leans close. His eyes glide slowly over my face. "Azriel is my little brother. My mother died giving birth to him. My father blamed it on him and disowned him. Since he is technically the son of one of the founding fathers of Kenya, he is still entitled, but not in my father's eyes. I was too young to take care of him until I turned fifteen and took matters into my own hands. Azriel lived with the housekeeper my mother employed to take care of us before her death until I was able to step in."

My heart aches for Azriel. It's why he feels so alone.

"I asked Azriel to bring you here and look out for you at the hardware store. That's why he was ready to defend you against that prick of an ex-boyfriend of yours. Why did he agree to go wherever you asked without making it obvious? They thought they would be able to kick my little brother's ass." Valen grins, but it doesn't reach his eyes. "I taught him how to defend himself, and I made a promise to him. No one would be able to hurt him, but he needs to keep to himself and not show up in places where they will recognize him. Azriel is a Vikiar, Melody. He's the legitimate son of a Kenyan."

"I thought you were the last son of your generation."

"Not the case for Azriel. Most people don't know he exists, and I plan to keep it that way. And he doesn't need to attend Kenyan."

I have so many questions I want to ask, but I start with, "Is this your house?"

"One of them. This is my main home. Azriel lives where I do, and for now, this is it. He wants for nothing, and he likes working at the hardware store."

"Who owns the hardware store?" I ask.

The suspicion of how everything is falling into place nags in the back of my mind.

"I do, Melody. I own the hardware store where you work, and it was my idea to have Azriel offer to have you live with us. It's not safe in the trailer. I didn't want your brother to find out what I'd done. I didn't want him to know how I felt about you."

His words nag in the back of my mind. *I get what I want. You'll see.*

I can see in his eyes that he's ashamed of his addiction. Everyone knows he sleeps around.

"Did you set me up? Mr. Crosby. The job at the store? Azriel?"

His eyes fall to my lips. "Not in the way that you think, but yes. I want you, Melody. Since the first time I saw you fighting for the wrong man, I've wanted you. I told you that."

Fear and anger wash over me, but the intense way he is looking at me has me holding back. I want to yell and scream at him. He doesn't have the right to control my life. I don't understand his motive. Is it sex? There is some twisted game he is trying to play.

"What do you want? Sex? A thrill to get you off? Is this a game you want to play? A campus prank for fun?" I shake my head. "I don't get it. Look at you. Look at me."

"I'm not following. I want sex, but not on a one-night stand. I brought you to the party the other day to show you my impulses." He pauses and goes on, "I'm not playing a game. Yeah, I did some shit to get you into Kenyan and away from Ohio. There are things you don't understand, Melody. All you need to know is that I want you. I want a normal fucking relationship with a girl. I've never had one that wasn't focused on sex."

"Explain it to me."

He leans over me. Everything is bright from the sun streaming between the curtains. The blue in his eyes is bright. My heart beats faster than a freight train.

"It is true that I suffer from hypersexuality, Melody. I like sex because it gives me a high, like a drug. I wasn't lying when I said it the first time."

"So the person who's with you has to accept..."

He rests his elbows on the side of my head. "No. I'm not saying that. I don't want to cheat on the person I'm with. That's what makes it so hard. After my mother died giving birth to my brother, my father spiraled. He blamed my brother for her death. My father can't look at him without remembering that she died. In his eyes, it's like he killed her."

"That is awful."

Poor Azriel.

"Mrs. Mallory took him in until I was old enough to send her money and provide for him. I had to keep him away from everyone, or my father would get angry. He would do anything to make him suffer because, in his eyes, he's suffering because of Azriel. My father never loved me. My mother was the love of his life and still is, but he spends his time having meaningless sex with random women. It's all I have ever seen. Different women." His eyes lift. "When I had sex for the first time with a woman my father brought, I liked the feeling.

I was fifteen, and it was the only thing that felt good. The only thing I didn't have to work hard to get. I don't know what love is because my father never showed me what it's supposed to be like. The closest I have to love is caring for my brother. I don't know how to love a woman in the real sense. The only relationship I know is through sex, and when I'm done…"

"You move on to the next."

He nods. "Except with you. I don't want that. I want to..."

"Want to what?" I am confused.

"I want to try. I want to be the one to take you to the dark sky and burn with the stars, Melody. I want to be that."

"So you don't want to have sex?" I'm confused.

"Right now, my body says... yes. But my heart says it's not ready, Melody." He looks away. "If you don't like me, I understand. I'll leave you alone. You can still go to school, and I'll look after you. I'll do that because I promised your brother I would, and I don't want to hurt you. I want…"

"Does he know?"

I do like him. I think he's hot, scary, and dangerous. I wouldn't know where to begin with someone like him. I don't know how far I can go without losing what's left of myself completely.

"Your brother doesn't know how I feel about you, Melody. I'm not going to lie. I'm not a good guy. I've done things I'm not proud of, but I want you." He gestures back and forth between us. "I want to explore whatever this is."

I don't know what to say. Valen Vikiar wants to date me. A guy who every girl on and off campus wants. A guy who every girl on campus has fucked. How do I compete with that?

I look away. "I didn't think I was someone you found attractive," I stammer. "I'm nothing…"

"You're gorgeous, Melody." He closes his eyes like he's in pain. "I want to show you, but... then you wouldn't believe me. It will put things in your mind you're not sure of, and when it happens, I want you to trust me. I want you to…"

"I don't know if I could, Valen. I trusted someone with my body, and they betrayed me in the worst way. I'm no good for anyone."

"He cheated because he's an idiot. I told him to stay away from you." He smiles. "He was jealous when he saw you with Azriel."

"They wanted to beat him up."

"Azriel would have handled it."

"Azriel would have handled it," I mock.

"My brother is nice, but again, like I said, he can defend himself. What kind of brother do you think I am?"

"I don't know because I don't know you."

"Get to know me."

"I'll think about it."

"Will you take our offer to stay here instead of the trailer?"

"I don't think that's a good idea, Valen." I look around the room, taking in the comfort and space compared to the trailer. What if he heard me having a nightmare or changed his mind and kicked me out?"

"I see the wheels turning in that pretty head of yours. Azriel is here, and so is Mrs. Mallory. You'll love her. It's safer. I don't like you staying in the trailer by yourself."

"What would my brother say if he found out?"

"You're renting a room. He doesn't know about Azriel."

"Who does?"

"Alaric. Only the sons of Kenyan and the founding fathers of the school know about Azriel."

"Jess?"

I regret saying her name as soon as it slipped out. I don't know why I mentioned her. It's the second time I've done it, but they have history.

"No." The curve of his mouth turns into a side grin. My cheeks heat. He knows I'm jealous. "I don't love Jess, Melody. Yes, I slept with her, but I was confused about my feelings for her. It's one of the reasons I'm holding back because I want more with you."

"I don't trust you," I admit. More to myself than to him.

"I know, but I want you to. I'm going to do everything I can so you will."

"We'll see."

VALEN

AFTER I DROP Melody off at the hardware store so she can get her car, I drive toward Reid and Jess's house. When the butler lets me into their sprawling mansion right on the outskirts of Kenyan, I find Reid seated on the sofa in the family room watching *Saw X*.

"Really, dude?" I say sarcastically. "Kids live here."

He waves me away. "I can't watch it when they're here. Gia took the little one shopping with Draven. She wants them to bond or whatever."

I sit on the loveseat. "Taking advantage?"

"Yep."

I look at the oversized television screen and then see Jess walk inside from the back patio.

"Hi," she says with a smile. "How's school?"

"It's good," I tell her. But I didn't come to talk about school, and the look she gives me tells me she knows it.

"What brings you by?"

"I wanted to talk to you guys. I haven't seen you since school started."

That part is not a lie.

"What's up?" Reid pauses the movie at the part where the guy straps himself to the chair, wearing two long plastic tubes over his eyes like a vacuum.

"I wanted to talk to you about a girl."

Jess sits next to Reid with a smile on her face. She hates that I have to marry Melissa, so this topic has all her attention.

I look at her now, and it's crazy that I don't find her attractive like I used to. I don't get hard around her or think about fucking her against the wall. Ever since Melody came into the picture, I don't think about having sex unless it's with her. I thought it was because I haven't, because she's forbidden, or because she's Prey.

"What girl? Who is she?" Jess asks with interest.

I glance at Reid. "It's Melody. Adam's little sister."

Silence.

You could hear the hum of the air conditioner as it turned on. The vent was blowing cool air on my flushed skin.

I said it. I admitted it for the first time to my closest friends. Friends that are like family, my secret. A secret I've carried since the first time I laid eyes on her.

"Valen," Reid warns.

Jess has her eyebrows raised in shock.

"I know. I-I know… she's…"

"It's not that, Valen," Reid says, concern etched in his tone. "She has been through a lot with school, and she's..."

"Prey," Jess finishes for him. "You realize that bringing her on campus in Kenyan makes her a target. It wasn't what we agreed. She has to choose, and you know how that turns out with everything else."

"What do you mean? It's not like before," I say, defensively looking between them.

I can protect Melody. I will protect her.

"If Melissa finds out, you know she will do whatever it takes to destroy her. She's delicate. She's young, Valen. And you're…"

A man with satyriasis

Jess doesn't say it, but it's there, floating above us in the room. I never thought Jess would be judgmental, given everything we've been through.

"Dude, she was kicked out of Ohio by the football team. That asshole, Zack, screwed with her future and put her brother in a bad place. He has to play, look at the asshole that fucked with his little sister's future, and play football with him. He humiliated her. Hurting her is the last thing she needs. She is not like the girls you hang around with," Reid says.

He means the kind I sleep with.

"Are you saying I'm too dirty for her? I'm too fucked up to be with a girl like Melody."

"I didn't say that," Reid says defensively.

"I like her."

"You like a lot of girls, Valen. Pick one on campus, have fun, and move on to the next. It's what has always made you happy. You used to be more outgoing. You didn't care about one girl when you could have your pick. This is your senior year. Yeah, it sucks that you have to marry Melissa, but she'll let you do it. She doesn't care who you fuck. She doesn't expect anything."

"So I can't have a meaningful relationship? You guys can, but I can't."

I can't believe this. I can't believe they think I'm incapable of loving someone.

I get up, having heard enough of this bullshit. I thought they would understand. I thought Jess would understand and encourage me to have a relationship with someone.

"Where are you going?" Jess says it with a concerned edge to her voice.

"I gotta go. I have practice. Say *hi* to the munchkin for me. She's gorgeous."

I do have practice, but it's in two hours. Reid is giving me a look that says he knows this.

Jess gives me a peck on the cheek that I don't return. I fist-bump Reid and walk out.

I'm walking to my Porsche when the front door opens, and Jess rushes toward me.

"Valen, wait…" She stops in front of me with a soft expression. "I'm sorry about what I said back there. I didn't mean it the way it sounded. I can't forget the way you were with me when I was going through my own shit. I'm sorry for the way I acted. It was insensitive." She blows out a puff of air. "Melody, huh?"

I nod. "Yeah, I like her." I look at the key fob in my hand and then at her. "I want to date her. I want…"

"What?" she asks. "What is it that you want?"

"I want to be with her, Jess. I want her to fall in love with me, and I don't know how, and I'll do anything to make that happen."

"Is that why you got her the scholarship? It was you that made sure she didn't get back into Ohio, wasn't it?"

"In a way. I didn't want her to be around that asshole. There wasn't enough to get him kicked off indefinitely, and his parents are lawyers. I didn't want people sniffing around. I didn't want to draw any more attention to Melody. She's…different."

She nods. "That makes sense, but what are you going to do about Melissa? And I know Reid isn't going to ask in front of me, but was it you?"

I snort. "You didn't think I was going to marry her, did you? And no, I didn't have anything to do with the dead kid. It wasn't me. It wasn't us. As for Melissa, I'll never marry that bitch. She's horrible and a jealous crazy bitch that doesn't know if she likes dick or pussy."

Jess smiles in agreement. "I couldn't agree more." Her smile falls, like she just thought of something bad. "Make sure she doesn't know about Melody, and if she does, make sure she stays away from her Valen."

"I know."

"Does Melody know about Melissa?"

"Not yet. It would kind of ruin my chances of asking her out on a date."

Technically, lunch at my restaurant was a date, but she didn't know that.

"I guess…yeah, it would." She tucks her hair behind her ear. "Have you two?"

"Had sex?"

She nods.

"I want to. I mean, she knows I want her, and I told her my problem, and she said... she would think about it." I rush out.

Jess grins. "She turned you down?"

"The first time, yes."

"I like her. She's making you work for it. I think she would be good for you, Valen. I saw her at the diner once. She's hot, and she doesn't know it. You'll have your hands full. If you need anything from me or from us, count us in. You know that, right?"

"I know. It's why I came to talk to you guys."

She gives me a hug, and all is right again between us. I feel better. I'm confident I can make this work.

She pulls away. "Do you know who killed that guy from Ohio?"

I look at her and give the only answer I can give her. "No."

After practice, Garret walks up to me while I'm changing in the locker room. I feel relaxed after pushing myself harder than usual. I'm worked up because I need to have sex. I want to come, but the girl I want to come inside of doesn't trust me. I can't jerk off in the locker room shower after practice around a bunch of guys. I'm frustrated. I'm so fucking weak.

"Hey, man. Are you going to the party?"

Normal Valen would smile and say hell yes to alcohol and easy pussy, but I'm not that guy anymore. I want to ask Melody Price if she will go to my house and watch movies so I can kiss her lips and then go to the shower and jerk off thinking about how they would feel around my ribbed cock.

"I can't. I have plans."

He smirks. "She still turned you down, huh?"

"No."

"Liar. I still can't believe you made me take that creative writing class again. We won't get credit for it, you know."

"Fuck you," I tease. "Like you care."

"I can't. I'm straight. Now I know why you did it, but it's not like you. I'm not going to give you shit about it. It's a nice class, and I like to hear the girls read about their fantasies so I can fuck them out of it."

I shove him playfully and pull my shirt over my head. For the first time, I hate what his comment implied. What everyone thinks of me. I'm a sex-crazed maniac. One that can't be with one girl.

I can't get over how perfectly we fit when I was leaning over her in the guest bedroom of my house. I waited for my brother to hopefully convince her to come over and see the house. I knew I couldn't do it myself, so my brother, the perfect guy he is, said he would do it if he got the chance. I almost fist-punched the air when he texted me, and he got her to come to our house. I want to keep her. I want to seduce her in every way. If she only knew what I planned to do to her body.

MELODY

AFTER WORK ON TUESDAY, I went to Ulta and bought the best acne treatment they had in stock. I didn't care if it was expensive. I researched the best one you could buy over the counter. I saw YouTube videos and came up with a skin routine for Azriel. It was the least I could do for him after he stood up for me Friday night. Valen put him up to it, but I ultimately invited him, so I was still on the fence about the whole thing.

Deep down, it was an excuse to see Valen. I don't have class with him on Tuesdays. On Monday, he was quiet and observant. I could feel the heat of his gaze on my back, but I didn't turn around. I tried to concentrate on what the professor was saying, but all I could think about was the scent of his skin. How close he was on the bed. The way his eyes tried to stay above my chin.

The old me would have let him fuck me. Old Melody would have arched my neck and let him kiss me. Old Melody would have lifted her hips slightly, letting him know what I wanted, but that was the old me. The new me is scared. Scared that I'll freak out and be unable to come.

There are tiny moments when I want to try. To test what I feel for him. Is it fear? Or fear that I would like it too much and want him all the time.

For now, I'll never know because something else nags the back of my mind in this school. The weird glances I get from the guys. The knowing smiles from the girls when I walk by. At first, I thought it was because I was new, but it's the same people.

I pull up to the gate to Valen's house, and it swings open.

Twilight cloaks the sky as the sun sets on the horizon. The lights on the pillars cast a glow on the driveway. I spot Azriel's truck, but disappointment fills me when I don't see Valen's black Porsche.

My stomach clenches, thinking he's out with someone else. I wouldn't be surprised. I haven't given him an answer. Then a part of me says, it was a test and if he's off fucking someone else, that I dodged a bullet.

The front door opens and Azriel appears with a smile. "Changed your mind?" he says with a grin.

I close the door to my car with the Ulta bag in hand. "Not yet, but I got you something."

His eyebrows raise in surprise. "For me?"

I walk inside. "Yeah. I hope you won't be mad, but I thought…" I trail off.

I didn't think about his feelings when the thought popped in my head. Shit. I hope he won't hate me after this. I meant well, but he could be sensitive about his acne.

Valen said he only had Mrs. Mallory as a mother figure. She's an older woman probably in her late sixties. She might not know what options are available for sensitive skin. Skin care has come a long way nowadays, but that doesn't mean he might not get offended.

"What's in the bag?"

I sit on one of the stools in the kitchen and begin taking out the items. The five-step kit, cleanser, night cream, wash pads, and exfoliator.

He looks at all the items spread out on the marble countertop. He picks up the kit and reads. I watch as recognition plays out on his features. My stomach clenches when he doesn't say anything and stares at the box. He slowly places it on the counter and then glances at all the other items.

"I thought this would be good for you to try. I hope you're not mad at me," I say in a soft voice.

He looks up. "I could never be mad at you, Melody. Thank you," he says with a soft expression. "How does it all work?"

I inwardly sigh in relief, open the box, and read the instructions. He sits on the stool next to me, and I place the items in order. I explain what each one does, how to use it, and when. He listens intently. After a skin test to make sure he isn't allergic to anything, I start to apply the cream to his skin.

After he washes his face, he sits in front of me, and I can't help but compare him to Valen. There are similarities and differences.

"Do you have a girlfriend?" I ask.

He shakes his head slowly, trying not to move so I don't get the cream in his eyes. "No."

"Have you ever had a girl…"

"No."

I pause with the cotton pad in midair. "How come?" I ask in disbelief.

He points at his face. "I don't think girls dig the pizza face."

"I've seen worse in high school. Trust me, girls would dig you."

He shrugs. "I'm not my brother."

I smile. "No, you're not. You're you, and that is all that matters. Besides, I think you're cute."

His eyes widen as soon as the words leave my mouth. "You think I'm good looking?"

I do. He is cute and sweet. He could have any girl if he would talk to one.

"Why would you think you aren't?"

"I thought I wasn't because…"

"Of you having acne on your face?"

"Almost all the guys I've come across at school have acne. Some more than others. Girls, too. Except girls are more self-conscious about the way we look all the time. We have makeup and a slew of products to choose from to cover it all up."

"I think mine is really bad."

"It's not that bad, Azriel. Nothing a good skin care routine won't fix."

"Thank you. How much do I owe you?"

"Nothing. It's my way of thanking you for the other night. You saved my ass."

"My brother did."

I wipe the side of his face. "Before…when Zack first showed up at the table."

"I knew something was wrong when he showed up. You tensed up, and the way he was looking at you, I knew it wasn't good." He pauses like he's trying to find the right words. "Did he hurt you? Physically. Did he...?" My hand pauses in midair. He looks at me, waiting.

I grab another cleansing pad so I can apply the cream to his chin. The silence is thick between us. I don't know how to answer without lying, but at the same not tell him the truth. He would tell Valen. Valen would tell Adam, and my parents would find out. I'll be humiliated. My parents would make a big deal and not let me out of the house or, worse, send me to a center for treatment. All of these would be useless because they don't make a wrong a right. It doesn't stop them from doing it again to me or someone else. The worst part is the humiliation. The pity.

They would make me tell them things about that night I'm not sure of. Things I hardly remember myself but know they happened.

Even if they confronted them, they would say I was stalking Zack and made it up. They would say I was mad that he broke up with me or spin it in a way where it was my fault. That I'm crazy and unstable. It's all of them against me.

I rub the cream with the cotton pad gently on his chin.

Our eyes meet. His friendly. Mine full of fear.

He sees the truth dancing in the depth of my eyes but doesn't say anything. There is so much silence can say that words don't. Sometimes the truth doesn't need to be said to know that something bad happened. You can feel it. It snakes up your skin and whispers in your ear.

"Does my brother know?"

"Does he know what? I ask dumbly, but I do know. He wants to know if his brother knows that I was raped by Zack and his friends. "Valen knows them. Probably better than he should. He goes to their parties. I've seen him there." I smile weakly. "Before, when I used to go to those things. The first time I went, Valen was there."

He lowers his head and stares at the ground like he's lost in thought. "You don't...go. Anymore?"

"I don't drink or go to parties anymore," I say quietly. "I don't date either."

He nods, and I think he gets it. I think he understands why I live in a trailer. Why I'm skittish. Why I don't accept his offer even though it's a good one. Because I can't trust anyone.

I start on his forehead and concentrate on his trouble spots before I have to clean up and then begin the next step.

The sound of a metal chain has me looking up. Valen leans on the wall, playing with his wallet chain with his fingers. His eyes shift between me and his brother. His jaw set. His blond hair flat and tousled. His shirt rides up, revealing the band of his Alexander McQueen boxers under his black ripped jeans and black combat boots. Valen is goth personified with his style while outside of work. Azriel is hot emo boy.

Similar but different.

"Hey, I didn't hear you come in," I say with a nervous smile.

His expression is blank. I hope I didn't overstep by stopping by without letting him know.

Azriel doesn't glance in his direction or greet him. I find it odd but don't point it out. I have no idea how they interact with each other when I'm not around.

MELODY

WHEN I SAW her car in the driveway, my heart was pounding in my chest. Did she change her mind? Is she staying? When I entered quietly and saw her with my younger brother, my heart sank. The way she was taking care of him. It didn't bother her that he has acne and is full of pimples. I was also surprised he let her touch his face. He doesn't let anyone talk to him about it. I've tried, but he always changes the subject or goes to his room to play video games. I felt bad. I wanted to take him to a doctor, but he always brushed it aside and said he was fine when I knew he wasn't.

I tried not to let my jealousy get me into a chokehold. It's a foreign emotion. One that I'm not used to. One that I have to get ahold of. He's my brother, but she's the girl I want.

The one with the hair I itch to touch. The skin I wish to lick and the pussy I want to fuck. And she is currently taking care of my brother while he looks at her like she's the girl of his dreams.

There is a knot in my throat when she slides off the stool to wash her hands.

My brother won't look at me, and I know something is wrong.

He's mad.

He does this when I've upset him, and that is the last thing I want.

"Hey, man. You invited her?"

I'm fishing for information. I could easily ask her, but I want an excuse to talk to him. To feel him out. Look where his head is.

"No, she stopped by to surprise me. She went and bought me this"—he picks up a bottle of acne cream—"for my face and came to show me how to use it."

The way he said it, I have a ball stuck in my throat.

I try to swallow and manage to say, "Oh, I had no idea she was stopping by."

"Is there a problem?" he asks with an eyebrow raised.

My lips twitch because of the funny way he looks with the white cream all over his face.

"It looks like someone jizzed on your face, but no, I don't have a problem."

"She did this for me."

"I did what?" Melody asks, walking back into the kitchen.

"Nothing," we both say in tandem.

I point to the sliding glass door and say, "I'll be outside while you two finish up."

"You don't have to go. I'm almost done," she says.

But she doesn't understand that I'm jealous. I'm jealous of her alone with my brother. I want to take her to my room, rip her clothes off, and claim her as mine. I don't want her taking care of his face or stopping by because of him. I want her to stop by because she can't stand not being around me. It's shitty of me to think this way, but there is something else that bothers me. She told him she didn't date. I caught that part when I walked in, but then there was silence. There was more I didn't catch. I want to know more. What did she say before I showed up? What did she tell him? What did he ask?

Did he ask her out, and she turned him down? Does Azriel want Melody for himself?

I jump in the pool after taking my clothes off and swim in just my boxers. I take my frustration out in the pool. Both angry and sexual. I thought of going to the shower to jerk off and think about her, but that would be weird. She's in the house with my brother, and I'm fucking myself in the next room at the thought of her.

I break the surface when I reach the end of the pool and see her watching me from the edge.

"Want to go for a swim?" I ask.

"I don't have a bathing suit."

I look down at my boxers, the imprint of my dick piercings visible underneath the water with bright red lights. "I don't either." She blushes and looks away. I take the opportunity to get closer to the edge so she can't see how hard my cock is. "Jump in. It's warm." Her eyes land on me. "There is nothing to worry about. I won't let you drown. I'm a good swimmer."

"I heard you're the best swimmer in Kenyan, possibly in the state of Ohio."

She isn't wrong. After the guys graduated, I was the best.

"You should come and see me sometime. Judge for yourself."

"You want me to see you swim?"

"Yeah, why not? Have you ever been to a swim meet?"

"I never knew a guy who swam competitively before."

"Now you do." I smile. "Will you come see me on Friday? Cheer for me?"

"You want me to cheer for you?" She laughs. "I think you have plenty of people to cheer for you."

"But I want you there, and..." I smile. "For you to tell me if I suck. If I don't, and win, you promise to let me take you out on a date."

Her smile fades, and I get nervous inside. I want her to see me swim. I want everyone to know she is there because of me. I also want to take her out on a real date with flowers and shit.

"I don't know, Valen," she stammers. I see something in her eyes. Fear. I would never hurt her. "I don't mind going to see you compete, but I'm not…"

"Are you afraid I will hurt you, Melody?"

Her eyes lift, and my stomach sinks. Dread slides in my veins. Air leaves my lungs. I've seen that look before. Not on her, but...

Her eyes are glassy. "I-I…"

No, no, no.

Who?

Then it dawns.

She is leaving her parents' house. *I don't drink. I don't go to parties. I don't date.* What she told Azriel when I walked in. At the restaurant, she was hesitant. She used to have this spark. It's what drew me in. Her fire. It's what I've been trying to find when I look at her, and I can't find it.

Rage burns in the back of my eyes. I tear my gaze from hers so she doesn't see what I feel. What I want to do.

"Who hurt you, Melody?" I ask in a pained voice.

She looks at the water, then at me. "I don't remember," she mutters.

She doesn't want to tell me or...

"Where?" I am confused.

She steps back and shakes her head slowly. "It doesn't matter," she says, giving me a tight smile. She's hiding from something or from someone. She doesn't trust anyone, but that's going to change.

"Come here," I demand.

She takes two small steps forward. I pull myself out of the water, not caring that she can see the imprint of my cock under my wet boxers plastered to my thighs. Her eyes roam appreciatively over my chest, down to my stomach, and lower.

Water drips on my skin, and my skin pebbles from the cool breeze. I reach with my hand slowly, not caring if I'm wetting her black top when I caress her bottom lip with the pad of my thumb.

"I would never hurt you, Melody. Whatever happened, I want you to know you could tell me. When you're ready, I promise, I'll make it right. You don't have to be afraid of me or Azriel. We wouldn't let anything happen to you." She steps closer. The heat from her skin caresses mine. Her lips are inches from the middle of my chest.

Her eyes dip to my erection. "I'm not going to excuse the fact that I want you," I say with a smile. "But I would never force you. I want that to sink in," I say, leaning close to her ear, "and when I find out who hurt you, nothing will stop me from taking what they loved the most. It will hurt, Melody. I promise they will remember."

She turns her head, and our lips meet. I cup her delicate face in my hands and slide my tongue between her lips, sealing my promise with my tongue. Her dainty fingers land flat on my chest. A whimper escapes her throat. I deepen the kiss, pressing my hard cock into her lower belly.

Kissing her makes me feel like time has stopped and reset. It can last forever, like a short circuit that keeps tripping over and over until I break the kiss, leaving her breathless.

Our chests are rising and falling. My heart hammers inside my chest. My cock begs for me to take her, but I won't. Not until she is ready. Until she accepts that I want her and she wants me, even if what I really want is to take her clothes off and get back in the pool so I can lay her on the lounge chair on the sun deck and lick her skin, watch her nipples harden as I suck one, then the other, while she gazes at the dark sky, recalling the moment when I caressed her skin with my tongue, just before I fucked myself and rubbed my cum over her tits like body oil.

I'm thinking this while she stares at me. Her eyes were full of lust, not wanting to let go. I was afraid of what I might do. I am afraid of what it would mean if she did it, but I need her. I need to feel her just a little.

She is the heroin, and I'm the addict, and I would do anything for a taste.

"Can I convince you to go in the pool with me?" I ask hopefully.

She must have seen the want in my gaze and the way my cock wouldn't calm down. She looks over her shoulder, probably worried that my brother will see her.

She looks back and bites her lip. "Umm..."

"You're wearing panties, aren't you?" I whisper.

She smiles and nods. It didn't matter if she wore them or not; I would still get a glimpse of her pussy and the shape of her tits. What I've seen so far is nice. Firm upthrust breasts I want to suck on. A plump ass inside her jeans.

"It's like a bathing suit." I look down at my thin boxers molded to my thighs and my hard dick. "Only thinner, but essentially the same concept."

She agrees because she removes her shirt. I stand hypnotized, not getting back in the pool in case she changes her mind.

She pulls her jeans down her thighs and takes off her shoes and socks. Her panties stay on, like her bra. They're hot pink. It reminds me of what her pussy must look like spread open along with the cheeks of her ass when I tongue it.

I look at the sky and smile when I see the clouds move and the stars appear. I still want to be the guy she first talked about in class.

The one who burns with her like the stars, but the guy who kills anyone who hurts her.

I tell myself that, in time, I'll find out. I'll start at the source. The one who called her ugly and body shamed her after she gave herself to him. The same one that looked at her like she still belonged to him. Zack.

She walks over to the shallow part of the built-in sun deck. She dips her foot to test out the water. The jets cause the water to bubble, like boiling water on a stove. It's warm, so I know she won't back out, telling me it's too cold.

I slide into the pool without making a splash when she steps in, and I feel giddy like a high school idiot about to get his first taste of pussy. She turns sideways, and my dick twitches when I notice she's wearing a thong.

She's gorgeous. Her stomach is flat and smooth, her hips flared slightly, and she has a perfect ass, with the tips of her hair hitting right above her nipples, plush lips, a straight nose, and dark lashes.

My eyes dip to the triangle part of her panties, tracing the outline of her pussy lips.

Melody is gorgeous.

"You're gorgeous," I admit. "Any man who tells you differently is a liar and doesn't want you to be with anyone else. It's what an insecure asshole says to a girl he can't keep. I think you're stunning."

"Is this your way of convincing me to sleep with you?" she teases with a grin.

"Maybe," I tease right back.

She sits in the lounge chair, touching the water bubbling on the surface with her fingers. I reach for her. My hands touch her smooth legs up her thigh.

"Is this okay?" I ask.

"Yes."

Her nipples are stiff under the thin fabric of her pink bra, sticking to her skin. Her breasts are big and firm. Perfect. She has a deep valley that I want to slide my tongue through.

My hands are on her hips. I'm on my knees, leaning slightly over her. My eyes trail her smooth skin. The strap of her bra hangs slightly off her right shoulder. I reach out and put it back in place when she surprises me by arching her back, and it falls right back. The cup of her bra barely contains her nipples.

My mouth is full of saliva. I'm fucking drooling over her. She looks hot seated on the lounger in the pool in only her pink underwear.

The tip of my tongue glides over her thighs. I savor the smell of her skin and memorize the way she tastes. A hint of strawberry and her. *My Melody*.

My tongue continues over her stomach until I reach her barely covered nipple. My eyes lift. I see the acquiescence in her gaze. I tease her soft skin with the inner part of her bottom lip. I lick. Her breath hitches, and I lick harder.

She tilts her head back and closes her eyes. I tug at her bra, freeing her heavy-set breasts. Fuck.

I suck on her tits until they are wet from my saliva and the pool water. I grip both in my hands and squeeze, sucking them like two juicy fruits. She whimpers and lifts her hips. I hold her steady and kiss her. I lick her lips, chin, neck, and then the little spot in the center of her throat.

"Play with your pussy, baby," I rasp on her skin. "Show me. Spread your cunt open for me."

She pulls her panties to the side and strums her clit. I watch, riveted, while her delicate fingers spread her pussy.

Her pussy is shaved. Lips are wet and pink. She's showing me her pink flesh. I'm dying to fuck her, but not yet.

"Mmm… Valen," she moans, her fingers working faster over her clit.

I lift my hips, pull my boxers down, and free my cock. Her brows rise in surprise. Her fingers pause, and she stares.

From the look on her face, she's never seen a pierced cock before.

I have six frenum piercings, also known as Jacob's ladder, from the base to the tip of my cock. I also have a prince albert and four rings along my scrotum, all evenly spaced, called a lorum piercing. I stroke my cock slowly. The moon caused the metal to gleam.

Her eyes lift. "Does it hurt?"

I smile. "There's only one way to find out." She licks her lower lip. "I've had no complaints," I admit.

"Did it hurt when you did it?" she asks curiously.

"The reward is worth the pain," I say, with my cock in my hand growing bigger the longer she stares at it. "You can touch it, Melody. I know you want to."

Her hand touches the first barbell, and I think I'm going to die. A drop of cum leaks from the tip. I'm so fucking horny. I want her so bad; it's taking everything in me not to take what I want.

"It's…gorgeous," she says.

I smile. "You think I have a pretty dick?"

She nods. "I think you're pretty everywhere."

"I would have preferred hot, but I'll take it."

She laughs, and I get a glimpse of her straight, milky-white teeth. She's suddenly shy, and it's refreshing. She pulls her hand away nervously.

"Can I kiss you?"

"Okay."

She looks up, and I lean in, taking her lips. "I meant whenever I want."

We kiss and kiss. I lean closer, hovering over her, my dick hard on the side of her stomach. I massage her nipples.

She whimpers, and I suck her lips, continuing to fuck her mouth with my tongue. I grind my hips, my cock rubs on her stomach, and she can feel the underside of my piercings, and it feels so fucking good.

"You feel so good, Melody. You're in control, baby. Tell me what you want."

She wraps her hand around my cock, jerking me off, surprised that she's taking control. I want to follow her pace. So I listen.

"I want to come," she says, "but..."

I'm reading her. She wants to come, but like this. No penetration.

Baby steps. I can do that.

I pull the soft fabric of her panties down her hips to her knees and spread her pussy with my fingers. My lips are a breath away.

"Is this okay? I ask.

"Yes," she says on a desperate plea.

My girl wants to come.

I eat her pussy. I take her slowly, licking her with my tongue, and hold her lips apart. She's tight as I continue with long strokes down to her asshole. She writhes and lets her legs fall to the side like she's straddling the lounger. She slides up so I can get in deeper. Her tits are wet and glistening under the moonlight. My tongue is hard. I drive it into her pussy and fuck her deep. Her hips lift, and she's now fucking my face. I play with her tits while I take her pussy deeper in my mouth. Her back is arched, and she looks beautiful. My face is full of her arousal. My chin, cheeks, and nose. She plays with her clit, my tongue sliding over her finger as I jerk my cock. Her breasts are rising and falling.

She trembles when she comes. Long and hard, causing her legs to shake. I don't stop until I suck her cum into my mouth. It's sweet.

I don't stop jerking myself off. I'm about to come and watch her spread out for me after I sucked her pussy like a mango, all swollen and ripe.

I'm on my knees, and I push my hips in when my balls tingle, signaling that I'm going to come hard.

"Melody?" I call out in a strained voice. "I'm coming."

She pushes up on her elbows. Her eyes are fixated on my cock, her mouth parts, and the first string of cum shoots out, hitting her mouth.

Fuck, that's hot.

I grunt, jerking my cock. More cum shoots out, painting her breasts. More lands on her neck.

With the head of my dick, I smear cum over her skin like the cream she was spreading over my brother's face.

When I'm done, I smile, looking at her perfect body painted with my cum.

Satisfied, I lean close and whisper, "You're mine now."

MELODY

I WAKE up the next day for school, looking at the stream of light coming through the small window. For a second, I forget where I am, but then I look at the small space.

I tentatively sit up and wince from the sharp pain in my lower back. I look at the sticky notes stuck on the plastic lining of the trailer. Reminders of the assignments I need to complete. How behind I am. Shopping, helping Azriel, and then...

Memories from last night cause my stomach to flip. The pool. His magnificent cock.

I brace for the guilt I thought I would feel, but it doesn't come. Touching his thick, hard cock and the...

I blush, remembering how it felt on my fingers. How he rubbed the head over my breasts, painting his cum over my nipples like lip gloss. I admit I was scared. I was afraid he would see how fucked up I was by my reaction. But Valen proved the little voice in my head wrong. He proved to my body that it could feel.

Now I crave his touch, and it terrifies me. *He* terrifies me because he hasn't been inside me, and if I let him, I know he has the power to destroy me.

I walk into my first class of the day, and when people stare at me, it's like they know about last night. I know it's all in my head, but it doesn't quell the feeling that they know what I did with the king on campus last night. It wasn't much, but to me, it was turning the page into a new chapter.

The professor drones on about math and how you should practice it every day to avoid forgetting the steps, blah, blah, blah.

All I could remember were the steps of what Valen did last night. I've been in a trance since he followed me home after I refused to stay the night. I can't bring myself to take their offer because that would mean he would be close.

Close enough to kiss and touch me when all I can think about is how it would feel if he wanted to fuck me. I want to feel his face against my legs. How thick his lips are against mine. How thick his wicked cock would feel when he stuffed it in my pussy and made me scream.

When he pulled it out, all I could think about were the barbells disappearing inside me one by one. Would it feel good, or would it hurt a little? Or would it hurt the first time, but not the second?

The next class slides into the next until it's lunchtime, and I feel like a zombie walking toward the quad on campus. My heart is in my throat, wanting to see if he's there or not. I'm not sure if I'm ready to see him so soon or if I should lay low so I don't look desperate. I'm not sure if I could handle more.

It was the first time I could touch my body and not feel scared or hopeless because I couldn't come. Last night was the first time I could do it, and it was because of Valen. He knew where to lick, suck, stroke, and kiss me.

I didn't notice I had already reached the table until I heard the familiar voices of his friends. If I'm like this after simple foreplay, I could only imagine the state I would be in if he fucked me. Is this how women feel after he fucks them? A sex hangover?

"Hey," a guy says, waving his hand over my face like he can't tell if I'm blind or not.

I look up, and it's his friend Garret.

"What?" I ask, confused.

"You can have a seat," he says with a smile. "I've been trying to talk to you, but you kept staring at me like I wasn't here. Is everything alright?"

I nod, looking around the table. I spot Charlie flirting with a girl. She must be a senior. They all must be seniors. My eyes scan the rest of the table, but it's just Charles, Garret, and the girl.

"Yeah. Everything is fine."

But I really want to tell him nothing is fine because his friend isn't here.

He's looking at me with curious interest, and I want to blurt. *I want to fuck your friend and can't stop thinking about his amazing dick, but I'm scared of what it might mean.*

"How was class?" he asks like he's interested.

"Fine."

He stares at me for a second longer than necessary. He nods like he's thinking of what to say next, trying to find the right words.

"He should be getting here in the next five minutes. His class is about to end in the next…" He picks up his phone and says, "Three minutes."

I try to play it off by giving him an "I don't know who you're talking about" expression, but it fails. It's as if he can see right through me, but it doesn't hurt to try.

"Oh, I wasn't."

He cocks his head. "Did you come here to see me?"

"I came to eat lunch," I correct.

He looks at the table and then at me. "Where's your food?"

"I haven't bought any yet."

"When are you planning to?"

"I can't sit here?" I say carefully.

"I never said that, but you're sitting in front of me, staring at nothing with no lunch, waiting for him to show up." He leans slightly over the table and lowers his voice. "It's obvious you like him."

"I don't…"

"You have nothing to worry about. He's into you," he says proudly.

"Did he say that?"

"I'm not at liberty to discuss." He winks. "All I'm going to say is that he's into you."

"How's that?"

"What did he tell you?"

He leans forward again. "Ask him yourself."

The wind picks up like nature senses his dark presence. I follow Garret's line of sight and see Valen walking from building two this way. The conversation stops when he approaches. They begin again when he passes.

He's wearing ripped black jeans and a charcoal gray hoodie, a contrast to the ink on his neck. One sleeve rolled up, revealing a tattooed forearm lightly veined. When he reaches the side of the bench where I'm sitting, he straddles it, facing me. My cheeks blush shamelessly, trying not to look between his legs. I could smell the scent on his skin. Citrus and cedar. He looks like a famous rock star. Dark and sexy.

"How was class?" he asks, ignoring everyone else seated at the table.

"Humdrum."

"Algebra, right?"

He knows my schedule. I wonder what else he knows.

"Yes."

"You find it monotonous because it's easy."

"Are you sure it's not because I find it hard?"

"You're perspicacious. I find that hard to believe."

If he only knew, I wouldn't. If I was, I wouldn't be here.

"I'm not."

"The fact that you know what that word means..." He raises his eyebrows. "What?" His eyes shift to Valen. "I've never heard you talk to a girl like that. You always tone down the fact that you're smart. Genius even."

"I'm not," Valen says. "I'm no different from any other student here."

Garret snorts. "Yeah, tell that to your GPA or, better yet, IQ test."

"Those are biased."

"You took it anonymously. I should know; my score was average compared to yours. It was not biased. Stop hiding the fact that you're fucking smart. You're here because you're bored. The same way she feels in algebra class."

"Is that true?" I ask.

"Now that you're here, I'm not bored." The breeze pushes a strand of hair into my face. "I'm"—he slides the rogue piece of hair behind my ear—"enraptured."

Chills glide over my skin like a tidal wave from his words. My eyes are lost in the shades of his eyes to see if I'm the cause.

"There you are," a female's voice says, interrupting the moment and taking a seat next to Valen.

Valen swings his leg over and faces Garret. The air around us shifts, leaving me confused.

"What's up, Melissa?" Garret says in a flat voice.

She leans forward. Her bottled platinum blond hair frames her face. The shape of her eyes, perfect brows, high cheekbones, and shimmery lips from her pink lip gloss. Melissa is beautiful.

I can tell Valen thinks so too, because he has suddenly avoided my gaze.

"I saw Valen sitting over here and thought I should come over so we could have lunch like old times. Right, baby? Like old times," she says demurely.

Garret's gaze swings to me, to Melissa, and then to Valen. My heart sinks, but my inquisitiveness doesn't allow me to assume. I want to know the truth behind Valen's words. What did last night mean?

I smile. "Hi, I'm..."

"Melody."

She knows my name.

"Yes."

Her smile widens, but it's forced. "Everyone knows who you are."

"Yeah." I glance at Valen. "Are you ready to get something to eat?" I ask purposely, ignoring her.

His jaw hardens, but he doesn't look at me.

"Sorry, but I can't." He gets up and looks down at Melissa. "Ready?"

Melissa gets up, and I try to swallow the needles in my throat, but it stings, and it feels like all my saliva has drained from my mouth to prepare for the tears that I'm holding back.

"Yes, baby," she says with a triumphant smile. She slides her arm through Valen's as he walks away and looks over her shoulder. "It was nice meeting you, Melody. We should all hang out sometime. Show you around."

I wait until they walk toward the parking lot and watch as he opens the door to his car so she can get in. Not once did he look back. Not once did he look up when he shut the door for her.

"It's not what you think," Garret says.

I grab my bag and stand. "It's okay, Garret," I say deliberately. "I don't have to think about anything."

"You're mad because you're jealous, and he turned you down to leave with her."

"Down?" I say to play it off. His words sting with the truth, but it's better this way. It's better I know now before falling into a trap.

"I thought you weren't waiting for him."

I shake my head. "You know what? Rose was right about you. You are an asshole."

I walk away, done with people playing games with me.

He is a sex addict, Melody. You know exactly why he left.

MELODY

TUESDAY

Valen: Can we talk?

Wednesday

Valen: I'm sorry about the other day.

Thursday

Valen: Will you answer me?

Valen: I went by your place, but you weren't there.

Friday

Valen: Why did you miss class?

Valen: Melody, please talk to me.

Valen: I can explain. She doesn't mean anything to me. It's not what you think.

"Are you going to answer? It's been going off again."

I grab my phone from under the counter by the register, open the messaging app, and block his number.

I place the phone back and look up. "Done."

"You want to talk about it?"

"No, Azriel. I don't," I say dryly.

I hate being standoffish with Azriel. It isn't his fault that his brother is an asshole. Valen was right about one thing: I am astute and keen. I knew the type of guy he was when I first laid eyes on him.

He didn't hide it, but, like always, I didn't listen to my instincts. I didn't listen to my brother.

Rose laid it all out that day at the bar about him. She didn't know me, and she had no reason to lie about the things she said about him. About Melissa. But I thought I was different. He knew what strings to play to get me to fall for the things he said. It didn't take much for me to take my clothes off like a desperate idiot in his pool. I could never hold a guy's attention.

I'm not *that* girl. It's why I'm fucked up. I can't remember.

"Melody?"

"Yes, Azriel."

"Are you okay?" he asks in a soft voice.

"I'm fine," I quip.

"Are you sure you want to come back, Melody?" Dorothy asks. "I mean, I love that you want to work for me, and you know I need the help, but..."

"Please, I can't work there. It's…" I trail off.

Dorothy isn't stupid. She knows I'm trying to come back because of Valen. I can't see the tortured look in Azriel's face anymore, and I hate treating him the way I have. He doesn't deserve it, but I can't be around him. He's going to expect me to talk about what is bothering me at some point, and I can't.

"Alright," she relents. "Come back. You are currently my best server, and good help is hard to find. But I'm warning you, Melody," she says in a serious tone, "he will show up. Running from him will make him chase you harder."

She means Valen.

"Who said I was running?" I lie.

"Avoiding him. Hiding. Whatever you want to call it, he will come, and he's not going to stop until he gets what he wants."

I scoff. "I'm the last thing he wants."

"You have your uniform?" she asks, and I'm grateful for the change of subject.

"Yeah."

"Good. I'm short-staffed. Can you pick up a shift?"

I smile. "Sure."

VALEN

"What's wrong?" I ask when I walk into the kitchen.

My brother sits at the dining table, staring mindlessly at the wall. I've had a shit week trying to get Melody to talk to me without pushing her away. It's the fourth day in a row that she isn't home. I could have shown up at the hardware store to speak to her, but then my brother would know what happened. I figured everything was okay if I explained that Melissa didn't mean anything, and I would take her to lunch, dinner, or both. Except that she won't answer my calls. She skipped class, which tells me she's pissed off at me.

"Nothing," he says in a flat tone.

I take a seat and notice he hasn't touched the bowl of soup on the table—it remains untouched and cold.

I pinch the bridge of my nose. "Azriel, if there is something I should know, it's not going to do any good if you keep it from me. Is it Dad?"

"I don't have a father," he snaps. "My mother is dead, and I just realized the brother I looked up to all my life is no different from the father who can't stand the sight of me."

"What the fuck is that supposed to mean?"

He gives me a pained look. "Why?"

"Why what?" I snap.

"Why her?" he growls.

I recoil. It's the first time he's been this angry with me about a girl. This is about Melody. Is he jealous? Does he know how I feel about her? Does he want her for himself?

"I don't know what you—"

"She quit," he interrupts.

I blink. "How? Did she tell you?"

"Don't worry. She didn't tell me how you hurt her, but she doesn't have to. Her silence says what you are too cowardly to say. Whatever the fuck you did, I can only imagine how you did it."

I clench my teeth. "Go ahead"—I slam my fist on the white Italian table, causing the soup to slosh out of the bowl—"say it," I taunt.

"You used her. You treated her like you treat every fucking girl in your life. You fucked her and then acted like she meant nothing."

"I didn't..."

"It's obvious that you did, just like the bastard who fathered me." His eyes are hard, and his jaw is clenched. "You hurt her. In her eyes, you're no different from the ones who raped her."

"What did you say?" I roar, swiping the bowl of soup off the table. The bowl crashes to the floor, my chair flipping backward behind me.

My blood is boiling, causing my anger to erupt like a volcano as I lean over the table with my face inches from his.

He grins sarcastically. "I'm surprised you didn't know. You're friends with her ex and his friends. The same ones live the college life while a beautiful, innocent girl suffers because she's not from a prestigious family and didn't know any better than to trust a guy who took advantage of her. Tell me, was it worth it?"

He stands up, and I can see the disappointment, anger, and rage swirling in his eyes, mirroring my own reaction to what he said. *Rape?*

"You said she was raped? Did she tell you who it was? Was it that piece of shit boyfriend?"

"She didn't say exactly. She said she didn't remember."

"When?"

"She didn't say, but I saw it in her eyes. She doesn't drink. She doesn't go to parties, and she doesn't date. It's fucking obvious, Valen."

"Did you ask her?"

"What do you mean?" he says, confused.

"Did you ask her out?"

"Out of all the things I said, that is what you asked me. Because you're jealous?"

"Do you like her?"

"Yes," he says.

I take a deep breath. "Do you want to fuck her?"

"That is easy to answer. You beat me to it."

I'm on the fence about telling him how far I went with her, but all I can think about is how I'm going to dissect the person who touched her. *There was laughter, not that he laughed.* She didn't have to use the word *they* in class. If it's more than one, the things I would do.

We lock eyes. He's challenging me while I plot. But most importantly, I need to find her.

"Where is she?"

He sits. "I don't know, and if I did, I wouldn't tell you. She obviously doesn't want anything to do with you. What did you do?"

I look at my boots. "Melissa. She tested me, and Melody was there."

"Tested you?" he asks incredulously.

I look up. "She wanted to know if I'm interested in her or if I'm fucking her."

"You are."

"I'm not… It didn't get that far. It's not because I don't want to. I'm…"

"I was waiting for her to choose, and now she isn't interested. You realize you're bringing her here because you can't handle your overstimulating sexual fantasies, which puts her in danger."

"I'm protecting her."

He scoffs. "Yeah, from who? You? Them? The way I see it, she is bait for the wolves, and she doesn't know it. You couldn't help yourself."

"I didn't know that happened to her, but I'm going to find out."

He laughs sarcastically. "Oh, yeah. You're going to walk up to her and ask. She's going to trust you because you have shown her that your prince is charming and has a key chain for a dick. You know what? Part of me loves that she will turn you down, but then there is a part of me that knows she is in danger if she doesn't choose wisely.

She's going to be in Kenyan for the next three years. I'm trying to figure out how she is going to survive because you can't see past the tip of your dick."

He's right. I fucked up. I didn't think because all I could see was her. She is all I could think about. She was young at the time, and I didn't pursue her because I'm not a sick fuck. I waited until she was older. It's a secret I kept because I couldn't balance love, sex, and a relationship. All I could do was wait.

"I know," I say, defeated. "I messed up and don't know how to fix it."

"What happened with Melissa?"

I told him.

"Where did you go?"

"I dropped her off at the stop sign and told her to get the fuck out of my car. Do you think for a second that I would choose Melissa over Melody? I chose Melissa to protect Melody from Melissa. She would destroy her, and you know it."

"She played you." He shakes his head. "She knew you would protect her. Melissa played you so that Melody would be vulnerable."

"You don't think I know that?"

"Does Melody know about Melissa? About…"

"No. She doesn't know, and what her brother does know is that he is sworn to secrecy and cannot tell her. She won't know until she chooses. She's Prey, Azriel. There are rules, and even I can't break them."

He leans his elbows on the table with his face in his hands. He can't help her, and he hates it.

"What do you plan to do?" he mumbles.

"She's Prey… and I'm the biggest predator."

"How about the other problem?" he asks, looking up curiously.

"That is where you'll help me."

He smiles, but it's like he knows something I don't.

"She's here for another reason, isn't she?"

Sometimes I wonder who's smarter.

"What do you mean?"

"She's different." He shakes his head and looks out at the pool through the glass window. "She's here because she needs to be. She's unstable right now. You know that, right?"

"It's why I'm going to need your help."

"Fine, but don't hold me back this time."

"Deal."

MELODY

"HEY, I didn't know you worked here." Rose greets me with a smile.

"You found me," I reply, mustering a grin.

She scans the crowded diner. "This is a productive way to spend your Saturday nights."

I need to make all the money I can until Zack and his idiot friends find out I'm back working here.

"What can I get you?" I ask.

"Um..." She scans the menu. "Sprite... and a salad, no dressing."

"I got it," I say, writing it down.

She looks thinner, but I don't point it out.

"Hey, want to hang out?" she asks, hopefully. "Not at a party or anything. I was thinking in my dorm. What time do you get off?"

I don't want to go back home tonight. I keep waking up in the middle of the night, not remembering where I am.

"Sure. I get off in about an hour."

After my shift, I follow Rose in my car. I've never been to the female dorms on campus. It's not like I was given the grand tour like you get at most colleges. It's dark and looks like werewolves and vampires live here rather than college students. The stone facade, weathered and worn like it's been here for centuries, exudes an aura of solemnity and secrecy.

"Welcome to Drury Hall," Rose says it like a tour guide, guiding me through the hallway.

Ornate tapestries line the walls, and vintage light bulbs that glow yellow replace the once-candle sconces, spreading over the walls and casting shadows as we pass.

When we reach the second floor, I follow her into her room. Her laptop glows in the dim light, posters of pop culture icons adorn the walls, and the faint aroma of instant Ramen noodles lingers in the air.

"It's not the best," she says in a tone hinting at sarcasm.

"You should see where I live," I say, looking at the '90s vintage Bush poster. "You like Bush?"

"Are you kidding me? He's hot, and his songs are a vibe."

"I agree. I think he was one of the biggest underrated songwriters in the nineties. I love grunge rock."

She places her phone on the charger and opens the music app to "Glycerin" by Bush. "That makes two of us. I also like metal—the good stuff, you know?"

"So what do you do after school?"

She sighs and lays down on the bed. "Besides arguing with my sister about my choice to accept the offer to attend here, I study. Here or the library."

I sit on the empty bed against the wall on the other side of the room. I'm surprised she has a room alone but don't point it out. I'm not sure how many people get a scholarship that includes room and board.

"Why doesn't she want you to go here? You told me she graduated from here." I turn on my side with my hands tucked under my cheek. "Didn't she get a good job after she graduated?"

"That is the million-dollar question she won't answer."

"She can't or won't?"

"Both."

"Isn't that weird?'

"This place is weird."

While pushing myself upward, I glance out the window and blink briefly as if an eyelash were lodged in my eye. Tall shadows are moving across the concrete. I turn my head to peer out further. The door to the church opens, and three cloaked figures walk out wearing bird masks. I look back at Rose, but she is busy trying to fix her nails.

I look back toward the church, and they're gone. I wipe my eyes with my fingers and blink, but there is no one.

Am I seeing shit?

I look left and right, but it's dark, and the wood door to the church is closed. I lie back on the stripped mattress, looking at the dark wood beams on the ceiling as Bush's "Glycerin" makes way to "If U Think I'm Pretty" by Artemas.

A distinct knock has me sitting up. Rose glances at me, and from the expression on her face, I know she isn't expecting anyone.

I open the door, but there is no one. I take a step and stumble over a large leather-bound book on the floor, resting against the chipped paint of the door. It is a worn leather-bound book.

I pick it up. "What is that?" Rose asks curiously.

I turn the thick leather book over. The cover has no title or author's name, simply the faint smell of ancient parchment and the weight of history.

Rose peers one last time out her door and then closes it. "Ass-holes. Whoever it was left it for us to find."

"Yeah," I say, taking a seat next to her on the bed.

My curiosity prompts me to touch the worn edge of the book.

"Open it."

I cautiously open it, uncovering pages covered with worn writing and forbidden rituals of flesh. The words leap off the pages with powerful impact, capturing my attention. One word jumps out from the title.

"Prey."

The single word hangs in the air, heavy with the weight of forbidden knowledge. Rose reads along with me. Her eyes move across the pages in sync.

With trembling hands, I trace the lines of text, each sentence unraveling the dark tapestry of the Kenyan University's past. It talks about secret societies, hidden rituals, and a chilling truth buried beneath the veneer of academic prestige.

A cold chill races over my arm, causing my fingertips to shake slightly. My heart quickens with each revelation as we read.

"Oh. Fuck," Rose whispers.

The underprivileged are pawns in a sinister game. They are the Prey, hunted by the privileged elite for sport; their lives are mere playthings to satisfy the whims of the powerful. To be chosen meant to be hunted, to be pursued through the halls and dimly lit corridors, until the predator claimed their prize. Prey are the property of the elite member the minute they accept the offer. A signature binding the agreement is in blood. No one leaves until they are claimed. Once claimed, the predator decides their fate.

I delve deeper into the pages, my stomach dropping with the weight of each revelation. Every minute is a crossroad, a choice looming like a phantom in the night. To turn away meant ignorance, to remain blissfully unaware of the dangers lurking. But to embrace the truth means to risk everything—safety, sanity, and your very soul.

"If a predator claims the hunted and the Prey chooses to stay, the Prey belongs to the predator and is immune to sins of the flesh otherwise forbidden."

"This has to be a joke," she says in disbelief.

I look up at Rose's stricken expression. "It's why your sister didn't want you here. She was..."

"Prey. She was Garret's."

"It's why the sons are married."

"What?" she asks, confused.

I lick my dry lips. "The sons of Kenyan are all married. I bet there is some rule." I flip through the pages. "As a rule, they have to marry before the hunt is over or they graduate. It makes sense. It's why they are all married. It's why they are all close in age. The timing. The scholarships."

It makes sense. It means Valen.

There are no innocents with privileges here, only predators and Prey. Deep down, I could no longer hide in the safety of ignorance. *Reason, not the whims of fate, had chosen them.* I turn the page. And now, Prey must choose—or the choice will be made.

"We're Prey," she whispers, the weight of the truth sinking in.

I nod. "Whoever left this"—I close the book—"is trying to tell us why we are here."

"Why would they…?" She shakes her head slowly, her eyes wide.

"At least we know why they don't have a football team."

They want us to know. They're watching us.

"Wait, wait, wait," Rose says, like something just dawned. "If the rich hunt for Prey, it means they are watching us. They know where we are, right?"

She's right. Like right now, they know we're here. The feeling when I walk on campus. The strange, knowing looks. The leers. That deep feeling I get when people stare at me like they know something I don't. Why my internal alarm went off the first day I walked on campus.

The worst part is that my brother has no idea what he got me into. There is no way he would have allowed me to set foot in this place if he thought I was in danger. A sense of dread rakes over my skin when I think about the night in Valen's pool. The night he said, *"You're mine, now."*

"Have you been with anyone on campus, Rose?"

"No."

"Are you…"

"A virgin? No. I slept with two guys in high school at a party. It's how I learned what assholes they can be once they get what they want."

"This is not high school, Rose. I don't think the people who run this place play high school games."

"Trust me, I think my sister quickly found out. It's probably why she left and didn't look back."

"And it's why you need to stay away from Garret. He's one of them."

"I don't think it's that simple."

"It is. Don't fuck the students who go here." I look out the window at the moon in the sky between the branches of the trees. "If they say they like you or you're pretty, it's a lie. This is a game to them."

"What are you going to do?"

"I'm sure you can't withdraw without owing your life. It wouldn't be that easy once you agreed to come here and then wanted to leave. The only way to survive in this situation is to play their game. Fuck or be fucked." I get up and drop the thick, leather-bound book on her desk with a thud. "And I'm tired of being fucked with."

MELODY

AFTER CLASS THE NEXT DAY, I'm seated at a table in Babylon. It's pointless to hide or return to the trailer where he can find me. If he shows up, which he is bound to do, he will never think to find me here. Waiting. Watching. It's not what Prey usually do. The Prey never becomes the predator. It's usually the other way around, and I've been preyed on before. I've been hunted by their kind. In the past, I was a victim of my own ignorance. Now, it's their stupidity to think I'm a victim.

I ordered the same thing. French fries and water. It is the most I can afford. I haven't told Mr. Crosby I quit the hardware store, afraid he will raise the rent. I was trying to buy myself some time to come up with more money before he found out.

I watch people trying to pick out the players versus the non-players. Basically, predator versus prey. I have come to the conclusion that all the guys are part of the predator club play pool. The girls and guys watching are all prey. Some girls are part of the predator club, but you can pick them out a mile away with their flashy designer handbags and clothes. All students that stay in the dorms are Prey.

"Is this seat taken?"

Melissa takes a seat across from me. Her glossy red lips over straight white teeth. Blond hair that spills around her shoulders. If you want to know what evil looks like, just look at Melissa, and you'll find it. Her smile reminds me of the mother in the movie *Evil Dead Rising*. The expectation is for a woman to embody goodness. Motherly, even, but not Melissa. You can tell everything she does has malicious intent.

There is something about her I don't like, and it has nothing to do with the jealousy licking my gut from the way Valen chose her over me. It's obvious they have something going on. I don't need an explanation or an excuse to see they have a special agreement. It is bigger than an alliance.

"How's your freshman year? It's an important year," she continues, like I give a fuck about what she has to say. "In my opinion, it's the most important. It's where..." She pauses, and she looks whimsical. "Where you break out of your shell and become an adult. A real grown-up compared to when you were in high school and every feeling was magnified, only to come to college and realize how juvenile it all was."

"Is that how high school was for you, juvenile?"

"In some ways, but the sex with Valen wasn't."

She watches me for a reaction.

"Oh, is this your way to warn me off him? Am I supposed to cry now?"

"Now, why would I do that?"

"Isn't that why you're sitting here?"

"Not really. I like you. I think you're pretty." She laughs to herself. "Weird, isn't it? You expect me to be some jealous girlfriend when all I want to do is get to know you better."

The server places the french fries I ordered on the table, and Melissa helps herself to the ketchup, dips a fry, and places it in her mouth. "Mmm... I forgot how something so simple can taste so good." She closes her eyes like she's eating a delicacy and not a greasy french fry.

I can tell it's all an act. Melissa says I'm pretty, and that could only mean one thing. She's into women, and I'm Prey. It's why she's sitting here, trying to intimidate me. To convince me. Feel me out.

"Have you ever been with a woman before? Or...a man and a woman?" she asks with a flash in her eyes.

"No," I say flatly. "I like big, pierced cocks."

She swallows thickly, almost choking on the french fry, and chuckles. "Oh..." She swallows.

She knows whose cock I'm talking about. If I let her think I've seen it, in her mind, it means I fucked him. I want to know what her deal is.

"So... have you been to any parties off-campus?" she asks, changing the subject.

"No. Why?"

She smiles, but there is a hunger in her eyes when she shrugs. "Oh, I don't know. Being a freshman and all, I thought you would have gone to one by now."

"What year are you?"

"Senior."

But I already knew that.

"How did you know I was a freshman?"

"I've never seen you around before, and you have the same look all freshmen do on campus."

"What look is that?"

"The fresh look."

She means the inexperienced look. The look of Prey. Who are these people?

"What are you majoring in?" I ask, acting like I'm interested.

"I'm majoring in communications."

I feel like someone is watching me lick my skin. I look toward the pool tables and see him leaning over the table to take a shot. He holds a pool stick and fixes his gaze on me. A disapproving expression.

Melissa turns around. "He is so jealous sometimes," she says with a gleam in her eyes, "ever since high school."

"Are you two going out?"

She laughs. "If that is what you want to call it..." She pauses. "I mean, we see other people, but we made a promise to each other once we graduated."

Interesting. He made no mention of a promise or her.

"Funny, I never got that impression, but what do I know? I'm just a freshman. I don't know any better, right?"

I know I'm being snarky. I'm jealous and pissed the fuck off. Why wouldn't he make a promise to a girl like her? She's gorgeous and comes from the same circle as he does. She is also older, and I'm young—too young, even if I'm legally an adult. Once he graduates, he will leave and get married as required, and I still have three years to finish college with these monsters. This is their game, and I'm just a pawn.

"I wouldn't say that. College is where you learn, right?" she says with a smile and looks over to where Valen is fixated on us. She turns around, and her smile falls. "Be careful, Melody. Valen doesn't play by society's rules. It's one of the reasons we have an agreement. Once he sleeps with a girl, he moves on to the next. You know how guys are? This is college. Guys want to screw around and have fun. I think girls should do the same. But, like I said, Valen has no heart and is physically available and emotionally unavailable."

"Except with you."

I really hate this bitch.

"Naturally. I've known him since we were kids, so I understand him."

"Of course you do," I say flatly.

She giggles. "If you've fucked him like you just implied"—she lowers her voice enough that I can still hear her over the music—"you're lucky if he lasts forty-eight hours before he fucks someone else. He comes with his own warning, unless you don't mind sharing him with everyone else on campus. The good thing about him is that he's not clingy, and you don't have to worry about him getting jealous if you hook up with someone else. He couldn't care less once he gets what he wants." I look behind her and meet his hard stare as she continues, "Ask any girl on campus; he's practically fucked them all."

I hate what she is saying, but I believe her. He has a sex addiction. He invited me to a party in the hopes that I would find it amusing to observe others fuck. The night at the pool. She is right. He won't stop until he gets what he wants. And like all the rest, he'll do anything to sleep with me. Like taking me to fancy restaurants and ordering me lunch and dinner. Offering me a room in his house instead of the trailer. Acting like a hero at the diner. He isn't going to save me. He did what he did in the parking lot because of his brother.

I slide out of the booth and drop five dollars on the table. "It was nice chatting with you, Melissa. Thanks for the advice."

She smiles. "Anytime. I love to help a girl out."

There is nothing in her expression that indicates she helps anyone out unless it's for her benefit. Melissa is manipulative and a liar.

"Oh, and be careful. They still haven't caught the killer."

Her smile falls, but I ignore her and glance at Valen before I walk out of the bar and tell myself there is one way to get him to forget I exist: give him what he wants.

I walk across the street to the sidewalk and head toward the parking lot. It's getting late, and I have assignments to complete.

"Are you going to leave without saying goodbye?"

I whirl around, and Valen stands in the middle of the sidewalk with his hands in his pockets.

"It looked like you were busy with your game."

He steps closer. "I would have stopped. What were you talking to Melissa about?"

"Worried that I'll cause a rift between you and your girl?"

He makes a face like he just tasted sour milk. "Girl?"

"Yeah, Melissa."

"What about her?"

"She told me you two have a thing. A promise. I get it. It makes sense. The other day at the quad. The way she showed up just now."

His jaw clenches. "What else did she tell you?"

"That you two have an understanding. It's college, right? You're both having fun, but once it's all over...

"Stay away from her. She's..."

"Why?" I say sarcastically. "Because that would make you a liar? A player?" I scoff. "Look, I think it's best we stay away from each other."

I turn around, but he grips my arm, holding me back. I look down at his hand, then at him. "I'm not a liar. Everything I said and did was real."

I pull my arm free. "I'm not saying that it wasn't. I just know that it's just your way of hooking up with a girl you haven't fucked." He flinches like I've slapped him. "Isn't that what you want? To fuck.

Scratch that underlying urge you have lodged in your mind. The one that doesn't mean anything."

"What the fuck did Melissa tell you? Whatever she said, she's lying. She's manipulative…"

I shake my head. "So you haven't fucked almost every girl on campus?"

"Have we?"

"But isn't that why you're here? Because you want to? Isn't that what you've been trying to do? At the pool? In your house? Right now?"

His chest is rising and falling. I watch his throat as he swallows. Melissa may be a vindictive territorial bitch who likes to play games, but she wasn't wrong about some of the things she said.

"What am I?" I press. "Number…eight hundred and fifty-three?"

"I…"

"You know what?" I walk backward. "Don't answer that. You wouldn't be the first asshole to use me for their sick games."

I turn around and hurry to my car because I don't want him to see how much it hurts me that he's no different from Zack and the assholes who hurt me.

VALEN

Valen: Follow he

I WALK into Babylon and scan the bar until my eyes land on Melissa, who is chatting up some girl.

I walk through the throng of people with beers and mixed drinks in their hands until I reach her, trying not to throttle her in front of everyone.

"We need to talk," I say, gripping her by the arm.

"Valen," she protests. Her eyes are wide. "What?"

I push her against the wall in a dark corner. "What the fuck do you think you're doing?"

Her mouth opens and stays stuck for a split second before forming a wicked smile. "So you do like her. How cute."

"What did you say to her?"

"A little of this. A little of that."

I slam my hand against the wall, causing a few curious stares, but I don't give a fuck. "What's your fucking problem, Melissa?"

She slides her pointed, manicured nail down my shirt, and it feels like acid is being poured over my chest. I can't stand her touch, smell, or hell, her fucking voice. If I hated a woman on this earth, it's this bitch right here. She's evil in ways no one can fathom.

The devil himself was present when they created Melissa.

Her laughter grates on my nerves. "You get so worked up over this girl. I never thought you liked the young ones."

"I promised her brother I would keep an eye on her."

"Keep telling yourself that. She told me..." She knows she's getting to me.

"Told you what?" I growl.

What did you say, Melody? Fuck. Telling Melissa anything is like telling the devil all of God's plans.

"That you fucked." My stomach sinks, and my heart sings at the same time. "Well, she mentioned she liked pierced cocks after we mentioned you, and I can only imagine if she said that, you two..." She sticks her tongue in her cheek and jerks her hand in a fist, making a lewd gesture. "That you fucked." She presses her small breasts against my chest, trying to get me worked up but failing miserably. Push-up bras with extra padding should be banned.

I smirk. "What's wrong, Melissa?" I lower my voice and lean close to her ear.

"Does it bother you that I want to fuck the freshman again?" I goad her with my words. "How much I like her sweet, tight pussy. It's so good." My nose inches from her skin by her ear.

Her nostrils flare.

Anyone looking at us this way might think we are having a moment. Maybe it looks like I'm feeling her up in the corner by the bar. I may have a sex addiction, but my cock has its limits when it comes to Melissa, and she fails to do it for me.

My cock has been in hibernation for other pussy since Melody showed up. I swear, I have blisters on the palm of my hand. I haven't jerked off this much since I was thirteen. I saw cum shoot from the head of my cock like a geyser and thought I witnessed a miracle.

With a menacing glare, I lower my voice to a dangerous whisper. "If you hurt her or if I find out you touched her, I'll kill you," I threaten.

The color drains from Melissa's face, and I release her, storming away before she can utter another word. She knows better than to push me further.

I walk back toward the back and spot a familiar face. It's the girl Garret kept eye-fucking the last time Melody was here. She gives me a look of disgust. I don't know what I've done to her. She's Prey, and it makes sense that she knows Melody. She looks behind me and then back.

Fuck.

She saw me with Melissa, and it looked bad.

Garret meets me out back and says, "She hates you like she hates me."

He's talking about Melody's friend.

"Why would she hate me?"

"It looked like you were practically fucking Melissa in a dark corner by the bar. It doesn't take a genius to know Melody likes you. Rose is her friend. Prey. You know, freshmen link up. Same classes. Like Gia and Jess did when Gia arrived. She saw you."

"It wasn't what it looked like."

"Look, Melissa is a conniving bitch. We all know that, but you're marrying her. It wouldn't be a surprise if you were..."

I unlock my car. "I'm not fucking Melissa."

"Then what were..."

"I was warning her to stay away from Melody."

"So you do like her more than normal."

"She's Adam's sister, and Veronica used to babysit her."

"She's too young for you."

"She's an adult, and I should say the same for you when it comes to Rose. Don't think I didn't see you eye-fucking her while pretending to play pool." I open the door and then remember something. "Didn't you fuck her sister?"

"I wasn't eye-fucking her, and that is none of your business."

"Trying to keep it in the family. That's messed up. But who am I to judge?"

"Says the guy who's fucked half the chicks at school. Scratch that. The school and the chicks at Ohio State."

He makes me feel like I'm a monster, but I hate that he isn't wrong. The first step to a problem is admitting you have one, and I do. I'm just not sure if it's a problem in general anymore or if it has turned into an obsession over one particular girl.

"I haven't—" I begin to protest.

"Lately," Garret interrupts, leaning casually against his sports car.

The back door of Babylon swings open, and Rose emerges, wearing an expression that could curdle milk.

"What's up with the face, Rose? Bad day torturing people," Garret teases.

"Why? Do you want to be next?" she retorts sharply.

"I can find plenty of ways you can torture me... ways you might like," Garret taunts.

She walks up to him and gives him a scrutinizing once-over. I like her. She reminds me of the type of girl who doesn't put up with shit. The kind of girl Melody was when I first saw her. But where Rose's eyes shine with a sardonic brilliance aimed at Garret, Melody's holds a pain. It is a pain that reminds me of Jess when I first met her.

When I look at the pain in Melody's eyes, it releases the evil I hide behind every joke and smile. Darkness no one sees coming.

MELODY

AFTER CLASS, instead of the quad, I find myself inside the library on campus. After Rose sent me the picture of Valen with Melissa at the bar, I knew I needed to stay away from him as much as I could. It meant not going anywhere where I might run into him. It meant avoiding him in every possible way.

I knew he wouldn't stop bothering me. He wasn't going to stop trying because that is human nature. To want something you haven't had is only made worse if you know you can't have it. I'm not trying to play hard to get or anything, I'm trying to get over him. Get over the attraction and the way he makes me feel.

I don't have much experience with guys, and the experience I do have isn't great. I thought of dropping out of school and moving somewhere. Away from my parents' judgment and start over. But it's easier said than done. I went to the financial aid office early this morning, and they said what I assumed. What I feared. I would owe them eighty thousand dollars, even if I supposedly had a scholarship. Some crap about my spot could have been given to someone else.

I looked at the lady behind the computer, wanting to punch her in the face because I knew it meant that they couldn't give it to another underprivileged student the rich assholes couldn't play a game with. This is how they strong-armed you into staying. The trap they set is to make sure you don't leave.

I look at the wood-carved gargoyles on the corner of each aisle and wonder how old this place really is.

My thoughts are interrupted. "Hey, is anyone sitting here?"

A guy with dark hair and darker eyes wearing a Kenyan black hoodie that reads Swim or Drown is staring at me, waiting for me to respond.

"No," I say, gesturing to the seat in front of me.

He smiles and takes a seat, taking out a history book and notebook. "You're Melody, right?" he asks.

Surprised, I nod. "How do you...?"

"I saw you sitting with Garret and Valen by the courtyard once. My name is Jeremy, by the way."

I pointed at his sweater. "You're on the swim team."

He nods. "Yeah. I'm a junior."

"Freshman."

He smiles. "I know."

"Who..."

"Doesn't? It's not like you can hang around the most popular guy at school, and it doesn't get around or get people talking."

"It's not." I pause. I thought the dead kid found sitting by the tree was a topic. They haven't found out who did it. It's all over the news, but I don't bring it up.

He opens his book and then his notebook. "I'm not judging. All the girls fall for Valen. He has a way to draw girls into his orbit." He snorts. "I thought he could get you at first, but you quickly proved me wrong."

"What is that supposed to mean?"

"Trust me, it's a compliment. It means..."

"What are you doing?" I look up, and Garret is looking at Jeremy like he wants to cut his head off.

"We're studying," Jeremy says slowly, but the tension thickens.

Garret glances at me, his expression inscrutable, and then glares at Jeremy. His voice sinks to a whisper, "You know exactly what I'm talking about."

Jeremy smirks. "What am I doing, Garret? Is there a problem?" he presses.

What is Garret's problem? Am I missing something?

Garret goes quiet, and they have a quiet stare off.

"Is everything alright?" I ask, raising my voice above a whisper.

Jeremy glances at me. "Everything is fine," he says unconvincingly. "I think Garret is under the impression that it's wrong for me to sit here with you." He looks at Garret. "I'm not breaking any rules."

I look up. Rules?

You're Prey, Melody.

The picture of Valen and Melissa is fresh in my mind. It's a game. What he said about me and Valen. He knows I didn't sleep with Valen. These guys know each other better than anyone. In everyone's eyes, or who was at Babylon last night, saw the same thing, or rumors are flying around campus. Valen moved on from the new girl. Me being alone in the library instead of the quad solidified it.

"What kind of rules?"

I know what they are talking about, but I need to play dumb. The way they expect me to be oblivious.

Jeremy smiles but doesn't look at me and says, "It's a team thing. We respect each other's girls." He picks up his pen. "And... last time I checked or from what I heard, you're not with any of the guys on the team."

I place a strand of hair behind my ear. "I'm not," I admit.

Garret glances at me with a solemn look. "Melody..." Garret pauses. "Be careful," he says cryptically before walking away.

I watch him leave the library. "What was that all about?" I ask.

Jeremy looks up. "I don't know. Maybe he thinks I'm going to hurt you or something. I'm not. I'm really a nice guy."

I snort. "Are you?"

"Why don't you find out?"

Jeremy is cute, but I know the game he's playing.

"Where are you from?"

"Upstate Ohio. My parents are lawyers."

"What kind?"

"The expensive kind."

"Let me guess, like most of the rich guys who come here, they want you to be a lawyer and take over."

He smiles. "Not really. I already own a percentage of the firm, and I don't have to be a lawyer. They took care of that part."

"Then why are you in college?"

His grin widens. "Because I'm bored, Melody," he says, going back to the book and flipping a page. "It would look bad if I didn't have a degree when I own a seven hundred-million-dollar law firm at my age."

"What kind of law firm is that? The kind that only hires graduates from Harvard. Like in the show *Suits*?"

He snorts. "No, the kind that shows results. Some are from Harvard; others are from Stanford and Cambridge. You can't have all your eggs in one basket. It would limit potential."

"What basket are you hatched from?"

He knows I'm asking what kind of lawyers his parents are.

"The kind that holds money, power, and influence. The kind that can send their kids to college and get a degree in basket weaving, and it wouldn't make a difference because where there is money, there is lineage. Graduating from Kenyan is enough. You have been given an opportunity of a lifetime."

"It doesn't seem like it."

"That's because you've been hanging around the wrong people."

"And you're better?" I say mordantly.

Jeremy is challenging and infuriating. He should go to law school and become a lawyer. He's got teeth and persuasion.

"I never said I'm the best or better. But I am interesting."

"Aren't you cocky? So you're saying you're better than Valen?" I challenge.

His left eye twitches. I've struck a nerve. "I'm not saying that. If you want to compare, you'll have to hang out with me and be the judge."

I grin. "Is this how you ask a girl out?"

"No." He smiles, and there is a twinkle in his eyes that I don't trust. He writes something down in his notebook, tears the paper, and hands it to me.

I take it, and it reads:.

There are ears everywhere here. I think you're gorgeous, Melody. A guy like Valen doesn't deserve you, and I think deep down you know it. Will you come to my next swim meet?

I write down five simple words and hand him the paper.

If you tell me why,?

He looks around nervously, like he will get caught in class for passing notes. He writes something down and slides the paper over.

My ex-girlfriend cheated on me. She slept with him at a party. Her name is Stephanie. Ask around if you don't believe me. I'm not interested in a girl who wants a guy like that.

What a bitch, and Valen is an asshole for doing it. I can't believe Jeremy wants to use me.

"I know what you're thinking," he blurts. "It's not to get back at anyone. I don't..."

"Want the same thing to happen again?" I finish for him. "And you think..."

I don't have to finish. I can tell by the look in his eyes that he thinks I'm different because I haven't slept with him. I don't think girls recover that easily. I got a taste, and look at me, hiding in the library. I shouldn't hide. It makes me look weak. Vulnerable.

"Alright, I'll go."

"Really?" he asks, surprised.

"Yeah, it's not a date or anything." His smile falls. "I don't date, Jeremy."

"Oh...that's cool. All about school, huh?"

"Yeah."

He shrugs, but I can tell he's bothered. He's good-looking, and he knows it.

Another time, I would have been flattered. Giddy with excitement. I'm just not that girl anymore.

It's Friday, and the air crackles with anticipation at the Kenyan swim meet. The scent of chlorine wafts through the venue as I navigate the crowded stands, my heart pounding with a mix of excitement and apprehension. I look around and see a couple of girls from my classes gawking at the guys with their hard abs. They all have perfect physiques without an ounce of fat on their sculpted bodies. I didn't think all the guys on the swim team looked like this under their clothes. I thought it was just Valen. Some have tattoos, but all have smooth skin. The guys from our school wear black shorts like a second skin molded to strong thighs instead of briefs.

“Oh my God...” someone blurts it out.

“He is so fucking hot,” the girl below me says, seated next to three other girls wearing skirts so short that it looks like they are sitting in just their panties.

I look up to see who they are talking about, and I’m not surprised. Valen is walking toward the bench with the rest of the guys ahead of Garret and Jeremy. My eyes fall to the bulge between his legs, remembering what his cock looks like underneath. Memories of that night at the pool play in my head, then the picture Rose took of him and Melissa at the bar the other night.

I tear my gaze away and meet dark eyes and a warm smile. Jeremy stares in my direction. I look behind me and find the seat empty. I turn my head, and his smile deepens. He waves at me, and my cheeks heat. There is a thickness in the air, making it hard for me to breathe.

I look a little to Jeremy’s left, and hazel eyes meet mine. My smile vanishes, and I look away.

I glance at Jeremy again, but he doesn’t look worried. He looks happy. Satisfied. I slide my hands under my thighs to keep them from shaking, trying to avoid looking at Valen, but I can’t. Valen makes sure he sits next to Jeremy. His eyes are aimed my way, not paying attention to whatever Garret is telling him. I can see his lips moving, but I can’t make out what he’s saying.

The girls keep whispering and giggling, thinking he is interested in them, but I know he isn’t. Not with the way he is staring right at me. Valen looks pissed.

He asked me that night at the pool to see him swim, and I never did. He knows I’m not here for him.

After a minute, he turns and glares at Jeremy. I don't get why he’s mad. He obviously chose Melissa over me. Whatever relationship they had is far from over.

I slide my phone out and pull up the picture Rose sent of Valen and Melissa. His mouth was close to hers like he was about to kiss her. His hand was over her head, flat against the wall, caging her in.

Her finger was on his chest. It is clear what they are into with each other. I didn't give him what he wanted, and she obviously was making a point by talking to me about him. It feels like a bunch of needles poke my throat. I hate that every guy I'm attracted to treats me like shit. They think I'm weak and stupid. I look at the picture and forward it to the last number Valen texted me from. I don't have to write anything. The picture says everything I need to say.

He's a manipulative liar.

VALEN

I WALK into the locker room, pissed off. I won, and I should be happy. I kicked ass and beat my lap time, but it was most likely due to the anger boiling in my veins under the surface. Not even the pool could extinguish it. I pushed myself harder and harder. All I could think about was drowning Jeremy in the fucking deep end of the pool.

I saw the way he looked at her. He invited her, and she accepted. She was there because of him.

I slam my locker, grabbing my towel and glaring at Jeremy. He knows not to look my way, or he'll end up like the last asshole.

I hang my towel and turn on the shower until the water is scalding, not caring if my skin will melt off. I want pain, or I'm going to kill Jeremy in the fucking shower like an inmate in a jail cell.

"I warned him," Garret says, walking in the shower stall to my right. "He said he wasn't breaking the rules."

I wipe the water from my eyes. "Oh yeah..."

Garret isn't helping, but there isn't much he can do when the girl I want won't look at me. She won't answer my calls and is obviously avoiding me at school and making new friends. Friends who are on the swim team and closer to her age with a fat bank account and obsessive tendencies. The last girl he went out with, I fucked, but that was beside the point. She dated him, but she complained that he was stalking her and was obsessive. I'm not far off the scale when it comes to Melody, but he's the weird stalker type. The kind that won't back off if you're not interested. That's why his parents sent him here. It wasn't so he could become a doctor. He can't go to a fancy law school, or it would draw attention if a girl went missing or someone brought a case against him. All that does is tarnish his family name and disrupt the Order.

His being here is what parents do to their offspring who can't make it in normal society after high school or during college. Guys like Jeremy need special treatment, and this is the way to cover up his transgressions until it's time for him to take over his family's legacy.

"Yeah, he said he wasn't breaking any rules."

He's breaking my rules, but I don't tell him that.

"Who said he wasn't?"

"Let it go, man. You can't get all worked up over this. She's single, and technically, you're not."

"Just because the girl you like hates you doesn't mean you get to stick your dick in my soup."

"It's rain on your parade. It's kind of weird talking about dick when we're in the shower."

"The fact that you pointed it out says a lot, Garret. It's okay if you've got a small dick."

He looks down at his cock. "It's not small."

"Yeah, whatever."

I haven't looked and don't plan to, but the whole Victoria Jess thing fucked up his insecurity.

"Hey, guys."

I rub soap on my body, keeping me from punching Jeremy in his smug face. If he touches her, I'll kill him. His parents wouldn't be able to prosecute anyone because I'd cut him up in pieces, and no one would ever be able to find him. It's all I could think about when he was staring at her like a lovestruck fool and waving at her like an idiot. She is oblivious to the danger of accepting anything that has to do with him. As much as there is a fire inside that no one can see but me, there is an innocence about her that drives me wild.

Jeremy walks to the far end of the showers. Neither I nor Garret acknowledge him. Garret doesn't like him, and in my eyes, he's an annoying fly buzzing around that I want to kill. He knows not to provoke me. If she's oblivious to what he is capable of, he's oblivious to what I'm capable of when it comes to her.

Garret shuts the water off and grabs his towel. I wait and do the same thing. Garret gets everyone out of the locker room, locks the door, and shuts off the lights.

"Hey, I'm still in here," Jeremy calls out.

I wait in the shadows until he emerges, his towel wrapped around him. A string of curses echoes off the walls.

"What the fuck?" Jeremy says, annoyed. "You fuckers need to grow up."

I hear his footsteps as he walks toward the exit so he can flick on the lights. I wait until I can get behind him. He doesn't hear me when I wrap my arm around his neck and cover his mouth so he can't scream.

"This is your only warning," I say in a hushed whisper. "Stay away from Melody."

He tries to say something, but his voice is muffled. I squeeze my forearm over his throat, cutting off his air so he gets the point. He struggles, trying to shake me off him, but he can't. I'm stronger and taller. The rage inside me won't abate. It feeds off his weakness and my desire to kill anyone who could hurt her. After a few minutes, he stops struggling, and I put him to sleep, letting his body fall on the wet floor.

Garret turns on the light, and his eyes fall to the body on the floor with no remorse in his expression. The past two years have made him harder. Colder.

"Is he dead?"

I shake my head. "No. I don't feel like cleaning up, and she will know it was me. It's not the right time."

"Alright, let's go."

I check my phone, and there is a text message from her. I grab my stuff, head to the parking lot, and sit in my car so I can open it without Garret around.

I open the message and see it's a picture. I wait anxiously as the picture downloads as I turn on my car. I almost drop my phone the same way my stomach drops and my vision blurs. How? I close my eyes, wondering how she got the picture. I replayed everything that night and know who it was, and I can't blame her for it. She is her friend. Rose saw me with Melissa, and it looked bad, but in Melody's eyes, Melissa was telling the truth. It's why Melissa played into it. She wanted it to look the way it did. She must have known Rose was in there watching. I was too busy threatening her and didn't notice she was playing me, so I would react and use it against me. She wants Melody to hate me to make sure I marry her.

It would make sense for me to tell her father the truth, but that wouldn't benefit me. He would make sure I married her to save face in front of the Order that his only daughter is a lesbian. There is no rule against being gay in the Order, but marriage and lineage between man and woman are requirements. What happens behind closed doors, no one gives a shit about.

Valen: I'm coming for you.

MELODY

I SLIDE my phone inside my apron pocket, reading the text Valen sent for the fifth time. I scan the booths looking for him, but all I see are Ohio and Kenyan students hanging out and some leaving.

For the past hour, more students have come together. Some leave other groups. I've had to keep tabs on all the checks to avoid someone leaving without paying since it comes out of my pay.

I know Dorothy would let it slide because she knows I need the money, but still, it's my job to keep tabs on checks and orders.

The bell dings, letting me know the food is ready from the kitchen. Tonight, we are swamped. My feet throb, but I'm making tonight what I made a whole week at the hardware store. My last check was for two months' pay, and I know it was Valen giving me money. I almost didn't take it, but I can't afford not to know about the possibility of Zack and his asshole friends telling everyone not to tip me when they come to eat at the diner.

It gets louder. When I turn around, my heart begins to race as my fear slams right into my line of sight. Zack and his friends walk in, taking a seat at the booth of girls I'm about to serve.

I take a deep breath and head over with my head held high even though inside I'm screaming from the nightmare. I can't seem to remember the night they raped me. I place the plates in front of the four girls, ignoring Zack's stare.

"Back again," Zack says playfully. "I knew you couldn't stay away." He reaches into his pocket and places a stack of twenties on the table.

I look up.

He smiles. "For all the times you didn't get a tip. I didn't know you moved out of your parents' house."

I ignore the money and glance at the other girls and his other two friends.

"Can I get you anything else?"

"A thank you would be nice, as would a date Saturday night," Zack says with confidence.

I glare at him like he's lost his fucking mind. "No, and you should put that money away."

I look back at the girls, and then a naughty smile appears over the one with blond hair. "Hi," she says.

It takes me a moment to realize she is not talking to me but someone behind me. I feel him before I can even turn to look at him. He rests his hand on my shoulder. I look over and meet Valen's gaze, full of determination. I try to shrug it off, but he brazenly slides his hand slowly over my ribs and stops at my hips. I can feel the heat through my uniform. Zack and his friend have both eyebrows raised.

"Are you ready?" Valen says, his breath fanning my neck. "I'm so hungry." I can see from the corner of my eye that his gaze is traveling over me suggestively.

"Find a booth, and I'll be right there."

"You're fucking him?" Zack asks, staring right at me.

"I don't blame you," the girl with dark hair says, and then looks at Valen. "We had some good times last semester."

"I'm sorry," Valen says. "Who are you?"

"Party? Last semester. Ohio State won against Penn State. We hooked up at the after-party. I'm Deborah."

"I don't know who you are, Deborah. I was loaded."

"Loaded?" she asks, confused.

"Yeah. I was coked the fuck out. I was going through shit, and I wouldn't have remembered what time it was. I've never seen you before."

Her smile falls when she realizes he's serious. That night was the night. I remember it because of the game. If Valen was loaded, that would mean he didn't know I was there. Zack's gaze shifts from me to Valen, then to Deborah, then to his friend, then to his other friend, before returning to Valen with a worried expression in his eyes.

"You were at the party?" Zack asks, surprised.

Zack didn't know Valen was there.

"Yeah, man. I was there, but I don't remember shit. I had Garret pick me up at around one a.m. I couldn't see straight. I was drunk, high, and drinking Coke. I wasn't in the right headspace. I went into a room that was spinning and got the fuck out. If Garret hadn't called me, I would've passed out. I don't party like that anymore."

"Oh... I never saw you there," Zack says with a look of relief. "Melody was there, though. I guess you really were loaded or would have recognized her."

I feel his hand tighten on my hip. "Oh yeah. Why is that?"

"Oh...yeah. It doesn't matter." Zack glances at me. "Melody had a few drinks, and I had to take her home that night. I was surprised you were there at all. She doesn't remember much either."

Liar. I hate him, and I never thought of seriously hurting someone until Zack and his friends. I drop the pen in my hands and notice they are shaking. Zack raped me. He raped me while I was with his friends.

I bend over, pick up the pen, and practically run to the back of the diner. I check my phone, grateful that my shift is over. I clock out and run out the back, where I find Valen leaning on my piece of shit car.

"In a hurry?" he asks.

"I need to go," I say in a shaky voice.

"Do you always cry when you see your ex?"

I swipe my face and notice my hands are wet. I'm crying.

"Leave me alone, Valen."

"We both know that's not going to happen. What's wrong?"

He isn't going to let this go. He's going to keep meddling until he gets what he wants.

He can't save me.

He can't change the past.

I walk up to him, defeated. His eyes fall to my face. I summon the inner me. The one that I locked away after that night. I need to let that version of me loose. There is only one way he will leave me alone so I don't lose myself entirely. I can use this as an experiment. A way to fix myself for when the right person in my life comes along.

That person doesn't deserve a broken girl. That man deserves the old me. The one with a smile and who is not afraid of life. The Melody who wasn't afraid to try new things. Have dirty sex. The Melody who wanted to fall in love. How could I ever expect to fall in love when I'm afraid of a man's touch?

I knew I was raped. I felt sore and violated. I got checked out at the free clinic, and I was relieved that I was okay. I didn't catch anything, but the damage was done. The fear of a man's touch was embedded in my skin. In my mind. What if I cried out when the guy I like touched me?

I step closer, leaving a small space between us, and look up. "I want you to fuck me."

He raises a brow. "Prove it."

I reach between his legs and grab his cock over his sweats, feeling it grow hard in my hand. I feel the barbells between my fingers.

"Fuck me."

"Why?"

"You said to prove it. I'm doing what you asked."

"Why the change of heart? What are you trying to prove?"

"I'm asking you for sex. Are you saying no?"

My chest squeezes. This is not going as I planned. He was supposed to be excited and take me to the nearest wall, hike up my skirt, and fuck me. Not interrogate me.

"I'm not saying that. I'm asking you why you want me to fuck you. You're not asking to make love or have sex. You said fuck."

"Do you know how to make love, Valen?"

"I'm not the kind who does, Melody. I'm the kind who makes you beg for more." He lowers his voice. "I'm the kind who fucks you in a dark corner while other people are unaware that you're getting fucked...hard."

"Like at the bar?" I fire back.

"I didn't fuck her. She wished I would, but I won't. I can't."

"Why?"

"Because there is a freshman I'm dying to fuck and make her mine, but she thinks I don't want her."

"What do you want?"

He grips my throat, eliciting a gasp. His eyes turn pitch black. "Whatever it is, you are willing to give me."

We stare at each other for a few seconds at the darkness inside us. His eyes were promising pain, pleasure, danger, and titillation. Mine promises the minefield of my worst nightmare and the girl I used to be. The one who would be face down on the back seat of my car with my ass in the air while he fucked me, begging me to be quiet.

"What do you want the most?" I ask.

"I want your fear," he says.

All I can think about is the fact that sometimes rebirth requires the death of the soul.

"Is that all?"

"I want your consent. I won't ask for it again once you agree."

"Condoms."

He grins. "Condoms," he mocks. "I don't have anything, but if it's pregnancy you're worried about..."

"It's not that. It's…"

"You think I'll sleep around."

"You don't owe me."

"I'm not going to fuck anyone else, and I'll give you peace of mind."

I drag my hands away from him reluctantly. "Like?"

He laces his fingers with mine. "Proof that I'm clean, and I need you to know that I have a dirty appetite, Melody. Right now, I'm like a caged animal."

"I'm your Prey, right?"

He smiles, but his eyes tell me he's surprised that I know that term and what it means.

"Since you set foot in Kenyan. I marked you. You're mine."

"I choose until you get bored."

"Who said I was bored?"

Let the games begin.

He removes his hand from my throat and tilts my chin up. The clouds moving over the moon cause the light to make his face appear sinister.

"I'm going to break you, Melody. I'm going to take everything inside you, including your breath, away. I'm going to be your new nightmare."

My fingers play with the band of his sweatpants, feeling his warm, smooth skin underneath.

"Why?"

"I've been waiting for you, Melody. When we first saw each other, there was nothing to say. Our eyes meeting was just enough." He takes my hand so I can feel his hard stomach. The deep grooves that make up his ab muscles. "You're not in high school anymore. You're not underage, but I promised your brother I wouldn't touch you." He smiles and lowers his voice, placing his lips over the lobe of my ear. "I lied." Sharp tingles slide down my neck.

MELODY

I TAKE the last step and turn right down the hallway, not wanting to miss out on getting something to eat. I end up at the vending machine, scanning the choices.

"Hey?"

Jeremy walks up, I know what he wants. For me to answer his calls. After my little agreement with Valen last night, he followed me home to make sure I was safe. Jeremy called me four times and left three text messages. It was a little excessive, but I did leave after Kenyan won and didn't say goodbye.

"Hey," I say, still looking at the chocolate chip cookies.

"I was worried about you last night. I didn't hear from you, and you left after."

I press D9 while watching the machine dispense the pack of cookies. "I had to work." I push the black opener and grab my cookies. "By the time you called, it was late," I say, giving him a weak smile. "Sorry."

He shifts on his feet. "That's okay. I was worried. You know, it's not safe out there."

I walk to the drink machine, find the Dr. Pepper, and slide in three single-dollar bills. "I'm good."

He places his forearm on the edge of the machine, watching me press the button, and asks, "I was wondering if you wanted to hang out?"

"I'm sorry, Jeremy. I don't..."

"Date," he finishes for me. "Right, but it wouldn't be a date. Just two friends hanging out."

I hate to turn him down. He seems nice, but I know the real reason.

"She doesn't need friends."

Jeremy looks back at me and straightens. The muscle in his jaw tics. Jeremy hates Valen.

The sound of the can dispensing like a bowling ball as it makes its way out breaks the silence. Valen bends and grabs the soda can.

"She can be the judge of that, but I'm surprised you care. I thought you would be fucking Stephanie somewhere."

Jeremy is obviously not over his girl cheating. I think he needs some time to get over her. I know what it feels like to be cheated on, and it sucks. I'm no expert, but he needs to be careful. I wouldn't provoke Valen. He looks calm, but I can sense something dark and ominous changing the air.

"I don't know. You should look for her since you're still hung up on her. I was high and don't remember what she looks like, to be honest. Stephanie is such a common name. In my mind, she could be anyone." Valen glances at me and asks, "What were you doing upstairs?"

"Nothing. I was curious, but the door was locked."

I didn't think anyone saw me. This place is vast, with certain areas designated for specific purposes. I haven't gone to the church and wonder who actually goes inside. The other night in Rose's dorm has been playing in my mind.

"Administration locks it during class hours," Valen says, ignoring that Jeremy is still listening.

"That makes sense. I'm going to head to the library."

"I'll go with you," Jeremy chimes in.

Valen grins. "The library is my favorite place."

When we walk in, it's practically empty, except for the couple in the back. The girls seated in front. I take the table to the far left by the encyclopedias. I place the soda and cookies on the desk, and Jeremy makes a beeline for the seat next to mine like a child wanting to sit in the front.

Valen pulls the chair out for me, which infuriates Jeremy. I think it's amusing how they are fighting over me because I know it's not because I'm gorgeous. It's part of their game. I should act flattered, but Valen would see right through it. So I act like it's normal and happens to me all the time.

After thirty minutes of hard stares between them, I walk to the back of the library, looking for a reference for an assignment.

It's quiet and dark back here.

The fluorescent lights make it hard to see the spines of the books. The one I need is on the last shelf. I try to reach for it—the feel of the cold air on the crease of my ass where my skirt has ridden up. My fingertips graze the leather spine of the book. I'm reaching as far as my arm will go, widening my legs a bit until I can get my fingernail to pull at the spine, so I slide the book out. I managed to get it. I pull the book back and fall to my heels.

Something wet and warm slides over my slit, causing me to gasp. I look down, and Valen is lying face up on the carpeted floor with his face pushed up between my legs.

His fingers grip my thighs, hooking my thong with one finger, and he spreads my lips apart. I look left and right, relieved no one can see what is happening. Heat runs up my neck. Nerves shoot between my thighs. He eats my pussy. I should push him off, but I can't.

It's hot and dirty. His face is wet and glistening. His tongue swipes up the crack in my ass and back to my clit. I ride his face, biting back the moan that wants to slip out.

I grind on his face. Faster and faster. My breathing is heavy. I drop the book and grip the shelf, my knuckles turning white. It feels so good. I grip my skirt in a fist with one hand so I can see his face.

His nose is shoved up in my pussy, and I feel him breathing. His nostrils are flaring with each lick. He fucks me with his tongue for a good five minutes, and when he slides his finger in my ass, I jerk violently as my orgasm slams into me like a gust of wind. I'm shaking, trying to hold on to the shelf to keep my knees from buckling.

"Oh fuck," I whisper when he holds my thighs steady and sucks the cum from my pussy.

When he finishes, I raise my leg to allow him to stand. I try to fix my skirt, remembering that Jeremy is waiting for me at the table, but he grips my chin and kisses me, rubbing his wet face all over my lips. I tasted myself on his tongue. It's sexy, and I want more. I want him.

"Your cunt is so pretty and tight. I'm addicted," he says, placing a soft kiss on my lips and walking away.

I watch him leave through the space between the shelves, not stopping by the table, and walks out of the library.

I make it back to the table, the book forgotten, wet between my legs. Jeremy looks up when I start to collect my things.

"Is everything alright?"

"Yes," I say, trying to hide the flush in my cheeks.

I didn't want him to stop. I wanted to keep going, but there are people. In the heat of the moment, no one existed, but in the back of my mind, I was worried we would get caught. It was a rush I never knew I needed. If he's addicted, I'm obsessed.

"You're leaving?" he asks.

"Yes." I hesitate. "I need to get home. I forgot I had something to do."

"Can we hang out later?" he asks hopefully.

"I'm sorry, Jeremy. I can't."

He lowers his head, but it's better this way. I can't lead him on when I'm not interested. I have to admit, I went to the swim meet because, deep down, I wanted to see Valen. I could tell myself a hundred times I didn't go because of him, but it's a lie. I want Valen. Since the first time I saw him.

I grab the rest of my things. "I'll see you later."

"I'm counting on it," he says before I walk out.

MELODY

I HEAR A TAP. I sit up and wince from the stiff muscles on my lower back. I need a thicker mattress to sleep on. Every morning, I feel like someone hit me with a car when I get up.

I look out the little window. The sky is dark. The moon hides behind the thick clouds. The fog is thick. I check my phone, and it's 2 a.m. I just fell asleep an hour ago. All I could think about was Valen and what happened in the library. I couldn't concentrate on the paper I have to write.

I hear it again. *Tap. Tap. Tap.*

I sigh and stand, grabbing a thick sweater that falls to mid-thigh. I slide my feet into my black boots and grab my phone. It must be something the wind dragged, and it's stuck against the side of the trailer, making that stupid tapping noise. If I don't pull it off, I won't get any sleep. I have school in the morning.

I push open the door, tap the flashlight on my home screen, and walk outside. The wind picks up, and I shiver from the cool air. It's getting colder.

All the lights are off in Mr. Crosby's house. He won't be back until Monday. He left to go visit his daughter in Maine.

The trees sway. The sound of an owl breaks the silence. I angle the light and walk around the trailer, looking for a piece of plastic or a piece of debris swaying in the wind and hitting against the wall of the trailer, but I don't see anything. I walk to the backside of the trailer, away from the street, but don't see anything. I glance behind me toward the tree line, a weird feeling snaking up my spine.

I keep walking, raising my phone so the light can shine on top. Maybe something is stuck by the window, making that annoying sound, but I don't see anything.

A shadow falls against the trailer, and I look to my right. It feels like my heart is stopping. Someone stands wearing a plague mask and a large robe with a hood over their head. It's the same kind I saw from Rose's dorm room window near the church entrance.

I blink a couple of times to see if I'm hallucinating, but I'm not. Whoever it is, they're standing and watching me. The eyes from the mask were pitch black and shiny, reminding me of the button eyes in the movie *Coraline*.

"Who are you?" I ask.

It shakes its head slowly.

I open the app to dial 911 when it comes at me, causing me to drop my phone. I run. I run so fast that the cold air invades my lungs like a whip, not letting me swallow. Not letting me scream for help. I can hear the footsteps gaining behind me. The sounds of feet hitting the ground like a horse.

I push through the branches of the trees, hitting my face. Some snag my hair as I run through the woods, kicking the leaves in my panic. I can feel whoever is behind me. They're close, and I'm tired. I don't run, and I'm not into sports. The air is thinner as I run deeper into the woods. My fatigue grips me in its embrace.

I snag my boot on the root of a tree, and I fall, hitting the wet leaves and dirt. My hair is blinding me when I look up.

Pain grips my skull when I'm thrown back on the ground. Strong thighs pin me to the ground as the man straddles me.

I hit his chest, feeling how hard his body was with each blow, but it's as if they are made of concrete. Every hit I land does nothing to diminish their power over me. Tears burned the backs of my eyes. Please stop.

"Please!" I scream. "Please…"

A gloved hand wraps around my throat and mouth, hindering me from screaming or calling for help. The beak of the mask runs over the skin of my cheek in a caress. I can't move. I try to move my thighs, but I can't. He has me pinned underneath him.

"Let me go," I demand.

He shakes his head and squeezes my throat tight enough so he can remove the hand covering my mouth and slide it up my thighs.

"Don't." The hand stops but then slides between my legs and rips my panties.

Two fingers pinch my clit, causing me to cry out. The trees rustle, and birds fly into the sky.

He pulls something out from under his robe, and I notice it's a ball gag. He swiftly wraps it around my head and shoves it in my mouth. I'm too exhausted to fight. Tears slide down my cheeks. My vision goes in and out. This has to be a dream. If I close my eyes, I'll wake up, and it will be morning, but when I open my eyes, he's between my legs, tying my hands above my head and tying the rope to the root of the tree. The same fucking one I tripped on.

I try to pull my arms free when I feel a surge of adrenaline, but I can't. He knew what he was doing, getting me to run. He wanted me to be tired and without enough strength to fight him off.

He's one of them. I can feel it. There is nothing I can do. He will find me. They will find me.

I can't speak. I can't move. His weight is on my hips, keeping me from kicking out with my legs.

His leather-gloved hands lifted my sweater, grabbing me by the hips. His thumbs are caressing my skin. He dips the beak of his mask, sliding the leather tip over my slit. I moan at how dirty and crazy it feels. My pussy is not in tune with the terrors crossing my mind. He plays with my clit with the tip of the mask.

I moan like I'm on the set of a porn flick. It spurs him on, and he moves faster until I'm shamelessly coming, looking up at the dark sky with tears in my eyes. I'm messed up.

I'm so fucked.

My sweater is shoved ruffly up to my neck, exposing my breasts. The air claws at my heated nipples after he pinches them.

I hear the rustle of fabric and then the feel of something hard between my legs. His cock is hot and heavy right at my entrance, teasing me. I close my eyes and then feel it when he roughly shoves his huge dick inside me. My eyes snap open, and I feel it. I feel him.

He fucks me hard. Savagely. My ass lifts off the ground. His thrusts snatch the air from my lungs. He growls like an animal. One hand grips my throat. My body was wet with sweat. Thick fog rolls in like a tie all around us, but he doesn't let up. Fireworks go off behind my eyes as I feel every inch of his cock.

He grips my legs roughly, spreading them wide as he takes me to the ground. The fog is a backdrop behind the bird mask as he looks at me through the shiny black eyes. He looks frightening. My tits bounce every time he pounds into me.

I can't take it.

I can't hold it anymore, and I come hard.

A strangled moan escapes my throat, muffled by the gag in my mouth, followed by a loud growl from his throat. He comes inside me, and I smile.

I bolted up from the bed, wrapped in a warm blanket. I look around, trying to remember where I am while my eyes try to focus on the sun streaming from the window. I see the dust motes floating above me. I look to my right, and my throat clicks, feeling the soreness of my throat, while my eyes zero in on the bird mask sitting on top of the Formica top.

I shove the blanket off, touch myself, and wince. I'm sore like a freight train was shoved up my insides.

It happened. It was real, but I don't remember when I got home or how.

I look around, but nothing is different except the scratches on my body from the trees and the soreness between my thighs.

The door behind me shuts with a loud thud in the church. The church is empty. There are four confessional booths to my right. I've never been a religious person, and my parents took me to church to get baptized and complete my confession, but other than that, I haven't set foot inside a church. I don't think I remember confessing my sins.

I walk over to the middle booth, see that the light is on, and then walk inside. The smell of rich wood, candles, and flowers envelops me. I see someone sitting on the other side through the lattice window.

The priest on the other side begins, "In the name of the Father and Son and the Holy Spirit..."

I glance up at the engraved message on the wood.

THEY'RE ALL LIARS. SPILL YOUR SINS SO THEY CAN HEAR YOUR PATH TO HELL.

"Are you with me, my child?" the priest says from the other side.

The words stick in my throat. The words I thought I would say were forgotten. My mind goes blank.

"Are you still with me?"

"Yes."

"Do you remember what needs to be said?"

"Oh, bless me, Father, for I have sinned."

"When was your last confession?"

I close my eyes, trying to remember, but I can't. It's all a blur.

"I don't remember," I say honestly.

"Well, it will come to you. It's something you don't forget easily. It's like driving a car or praying for your sins. You remember that, don't you?"

"Yes, I guess I do."

"Well, what are your sins so you can ask God to forgive?"

"Umm… I had sex last night."

"I see. Out of wedlock, I'm assuming."

"Yes."

"Is the other person married?"

"See, Father. I think I know who he is, but I'm not sure. I don't remember. I thought it was a dream, but it wasn't."

"Who do you think it was?"

I pinch my brows and reply, "How bad is it?"

"Depends on whether it was real or not. If it happened, if it did, you committed a sin of the flesh. Fornication is a sin. If it didn't, and it was all in your mind, it's still a sin, but not as bad. Sometimes the thought of sinning can be placed in a person's mind, but as long as the thoughts don't lead to actions."

This priest is weird. This feels like an interrogation.

He goes quiet for a few seconds. "Is there anything else you want to tell me, Melody?"

A chill runs down my spine.

"I didn't…"

I slide the door to the confessional booth open and run out. I rush out the door and into something hard. I look up and sigh.

"What's wrong?" Valen asks, holding me close.

"I went to confess and..." I swallowed thickly, trying to catch my breath. "He knew my name and asked me things."

"Wait here," he says calmly and walks inside.

I look around and catch the entrance to the cemetery. The tombs look old, like they were here for centuries. I wonder who they have buried there, and why does the school have a cemetery next to a church?

The door to the church opens, and Valen walks down the steps.

"What happened?" I ask.

"Where were you last night?"

"I was home, but you didn't answer my question."

"You don't know."

"What? I'm not following."

He pulls out my phone, and I look at the news article.

ANOTHER OHIO STUDENT DEAD

It says Jacob Macnab was found dead in the woods, four miles from campus. His body was mutilated.

I look up, handing him his phone back. "He plays football."

"He was also at the diner with Zack when you ran out crying. Do you know him?"

"No," I lie, but I think I do.

He was with Zack that night. He said it when that girl claimed to have screwed Valen the same night he said he was loaded. I don't remember how, but I know he was one of them.

"Is there something you need to tell me, Melody? You can trust me, baby. I need you to tell me what you know."

"Where were *you* last night?"

He looks at his phone.

"Home with Azriel finishing school."

My phone vibrates in my back pocket. I take it out and see it's a text from Rose.

Rose: Come to my dorm room.

Melody: See you in five.

"I gotta go. I need to see Rose. What did that crazy priest say?"

"Nothing." He shakes his head and pockets his phone. "He didn't say anything. He was waiting for you to finish and said you ran out like the booth was on fire."

The guy is a liar, but I don't tell him that.

I pocket my phone, and then it goes off from another message.

I pull it back out and open it.

Valen: Don't go inside the church without me.
It isn't safe.

I look up. "I'll meet you outside of Drury Hall in an hour," he says, nodding slowly.

"Hey," Rose greets me when I walk in.

"Did you hear about the Ohio student turning up dead?"

"Yeah, but that's not what I wanted to talk to you about," she says with a slight frown.

"What is it?"

She pulls out her phone, scrolls through it, and hands it to me. "I was looking online through social media and found these. It doesn't make sense because of the dates. I couldn't make sense of it."

I scroll through screen shots of pictures of me at a party, but these are dated three years ago. I was still in high school. I keep scrolling, and I see Madison with me in one of them. I hated that we looked different. We don't look related at all, but I stop scrolling when I see one of Valen and me.

"Where did you get this?" I ask, holding up the phone and pointing at the picture.

"That's why I texted you to come over. Did you know Valen from before?"

I shake my head. "No. I mean, I saw him at a party once when I was still in high school."

I tell her about Zack and why I was there.

"But why does the picture before show you wearing an Ohio State sweater? Based on the dates of these pictures, you should be a senior, not a freshman. It doesn't make sense."

It doesn't. I look through the pictures, and it's me, but not me, if that makes sense. Like I have a doppelgänger.

"Have you shown these to anyone?"

She shakes her head. "Good, don't."

I hand her phone back and open the door.

She looks up with a worried expression. "Where are you going?"

"I'm going to ask the only person who can tell me the truth."

VALEN

I EAGERLY WAIT for her to come out of Drury Hall like a caged lion. I can't take this anymore. I miss her. I miss my girl. I know I said an hour. I keep checking the time on my phone to keep me from barging in there and dragging her out so I can take her home, but I can't.

I look up when the door opens, and she walks out. "Valen?"

Fuck, she's gorgeous. I can't get her off my mind. "I'm sorry. I know I said an hour, but I saw you run out of the church, and then I texted you and didn't want you to freak out."

She smiles, and that's her. "Why would I be afraid? You're here."

I walk up to her and kiss her hard and deep.

She pulls away with a laugh. "Are you here to take me home?"

I nod like an idiot because I love to hear her say that. Home.

When I walk inside my house, I don't waste time and drag her to the bedroom. I shove her short skirt up her thighs and tear her pantyhose.

She pulls out my cock and surprises me by dropping to her knees.

She looks up. "I love you," she says for the first time, and my heart breaks.

She takes me inside her mouth, and I close my eyes, feeling her tongue on my cock like the first time I met her. She takes me deep, and I almost come on the spot.

"Fuck!" I growl and grip her hair, fucking her mouth.

She draws me in with her expert mouth. I pull out and push her face down on the bed, grip her thighs, lift her feet off the ground, shove my cock inside her wet, dripping cunt, and fuck her.

"Yes, Valen," she says and then moans. "Mmm...deeper, like last night."

I smile. She remembers.

I fuck her hard, our skin smacking against each other. The bed bangs against the wall with each forceful thrust. I pull her hair, causing her back to arch.

"Are you going to tell me?"

She smiles wide and pushes against me as my cock slides deep. "And ruin all my fun?"

I grin because this version of herself is unpredictable. Powerful. "I love all the parts of you, Melody."

She undulates her hips. "Do you?" she says in a naughty voice.

I squeeze her hips, slowing down. She knows how to make me come. She rolls her hips faster, and a drip of sweat lands on her lower back.

I squeeze my eyes shut, savoring the moment right before I explode inside her. "Fuck, baby," I grunt as hot cum shoots inside her.

When we're done, I clean her up and toss her pantyhose in the trash. She looks at her fingers and pouts.

"Where is my ring?" she asks.

I smile and open the drawer. "You put it in here last night before you went to bed."

I hand her the five-carat pear-shaped solitaire.

She slides it on and smiles. "I did put it there, didn't I?"

"Yeah, you forget sometimes."

She walks up to me naked, except for the giant rock on her finger, and wraps her arms around my neck. "What else do I forget?"

"Your homework. You have a bad habit of forgetting to do it."

She angles her head like she is lost in thought. "But I don't have any." She furrows her brow like she has figured something out. "I graduated, remember?"

"Almost, you have three more classes. The ones you missed, remember. When you were sick."

I try to blink back the sting from my eyes. I hate this part. The part that she won't tell me. The part I have to hide from everyone. The part she won't tell me because it hurts.

"Hmm…is that why I was at the dorm?"

"You were visiting a friend." She giggles. "How come I forget things?"

"Sometimes, we forget things because they remind us of things that happened. There are things that hurt, but we have to remember the things that make us happy."

"You make me happy. Do I forget about you?" She says it in a little voice.

"You can never forget me because I want to fall in love with every part of you." I squeeze her ass and press my hard cock against her belly. "Even the forgetful ones," I say with a smile and whisper, "Let's go to bed."

"Don't we have class?"

"Not today."

I stare at the tiny picture. My soul is breaking into a million pieces. The pad of my thumb tracing the glossy surface of the black-and-white picture.

"You alright?" Azriel asks. I nod and place it between the pages of the little black book. "How is she?"

"Asleep."

"You're not going to take her back, are you?"

"I can't leave her there. I can't sleep in my car forever. I also can't ask you to keep doing it either, and I don't trust anyone else when it comes to her."

"Does she remember?"

I shake my head. "No, and when something is triggered, another asshole ends up dead."

Azriel smiles. "At least she has help."

"It would help if she would tell me what happened."

"She was looking for you. Well, the other part of her was. Now that I know the truth."

"I'm sorry I didn't tell you. How could I?"

"I get it. I'm not upset, but you could have told me you loved her. It would have all made sense."

"No one knows except you."

"It means a lot, brother. You trust me enough to tell me something that is not easy to admit." He smiles. "I loved that she was doing things like before."

"You mean you got her to watch scary movies again?"

"Hell, yeah. She loves the scary ones. She likes M&Ms in her popcorn, and I made sure to buy all her favorites. I want her to think it was all my idea."

I shake my head. "You're making me jealous."

"Do you think she will be mad if I tell her that I've seen the same movies with her before? I mean..." He pauses. "You know what I mean."

"I want to tell you something important." He looks up. "I have never cheated on Melody."

"Does she know that?"

"I think part of her does. The deep parts, the one that counts, but there is something else I need to tell you. Something no one knows. Not yet."

He gives me his full attention, and I begin.

MELODY

MY EYES FLUTTER OPEN, and I yawn. It feels like I'm floating on a cloud. My throat is a bit sore, and my tongue is stuck on the roof of my mouth, but something is different. My back doesn't hurt, and I'm not in the trailer. I take a deep breath. The familiar smell of citrus and cedar.

I look to my right, to my left, and then at the ceiling. Where am I?

I sit up and notice the expensive furniture. The huge bed I'm in.

I lift the comforter, and I'm naked. My hand snags on a thread from the sheet, and I see a huge diamond ring on my finger. I extend my fingers and see the way the stone glitters in the light coming in from the huge bedroom window.

I glance at the nightstand and notice the picture frame of Valen and me. I don't remember when it was taken. I open the drawer and find two cell phones on a wireless charger. I pick up my phone, then the other. I look at the late-model cell phone, guess the code, and it unlocks.

I notice it mirrors my phone, except there are messages from my sister Madison from yesterday asking how I'm doing. Messages I don't remember sending.

I scroll to Valen's name and open the thread messages.

> Valen: You look beautiful when I'm inside you.

> Valen: I love the color of your hair when the sun rises in the morning. I think it's one of my favorite things when I wake up next to you. I hate that there are times when you forget how I feel about you. How do I feel about us?

Melody: I could never forget you. I could never forget us.

Valen: You're my favorite part of my day, Melody. Don't forget to come home to me.

Melody: Always.

The bedroom door opens.

"You're awake."

"Veronica?"

"Of course, it's me." She takes a seat on the bed. "Who did you think would barge in on you and not care if you're naked?"

I remove the sheet and cover myself. "How did I get here?"

She gives me a sympathetic look. "I'll show you." She gets up and opens a drawer, handing me one of Valen's T-shirts. I pulled it over my head. "He loves when you wear his clothes."

I close my eyes, briefly loving the scent of him still clinging to the fabric. When I open my eyes, she places a book on my lap. I sit cross-legged on the bed, and she begins, "You told me to give this to you when the time is right, and I think that time is now."

"What do you mean? It feels like I haven't seen you in forever."

She laughs. "You were with all of us the other day. You don't remember because the Melody that was with us was the older version of you."

She pulls out her phone and shows me a picture of her, Gia, me, and then another one of Jess and three gorgeous kids. There is something wrong. I don't remember going there. I don't remember any of it.

Tears run down my cheeks. "What's wrong with me, Veronica?"

"You have DID, or multiple personality disorder. You have an alter. I'm not an expert, but in a nutshell, you have a younger version of yourself and an older version of yourself. The problem is you don't remember what the younger one does when the older one is present, and vice versa." She hands me a designer wallet. "Open it," she demands.

I open it, and I look at the driver's license and credit cards, all in my name. "I've never seen this before."

"Of course you have. The other you. Look at the date of birth on your driver's license."

I do, and I'm older. The pictures Rose showed me and the one on the nightstand. Veronica is right.

"And Valen?"

"He knows. He's…known."

"The whole time?"

"Yeah, the whole parents' thing and babysitting thing makes sense now that I saw for myself how wild the older version of you was, but something happened."

I sniff. "It did, but I don't remember all of it."

"Tell me what you know before more bodies turn up, or your man decides to kill the entire football team and leaves your brother as the only player on the field."

"It was him?"

"He says it wasn't, but I'm not sure. He would do anything for you. I think it's safe for you to tell me what you know."

I tell her.

When I'm done, my hands are like two balls in my lap, and I'm rocking back and forth.

"He doesn't know, does he?"

I shrug. "I don't know how much he does know."

"He's not friends with them, Melody. He was at those parties because of you, and believe me, the older you are, the more in love you are with Valen."

"And the younger? Me…the one here right now?"

"Are you?"

I look at my hand and see where the diamond is on my finger. "I don't know. The more I read the back-and-forth texts between me and him, the more certain I become. I love him, but there is a doubt. I have a small, lingering doubt, and I don't know why."

"It's because he doesn't know what Zack and whoever was responsible for raping you did. There is something the younger you do not know. It's what the older you are protecting you from. It's the way the mind protects itself."

"Tell me."

"It would change everything, Melody," she says with a pained expression. "It could destroy you, but it could help you all at the same time. Things will click, but he would hate me for it."

"Why?" I am confused.

"He wants the younger you to fall in love with him the way the older you already is."

"The ring."

"I'm going to guess, but that rock on your finger can only mean one thing. One thing that you two share. A big secret."

"Like Azriel."

"Like Azriel."

"We're married, aren't we?'

She grins. "Yes, Melody. As of eight months ago, you are Mrs. Vikiar."

"It's why I'm in Kenyan?" I ask, trying to piece everything together.

"Among other things."

"I'm not a freshman, am I?"

"In your mind right now, yes. Technically, no. You're a senior."

She scrolls through her phone and shows me countless pictures of dates, the restaurant he took me to, and us kissing passionately. The smile on both our faces tells me we are so hopelessly in love with each other.

"What am I protecting myself from?"

The look in her eyes tells me that whatever she is going to tell me will break me.

"You were pregnant, Melody. You lost the baby, and the younger you took over."

I gasp. "When? How?

No, no. How could I? But it's possible. The clinic.

"I think you know, baby."

"How did they..."

Someone knew. They knew I was pregnant.

"Valen knew you were pregnant, and he spiraled. Drugs and alcohol, but he never cheated on you. That I can guarantee. He is so worried about you," she says, and then sobs. "I have never seen him like that." Her voice grows thick with emotion. "He would follow you everywhere. He would hire people. He would ask Garret. I mean, he would let you be you, but he was always there, waiting for you to come back, and when you didn't..."

"When did we start dating?"

"He saw you at the party that night, and then he was obsessed. Then he met the older you. The one Adam was trying to look after at school. Your sister. Your parents. I didn't get it at first, and then they told me the truth. You're adopted, Melody. Your mom abandoned you when you were five, and you showed signs of DID around ten, and then it stuck. Your mind created an altered way to deal with the trauma. It's why you have a hard time remembering, but Valen didn't give a shit. We have our crap. He has his, right? When he saw the older you, I guess you guys had a thing. Then he saw you at the party with Zack, and he was stunned. He was confused, and Adam explained it to him, but you were young. This version of you had to grow up."

"He had to wait."

"Yeah, it was hard for him, but he waited until you were eighteen and swooped right in and made the older you and him official in secret."

"The younger me had to feel the same way."

"I think it's what the doctors said. After the miscarriage, you shut down. You left your parents' and moved to the trailer, and there was nothing no one could do but give you time."

It all makes sense.

"And now?"

"Now you tell him the truth about how you lost the baby before you do something crazy."

"Like what?" I am perplexed.

"Like find another dead kid sitting at a tree with his throat cut." She leans close and lowers her voice. "You didn't think he was there by coincidence, did you?"

"The other one found in the woods?"

She smirks. "Your husband hates to see you cry. He also hates when you work or when an asshole insults you."

The diner. Jacob was at the diner. It means Zack is next, but there is something I'm missing. There is something that doesn't make sense. Why? If they knew the older me was with Valen, why would they drug and rape me?

"Did Zack know about my disorder?"

"I'm sure he did. Why?"

I get up and hastily get dressed. "He was part of it, Veronica. He was there, and I remember another name. Sam. There was a guy named Sam, but I was drugged and was in and out. The fact that the other me doesn't remember what the younger me does doesn't help."

"Tell him, Melody."

"I think he knows, Veronica. It's why I'm here and not at the trailer. It's why you're here suddenly, talking to me about this."

She smiles. "He did say you were smart as fuck."

VALEN

TAKING a seat in front of the other members of the Order and Consortium, I smile. I watch as Melissa squirms in her seat. Melissa is attempting to understand the reason for our current seating arrangement. Why did the Order call for this meeting? It's too early to announce nuptials with graduation still far away. We haven't had our annual gala yet. She so fondly loves to remind me that we are about to get married.

"Vikiar!" Riordan calls out. "Begin."

"I want to announce my decision to withdraw from my alliance with Melissa. It is null and void."

She stands. Her mouth is opening and closing as her father looks at me like he wants to murder me with his bare hands.

"How is this possible?" her father asks, bewildered, looking around the room.

"It's simple," Dravin says. "Valen Vikiar is not marrying your daughter."

"Why the hell not?"

"Because she drugged and violated Prey. A Prey that happens to be his wife. It's not the first time she has done it."

"That's a lie," her father bellows.

"It's no secret your daughter is a lesbian," Reid points out. "Ask my wife." Reid glances at Garret. "Ask Garret. We have witnessed her having sex with women."

"You're all a bunch of liars."

The door to the church opens, and Melody walks in, with Rose close behind.

"She can't be here," Garret interjects, pointing directly at Rose.

"She is, and she will stay. She is Prey, and if I want her here, she stays." Garret sits down but glares at Rose.

Melody glances at me, and I smile with pride at my wife. I nod for her to continue.

She opens the leather book from the Order to a page, but I don't miss the darkness in her eyes.

"It says here that if a member causes the death of another, the punishment is death, is it not?"

"It is," Old Man Caruthers chimes in. "Who are you?"

"Mrs. Vikiar. Valen's wife."

"You are a lying bitch!" Melissa screams.

Melody smiles maliciously. I can see the hunger in her eyes. She walks up with a serrated knife and, in one motion, slices Melissa's throat. Blood shoots out like a geyser.

Rose screams in terror.

"Holy shit." Mr. Bedford says in dismay.

"That was for my baby, you bitch. It was you in the room with them." Melody stabs her eyes, and they pop like eggs. Blood is splattering everywhere. She continues to stab her face. Blood continues to squirt for about five minutes.

"Stop her!" her father yells in panic and then tries to grab her, but I'm faster. I shoot him point-blank in the head. He falls over the pew.

I stand. "Touch my wife, and I'll cut you to pieces." I glance at Garret. "Get Rose out of here."

MELODY

"SO HOW ARE YOU, MELODY?" Dr. Wick inquires. "How's school?"

"Three years, and I graduate."

"Good, and married life?"

"Oh, um, okay, I guess."

"You know that you are married, right?"

"Of course," I lie.

She doesn't know which version of me she is talking to right now.

"Hmm, and your boyfriend?"

I smile. "Valen is great. We're good?"

"How about your sister, Rose?"

I pinch my brows. "My sister, Rose?"

"Your sister. She attends Kenyan."

"Rose isn't my sister. Dr. Wick. I just met her."

She smiles like she knows something I don't. Like those pity smiles you give to people who are sick and don't know they are dying.

"You're her only sister, Melody."

"Her sister graduated. My sister's name is Madison."

"Yes, but that is not your biological sister, is it?" I look around the room, and it sways. I feel dizzy. The ground rushes to the ceiling, and everything goes black.

I wake up in my Valen's bed—my bed.

"You're awake. Are you okay?"

I place my hand over my forehead. "I had this crazy dream. I was in a psychiatrist's office, and her name was Dr. Wick, and she said Rose was my sister."

He caresses my face and places a soft kiss on my lips. "I love you, Melody." He places the palm of his hand over my belly.

"I love you, too," I confess. I do. I love him.

He smiles. "I've waited a long time for you to say that."

"I'm sorry you had to wait so long."

"It was worth it," he says, caressing my stomach.

"Is my stomach upset?"

"No. It's"—he swallows—"growing."

"What?"

"You're pregnant, Melody. Two months."

He reaches for a book he keeps in the drawer on the nightstand and hands me a sonogram. "I can't believe it. Isn't she beautiful?"

"How do you know it's a she?" I say it with a smile.

I read the sonogram, and I am. I'm pregnant. My heart melts. I see the small pea in the black-and-white picture. Melody Vikiar with my birthdate and the date of the sonogram taken the day of the library. I remember because it was the day he ate my pussy when I was trying to reach for the book.

"Daddies know these things. It's a girl, and I'm going to pay for everything I've done because she is going to bust my balls."

I laugh and place my hand over his while he caresses my stomach. "I love you, Valen."

"And I love you," he says with such depth to his voice.

"What did the doctor mean about Rose?"

He caresses my thigh, making circles with his finger. "You fainted. I guess the stress and the pregnancy. According to the doctor, you can switch at any given time. The safest thing is for you to be aware of everything and everyone."

"It's why you waited."

"If I was going to love you, I needed to love all of you. Every part of your mind and soul. The same way I gave you all of me."

"What about your problem?"

"I get to have two girls with the same name," he teases. "It's enough, trust me."

I snort. "I fuck different or something?"

He stares.

"I do, don't I? Is it bad?"

He shakes his head with a smile. "No. It's fucking crazy and hot as hell."

"Was it you in the woods?"

"You love the mask? The older Melody likes me to fuck her with it."

"The younger one does too."

"Which one…"

"You fucked us both. The beginning was me, and the ending was..."

I close my eyes, and I can see him over there. A memory of that night. The piercings of his cock rubbing between the folds of my pussy. I'm moaning, but the gag is in my mouth, keeping me from screaming. I arch my back, and he is fucking me with two fingers in my ass. I buck when I come, and then he rips his mask off. I can see the sexy smile on his face while a string of spit lands on his gloved hand before he continues to fuck my ass with his fingers.

"What do you remember?"

I open my eyes. "Everything. You fucked me."

His gaze glides over me and says, "Everywhere. I fucked you everywhere for hours."

"And what about Rose?"

He sighs. "Rose is your biological sister, but the sister she thinks graduated died."

My heart breaks. "How?"

"She was in a car accident with her parents, and none of them survived."

"How did she get into Kenyan, and how is Rose my sister?"

"Your mother had two girls. CPS took you both after she abandoned you. I tracked Rose for you because she is your only living family, and I got her a scholarship after she applied ten times when she was seventeen. Rose has an ugly past, Melody. She was sent to foster care and then got a break with a family, but they all died on a trip to visit her here. Rose was adopted like you were, but in her case, happened twice. The sister Rose thinks graduated, died, and she was sent to foster care at seventeen."

"Who adopted Rose? The second time?"

"Garret's family."

That is why she hated Garret. She thinks he was with her sister when his family adopted her.

"Why Garret?"

"Do you have a better option?"

"His parents do whatever he asks. He asked to help a girl in trouble, and they agreed."

"She's sick."

He nods. "Yes, baby. I love you too much to leave her out there all alone like that."

"Thank you," I say softly.

"I think a part of her inside is drawn to you. She loves you, even if she doesn't realize it."

I look down at our hands. "What about Zack and Sam?"

"What do you mean?"

"Where are they?"

He pulls out his phone and hands it to me.

The article reads: There is a heightened police presence in Ohio. Two Ohio students were found decapitated in their car, with their bodies sitting on the hood of the car outside a frat party house with two red Solo cups with HE DID IT written in blood on the windshield. They discovered their heads in the front seat, their eyes severed.

The killer is still at large. Homicide detectives are now calling it a serial killing. The serial killer is targeting college football players. They have no leads, but students are strongly urged to stay vigilant.

I hand it back. "Was it…?"

"You didn't think me and my little brother were going to let it go, did you?"

MELODY

UNDER THE GRAND arches of the church, the air hummed with softness, and the voice of Lana Del Ray's "Say Yes to Heaven" played like an ancient organ.

Stained glass windows, alive with vivid hues of sapphire and crimson, cast a kaleidoscopic light across the stone floor. Between the towering pillars, the guests stand. My parents and Valen's father. My brother and the rest of the founding fathers of the Order.

At the end of the long, petal-strewn aisle stood the altar, bathed in the ethereal glow of candlelight. The shadows flickered and danced, creating a ballet of darkness and light on the ancient walls. Above, the vaulted ceiling soared, whispering echoes of the lyrics as I walked down the aisle.

Valen stands with pride, donned in an elegantly tailored suit of midnight velvet. Azriel stands beside him as the best man.

A hush falls upon the crowd as I take off my gown, which is completely inside a masterpiece of lace and whispers of tulle, trailing me like a silvery mist. My veil, a delicate web of the finest silk, barely conceals the excitement and love in my eyes. With each step, the echo of my heels on the stone sings in rhythm.

The priest stands, with a voice both clear and reverent, as he begins. My husband, breaking tradition, lifts the veil and places a soft kiss on my lips, a seal of love and a promise of forever. The applause renders the priest speechless for a minute.

When it's our Valen's turn to say our vows, He clears his throat with my ring on the tip of my finger. He looks at me with his eyes glistening and begins, "In the quiet shadows of our solitude, we found each other, seeking the part of us that was missing. I vow to be the keeper of your secrets and the partner of your soul. I vow to love you beyond the final breath of stars, in the spaces where darkness whispers its truth. When night falls and the world sleeps, you are my love, and I promise to love every part of you. Where you forget, I'll remember for us both. If you get lost, I promise to bring you back so I can love you harder and longer until we both rest peacefully on earth." He slides the ring the rest of the way. "Forever in your embrace."

My eyes blur. "I do," I say with a smile. "I love you, Valen Vikiar, with everything that I am. Every part of me is yours forever."

THE END

Want more of the Prey Series?

Preorder

Prey Series Book 6

Envy

The Envious... Covet the Prey

2/6/25

Rose and Garret's Story

Don't forget to sign up for my newsletter and follow me on my socials to keep up with all my new releases scan the QR code on the next page.

Check out my alter ego Delilah Croww

Erotic Horror

Whispers in the Dark

Circle of Freaks

www.delilahcroww.com

www.carmenrosales.com

For readers 18+ with no triggers

THE PREY SERIES

ENVY

Sold into slavery to a depraved man, I was meant to serve. To obey. To deceive.

But when the Order uncovered his secret, they gave him a choice: send me to Kenyan University, or he'd lose his claim over me.

At the university, I wasn't just a student. I was Prey—a label that marked me as less than human in their brutal hierarchy. Unlike others marked the same, though, I couldn't be hunted. I couldn't be caught. Everyone thought they knew me—until my lies unraveled. Branded a liar, I became an outcast in a world where power thrives on manipulation and deception.

But then came him.

Garret Nox.

Manipulative. Vicious. Addictive. He is a predator disguised as perfection, a psychopath hiding behind the mask of a golden boy. Despite the warnings to avoid him, his fixation on me is unavoidable.

They say envy consumes everything it touches. And Garret? He's the embodiment of it.

Now, I'm caught in a dangerous game where the envious don't just covet the Prey—they destroy them. The only question left is: Will I survive his obsession?

ROSE

THE VOICES NEVER STOP.

The whispers. The lies.

Conversations float around the room as I sit here like I'm nothing. Because to them, I am nothing. I'm something you buy. To use. To discard.

I was bought and paid for because no one wanted me. They still don't. They never will. Especially the one who owns me.

John.

He doesn't see me as human. To him, I'm his sick fetish in the flesh—the kind of men like him try to hide, but always fail. Because secrets always come to light.

"She needs to go, John," David, his lawyer says, pacing the room.

"You can't have her go anywhere else," Mary says. Her ice-blue gaze burning into me like acid.

Mary.

If there is one person in this world who would love to see me gone or dead, it would be her. When she married John, she learned the truth. That her husband's interest in her was never real. That she was nothing but a public mask to cover his depravity.

And that I exist.

At first, I thought she would help me. Free me.

But instead, she hates me. More than anything.

She never lets me forget how much. Sometimes, I wish she would end it and be done with me. It would be better than what John does behind closed doors. It would be better than the pain.

I tried before.

Cutting. Hanging. Even stepping out of a moving car.

Each attempt—stolen from me.

John made sure I didn't succeed. And each time I fail, he makes sure he makes me pay in ways no human should inflict on another.

After a while, hope seems like something I should have abandoned a long time ago.

Suicide was the only answer plaguing my mind ever since John appeared in my life: How could I end it? What would be the quickest way I could die so it could all go away? For the voices to stop.

The desire to kill oneself is not as hard as some people think—not when you don't have a choice. It's not what I really want, but it's the only thing I can think about when I want the pain to stop. Wanting to die is a choice for some because there isn't a better option when living is too painful. For others, it's an imbalance in their brain for which they don't have a cure. But not for me. For me, it's freedom from this invisible cage.

"I know," John says, exhaling through his nose. "She will also get the care she needs there, but…"

"You don't want her running off with someone or getting any ideas if she goes to Ohio State, do you?" Mary tilts her head, voice dripping with concern like she gives a shit.

John presses his lips together.

"If she doesn't go," Mary continues, "people will start asking questions. The board members are not asking. The media isn't helping." She sighs. "We gave a statement. We said we adopted her internationally. It's what they wanted to hear."

I remain still.

Mary keeps rattling off excuses and lies. I'm trying to understand what they want to do with me. Where will they hide me next?

"Kenyan University will not accept homeschooled students," Mary says, "because she doesn't have any record of academic achievements. She doesn't qualify for a scholarship anywhere else. She doesn't have the test scores or the grades."

"But she won't be like the others," John retorts, leaning back on his wooden office desk and staring straight at me.

I can still taste the tang from the maple syrup on my tongue from this morning, making me want to vomit all over his designer shoes.

"She'll have to stay in a dorm when she starts her freshman year.

She doesn't have lineage," Davids says like a warning. "John?" David voice cuts through the room, hesitant.

John's gaze darts to his lawyer.

David's gaze dips to my legs waiting for him to respond.

My fingers itch to pull the hem of my dress down my thighs like a rash needing to be scratched, but I know better.

I don't move.

I don't react.

I stare straight ahead, wishing I wasn't in the room. To them, my voice, my thoughts, or feelings don't matter. To John, it's my body that holds value. It's what I wear. How I move. How I obey.

"David, are you sure Rose can go through with what we discussed?" John asks, his voice oddly light.

David's cold stare locks onto me. The massage clear. I don't have a fucking choice. "She will."

"Look, I know how you feel about Rose going to Kenyan Prep High School as a senior, but it's the only way she can get into Kenyan University without raising questions and to comply with what the board wants," Mary says. "She will be in good hands,"

My stomach twists. But I don't know if I'm being sent somewhere worse. For the first time, I might be finally leaving this house.

"There is one subject we haven't covered," David says.

My ears perk up.

"And what is that, David?" Mary asks, sounding bored.

David's gaze flicks to me. Then to John. Then, finally, to Mary. "Your son."

John's expression hardens, filled with warning—a warning I don't understand because I've never met Mary's son.

I've heard snippets here and there. I've only heard his name a couple of times. Apparently, he's trouble. The bad kind. The kind that pisses people with money off.

Mary was a widow before she married John and has an older son, whom he is not quite fond of.

Garret.

Mary slowly crosses the room. She bends down until she is eye level with me. "That won't be an issue, gentlemen," she says, her tone full of hatred slicing through me.

I know not to speak. Not until John says I can. Mary knows this. Garret doesn't know I exist, but obviously, when I arrive at Kenyan, he will.

She lets the silence stretch before she leans in, her perfume filling my lungs like poison. "My son Garret is off-limits to you," she whispers. Her fingers tighten around my wrist. "If you so much as touch my son, I will have you raped and beaten."

John steps forward once she pulls away. "If you so much as allow another man to touch you, I will bring you back here myself." His breath is hot against my skin. I go still. My stomach turns. The sound of his zipper causes my lungs to seize.

I close my eyes. Then softly—loud enough for him to hear—I whisper the only words I'm allowed. "Yes, master."

"Good girl." He undoes his belt, the brass buckle clanking like a bell. "Mary, you can watch or you can leave. The choice is yours."

Her heels thud on the wood floor. Her Chanel No. 5 perfume wafts away like a breeze, replaced by the scent of leather and sandalwood—two scents I hate, splitting my stomach in half.

The sound of the door swinging open makes my heart thud rapidly as she leaves. "Make sure she understands, John. It's bad enough I've had to deal with her filth in my house." The door slams shut with a thud.

"Open your eyes, Rose," John demands. My eyes open, and they focus on his hand fisting his cock, the tip inches from my nose making me gag.

David watches every second, his arms crossed and his cock tenting his black slacks. *Pig. All of them.*

"Open for me," John demands.

"Yes, master," I whisper reluctantly.

"You won't need another man when your mouth is full of me." He grips my hair savagely, tilting my head back, and shoves his cock into my mouth to the back of my throat, eliciting a choking sound. I try to suppress my gag reflex, trying to blank out the stinging pain.

My eyes roll back in my head as my lungs fight for air. Pain smothers my shame as I refuse to let him see my tears, but they slide down my cheeks anyway.

"That's it," he says, thrusting in my mouth. "That's my girl. Take it. You were born to serve me and only me. Touch another man, and I'll fuck your bleeding corpse."

I'm choking, but he doesn't care. The inside of my throat is on fire. My skull throbs in pain while his nails dig into my scalp. He won't stop until I pass out or he comes.

There are times I've woken up naked on the floor, and he's fucking me. There is no question he is good on his threats. John is evil—a pedophile of the worst kind. Sick and twisted and this time won't be different.

ROSE

Present Day

"ARE you sure you're not my sister?" Melody's voice is calm, but I hear it—the crack beneath her words, the disappointment behind the question.

I know her mind is fragile, but when she's in this state—the one where she remembers—it's better to give her the truth. "I'm sure."

It's the only thing I can admit.

She exhales sharply. "Well, shit." A loud sigh escapes her. "How did you know?"

I shrug, not wanting to say the words. Valen must have found out. Maybe it was David—the biggest fucking liar the devil created. Who also happens to know Garret. A little detail John and Mary left out.

It was all part of the plan. A way to make me fit in. A way to get me close enough to them. I had to go along with it. It's not like I ever had a choice.

"Do you know who—"

"My parents are?" I finish for her. I let out a puff of air, wishing I had an answer. "All I remember is being in a place with a lot of kids. I was about ten."

I leave out the part where all the girls—including me—were drugged inside a room in some building in the middle of nowhere. "All I know is that John Strauss adopted me."

"Garret's stepfather," Melody mutters.

Garret.

Mary's spoiled son. The one who inherited a fortune and lives like a crowned prince, fucking his way through Kenyan university. A mask of perfection. He parties as hard as he deceives. Drugs, sex, and power.

But I saw it the moment I met him. The truth beneath the mask. He is not what they think.

He is undeniably beautiful: dark hair, chiseled jaw, and a cocky attitude. Melody warned me a couple of times that he didn't take anything or anyone seriously. He's the life of the party. And at one time, girls didn't go for him because he wasn't popular but now, he's all they want.

There's a darkness inside him that rivals John's. And once he learned who I was—that I belonged to John Strauss—his mask slipped. The air in the room felt like it was sucked out and replaced with hate. Unadulterated hate. I was John and Mary's dirty little secret, and I'm not to be trusted. We were enemies.

"We all graduated," Melody says to Valen as if I'm not in the room. As if I don't exist.

"I know." Valen's tone is careful, trying to avoid looking at me while softening his gaze on Melody. Nostalgia hitting me hard in the ribs. I wish someone looked at me that way. It's possessive—but the good kind. The kind you wish for.

I shift on their couch, letting the familiar feeling of being unwanted settle in my chest.

I'm a liar.

An outcast.

Prey without protection.

It's what she's telling me without saying it. I'm not her problem. I have no ties to her or her friends.

"Do you know what that means, Rose?" Her gaze locks on mine.

"I do." My voice barely makes it out.

Valen stiffens. "I think it's best you leave." His tone final.

He doesn't know why I lied, but I'm not his problem for him to give a shit. His priority is Melody, as it should be.

At first, I didn't see how all this would affect me. How it would affect anyone. I've never had friends or felt love from anyone.

But this is what John wanted—a way to sever any hope that I

would find someone who would care about me. But most of all, he wanted to make sure I wasn't protected by the sons of Kenyan.

I get up and reach for my sweater. The only one I own. A cheap contrast to the designer one Melody wears. It says Kenyan University—the same one they give all Prey. A way to distinguish us from the rest. I'm sure Melody got one too. And I'm sure Valen never let her wear it. Because Melody is not me.

She's the opposite of everything I represent.

I was bought.

She was chosen.

I am hated.

She is loved.

I want to die.

She wants to live.

I am nothing.

She is everything.

"I'm sorry," I say softly. My stomach sinks when she looks away.

The front door shuts behind me like the final nail in my coffin.

The sun is painted in twilight when I pull my phone. I type out the message as instructed.

Rose: It's done.

M: Good.

A voice cuts through the silence. "Do you need a ride?"

I jolt. The phone almost slips from my fingers. I turn. Azriel leans against a pillar, taking a slow drag from his vape.

"You scared me," I exhale.

He tucks the vape into his pocket and steps forward. The setting sun bleeds against his face, painting in molten gold. "I didn't mean to."

His face has changed. The acne gone, thanks to Melody. And thanks to his brother, he's not as quiet anymore. He's nicer. Handsome, too. Lean. Tall. Strong jaw. Dark brown eyes. Tattoos on his neck that weren't there before.

"It's fine." I clear my throat, knowing I need to go. "I gotta go."

"How do you plan on doing that?"

I blink. "Excuse me?"

He arches a brow and points to the driveway.

"How are you gonna leave? You don't have a car."

"I was going to order a ride." I leave out the part that I don't have money to order one. I was about to ask John to add funds to my account.

The pity in his eyes is sharp. "No need. I'll drive you." He's just being nice. Or maybe, he's like the rest of them.

"That's okay."

"Why not?" His tone shifts. His eyes are pools of chocolate, like he's morphing into someone I should be afraid of.

I clutch my phone tighter. "I don't think your family would approve." His eyes drop to my hand, then back to my face.

"Honestly," he muses.

I think they want me gone as soon as possible."

"Then me taking you would be the logical choice. Why make things more difficult when I could just drop you off?"

He has a point, but I'm unsure of his motives. Is it out of pity? Does he want me gone?

A shiver runs down my spine. Maybe they want me gone, like dead?

Maybe, I'll finally get my wish. A way to fuck over John.

It's what prompts me to agree. "You're right. that does make sense."

He walks to his blacked-out truck, parked on the far side of the driveway like a hearse waiting for me to get in. The twilight sky darkens everything around us like a blanket revealing the stars.

"I'm not like my brother or the others," he says.

I don't say anything as I stare straight ahead. My opinion doesn't matter.

"I'm sure you had a reason to lie. It's none of my business to ask you why you did, but you do understand that Melody is like a sister to me, and whoever hurts her…"

I blink back tears. The reminder of what I've done feels like splinters pricking my skin. I still don't answer. I don't look at him. I don't even say thank you when he stops in front of my dorm because I know he's too good inside to do it and I'm not worth it.

"Rose?" He clears his throat. School starts on Monday—"

My phone vibrates in my lap, interrupting what he was about to say. The screen lights up with the notification. Azriel's voice fades into the background as pure panic sets in when I read the message.

M: Get out of the truck.

I swallow thickly, my throat is like sandpaper. The mistake of getting in his truck hits me like a bug on a windshield.

He's always watching. I shouldn't have involved Azriel like this.

My phone buzzes again.

M: Now.

I close my eyes and grip my phone. I pull the handle, hoping for a split second that Azriel would drive off, but I know he won't.

I can feel his gaze burning like the sun. "Rose, are you okay?"

I push the door open, jump out, and run toward the doors to get inside the building. My lungs burn. My heart pounds in my ears, drowning out Azriel's voice follows me. "Rose!"

I open the door and run down the hallway. My thighs burn. My vision narrows like I'm in a tunnel. A hand clamps over my mouth. The scent of ether and chemicals fills my lungs.

I kick.

I thrash.

"Come on," a man's voice says.

I can't see behind me. I'm dragged to the back exit. I try to kick, but the arm wrapped around me is too strong. I feel the air shift. I'm outside.

A black SUV skids to a stop. The back passenger door is flung open. I'm pulled inside. All the air whooshes out of my lungs when something hard hits my head. A crack of pain explodes in my head and darkness swallows me whole.

ROSE

MY EYES FLUTTER OPEN, and I sputter from the cold water. Shocks me back from the abyss. The pain in my wrists. The bite of the restraints. A red light.

John's voice slithers through my mind— a never-ending nightmare. His hot heavy breath against my skin. The weight of him. This time, he drugged me. I remember slipping in and out—wishing I'd stay in the dark. But the cold water keeps pulling me back.

The spray stings, electric against my skin, and I gasp as reality slams into me. Off-white tiles. Metal brackets from a stall. Fluorescent lights. I'm back in my dorm's shower.

Something warm pools between my thighs causing my muscles to lock up. For split second, terror seizes me but then I realize I'm peeing. The drugs are wearing off. I wiggle my fingers, testing. Movement comes slowly. I press my palms against the cold tiles, trying to drag myself away from the water. A sharp spike of nausea coils in my gut.

A puff of air escapes my throat. Pain erupts through my ribs. I sob. Fuck. I try again, but my body doesn't move. It's all in my head.

I stare at the same crack in the tile, my vision blurring in and out. A frustrated moan rumbles from my lips when I realize I haven't moved an inch. It's all in my head. Then—

Thud.

Thud.

Thud.

Footsteps.

My eyes roll back. *Someone is coming.*

I try to call for help, but my throat is raw.

I try again. Nothing.

The fluorescent lights swirl, tilting beneath. And then, I float.

Something warm presses against me. Heat melts into my frozen skin, chasing the cold away. For the first time, I don't fight it.

If this is death, I'm home. Because living is my true hell.

I'm weightless, suspended on a cloud. For a second, I savor the quiet. I count to five. Then open my eyes. Two black orbs stare back. Blink. Something wet, leathery, breathing. It blinks again. Metal. Spikes. A growl. My pulse spikes. It's a fucking dog. A big, black dog. With pointed teeth and bared teeth.

I yelp—my voice hoarse, broken. I bolt upright. Catching the soft black sheets, clutching them to my chest, trimmed in gold. The bed is enormous. And I'm naked.

Where am I?

My head whips around, the room is huge and unfamiliar. Black oak floors. Dark furniture. Monochrome colors carefully placed by design. The windows are covered in heavy drapes. The air smells different. Not like John. Not like the others.

A sharp growl pulls me back. The dog sits in front of the door. A Doberman Pinscher. Large. Watching. Waiting.

I test a slow movement, pausing the growl deepens. Shit. Whose fucking dog is this?

I try again, inch by inch. The Doberman raises its head. I sigh and lean against the headboard, staring at the beast. "Who do you belong to?" I ask.

The dog's ears flick. It watches me without blinking. Minutes pass. My heartbeat slows.

I scan the room—really scan. Ni chains. No cuffs. No red lights. This is not John's house. I would be locked in a small room with a twin bed, not in a room this luxurious. And John would never leave me alone. He would never leave me with a dog either.

Desperation sets in after sitting still for so long. I wonder how long I've been here. The smell of cologne on the sheets doesn't help. It's not one I'm not familiar with. It's how I learned who John let in.

Their cologne. Their sweat. Their sickness. I knew which ones were violent, cruel. Which ones would use me the worst.

It's how I could tell what kind of day I was having. It's funny how quickly you tune in to your other senses when you're tortured —raped, hit, slapped. I knew them by their scent when the drugs kicked in and my vision blurred. And this scent isn't his.

A whine snaps me back to the present. The Doberman circles, then sits again. It watches me with the same unreadable expression. I shift lightly. Another growl. I sigh.

"You're trained," I mutter. The growl stops. I raise brow. "You're not attacking me. You're keeping me here." Black eyes shimmer under the dim light of the chrome lamp.

Talking then.

"I never had a pet," I continue, studying it. "Looking at you, I don't think I'm a dog person." He whines, stretches, then stretches its long leg as if I'm about to tell him a story, and he's going to be bored.

I pull the soft black sheet to my nose, causing his head to rise in curiosity. I pause. He does too. I sniff. Wood, floral, and a touch of amber.

Nothing I recognize.

The door opens. My breath hitches. All the oxygen in my lungs rushes out. My fingers fist the sheet. I stare at the last person I expect steps inside.

ROSE

"WHY THE FUCK AM I HERE?" My voice cracks, choked and raw.

Garret snaps his fingers. The dog obeys, slipping out the door.

He tilts his head, black hair falling over his brow, a slow smirk tugging at the corner of his mouth. "I knew you had venom in there somewhere." The smile isn't friendly. It's calculated. "You know"—he crosses his tattooed arms over his chest—"you should be thanking me."

I grip the sheet tighter, the soft fabric the only thing shielding me from him. "What do you want from me, Garret?"

The playfulness vanishes. His expression shifts, the light in his gaze flickering from golden boy to something colder.

Darker.

Like a switch flipping, light to dark.

He moves to the side of the bed. I pull away, pressing into the headboard, hating how I cower. But I know evil when I see it. And Garret?

He's worse than evil.

He's deceptive.

A manipulator.

He lets you think you're in control. Lets you believe you've figured him out. When in reality? You were playing his game all along.

"You're clutching that sheet really tight, Rose."

My heart pounds, hammering against my ribs. A slow trickle of sweat slides down my spine.

"I've already seen what I wanted to see."

"Fuck you."

He laughs. A sharp, maniacal chuckle. "Uh, no. I don't fuck dirty cum rags. I like mine clean."

I flinch, but I don't look away. "Then why didn't you leave me where you found me?" I challenge. "Why go through all the trouble?"

His gaze flickers—brief, unreadable. Like a serial killer caught mid-thought. You think the answer he gives you is the truth, but it never is Garret doesn't act without reason. He's been waiting. Watching. Every time I was with Melody and the others.

Evil men like Garret don't operate in chaos. They operate in silence. In the shadows.

He smiles, but his eyes stay cold. "I had to see for myself what the fuss was all about."

His gaze drops—slow, deliberate. Down my chest. Further.

Heat crawls under my skin. Then, hot and cold at the same time.

He didn't touch me. Didn't fuck me.

He just said he didn't. Besides, Garret doesn't need to drug women to have sex. That's not his style. He wants you to know it's happening. Because what he really fucks is your mind.

"And?" I force out.

The corner of his mouth lifts. Not a smile. Something worse. I want to run.

Crawl my way out if I have to. But I can't. I can scream, but no one will hear me. I can fight, but he's stronger. And I've learned one thing about rich men with power. Running only makes it worse.

Garret leans closer. Bends at the waist until his mouth is inches from my cheek, his breath candy-sweet against my skin. "Take your fingers," he says slowly, "and run them above your slit."

My pulse skitters. His gaze drops to my hand.

"I'm not going to ask twice."

Fucking asshole. He's trying to tell me something, but he wants me to find out his way. The most humiliating way possible.

I hesitate. Then do as he says. My fingers slide beneath the sheet. His gaze stays locked on mine. I expect prickly hair. Rough skin. But it's smooth. Buttery soft. Bare. Shaved. The realization hits me like a freight train. Garret shaved me.

He bathed me.

I haven't had a razor in weeks. And John, he liked it grown out. He said it made me more of a woman. Sick fuck.

But Garret? Garret had a different reason.

I drag in a breath. "Congratulations." My voice drips venom. "You've seen me naked and decided to be a creep, so what now?"

He sits at the edge of the bed. But with him there, it feels small. "For the record," he says, "we both know I'm not a creep." I hate how perfect he is. How beautiful. "I cleaned up my stepfather's cum from your pussy." He pulls the sheet back. And stares at the tattoo on my left shoulder. The numbers. My cattle brand.

His eyes narrow. His tongue drags over his bottom lip. His fingers skim the numbers causing my nipples to go hard. "Does it mean something special, Rose?"

It's the date I was enslaved. Written backward.To some, it's just a set of numbers. To me, it's the day I was destined to die a slow death.

But I don't say that.

I lift my chin. "If you know, you know. It doesn't matter what you think."

"I think what most people in Kenyan think," Garret says, leaning back. "You're a liar. And you're Prey."

My stomach sinks.

"You are fair game," he continues. "On campus, you belong to us."

My blood runs cold. "Us?"

"It's no different than what you like to do with John."

Rage churns inside me. He doesn't know. But it's killing him. And I can't tell him. I lift my chin. "Your mother made it clear to stay the fuck away from her son."

Garret's jaw tics. His mask slips—just slightly.

I snort. "Lucky for her, she never had to worry." I lean forward, mirroring him. "I'd rather fuck a corpse than an entitled prick like you."

I struck a nerve. His gaze darkens. His lips curl. "Spoken like a true whore."

"You shaved me while I was unconscious," I mock, "because deep down, you know I wouldn't give you the time of day."

His smirk vanishes. "I forgot to add," he says slowly, "a drug-addicted whore."

The words cut deep. He leans back, watching me crumble. "You're so disgusting, your pussy stinks."

I swallow the pain. Forcing my tears down.

Garret stands. Grabs a set of clothes from the dresser.

"You figured me all out," I say, voice flat.

He tosses me a sweatshirt and sweatpants. I pull them on, the fabric soft against my skin. They smell like him.

It's a shame. I'll have to burn them.

ROSE

I STARE at the lettuce sticking out of my sandwich, the edges turning brown from sitting out too long.

I haven't touched it. I'm sitting in the far corner of the cafeteria—the only seat far enough from anyone else.

Another twenty minutes until my next class. I keep my gaze down, but I can feel the stares. It's been like this all week. And every time I hear someone bring up Garret—Kenyan's richest student. Senior. Gorgeous. Star of the swim team.I turn and head in the opposite direction.

I don't want friends. There's no such thing when you're Prey. Especially after everyone heard about the fallout between Melody and me. How I'm not in their circle anymore. How I'm adopted but don't have the right bloodline. Why I'm in the dorms instead of a mansion.

The table shakes. Someone just sat down. I should leave before—

"Hey." A male voice.

I pretend I didn't hear.

"Hey." I look up. Intense brown eyes. A grin, the kind that makes his top lip thinner than the bottom. I don't know him. But apparently, he knows me. "You're Rose, right?"

Laughter pulls my attention to the right. A group of seniors. I can tell by the way they carry themselves. Not Prey. Rich. The kind of troubled kids you don't send to Harvard. The kind you send to an Ivy League school built for the one percent. Some say it wasn't built, but found.

I recognize some from Babylon—the off-campus hangout.

The two blondes and one brunette. Their skirts are so short that if they bend an inch, they will reveal what type of panties they're wearing, if at all—fall weather in Ohio be damned.

When the blondes shift, the brunette leans in. Her sultry smile practiced, perfect. She pulls her sweater low, the neckline dipping.

Her breasts push together, aimed at one target.

Garret.

He stares. Not interested. Not disinterested. Just watching. Her lips move, but he barely listens. He tilts his head. Like he's deciding something.

"That's Cassie."

Almost forgot someone was sitting across from me.

"I'm Luke."

I don't respond. Cassie licks her blood-red lips. Garret smiles. Something twists inside me. I don't want him. I hate him. Right?

"They hook up sometimes," Luke says, watching me. "Garret gets around."

My eyes stay locked on him and Cassie. They have chemistry.

Luke shifts. "Do you know Garret?"

I rip my gaze away, meeting his stare. Like he just asked if I'm friends with a celebrity. "No."

Luke lowers his voice. "You like him, don't you?"

I scoff.

"All the girls do."

I shake my head.

"You can't blame them. He's filthy rich. Captain of the swim team. Good-looking. He's like a walking lottery ticket."

I look him dead in the eye. "Well, I'm not one of them."

Luke searches my face. He's not convinced. But he's not wrong, either.

Garret is tall. Gorgeous. Dangerous. The kind of man who could make a girl lose herself. But I don't want him.

I want freedom. A place to start over. Somewhere where people don't ask questions. Where I can say "no" and it will actually mean something. Where I can be just a woman. Where a man will ask my name, and I can give him one I chose.

Where he'll smile and ask how my day was. He'll never think of me as polluted. His scent won't remind me of something dark and he will never touch me without permission.

"You're not interested in Garret?"

I roll my eyes. "No, I'm not."

Luke leans in. "You like women, then?"

"No."

A pause. "Do you like anyone?"

I exhale. "No."

"So what's it gonna take for you to go out with me?"

There it is. His real reason for sitting here. I push my plate away. "I don't date."

"Are you a virgin?"

I go still. Then I look at him, tilting my head. "Are you?"

Luke chuckles."No. But you already knew that."

I arch a brow. "How observant of you. Are you going to show me a trick?"

He laughs. But it's not funny. "You know what? I like you."

I raise a brow. "How is that? You don't know me."

Luke leans forward. "There's a party this weekend. At Garret's house."

My stomach clenches. The memory of his bed. His sheets. The way he promised to burn them after I touched them. "I don't like parties," I lie.

I've never been to one. Never been asked out, either. Not even in high school. Back then, I was too socially awkward. The only kids I knew were hopped up on drugs, waiting to be sold.

And Luke? He's not asking me out. He has a motive.

He places his forearms on the table, and it's then that I notice his jacket with the Kenyan swim team logo. He's on the swim team with Garret. "Come on," he says. "It'll be fun."

Garret wouldn't want me there. "I wasn't invited."

And I wouldn't want to go.

"I can change that."

I freeze. My eyes widen as Luke turns, calling out. "Hey, Garret."

I stop breathing. Garret's gaze locks onto me. Cassie? Forgotten.

Luke grins. "I wanna bring a friend this weekend."

I wait for Garret's rebuttal. For him to say, "Hell no." For him to humiliate me. But instead—

Garret smiles. Like a Cheshire cat. "Sure," he says, too smooth. "Bring lots of condoms." He lets the words sink in. "And a bathing suit."

How about a knife to cut off your dick?

My stomach churns. Garret is inviting me. Not because he wants me there. But because he wants me to see. Sex. Money. Drugs. His world. And I just walked right into it.

Friday arrives, and I have no intention of showing up at Garret's party. Invited or not, he'd have to kidnap me to get me there.

John owns my weekends and after that, they consist of recuperating. Of trying to piece together what happened the last time he forced me to do whatever he wanted. Half the time, I don't remember. The drugs ensure that. Except when it's just John and me. Then, he prefers me sober. He wants me to remember him. And only him.

Those nights are the worst. When he calls me his good girl. When he pets me after he's done. When he whispers how he loves me. Those are the nights I cry the hardest in my sleep. If it were possible, I'd take a scalpel and scrape every trace of him from my mind.

I walk into the library, trying to forget the weekend is almost here. The girl behind the desk looks up.

"Hi, I'm interested in signing up for tutoring."

She nods and moves around the desk, looking for something. I take the moment to scan the library. It reminds me of a cathedral, except instead of saints and angels, gargoyles perch on the tops of shelves. I inhale deeply. Books. Old wood. Ink. A scent so unlike John's house.

I've been meaning to check some out. To get better.

I struggle in class. Because I was never homeschooled. John and Mary lied. I can barely spell, write, or solve equations. John must have paid off the teachers because my grades were low.

I'm here because I need a tutor. If I don't keep up, Kenyan will kick me out.

And I'll end up back in John's house.

She places a clipboard on the counter. "Here you go."

I scan the names. The only available tutor is A.

"Who's A?"

She shrugs. "Most tutors are hybrid students. This one just goes by A, I guess."

I didn't even know Kenyan had hybrids. Doesn't matter. I write my name, circle a time, and push the clipboard back.

"You're all set," she says. "Tutoring is at the table behind the computers. If you're ten minutes late, you forfeit your time. Three no-shows, and you're out for the semester."

"Got it. Thanks."

I drift toward the literature section. I need a book on the Renaissance era for history class. I scan the shelves, fingers tracing the spines. I pull a book when—

Thump.

A grunt. I freeze. Heavy breathing.

Slowly, I move to the next aisle. My stomach drops.

Muscles taut as a rope as a strong arm braces against the top shelf.

Below him—

Cassie. Her mouth stretched wide, lips stained red, struggling to take him in. She gags. Not in protest but with determination.

Garret thrusts harder, a silver flash catching the light on his watch.

She whimpers. He grips her hair. "Shh…" The command is dark.

His eyes flick to mine. My stomach knots. His gaze doesn't waver.

Cassie follows his line of sight, noticing me. Her face flames with humiliation. Garret doesn't look away. He doesn't stop. But I can't look away either. I should run and pretend I didn't see. But I stand there, book clutched to my chest. Hating that I'm watching. Hating that I'm curious.

Garret's lip curls slightly. Like he knows. Like he's inviting me deeper. He grips her hair harder. "Go."

Cassie stumbles back, wiping her lips. Her glare burns into me before she leaves. I should go too. But—

His hand moves faster, still gripping himself. He steps closer. I step back.

A silent game. A slow, calculated chase. My back hits the bookshelf. He stops, towering over me. The light from the window casts a halo over his dark hair. Like an angel descending. But he's no angel. He's a demon. A predator. And I am prey.

"Garret…" His name escapes my lips like a plea.

He doesn't stop. His fingers move faster. "You like watching, Rose."

My fingers tremble. The book nearly slips from my grasp. A book on love.

He sees the title. His smirk widens. "You're wishing for love?" His breath fans my lips. "For someone to read you sonnets and poems?"

He's mocking me. But his eyes are dark. Wanting.

His forehead presses against mine. The pressure sends tiny pricks down my spine. I should push him away. But I can't.

He smells different. Not like John. Not like any of the men before.

The scent of his skin mixed with cologne envelops me. His forehead pushes against mine, and the pressure sends tiny pricks across my skin. His breath teases my lips, but I'll never kiss him,

"Have you ever wanted something so badly, Rose?"

The words are a prayer, a curse. I clench my hands. The book bites into my palms. "Yes," I whisper.

I won't tell him it's death.

His breath shudders. He licks his lips. "Fuck." His jaw tightens. His body shakes. His forehead rolls against mine. "I'm going to come, Rose."

The pupils in his black eyes expand. A surge of heat. Then—

His cum. I freeze. Hot liquid hits my hand.

My book.

My sweater.

He wipes the tip of his cock on my hand. Tucks himself away. Grips my chin. His cum-stained fingers digging into my skin. "I think you should get yourself cleaned up." His voice is smug, wicked.

I shove him away. "You're disgusting."

He steps forward. "I think we've established how we feel about each other. It looked like you wanted a front-row seat; I gave it to you."

I push him away, trying to wipe my hands on his black sweater, feeling the hard wall of muscles as he steps back to let me pass. "You're an asshole."

"At least I'm not a liar." I walk down the aisle to the back exit. "Don't come to my party and stay away from my friends. It's your only warning."

I push the door and run outside, not caring if I didn't check out the book. It's not like I could hand it to the girl sitting in the front, covered in his cum.

I finally make it to my dorm building with tears streaming down my face. When I reach the bathroom sink, I assess the mess on my hands and my sweater. It's everywhere. He's everywhere.

I scrub my hands and face raw, but it's like he's embedded in the pores of my skin. The musky scent of his cum mixed with cologne. He doesn't smell like smelly sex or spit.

I'm repulsed with myself for not wanting to gag; for not finding it disgusting. I look up and catch my reflection in the mirror, my eyes are puffy from crying. My cheeks are red and splotchy. I hate myself for not running sooner, for not screaming for help when he caged me.

"I'm sick," I tell myself.

How could I like the smell of his cum or his skin? Why do I still crave his kiss?

ROSE

I SCRUB MY SKIN RAW, trying to erase Garret's last words. A warning. A threat.

A reminder to stay away. The words replay in my mind like a catchy hook from a song.

I never showed up at his party. He wanted to scare me off. It worked.

After cleaning the library book as best I can, I sit cross-legged on my bed.

The dorm room is silent. I glance at my phone. 2:00 a.m.

I flip through the book. Sonnets. Plays. I try to read, but as always—

I struggle.

The words blur together. I attempt to read aloud. But I sound horrible.

It reminds me of that day in high school. The teacher called on me to read.

I tried. I stumbled. She made a face and told me to stop. That was the day I realized I couldn't read at the same level as the others. I couldn't multiply or spell.

I was useless.

John wanted it that way. Dependent on him. A girl with no future. He ensured I would never escape.

I flip the page and try again. Tears pool in my eyes. The words won't stick. I can't read a full sentence without stumbling.

I slam the book shut. A sob rattles from my chest.

Knock. Knock.

I freeze. A slip of paper slides beneath my door.

I wipe my face. Heart pounding. I don't move to open the door. What if it's some creep?

I unfold the paper. The ink is delicate. The handwriting elegant. It looks like a poem.

I had stayed in my room all weekend, only going to the vending machine for snacks. John gave me twenty dollars a week on a loadable card, claiming it was for tampons and toiletries. It was minimal, but there was nothing I could do. Some people think that if you're adopted by a wealthy family, you're provided for, but not in my case.

John didn't call me the whole weekend, and I was relieved. I hardly slept staring at my phone waiting for the unwanted text to pop up. Trepidation and fear running rapid in my mind.

Maybe he realized he went too far last time and that I needed time to recuperate. I received a text about an upcoming appointment at the campus health center this morning scheduled for 4:00 p.m.—two hours after my scheduled tutoring session with the mysterious person named A. I wouldn't put it past John being behind it and there was no way I could ignore it.

I tried all weekend to improve my reading skills. My phone doesn't have internet access, and I was afraid to walk into the library after the incident with Garret. I had never stolen anything before, and I was petrified. I didn't know what to do, but I needed a tutor for math. Hopefully, no one noticed it was missing.

I walk in ten minutes before my scheduled appointment, relieved that there's a guy at the front desk and that the redhead from last time is nowhere to be found. I tell him I have an appointment with Mr. A.

"He's waiting in the back," he says without looking up from whatever he's reading.

I walk to the designated tutoring table and freeze. An overwhelming urge to run away suddenly washes over me. Garret is sitting at the table where my tutor is supposed to be.

There must be a mistake.

His chiseled jaw and perfect lips move when notices me and asks nonchalant, "Waiting for someone?" His white designer sweater is snug around his arms as he leans back in the wooden chair. His dark hair almost obscures his eyes.

"You're not my tutor," I reply, hoping he isn't because I would be screwed. There's no way I can have him as my tutor.

"No, I'm not." A sense of relief washes over me, steadying the rapid beat of my heart. He points to the chair across from him. "Have a seat, Rose. This will only take a second."

I sit, clutching my bag to my chest as if it will protect me from him. He stares at it with a blank expression. A blush stains my cheeks. The thread at the corners is unraveling, and there are scuff marks and stains on the front even though it's black. I'm sure Garret has never known what it's like to use a bag from a donation box.

He looks up, and I quickly avert my gaze, staring out at the glass windows that overlook the hallway, hoping to catch my tutor to rescue me. As if that would save me from Garret.

Having hung out with Melody a couple of times, I know he's part of the Order and the Consortium. I know they have the power to eliminate whomever they want. They're killers with money and power, and Garret—he's unhinged. I can see it in his eyes—how he struggles with the darkness inside him.

He reaches for the chair beside and lifts a plastic bag placing it on the table. It's from the café on campus. I didn't know you could bring food into the library, but then again, this is Garret.

"You're no use to us if you don't eat."

The delicious smell wafting from the bag makes my stomach growl, but I push it down, letting his words sink in. "What I eat and when is none of your business."

He leans forward. "That's where you're wrong. As long as you're on campus, you are my business. I think I've made it very clear to you."

"I didn't ask to be here, and I'd appreciate it if you'd leave me the hell alone." I glance at the bag reluctantly. "Take your damn handout with you." I'm seething now, but this is my chance to make my point and push him away. "I don't want anything from you."

"Funny, I didn't see you running for the hills on Friday. You waited until I was finished." He stands and leans over the table, making me feel small as he towers over me. "Eat the fucking food, Rose. Don't make me feed it to you."

Suddenly, I'm lightheaded, and I can't breathe. I can feel my mouth getting thick, as if my tongue is swelling, and soon I won't be able to swallow. Flashes of white and silver. My mouth being stuffed with force. The taste of something runny and cinnamon. My mouth burning. I lean back in my chair violently, my eyes wide.

"What the fuck… Rose." Garret is staring at me, confused.

My skin feels tight.

There's another voice I recognize coming from behind me.

"Rose, what's wrong?"

Azriel.

I shake my head violently, but all I see are flashes of a spoon being force-fed. "Please…" I whisper. I have to calm down and stop this feeling, or they'll know, and then he'll make me pay.

Azriel comes into view, glaring at Garret. "What are you doing, Garret?"

"I should ask the same," he replies icily.

"I'm her tutor."

"I'm fine," I say to no one, but try to sound convincing.

They both swing their gazes to me.

Azriel is the first to speak pulling a chair. "I think it's best we get started."

I'm still at a loss for words. He's A. But how or why? What are the odds? He's a hybrid student. I just never thought of Azriel as being a tutor or having the time to be one with his job.

Garret moves with no intention of taking the food. Instead, he gets in Azriel's face, and they stare at each other, communicating something with their eyes that I can't make out. "Make sure she eats," he drawls disturbingly and walks out.

I stare straight ahead, trying to figure out what just happened. Azriel sits in Garret's chair as if nothing happened. As if this is normal.

"So, you need help with math," he states as he pulls out a notebook, pencil, and calculator.

I open my bag slowly and pull out the book and the notebook with the problems I'm having issues solving.

He pauses, watches me for a few seconds, and then asks what I was expecting him to ask, "What happened the other day?"

I haven't seen or heard from him since John took me, and I didn't expect him to. He made it clear where his loyalty lies. I'm not his problem, and I'm not his friend. I get it.

"Nothing. You gave me a ride," I reply, as if it's perfectly normal.

"I came to your dorm to see if you were alright the next morning, but you didn't answer," he says it almost accusingly, as if I did something wrong or let him down.

"I was probably sleeping," I lie, but I can tell he doesn't believe me and lets it slide.

Who cares at this point if I don't tell him the truth? It's not like he doesn't think I'm a liar, like everyone else. I don't feel guilty anymore.

"I was worried and..."

"Why?" I interrupt.

He pauses as if there's something he wants to say but can't.

"I just am. I can't explain why, but I'm here now, and you need help." He picks up his pencil and takes my assignment.

Time passes quickly as he explains the steps, helping me make sense of the material. I love how easygoing and patient he is when I ask questions. I'm embarrassed to tell him that I struggle with reading the problems.

"There are videos to help you if you get stuck." I look up from the example he wrote down, trying to think of an excuse but coming up empty. "Online."

"I don't have internet on my phone," I finally admit.

Why lie about it when he's helping me not to fail? I probably should be in remedial classes, but those classes aren't offered.

"Oh," he says, surprised. "There's Wi-Fi. Can't you connect your phone to it?"

"I don't know the password, and I'm not sure my phone is capable."

John gave me a phone when I started school, but it's limited in what it can do. It's the type you see at Walgreens—plain, with a simple screen. It's not the fancy kind I've seen the kids on campus have. I don't even have apps or the capability to listen to music.

"I'll take a look if you don't mind," he says gently. My stomach churns at the thought of him seeing the text messages on my phone. "I mean, if you want."

It feels as though he can read my mind. I want to see if he can help figure it out. I would love to watch videos. Listen to music online but I can't risk it.

"That's okay," I deflect. "I'll figure it out."

"The password is KCAMPUS."

I write it down and then slide the book and notebook into my bag. A piece of paper slips out, and he catches it before it falls. I'm about to reach for it but my stomach drops when he reads it. I'm still wondering who would have slipped it under my door.

"Did you write this?"

I almost want to laugh. I can barely spell at a college level. "No."

He watches me for a few seconds, waiting for me to say more, but I won't tell him that someone slipped it under my door, and I won't admit that I don't understand the meaning behind what it says.

He doesn't push, and it's like a weight has lifted from my chest. "Do you mind if I read it aloud?"

I turn around and scan the library to see if anyone is around, but I find it empty. I really want to know what it means, so I face him and nod.

"It's a sonnet." He clears his throat and begins.

Beneath the moon's cold light, your shadow sleeps,
A ghost spinning the thread of fate.
If you whispered words through purged lips, you chain my eager hands,
And reawaken my cold heart.
Your touch, a thorn that bleeds both sadness and beauty.
A curse I'd endure until the world ends.
Each stolen breath ignites my soul, begging for a poison-laden kiss.
The scent of your skin feeds the darkness within me.
A haven carved from fire and sin.
Though every word you speak is laced with lies,

I'd burn for you and take the blame.

For love that lingers close to ruin's edge,

Is love immortal, bound by the blood that's bled.

The way he reads is perfect. What he read was dark and passionate. Each word knocked on my heart, wanting to get in, but who would write something like that?

Azriel furrows his brow and hands me the lined notebook paper. "Who wrote that?"

I shake my head, looking at the delicately written words. The handwriting is perfect. "I don't know. Is it from a book or something? Maybe someone copied it from a famous writer."

"I don't think so, Rose. I've never heard or read anything like that. Whoever wrote it is…"

I slip the paper delicately into my bag, careful not to ruin it. "Is what?" I press. "What does it mean?"

My stomach twists in anticipation and trepidation. I don't have a boyfriend. There is no one I can think of that would write something like that but I want to know what it means.

"Well, whoever wrote it is dangerously obsessed."

"I found it and thought it was interesting."

The look in his eyes tells me he is not so sure. "What's with you and Garret?"

I shrug glancing at the bag of food. "I have no idea. "Why?"

"Because he's dangerous," he warns. "I don't want that for you, Rose. I know there is something behind all this and I don't expect you to trust me."

There's no way he knows the truth. "Why do you say that?"

"There always is and remember"—he glances at the bag of food one more time—"there is always someone watching. As for Garret, stay away from him."

ROSE

I TAKE the elevator to the fourth floor of the student health department and check in with the nurse at the front desk. She says I'm here to see a therapist. I nod as if I understand, but I don't know why John would make me an appointment when I've already lied to the last one about using drugs, having nightmares, or being in a harmful relationship.

I sit in one of the empty chairs closest to the exit. I expected to see more people, but the entire waiting room is deserted. The walls are painted white, like a glass of milk. There are no pictures, no table with magazines, or anything to keep you entertained. There are only two doors and one window: one door for the exit, one for the back rooms, and the window looks out at an elderly woman who appears to be a grandmother.

When my name is called, I walk in and see a woman seated behind a cherry wood desk. Her hands are neatly folded on top, as if she's praying. She wears a red silk blouse and pearls around her neck, her expression serious, as if this is the last thing she wants to do.

"You must be Rose."

"Yes."

She points to the only available chair against the wall. I find it odd that it's so far away from her desk. She doesn't have the customary two chairs facing her desk, as I've seen in other offices.

I sit.

She leans back and doesn't say anything, watching me like I'm an animal she's studying.

"I'm Dr. Wick."

"I'm Rose."

"I think we've established that."

I want to tell her that I was informed I would see a therapist, not a psychiatrist, and that there must be some mistake about why I'm here, but I keep my mouth shut. The last thing I want is for John to find out I'm asking too many questions. There's no such thing as client privacy when it comes to me. Girls like me don't have human rights. We're selected like cattle and then caged.

"I would like to ask you a few questions, and then you can ask me anything you like."

"Okay." The faster I get out of here, the better. I don't trust this woman. She works here and is hired by monsters who run this place. Who knows what her angle with me is?

"There have been reports from dorm security that you have had issues sleeping?"

I blink a few times, convinced there must be some kind of mistake. How could dorm security know anything about my sleeping habits? My door is always closed, and I hardly see security. There are times I didn't even think we had any. I'm still trying to figure out how Garret found me, but he's not someone you can easily ask questions.

"I'm not sure what you mean."

"It's not uncommon. There are students who have nightmares. They scream in their sleep without being aware, and out of concern, other students report it. Security sends it to the school, and then it's forwarded here to the health department. We take these types of reports seriously."

I want to laugh in her face. Does she know what kind of school this is and what they do to the less fortunate trapped here under the pretense of higher education and a promise of a better life? Of course she does. This woman is no better than a demon foaming at the mouth, telling you to screw yourself for her enjoyment. There is no question; this bitch is evil. How dare she call herself a doctor.

I raise a brow. "And? I had a stupid nightmare. What's the big deal?"

"Does this happen often? If so, what do you have nightmares about?"

"I don't remember," I fib.

Of course, I remember John violating me. I remember being force-fed when I refused to eat, raped, humiliated, touched, and drugged. But is she going to do about it?

"Do you have trouble sleeping?"

"You just said I have nightmares."

Is she dumb?

She lets out a frustrated sigh. "How was your childhood?"

She wants to go there. What a bitch.

"I was adopted." I smile sarcastically. "But I'm sure you already knew that."

She smiles back, but the lines don't crease around her eyes. "I did, but I want to see what you remember about your past."

I shrug. "Nothing really. I was adopted when I was a kid."

"Do you remember your parents?" she asks, ready to type my answer on a keyboard.

Pain slices through my chest, wishing I knew, but I don't. I never will. The numbers on my skin told me the truth a long time ago when I pieced it all together.

Girls who had fallen pregnant when they were taken by rich sick fucks would give birth, and those babies were taken to a building in the middle of nowhere with minimal care. The children were undocumented—boys, girls, it doesn't matter.

When they're old enough, they're placed in a room to be drugged and raped. When they're selected to be so-called adopted by a rich family, documents appear, and the child thinks this family is their savior. The father a hero, the mother a saint. But none of it is real. There is no hero. There is no saint. It's just one sick man from hell with a twisted appetite. Then they take you wherever they came from. As for me, they brought me to the states.

"No, I don't."

She asks me how much money I have while I'm on campus and whether my meals are covered. I find her questions a bit odd, but I answer them as best I can. She inquiries about my last physical. I've never had a formal one, so I tell her I don't remember.

She then sends me to the next room to get one and to see a gynecologist for birth control. I should fight her on this but in my case, it isn't a bad thing. I would like to be checked anyway.

A woman with dark brown hair walks in and say her name is Dr. Mullen. I mention that I have an IUD, but says, she will check anyway. Maybe it's because I'm Prey, and this has nothing to do with John but rather the order. Perhaps they require all females to be on some type of contraceptive. I imagine the last thing they want is a bunch of poor kids with rich babies in their stomachs, messing up their bloodlines.

John told me he had one placed when I was unconscious so I wouldn't get pregnant. I felt relieved. I overheard some girls had their reproductive organs removed.

I'm on the examining table; the woman's head is positioned between my legs, with my heels resting on two metal supports at the end of the table. I feel a tug between my legs. I tilt my head to the side, and watch her as she removes her gloves, but catch a glimpse of bloody fluid on the tips.

"Is there something wrong?" I ask in alarm. Maybe John or someone ruined my insides, or I have some type of disease.

"Everything is fine. The bloody discharge is normal. Your IUD is intact. If you want to regulate your period, it's best to start taking your birth control at the beginning of your cycle."

I want to tell her my cycle is fine, but I'm eager to leave. I'm uncomfortable and want to take a shower. I never expected this visit and don't know who to believe.

I grab my pills from the lady at the front and head toward my dorm building. My stomach drops when my phone goes off. I stare at the screen in horror.

John: Get in the car outside your dorm building.

I look up at the loading zone in front of the building and see a blacked-out Escalade idling.

The SUV drops me off in front of the massive entrance of John and Mary's home. I stare at the dark brown double doors like it's a prison and I'm to be sent to the electric chair. I'm not sure why he wants me here during the week. He said weekends, but he skipped last weekend, so maybe he wants to make up for lost time.

The door opens.

The woman who cleans the house doesn't look me in the eyes. She must think I'm disgusting for the things John does and says when she's hovering around. She must think I like it because I don't protest when deep inside, I'm screaming to die.

"Hello, Georgina," I greet, like I do every time.

She turns around, dismissing me like she always does, but I don't care. I hoped maybe one day she would have mercy on me, but I know she won't.

The faint smell of food and coffee makes my stomach churn. My appetite is gone. It's a familiar feeling I've grown accustomed to when I'm in this house. Who would feel hungry when they're a sex slave?

My hands tremble around the torn strap of my bookbag. The deeper I follow her down the long hallway, the louder the voices.

She turns into the dining room with the massive table for fifteen. The cream marble floors with blood-red veins. The grotesque red curtains Mary insisted on draping over the oversized windows.

I hate this house.

I hate the people and the furniture.

"There she is," John says when Georgina moves to the side.

"You didn't tell me, Mother, that my sister was so petite and small," a voice that could only belong to Garret says warmly.

My throat goes dry remembering the taste of his breath. The look on his face when he came. This is a joke. I've never seen Garret set foot in this house. We both know he doesn't see me as a sister.

"Sit," Mary says, coldly watching me like I'm a fly she wants to squash. "I wouldn't call her your sister."

"Well, step-sibling," Garret says with a smile, but I can tell he doesn't find it amusing.

He's wearing a fitted blue sweater that outlines the muscles of his pecs, doing nothing to hide the mural of tattoos on his neck reaching his jawline. I sit across from Garret, next to John, but he isn't having it.

"Why don't you sit next to me so we can get to know each other better?" Garret's gaze slides to John. I can feel the tension radiate between them. John's eyes turn cold, like he wants nothing more than to reach across the massive table and rip his throat out, but Garret doesn't seem fazed. He continues to watch John closely, daring him to object.

Mary smiles triumphantly. And me? I don't know if I should be happy or terrified. One monster or the other. Two of Satan's most powerful demons facing off.

I don't have to be told to move to the other side and take the seat right next to Garret. I sit, and when I inhale the scent of his cologne, my heart starts to beat like a thousand drums in a parade. He moves his hands from the table to his thighs.

My gaze drops to the back of one of his hands with a skull. The veins disappearing under the edge of the sleeve. His clean fingernails. The black nail polish gone, replaced by a clean manicure.

"Have you seen each other on campus?" Mary asks, but I know why she's asking.

"It's obvious I haven't. I've been busy with swimming and…"

"The orgies at those parties you like to throw," John interrupts. "You've heard," Garret replies, but his gaze is scrutinizing him like darts aiming at a bullseye. "You can come if you want to, John. It might be your kind of party."

Mary sucks in a breath.

I swallow, staring at the plate in front of me as Georgina comes beside me and places a piece of meat that smells like dirty socks on my plate. John glances at me and then at Garret, measuring the distance between our chairs. Jealousy and possession drip from his scrutiny like a blazing fire. "Oh, Garret, you're so funny sometimes," Mary chuckles, trying to play it off like it's a joke. Garret tilts back his head and laughs, and it strokes my skin like a caress. How can a laugh be so beautiful yet so dangerous? "I'm fucking with you, John," he says, but I'm not sure John's convinced. This is the first time I've seen John uncomfortable, and it's almost like he's terrified of Garret. "How's school and swimming? Any girlfriends?" Mary asks genuinely, her knife and fork cutting into the meat with precision. I think she cares about Garret and what he thinks, but with who she married, I'm not so sure. I wonder what Garret's father was like. Was he like Garret or John? "I'm beating my time. I think we will go all the way again this year. And her name is Cassie."

The bitter taste of his lie burns, like embers smoldering beneath my ribs, flaring into something foreign. He lied! My stomach clenches. What type of girlfriend lets her boyfriend stay in the library with his cock out with another girl after he dismisses her? "You have to bring her by so we can meet her," Mary gushes, as if he just told her he's getting married. I stare at my plate but feel empty. A waste of space. I don't even know why they bother letting me dine at the table with them. I'm always sent to my room to eat. I don't even know which fork goes with what or why the hell this meat looks like human brains. "Rose?" I look up and meet John's impenetrable gaze. "Eat," he scolds, like I'm a child. I pick up the smallest fork. "Wrong fork," Mary snaps. I drop it like I've been slapped. "I-I'm sorry," I stammer, knowing that John will make me pay for it later. "Mary." But it's not John scolding her; it's Garret. "Give her a break."

"She needs to eat. I've told John she needs to see a doctor for her eating disorder. She's skin and bones." John stares at her like she revealed a secret, but she goes off, knowing John wouldn't disrespect Mary in front of Garret. "He's complained about it before." John turns his focus on me like he's just found out I stole his car as she continues her rant. "She's always had a problem eating since she was little."

"Isss that sooo," Garret says, his voice dripping with sarcasm, each syllable stretched out like a rubber band being pulled. His gaze flicks to me like I'm under a spotlight, the heat of his stare sinking into my bones. His hand is on my thigh, and I swear my breathing stops. "I'll have to make sure she eats then," Garret says, like I'm not even in the room. The heat from his hand spreads like smoke between my thighs. He's so close yet so far. I don't know if I should shove it away or stand. But then, John will know, and he'll make sure it won't happen again. "I give her money for meals, and she's on the meal plan at school," John counters.

"The food at school is disgusting," Garret states. He isn't wrong. The food looks like it's about to expire. It's not meant for the wealthy but for prey. "How much money are you giving her?"

"I beg your pardon?" John says accusingly, like his card was just declined. "Money?" Garret says, as if he's stupid and hard of hearing. "How much money are you giving her?"

I want to hide under the table.

He could ask me, but Garret knows I won't tell him, and I'm trying to figure out why he suddenly cares. "Enough," John bellows harshly.

"Oh honey, she has everything she needs. I know you always wanted a sister or brother, but…"

"You were too busy taking them out of your stomach so you wouldn't get fat," Garret interjects, taking a sip of his wine.

Mary places her knife down with a clank. "It's not my fault I'm fertile. Your father wanted more children and forbade me to be on any contraceptive. I had a son like he wanted."

"What is so wrong with him wanting more?"

I can feel the anger building, a ten-foot wave wanting to destroy the little fake charade she has going with John. I glance at Garret's plate. He hasn't touched the food either. "I've had enough of you." She's an even bigger monster when she smiles at John as he pours himself another scotch. "John understands. He doesn't want children. Besides, we have Rose."

I want to gag. She's delusional.

Garret throws his napkin onto the meat, the blood bleeding through the white linen. "I gotta go."

"Already?" Mary cries. "But…you just got here."

"I've been here for the past hour, Mary."

"But you haven't eaten your food," she whines.

"It looks like shit."

"It's liver," she explains as if it's a delicacy. "And I'm sure it tastes like shit," he replies dryly. "It is why Rose hasn't touched hers, and I don't blame her." The chair screams when he pushes it back to stand. "I'll drop off Rose."

Why is he defending me?

"That's unnecessary," John argues, placing his scotch glass on the wood with a thud. "I don't think you have a choice," Garret replies scathingly.

Mary glances between John and Garret with wide eyes.

"Let's go, Rose." And he walks out. I don't wait; I grab my bag from the floor and rush out before someone stops me.

The front door slams behind me. I look at the massive driveway and spot him getting into a shiny blacked-out car with two huge letter Rs on the hood. I move to the passenger side and hesitate to pull on the handle. The engine rumbles, and then he's stepping out and walking around the front. He pushes me back gently, pulls the handle, and the smell of rich leather hits me like a caress.

I look up, and his face is hard. Angry. "Get in," he demands.

I slide in, not knowing if this is what I should be doing. My mind and body battle over what is the right thing to do: leave with him or stay and face John. I don't get to decide because Garret is placing the car in drive, pulling out of the driveway. I stare at the screen on his dash, then at his hands and the way they grip the steering wheel. The skull tattoo mocks me with its smile. I sit rigid, afraid to lean back and tarnish his car. It's beautiful, like him. It reminds me of an enchanting, rare black butterfly that's poisonous if you touch it.

"Just so we're clear," he mutters harshly. "I'm not your brother."

GARRET

THERE IS something about Rose I can't figure out. She occupies my thoughts every waking moment, even when all I want to do is ruin her—break her into pieces so I can create the perfect version of her. But I can't, because she is beautiful the way she is. Lies and all.

What if I ruin the look in her eyes that she reserves only for me? The tremble in her hands when I'm near her. The look that battles between lust and hate.

I sit outside her door, listening, hoping that my name slips from her lips. But it doesn't. It's always "stop," followed by the sadness in her cries—cries that fill my soul.

I'm fucked up. I know I am, and it's no secret. I'm a killer, and I enjoy pain.

I was ordered to kill her—an order given when a Prey knows too much. She's a liability, but I can't.

John still doesn't know the real reason for my visit. All he knows is that the Order sent me to meet her. They know we've talked on campus. There are cameras, and I don't care if they saw me come all over her hands. They've seen worse.

But I couldn't help myself. I want to degrade her, show her how my hate spills from my cock for wanting her the way I do. Even if I can't fuck her because she'll ruin me if I did.

"Where are you taking me?" she asks in a fragile voice pulling me from my thoughts

I wish I could tell that I'm going to kill her and be done with it, but I can't. Not yet.

I had a spot picked out near the abandoned house the consortium uses for its victims. The others don't know the Order wants her dead. Not Valen, the twins, Reid, Azriel, Melody, Veronica, Gia, or Jess. They're not supposed to. All they know is she's on her own until she graduates, but what they don't know is that they signed her death warrant.

"Wherever I want," I say instead.

She looks away, staring at the dark-tinted window. The silence is thick with tension, unlit, waiting for the right spark. I'm not sure what I'm even doing being this close to her.

All I know is that I couldn't leave her there with him. The way he looks at her disgusts me. It's like the sharp end of a knife slicing my skin open.

I pull into the famous diner where all the sons of Kenyan have taken their wives. Except she isn't going to be anyone's wife. Ever.

"You didn't have to offer," she says suddenly. "I couldn't have stayed."

"You like the attention John gives you?" She glances at me with sadness and hate in her eyes every time his name is mentioned, and I don't know why she doesn't leave. Why she accepts the way he treats her for money. Why she told the biggest lie to the only people who could protect her.

And I hate her for it.

"Let's go." I get out, not waiting for her answer. It's probably just another lie, and I don't want another reason to kill her.

Walking up the steps, I turn around, waiting for her to get out of the car. I'm not chivalrous. I surprised myself when I opened her door to begin with. I wait a few seconds while she contemplates getting out of the car. I press the unlock button on the key fob, hoping she gets the hint from the clicking sound. A few guys from Ohio State Walk up in their letterman jackets right when she steps out of the car.

The guys stop whatever they were saying, and one of them mutters, "Damn," staring at the car. But when she straightens her faded sweater, trying to cover the sliver of skin on her small waist because it's a size too small, outlining the generous amount of breasts underneath, I notice it's not my Rolls Spectre they're looking at, as I'm used to, but her.

The feeling of possessiveness when another man looks at her drives me insane when it shouldn't. The way their greedy gaze slides over every curve, thinking of all the ways they could fuck her. The way these assholes are doing now. The way Luke did when he asked her to my party. What I had to do to Luke's face when he said he was going to fuck her. Why I marked her with my cum and warned her not to go.

The one wearing a fucking cowboy hat steps forward and says, "Hi." I recognize him. He's this year's new quarterback for Ohio State from Texas. She smiles awkwardly, and annoyance settles in the pit of my stomach. "Nice car."

What a loser.

"It's not mine," she says truthfully.

"Ahh… boyfriend," he says, fishing for the truth. She shakes her head. I watch in slow motion as his eyes light up like she gave him the greatest gift in the world. Her voice and an opening to keep talking to her. Stealing her eyes, her voice, and her time when they weren't his. "I'm—"

"In the way," I interrupt him scornfully. He looks up, and so do his stupid friends. I watch his expression turn to shock when he recognizes me. "What's up, Garret?" he says nervously, looking between me and Rose. "Could you move? I'm kind of hungry." I open the door wider, forcefully holding it open, arching my brow at Rose to hurry the fuck up before I stab him in the eyes, break his fucking hands, and cut out his tongue. Rose doesn't argue and moves like it started to rain.

Dorathy smiles when she places the menus on the table, her matchmaking eyes shifting between me and Rose. "I haven't seen you here in a while, handsome," she smiles. "Who's the pretty lady?"

Rose grins awkwardly, not knowing what to say, and I'm pissed at the way the asshole keeps looking this way. If it weren't for Dorathy, I would have walked over there. I grab the menu and scan it like I don't know what I want. "Her name is Rose."

"Hi, Rose," Dorathy says brightly. "I'm Dorathy."

Rose smiles, and my chest tightens at how gorgeous she is when her lips stretch, showing her white teeth. One is slightly shifted, and I want the imprint of her bite on my skin. "It's nice to meet you, Dorathy," she replies gently. Dorathy looks at me with pride in her eyes. "She's gorgeous, Garret."

"She's not my girlfriend," I point out.

"Well, I guess some other guy will be lucky to have her then."

Rose looks down at the menu. We both know that isn't going to happen for very different reasons. I place my order. Dorathy patiently waits for Rose. Rose bites the corner of her lip. It's so innocent. I'm not sure she knows she does it. She looks at Dorothy like she's summoning the courage to speak. "Can I have a glass of water and fries? The small basket, please?"

I frown, scanning the menu and finding the small basket of fries where Dorothy created a value menu. A small basket of fries is $2.95. What the fuck? "She'll have the special, Dorothy," I order. "Burger, large fry, and a strawberry milkshake."

Dorothy smiles, ignoring Rose's panicked expression. "There we go," she says, taking the menus. When Dorothy is out of earshot, something flashes in Rose's eyes. "Why did you do that?"

"Because you're too skinny, and you need to eat."

"Why the fuck do you care?" she says, as if I offended her.

"Hmm… I like this side of you so much better. You should let out whatever the fuck is keeping you from speaking up. I know there's a wildfire inside waiting to be lit."

She rolls her eyes.

"And you're the fucking match, right?"

"Is that what you want, Rose?" I lean close. "You want me to be your match?"

Her pupils go wide. Her brown eyes are so rich, I would pay anything to drown in them.

Her straight hair frames her face, so pretty and delicate. I bet my hands would leave dents a flat iron couldn't straighten.

"Why are you doing this?" she asks, looking around the red-and-white decorated diner like she's never been to one.

"I don't know what you mean. I was hungry and bored with

useless people. Don't read too much into it. I said I would make sure you ate, and unlike you, I keep my promises."

"Like you did to your girlfriend, Cassie," she says sardonically. I smile when I see jealousy the spark of jealousy in her eyes. "I thought we talked about this. I don't have a girlfriend."

"But you told your mother…"

"I said I kept my promises. I never said I didn't lie."

"What promise is that?"

I lean back. "Well, that depends."

"On?" she presses, trying to sound tough.

"What I want," I say truthfully.

"What do you want?" she asks, curiously, but I can tell deep down she's afraid of the answer.

Her eyes tell me what her words can't. She's afraid I want her. That I would break the wall we've built between us. A wall we couldn't break because we weren't sure if we would survive once we crossed it, but I have to kill her.

And then there's the part of me that can't end her without me in it.

ROSE

AFTER WE ATE, I was glad the guys from Ohio took the hint. I don't know what came over Garret or why he decided to order me so much food. How did he know I would love a strawberry shake?

I lean my head back and stare at the stars twinkling on the black ceiling of his car. I didn't think cars were equipped with stars on the ceiling. It's dark but alive at the same time—beautiful with minimal light.

"They come with the car," he says, as if he's reading my thoughts.

I look out the window instead, watching my dorm building flash by. "Where are you taking me?"

"I need to stop at my house first," he replies, as if he's just going to sleep over.

"You could drop me off, so you don't have to go back," I reason, trying to hide the panic threatening to rise in my stomach.

I don't want to go to his house, where it smells like him. Where I know what his sheets feel like, only to see them gone. Where I remember him bathing me and shaving me bare, where he told me I was disgusting.

He doesn't respond, and it enrages me further, but I don't push. I'm afraid he'll snap.

He pulls into his driveway, and the garage door automatically opens to reveal a row of cars I've heard people talk about around John, like their precious collectibles. Different makes and models, but all share the same color: black. There are at least five or six, including the one we're in. He parks in the empty spot and shuts off the car.

He closes the garage, and I watch through the rearview mirror with horror as it descends like a trapdoor.

"Get out," he says, his voice a deep whisper that sends goosebumps erupting across my skin.

I do as he says, taking my bag and following him inside.

A shiver runs down my spine. What would John do to me if he found out? How would I survive his jealous wrath? "How long is this going to take? I have class tomorrow."

He looks over his shoulder, and the intense look in his eyes makes me shudder. "As long as it takes." His words float above me like dust in the late afternoon sun, with nowhere to go.

I walk to the couch in the living room and sit, avoiding the hallway he disappeared into. His house is grand and opulent like John and Mary's, but decorated differently. I can tell things have been removed and replaced. There's a cream and red chair that Mary would have picked out, with giant black letters spray-painted across it that read, CUNT.

Anyone could tell a man lives here. The rest of the furniture is black and gold. It looks Italian—modern, with a mix of traditional pieces like gilded mirrors and frames on the walls. Italian chairs surround a large rug with the same baroque details as the sheets in the room.

The rich black leather couch is modern yet comfortable. I take a deep breath, and a sense of calm washes over me. I can see myself in a house like this, with a man who loves me—sitting right in this exact spot, reading a book and waiting for my husband to come home from work to kiss me. A fairytale I could get lost in.

I wake up with a jolt and a shuddering sob. I look around and remember I'm not in my dorm. The smell of cinnamon teases my nose. The room spins, and I blink rapidly, hoping it will stop. I clutch my stomach, telling myself I'm safe and that I fell asleep, but then I remember that I'm in Garret's house, and he never took me back to my dorm.

He disappeared.

It's dark except for the light from the glowing flames of the electric fireplace. I grip the sheet covering my body and notice it's the same one from that night.

"Do you always cry when you sleep?" My heart threatens to burst out of my chest. I wipe the tears off my cheeks with a clammy hand.

Garret is sitting in a single chair deep in the shadows, watching me.

Studying me.

"What time is it?" I ask, my throat raw.

"A little after one a.m."

The last thing I want to tell him is about my nightmares. I pull the sheet away. "It's really late. I should be heading back."

"I didn't want to wake you," he says, as if he cares.

"So you watched me sleep?"

He gets up, and I try not to cower when he walks toward me. "Come," he says, then turns around, heading down the same hallway he disappeared from, illuminated by long black modern sconces on the wall.

I grab my bag and sheet, dragging them along with me until he stops in front of the door. There are so many down the long hallway; I don't remember which one I was in the last time I was here. All I could think about was leaving when the Uber arrived.

When he opens it, familiarity blankets me. The king-sized bed that felt like a cloud sits in the center of the room, like a bottomless pool of comfort.

I walk in and freeze. Something black moves toward me, and I step back in fear when the dog with the spiked collar growls.

I step back further.

Then a few steps more until my back hits something warm, hard, and solid.

"Shhh…" His breath fans my hair, causing goosebumps to spread along the side of my neck. "Don't show him fear. Fear is what feeds the attack. Fear is what breaks you inside."

"That's because he isn't about to shred you into pieces."

"It's his protective instinct."

"That's why you need to take me home," I argue.

The massive Doberman seizes the moment to run up to me and sniff the sheets, then my legs. I turn my head to the side, a scream threatening to rise from my throat. The dog looks up, the dark orbs of his eyes resting on me as he sits on his back legs, analyzing whether I'm a threat.

Garret snaps his fingers. "Ace, stay," he commands. The dog walks back to the foot of the bed and lies on the floor. "He knows your scent," Garret rasps, inhaling the aroma of my skin. Heat spreads over my body to the juncture between my thighs. I can feel the stubble from his cheek against my temple, his breath fanning my ear. "You have nothing to be afraid of. Watch."

The dog observes

us, his eyes following Garret's hand as it slides around my throat. "Ace is a good judge of character. He keeps coming back to this room looking for you."

I don't know how to interpret that statement or how I should feel about it.

The dog growls when Garret's hand tightens around my neck, stealing my breath. I should shove him away, but I'm terrified of what the dog might do. Will he attack? Will he shred me to pieces before Garret can stop him?

"He's not growling at you, Rose. He's growling at me for touching you." The dog's ears point to the ceiling, and his snout is wet. Garret is right; he doesn't look happy.

"How is that possible?"

"Ace is moody and overprotective when he sees something he likes—something worth protecting." The dog whines and lowers his head, unsure of what to do. "See, even my dog wants you, Rose." His lips skim my neck, causing my nipples to harden. My knees threaten to buckle. "You're safe here."

He releases me, and it feels like stepping into the dark, cold night when he moves away.

"If you want to take a shower, it's through the door to your left," he says, pausing at the threshold. "There's a robe and a towel in the warmer. I'm sure you know how the shower works."

I turn around, but he's already gone.

"Read this part here," Azriel says, pointing to the paragraph.

I'm struggling in my Literature class. I thought math would be a problem, but once the professor told us we had to write an analysis on a selection of written works, I didn't know what to do. I had no choice; I had to sign up with Azriel for more tutoring.

I begin, but I struggle by the fourth word. I stop and glance at Azriel. My heart sinks when I see the grimace on his face.

"It's bad," I say with a frustrated sigh.

"Has it always been like this?" Azriel asks softly, a pitying look in his gaze.

"I struggle a bit," I confess, placing a strand of hair behind my ear.

He stares at my assignment, and I know he must be thinking there is no way I'll pass. There are times I want to give up and let them fail me, but my pride gets in the way. I know that if I had the right schooling, the right opportunity, I would succeed. I get the assignment, but I have to read to understand it. It's like trying to fix a car with no tools.

He scratches his brow. "Do you have friends in your class that you can study with? Someone in the dorm who can help? Read it to you?"

I hadn't thought about making friends in my classes for the purpose of studying. I can't think of anything, knowing I'm on my own in a place like this, considering what I do. Who do I trust?

You trust Garret enough to stay in his house.

He took me to school instead of ordering an Uber this morning. He dropped me off in front of my dorm without a word and then drove off.He also made sure I had a bowl of fruit on a tray in my room in the morning, as well as new clothes in my size.

I don't know what to think or why he did it, but I'm grateful.

"I didn't think I could make a friend." He looks up. "You know, after everything." I scan the library as if someone is out to get me at any second.

"It doesn't work like that," he says, lowering his voice.

I lean forward. "How does it work exactly?"

Any help I can get will be welcome at this point. Staying at Garret's house has clouded my judgment. John hasn't texted me. It's as if Garret has the power to keep him away, and I don't know what to make of it.

"Keep to yourself and don't fall into a trap."

"What do you mean?" I ask curiously. I don't have a guy in the Order who is in love with me and will keep me safe.

The current one ruling the school hates my existence. Garret doesn't want me; he wants to destroy me.

"You say no at all costs, Rose. Do you hear me?" I nod. "If any asshole corners you, you say no. And you don't go anywhere where you might find yourselfalone with them, especially Garret."

"What about me?"

My stomach flips.

Garret takes the seat next to Azriel, looking at him as if he wants to slit his throat and play with his vocal cords.

Azriel looks at him unfazed and then at me. "I was warning Rose to be careful on campus."

"I heard my name," Garret points out. Then he glances at the designer sweater he left on the dresser this morning, as if he's peeling it off my chest. "Nice sweater." He gives me a wink.

My cheeks flush. Azriel looks at me and then back at Garret. "What are you doing, Garret?" Azriel says in a hard tone, like he's scolding a child.

"I came to say hi." He glances at my assignment in front of Azriel. "You need help?"

"No."

Ignoring me, Garret picks up the paper with the list of works to choose from for an analysis. He scans the list and places it on the table, turning it around to point. "Edgar Allan Poe's *Annabel Lee*."

Azriel looks at me. We both know it would be difficult for me to read and analyze.

"She's going to need a lot of help with that one," Azriel begins.

"I'll help her," Garret says, snatching the paper. "You can help her with the math and stuff. I'll help her with this."

I'm about to protest, but Garret gets up and walks out as if his word is final and I've agreed to let him help me.

"Fuck," Azriel says, rubbing his eyes.

I watch Garret through the glass window, wanting to stab him when he smiles at a group of girls.

"Why?"

"Because he's fucking crazy," Azriel mutters, as if that's supposed to make me feel better.

"What do I do now?"

"Nothing," he says. "There's nothing you can do, Rose. The guys messed with him when he was younger. He got into some trouble and was always the crazy kid left alone in his big house, getting whatever he wanted. Then his father died two years ago, and he spiraled. He was put on medication. When his mother remarried after being left with nothing, he went dark. It was as if the lights were on, but no one was home. No one—and I mean no one—could change his mind once he set it on something. He smiles, laughs, plays along. But some of us know it's all a lie. Garret doesn't give a shit. He does whatever he wants."

"What makes him so different from your brother or…the others?"

He exhales forcefully through his nose. "Simple. Garret doesn't answer to anyone. He doesn't have a father to respect because he's dead. His mother even less, because all she cares about is her Bentley and how much is in her bank account. He basically grew up fending for himself in his father's mansion, and it's no different now that he's dead. The only people he answers to are the Order. He has everything at his disposal." He snorts. "Garret has so much money that there's no way he can spend it all in three lifetimes. What does a man with power and an unlimited bank account do?"

The most I've had was twenty dollars to last me three days before I had to spend it. "I wouldn't know."

"Whatever the hell he wants. The Nox family has power and connections, and he's the only Nox left. That is what makes Garret dangerous, Rose. He can do anything because his father made sure of it."

ROSE

THE ROOM FILLS with students when the professor walks in. I make my way toward the back, where a girl with strawberry blond hair sits.

She takes out a notebook from her bag.

Being around the others last year, I can tell she's prey. Her clothes are not designer, and the deer-in-the-headlights look she gives the others gives it away. The privileged here are cocky and stand out. They know everyone, and if you stay in the dorms, you'll recognize certain faces. I've seen her a couple of times but never thought to talk to her until now.

I'm sure Azriel is taking a huge risk in helping me. I still don't know why, but the least I can do is help myself. This is something I can control. That gives me hope. Garret knowing I could barely read and write is too much of a risk. He isn't going to be there when John finds out and gets ahold of me. It also shows weakness—a vulnerability that isn't wise to share with someone like him.

The intense way Azriel looked at me when he spoke about Garret set off an alarm bell in the back of my head—a warning I recognize when something bad is brewing. Garret showing up wasn't a mere coincidence. He's watching me like a predator does when he's already caught his prey and is waiting for the right time to kill it, and Azriel, he's doing his best to try to warn me.

"Is this seat taken?" I ask. She looks up with wide eyes and then grins.

"No, go ahead." A sense of relief washes over me.

"Great." I'm awkward around others, and I hope I can pull this off and she doesn't find me weird.

I take out my notebook and open it to the page where I wrote Edgar Allan Poe's name.

"Oh, are you working on that one?" she asks.

I nod. "Yeah," I say, glad for the opening I need.

"That's a tough one, I think. I'm doing this one." She points at the sheet Garret took the other day—the one I need to get back. I can't read the one she's pointing at because she pulls the paper away before I can make out the words. Fuck. This is not going the way I planned. "Hey, if you want, we could go over it together."

I raise my brows hopefully. "Alright."

"We could critique each other's work. Maybe hang out."

It's like a huge weight has lifted off my chest. She gives me her number and tells me her name is Amy. She asks where I hang out and what my dorm number is. I tell her I don't have a specific place. I agree to her invite to a small party off campus.

I forget about John and Garret. I forget about my past and my nightmares.

For the first time, it feels like I can breathe. I don't have to lie to this girl. I don't have to pretend. I listen to every single word the professor says, trying to take notes the best I can—in a way I can understand. He drones on about what is required for the assignment and, of course, a reminder of when it's due—two weeks from today.

I'm about to walk to my dorm room after my last class when my phone goes off.

Unknown: Meet me after class. Pool.

I don't have to guess who it's from, and I won't bother to ask how he got my number. I also don't want to piss him off, so I walk toward the indoor pool on campus. I've never seen the guys at swim practice—not with Melody or the others. We always met up in the quad or at the bar across the street.

I don't know what to expect, but when I pull the door open and the smell of chlorine hits me in the face, it isn't this. The bleachers are filled with people—mostly girls fangirling over the guys wearing swim trunks. I can't blame them. Their bodies are perfection.

There isn't an ounce of body fat on them, but then I notice this is not a practice but a swim meet. On the other side of the pool, there are more guys half-naked—abs and muscles made to snatch a girl's attention. Someone whistles, snagging my attention, and I realize it's the coach from the Kenyan swim team getting the team together. I spot Garret, and my heart almost stops. He's gorgeous. My mouth goes dry. He stands above most of the guys, but his tattoos ripple along with his muscles when he moves. I've only seen him with his clothes on, and I knew he was ripped, but the man is dangerous in every way. It's hard not to stare. I walk up the bleachers on the home team side and sit in the empty row on top to get a clear view of the pool.

"Let's go, Nox!" a girl screams. Garret turns around and grins. My heart sinks when I see it's Cassie. She blows him a kiss, and I get the sudden urge to grab her by the hair and drown her. I don't know why he asked me to come. He obviously has plenty of fans. I'm about to get up, but then someone waves in my direction while standing next to Garret. I notice it's Luke. I look behind me and then back. He waves again, catching Garret's attention. I notice he has a large cut on his lip and wonder how he got it, but then I feel Garret's gaze on my skin. He shakes his head slowly in warning. I sit, letting him think I'm staying. I don't like the attention I'm getting from everyone.

Cassie looks over her shoulder; when she spots me, she sneers, "Don't think about it, bitch. I saw you watching us like some kind of creep." People turn and stare at me like I'm a stalker. I could pretend that her words don't sting, that the laughter from her friends doesn't crawl under my skin. The mocking glances from the others as they whisper only heighten my discomfort. I keep my head down, knowing there is no point in telling Cassie to go fuck herself. There are more of them and one of me. There is no one who would help me or come to my defense. Like always, I have no one. Tears burn behind my eyes, but I make sure to look away. "Is she going to cry?" Cassie says loud enough for everyone to hear. I get up to leave before the last bit of my pride snaps, and I do something I will later regret. I shouldn't have come here. Fuck her. And fuck them. These entitled pricks aren't worth it. I walk out, the cold air smacking me in the face. I take a deep breath to steady the hammering of my heart. The weight that was lifted earlier slams back on my chest, trapping me inside. I head for my dorm and decide I will stay inside until school tomorrow morning. I can get something to eat from the vending machine. I'm down the hall, about to turn left to get to my door when my name is called.

"Rose?" I turn around. "Amy?" She smiles. "Hey, I was about to knock on your door. Want to grab a drink or a bite to eat across the street?" I smile like she's my savior. "Yeah, I would like that a lot."

Babylon is not as packed as the few times I was invited by Melody, most likely because of the swim meet on campus. I'm sure it's only a matter of time before students start pouring in to head to the bar and the pool tables. "Do you know what you're going to wear to the party?" Amy asks after we are shown to a booth. I haven't thought of the party or what I'll wear. The truth is, I have nothing to wear. "I'm not sure." I stare at the small menu on the table, mentally calculating how much I have on my card. The waitress with six piercings on her face and orange hair stops by. Amy orders a beer, and I opt for water. "Oh, no," Amy says with a grin. "Make that two beers."

Before I can protest, the waitress scurries off. "I don't drink."

Amy leans forward. "Please tell me you've had a beer."

I haven't, but I don't want to sound like a prude, so I let it slide. The most I've had is Scotch—a drink I hate as much as the person who gave it to me laced with drugs. It was either needles or Scotch. Both I detest with every fiber of my being. "Not really. I'm not twenty-one."

"I am. I started school late, and my birthday was last month. Besides, she doesn't look the type to ask or give a shit either way."

I'm sure they are told not to when it comes to Prey. There is a different set of rules when it comes to anything involving Kenyan, Babylon included. The waitress comes back with our beer and my water. I take a sip of the amber liquid and hold back a wince from the bitter taste but play it off before she notices. "Who's the guy I saw you with at the library?"

My stomach drops. My thoughts fly to the afternoon on the shelves with Garret. "I'm not sure..."

"Not the swim team captain—the other one."

A sense of relief washes over me like a gust of wind. "Azriel."

Her eyes light up with interest. "So that's his name. I didn't think he went to Kenyan."

"He does, but he's a hybrid student. Mostly online. He tutors."

"He is so cute."

I should tell her to stay away, warn her, but who am I to tell her anything? It would also mean I would have to explain why. Then she would get scared and tell me to fuck off. Two things I can't risk. Azriel is nice, and he isn't evil like the others. He hasn't given me any reason to worry, but that doesn't mean he isn't. He's Valen's brother, after all. I'm sure he's part of something. They all are. "He is nice to look at," I tell her truthfully, and then a sense of protectiveness settles in my gut. I don't know where it came from, but I see Azriel like a brother, the same way he sees Melody like a sister. I shouldn't feel this way after the way things went, but Azriel has been the only one to help me, to warn me. He's shown me that he cares, even if it's stemmed from pity. "I guess I'll have to sign up for tutoring then."

"Be careful; he's a heartbreaker." I don't think I've ever seen Azriel look at another girl, but it's the only thing I can come up with. "You know, I thought he was your boyfriend at first, but then the other guy showed up… Garret is his name, right?"

"I don't have a boyfriend. He was there for Azriel." I hate lying. It's like a disease that acts up when you least expect it, but I don't want to talk about Garret. I came along to make a friend and forget about him. "So, about the party. What are you planning on wearing? I heard it's fun and it's where both Kenyan and Ohio students go to hang out without killing each other."

I've heard of it but have never gone, most likely because my weekends were occupied or I was unconscious. "I've never been invited."

"I haven't gone either. I transferred from another school."

I'm curious to know where she came from. I didn't see her in any of my classes or on campus last year. "What school?"

Her eyes dim, and I can tell there is a story she isn't ready to tell, so I keep it light. I guess we all have stories we are afraid to tell and sometimes ones we can't. "Delaware."

"I've never been."

"Boring. You're not missing anything special." Definitely a story back there. "I applied for a transfer, and this place offered a scholarship based on my GPA. I couldn't say no."

I don't want to rain on her parade and reveal the real reason. It would scare her off, and they wouldn't let her go either way. These people are evil. Once you accept, it's like you've pledged your life in blood, and you didn't even know it. They make sure she will never graduate anywhere else—probably blacklist her wherever she goes. That's why I keep my mouth shut and make it my mission to look out for her. One good deed to erase the lies I've had to spill. She talks about the things she likes, her favorites. I tell her I have none because I don't. There wasn't much to compare anything to with my limited experience, and everything I did try was part of an act I was forced to endure. If it was food, a song, a drink, a smell, or a feeling, I ended up hating it because it reminded me of the time I had to try it.

Music starts to play, and then voices get louder. Within the hour, the place is crawling with students. My guess is the meet is over, and judging by the happy faces, Kenyan dominated. "Oh my God," Amy says with excitement, bopping her head to the intro. "I love this song. It's 'Everything I Do Is for You' by Amira Elfeky." She glances at the jukebox to see who selected it, and my heart feels like it's going to stop. Garret is standing like a skyscraper. His tall, muscular back underneath a tight long-sleeved shirt molds to his frame. The band of his sweatpants sits on his hips. I can tell he's fresh from a shower. The black strands of his hair on the back of his head are dark like ink from a black marker.

"Is that..." Amy trails off when he turns around, pushing the long strands of his straight hair off his face like a model in a commercial. His face is smooth. His chiseled jaw does things to my insides—the memory of his lips on my skin when he spoke, his breath causing heat to spread to my thighs. It all evaporates when Cassie walks up, standing on her toes and causing her skirt to lift almost above the cheeks of her ass. She is everything I'm not: beautiful with a nice body that guys drool over. He can keep lying all he wants—he's into her. You wouldn't have caught her sucking him off if he wasn't. I tear my gaze away. "Yeah, it was him. Garret."

"He's looking this way," she says, but I don't care. I'm focused on drinking my beer for moral support. I could care less if he told me to meet him after his swim meet and I left. I'm done being humiliated. "What's going on between you two? The girl with him is glaring this way."

"There is nothing going on. I was friends with him, and now I'm not. They graduated, so… it doesn't matter anymore."

"I don't think he feels the same, judging by the way he's staring. It looks like he wants to kidnap you."

She wouldn't be wrong, but not in the way she thinks. He isn't into me. He's playing games, like they all do to prey, and I'm on the menu. "I don't think his girlfriend, or whatever she is, will be happy about it. She already showed me her claws after I caught her sucking him off in the library." I take a large sip of my beer and place it on the table, letting the heat from the alcohol calm my anxiety. "If you hear about it in the morning, that's what happened. I don't think she was so happy about it."

"Is it because he's ignoring her and staring right at you?"

I sneak a glance. I can't help it. Sure enough, he's leaning on the jukebox like he owns it and staring at me with his black eyes. The heat from his gaze feels like it's threatening to melt my skin.

He heads this way after ignoring Cassie's attempt to grab his attention and storms off. Shit. I stare straight ahead at Amy. I can see apprehension in her expression when he walks up and slides into the booth next to me. "Why did you leave?" he asks, his mouth inches from my cheek. I can feel his eyes rolling over my skin. I turn and stare him down. "Why don't you ask your girlfriend?"

He smiles, but it's not friendly. "She's not my girlfriend."

I arch my brow. "Could have fooled me."

"Yeah, now everyone thinks Rose likes to watch you get it on in the library," Amy chimes in my defense. "Looks serious to me."

Garret shifts in his seat and faces Amy with an unreadable expression. "And you are?"

"Amy," I reply. "She's in my Lit class. We're catching up. We have to study for our current reading assignment."

"Is that right?" he drawls, still looking at Amy. She shifts in her seat under his scrutiny and grabs her beer, chugging the rest in one go. "What do you want, Garret? Don't you have someone waiting for you to nail them to a cross?"

He chuckles darkly. "What a great idea, my little Darkthorn."

"I'm not your anything," I sneer, my tone curling like smoke. I'm done playing this game with him. I won't let him ruin my every waking moment. I have enough with John and his shit. I don't need to add Garret to my mountain of fears. "Hurry up with your little friend," he says dismissively. "You have class tomorrow." He gets up, grabs my half-empty glass of beer, and walks off in the direction of the bar.

"What was that about?" Amy asks after a few seconds.

"I don't know."

Garret heads to the pool table area where Cassie and her friends are hanging out, drinking shots. He says something to her, and judging by the look on her face from where I'm sitting, she isn't thrilled. She glares in my direction when he walks away and heads back over. "I think I'll see you tomorrow," I say as I get up.

"Sure."

I stop the waitress when she passes by. "Can I have the bill, please?"

"Oh, your boyfriend took care of it," she announces with a smile and a wink before she walks off with her tray. My eyes dart to Amy. "Don't stay up too late," she beams, as if I'm going to hook up with a celebrity. If she only knew.

GARRET

"SHE DOESN'T HAVE the right blood, Garret. You know the rules."

"Neither did Veronica," I reply.

Alaric's gaze hardens. I struck a nerve. He hates when another man speaks his beloved wife's name. But I saved her—more than once. Not in the way he would like. But in a way, she saved me.

It's true. She was supposed to be in the dorms, but the sadistic bastard her mother married wouldn't allow it.

"True," Caruthers agrees. He's the oldest one in the room so he gets the final ruling when it comes to Prey.

But I can see the wheels turning in the old man's head. He's playing right into my game. And he doesn't even know it.

"And what do you propose?"

I don't hesitate. "She stays with me."

"Absolutely not!" John roars.

I smirk. It's not up to him. No one but Caruthers and the others—the real players in this game—know why I have to be involved.

Valen and Reid watch me with interest. They haven't decided how they want this to end. But I have.

Rose is mine. I want to peel her apart, layer by layer. She only gives me glimpses. But she's pulling away. I can see it in her eyes—She's giving up on me. A girl like her doesn't stay interested for long. She's taught herself not to trust. It's what people do when lying is their only choice.

"It's not up to you, John," Caruthers says. "It's up to me. You're lucky we don't kill you for the deception."

John's face darkens. "She gets nothing." He looks at me triumphantly.

I want to laugh in his face. "You think I'm conspiring, John?" I grin. "I have more money than your entire pathetic existence—your forefathers included—sitting in my bank account. I wouldn't burn through that amount if I died four times and came back. So please, don't insult yourself. I can smell your shit from here." I glance at Caruthers. "She stays with me. Until I see fit."

Caruthers exhales, impatient. "Fine." His voice cuts through the tension like a blade. "Enough talk about a girl with no future in our organization."

John's fury ignites. "You won't get away with this, Nox." He glares, seething. "I own her. She's mine."

I pick up my plague mask from the pew. "Please, try and stop me." My tone is dry, amused. But inside— I want to smash his face in.

I want to gut him open and play jump rope with his intestines.

Alaric meets me outside after the others leave. "What the fuck, Nox? You want your bloodline to die?"

I shrug. "I didn't mean to mention her. But it was the only way."

He adjusts his tailored suit jacket, the red Louis Vuitton tie unmistakably Veronica's choice. He never would have picked that out himself. Let alone worn a fucking tie. "A way to get your little toy out of the playpen?"

I scoff. "You would've done the same." I pause. "I need a favor."

He snorts. "What? You want my fucking balls? My cock? You want that too?" "I need Veronica to stop by the house."

He laughs. It's murderous. "Like fucking hell. You had a better chance with my dick."

"It's not for me. It's for her."

He rolls his shoulders."Ask any other asshole's wife you've fucked in the past. Why does it have to be mine?"

I exhale. "Jess is eight months pregnant. Melody wouldn't understand. And the twins don't let Gia out of their sight." I meet his gaze. "Veronica's the only one I trust."

He studies me. "Why her?"

I give him the real answer. "She's the only one who understands me."

Alaric walks to the cemetery entrance. The clouds shift, revealing the full moon. He sighs. "I should have hit you harder that day." His voice is flat. "I thought the pills we slipped you would teach you a lesson."

I shake my head. "That wasn't funny." He smirks. "I thought I had small dick syndrome for a year until the doctor told me about the side effects."

He grins, unrepentant. "You should have kept it in your pants before you fucked with Jess. It was Reid's idea."

Fucking assholes.

I shake my head. "Tell him he owes me."

"I think knowing you've tasted our wife's pussy is punishment enough."

I glare. "I said I was sorry."

Alaric exhales.

"What is it with you and this girl?"

I don't respond.

He continues.

"Melody wants to reach out to her. You said no. Repeatedly. And now this."

I hesitate. "I don't know yet. But I need you to find out where John adopted her from." He goes still. "There are no records. Something doesn't add up."

Alaric leans against the stone pillar. The moonlight catches in his dark eyes.

He finally nods. "Well, for one thing—John's a liar." He straightens. "It's obvious he's possessive of her."

"She has nightmares." I exhale. "The way she cries. The way she pleads."

Alaric's jaw tics. "Like Veronica did?"

I stare at my father's grave. "Yeah."

The tombstone doesn't say beloved father. Or beloved husband. Because he was neither.

He became a monster the day my mother terminated every child he put inside her—except me. I thought he hated me for being the only one she chose to keep. But it wasn't hatred. It was pity. He used me against her.

He was a liar, a killer, a deceiver. But he loved his legacy. And that meant, in his twisted way—he loved me.

I was his sole heir to the Nox estate, the fortune, the company—mine.

No stipulations. No forced marriage. No need for heirs.

I could have walked away. But then Rose showed up. She witnessed corruption. She saw death. And didn't run. She took it and it means she's seen it before. It means she's suffered.

The Order sends students to Kenyan because they have some type of mental condition. Me included. But what if the Order made a mistake? What if Rose is the sanest one of us all?

ROSE

THERE IS a knock on my door. I place the bag of potato chips on the old nightstand next to the soda. I mark the page of the passage from *Edgar Allan Poe* and get up.

There is no peephole. Someone messed up the hole, and I can't see who it is.

I've told security multiple times, and they said someone from maintenance should have come up to fix it, but no one has arrived. I gave up after the third request.

"Who is it?" I call out.

Nothing. It's not Amy because she said she would call me tomorrow to go shopping. I didn't want to tell her I didn't have money to buy anything, but I didn't want to miss out on some girl time. She wouldn't just stand there and say nothing. She comes in like a ball of energy the few times we've hung out.

They knock again.

"Who is it?" I repeat.

Nothing.

I kick the door. "I guess you can keep knocking because I'm not going to open the door until you tell me who you are."

Knock. Knock.

I sigh in frustration. "Who's there?"

A paper slides under my door. Is this some kind of joke?

I pick up the sheet of note paper. I DON'T KNOCK.

"What?"

The lights flicker off, and my blood turns cold.

"I'm already inside." Garret's breath floats over my skin. He's right behind me.

Sweat trickles from the nape of my neck down my spine. I whirl around, but I can't see him. It's dark, but I can smell him.

"What are you doing?"

"I came to tutor you."

Like hell he is. I walk toward the light switch, but he grabs me and tosses me onto the small bed. "Get off me," I yell. His weight is crushing me on the mattress, but it's not enough to stop me from breathing.

"This will only take a second." He pulls the string on the lamp on the nightstand. I swear he must have night vision because I wouldn't have known where to pull.

Warm light spreads around the room like the glowing sun. The only darkness comes from the dark eyes pinning me to the mattress. His gaze trails over the T-shirt I use to sleep in, stopping at the two points of my nipples.

"It's cold," I reply.

He looks up, and his pitch-dark eyes are like two moons during the phase of an eclipse because of the light. "Then I should warm you up," he breathes. His mouth is on my neck, his hot breath warming my skin. I try to squeeze my legs together, but all I do is straddle his hips, pushing him into me. His mouth trails over my left breast, hovering over my nipple beneath the thin T-shirt. "Is this how you study?" His eyes pause on my hard nipple. "Dressed like this?"

I can smell the scent of his shampoo from his hair tickling my chin. His cock is pressed against my panties through his black jeans, causing my pussy to ache.

"Garret," I croak, not knowing what to say or how to move.

How did he get in here without using the door? It means he could get in here whenever he wants.

"Yes, my little Darkthorn?"

I swallow thickly, wondering why he calls me that. "Why do you call me Darkthorn?"

He arches his back and removes his shirt in one go.

My eyes are lost in a world of black ink. It's everywhere except on his gorgeous face—angels, skulls, demons, and flowers. It's almost too much until I stop on his heart: the petals of black roses with large thorns piercing a heart. The heart is bleeding black ink.

He grabs my hand and places it over his heated skin, right where the thorn pierces the heart. Right where his heart beats. "I have never been in love," he says, his hand warm and firm over mine. "I thought I had, but it wasn't love. Because the greatest love hurts. It's kind of like the feeling when you lose a parent. I imagine when it finds me, it will hurt. It will come from something beautiful—a rose with hidden thorns. Painful if touched, yet impossible to resist. I will bleed, and it will consume my soul." He pauses, and his expression darkens. "You remind me of a Darkthorn."

"It's best if you don't touch me then."

He pushes away from me, taking his scent and warmth with him, leaving me feeling empty.

I pull the hem of my t-shirt down to cover my thighs and sit up. He moves to the small closet. "What are you doing?"

He slides the brown door open. "Getting your things."

"For?"

He turns around, glancing around the room before looking back at the closet. "Where's the rest? A suitcase?"

I grab my black backpack from in front of the nightstand and place it on the bed. "This is it. Now tell me why you need to get my things."

He stares at the black backpack, then at me, as if he thinks I'm joking. I wish I weren't. There isn't much I was given, but why should he care?

He hesitates, then grabs the bag and stuffs the few items I have hanging on the mismatched hangers the previous student left. Once he's done, he looks around the room as if he's about to be evicted, grabbing papers and notebooks from the small desk.

"Toiletries?" I point to the small shower caddy from the dollar store. He picks it up like he's checking for rotten potatoes and drops it on the desk with a thud. He scans the room one more time. When he's satisfied he didn't miss anything, he says, "Let's go."

"Where?"

"To my house." A fluttering sensation fills my lower belly. "You're not staying in the dorm anymore."

"Who said that?"

"The Order."

I almost choke on my spit and stammer, "T-the Order?"

"Yeah, the people who run things around here, and that includes me. You're stay with me."

"Until when?" I ask. "What if you throw me out, and I don't have a dorm to go back to? How about John?"

He pushes his hair out of his eyes in frustration. "Relax with the word vomit. It's getting late. We still have to study, and you need a shower."

"Are you saying I smell?"

He snorts and points at the shower caddy he discarded like a sack of potatoes. "No, but you can't call that soap. It should be illegal in all fifty states."

"Tell that to John and the twenty bucks he gives me a week. What am I supposed to do?"

He glances at the half-eaten bag of chips, and a look of disgust crosses his features.

Yeah, not everyone is born with a silver spoon in their mouth.

I'm back in his car, heading for his mansion four blocks away. It takes about six minutes to reach his house and another three to finally park in his garage. A thought crosses my mind after he puts the car in park and shuts the garage door.

"Where will I go when you throw one of your lavish parties?"

He opens the door. "I haven't thought that far yet."

Flashes of him with girls like Cassie in the king-sized bed make me want to throw up. I slam the car door shut harder than necessary.

"What's wrong, my little Darkthorn? Your thoughts getting ahead of you?"

It's like he knows what I'm thinking. Am I that transparent? Does he see the way I look at him, the way he unravels me with his dark gaze?

"I don't have any thoughts when it comes to you," I snap and walk inside as if this is my house.

I head down the hallway, remembering the bedroom he always

takes me to, but then I recall the flash of black and the pointy ears. I pause at the threshold and scan the room.

Awareness skates down my spine. "You like this room, don't you?"

"It's the room you always leave me in."

I haven't had the chance to explore the huge house, something I might do when he isn't around.

He chuckles, and I feel it all the way to my toes. "Whose room do you think it belongs to?"

My heart races as I stare at the bed that belongs to him. It's why the sheets smell so good—they're slept in by him. The decor and the painting all make sense, but why would he bring me to his room and let me sleep in his sheets? Sheets he didn't burn because they are still here.

"You didn't burn the sheets."

"I planned on bringing you back. I had them washed instead."

I didn't burn the clothes he gave me either. I kept them like precious souvenirs because I knew I could never afford something so luxurious, but deep down, the real reason was that they were his. No one had to know, but I'm sure he noticed when he grabbed my things.

"Why? The last time, you seemed hell-bent on getting rid of me. Won't I contaminate them?"

He moves past me, pulls clothes in my size from a drawer, and places them on the made bed. "I'll take my chances."

It's another designer hoodie and a pair of black leggings. This is the sixth outfit he has chosen from the closet. A tiny flutter rises in my stomach knowing he picked them out and placed them in a drawer in his room.

"Where are you going to sleep?"

He steps closer, his scent a breeze that permeates the air between us. "In the bedroom next door."

"Why not put me in that room? Why this one?"

Why does he want me in his room, on his bed? The thought of sleeping in his sheets feels personal. I'm not sure what to make of it.

"Because no one comes in this one except Ace. Not the housekeeper, not a friend if they show up, not when I have a party, or a girl I want to fuck."

At least I'm not sleeping in cum-infested sheets. I should be grateful, considering it's him. Who knows how many women he's been with?

"At least I won't catch anything."

He smiles, and I think my heart skipped a beat or slowed down. "Funny, that is the part you're most worried about—me fucking someone else."

"No more than you. I distinctly remember you pointing out my pussy. I also want to note that you made sure you shaved it."

"Correction, I bathed you. Thoroughly."

"I was unconscious. You're lucky I didn't claw your eyes out."

He leans close, his breath skimming my ear. "We both know you would have let me."

I push him away, and he laughs. The motherfucker laughs.

My blood boils, threatening to explode inside my veins. "Am I a joke to you?"

He stops laughing. His sexy mouth hardens, and his darker side makes an appearance. I wonder how many people have seen this side of him. It's terrifying. His eyes grow hard, like an animal in the dark, ready to pounce.

I step back, cursing myself for letting my mouth get the best of me. An uneasy feeling replaces the flutters in my stomach.

"You being here is not a joke, Rose. You should be nice to me. After all, I'm keeping the monster that keeps you awake at night inside his cage. I'm also generous enough to give you better accommodations."

He means John, but I don't buy it. My internal alarm is going off. There is something he isn't telling me, and I have a nagging feeling in the back of my mind. I've been taken from one trapped door to another. My fate is sealed.

Garret is a psychopath. He is popular but hides his true nature from others. He is cold. The way he dismissed Cassie after he'd been intimate with her, not caring if he hurt her feelings, speaks volumes. His impulsivity in bringing me here that first night shows he lies and is manipulative. Flashy cars and the over-the-top designer items he buys, are just a way to inflate his ego.

It's why he's at Kenyan.

"Your mind is turning," he says with a smile, but his eyes are distant. "I can practically hear the wheels turning in that pretty head of yours."

"You're going to kill me."

He angles his head to the side. "Is that what you think?"

Dread pools in the back of my eyes, forming tears that threaten to fall. There is a huge ball lodged in my throat, robbing me of speech. I nod.

He claps. "Congratulations. Now you know the reason you're here." He moves to leave. "Don't forget to wash up. I'll order you something to eat."

"I'm not hungry," I blurt, thankful I found my voice.

He pulls open the door wider, allowing Ace to saunter in, his nails clacking on the marble floors. "I don't think you have a choice." He snaps his fingers. Ace lays on the floor at the foot of the bed. "Promises, remember?"

"Fuck you." I'm past caring. If he was sent to kill me, fine. It's what I've been wishing for anyway. At least he has the balls to do it. I'm sure he wouldn't lose sleep over it.

I still can't believe I agreed stay here with him. Maybe it's self-preservation knowing that John wouldn't show up. There is something freeing knowing that I'm safe from him while I'm here. John is afraid of Garret. I don't know why but maybe I do if Melody's actions that day with Melissa is a hint of the depravity Garret is capable of. Images from the day Melody stabbed Melissa to death flash like a horror movie thinking of all the ways I'll be his victim.

I'm crying for not being strong enough. I don't care if he sees. Psychopaths don't feel. I could cry and sob my heart out, and he wouldn't flinch—just like he isn't now.

"I think we've established how I feel about your cunt."

How could I forget?

I smile. He must think I'm unstable—crying and smiling at the same time—but I won't go down without a fight. Even with my limited ability to read people, I've managed to figure out the basics about those who are mentally disturbed. I wanted to understand what I was dealing with when it came to John and the others; Garret is the classic type of psycho.

"What's so funny?" he asks.

He's trying to hide his confusion, but he's failing. I'm supposed to be crying and trembling, not smiling and laughing when he's about to leave the room. "This whole time, I've been around the one person who would kill me and end all my problems."

"What the fuck are you saying?"

"You asked me the other day if there was something I wanted more than anything. Death."

He flinches, not expecting my revelation. He thought I wanted white picket fences and a savior.

"Death is the one thing I want more than anything, Garret. You killing me is my greatest wish. I'm hoping you can bury me in Kenyan's cemetery right next to the church that decides my fate. I have a spot picked out."

He storms out, slamming the door behind him. The force rattles the painting representing envy on the wall. I walk up to it and trace my finger over the bone on the woman's hand.

GARRET

SHE WANTS TO DIE, and she's okay with me being the one to do it. But why? It's not what I expected her to say. Who the hell is okay with dying? She didn't cry out or scream like I thought she would, and none of it makes sense. Why would she go through all the trouble with John if she wanted to die? She could've just jumped off a roof or something.

You would stop her. Someone would. There are cameras everywhere.

I close my eyes, pushing the thought away.

My phone vibrates in my front jeans pocket.

I fish it out.

Alaric: Make sure you go to class. I have the info you asked for. My assistant will be in shortly to explain. I trust it will be an educational experience.

Garret: I thought you graduated like a million years ago.

Alaric: Stop hating because I'm smarter than you, and don't disrespect your elders.

Garret: Yes, Dad.

Alaric: I can be your daddy if that's what you want.

Garret: I guess you want to die and be buried next to the last Nox.

Alaric: After your next lesson in class, I think you'll want to save those thoughts for someone more deserving.

The thought of killing her sits like a hot coal in my stomach, burning my insides after she admitted the last thing I expected.

I imagined material things—money, an education, sex. It definitely wasn't the wish to die. Or for me to be the one to carry it out.

I'm practically running to class to find out what Alaric doesn't want to tell me over the phone. What's so *educational* that involves Rose?

The smell of her skin still lingers in my sheets. I snuck into the bedroom this morning while she was eating the breakfast I ordered. There was no way I could get rid of something that smelled so beautiful.

She reminds me of the lingering scent of a black rose. My little **Darkthorn.**

I knew if I touched her, she would consume me. And I couldn't let that happen.

I walk into my International Relations class and take the seat closest to the exit. I like the freedom to leave without making a fuss. Not like the professor would question me for ditching early, but still, I like to make things easy.

The fact that Alaric chose this class to tell me something doesn't sit right. International laws, globalization, human rights—nothing in this class should have anything to do with Rose. It's an easy course, one I took only because I had to stay my entire senior year when I could have graduated early and been sitting behind a desk, barking orders in my late father's building downtown.

I stretch my legs, ignoring the glances girls aim my way as they file in, staring at the time on my phone and waiting for class to start.

I only look up when the professor walks in—thick glasses, a porn mustache—waiting for him to announce that we have a *special guest.* My leg starts shaking.

Anxiety gnaws at me as Professor Mullen takes his time extracting a leather folder from his attaché. He notices me. Or maybe it's the tapping noise I'm making with my sneaker, repeatedly hitting the metal chair leg. I want to grab his head and shove it inside the damn thing so he gets the hint and hurries the hell up.

The door swings open, and my blood pressure skyrockets. Azriel. The last person I want to see. What the *fuck* is Alaric thinking?

Valen's younger brother doesn't belong in a place like this. He's good—better than most—but he's been doing questionable things lately.

Like caring too much for the girl who lied to us all. I see the way he looks at her. He *likes* her. Maybe he'd sleep with her if she showed any interest.

But I know she doesn't. She's still conflicted about whether she should trust him. And right now, she has every right to doubt him. Rose is an addiction for someone like me—a *psycho*.

I want to cage her.

Dominate her fucking mind.

Terrify her.

But at the same time, I want her to desire me.

She brings out the dark, unhinged version of myself that I keep locked away—the version I reserve for others when I want to wipe them off the face of the earth.

"Today, I want to go over human rights and globalization," Professor Mullen begins. "As you can see, I've brought Mr. Vikiar. He has conducted extensive research on the matter and would like to share his findings. This is an opportunity to spread awareness about the issue. He will cover human trafficking and the context of migration, labor, and exploitation."

Panic rises in my chest, forcing me to sit up.

Azriel's gaze lands on mine.

There's something in his eyes. Pity. Guilt. All I see is red. I want to strangle the knowledge from his mouth.

"My name is Azriel Vikiar. Some of you may not know, but I'm a hybrid student. I would like to share the results of my findings with you."

The class grows quiet. He shuts the lights. The projector flickers on. The bastard has a whole presentation prepared.

My eyes dart across the screen as he flips through images—buildings in the middle of nowhere. Then, an image stops me cold.

Young girls. Barely ten years old. They're dirty, malnourished.

Their eyes hold a drug-induced daze—similar to the way I found Rose on the shower floor.

My stomach churns.

The bruises. The scars.

Track marks etched into their delicate skin.

Needles.

Drugs.

Girls sprawled on filthy mattresses in different rooms.

"This is where human traffickers hide their victims," Azriel says.

Gasps echo around the room. Some students watch with blank faces, unfazed.

It makes me sick.

"I know there are stories and reports of women and young boys being trafficked, but I would like to share this topic with children."

I only pick up bits and pieces of his words. The ones that matter. The ones Alaric *wants* me to hear. The ones that involve Rose. If that's even her real name. Because she might be nameless. No parents. Because these fuckers impregnate them to produce more. To sell them. Like animals.

Then I see it.

An image of a young girl with soulless eyes—

And a tattoo of a set of numbers.

I tear my gaze away. Bile rises in my throat, threatening to spill out of my mouth. No one knows what the numbers mean, but it's how they mark them.

To be used.

To be owned.

To be sold.

I bolt out of the chair. Rush into the men's bathroom. And throw up.

That motherfucker bought her like a dog.

ROSE

"LET'S head to my dorm. We can get ready and then go to the party," Amy says with a smile as we exit our lit class.

I don't know how to tell her that the only decent outfit I have is a hoodie and leggings—the same ones I wore earlier this week. I really want to go, and in a way, I should make the most of my time before Garret comes for me. And it won't be just to tell me he has breakfast waiting in the kitchen.

He's been avoiding me all week. I hardly see him except when he feeds me and drops me off at school. The rest of the time, he's nowhere to be found. Not that I'm looking for him. Who would want to see the one person who is going to kill you?

Maybe he's giving me space.

There isn't much I can do.

"Um . . . I didn't bring any clothes to change into."

"No worries! I have something that would look great on you. I don't mind."

"Are you sure?"

No one has ever offered to let me borrow anything. I can't shake the feeling that I might be overstepping. I don't really know her that well—aside from the time we went to Babylon and our classes together.

"Yeah, I have this perfect dress with a black leather jacket that would look sooo cute on you." Her eyes sparkle with excitement, and I can't help but smile.

I check myself out in the bathroom mirror of the dorm building. I look different. Amy applied eyeliner and a layer of foundation to my face. I'm wearing a tight dress with over-the-knee boots. I'm grateful for the jacket, but I'm unsure about showing five inches of thigh between the hem and the edge of Amy's heeled boots.

"Are you sure about this?" I ask nervously.

I've never intentionally dressed up for anything. The few times I had no choice were for reasons I prefer not to think about right now.

I'm sure Garret wouldn't care I didn't show up. But maybe he might. He never said I had a curfew or that I was obligated to wait for him after his swim practice. I simply didn't show up and ignored his last text asking where I was.

"You look gorgeous, Rose."

I catch Amy's red-lipped smile in the mirror's reflection. "So do you."

Amy is wearing skintight black jeans and a pink crop top that highlights her trim waist. Her strawberry-blonde hair is a cute contrast to her outfit.

As I shut the passenger door of the Uber—Amy insisted on paying for it—my legs shake. I watch the two red lights disappear down the road as the sun sets.

The volume of the music blaring from the house fluctuates, fading each time the front door opens and closes.

"Come on," Amy says, grabbing my hand. I stumble as she practically drags me toward the front door.

A couple of guys hold the door open with wide smiles when they see us. "Welcome, ladies," says the one with freckles, stepping behind us.

My internal radar kicks into full force as the smell of alcohol, heat, and perfume *hits me like a wave* from all the people crammed into the living room.

People dance to the beat of Kendrick Lamar's *Not Like Us*, singing the lyrics.

"Holy shit," Amy says over the music. "This is crazy."

A guy holding a keg of beer cheers while a girl underneath it tries to drink as much as she can, not caring that beer is pouring down her shirt—her nipples visible through the soaked fabric.

Two guys stand on either side of one girl as she takes turns French kissing them.

A ping-pong table is in the back. The girls are topless. Their breasts bounce harder than the ball every time they swing the paddle.

If this is an Ohio frat party, I can only imagine the type of party Garret throws. Orgies must be an understatement.

"Let's get a drink," Amy suggests, pulling me through the throng of people.

Curious glances follow me as Amy pushes through. They all must be from Ohio, because I have yet to see anyone from Kenyan.

Amy reaches the kitchen and grabs two beers from a bucket of ice. She pops the top off with a bottle opener and hands me one while she chugs the other.

A guy with light green eyes looks over. It's hard not to get lost in their bright depths. I'm not sure if it's a trick of the light. A guy with brown hair slaps him on the shoulder playfully.

Green Eyes nudges his head in our direction, says something to his friend, and they both head over.

"Do you know them?" Amy asks, taking another sip of her beer.

"No."

"They're kind of cute," she says. "They have to play football."

I understand why she made that assumption. These guys are not small by any means. They are big—with large hands and wide necks —the type that play football.

"Hey," Green Eyes says when he reaches me.

His friend watches Amy with interest.

"Hi," I reply a bit awkwardly.

I tune out Amy and the other guy. We stare at each other for a few seconds.

I'm not sure why he walked over, but all I can think is that he must want something. Or he's just curious. Recognition wraps around me like a blanket. It's like I've seen him before but never *really* paid attention.

My focus sharpens on the guy in front of me—his green eyes, the tiny freckles on the bridge of his nose. The way his mouth lifts higher on one side when he grins. He's not Garret by any means. He doesn't make my heart hammer in my throat. He doesn't make me wonder how it would feel if he kissed me. If I was the Darkthorn he called to make him bleed.

This guy is different in every sense. He doesn't know who I am. He doesn't look at me with disgust. He's looking at me like I'm human—a girl at a college party.

"Your name is Rose, right?"

How does he know my name?

Then his voice *digs the memory out*. The diner. The guy with the cowboy hat.

"Yes," is all I manage to say.

"I'm sorry about the other night. I didn't get to give you my name since we were so rudely interrupted."

He holds out his hand, and I take it, almost dropping my beer. If he notices, he doesn't point it out. His hand is rough but firm.

"I'm Leo. Short for Leonidas."

"Spartan!" his friend chimes in.

I arch a brow. Leo smiles. "My mom had a thing for the movie *300*."

I have no idea what he's talking about, but I nod. I've never watched the movie, but I don't want to sound clueless.

"Where's your cowboy hat?" I ask instead.

If anyone looked good in one, it would be him.

"You like the hat?"

"It's different. Kind of like your name."

His gaze drops to my beer, already getting warm. "Do you like beer?"

I shrug. "It's what everyone is drinking."

I tilt the bottle and wince at the bitter, lukewarm taste.

He chuckles, grabbing it from my fingers and tossing it in the trash. "Let's get you something that doesn't taste like piss." He flips the lid from a nearby cooler and hands me a Coke can. "I like my girl sober."

His words wrap around me like a warm embrace. For a moment, it doesn't matter that I have an ugly past. Or that after tonight, I will never see him again. He is a moment. Normal in all the ways I couldn't be.

So when he asks if I want to dance . . .
I don't hesitate.

GARRET

"YO, GARRET?"

I turn my head to the left. It's Clay from the team.

"What's up?"

I face the tiles, the hot water from the shower easing my aching muscles. I've been drowning out my conflicting emotions about Rose in the pool, punishing my body because there's no way I can look her in the eyes. I can't take the words back—the ones that replay in my head like a badly written song.

"You going to the Ohio frat party tonight?"

"Nah, man. I think I'll pass."

I continue to stare at the tiles, pretending to listen. The last thing I want is to go eat shit at an Ohio party. I texted Rose and almost flung my phone against the wall when she didn't respond. It's like I can't demand anything from her—not after what I learned.

"Some of us are going," Clay drones on. "Prey will be there."

Luke laughs. "Yeah, man. You don't want those fucks from Ohio to get dibs."

Some of the guys in Ohio are part of the Order. They don't have power like I do or like the sons of Kenyan, but they follow the same rules and are rewarded handsomely for it. They also have dibs on Prey, and the guys love to show them that we have the power to show up and do whatever the hell we want.

"Like that girl you bring to school," Clay says.

My vision narrows like I'm going through a tunnel. A loud sound goes off in my head, like nails on a chalkboard.

"What did you say?"

"That girl," Clay says, glancing at the other guys in the shower. Some look away. Luke swallows hard, his face almost healed from when I hit him after he talked about Rose.

"What about her?" I growl, shutting off the water and snatching my towel.

Clay's throat moves slowly as he swallows. "She went with that girl in her lit class. I overheard them talking about it in the hallway."

"Are you sure?" I press, imagining some asshole touching her, breathing in her scent, not caring if she wants to or not. Getting her drunk enough to sleep with her.

My vision goes red, the piercing sound of my rage boiling in my ears. I barge out of the shower, grabbing my bag from my locker, the metal door slamming shut like a cannon going off.

"What the fuck? Is everything cool, man?" Clay asks tensely. "Did I say anything wrong?"

Zipping my bag, I grab my hoodie. "No. Thanks for the heads-up."

I walk out and head to my car. The powerful engine roars as I press on the gas, but it's not loud enough to drown out the different ways this will end. They all have one thing in common: they end with me murdering someone.

I drive up the sidewalk, not caring if I fuck up my car. I park on the grass, over the pathway leading to the front door, and jump out, ignoring the gasps and wide eyes when they see me.

"Nice car, man," some idiot shouts.

I push open the door and scan the crowd. The moment I see her, the air grows thick. Her hands rest on the quarterback's shoulders. His fingers press into her small waist. Something sharp twists under my ribs. Clarity slices through the noise. I should leave. Pretend this never happened.

Instead, my vision clears. His hands don't belong on her. They should be pinned to the wall so the next asshole knows exactly what happens when he touches something that isn't his.

He says something to her. She tilts her head back and laughs. A knife lodges itself in my gut. It takes me a moment to recognize what I'm feeling. Something I should have buried with the rest of my mistakes.

Jealousy is a poisonous thing. Envy is the vine that feeds it, curling under my ribs, constricting until I can't breathe.

It's why she didn't answer my calls or texts.

"Hey, Garret! My man . . . you made it." Billy walks up, slapping me on the shoulder like he always does, oblivious to the way I'm feeling. "You check out my man Spartan? Since that night at the diner, she's all he talks about. The one that got away. The girl of his dreams."

He laughs. I want to deck him in the throat, but I don't. What would be the point? He has no idea what's racing through my head—how dangerous he and his friend are from being cut to pieces.

"I saw some of the girls out back."

He means the ones I mess with, but there's only one I have my sights set on. And I'm the last person she wants to see.

"I'm not here for that."

Billy follows my line of sight, then his eyes widen. "Shit! Hey, man. Listen—in his defense, he didn't know. We don't want any trouble."

I can't blame Leo or Billy. This is my fault. I should've noticed the signs. But I failed. The same way I failed with Jess. With Veronica. And now with Rose. My pulse pounds as I watch her.

Still laughing.

Still touching him.

I flex my fingers and count.

One.

Two.

Three.

Then I move.

ROSE

"YOUR NAME, ROSE. IT FITS."

"How come?"

I can't stop smiling. My face hurts from doing it so much. But I don't care. The things he says… No one's said them to me before and I don't want it to end.

"You're small. Delicate." He leans in like he can't get enough. "And you smell like flowers."

"You can thank the dollar store."

He leans back, giving me a funny look. "You're kidding?"

I shake my head. "I wish I was .But it's what I could afford."

"Well, it's smells nice."

"You're just trying to be nice."

He spins us around. "I don't joke about a girl and the way that she's smells."

I scan the crowd, searching for Amy. I find her smiling at his friend. Awareness creeps up my spine. My stomach clenches. I feel it before I see him. Garret.

He's watching me like a serial killer. Dark. Angry. He leans against the wall, arms crossed, eyes locked on mine. I wonder how long he's been standing there.

His gaze dips to Leo's hands on my waist. Suddenly, they feel wrong. Like flames burning my skin. Everything grows heavy.

"Is everything alright?"

I swallow hard. "I-I have to go."

Concern flickers across his face. "Why?"

"Because my ride is here." Is the only excuse I can come up with. He'll understand. Once he sees Garret.

"Where—"

"Times up, Loverboy," Garret cuts in, his tone sardonic.

Leo looks between me and Garret. "Oh, hey man." His tone is easy, but his eyes stay on me. "She doesn't need a ride. I can take her home."

"You want to come to my house?" Garret muses. Leo's brows pull together. "Because that's where she stays. It's where she sleeps." Garret pulls a joint from his pocket, lights it, and blows smoke in Leo's face.

"Garret…" I warn.

He holds up his hand. "Not yet, my little Darkthorn."

Leo swats the smoke away. "Is there something I should know?"

"Depends," Garret says, smoothly, the joint dangling from his lips.

Leo squares his shoulders. "On?"

Leo is about two inches shorter, but Garret but Garret is more intimidating More muscle. Tattoos. Darkness. More power.

"On what she wants to tell you." Garret grins. "I'll let her decide."

Bastard.

He's forcing me to walk away because we both know I can't tell Leo the truth.

"I'll see you later," I tell Leo.

He studies me. He must see it, that I have to go. That nothing he says will change my mind. "I'll call you."

I nod. gave him my number earlier, when we took a break to grab some water. We talked about his family in Texas. The ranch he grew up on. How is father is into oil. He offered to show me sometime. Even if I knew that would never happen it was nice to imagine I could. Then Garret had to show up and ruin it.

"Alright," I say weakly, knowing I'll probably never see Leo again after tonight. I'm pretty sure Garret will make sure of it.

Leo leans in, aiming for a kiss on my cheek but Garret shoves him back."Let's go." He grabs my hand, tugging, dragging me toward the exit.

"You didn't have to be such an asshole," I snap, yanking my hand free.

"I was saving you from heartbreak."

"How would you know? You don't have a heart." I pause, remembering I came with Amy. "My friend—"

"I ordered her a ride."

I blink.

"Told her she had to leave."

"Why?"

He shrugs. "Because I said so."

We step outside. I freeze. His car is inches from the first step. "Are you insane?"

He opens my door. "I think you figured put what I'm capable of." His voice lowers. "Even had glimpse with my friends." He holds the door. Waiting. Now, get in the car."

I fold my arms. "Or what?"

A shadow of amusement crosses his face. Then it disappears. He steps forward. His body cages mine.

I tilt my chin up. The back of my neck hits the edge of the door.

His eyes burn into mine. "I'll make sure our audience knows how wet you get when I press my cock over that hot cunt of yours."

Heat spikes up my spine. "You wouldn't." I challenge him. He smirks "I disgust you, remember?"

His eyes don't waver. They pin me in place. "Get in the car, Rose." Then he walks to the driver's side.

I don't move. I don't get in the car. Not until my pulse slows and my hands stop shaking.

ROSE

SINCE ARRIVING at Garret's house, he's been a ghost. The bedroom door was left open—a silent invitation, or maybe just indifference—but the space around me feels suffocating. Like the drive over here.

He didn't say a word. No cruel remarks. No taunts. No surprises. Just silence.

He drove the short distance like I wasn't there. But that wasn't what unsettled me. It was the restraint. The tension.

Garret opened the car door for me, a gesture so unexpectedly chivalrous that I hesitated before stepping out. But that was as far as his civility went. No instructions. No threats. Just an unreadable gaze that sent a ripple of unease through my chest.

And now, I don't know how to feel. Am I angry that he dragged me away from Leo? That he ruined the brief glimpse of normalcy I'd let myself enjoy? Or am I conflicted by something else—that it *bothered* him? That he *saw me* with another guy and reacted?

I don't want to sit in this room and let my thoughts eat me alive.

Carefully, I push open the door and step into the hallway, my bare feet silent against the cool marble. The house is eerily quiet. No Ace. No sounds of movement.

I exhale, telling myself maybe Garret went to sleep. Maybe he left.

I move forward, curiosity leading me down a hallway—one I haven't explored before. The house is massive, a maze of intricate woodwork and cold stone, like a living museum of wealth and legacy.

I pass a library filled with books stacked to the ceiling, a ladder affixed to a rail. It reminds me of the one on campus, and for a moment, I pause, about to step inside.

Then I hear it.

A low splash, followed by another.

My heart jumps.

Music plays faintly, its haunting melody curling through the air like smoke. The intro of *No Time To Die* drifts through the open space, growing louder as I follow the sound. My pulse quickens when I step into the indoor pool area.

The water glows deep crimson beneath the submerged lights, sending ripples of red through the high-ceilinged room. Steam rises in soft wisps where the warmth of the pool meets the crisp night air filtering through the partially open roof.

And then, there's *him.*

Garret slices through the water with sharp, precise strokes, each movement smooth, controlled, devastatingly powerful. The muscles in his back shift with every stroke, his tattoos morphing like ink on liquid, his body moving like it was carved from stone.

I should leave.

I should turn around before he catches me watching.

But I don't.

My feet carry me closer, the marble beneath me cool and slick. I inch toward the edge, my breath shallow, drawn in by the mesmerizing sight of him—like a predator lost in its natural element.

The surface ripples hypnotically, lapping at my toes. I lean in just a little more, peering into the water, wondering how deep it is.

Then—

I *slip.*

A startled gasp escapes my lips, but it's swallowed instantly as I plunge into the water. A rush of warmth engulfs me, my body sinking, panic slamming into my ribs like a hammer. Water floods my nose, my throat, burning like fire. I try to surface, try to kick, but I can't find which way is up. The weight of the water presses against my lungs.

I can't breathe.

Then, a force like a wrecking ball collides into me.

A steel grip yanks me through the water in a powerful wave, and suddenly, I'm *airborne.* I choke, spluttering as my body is flipped onto its side, coughing up water while heat—warm, strong, *alive*—surrounds me.

"Rose! Fuck." Garret's voice is sharp, laced with something I can't name.

His arms are locked around me, his hand pressing against my back, rubbing slow, measured strokes as I struggle to breathe.

His touch is solid, grounding, his body radiating warmth as he holds me against his chest, keeping me *here*.

"Breathe," he commands, voice raw.

I do. A ragged, painful inhale that fills my burning lungs with precious air. I cough, my throat raw, my chest tight, but I *breathe*.

His fingers tilt my chin up, forcing me to meet his gaze. "You don't know how to swim?"

I shake my head weakly, still trying to process what just happened.

I could have drowned.

But he saved me.

"Why did you save me?" My voice is hoarse, barely a whisper.

His eyes flicker with something unreadable—something fierce. His grip tightens around me, his chest rising and falling like he just ran a marathon.

"You could have let me drown," I murmur, my voice hollow.

His expression darkens. His gaze drops—to my lips, to my throat, lower still, pausing just beneath the waterline where my soaked tank top clings to my skin.

When his eyes meet mine again, there's no hatred.

There's *fear*.

Before I can react, he shifts. His strong arms lift me effortlessly, my legs instinctively wrapping around his waist as he carries me through the pool. Water sluices off his skin, glistening under the dim lights.

I don't fight him.

I don't *want* to.

He lowers me onto the built-in ledge at the shallow end, the water lapping at my ribs. The cool night air brushes against my damp skin, sending a shiver through me.

His hand cups my cheek, his thumb tracing my jawline. His touch is gentle, contradicting everything I know about him.

"I'm okay now," I whisper, though my voice betrays me.

His gaze drifts lower. My chest rises and falls rapidly, my skin flushed from the heat of the water.

"Are you?" he murmurs, his tone unreadable.

I don't answer.

I *can't*.

Because the way he's looking at me—studying me like I'm something fragile, something *his*—makes my heart stutter.

I should pull away.

I should shove him back, remind him that I hate him, that I don't *want* this.

But I don't.

Because when he leans in, slow and deliberate, I realize I *do* want this.

To *feel*.

And Garret makes me *feel*. He makes me want to experience life another day.

His lips brush against mine—hesitant, waiting. *Testing*.

I don't stop him.

Instead, I fist my fingers into his shoulders, silently granting him permission.

A low groan rumbles from his throat as he deepens the kiss, his tongue sweeping into my mouth, claiming me with a slow, intoxicating rhythm. He tilts my head back, his hands tangling into my wet hair as he devours me, like he's trying to drown me in something other than water.

His mouth trails lower—to my jaw, to the hollow of my throat, his breath hot against my damp skin.

"Tell me to stop," he rasps against my collarbone.

I don't.

I *can't*.

Instead, I whisper breathlessly, "Don't."

His mouth crashes against mine again, hunger igniting between us like gasoline to an open flame.

My back arches into him, my body betraying every rational thought in my head. His lips move lower, his hands mapping my body beneath the water, like he's discovering something forbidden, something he *never* planned to want.

I was breathless. His mouth devoured me—possessive, claiming, relentless. His tongue teased, his teeth grazed, and I could do nothing but surrender. There was nothing I wanted to think about except him.

He pressed against me, his body hard, unyielding. Heat radiated between us, searing through the thin barrier of fabric. Every deliberate roll of his hips sent a delicious shudder through me, and I arched into him, seeking more, needing more.

A groan rumbled from deep in his chest, primal and raw. His lips found my neck, and then—he bit me. The sharp pleasure sent a cry tumbling from my lips.

My fingers slid between us, wrapping instinctively around the rigid length of him. A bolt of heat shot through me, intoxicating and dangerous. And then he froze.

His breath hitched. His muscles trembled beneath my touch. His hands clenched at my waist like he was holding himself together by a thread.

"Run," he rasped, voice hoarse and strained, like the single word cost him everything. His throat worked as he swallowed. "Rose…"

The sound of my name on his lips shattered something inside me. I let him go like I'd been burned, my fingers tingling from the loss.

My legs slid down his hips, the heat between us cooling with the weight of reality pressing down on me. My heart pounded in my chest, the truth slamming into me with brutal force.

If I let this happen, what then?

I would be exactly what he said I was.

I staggered back, my breath coming in quick, uneven gasps. His gaze stayed locked on mine, dark and unreadable, but the tension in his body told me everything.

I had to leave.

ROSE

I BURY myself in the book I still haven't officially checked out from the library—sonnets, poetry, pieces of love and longing that feel like fragments of a world I'll never belong to. It's the only way to push away the memories of last night but at the same time it makes me wish it never ended.

The way his lips swallowed me whole. The way my body burned against his. The way I wanted it.

I don't care if I skip over words that are too difficult to read. I just need something to keep me from overthinking.

I brush my teeth and curl up on my bed, pulling my sweater over my knees. I don't have the courage to leave the room. If I go to the kitchen, I might run into Garret. And I have no idea how to face him—how he'll look at me.

Does this mean he likes me?

Does this mean he still hates me? The last thought makes my stomach churn, so I focus on the book, forcing my eyes over the words.

Then my phone chimes.

Leo.

Leo: Good morning, gorgeous. I hope you haven't forgotten about me.

Guilt crawls up my spine, a million tiny ants swarming, biting at my insides. I force a smile when another text comes through—this time with a cowboy hat emoji.

Rose: How could I? How many guys do you think I know that look good in cowboy hats?

Leo: I'm hoping it's just me. ;)

"Are you ready for your tutoring lesson?"

The deep voice makes me flinch. My phone slips from my hands, landing on the bed like a hot coal.

Garret stands at the foot of my bed, staring at the screen. At Leo's name. At the text.

He's shirtless.

Every sculpted muscle of his chest and abdomen is carved with shadows, disappearing beneath the band of his black sweatpants. His damp hair curls at the ends, fresh from a shower, the scent of his soap teasing my nose.

I swallow hard.

"Good morning," I murmur, my voice barely above a whisper. "I… I didn't think you were serious about the tutoring thing."

"You haven't eaten," he states, like it's fact, not concern. "I was waiting for you in the kitchen."

Warmth unfurls in my chest, slow and foreign.

No one has ever cared if I ate.

"I didn't think you noticed."

His eyes flick to my phone again before locking onto mine, his voice cool and unreadable. "I notice everything."

Heat spreads across my cheeks. Did he read Leo's texts?

I close the book, marking my place before pulling the hem of my sweater down my thighs. "I'll be right there."

But he doesn't move.

His eyes travel down my legs, stopping at my bare feet.

"You should wear socks," he mutters. "Or slippers. The floor is cold."

I blink. Garret doesn't care about things like that.

"I don't have clean socks," I admit quietly. "I don't own slippers."

His frown deepens. His gaze sweeps the room before landing on my backpack. The only thing I own.

"Do you want me to grab some clothes for you from the house?" He means John's house.

I shake my head. "What you saw in my dorm room? That's everything I own."

Something flickers across his expression, something I can't quite read. Without a word, he moves to the dresser, pulls open a drawer, and takes out a brand-new pair of socks.

"Sit." His voice is quiet but firm.

I hesitate, but my body obeys.

He kneels in front of me.

"What are you doing?" My voice is barely a whisper.

He looks up, his expression unreadable. "Making sure you don't get cold."

His fingers wrap around my ankle, warm and firm, as he pulls the sock over my foot. The oversized fabric slides up my calf, covering my skin. Then he does the same with the other foot, his touch surprisingly gentle.

I don't know how to stop the goosebumps trailing up my arms.

"Thank you," I murmur.

He doesn't respond, just stands and nods toward the door. "Let's go."

When I step into the kitchen, I freeze.

The island is covered with food—fresh pastries, soft bread, butter, muffins, colorful fruits arranged in careful rows.I've seen this spread every morning, but I always reach for the same thing.

Strawberries.

They're safe. Familiar.

Garret moves to the espresso machine, his broad back flexing as he grabs a cup from the cabinet. Effortless. Controlled.

He presses a button, and the scent of rich coffee fills the space.

Then, without turning around, he asks, "Do you want some?"

I stiffen.

"C-can I?"

He spins around to face me, his gaze locking onto mine.

"Why would you ask me that?"

I swallow hard.

"Because I wasn't sure if I was allowed one."

His jaw tightens. "Have you ever had coffee before?"

I hesitate. Then shake my head. "No."

The espresso machine hums. The silence between us is louder.

Then, barely audible, he murmurs, "You like strawberries."

I nod.

"Is there anything you don't like?"

I glance at the pastries, my throat tightening. "Cinnamon."

His brows draw together. "Why?"

I fight the bile rising in my throat. "I just don't. It's disgusting."

He doesn't push. Just nods once. Then, without another word, he walks over to the island and—one by one—starts removing selected pastries, cakes, and muffins.

My chest tightens. "What are you doing?"

"Making sure you don't eat something you hate."

I stare at him. "Why are you being so nice to me?"

He doesn't answer. Instead, he wraps the discarded pastries in plastic and slides them into the fridge. "For my housekeeper," he explains. "I'll make sure to order nothing with cinnamon."

I don't understand. After last night, something has changed. I don't know what to do with this version of him. "You don't have to go to all the trouble," I whisper.

Garret turns. Walks toward me. Lifts me off the floor.

"Garret!"

My stomach somersaults as he places me on the counter, stepping between my legs. His warmth presses into me. "What are you doing?"

He reaches for a square of pineapple, lifting it just before my lips. "Open."

The juice drips down his fingers, a golden trail glistening against his skin. Heat curls low in my stomach. I part my lips, biting the fruit from his fingers.

His gaze darkens as he watches me lick the lingering juice from my lips. "You like it?"

I swallow. "Yes."

His lips curve.

For the next thirty minutes, he feeds me, learning what I like, what I don't.

And for the first time—I feel seen.

ROSE

THE WEIGHT of uncertainty over Garrid's motives dissipates as he settles beside me on the couch. He keeps a small distance, just like in the kitchen earlier, but not enough to stop the shiver from crawling up my spine or the goosebumps from appearing on my exposed thighs. If he notices, he doesn't show it. His gaze lingers but never for too long. He also doesn't mention what happened between us last night.

It's as if it never happened. As if he never threatened to kill me. As if he never decided, for reasons I still don't understand, that my life was worth saving.

"Alright, try this one," he says, pointing to a page in the book. "It's easier."

I glance at the poem—it's short. Manageable. I hesitate, taking a deep breath before beginning. The fourth word tangles on my tongue, and he corrects me gently. Patiently. I push through the rest, stumbling, fumbling—but he never makes me feel stupid.

"If you ever get stuck…" He unlocks his phone, pulling up Google Translate. "Type the word in. It'll help you pronounce it and show the meaning."

"Azriel told me I could look things up, but my phone doesn't work like that," I admit.

He flips the page. "I can fix that."

I glance at him. "How?"

"Don't worry about it." He nods to the book. "Try this one."

I lick my lips, reading the lines silently before daring to say them aloud. I don't push the issue about my phone. In the back of my mind, I keep waiting for him to snap out of whatever this is and go back to the way we were.

"Good," he says when I finish.

I laugh. "Are you kidding? I suck."

"No, you're just not used to it. But you'll get better. The more you practice."

I sigh. "I'll need a ton of books before I can read one page without tripping over my words. Half the time, I don't even know what they mean."

He chuckles. "Rose, there are plenty of people who don't understand what they're reading—people who read every day. They just pretend they do."

"But they're not in college, where it counts."

"I'll worry about that part. And I have a ton of books."

I glance at him nervously. "You wouldn't mind if I borrowed some?"

"I don't think anyone would object."

His fingers brush against my cheek as he tucks a strand of hair behind my ear. A tingling warmth spreads down my neck at the soft touch.

"You can have as many as you like," he murmurs. "You can go anywhere you want—except the pool." A gleam of amusement flashes in his eyes. "I think it's best you let me know if you decide to jump in again."

I smile shyly. "Probably a good idea."

A hot breath tickles my face, followed by a wet swipe across my nose.

I bolt upright, heart hammering.

Ace stares at me, his dark eyes steady, before laying his head back on my pillow like he belongs there.

"A little warning would be nice," I scold, wiping my nose.

He lets out a small whine.

I swallow hard, slowly reaching out to pet his head. He lifts it slightly, and I flinch, snatching my hand back.

"Don't show him fear," I whisper to myself.

Ace watches me. Waiting.

I exhale, repeating it again. "Don't show him fear."

Tentatively, I extend my hand once more.

He leans in.

The moment my fingers sink into his soft fur, I let out a triumphant little giggle. He licks my fingers, nuzzling into my palm, his massive head heavy against me.

"Good boy," I murmur, scratching behind his ears. He rolls onto his back, paws up, demanding a belly rub.

"He likes you." Garret's deep voice makes me tense.

I glance up to find him leaning against the doorframe, shirtless, his toned body bathed in the early morning light. I swallow, my mouth suddenly dry.

"I hope you don't mind, but I think he likes sleeping with you. He's protective."

I shake my head, still running my fingers through Ace's fur. "I don't mind. He scared me, but I think he's making up for it."

Ace lets out a satisfied groan, pushing his head against my palm.

"What would he need to protect me from?" I ask absently, scratching behind his ears.

Garret's expression darkens. "You never know. Maybe he doesn't like when you have nightmares."

I freeze.

I lower my gaze to Ace, my fingers slowing. My nightmares are nothing new. I've had them for as long as I can remember.

But if Ace was with me last night, watching over me…

Who else was?

"Did I keep you up?" My voice is quieter now.

Garret doesn't respond immediately.

After reading with him yesterday, I was exhausted. I don't even remember falling asleep. But I remember feeling warm. Safe. Wrapped in something I didn't want to wake up from.

I look up at him, our gazes locking across the room. And in his dark, unreadable stare… I know.

Ace wasn't the only one in my room last night.

ROSE

AFTER SCHOOL, Amy begged me to come to Babylon to catch up. After the party, she assured me that Garret had gotten her back to the dorm safely.

"So, what is up with you and the swim team captain?" Amy asks, narrowing her eyes playfully over the rim of her beer.

"I should ask you the same about Leo's friend."

She waves a dismissive hand and takes a sip. "Friends. He's a player, and I'm not interested. I know the type," she says, her voice dropping on the last part. I catch the shift in her tone but don't push.

"There's nothing going on," I say, but even as the words leave my mouth, I know they're a lie. Not when I think about how Garret made sure I ate breakfast this morning—and how much I liked it. Not when I replay the way he opened every door for me as if it were second nature. The way he kept checking in on me on the drive to school, asking if I was okay, again and again.

"Didn't look that way to me at the party," Amy quips. "He practically threw you over his shoulder caveman-style when he saw you with Leo."

I shake my head. "He was just upset that I was avoiding him. His mom is married to the man who adopted me and... I'm also staying with him."

Amy's eyes go wide, her beer freezing mid-air. "You're kidding?"

"I wish I was."

Not many people know, but it was the only excuse I could give her. There's no way I could tell her the real reason I'm staying with Garret. No way I could admit that we kissed. That he saved me from drowning in his pool. That I liked it. That I still have the bite marks to prove it.

"How is he when you're alone?" she asks, lowering her voice. "I mean, he's always the life of the party, but he also has this dangerous quality. You know, 'don't let the nice act fool you' type of thing."

She isn't wrong. I thought I was the only one who noticed. But since that night at the party, Garret has me wrapped up in him. In his kindness. In the contradiction of him. And I can't get enough.

But he hasn't tried to kiss me again.

I thought it was guilt. Maybe regret.

I don't know what I'm feeling, but I can't ignore the way my body reacts when he's close. The anticipation of his touch. The way his gaze lingers in a room full of people.

And just when I convince myself it's all in my head, he does something that takes my breath away—like getting me a brand-new smartphone. Showing me all the features and how I could use it for my assignments. He didn't expect anything in return, just said it was a gift. A simple gift to help me out.

For the first time, I saw kindness in the dark depths of his eyes. A kindness I don't think he shows just anyone.

It felt like a rare gift—an eclipse of the moon.

I didn't know what to say, just thanked him over and over. And he just stared at me, his gaze deep, like he was committing the moment to memory.

"Is that why I haven't seen you in the dorms?" Amy asks.

I nod, wondering how many people had noticed. "Yeah. I don't know how he convinced his mom and stepfather, but I guess they agreed."

I leave out the part that he was ordered to take me in. That he didn't have a choice. Not that it mattered. No one goes against the Order.

And I still don't know if Garret's behavior is out of obligation. Or pity.

The bar grows louder as more people filter in. The sharp crack of a pool stick against a ball pulls my attention. My chest tightens when I spot a group of guys from the swim team—including Luke. But Garret is nowhere to be found.

I check my phone, but there's no text. Not that I expected one. He told me not to wait up for him after class.

"Do you know them?" Amy asks, catching me staring.

I snap out of it, shaking my head. "No."

She raises a brow. "Aren't they on the swim team with your boy?"

"He's not my boy," I say too quickly.

"He's not your brother either," she points out. "You're not related by any means. You didn't grow up together, right?"

"You sound like Garret. He says that all the time."

Her grin turns knowing. "That means he likes you."

I want to laugh at her assumption. Garret Nox might screw anything that moves, but liking me? That's something I don't think he's capable of.

I nod, wondering how many people have noticed the same thing. How obvious is it?

"Yeah. I don't know how he convinced his mom and stepfather, but I guess they agreed," I say, leaving out the part that Garret didn't have a choice. That he was ordered to take me in. It doesn't matter, though. Nothing could have changed it. No one goes against the Order.

And yet . . . I wonder if Garret's behavior is out of obligation. Or pity.

The bar grows louder as more people filter in, the air thick with laughter and the clinking of glasses. The sharp crack of a pool cue against the ball pulls my attention. My chest tightens when I spot a group of guys from the swim team—including Luke. But Garret is nowhere to be found.

I scoff, shaking my head. "He might screw anything that moves, but liking me? Not a chance."

Still, I keep checking my phone, hoping I didn't miss a message. Where did he go? There wasn't any swim practice today.

Last Sunday, he told me to take an Uber home and gave me the code to his house. Why? He was never this lenient before. He always had specific instructions—when to leave, when to arrive, when to wait. Now, suddenly, he trusts me?

Maybe it's nothing. Or maybe it's everything.

I can't stop the dream from creeping back into my mind.

Melody, a knife in her grip, stabbing wildly—but not at me. It was Melissa at the church. Then, another dream.

John.

I'm trapped in a dark room, my body frozen, terror rooting me in place. But then—there's someone else. A man in a mask. He saves me. But I don't know who he is.

"Where do you think he is?"

Amy's voice snaps me back.

"What do you mean?" I ask, though I know exactly who she's referring to.

A knowing gleam dances in her eyes. "You know who I'm talking about."

Before I can respond, a voice cuts through the din.

"Hey, ladies."

I glance up, and my stomach drops.

Luke.

Amy throws me a look—one that says, Why is he talking to you?

"Amy, this is Luke. Luke, this is Amy," I introduce half-heartedly.

Amy offers a weak smile, unsure how to react.

Luke barely acknowledges her before turning his attention to me. "I haven't seen you at lunch in a few days. You didn't answer my call about our date."

Amy arches a brow.

"I wanted to see if everything was okay," he adds.

I force a smile. "Oh, I'm sorry. I forgot Amy had asked me out first, so—"

"That's okay," he interrupts, but there's something off. A flicker of unease. His eyes keep darting toward the entrance.

I cross my arms. "I figured you'd understand. That's why I didn't bother to call. I'm sure there are plenty of other girls you've asked to come along."

I don't like how hard he's trying. I haven't given him a reason to pursue me, not even the slightest hint of interest.

Luke shifts awkwardly, running a hand through his hair. Silence stretches between us.

"I've heard you've been hanging around Garret," he finally says, rubbing the back of his neck.

My pulse spikes at the sound of his name. "Where did you hear that?" My voice is steady, but inside, I'm unraveling.

"I saw you two leaving after practice. It's been happening for a couple of weeks now."

Has he been watching me? Does he know John? Do the others know?

"Stalking is a crime, you know," Amy interjects, unimpressed.

Luke smirks. "It's not like I don't have eyes. Besides, everyone knows where Garret is—on campus and off."

Amy leans forward. "Oh yeah? Where is he now?"

I could kiss her for the way she asks it—like she doesn't give a damn, but like she knows I do.

Luke hesitates before shrugging. "I think he's with Cassie. They're off and on. You know how it is. Garret doesn't take anyone seriously."

A slow burn ignites in my chest, spreading like wildfire. I don't respond. I just stare at my beer, willing the words away. But they settle in my bones.Garret. Cassie. Of course.

Amy touches my arm gently, but I don't meet her gaze.

I feel sick. That night—the way he touched me, kissed me, made me feel wanted—it meant nothing. And I was stupid to think otherwise. When you've been shown cruelty your whole life, you cling to anything that feels different. Anything that makes you feel *human*.

I check the time on my phone, my fingers tightening around the device. I should throw it across the room. Should erase the reminder of him.

But I can't.

Because when you're desperate, when you have nothing, you don't let pride get in the way. It doesn't matter how much it hurts. Or who it came from. It's survival.

"It's getting late," I announce, glancing at Amy.

She understands instantly. "Yeah, we have a paper to work on," she lies, pushing out of the booth.

Luke gives me space to stand. "I guess I'll see you around?"

"Oh, sure," I murmur, my smile barely there.

We slip out the back exit, away from prying eyes. The night air is cool, thick with the scent of damp earth. Streetlights flicker, casting long shadows against the pavement.

A car door slams. I freeze. Laughter A voice. His voice.

Cassie walks ahead of Garret, her heels clicking against the wet pavement.

Amy must sense my hesitation, my urge to disappear. We stay hidden, watching as they round the building toward the entrance.

Garret isn't wearing the same clothes he had on this morning. Luke was right. He was with her. And that's why he told me not to wait.

A bitter taste fills my mouth. "Can I stay with you tonight?" I whisper, my voice barely there.

Amy doesn't hesitate. "Yeah, of course."

Garret doesn't owe me an explanation. We are nothing. But I can't face him tonight. Not after this. Not after realizing how foolish I've been.

I had one night. One fleeting moment where I let myself dream of something different.

He said my name like it was something precious.

He said I smelled like flowers.

He said I was beautiful.

ROSE

"ARE YOU GOING TO GET THAT?" Amy asks, shifting on her bed to face me.

Her dorm room setup is different from mine. She's on the third floor, in a space meant to be shared, but she doesn't have a roommate. There's an empty twin bed against the far wall, sheets folded neatly at the foot. She gave me a spare blanket, and though the room is small, it feels warmer than mine ever has. A tiny desk sits against the window, cork-board pinned with notes and photos, fairy lights strung above it like a halo, casting a soft glow across the walls.

It's the only light in the room.

My phone vibrates against the chipped nightstand, buzzing like it's possessed. The screen flashes with another missed call from Garret, followed by a series of texts.

Garret: Where are you? You never made it home.

Garret: Rose, answer the phone.

Garret: ?

The screen lights up again, the glow hitting the ceiling like a flashlight in the dark.

I sigh, my fingers hovering over the power button. He could make me pay for ignoring him. Just like John. Garret acts like his house is my home, but I don't have a home. Never did. Never will.

He should have let me drown in his pool.

It would've been a perfect way to get rid of me—an accident, my own fault. Not at the hands of the people who have already planned my death.

I press the button, watching as the screen fades to black. A silent rejection.

I don't want to hear him threaten me. I don't want to listen to whatever excuse he has, don't want to see whatever expression he'll wear when I finally face him.

Not yet.

I drop the phone onto the nightstand with a thud—like shutting the final page of a book, a chapter closed.

"Don't want to hear it, huh?" Amy's voice is quiet, mirroring the storm inside me.

Anger. Regret. Defeat. Acceptance.

"What's the point?" I turn on my side, resting my head against my palm. "Thank you."

"For what?"

"For being a friend when you don't even know me. For letting me stay here."

She exhales, stretching her legs under the blanket. "I'm glad you asked. I hate being alone."

"Trust me, it's better than bad company," I say softly.

Amy hums in agreement. "Then you should surround yourself with better company."

"I am."

Her face lights up with the smallest smile, like I've given her something precious.

"Promise me something?"

"Anything," she says, her tone full of sincerity.

I swallow, my throat tightening. "When you graduate, find someone that makes you happy . . . after you land a job that lets you live in one of those apartments where you can see the stars and the city lights at the same time."

She laughs.

"And when you find that someone, make sure he tells you he likes your name, your smell, and that you're beautiful."

Her smile falters for the briefest second, sadness flickering in her eyes before she quickly masks it.

I wonder if she dreams of the same thing. I want that for her.

Hope.Even if I don't get to live my dream, I can at least encourage her to live hers.I might not make it out of here alive. But she will.

"Why can't we do that together?" she asks, her voice tentative.

I can't tell her the truth. But I can give her hope.

"Yeah. Maybe we will. We just have to keep our heads straight and not fall for any of the assholes here."

She exhales, rubbing her palms together. "I don't get the best vibes from some of the people on campus."

I know exactly who she means. Luke. The others in class. The way they watch us. The stolen glances when they think we aren't looking.Like predators circling their prey.

"Same," I mumble.

What else can I say? That they want to use her? That they want to fuck her mind as much as her body? That they enjoy breaking people like us? That they bring girls here just to finish what our lives already started?

The next morning, I avoid large crowds and anyone who knows Garret. I steer clear of the places he hangs out, walking with my head down, adjusting the skirt and leggings Amy let me borrow. I'm grateful they fit—and that they're not as short as the ones most girls here parade around in.

I had been about to object when Amy pulled out the black pleated skirt and tights, but I didn't want to seem ungrateful. She's the only person I talk to, the only one I can sit in silence with who doesn't ask questions. It's like she's trying to break free from the chains of her past, while I'm desperately trying to escape my present.

But I know it's no use.

I can't run.

I can only dream—and hope that she'll be the one to live them.

For her. For me. For every poor soul walking through these dormitory halls, clinging to the illusion of a better life.

And me?

I just hope to live longer than the other girls who were in that room when John took me. I've heard the rumors—most of them don't make it. They die from overdoses, from trauma, from the beatings, or they simply disappear, never to be heard from again.

A breeze rustles through the trees, carrying the crisp scent of fall. My stomach growls, but I push past the hunger, opting instead for my favorite chips and a soda. I skipped breakfast—too afraid of running into Garret.

I find a spot near a tree by the church.

It's not really a church, but everyone calls it that—even though more people die inside than pray.

This spot is usually deserted. Amy's schedule doesn't align with mine on Tuesdays, so I eat alone.

"Keeping your phone off isn't smart."

Garret's voice slices through the breeze, making me jump. My bag of chips nearly spills onto the ground.

Fear curls in my stomach.

"Are you tracking me?" I ask, already knowing the answer. John did it. Why wouldn't Garret?

"Something like that." His tone is sharp, edged with restrained anger.

I sigh. "Can I finish my lunch before you do whatever it is you plan on doing?"

He steps in front of me, forcing me to crane my neck to meet his gaze. He's wearing a fitted sweater, black jeans, and dark sunglasses, but I can still feel his eyes burning into my skin, like the sun breaking through a cloudy sky.

"And what do you think I plan to do?"

"Kill me." I gesture toward the cemetery. "I can even show you the spot I picked out. It's far enough that no one will notice—or remember me."

He stiffens.

Despite the cool breeze, it feels like all the air has been sucked from the world.

The silence stretches between us, heavy, suffocating. The veins in his forearms flex as he clenches his fists.

Then, he kneels in front of me and pushes his sunglasses onto the top of his head.

His black eyes bore into mine, so intense it feels like lightning is about to strike.

"I'm not going to kill you."

"You're going against the Order?" My voice is flat, disbelieving.

"Let me worry about that."

"Then what is it you want?"

His answer is immediate.

"You in my house when I expect you to be. In my bed when it's time to sleep."

I swallow hard.

"I'm not fond of sleeping in your bed. It's a bit too crowded."

His jaw tightens, but I keep going.

"Besides, I gave you the night off from babysitting me. I thought you'd be grateful to spend time with Cassie."

Something flashes in his expression, but I don't stop.

"I was at Babylon last night. Don't worry, Luke cleared it up for me—and I saw for myself when you both arrived."

His face is unreadable, but his body is taut, coiled.

"What did you see?" His voice is controlled, but there's a sharpness beneath the surface.

I expected guilt.

But all I see is anger.

Why would he be angry? That I know what he was up to? That I think he's full of shit when he insists Cassie and he aren't serious?

"I saw what I needed to see," I say, my voice hollow. "I read what I needed to read in the messages you sent."

His jaw tightens.

"I'm just a puppet to you. A toy for your dog. I'm not important. So cut the shit and just get it over with. It wasn't like I didn't expect it."

I push myself to my feet, chin high, challenging him.

"You can drop the nice-guy act and be the monster we both know you are."

His nostrils flare.

His chest rises and falls with deep, measured breaths.

"Is that what you think?" His voice is low, dangerous, laced with something I can't decipher.

Anger seeps into his expression, into the hard set of his mouth, the rigid lines of his posture.

I brace myself. Because I know what happens next. I've seen it before. My reality is about to shatter.

And I'll be at the mercy of the monster.

"Let's go," he says with a finality that leaves no room for argument—like I'm a child who needs to be scolded for making the wrong assumption.

But I know what I saw.

I follow him to the parking lot, stopping when he halts in front of a sleek black Range Rover. I don't have to ask whose car it is—this is one of many parked inside his massive garage.

"You're driving."

I freeze in front of the hood. My panic must be written all over my face because he frowns.

"What's wrong?"

"I don't know how," I admit. "I don't have a driver's license."

His jaw tightens. "John really wanted you to be clueless, huh?"

Dumb is more like it—but at least he's finally catching on.

"Get in."

My eyes widen. "I can't."

Letting out a frustrated growl, he walks around to the driver's side, yanks the door open, and gives me a look that makes my stomach drop. "Get in the fucking car."

I don't argue.

As I step forward, he slides into the driver's seat and grabs my waist, lifting me onto his lap like I weigh nothing.

A gasp catches in my throat. The heat of his muscled thighs burns through my tights, igniting those damn butterflies in my stomach. My body betrays me every time he's near, and no matter how hard I try to push it down, the sensation lingers.

I tear my gaze away and stare at the massive screen on the dashboard. It reminds me of something from a spaceship I've seen on TV.

The car door shuts with a solid thud.

He presses his foot on the brake, pushes a button, and the soft purr of the engine fills the silence—along with my erratic heartbeat.

Then, his hands move. Slow. Purposeful.

Heat erupts across my thighs as his palms slide over the black tights stretched over my skin.

I squirm.

And that's when I feel it.

The hard length pressing against my ass—thick and growing by the second. "Keep squirming like that, and I'm going to fuck you in the school parking lot," he rasps.

I freeze.

My breath is trapped in my throat, my body betraying me again. My mind flashes to him flipping my skirt up, burying himself inside me, deep and rough.

Would I scream?

Would I like it?

Would I claw his eyes out?

No. I already know the truth.

I would let him.

Because Garret is not John. He is not David or the others. If Garret wanted to take me, he would have.

But he hasn't.

His need isn't about control—it's about me letting him.

And I did.

I let him kiss me.

I let him touch me.

I let him sink his teeth into my flesh and mark me.

And I didn't fight.

I didn't tell him to stop. I let him do things I never thought I'd let another man do—but him.

The shift in the air is suffocating, but he doesn't push me further. Instead, he places the car in reverse.

The screen shifts with a live feed of the rear camera, beeping softly as he maneuvers the vehicle with effortless precision. "This is reverse," he says, his voice calm, controlled. His large hands rest lightly over mine, guiding them to the wheel. "This is drive."

My fingers tremble beneath his.

"Relax," he murmurs against the back of my neck, his breath a dangerous caress. "I got you. You're doing great."

I forget that I'm sitting on his lap.

Forget the way he feels against me.

Because I'm driving.

A slow smile spreads across my lips.

"I'm driving," I breathe in awe.

It must sound childish, but I don't care.

I've wanted this for so long—for someone to show me I'm more than just a body.

"When you brake, press it slowly," he continues, guiding me. "If you stop too suddenly, someone tailing too close might rear-end you, or you'll be thrown forward. It happens, but only if you're trying to avoid hitting something—or someone."

A shiver runs through me. I tense, suddenly afraid of messing up.

His hands smooth over my thighs in slow, measured strokes.

Soothing. Grounding.

My leg shakes less.

We pull into an outdoor shopping mall. As the car rolls to a stop, a valet in a crisp red shirt immediately opens the door. "Welcome, Mr. Nox."

The valet's expression remains neutral, as if it's completely normal to see me sitting on Garret's lap.

"Park it in front," Garret orders. "I want my car ready when we're done."

We?

The word lingers. I don't think I've ever been included before. My pulse stutters. I've never been out alone with a guy before.

"What are we doing here?" I ask. "Don't you have class?"

"No," he says, unbuckling me like he does this every day. "And we're here to shop."

I blink, caught off guard.

I imagine he wants more things for himself—Garret never wears the same thing twice.

I've noticed.

His closet is the size of my entire dorm room floor—maybe bigger.

I wonder where he puts it all when he's done. Everything he owns is brand new—his socks, his underwear, his fucking bedsheets.

Always black.

Like his cars.

His kitchen.

His dog.

His heart.

ROSE

GARRET TAKES me into nearly every store.

I don't ask how much anything costs. I just stand there while he speaks with the clerks, watching the way their faces soften when they look at me—not because they care, but because he's buying something.

"She looks like a size two."

"I want the latest collection," he replies.

The woman behind the counter blinks slowly, reminding me of a sleepy cat. "Which one?"

Garret picks up a black leather boot embossed with two interlocking Cs in white.

"All of it," he says, as if she's new and doesn't understand his language yet.

Her eyes widen slightly before flicking to me. "Are you sure?"

Garret tilts his head and nods. "I'm sure. Also, if she touches it, add it. Spare no expense."

I swallow thickly. Did he just say he doesn't care how much everything costs? I lean over a nearby display, running my fingers over a small leather bag—one Amy would love. My eyes flick to the price tag.

Fifty-seven hundred. I snatch my hand back like it burned me.

"Do you like this one?" Joan—the store clerk, according to her name tag—immediately lifts the bag, eyes expectant.

I glance between her and Garret, panicked. "I was looking for a friend, but I changed my mind," I say quickly, hoping to escape the moment.

"Get a new one. Gift wrap it."

I snap my gaze to him, stunned. Is he serious?

The corner of his mouth lifts in a slow, knowing smirk, and I swear my heart stops beating altogether.

By the time six rolls around, I want to collapse—preferably into the fountain at the center of the promenade. "How much did you spend?" I ask, panting slightly from exhaustion.

Garret laughs like it's nothing, but I know it isn't. His arms are loaded with glossy designer bags, the strings looped around his wrists like bracelets. Every time I offered to carry something, he refused.

"A lot," he finally says.

"How much is on that card?" I press.

"There isn't a limit."

I stop walking. "What?"

I've never heard of a card without a limit. Whenever I tried to buy something and miscalculated in my head, my card would decline. "That's not possible."

He shrugs, unbothered. "It's not going to be a problem for you anymore."

My stomach clenches. He makes it sound so simple—like I'm his responsibility now. The moment I've been dreading all afternoon finally arrives.

I inhale deeply. "How can I pay you back?"

Every store he walked into, he dragged me along. Every luxury brand, every exclusive collection, he bought it all. Shoes. Clothes. Perfume. Handbags. Silk underwear. His SUV is stuffed to the brim, overflowing with shopping bags.

He spares me a glance, then effortlessly shifts the car into drive. "I want you to smile. That's how can pay me back."

My insides melt into liquid fire.

A smile. That's all he wants in return.

I was so sure he was evil, but now… I hope he's not.

The next day, the hope doesn't last long.

I see it before I even step onto campus—the flashing red and blue lights, the cluster of news vans parked in disarray, the yellow crime scene tape stretched across the quad. The main entrance is blocked off. Cops won't let anyone through.

I don't know who did it. But I have a very good idea.

Luke was found nailed to the cross outside the church—upside down, naked. His eyes were missing. His tongue was cut out. The words "A LYING TONGUE IS A PERSON WHO SEEKS DEATH" were carved into his chest.

I shudder violently.

The police are asking questions, but they don't have any leads.

I do.

Because I know who could have done it. And why.

Garret.

I don't know how I know, but I do. It was Luke who told me about Garret and Cassie. It was Luke who made me confront Garret. It was Luke who couldn't stop looking at the door that night in the bar.

Amy rushes up to me in the hallway, breathless. "Did you hear about Luke?"

People are crying. A makeshift memorial is already set up on campus—flowers, pictures, candles.

I nod, but her expression tells me everything. She knows—or at least, she suspects. "Yeah, it's crazy," I say. "One minute he was there, and the next, he…"

"Got nailed to a fucking cross," Amy supplies. "I wasn't fond of him. He was a little pushy, but shit… that's a fucked-up way to go."

My stomach twists violently.

What if Garret changes his mind about me?

"Hey."

I turn around. Garret is standing there, watching me with soft, careful eyes—like nothing happened. Like today is just another normal day.

"Hey," I reply, wrapping my arms around myself, suddenly grateful for the new sweater he bought me.

He leans in, pressing a kiss to my cheek, and I swear my toes curl inside my new designer boots. "Did you give your friend her gift?" he asks, expectantly.

Amy perks up. "She did! I keep asking if she won the lottery."

Garret smiles—a slow, knowing curve of his lips, like the cat that got the cream. "I think she did. She just doesn't know it yet."

My stomach tightens. What the hell does that mean?

"Anyway," Amy chimes in. "I hope you don't mind, but I'd like Rose to hang out at the Babylon tonight. My treat."

I glance between them.

Amy is waiting for his permission.

Garret smiles, but it's calculated—like he's plotting something. "Sure," he says, sliding his hands into his pockets. "I'll meet you there."

"Okay."

Before I can react, he presses a second kiss to my neck—lingering just long enough for his teeth to graze my skin. I swear I feel him smile.

He walks away, completely unbothered, as if he didn't just claim me in front of everyone.

"Damn," Amy mutters, watching him go.

"What?"

"That boy is crazy about you."

I almost burst out laughing. *If she only knew.* "Why do you keep thinking that?"

"You should see the way he looks at you. When I asked if we could hang out, he wanted to murder me for taking you away."

I shake my head. "You're imagining things. We both saw who he was with, remember?"

Amy doesn't look convinced. But deep down, neither am I.

Because something about what Luke said doesn't add up. And now, Luke is dead. His body was carved with a message.

A LYING TONGUE IS A PERSON WHO SEEKS DEATH.

Was it Garret's way of telling me Luke lied?

Or was it a warning meant for me?

Instead of Babylon, Amy decides we should go somewhere else.

We take an Uber across town to a dive bar near Ohio State. The place is smaller than Babylon but looks bigger from the outside. Inside, it's evenly spaced out with a rustic, lived-in feel—mismatched tables and chairs, two pool tables, an area for darts, and a bar positioned at the center. The music isn't bad either, probably because people pay to hear what they want.

"I thought we needed a change," Amy says, sliding into a booth just as Timeless starts drumming through the speakers.

I text Garret to let him know. I don't bother sending the address—I know he'll find me anyway. The tracker he has on my phone makes sure of that.

Except for the night I stayed in Amy's dorm.

I have a feeling he knew, but he didn't mention it. That's the thing with Garret—he's quiet. Unpredictable. I never know what he's going to do or what his motives are.

The thought of Luke still lingers in my mind.

I should feel bad. I should feel remorse.

But when you've lived around death for as long as I have, when you've been surrounded by people who do nefarious things, a dead body isn't shocking.

It's a norm.

I've seen worse.

Amy stiffens suddenly, her eyes widening. "Oh my God."

"What?"

"Don't look now, but that guy—Leo? He's here. Right behind you. Playing darts."

My spine stiffens.

Slowly, I turn over my shoulder.

Leo's laughing with one of his friends, smiling as he bends to pick up a dart from the floor. His shirt clings to his broad chest, the words OHIO FOOTBALL printed across in bold white letters.

Our eyes connect.

Shit.

I whip back around, praying he didn't notice me.

"Shit," Amy mutters, lowering her head. "He's coming this way."

"Hey, beautiful. Aren't you going to say hi?"

Leo's grinning down at me, easygoing as ever.

I hadn't expected him to walk over. He hasn't called or texted my other phone—not once.

I check it every day, but not for him.

For John.

And deep down, I have a terrible feeling that one day, he's going to show up.

That I'll have to pay for staying with Garret.

Or worse—he already knows my fate.

And he's simply stopped caring.

"Hi," I say, forcing a polite smile. "I didn't want to bother you when you were busy with friends."

Leo leans against the booth, bracing his hand against the top of the seat behind me. His smile deepens, cocky and sure. "You could never bother me."

Amy's brows shoot up at his confidence, but then her gaze shifts past him, locking onto something behind me.

My stomach drops.

I don't have to turn around to know. I sense him before I smell him—Garret's exotic cologne drifting through the air.

"You're in my way," Garret says scathingly.

But he's not alone.

Leo straightens, stepping aside to let him through. He doesn't expect Garret to slide into the booth right next to me, nor does he expect the seething glare Garret sends his way. I barely have time to process before my eyes shift to Azriel, who's standing beside him.

His gaze flickers between Amy, me, and Leo, assessing the situation. "Aren't you going to introduce me to your friend?" Azriel asks, his gaze trailing over Amy's face—lingering a little too long on her chest—before snapping back up to her eyes.

Whoa.

I've never seen him act this cocky before.

Amy's face flames bright red.

"Amy, this is—"

"Azriel," she cuts in, rolling her eyes dismissively. "I know. I tried signing up for tutoring once, but he said he was too busy."

Azriel doesn't flinch.

"I was," he replies dryly before turning back to me.

"Are you okay?"

His eyes narrow playfully, but I know what he's really asking.

I meet his gaze with a knowing smile. I see what you just did.

Azriel's protective instinct is kicking in.

I like him, but I know where his loyalty lies.

And Amy? She's Prey—just like me.

"Hey, man."

Leo claps a hand on Azriel's shoulder, greeting him like an old friend.

Azriel doesn't so much as blink. He merely lifts his chin, utterly indifferent.

Leo doesn't take the hint.

Instead, he slides into the booth next to Amy, making himself comfortable.

Azriel's jaw tics, but he doesn't say anything.

A small smile tugs at my lips.

"Aren't you abandoning your friends?" Azriel asks, gesturing toward Leo's crew across the bar.

Leo doesn't miss a beat. "They're fine."

I swallow hard as my eyes dart toward Garret.

He's watching Leo like a predator. Unblinking. Seething.

Leo, for some reason, seems immune to the death glare currently directed at him.

Then, just to fucking test fate, he smirks and winks at me.

"Wink at her one more time, and I'll rip your eyelids off."

Garret's voice is low. Deadly.

"That's your only warning."

"Garret—"

But before I can stop him, he yanks me out of the booth.

Drags me outside.

Pushes me against the brick wall of the building.

The sun dips below the horizon, casting the alley in shadows.

Time slows.

His body presses against mine, heat radiating through my clothes.

"Because you're mine," he growls.

Before I can speak, his lips crush against mine.

I gasp—and he takes advantage, plunging his tongue deep into my mouth.

His hands grip my thighs, lifting me off the ground, and I wrap my legs around his waist without thinking.

"Mine."

He squeezes my ass, his fingers digging into my flesh.

"He doesn't get you," he murmurs between kisses.

"I get you. I want you. I need you. I'll save you, Rose."

His words are a promise. A plea. A curse.

"What's it going to take, huh?"

His breath is ragged. His hands shake with restraint.

"For you to see it?"

I can't think.

I can't think when he's like this—dark, feral, unhinged. When he presses his cock against me, rolling his hips so I feel exactly how hard he is. "What about—"I start, but he cuts me off.

"I'm not with her. I'm not with anyone. Can't you see, Rose?" His voice is wrecked. Desperate. "I can't be with anyone else. I can't come with anyone else." He bends his knees, grinding against me. "Feel that…my little Darkthorn. His dick is big and hard pushing between my black leggings. The rubbing my clit. "Fucking feel that?"

My head spins.

"I have to beat you out of my dick knowing you're sleeping in my bed every night." He presses harder. I ache. "Do you know what that's like?"

My body wants him but my mind doesn't understand logic. It only understands him and his words. "I want to fuck you, but I can't. Not until you want me. Not until you say yes. Because I can't hurt you, Rose. I'll die…I'll die knowing you're not breathing."

I don't stand a chance. I know it now. I'm falling for him.

ROSE

GARRET DRIVES like a madman through the streets of Kenyan, his grip tight on the wheel, the low growl of the sports car vibrating through my bones. He doesn't speak. Not once.

When we reach the house, the doors swing up, and he's rounding the car before I even unbuckle. His hands find me, lifting me effortlessly as if my hesitation doesn't exist.

Azriel assured him Amy would make it back to the dorms. I wasn't worried. Azriel, despite being a son of Kenyan, has a heart. He wouldn't hurt Amy. But I don't trust him with her heart.

Garret makes a sound of frustration at my sluggish pace and picks me up, carrying me through the threshold and straight to his bedroom. I don't have time to think. I barely have time to breathe. He sets me down on the bed, stepping back only long enough to pull his shirt over his head.

My mouth goes dry.

He's perfect. The hard planes of his muscles flex beneath inked skin, each tattoo an untold story. Thorns curl over his heart, inked deep. Dark and possessive.

His gaze locks onto mine ."Tell me," he rasps, voice rough with want. "Is this okay?"

He's asking for permission. Tears sting my eyes.

His expression tightens when he sees them. "Don't cry, Rose. I'll stop."

I shake my head, pressing my lips together to keep my emotions in check. "No, please. Don't," I whisper. "I'm just… happy."

His brows furrow slightly, as if he's trying to decipher whether he's hearing me correctly. "Are you sure?"

I nod, breath hitching.

His jaw flexes, shadows darkening his features. "I'm not gentle,

Rose. It's why I've tried to stay away. I've tried to keep my distance, but once you say yes..." His voice drops, guttural. Dangerous. "I'm going to fuck you. I'm going to fuck every man from your memory."

Shame burns through me at his words. The memories—the past I can never erase.

"I know how you got your tattoo."

My breath falters. The pieces click together. That's why he changed.

His hands slide up my thighs, his thumb pressing against my clit, sending a shockwave of pleasure through my body. His tongue darts out between his lips, wetting them as he watches me.

"I'm sorry I judged you," he murmurs. "But I don't regret shaving your pretty pussy."

A strangled gasp escapes me as I press my hand over his, pushing harder against the pressure of his thumb.

"Fuck, Rose," he grits, the muscle in his jaw contracting.

Heat pulses between my legs, an unbearable ache. My body betrays me, hips rolling in a slow grind against his hand. He watches me come apart for him.

His fingers find the band of my leggings and tug. He slides them over my hips, down my thighs, stripping me bare, tossing them behind him. His eyes flick to my panties—silk, thin lace, already wet.

His nostrils flare, dark hunger twisting across his face. "I can smell you," he breathes, voice thick.

"Then let me feel you."

His lips part slightly, eyes flicking up to my sweater. His fingers find the hem, and I let him pull it over my head. My bra follows.

He moves slow, calculated. Holding himself back. I know he wants to tear my panties away, to claim me completely—but I make him wait. Because this moment isn't just sex.

It's ours.

"I've made a lot of mistakes in my life, Rose," he murmurs, stripping the last barrier between us. His cock stands proud, thick and heavy, silver barbells piercing from tip to shaft. He strokes himself, watching me watch him.

He's beautiful.

"But you…will never be one of them," he says.

His words shatter me. Because I know what it feels like to be a mistake. I've spent my whole life feeling like one.

But as he kneels between my thighs, inhaling me like I'm the only thing he's ever wanted—I believe him.

"Fuck," he whispers, voice wrecked. "You smell so good." His head dips, the flat of his tongue dragging over the lace, over the heat of me.

Pleasure explodes through my body like a wrecking ball. My nipples tighten, aching. My legs tremble as my breath stutters out in a desperate moan.

"Garret…" I gasp. "Please… more."

He smirks wickedly, straight black hair falling over his brow, his pitch-dark eyes, the white part visible glinting up at me like the devil himself. Then, he flicks his tongue. A strangled sound rips from my throat. He doesn't stop.

He grips my hips, holding me in place as I writhe beneath him. My hands fist the sheets, my body arching into him as pleasure tightens in my core. I want him to rip the lace but I break.

My climax crashes through me, a scream tearing from my lips as my vision blurs. My body convulses, tremors rolling down my legs as wet heat floods me.

Garret groans. He rips my panties off. Clamps his mouth over me. Drinks me in.

I'm still gasping when he rises, fisting his cock, pressing the tip against my slick entrance. My heart stutters at the delicious pressure, my body aching for more.

Our eyes lock.

I don't look away. I don't blink.

He pushes inside me. A strangled cry escapes me, my thighs trembling. One of his hands flattens against the mattress by my head; the other grips my leg, holding it over his hip.

He moves. Slow. Deep. Hard. Raw.

His gaze never leaves mine. Consuming.

His jaw clenches. "I didn't use a condom," he rasps.

I know. I can feel everything.

"I'm clean," he adds, voice tight, rough. "But I'm coming inside you, Rose. Do you understand?"

I nod, breathless. "I'm on birth control."

A wicked smile curls his lips. "Okay." He flips me onto my stomach, pulling my hips up, slamming into me from behind.

A shocked moan escapes me as his fingers tangle in my hair, pulling my head back. His teeth scrape over my shoulder, his tongue soothing the bite.

"You're so fucking beautiful," he groans. His hands roam—skimming over my breasts, teasing my nipples as his thrusts slow, deep, measured. He rubs his nose over my cheek, breathing me in. "This pussy," he growls, thrusting harder. "Is fucking *perfect*."

I cry out, gripping the sheets, lost in the rhythm of him. His lips find mine, devouring me as he fucks me—owns me. His thrusts turn frantic. His body tightens.

"Fuck—Rose, I'm gonna come."

His words slur against my lips, his voice desperate, wrecked. His movements become erratic, his fingers digging into my hips, his cock pulsing—hot, thick, endless. My body clenches, milking him.

He keeps moving. Keeps fucking me. Keeps worshipping me.

His arms wrap around me as he rolls us, my back pressed to his chest as he fucks me slow, lazy, deep—like he never wants to leave.

Billie Eillish's *Lovely* plays through the house speakers as he kisses my neck, whispering words against my skin. "You're perfect, Rose." His breath skims my ear, fire erupting in its wake. His hand presses over my heart. "I promise," he whispers. "I'll never let anyone hurt you."

I turn my head, catching his lips. And for the first time…

I believe him.

GARRET

"I HEARD you've been spending time with a Prey around town," Draven's father says, lighting a cigar.

The other members of the Order watch me, waiting for a reaction. The old man is bringing it up to make a point—Rose is off-limits. It's been three weeks since I first tasted her, and I can't get enough.

"I have," I admit easily.

John shifts in his seat, his anger a live wire beneath his skin. He watches all fifty members in their respective chairs but says nothing. He knows better. Someone else needs to take his place—someone more deserving. Because John Strauss doesn't deserve to sit here. He doesn't even deserve to breathe for what he's done to my girl.

I scan the room, noting the familiar faces. All members of the Order are present, but there's one other person I'm interested in seeing. Leonidas, he looks away but he's getting it now.

"Nice piece of ass," Alaric's grandfather comments, exhaling a slow puff of smoke.

I let it slide.

He must have helped Alaric uncover Rose's past, so I'll let him talk. He doesn't mean anything by it, and I can't blame him.

Rose does have a nice ass. And I've been fucking that ass all night, every night.

Still, baby steps.

She needs to trust me before I introduce her to my darker tastes.

John grunts. I turn to him, my glare cutting like a blade.

"Problem, Strauss?" I ask, my voice deceptively calm.

"She's not yours," he states triumphantly, his chin lifting.

I smile.

I can see the flicker of uncertainty in his gaze.

"Right now, my DNA dripping between her thighs says otherwise," I shoot back smoothly.

Laughter erupts around the table. The twins, Reid, Valen, and Alaric throw their heads back, their amusement filling the boardroom. Even old man Bedford chuckles. They all know what I mean.

Touch her, and I'll kill you.

Clearing my throat, I shift my focus. "I have a matter to discuss." My eyes flick to Valen, then to his father. Old man Vikiar is going to be pissed. But I don't give a fuck.

It's time.

"What is it?" Alaric's grandfather asks, the room quieting as all eyes turn to me.

"There's one son missing from this table," I state, my voice measured but firm. "He needs to be here. It's his birthright."

"How dare you?" Valen's father spits, his face going red, like he's seconds from a heart attack.

The other elders glance at him, some raising their brows at his outburst. He quickly composes himself, adjusting his tie with a forced calm. Then, begrudgingly, he concedes.

"Yes, but he's right." Alarics's grandfather turns to me and Valen, reluctant but resigned. "Next meeting, Garret. Valen. Bring him. He needs to be here, as his birthright."

A slow smile spreads across my face.

Finally.

But John isn't done.

"And the issue with the girl?" he prods, his voice sharp. "The Prey."

I flick my gaze to the piece of shit across the table. I wish I could end him now—but patience.

"What about her?" Bedford asks through a slow drag of his cigar, the smoke swirling like a raincloud above his head.

"He has to let her go if he can't do what was asked," John insists.

Reid's gaze sharpens. I know exactly what he's thinking. *Kill him now and get it over* with. His eyes dart to mine. I give a subtle shake of my head.

Not yet.

I have a plan.

I've had one since Rose first arrived. I hated that she lied, but I knew something wasn't right. Valen knew too. But we didn't have proof—until now.

John bought her. The Order doesn't condone human trafficking. Children are off-limits. It's messy. Disgusting. But we still need evidence. Not that it matters—John doesn't get a free pass. He's already dead.

I promised Rose. I promised myself when I first laid eyes on her, when I first heard her snarky mouth. Rose was mine before she even knew she was.

"She's chosen to stay, John," I remind him. "She's a student on campus. You know the rules. Besides, why do you care?"

"I'm her guardian," he sneers.

"She's an adult."

"Who's going to provide for her?" he challenges.

I will.

I have.

"It's no trouble for Garret," Bedford cuts in. "He has more money than you." He leans back, tapping ash from his cigar. "Find another woman to park your dick in, John. I'm sure Mary won't mind. Buy her a Rolls and a trip to the Maldives. She'll look the other way."

I let the jab at my mother slide. Everyone knows how I feel about her.

I don't give a fuck.

"Let it go, John," Draven speaks up, scrolling through his phone. He's bored, itching to get back to Gia and the kids.

John doesn't take the hint.

"So, does anyone have anything to say about Luke?" he asks, bringing up the real reason we were called here. "The boy's father is distraught."

"He shouldn't have stuck his nose where it didn't belong," I say flatly, my tone devoid of emotion. "He was warned, John. Drop it."

John snaps. "You son of a bitch!" he roars, lunging out of his seat.

I grin. "You're not wrong," I reply lazily. "But then again, you married her."

The chair behind him topples over, slamming against the floor-to-ceiling window.

Silence blankets the room.

Reid sighs, shaking his head. "Pay him," he says simply. "If he starts any trouble, the Consortium will take care of it."

We all know what that means. We'll take care of it.

John's face twists in rage, but he knows he's lost. "You won't get away with this," he spits before storming out of the boardroom.

Coward.

"Handle it," Old Man Caruthers orders. "The girl is your responsibility, Garret. Do what you want with her."

His tone leaves no room for debate. "Alaric already briefed me." Then, he lowers the gavel. The meeting is over.

We all rise.

Valen's father turns to him, eyes filled with fire and hate. "He's your responsibility now," he seethes. "You got what you wanted." Then, he storms off.

Valen meets my gaze. Azriel is officially a son of Kenyan. But people don't know the truth. As nice as they think he is, there's a part of him his father doesn't want the world to see.

He's a patient from the fourth floor.

And someone had to help me nail that fucker to the cross.

ROSE

FOR THE THIRD time this morning, I retch into the toilet, my stomach twisting violently. My nose runs, snot dripping, as I clutch the rim, feeling like my insides might spill out through my mouth.

Leaning back against the cold tile wall, I wipe my mouth with the back of my hand, sweat slicking my brow. My ribs ache from the force of vomiting. Maybe I ate something bad. Or maybe I caught a stomach bug.

I exhale shakily and glance at the small teak table near the sink, where a folded note waits for me.

Garret's handwriting. My heart clenches. He was the one behind the first note. Who would've thought Garret Nox was a romantic?

Smiling softly, I pick up the letter, pressing it to my chest. I love him. The forever kind. The kind that roots itself so deeply inside you, no one could ever measure up.

He's embedded in me like vines creeping through cracks, wrapping around my heart, refusing to let go.

I unfold the letter, my pulse pounding as I read:

You have broken the darkness around my heart with a kiss.
Your warmth, the scent of your skin.
The essence that is you.
It is only you that it beats for,
When death comes knocking, I'll answer.
I'll surrender.
To save the Darkthorn I bleed for.

I press the paper against my chest. Still lost in my thoughts, I pad toward the kitchen, craving something light to settle my stomach.

But the moment I hear laughter, I freeze. A woman's laughter. A sharp, ringing sound puncturing my ribs.

Then, his voice—low, amused. Laughing with her. Jealousy spikes through my veins.

Steeling myself, I step forward. Garret stands shirtless, smiling at a woman—a woman so stunning she could crush me with a glance.

Long, inky-black hair cascades down her back, skimming a slim waist and wide hips. Her lips full, glossy curve in a knowing smile.

She's been with him. I can tell.

She lifts a delicate hand, feeding him a bite of cake from her fingers.

The intimacy of it makes my stomach churn. I no longer feel hungry. I no longer feel anything but a sick, twisting knot of realization: This isn't new.

The way they stand too close together. The way her manicured nails brush his wrist as he takes the bite. The way her dark eyes drink him in. Playful. Too friendly.

She isn't Prey.

She isn't like me. Her dress is designer—black, mid-thigh, expensive. She belongs to his world.

"It tasted better last time I made it," she says, solidifying my thoughts.

Garret grimaces, chewing slowly. His expression shifts. "It tastes... off." He shaking his head. "Not good enough."

I clench my fist so tightly I don't realize I'm still holding the note.

Her eyes find mine.

I look away in defeat.

I move toward the trash can, wave my hand over the sensor, and crumple the note into a ball.

Garret steps back from her, but not far enough.

"Hey..." He clears his throat. "Did you sleep well?"

The black steel lid lifts.

I force a smile. "Yeah." I drop the note.

The lid closes.

"Hungry?" he asks.

I shake my head. "Not really."

I don't look at him.

Instead, I turn to her. The woman he didn't introduce me to. The woman he let feed him. "Hi," I say smoothly. "I'm Rose."

Her smile is perfect. "It's nice to meet you," she says. "I'm Veronica." Then she glances at Garret.

Veronica. Even her name is beautiful. A perfect, glossy, effortless Veronica.

I glance at the cake. Garret never asked me to bake for him. Granted, I don't know my way around a kitchen. But I would have tried.

I would have learned. I would have done anything for him—if only he had asked.

But he asked her.

He was here with her while I was upstairs, puking my guts out. He didn't even know.

The tension thickens. It smothers me like a heavy fog. I know Garret has a past. And I know mine isn't pure. But watching him parade it in front of me—or worse, knowing he might still be fucking her, rips something apart inside me.

We never talked about what we are to each other. I was stupid to think I was special. Garret can have whoever he wants. Why would he waste his time with me?

A wave of nausea rolls through me. My hands turn clammy. My stomach lurches. I need to get out of here.

Garret grabs a plate of strawberries. "You sure?" he asks.

Veronica smiles and plucks one from the plate. "Aww…you remembered?" she says, softly.

Acid burns my throat.

"I try," he says, as if I'm not even in the room.

I swallow hard and clear my throat. "I'll leave you two to finish."

Veronica hesitates. "Oh, I can go—"

"No, stay." I force my best fake smile. "He invited you." I lie through my teeth. "I have a paper due. You can keep him company." I turn away before my voice cracks.

"Rose?" Garret calls.

I pause. I don't turn around.

Tears silently streak down my cheeks. "Yeah?"

His voice is soft. "Call me if you need help."

I nod, swallowing the lump in my throat. "Yeah. Of course."

I make it to the bedroom, shaking. I grab my black book-bag—the same one I came here with. The one thing that still belongs to me. Then I start collecting my things. The ones I didn't throw away.

A reminder of who I was before him.

GARRET

VERONICA SMACKS me on the arm. "What the hell is the matter with you?"

"What?"

"You don't know?"

I scratch my brow. "You're talking in tongues. First, you fucked up the cake I wanted to surprise her with, and now you're berating me for God knows what." I pick up the plate.

"She's gorgeous," she states. "And very pregnant."

I almost drop the disgusting cake. "What?"

She's been pale for the past couple of days. I count the days. Subtract. Then count again. A slow, proud smile spreads across my lips. She hasn't been eating like she usually does, and she looked at the plate of strawberries like it was covered in mold.

"You think?" I ask, but I already know the answer.

"Yes. And she's also jealous that I'm here." Veronica crosses her arms. "And she knows."

Knows what?

"That we've..." She tilts her head to the side, avoiding the words.

We don't talk about it. It was a mistake, but it happened, and at the time, it helped both of us.

She's happily married and in love with Alaric. And me? I'm in love with the girl who's more than likely pregnant with my child.

"I guess I have to change that."

I wave my hand over the trash. The lid lifts with a soft whir. Reaching in, I pull out the note she threw away. The note where, in not so many words, I told her I love her.

Yeah, I haven't outright said it, but I didn't think I needed to. I was wrong. I was wrong not to introduce her first. And, if I'm being honest with myself, I was an idiot for inviting Veronica in the first place. I didn't think about how she'd feel. I should have.

But I wanted to bake her a cake. To celebrate her birthday. Or at least, the birth date Alaric found for her. It wasn't real—he could only confirm the year, not the month or the day—so I thought of letting her pick one if she wanted.

I didn't want to buy a cake. I didn't know which one to get. I wanted her to taste different flavors and find out which one she loved best. What color she liked. Buttercream icing or whipped? Chocolate, velvet, vanilla, or birthday cake?

But again, I didn't think. I should have never let her walk away. I should have explained. Told her that I love her. That it will always be her.

"What do I do?" I ask, dropping the ruined cake into the trash.

Veronica peers over at the note in my hands, then at me. "What a man should have done a long time ago," she says flatly. "Kill that asshole. Marry her. Create a fucking legacy with her. Fill this house with children of your own."

I smile, imagining a little girl with her smile—Rose wearing my ring.

ROSE

A FLASH OF RED LIGHT. I groan. My head feels like it's being plowed by a bulldozer. One minute, I was walking out of my dorm, putting my things back. The next, I was rushed from behind—something hard slammed against the side of my skull.

Pain throbs behind my left eye as I struggle to peel my eyes open. That damn red light.

The stench in the room makes my stomach twist violently—a foul mix of dirty socks, sweat, sex, and cologne. I gag. Then I vomit. It burns its way up, acid and bile hitting the floor.

"Fucking hell. She threw up again."

David.

His voice is annoyed, disgusted. I inhale through my nose, and my stomach lurches again.

"What the hell is wrong with her?" David asks, irritated. "Is she sick? Did you hit her too hard? She might need a doctor."

No, you piece of shit. I don't need a doctor. I need you to fucking die.

"She's fine," John replies, impatient. "We didn't give her the drugs this time."

John.

John took me. He wasn't supposed to. He broke the rules. But John doesn't give a shit about rules. He's been waiting for this moment. Watching. Plotting. He saw an opportunity, and he took it—like the sick pedophilic fuck he is.

But something isn't right with me. I've felt off since Saturday. I missed my period before I could restart my contraceptive pills. I thought I was safe. I have an IUD. But maybe it failed. And I think I'm pregnant. I won't tell them. It wouldn't save me. I need to be strong.

I pull at my wrists. Nothing. The restraints bite into my skin, tight as ever.

I take a deep breath, swallowing nausea, trying to recognize the scents. John. David. Just the two of them.

I still have the phone Garret gave me. I didn't leave it behind. Just in case. I was right. I can only hope Garret looks for me. If he hasn't given up. Maybe he was waiting for me to leave. Maybe he already got what he wanted. Control.

John curses.

"What's wrong?" David asks.

"The cameras are out."

"Want me to check?"

John exhales sharply. "No. Stay here with her. Clean this shit up."

The door slams. I close my eyes. This is the part David loves. The fact that I'm restrained. The power in forcing me to submit.

He grips my hair. Yanks. Pain splits my skull. The clinking of his belt buckle is unmistakable. And then, the smell. Cinnamon.

I gag.

He rubs cinnamon on the head of his cock. "Stop it and be a good little whore."

I scream.

His hand cracks across my cheek. The burn spreads across my skin, a fire consuming me.

I turn my head away. I inhale deep. He presses closer. I bite. Hard.

The taste of copper explodes in my mouth. David screams.

His hands cup his junk. "You fucking bitch!" he snarls, slapping me again.

Stars explode behind my eyes. I spit in his face. "Fuck… you," I manage, panting.

The door slams open. David freezes. I turn my head. A man in a plague mask stands in the doorway. Dressed in a black long robe.

David starts screaming. My eyes lock on the object in the masked man's gloved hand. John's head. Severed. Dark red muscle and bone hang in shredded tatters.

David chokes. "Who…are you?" His voice shakes with real fear.

The masked man steps forward, the head swinging from his grip.

David glances down, then back up. "She bit my dick," he whimpers. "She bit… I—"

I follow his gaze. John's empty eyes stare at the ceiling. Blood seeps from his ruined skull. Tears leak down my face. I'm going to die. He won't let me live. I know too much.

"Please," David begs. "Let me go. I'll pretend none of this ever happened."

He looks at me. "You can have her. Just let me go."

The man in the mask shakes his head. And lifts John's head like a prize form a hunt. An offering.

David sobs. His hands shake as he cups himself, still bleeding out. "Please…" He holds up the bottle in his hand. "It's cinnamon." Like it's a fucking peace offering. "See?"

The masked man opens his fingers. John's head thuds to the floor. It rolls like a bowling ball.

A long, gleaming knife slips from the man's sleeve. David screams right before the blade swings down. Clean. Precise. David's dick hits the floor. His shrieks shake the walls. He drops to his knees. Tries to grab it. The blade swings again. Vertically. The cut leaves his head in half. Red blood spray paints the walls. David collapses.

The man sheathes the knife.

I lift my chin. I know my fate. This is how I die. I exhale. "If you're going to kill me," I whisper, "make it quick." He pause like he' s listening. Waiting. "And tell Garret…" I swallow hard. My voice drops to a whisper. "That I love him."

I close my eyes. Silence. Then—soft pressure on my wrists. The chains loosen. I wait for the pain. For darkness to drag me under on last time.

I let myself dream. Of a different life. Of Garret. Of our child.

Something cold and damp wipes my lips. The cinnamon is gone. My eyes snap open.

He's there.

Just like in my dreams. The man with the mask. Dressed in black. With no face.

He leans close, his voice soft—so soft, I almost miss it. "I promised I wouldn't let anyone hurt you." His glove drops to the floor as his bare hand presses against my lower belly. His touch is warm, possessive. "This is me saving you, my love." His lips brush my ear. A whisper. A decree. "Welcome to the Order, Mrs. Nox." My eyes widen when he lifts me.

A loud voice cuts through the heavy silence.

"The fuck, Garret? Is she okay?" Melody's voice shakes as she rushes inside, flipping the light to a harsh white. The sudden brightness burns my eyes.

She falls to her knees beside me, her fingers trembling as they brush my face. Her eyes brim with tears, her lips parting in a silent apology. "I'm so sorry…"

She turns to the shadow in the doorway.

"Valen!" she calls out, panic lacing her voice.

A familiar figure steps forward. His voice is calm, but the edge in his tone slices through the air like a blade. "He has her, Melody. Chill."

Want more of the Prey Series?

Scan the QR code on the next page to Preorder RAGE (Azriel and Amy's story.)

ABOUT THE AUTHOR

Carmen Rosales is a best-selling Dark Romance and Latinx author. She loves to write in different genres of Romance and erotic horror under her alter ego, Delilah Croww. Beyond her writing, Carmen is a devoted wife and mother who loves spending time with her loved ones. Join her VIP list at www.carmenrosales.com

Join her VIP list- www.carmenrosales.com

.

Scan the QR code to follow her on Social Media, sign up for her Newsletter, and for preorder links for upcoming releases:

Carmen Rosales

www.ingramcontent.com/pod-product-compliance
Lightning Source LLC
Chambersburg PA
CBHW020720310726
48979CB00004B/994
* 9 7 8 1 9 5 9 8 8 8 5 9 8 *